KU-539-029

The Ringed Castle

DOROTHY DUNNETT

SPHERE BOOKS LIMITED
30/32 Gray's Inn Road, London WC1X 8JL

First published in Great Britain by Cassell & Co Ltd 1971
Copyright © Dorothy Dunnett 1971
First Sphere Books edition 1974

TRADE
MARK

Set in Intertype Baskerville

Printed in Great Britain by
Hazell Watson & Viney Ltd
Aylesbury, Bucks

ISBN 0 7221 3128 3

With love, for Dorothy Eveline Millard Halliday to whom both Francis Crawford and the author owe their present delightful existence

Author's Note

No one could write of the remarkable events leading up
to the visit of Osep Nepeja without mentioning a profound debt to the published studies of Professor T. S.
Willan of the University of Manchester.

Apart from Lymond himself, his family and his immediate
associates, all the characters in this novel are historical,
as are all the principal events.

The verses of the Song of Baida have been translated from
the Ukrainian for this book by Yaroslav Baran.

PART 1

CHAPTER ONE

Not to every young girl is it given to enter the harem of the Sultan of Turkey and return to her homeland a virgin.

The most prosaic schoolgirl in England, Philippa Somerville arrived home from Stamboul in the summer, having travelled stoically through Volos, Malta and Venice where she received, with mild distaste, the unexpected bequest of a fortune. From Venice, she crossed Europe to Calais, and at Calais she took ship for Tynemouth, whence she set off for her home in Flaw Valleys.

With her rode her henchman, guide and protector, a Scotsman called Abernethy. And on Archie Abernethy's stout arm, complaining, was a two-year-old boy named Kuzúm.

Sir Thomas Wharton and his company came across them all just outside Newcastle, and since there seemed to be a great many sumpter mules and a large number of hired soldiers guarding them, he gave himself the trouble of investigating. The sight of the Somerville child, returning after two years' absence on unexplained orgies abroad, was the reward of exemplary vigilance. His companion, a fledgling nobleman from Northumberland, was inclined to be more sentimental, but Sir Thomas quite rightly ignored him. Sir Thomas halted Philippa dead in her tracks, and made her vivaciously welcome.

It was a chaste encounter, conducted with grim efficiency by Archie Abernethy, with Philippa brazenly helping him. Yes, she remembered the Whartons, beside whom her late father had often fought. And yes, she remembered Austin Grey, Marquis of Allendale, although from a viewpoint four feet high, to a target not very much higher.

The Allendale estates were not far from Flaw Valleys. At twelve, this boy had been packed off to Padua and was now returned, dark, engaging and fragile in a doublet clearly fashioned in London. Peering from under her hood, Philippa favoured Austin Grey with a generous smile and returned to the business of supporting the lies Archie Abernethy was telling.

Yes, they had just come back from Malta. Yes, Mistress Somerville had been travelling abroad with a party, including her mother's friend, Crawford of Lymond. And that – indicating the now sleeping Kuzúm – was Mr Crawford's motherless son, being taken home to his grandmother in Scotland.

They looked at Mr Crawford's motherless son. 'Who's his mother?' Sir Thomas said with blossoming interest. 'Don't tell me Lymond married before he left Scotland. Too busy with other men's sisters.'

Archie said, 'No. He didna marry Kuzúm's mother. She's deid.'

Which was true. With a charming artlessness, Philippa squashed Tom Wharton's further inquiries and, prattling, prepared to detach herself. Austin Grey said, 'You aren't going home to Flaw Valleys?

For a moment, staring at him, she thought of disaster. Her home was burnt down and Kate dead? The Scots had come over the Border and levelled it? Kate had married again without telling her? Philippa said, 'Yes. Why not?'

And Austin Grey said quickly, 'It's all right. Your mother is quite all right. She isn't there, that's all. She's gone to stay at Midculter Castle in Scotland.'

Which was how, wheeling about, the small but resolute migration from Turkey abjured the delights of home and Flaw Valleys and turned up six days later in Scotland.

Austin Grey, as it happened, reached Scotland before them. Voluntary and kind-hearted harbinger, he took his horse over the Border and traversing the hills of the Lowlands reached that part of Lanarkshire west where the castle of Midculter stood. There he called on Sybilla, the Dowager Lady Culter, and delivered to her certain papers at Philippa Somerville's behest.

Sybilla welcomed him in. White-haired, blue-eyed and urbane, she was quite capable of dealing with diffident young English noblemen and putting them instantly and disarmingly at their ease. Only after he had settled in front of her beautiful fireplace with a cup of her equally desirable wine in his hand did she glance at the packet he had given her and say, 'But it is for Mistress Somerville of Flaw Valleys?'

Austin Grey said, 'Yes. I thought she was here?'

For an elderly lady, the blue eyes confronting him were

disconcertingly shrewd. 'Yes, she is,' Sybilla said. 'May I know who this is from?'

'I felt,' said Austin Grey, 'that you should break the news, Lady Culter. Mistress Somerville's daughter is home. She is travelling north. She should be with you in two or three days. The letters are from Philippa to her mother.'

Sybilla's eyes had become very bright. Then, 'You've seen her, Lord Allendale?' she said gently.

Austin said, 'She is in good heart, and travelling well. Only slowly, because of the baby.'

Lady Culter said nothing. She sat and looked at the young English messenger, with her lips parted and her eyes rather wide, so that the white skin of her brow was finely pleated. He hesitated and said, 'Your son's child. Mr Crawford's small boy called Kuzúm.'

'They found him,' Sybilla said.

He said, carefully, 'I don't know the story. But they have him quite safe, Lady Culter. If I may say so, he has just your colouring.'

'And my son?' Sybilla said finally.

'I gather . . . Perhaps the letters will tell you,' said Austin Grey. 'I gather he is still overseas.'

He left soon after that. But not before a light, brown-haired woman entered, whom he had seen all his youth about Hexham with her late husband Gideon Somerville, and her one small unkempt daughter Philippa. Kate Somerville came forward to greet him and was forestalled by her hostess the Dowager. 'Kate, he has letters from Philippa. She's safe, and on her way here with the child.'

But since women's tears, suppressed, made him uncomfortable, Austin Grey left as soon as possible after that.

By the time Philippa arrived at Midculter her mother and Kuzúm's grandmother between them knew the contents of the letters and diaries by heart and still could not reconcile them with the undersized fifteen-year-old who had left her uncle's home in London two winters ago, to plant herself willy nilly in the unsuitable company of Lady Culter's younger son Francis . . . Francis Crawford of Lymond, the hard-living leader of mercenaries whose by-blow Kuzúm had been snatched and used in a game by his enemies. Until he had caught up with and killed their leader, Graham Reid Malett.

It was typical that, in the wild hunt through far lands

which followed, the main concern of Crawford of Lymond had been to kill Malett, not necessarily to rescue the child. And typical that, suspecting it, Philippa Somerville had stuck grimly to him, and biding her time, had found the child and brought it back, too.

It was at the first reading that Kate stopped and letting her hand fall, with the letter in it, said in tones of failing belief, 'But she was in the *harem*!'

Sybilla said calmly, 'It doesn't matter. If she says she was untouched, she was untouched. And no one else need know anything of it.'

'In Flaw Valleys?' Kate said. 'They'll ask her about the pattern on Suleiman's nightshirt. And I cannot believe that Francis was not fully capable of extracting his own son without Philippa's help. She was probably an unqualified nuisance.'

Sybilla turned over one or two pages. 'Certainly, she has remarkably little to say in his favour.'

Kate said glumly, 'I don't suppose they were speaking to one another. All she did was saddle him with two children to look after instead of one. She says he sent her straight home from Volos, and I can't say I'm surprised.'

'Well, at least she went,' said Sybilla comfortably. 'It says here he sent her straight home from Algiers as well, and she made Archie Abernethy turn back so that she could continue her hunt for the little one. I think we owe a great deal to your Philippa.'

'Grey hairs,' Philippa's mother suggested.

But it was Kate, daily tramping the battlements, who first saw the long line of dust which announced her young daughter's arrival. By the time Philippa's cortège arrived, they were all on the steps of Midculter : Kate, Sybilla and Richard, Sybilla's other older, responsible son, with his wife and young children beside him.

There seemed to be a great many mules. Straining her eyes as they turned in at the gates, Kate studied them vainly for Philippa. In the lead was a small bearded man bearing a bundle, and beside him a stylish person in a cloak and hood trimmed with lynx, at whom Kate cast a wistful glance, since she could not imagine her having much time for her bedraggled Philippa. Then, looking again at the smooth, polished face and the coils of intricately pleated shining brown hair, she saw that it *was* her bedraggled Philippa. She walked forward, slowly.

Philippa reined in and looked down at her mother. Sitting like the Queen of Sheba, with her face green with fright she said, 'Did you get my letters from Austin?'

Kate nodded. Clearing her throat, she said, 'Kevin and Lucy were expecting a nose-veil and curly-toed slippers.'

Her daughter's youthful brown eyes, losing their starkness, became visibly pink round the edges. 'They're in my luggage,' Philippa said. 'With my prayer mat. I thought you would show me the door. Perhaps. That is, one shouldn't think of other people's babies before one's own mother. I knew you would stop me.'

'I can't think how,' Kate Somerville said. 'Gunpowder? It was more than Mr Crawford evidently could do.'

'There were a few unpleasantnesses,' Philippa said guardedly. She stared at Kate, trying not to think of Mr Crawford's unpleasantness. Her nose, also, was growing faintly pink.

'There are times,' Kate said conversationally, 'when one wonders where that gentleman's habits came from. Are you going to come indoors *on* the horse, or can I help you . . . ?'

At which, giggling, Philippa Somerville slid, with her eyes overflowing, into her mother's damp and convulsive embrace.

Presently, there was the other meeting, with Lord Culter and his wife on the steps. Presently, too, came her first encounter with Lord Culter's mother Sybilla. But before that the Dowager, the soul of discretion, had wandered into the courtyard to speak to her old friend Archie Abernethy. 'We are so glad to see you. David will look after your men. Won't you give him your horse, and come inside with us? And—'

For the first time, with courtesy, her gaze dropped to the rug-wrapped pack in his arms. '. . . And this is Khaireddin?'

Archie looked down, swore, and then apologized. 'We had him all nice,' he said. 'But he wanted to play Turks hiding in ambush. *Kuzúm!* It's your grannie!'

The bundle heaved, and Archie snapped, 'And you've made a right mess of your hair.'

A feathering of silky fair hair shot up from the core of the rug, followed by a round vermilion face with a belligerent blue stare. 'I want a shot of Fippy's horse,' the object said.

15

Archie said peremptorily, 'You're not having a shot on anything; we've stopped. You're there. You're at your grannie's home in Midculter. Here she is, waiting.' And his attention drawn for the first time from the child Archie looked, a little anxiously, at Lymond's mother, who had said nothing at all.

And as though she felt his gaze, Sybilla raised her eyes from the silvery hair and blue eyes and charming, over-heated two-year-old face, and smiled at him, and then said to her grandson, 'Hullo. Is your name Kuzúm?'

Kuzúm, abandoning the Turks, stared at her critically. Then he said, 'My rug's all crumply. Lift down me to walk?'

So Archie lowered him, and she received the solid weight and placed him on his two feet and then, kneeling, steadied him. 'Not Khaireddin?' she said to Archie.

'Kuzúm's his pet name. It means Lambkin.' Dismounting, he held the child by the shoulders. 'Mr Crawford's all right, my lady. Ye'll not expect him home yet: he's not a man for mentioning plans. But the bairn will make you good company.'

The bairn, tugging himself free, set off at a trot towards Philippa. Following slowly, 'Where is Mr Crawford?' Sybilla said.

'God – That is, we're no' all that certain,' said Archie. 'We left him in Volos, Greece, a wee bit overcome by the weather. Then we heard he had gone. . . . You'll see a change in the young lady?'

'Yes,' the Dowager said. They had reached the rest of her family. Holding out her hands to the new, self-contained Philippa she said, embracing her, 'Although I don't know how we are going to explain it.'

'We met Sir Thomas Wharton,' Philippa said deprecatingly.

'So it will be all over Hexham,' said Kate. 'Since that man went to court he's been worse than a midwife. You won't be dull, Philippa mine. We shall have plenty of callers.'

'Mostly male,' Richard said, grinning.

'Isn't it queer?' Philippa said. Standing at the top of the steps, she caught Archie's eye and then removed her gaze from him, unfocused. 'It didn't occur to me that people might gossip. It was Mr Crawford who warned me.'

'I'm glad he took the trouble,' Sybilla said tartly. 'To

16

allow you to travel home on your own, after treating you, so far as I can see, like one of his own underpaid mercenaries, must be the abominable highlight of a strictly egotistical career.'

Kate, better acquainted with her daughter, said, 'How did he warn you?'

Philippa gazed again round the courtyard. The chests were being shouldered indoors. Archie, lifting Kuzúm, had carried him across to young Kevin and Lucy. The horses were being led away. Richard was looking at her: the 3rd Baron Crawford of Culter, more heavily built than he had been, but still level-headed and pleasant: running his home of Midculter, raising his children, sustaining, year after year, the blows which fell without warning, the traps which opened, the doors which shut in his face because of his brother Crawford of Lymond. Richard smiled.

Philippa said, 'He suggested I should get married.'

Kate, whose hair was coming down in the wind, gave a groan. 'A profound offering of typical masculine subtlety,' said Philippa's mother. 'I might have known it. Come inside. I want to look at your earrings.'

'So I did,' Philippa said.

There was a mind-cracking silence. 'What?' said Richard.

'I did marry. On paper. To give me some standing at first, especially because of Kuzúm. Of course, it will all be annulled in a moment. It was,' said Philippa again, austerely emphatic, '*strictly* on paper.'

It was Sybilla who walked slowly forward and, taking the girl's manicured hands, held them both, firmly and coolly in her own. 'Philippa. You are not to worry. We are all here and ready to help you. But tell us first, whom did you marry?'

'Mr. Crawford,' said Philippa bleakly.

Kate said '*Philippa!*' and it fell on the air like explosive. But Lymond's mother, still holding Philippa's hands in her own, carried them after a second to her cheeks, where the colour had come flooding back, and said, 'Of course he would do that. *Strictly* on paper?'

'Well, my goodness –' Philippa said. She was trembling. 'He could be your uncle. I know. And there was no one else handy.' She turned, her blue eyes alight, to Kate Somerville. 'Kate, you seem to be Francis's mother-in-law.'

Philippa's mother was not smiling. She said, 'There was

no need for that. How could there be? Philippa is a child.'

'I don't want anything,' Philippa said. 'I have my own money. I don't want any formal recognition. I may be divorced already for all that I know. He said I must do it and you know what he's like. You *do* know what he's like.'

Richard Crawford had begun, slowly also, to laugh. 'Francis! My God, the complications,' he said. And then seeing Kate's face, 'But it's all right,' said Sybilla's reliable son, and, putting his arm around her rigid shoulders, smiled at Philippa's sensible mother. 'Welcome to the clan. Philippa will stay with us for a bit, and we shall look after the legal side. The annulment will be no trouble at all.'

Philippa went to her mother. 'It *is* all right. I promise you.'

Kate Somerville looked up.

Concern surrounded her. Above her, the pleasant, middle-aged person of Richard. Below, peering at her, Philippa's overcast and luminous face. To herself, *I am a widow*, said Kate Somerville grimly. *A widow with one married daughter*. And to Philippa, 'I'm sure it's all right. At least it's a novelty,' her mother said flatly. 'You'll be the only divorced child-bride in Hexham.'

They began, at last, to walk up the steps. 'All the same,' Richard said. 'I should like to know where Francis is.'

No one answered him.

'Or even who he's with,' pursued Lord Culter reflectively.

Archie Abernethy looked across Kuzúm's head at Philippa, and Philippa said prosaically, 'We know who he's with. He's with Kiaya Khátún.'

'Kiaya Khátún?' said Sybilla blankly.

'Kiaya Khátún,' said Philippa patiently. 'Head of the harem, and until recently Dragut Rais's mistress. The Diane de Poitiers, as you might say, of the East.'

At which, despite herself, her mother began, rather helplessly, to give way to laughter.

*

There were no children with Kiaya Khátún, on the other voyage from Volos, whose character was infinitely more worldly and which partook more of the nature of an exodus.

In the heart of the mule-train travelled the four mummy cases painted with lotus flowers and the names of pan-theistic God-triads : Ptah, Sekhet and Imhotep; Osiris, Isis and Horus; Magna, Horus and Harpoctates, and beside them the crates of innocent merchandise : the poor silk, the dried fruit, the sacks of sponges and screws of spoiled amber, turgid as egg in blown glass.

Among the muscatel raisins heady with syrups were the Mistress's rubies. Behind the wagons, suitably altered, rode Kiaya Khátún's private household : her cooks, her physician, her chamberlain, her maids, her secretary and those men at arms who were not already discreetly bestowed at the caravan head.

There the Mistress also rode, in a felt cloak and two fustian overgowns covering a shift which had taken twelve women three painstaking months to embroider. Without undue haste, unassuming as a cut of rye bread, she passed through the late winter mud of the Balkans and was taken for what she appeared to be, a woman among petty Syrian traders, and not what she was, Kiaya Khátún, late harem keeper to Suleiman; the powerful mistress whom the corsair Dragut knew as Güzel, and owning a ransom in gold beneath the false base of each wooden cart.

It amused the distinguished nobleman who, from Sofia onwards, had offered her his protection. Prince Dmitri Ivanovich Vishnevetsky was also new come from Turkey where he had been carrying out a small and unpublicized task for his master. He had seen Kiaya Khátún in the Seraglio. He had even, to his surprise, found her of decidedly practical help. His mission had failed, but he was inclined to believe she might favour him on another occasion, as she had favoured others, equally gifted and perhaps equally blessed in appearance, in her long and notorious career.

Meeting her again, not entirely by accident, in Sofia he thought again what a magnificent pair they made, he and she. He helped her pay her small dues at the barriers and decided after all to give her the benefit of his company and that of his men. As Governor of Cherkassy he had standing outside Lithuania and authority within it. Religious houses made him welcome. Mudwalled villages gave of their biscuit, mutton and rice. And when, on their last day in Turkish-held land, they overtook the camel string of a colonial Pasha, with six cloth-of-gold wagons for his wives and his catamites and a consort of reed pipes and tambours and brass dishes to knit up the travail of their passage, the Turk neither approached nor molested them.

That night, in the hide tent they raised for her, Vishnevetsky shared her supper and ventured a question, which he expected her to avoid.

Instead, she was frank. 'Roxelana the Sultan's wife became jealous. It was needful to leave.'

'You have left Turkey for ever? And Dragut?'

Her hair shone and glittered like coal: her brushed eyebrows gleamed above the moist coffee shells of her lids. Her nose was Greek and short; her warm cheekbones and brow a smooth sun-ripened olive. In Stamboul she had been tinted and gemmed like a Persian painting. She said, 'Dragut Rais understands these things, as men of stature may do. No jewel can remain in the same box for ever.'

'And the next owner?' said Prince Vishnevetsky.

'Ah, you mistake me,' said the woman called Güzel; and lifting the four pointed nails of one hand, ran them down his white sleeve and over the flesh of his hand, lightly scoring, so that the blood sprang sudden and scarlet in beads. 'I am the owner. And I have chosen my jewel and my box.'

He could not get her out of his thoughts. He spent his last evening with her on the frontier, but could not touch her or obtain any satisfaction but word-play. But she was well disposed towards him and at the end rose from her meal, and took one of her keys, and sent her steward to where the merchandise stood ready piled, to pass out of Lithuania in the morning.

Among the rest stood the stacked cases of Ptah, Osiris and Magna, with the customar's mark still upon them. Key in hand, the steward approached, while Prince Vishnevetsky and his hostess observed him. 'What a curious fashion it is, this craze for embalmed bodies. If there were tax to pay,' he said, 'would we import them, I wonder?'

'For every pleasure, one pays,' Güzel said. 'Come. I have in mind a small gift for you.' And they crossed to the coffins.

He laid his hand, a tough, soldier's hand on the top one. 'A handsome box, for an Egyptian.'

She glanced at her steward. 'The first is a gift for the Emperor. The one below may be opened.'

It was unlocked. The bandage shroud, delicately disarranged, revealed a custom-free fortune in spice-bags. Half a dozen changed hands, and the rest were repacked, rebound and coffined. Vishnevetsky was smiling. 'I hope you will remember,' he said, 'the small benefits which may have accrued from my presence.'

'And the pleasure,' said Kiaya Khátún kindly. 'For the rest, it is not I who shall remember, but the Emperor.'

They parted company the following day, and he stood on the town walls and watched her pass through the gates with her wagons, before he collected his men, and turned them, and resumed his own journey thoughtfully.

He did not see therefore her arrival at the first post-house; where a group of the Emperor's men were awaiting her. Nor how she was conducted from station to station, and used with deference but not with ceremony, as one might receive an august employee, but not a person of the first reputation or rank.

Nor how his place at her side had been filled, quietly, as of right, by one of her anonymous entourage. A man he had never observed who had travelled, discreet as their cargo, from Volos and was now placed by Kiaya Khátún at the head of her household, which found it expedient very quickly to humour him.

Far from his troublesome homeland of Scotland, and from the courts and battlegrounds, boudoirs and souls he had ravaged, Philippa's husband Francis Crawford of Lymond was riding. If the climate had affected him at Volos, it did so no longer. If he remembered friends or family, wife or commitments, it was quite unapparent. Instead he led his mistress's caravan and ordered it in every rigorous detail; using his many tongues, and the new one he had in seven weeks already half mastered.

With Prince Vishnevetsky, Güzel had employed her beauty and her experience, and had let him feel her strength, both of wit and of will.

With the man who was known simply as Lymond, she used none of these. They rode together in company, but spoke rarely, and then on affairs of the journey. Their meals were formal. They slept and took their leisure at all times apart.

She knew her household, watching, were mystified and, self-sufficient as she was, it gave her no concern. To be with her, Francis Crawford had come a long way, in mind and in body, and had to travel still farther yet. A patient

21

woman, Güzel was content to wait and to watch, and to allow him what power he wished to exert.

They were then no more than a week's journey from their destination. Spring was coming. The sun dried the quagmires and ditches and the bogs platformed with fir trees. Birds whistled in the thick, reeded rivers and women stood watching outside the thatched villages of wood-pinned bark houses, with their ditch-and-stake fence against bear and boar and the marauding bands of wild horsemen, who rode by with undressed furs on their mares' buttocks, and chains of silver and gold swinging bright from their ears.

They were nearly there, and she could be forbearing as she had been after this man had joined her, as bidden, at Volos. When at length, since he had not asked, she had told him the name of the land he was bound for.

Or rather, she had described it all, watching him. 'A land other than yours, baptized and blessed by St Andrew. A place of black wolves and white bears, of marshes, rivers and forests, of wide skies and flat vales of cherries and tall trees all running with honey : the sweat of heaven, the spittle, they say, of the stars. The sleeping cold of the north, which is the mother of whiteness. The land whose Emperor is Ivan Vasilievich of Vladimir, Novgorod, Pskov, Tver, Yogorsk and Smolensk, Duke of Muscovy and Tsar of all Russia.

'My friend, you are going to Moscow.'

And he had been acquiescent and civil as ever, at which she had concealed every trace of relief.

For greater than all her gold or her spices was this gift she was bringing to Muscovy.

CHAPTER TWO

'Russia! Christ!' said Danny Hislop. 'What in hell is he doing in Russia?'

'Waiting for us,' said Alexander Guthrie in the level tone of precarious patience exercised over the years with lesser scholars and fighting men both.

It took more than that to deter the band of free fighting men known as St Mary's, at present concluding an engagement in France. It took a great deal more than that to

22

put off Danny Hislop. 'I thought,' said Danny Hislop emotionally, 'that *I* was the mother ship and *he* was the bloody dove with the twig in its beak!'

Elbowing off the heavy-breathing crush of his officers, Alex Guthrie looked again at the astonishing communication from their absent and unaccommodating commander. After twelve months of private vendetta, Francis Crawford had been reminded, it seemed, of the fighting force he had left under Guthrie, on lucrative hire to the monarchs of Europe.

Lymond had left Turkey, it transpired, for Moscow. And now was inviting the pick of his captains to follow him.

'Well?' said Guthrie. 'He says the prospects for trained men seem excellent.'

The legal mind in the group was affronted. *'Prospects?'* said Fergie Hoddim. 'Yon's a sore outlay, travelling to Russia and back for a prospect. They're a coarse, jabbering, ignorant people, and ye canna issue a complaint against wrangeous and inordinate dunts if ye're lying down deid on your baikie. I'll not move a step but a contract.'

They left at the end of a week: eight well-balanced and reasonable mercenaries, who had made up their minds to this exploit before even finishing that laconic letter. And Fergie Hoddim was one of their number.

They were bound, it seemed, for an unknown and barbarous country, ignorant of modern warfare and backward in weapons and tactics, there to offer their specialized services for what they were worth to the Emperor.

The recompense might be large. It might be more than they dreamed of. Or they might be spurned by the boyars. Or never reach Russia at all, through the ring of unfriendly lands which surrounded her. So the letter had said; nor had its summing-up any message of feverish bonhomie. *There is a prospect of employment, entertainment and riches, but I can guarantee none of it, and least of all your personal safety. You have the facts. I merely place the proposal before you.* And it was signed, CRAWFORD OF LYMOND AND SEVIGNY.

'Sevigny?' had inquired Ludovic d'Harcourt.

And Guthrie had answered. 'He has a French comté.'

'But no scent,' Danny Hislop had said, and had withdrawn his tiptilted nose from the pages. 'This is a clever

23

bastard, my friends. I like that word *entertainment,* for instance.'

And d'Harcourt had said, 'We thought you would,' and tripped him up with casual competence.

But the four who knew and had been trained by Francis Crawford had been tactfully silent. To Danny Hislop, they were aware, the word conveyed Tartar maidens in wolf-skins. To Lancelot Plummer, a land where he could preside, an architect among builders of cabins; to Alex Guthrie, a scholar and Latinist, a new nation to study in genesis, all patched together from snatched states and princedoms. To Brown and Vassey and d'Harcourt, their Knights of St John, a high Church which called itself Christian but spurned so far both the advances of the Protestant lords and the Pope. And for Adam Blacklock the artist, older, wiser, and perhaps less vulnerable than once he had been, a chance to assess from maturity a person whose maturity was and always had been a thing disconcerting to witness.

For what, after these violent years, would entertain or even interest Francis Crawford, Blacklock found he had no idea.

They travelled each in his own way to Muscovy, the eight chosen men summoned by Lymond. They came by sea and by road; through Lübeck and Riga, by Vienna, Silesia and Moravia, across the Danube and past the walled city of Vilna in its high wooded hills. They traversed forests and marshes and rivers and saw bison and buffalo, and herds of light-footed wild horses, and the small sheep of the mountains with their high-stretched ringed horns. And at length they foregathered in the oak fortress town of Smolensk on the western extremity of Russia.

There they found lodging prepared for them, and guides waiting who gave them little respite but hurried them on their journey, answering their queries with nothing more than sign language and smiles. Which was something, as Fergie Hoddim was heard to remark sourly. But he would be damned glad when their meat, their fleabites and Danny Hislop's ill-organized appetites could be dealt with in civilized English.

It was after they had left the insect-ridden banks of the Dnieper that Danny Hislop reined up beside his friend d'Harcourt and said, 'What intelligent remedy, like jumping in the river, do you suggest if we find this man Lymond irreconcilably dreadful?'

Ludovic d'Harcourt was not the man for extravagant phrases. He smiled and said, 'I assume that if Alec Guthrie serves under him, then he is better than Alec Guthrie.'

'In the field maybe,' Danny said. 'But I suspect the passion with which they don't discuss him.'

'They are afraid of him?' D'Harcourt raised his comedian's eyebrows.

Danny Hislop's bright teeth flashed in his hairless, unremarkable face. 'If they were afraid, they'd tear him to pieces like schoolgirls. My guess is that he's gorgeous. A terrible tease and nasty at moments, but oh Maeve, he has such a way with him. . . . Is he gorgeous, dear Adam?'

Adam Blacklock, thus addressed, said quietly, 'Undoubtedly gorgeous.'

Ludovic d'Harcourt bent his innocent gaze on his companion.

'Hislop,' he said, 'Adam is humouring you. But be careful. I do not think the Russians will humour you.'

Danny Hislop shook his fluffy head of sparse hair. 'Where, gentlemen, is your backbone? You see someone before you who is not afraid to say what he thinks, provided he is in a position of ascendancy with a door open behind him and a knife gripped in each hand. Besides, I love gorgeous people: they make me feel gorgeous as well.' And he kissed Adam, who had been expecting it and did not flinch.

'I think you should settle down,' said Alec Guthrie's dry voice just behind them. 'These are the towers of Moscow.'

They had stepped out of the forest. Around them flowered the silk skies of sunset. The air, clear and warm, slipped against the clogged wool and sour metal and scuffed, sweaty leather of tired men and horses, and brought them the smell of spring grass and fresh earth and the still, breathing leaves of thin birch trees, the new stars like birds in their branches.

On the horizon, palisaded in wood, enclosed in long walls of russet-red brick and enthroned in the elegant scrolls of her rivers, rose the small hills of the city of Moscow, larger than London; the second Rome; the refuge and shrine of the church which the infidel drove from Byzantium. And within the walls, leafed and spiralled and knopped with bossed gold like an ikon, the Kremlin towers, globe thick upon globe, hung burning upon the iconstasis of the whole airy sky.

That night, by order, they spent outside the walls. The next day, a bright morning in the middle of May, they crossed the ditch and were led by their escort through the several walled suburbs of Moscow, the gates opening smoothly before them.

Riding over the grey wooden logs, they were silent. They saw a city, mellow, irregular, low, of weathered log houses, thatched, or roofed with layers of silvered wood battens, undercarved and flocked over with a wandering of vine and fruit tree and tangled greenery, assorting with swine and thin poultry and bushes of heavy, washed linen in the wooden fenced yards. There were shop booths, and buildings of board, and on the slope of the ground to the river, a handful of taller brick mansions set among the high walls, red and white, of rich convents and the squat shapes of churches, with their deep painted doorways and buttoning of assorted gold domes. Below them, half the width of the Thames, was the busy blue stream of Moskva. And on the banks of the river the triangular wall with its twenty fortified towers which they had seen from a distance : the russet fifty-foot wall of the Kremlin, the High City where the Tsar lived.

They were taken not to a khan but to a smaller square building of brick, with stables lining two sides of its yard. There, men in wide, booted breeches came to lead off the horses and others to unload the packmules and show the way up the staircase, built Scottish-style on the outside, which gave on to their rooms on the first floor.

These were not luxurious, consisting of no more than two parallel chambers with a door in the long wall between them. The front room, with windows on to the yard, was entered direct from the staircase, and contained inside it another flight of steep stairs which appeared to lead down to the kitchens. In the room was very little : stove, table and an assortment of benches and stools. Here no doubt they were meant to take meals.

The inner room, of identical size, had no outside door and its windows looked out to the rear. Typically, it was lined with a wood sleeping-bench, supplemented by some chests and a number of new-made and un-Russian beds.

They had come a long way, through foul and difficult passages; suffering gross meat and sour wine, stinking drink and filthy straw for a bedding; travelling in small barks and loose, jolting wagons. There was not one of them who

26

had not been forced to fight for his money, his life or to preserve his fictitious identity : Plummer had a cracked rib; Guthrie a scar from a Janissary run drunk-wild with a mace. They had been blackmailed by ferrymen and cheated by inadequate guides and faced philosophically the unpleasantness of travelling at night through forests harbouring boar and plains ranged by wild cat or wolf.

By comparison, this was harbour and comfort. They had perhaps hoped for more, but they had been promised nothing. And being professional men they made, caustically, the best of it with the help of Danny Hislop's sharp tongue. They threw down their saddles and baggage; they moved about, examining the appointments and stood at the windows, discussing what they could see. There was no sign of other quarters attached to the lodging, and no sign at all of the man they had been summoned to meet. But presently a door opened somewhere and the smell of hot meat filtered up from the steep kitchen staircase. And a moment later a tousled head rose from it and they were offered unexpectedly a tray full of rough bowls of broth.

They had breakfasted already at the monastery, but none the less it was decidedly welcome. They kicked stools up to the long oaken table or ate standing, their exuberance quieted, so that they became aware of the noise of the city; of the broken rumble of wagons on the long laddered paving of timbers; of the discordant clanging of bells and the whining of vendors and the harsh spoken artillery of the Russian voice, with its scooping vowels and hard bitten consonants.

Adam Blacklock found it soothing. He spooned his broth, absorbing it, thinking of nothing, and suddenly among the sounds in the yard was another voice, light and clear and demanding, which he had not heard for a year and a half. It spoke in Russian, once, and then again, giving an order. And then was followed almost at once by a quick running step, scaling the stairs outside the house.

There was time to glance once at the others, sitting arrested, and then the door opened and Francis Crawford stood on the threshold.

For a moment Lymond remained there, surveying them. His eight officers, staring edgily back, saw a delicate-looking gentleman in a pretty paned and pinked tunic with the finest voile shirt bands and a link-belt of Italian enamel work. A man whose yellow hair, dry and light and unevenly tipped, eclipsed the sunlight behind him, and whose attic profile and unoccupied, long-shafted hands caused a small moan of ecstasy to burst, very circumspectly, from Mr Hislop's baby-pink lips.

He was the same. Or very nearly the same. Relief flooded through Adam, and beside him Alec Guthrie smiled also, and said, 'Francis!'

The wreathed, sapphire gaze rested on him and then moved, with perfect courtesy, along the haphazard grouping of faces. 'So you have all arrived safely. I am glad. Don't rise, gentlemen,' Lymond said pleasantly. 'I am sure you have worked hard for your breakfast.'

Which brought them all, untidily, to their feet as Lymond pressed the door shut and walked to the head of the table. There he tossed down some papers and, hooking the master chair to him, said, 'Please sit. We have a great deal to get through this morning. I know four of you. Guthrie, will you kindly introduce me to the others?' And stood, knee and elbow supported, while Guthrie, level-voiced, described them one by one. Roger Brown of Kirkcudbright. Hislop, from Renfrewshire, who had joined them when Hercules Tait left for Venice. And the two former Knights of St John, Alan Vassey and Ludovic d'Harcourt, a Frenchman of Scottish extraction who had come to replace Jerott Blyth.

'Also departed,' said Frances Crawford. 'The beauty of worthy things is not in the face but in the backside, endearing more by their departure than their address. Daniel Hislop, the son of the bishop?'

'The Bishop's bastard,' said Hislop, with a cold-eyed assumption of coyness. 'Sir. My lord. Jesus.'

Lymond's eyes turned to him, open. Then changing position, he seated himself, and placed his hands gently on the table before him. '*Sir* will do,' said Lymond calmly, 'unless you receive divine witness to the contrary. I thought all our Knights of St John had hastened back for the Grand Master's election on Malta?'

D'Harcourt answered : a burly, soft-footed man with wrestler's features and a schoolboy tangle of pale, tightly curled hair. 'Malta will manage without me. I wished to fight Mohammed in Russia.'

Lymond was watching his fingers. 'And if the Tsar in

his wisdom decides to fight the Lithuanian Christians and not the Koran-worshipping Tartars?' He looked up.

'I will fight,' d'Harcourt said. 'I am a mercenary, and I fight for the leader who pays best.'

'So are we all mercenaries,' Lymond said. 'I would have you remember that, all of you. There is no precedent for what we are about to do here. We are about to offer this kingdom an army, and there will be no place whatever for anyone's private crusade.'

'An army!' said Alec Guthrie.

'Can you possibly imagine,' Lymond said, 'that I brought you all from France to rush about on demand, killing Tartars?'

'Eight of us?' said Adam diffidently.

'Nine of us,' Lymond said dryly. 'To find out what exists, and plan what we want to exist. To create the prototypes, and instruct the instructors. And then to muster and train and equip a national army.'

'Dealing meanwhile with such aggravation or re-aggravation as molesting invaders may offer us,' said Fergie Hoddim. 'Yon's a long business, sir.'

'Yon's a lifetime,' said Danny Hislop. 'Fergie's all right. *He* isn't married.'

'Neither are you,' said Adam sharply.

'No, but the women are all the right shape for Fergie,' said Hislop.

'Then you will have to decide, won't you,' said Lymond, 'between women and money? It will be a stay of five years. Are you prepared for it?'

Guthrie said, 'Are you staying five years?' And his blunt, bearded face turned squarely to Lymond's.

Lymond said, 'I am not staying anywhere unless we are granted fees on a scale greater than anything we might earn in Europe. That, on your behalf, I can promise. In return, I shall offer the Tsar five years from this spring of our services. After that, you may take your fortune and go.'

'And you?' said Guthrie again.

'You need not, I think, concern yourself about me,' Lymond said, his brows lifted slightly. *'D'Harcourt!'*

'It was me,' said Danny Hislop. And as Lymond continued to look at him, he added bright-eyed, 'I only said you were gorgeous.'

Francis Crawford threw down the card he was holding.

'The buffoon of the party,' he said. 'You have, I am sure, enlivened the long summer evenings round the camp fires. Your men, I am certain, find your quips irresistible and your effrontery something to talk about, slapping their knees with their girl friends. With me, you refrain.'

Danny Hislop, hanging his head, was mouthing a long and inaudible apology. Guthrie half rose to his feet but sank back at a brief glance from Lymond. Lymond said, 'Since you are still with St Mary's, I assume your ability is unquestioned and your performance impeccable. It would be a pity to have to take both unsung back to the Bishop. This is a country with no middle degree. Between the top rank, which you will hold, and the bottom rank, which you will be controlling, there is a chasm. If you bridge it this way, you will bring yourself and your friends into ridicule. The proceedings in this room are formal because I intend all our proceedings in Russia to be conducted with the utmost formality. Whatever has been the custom before, in this company we shall use surnames only; and that applies to you all. We are a coterie of foreigners in an old and alien and bigoted society, and to conquer it, we must move away from each other and employ no codes and forget even our language. . . . What are the defences of Moscow?' He was looking at Danny.

'Us,' said Danny. After a second he added, 'The walls and the rivers.' His colour was high.

'What walls?' Lymond said. 'Tell me how they are manned. And the names of the gates and the bridges.'

He had picked, as it happened, the most observant man in the company. Danny Hislop pursed his lips, aware of the ranked eyes around him, and then, drawing breath, reeled off with care all the details which Lymond had asked for.

'Good. And the house we are in?' said Lymond kindly. 'How would you defend this house, Hislop?'

'Given weapons?' said Danny. He was recovering, but kept any hint of the caustic most rigorously out of his voice. 'Assuming hand guns and bows and all that goes with them, but nothing else except for your knives and your swords.'

Danny glanced round. 'Against what sort of attack? It's not very defensible.'

'It isn't, is it? Against an attack by fifty men, with bows and inferior small arms,' said Lymond.

'Christ!' said Plummer. But Danny, thinking it out as

30

he spoke, produced, in snatches, the scheme for defence he had been asked for. Then, restored, the bland hazel eyes rested on Lymond.

'Thank you,' said his commander. He looked round. 'I hope you all heard it. I further hope you will all obey to the letter the instructions I have laid down on conduct. Because if you make a mistake with these people, you can expect neither to survive in this house, nor to escape through the walls of the city. Is it possible,' said Francis Crawford, 'that we might now carry on with our business?'

Much later, when their discussions were ended and the afternoon was half worn through, Lymond touched Guthrie on the shoulder and walked with him to the window, where they could see the courtyard and the crowded brown ranks of log houses, and beyond them, the walls of the Kremlin. Lymond said, 'They've been in good hands. They will still be under you for all day-to-day purposes.'

Alec Guthrie said, 'I should have got rid of Hislop.'

'No,' said Lymond. 'We've had the cleverness thrust down our throats. Let's see what other quality he has. Where have you been fighting?'

There was a year and more to describe, telling of the long power struggle between Henri of France and the failing Emperor Charles with his over-extended possessions in Spain and Burgundy, Italy and Peru, Sicily and The Netherlands. Guthrie reported, and Lymond asked all the questions. 'And the Pope?' For between these two empires the Pope, or design, held the balance.

Dryly, Alec Guthrie quoted the words of the Emperor. 'Our custom has always been to speak with respect and moderation to Popes, whose goodwill we need on account of concessions and other favours we are frequently obliged to demand.'

'Where did you pick up that jewel?' Lymond said.

'Hercules Tait. You remember. He's in Venice now, and has a very dear friend in the Council of Ten. From his letters you'd think he helps the Doge with his spelling. He says the Emperor Charles will marry his son to Queen Mary of England.'

'It seems unfortunate,' said Lymond idly. '. . . I wonder if Hercules Tait would write to me? I have a great deal of time for the right kind of gossip.'

'Yes,' said Guthrie after a moment. 'I believe that he

31

would.' He paused. 'I thought you were confident that the Tsar would want our services, and for some time, at that?'

'I am still confident,' said Lymond briefly. 'But we have a virgin nation here on our hands, with no more than two generations of cohesion behind it. Nothing is going to be quick. And what happens in west Europe meantime may well determine what happens to us here in Moscow. When we are called to the Tsar, I shall let you know. If you want me, this is how you can reach me.'

Alec Guthrie looked at the paper he was being given. 'You are not living here?'

'No. I saved to the last,' Lymond said, 'my piece of gossip, which you can retail later for the undoubted edification of Hislop and d'Harcourt and the rest. I have no financial resources. Your journey to Moscow has been paid for by a woman now living in Moscow. She is no concern of yours, but she is in partnership with us in so far as we are in her debt until our present expense is repaid. Her house is mine, and that is the direction.'

Alec Guthrie's eyes remained bent on the paper. 'And her name?'

'Her name is Güzel,' said Lymond. 'But you will refer to her, if you please – you will enjoy referring to her, I am sure – as the Mistress.'

He was smiling, Guthrie found, although he did not greatly care for the smile. He said, 'As you say, it is none of my business.' And then, because of what had once been between them, Alec Guthrie said, 'She's Dragut's woman, and she's a kingmaker. You know what Graham Malett became. You know why he wanted St Mary's.'

'Perhaps,' said Lymond, 'it escaped your notice, but we have already covered the subject. You are a mercenary. I am a mercenary. If you object to my money, my rule or my ethics, you have a remedy. You simply open that door and walk out of it.'

'No,' said Alec Guthrie grimly. 'I knew the risks when I came. I'll stay with you. If they accept us.'

'But you didn't know about the woman, dear Alec,' said Danny Hislop at supper that night, when Lymond had walked down to his horse and departed. 'Nobody told us about the woman. Güzel. The Mistress. What if they have a tiff and she withdraws all her assets before the Tsar has decided to keep us? What,' said Danny dreamily, 'if she takes against our coarse ways when she meets us? Or decides she'd prefer one of us to sweet Francis? . . . Jesus . . . Sir?'

'Presumably,' Plummer said languidly, 'it will keep him at least off your neck, Danny Dare-all. My saints, it's a dedicated hunt for experience. Remember Joleta?'

'Joleta?' said d'Harcourt.

'Graham Malett's sister Joleta. Lymond bedded her before he killed her and her brother; did you know that, I wonder, dear Ludo? And her baby went the same way in Turkey.'

'My God,' said Alan Vassey with reverence.

'Now then,' said Fergie Hoddim. 'Ye want to be careful with that sort of pronouncement, or ye can find yourself in the middle of a fine juicy action. Lymond killed Graham Malett. He engineered the death of Joleta, but didna just hold the sword personally. And he had to choose between Joleta's boy and his own. Or so Jerott Blyth says. So he saved his own, and that's only human.'

'So it is,' Danny said.

Ludovic d'Harcourt, looking somewhat dazed, said, 'Do I gather there were two children at risk?'

'That's right,' Said Fergie Hoddim approvingly. 'The mutes were going to kill one or the other, so he chose to keep his own boy. God, it's a terrible system. Consuetudo, consuetudo, consuetudo, and no' a good statute law on the ledger. The Court of Session would never be happy in Turkey.'

'And then by all accounts,' said Plummer sweetly, 'he married.'

Six heads shot up. Adam Blacklock said, *Married!* and Guthrie, who had been minding, at some cost, his own business, put down his spoon and said, 'Yes, married. What does it matter? It's nothing to do with our prospects here.'

'A bath girl?' said Danny. His eyes were shut, his expression deeply seraphic. 'A duchess? A very rich Mother Superior? How do you know?'

Guthrie said, 'It was in Hercules Tait's latest letter. Crawford spent a night with the girl in Stamboul. She was caring for one of the children you talked of. Her people will have it dissolved.'

Joleta Malett had been — what? Sixteen? Adam, his appetite gone, said, 'Who was it?'

And Plummer said, 'Philippa Somerville. Do you remember, Adam, in England? The girl from that big steading near Hexham. She followed him, poor dear, out to Turkey.'

33

Adam got up from the table. He said, 'She's too young to bed with.'

'Not quite,' said Guthrie dryly.

*

Later, lying on his extremely hard bed, Danny Hislop thought it all over and produced, for his own satisfaction, a verdict.

'Gorgeous I called him and *that* he is, Maeve; you'd be surprised. And nasty I called him, and that, Maeve, was a shrewd piece of insight, for nasty he certainly is. And a clever bastard, I called him. . . . Not to his face, dear. We're not all born to be heroes. But what he may not know, Maeve, is that I'm a clever bastard as well.'

CHAPTER THREE

The summons from the Sovereign Grand Prince Ivan Vasilievich, Duke of Muscovy and Tsar of all Russia, reached Lymond three days after the appearance of his eight officers in Moscow, an unusually brief interval. In the preceding three days the eight had talked, eaten, rested, viewed with unconcealed curiosity and some foreboding the amenities of Moscow, city of churches, and had discovered, by dint of some highly skilled shadowing, just where Lymond was living and – curiosity being equally potent in east and west Europe – what Güzel, Dragut's mistress, looked like.

'A handsome woman,' Fergie Hoddim had opined, stroking the sad brown moustache he had been attempting to cultivate ever since Lübeck.

'Going by what?' Lancelot Plummer had inquired. 'She was wearing a veil and a cloak to her ankles. I grant you the jewellery was handsome all right.'

'Enough to keep us for another few days?' asked Danny Hislop. 'I thought they had a light hand with the mutton at supper. Did she look exhausted?'

'She looked,' said Alec Guthrie dryly, 'like a clever woman who was not unaware that five ill-dressed passers-by were displaying an unhealthy interest in her personal life.' But he spoke without rancour, because he shared the con-

34

cern of the others. In this unknown country their standing and fortune and future were precarious enough as it was, without depending as well on the whim of a well-furnished hetaera.

They were not present however at the brief encounter between Francis Crawford and Güzel when, on the day of the audience, he took leave of her on his way to collect Guthrie, Blacklock and Hoddim, who were to accompany him to the Kremlin.

He wore a doublet her tailor had fashioned for him from woven Indian silks of all colours; and over it a sleeveless coat cut with cunning, the seed pearls glimmering as he moved in the warm morning sun. She came to meet him and considered him, standing in silence, while he watched her with unmoved, cornflower eyes. 'The word,' he said, 'is "gorgeous".'

She raised her arched eyebrows.

'. . . But it is axiomatic to select the right armour, whatever the battle. An overplus of rings, would you consider?'

'No,' she said. 'The Tsar is the supplicant.'

'I trust he knows it,' said Lymond. 'But you have no doubts.'

Her smile, cool and subtle, was celebrated.

'No. Neither have I,' Lymond said. 'Which is fortunate, perhaps, for us both. If you want Russia, mistress mine, you shall have it.'

*

Alec Guthrie had paid fifteen gold florins for a boyar's cap trimmed in black fox, and wore it doggedly, his short beard combed, above a new velvet cloak with gold braiding. Fergie and Adam Blacklock likewise had spent the morning, to the marked admiration of their less fortunate fellows, struggling with new clasps and unfamiliar belts until Hoddim offered, red-faced, to replace an oral process with a physical one. Then, joining Lymond in the cavalcade of liveried horses waiting outside, they trotted, stiffly correct, up to the drawbridge which led to the square red Frolovskaya Tower, the principal entrance to the Kremlin.

Adam Blacklock, riding behind his commander's uncompromising back and the swaying gold fringe of his horse-harness, wavered between a savage excitement and a deadly desire to be safely in Renty, speaking bad French and facing the guns of the Emperor.

He recited to himself, and saw by Fergie's set face that he was doing the same, the remarkable briefing they had received from Francis Crawford :

'Ivan Vasilievich has been Tsar since he was three. He is secure on his throne : has dealt harshly with the boyars who repressed him as a youth and has turned his attention to this inheritance. After more than two centuries of Tartar subjection, Greater Russia has come into being, largely through Ivan's father and grandfather.

'There remained three Tartar kingdoms unconquered. Two of these, Kazan and Astrakhan, Ivan has successfully dealt with. The third, the kingdom of the Crimean Tartars, still remains a marauder within his southern frontiers whose raids have the support of Ottoman Turkey. Ivan must conquer the Crimean Tartars. He also wants to recover those lands lived in by Orthodox Russians and seized by western neighbours while the nation was engaged with the Tartars. Then he wishes to enter Europe and the civilized world through trade to the west through the Baltic.

'Some of this he has done. He took Novgorod, and brought back to Moscow three hundred sledges of treasure. Three years ago he conquered Kazan. Soon he will turn to Lithuania, Livonia and Poland, and for that he must have a trained army.

'In Russia none has ever been organized. The Tsar appoints a general, or Voevoda, who may be a leading member or even the chairman of the council, the boyar duma. For his officers, he counts on the Moscow boyars and his own many relatives, who appear on demand, and on the service princes, who occupy estates in return for their duty. Also, after Kazan, the Tsar created the Streltsi, the first permanent force of hackbutters. He recruits men of ability, and gives them in return grants of confiscated land. And sometimes he can call on the Cossacks, free settlers, who live under their own chiefs on the frontiers.

'Since he lacks artisans and engineers, he has tried to import these from the west, together with armour and weapons and powder, but most of this traffic has been blocked, as we know, by the western states on which he will use them. The people have valour and endurance, but no discipline, no method and no drill. Nor, by tradition, is the

Tsar himself a leader in battle. Since the days of Dmitri Donskoi, no Duke of Muscovy has gone into battle. The tradition has been the oriental one until now : to save face, and to delay by negotiating.

'We are negotiating now to become the first foreign paid leaders of the Russian army,' Lymond had said coolly. 'Bear in mind that you are not dealing with an Englishman, an Italian or a Scot. You are dealing with a nation more accustomed to the traditions and commerce of the east, and with a man whose upbringing has left him distrustful of people. He is given to violent outbursts : his brother Yuri is an idiot. The greatest restraining influence in his life is his wife, and his young family. He is educated and widely read, but irrationally so. He thinks quickly, and expects it in others. He has great personal wealth. He is deeply and romantically religious, and sees his country as the custodian of a sacred trust – *Two Romes have fallen, but the third stands, and a fourth there will not be.* But though there is a Metropolitan, there is no powerful Church with secular powers. There is no social system; no feudal arrangement; no chivalry. Only the boyars, corrupt and violent whenever the Tartar threat is removed, and the descendants of the old appanaged princes.

'He is to be cultivated as the hawk is to be cultivated. We have also to enforce the friendship and confidence of his favourite, Alexei Adashev, risen from the minor gentry to become keeper of the Tsar's bedchamber and of his personal treasury, and the Tsar's chief adviser, in council and out of it. Together with him you must impress the monk Sylvester, who succeeded the Metropolitan Makary as the greatest influence, until last year, in the Emperor's life. And after them, you must deal with the Russian commanders – Princes Mikulinsky and Pronsky-Shemyakin and Vyazemsky, Mstislavsky and Andreevich, Peter Morozov and Ivan Sheremeter and the most learned, idiosyncratic and skilful of them all, Prince Andrei Kurbsky, Adashev's particular friend. . . .'

Sweat broke out on Adam Blacklock's pale brow, and he reined in abruptly, just in time to avoid the hindquarters of Lymond's horse. Lymond had dismounted and, pulling off his flat cap, was saluting the ikon over the gateway. Adam, without looking at anyone, did the same; and remembered to keep his hat in his hand as he walked, with Hoddim and Guthrie, over the threshold. There, Viscovatu met them: the monk who was Ivan's Chief Secretary, and led them past the ranked guards and up the slight, crowded rise of the hill.

For four hundred years, the ancient high city of Moscow had stood within its ramparts above the River Moskva, and within it, century after century, had flowered the palaces of the prince and his courtiers, the storehouses, the kitchens, the stables, the workshops; the markets, the painted churches in brick and in timber, the hooded arches of convent and monastery; the blessed walls and chapel which sheltered the Metropolitan, who was next unto God, our Lady and Saint Nicholas only excepted. Walking between the monasteries of St Nicholas on his right, of Constantine and Helen on his left; past the square belfry where, on Easter night, the great bell of Moscow would set off the carillons of three hundred and fifty churches in the low city outside the walls, Adam Blacklock, the artist, was gripped by an open-eyed silence, as if a volume of miniatures had surrendered to him, and was submitting, book by book, to his advance.

This garden of towers: this confection of wrought stone and round tulip heads, copper and gold, spiralled and lobed in a frilling of leaved stone and damascened roof-planes; this ancient assembly pleated with steps and fretted with a nonsense of archways and ivorine galleries; dissolved in fire; lost in neglect; masked; altered; rebuilt; painted; carved; gilded; dressed within and without to a thousand different tastes, stood at the headwaters of four civilizations, and the sunlit white scallops of Italy smiled daisy-fresh down on the squares, garrets, towers, steps, passages, shafts and deep frescoed arches of the earlier ages, spanning two hundred years to the low-stalked domes and squat shapes of St Saviour with its budding of chapels fit, one felt, to be stood in the palm of one hand.

Then Lymond said briefly, '*Blacklock!*' and he found that they had passed the cluster of cathedrals, and the dust of a tall church rebuilding, and had arrived before a square wooden pavilion, resting among the newly sprigged bushes and trees running down to the slope of the Moskva.

It seemed an unlikely presence chamber for the Tsar of all Russia, until you remembered the fire of a few years before, which had destroyed so much of Moscow that the Emperor had moved from the Kremlin to Vorobievo, ruling from over the river, and seventeen thousand of his subjects had died. Then they were inside, their heads covered again, as was the custom, and standing waiting in a room lined with guards, their axes lifted shoulder high against the white fur of their hats; their white velvet gowns brushing the smooth wooden floor, laid with fine carpet. They stood there, Viscovatu, Guthrie and Lymond sustaining a weird conversation in Latin, embellished with gems from Fergie's professional repertoire, until the interpreter arrived, twenty minutes later, and at the end of the room the carved double doors were flung open. The interpreter, a cheerful monk called Ostafi, shook them one by one by the hand as they were ushered forward, and grinned even more widely when Adam addressed him in English.

'My dear man!' said Guthrie sardonically. 'Wherever would he learn English? Our friend here speaks Russian and Latin and Greek, and if you can't teach yourself one of them quickly, you'll have to become the world's leading exponent of mime.' And so he walked, deaf and dumb, after the others into the Audience Chamber, and became aware of space, and a high tented roof, of carpets and benches and a standing group of men dressed in identical robes of gold tissue, and of a high dais at the far end on which was a state chair of gold on which a crowned man was seated, surrounded by a handful of courtiers more richly dressed than the others, and a bearded man in the black hat and robes of a priest. Then Ivan IV, Tsar of Russia, lifted his heavy, ringed hand and they moved forward, coming to rest below and before him while in clear, echoing Russian the interpreter began his preamble.

The windows, some glass, some latticed, were small. But shafted sun danced on the walls, reflected from the gold tissue, and gathered itself to blaze and glint on the sceptre, the tiara and gown of the Tsar. He was wearing, as Adam learned later, the Kazan cap of state, a sable-based pyramid of foliated gemmed gold; and the fabric of his robe was gloved with wrought gold : blocks of pearl-bordered metal with inlaid figures of brilliant enamel, all joined with a network of heavy, natural jewels.

But it was the man within the harness at whom they all looked. A man tall, wide-shouldered and young, with blue eyes and a long, flattened nose and a moustache and beard of fine, thick auburn hair, who spoke Russian in a bass voice, and waited while Viscovatu translated, and Lymond, baring his head, answered in neat, balanced Latin.

39

Ivan was young. This Adam had not known. Young as himself; younger than Fergie; younger by far than Alec Guthrie. The man who planned the conquest of Kazan and had outfaced the boyars, who was bending his mind to the new laws, the new schools, the new tutors and the new printing which must drag Russia from its barbaric enslaved history could be in age very little more, or little less than the other man standing before him. In years, in ability and, it seemed likely, in pure intellectual arrogance, there was not all that much to choose between Francis Crawford and the Sovereign Grand Prince Ivan Vasilievich.

A shiver of foreboding travelled up Adam's spine. There was more talking. He saw Lymond turn towards him, and bracing himself, he moved forward in his turn and paid his respects, in European court fashion, to the Tsar. Then the Chief Usher moved forward and he saw that the chest containing Kiaya Khátún's present, of which he had heard, was being passed from him to Viscovatu and thence, on one knee, to the Emperor. There was a waft of spices, and Ivan lifted the narrow lid.

Inside were a number of long objects wrapped in soft linen. Adam, standing close to him, smelt the frankincense in their folds and knew, with sudden finality, that the aroma was all of spice that the fine chest contained. Instead, lifted out one by one by the secretary and examined one by one by the Tsar, were the objects which the woman Kiaya Khátún/Güzel/the Mistress had brought with her from Stamboul in that coffin painted with lotus flowers and the names of Magna, Horus and Harpoctates : the prototypes, in perfect small, of six of the newest field-pieces and hand-guns from the West.

He felt himself go red, and saw Guthrie had flushed also. Given the smiths and the metal, these guns in their proper size could be dealing death on the field in six months. Death, perhaps, to the Tartar and Turk. But death later to whom?

And then he thought, 'But in himself and us, Lymond has already placed a weapon a thousand times greater than these in the Sovereign Prince's hand.'

Ivan was speaking. Lymond replied, through the interpreter and Ivan uttered again. Neither man smiled : there was no change and no softening in that unexpected bass voice. Then the box was closed and taken away, and the Tsar lifted his heavy, chased sceptre again, holding it loosely in his well fleshed, metal-soiled fingers, and, echoed by his interpreter, began to voice a string of uninflected, flat questions.

Lymond answered. He went on answering while Adam, the blood alternately flooding and leaving his veins, tried to stand at ease, without swaying or stiffening, and with mounting anxiety, to follow the mood of the exchange. On the Tsar's side, there was, if anything, an added brusqueness by now. The questions came without cease : he had, it was clear, a precise catalogue in his mind of what he wanted to know and only once did the man on his right – Adashev? – with the cloudy brown beard lean forward to murmur to him.

His next question was pointed. Lymond took a moment longer than he need have done to volunteer a reply. When he did speak, it was in Russian. He had been asked, Adam supposed, how he could hope to control thirty thousand assorted men through an interpreter, and with no humility had demonstrated his answer. It would also, he knew, be in excellent Russian. Given, single-minded, four months in which to learn a new language, he would back Lymond against any linguist on earth.

In any case, it had given him at this moment the ascendancy he needed to change briefly the lead of the interview. Having begun, he went on speaking in Russian while the Tsar sat staring at him with those curious china-blue eyes. Elegantly scented with spice like his pistols, the requirements and demands of St Mary's.

The Tsar heard him out. If he had a reputation for violence, there was no sign of it here; but no sign either of a weak or a yielding personality. He received Lymond's words without interruption, and, at the end, stared at him for a long time without speaking. Then, lifting his voice, he made a single harsh comment.

Hard and fast as a ricochet, Lymond answered him, displeasure distinct in his face. The Emperor replied with three words; and then, turning his shoulder, began to address the black-attired man on his left. The secretary, approaching Lymond, spoke in a murmur of Latin. 'You and your men are dismissed.'

Lymond lifted his eyebrows, but made no audible rejoinder. Turning to the dais, he bowed, and Blacklock, Guthrie and Hoddim in turn did the same. The Tsar, still chatting, half lifted his right hand in acknowledgement. They had almost retired to the doors when he turned fully round, raised a finger and said something with mild force to Adashev. The courtier rose, bowed, and walking smoothly, caught up with Lymond. Adashev smiled, and spoke.

'Oh *Christ*,' said Adam under his breath, cut off like a deaf mute from all adult comprehension.

Guthrie, beside him, grinned and murmured, but not loudly enough to be overheard, 'It's all right. Lymond has been commanded to Adashev's house for further discussion, while we are to return to our quarters. You aren't dealing with Scots or English or Italians, you know.'

It was Guthrie also who enlightened them all, back in the building they shared, and answered Adam's questions, and those of Plummer and d'Harcourt and the others who had not been present. 'The contract is still open. Ivan won't decide until after Adashev's meeting with Lymond.'

'Christ,' said Danny Hislop, 'with the Angry Eye?'

'What?' said Guthrie sharply.

'Boyar Plummer here,' said Danny, 'was anxious to know. Were you in the Uspenski? Did you see the Rublev frescoes? The Virgin of the Don? Christ with the Angry Eye?'

'Which was the Uspenski?' said Fergie Hoddim with interest. 'Yon tall, plain one at the end with the five gold-leaf onions?'

'Fioravanti,' said Lancelot Plummer, driven to intervene in the interests of culture. 'The Uspenski Cathedral, re-designed seventy-five years ago by Aristotle Fioravanti from Bologna in white Kama sandstone and used for coronations and all State ceremonials. My God, you must have noticed it.'

'From Bologna?' said Fergie, surprised. 'Think of the price! Had they no Russian architects?'

'The Cathedral of St Michael Archangel,' said Plummer kindly, 'built by Alevisio of Milan. The Granovitaya Palace and the Kremlin walls, built by Marco Ruffo and Pietro Solario. They had Russian architects begin work on the new Uspenski before they called in Fioravanti. They called in Fioravanti when the new walls fell down.'

'If,' said Adam, 'we could get back to the Tsar . . . ?'

'Well, you saw what happened,' said Guthrie. 'He asked the sort of questions any hard-headed statesman would think of. Where had we all learned our profession; how long had we been together; what nationality were we all; what battles had we taken part in, and whom had we fought for. What religion did we subscribe to. Were we traders. Why had we left France in the first place. And what had Lymond been doing in Turkey.'

'*Mon dieu,*' said Ludovic d'Harcourt gently.

'*À l'oeil fâcheux,*' said Danny Hislop. 'What did he say?'

'The truth,' Guthrie said placidly. 'More or less. That we owe allegiance to no single master. That we fight for money and France has not enough money to satisfy us. That we have never taken arms against the Scottish nation, to which many of us belong, or for the Turk, whose faith none of us holds, but that were we to be munificently paid, we might do even that. And that we have no interest in trading.'

'Speaking for himself,' said Lancelot Plummer.

'Speaking for all of us,' said Guthrie bluntly. 'The English have opened up a new shipping route by the Frozen Sea to the north coast of Russia. Their pilot Chancellor was in Moscow last year. Ivan doesn't want a hopeful new prospect blighted by local disputes with the natives. If the English want to trade here, we help them.'

'There's a point,' said Fergie Hoddim, 'that I'd advise ye to give suit and presence to before you argue much further. If Lymond has asked for more money than the Russians are willing to pay, you don't suppose they're going to stand by and watch us stroll away to offer our catholic services to Poland or Lithuania or Turkey?'

'That, of course, is the risk,' said Guthrie blandly. 'It all depends on whether our friend has judged the market correctly. I won't tell you the conditions he laid down. It would upset your digestion.'

They were in their dining hall, sitting or standing about him as he leaned half-hitched against the long table. Adam said, 'My digestion died on me as it is, somewhere in the Baltic. What went wrong? Why the bristle and snap at the end?'

'The Tsar,' said Alec forbearingly, 'said that no high-born prince in his realm, or even the Blessed Head of his Most Holy Church, had ever laid claim to fees of such magnitude.'

'And Lymond?'

'Said that this was possibly why, as he had observed, the Crimean Tartars had been driven out neither by a princely campaign nor by a miracle.'

'Oh Mary Mother of God.' Adam closed his eyes.

'He wished to make an impression,' said Hislop, with a blandness quite equal to Guthrie's. 'Let us hope . . .'

He broke off. Adam looked at him quickly.

'. . . that he makes the right one?' said Guthrie, smoothly filling the pause. He had risen from the table, raising his hand. At the unspoken signal, Plummer rose also and swiftly and silently took his place by the door to the staircase, while d'Harcourt and Vassey moved to the head of the steep inner stairs to the kitchens.

Danny Hislop said, 'What's more, I suppose we have to wait dinner until his lordship returns?'

And Adam heard again what had barely reached him before: the finest paring of sound from the inner chamber: the long room where their bedding and all their possessions were stored, and whose high casement windows gave on to the back yard alone.

When they had all gathered here, they had left the inner room empty. A thief, then, after the foreigners' money? Or the weapons left in their store-chests?

Except that they were wearing their weapons, and wore them day and night, wherever they were, muffled under their cloaks and their clothing, since the day when Danny Hislop had propounded a certain hypothetical scheme of defence and Lymond, not hypothetically at all, had desired them to keep it before them.

So now, Danny Hislop, his hazel eyes sparkling, took up his position on one side of that closed, inner door, with Fergie Hoddim grim at the other; and Adam himself, keeping out of the line of the windows, edged beside Plummer and looked down through the small opaque casement, at the outside steps which led to their door.

The steps were deserted, and so was the yard. But as he watched, the cold spring light glinted, for a second, on something hard and metallic which glanced past the balustrade and then vanished. Then the sun struck through the cloud and he saw, for an instant, a dancing pattern of light on the rough brick wall of the yard, which made him throw up his hands to draw Guthrie's attention through the covering patter of chat, and then open his fingers to denote numbers. Not a sneak-thief. Not a raid by underprivileged Muscovites. But a full-scale attack by three to four dozen men under arms.

And the only armed men in Moscow were the Streltsi, the hackbutters of the Sovereign Grand Prince of Russia.

Plummer, sighing, left his post at a signal and helped them lift the oak dining table against the outer door he had

44

been guarding. 'I fear,' he said, 'our dear commander has committed some blunder.'

Their hackbuts were in the inner room – all except one, with its stand and charges which had been hidden with care in this chamber. It was already out and charged and d'Harcourt was standing beside it, match in hand, when Guthrie gave the signal, and Fergie flung open the door.

Their handgun looked straight into the mouth of another, already set up in their sleeping chamber, with half a dozen fully armed men crowded about it, and more climbing in through the windows. Then Guthrie said, 'Fire!' And in that first shattering moment of surprise d'Harcourt's hackbut exploded, blowing up the Muscovite weapon in a roar of red flame, and hurling the helmeted Streltsi back shouting against the walls and the beds. Then Guthrie sprang through the doorway, and, followed by the small silent team from St Mary's, set upon the intruders with dagger and sword.

They were trained to kill. They were trained to fight at close quarters against curved swords and straight; and against no weapons at all. They were trained to study other men's minds; to watch their eyes; to forestall their actions. They fought, guarding each other's backs, with heavier swords and faster dagger hands : they trusted one another to fight, choosing and passing on victims as fitted the chance of the moment; and reached and cleared the window in the first three minutes of action, thrusting down the tall ladder which scaled it and sending the last climbers shouting into the yard. And at the same time, they watched and listened behind them, so that when Plummer called they were ready for brisk part-withdrawal, leaving four of their men fighting the dwindling numbers in the bedchamber while the rest raced back into the dining hall.

'Another dozen, perhaps, on the steps,' Plummer said, his face quite composed. 'And a group of archers have appeared in the yard. Waiting for us to rush out with our foreign tails burning.'

The sound of fighting was less in the inner room. Fergie Hoddim appeared, with the clacking of swordblades behind him, and said, 'That's them all, just about. The other two jumped out the window. Danny Hislop's getting the hackbuts.'

And so it came about that when the Streltsi swept up the

45

steps and launched their first open attack on the main first-floor doorway, they were met with the thundering mouths of St Mary's hackbuts at each casement window, followed by the whistling flight of their arrows, so that they withdrew, pulling their wounded men with them, and re-formed out of range for the next move.

They had a dozen handguns between them, and a fair store of matches and powder; their swords and a bow each, with arrows. Alec Guthrie recharged the hackbuts and set bows to guard every window, pushing the Muscovite dead and wounded out of the way and clearing the shattered remains of the hackbut, while they reviewed the situation between them.

They had suffered no serious casualties. Unless the Streltsi brought heavy-bore cannon, they could hope to beat off meantime any attack from the front or the rear. No attempt had been made to enter from below, and there seemed no point in trying themselves to descend to the kitchens : it was certain death to step into the yard. And even if they could fight their way to the horses, there were still the streets to get through, and three sets of gateways, all of them guarded. How well, they had good reason to know.

'So?' said Danny Hislop. 'Our powder and arrows are going to run out on us some time. And so are our food and water and joie de vivre and good books and everything. Why not walk out now and get made into somebody's favourite slave?'

Alec Guthrie said, in his brittle, lecturer's voice. 'It's simple. If the Tsar isn't going to accept us, then we're expendable, and nothing can save us. If, on the other hand, he is not yet decided . . .'

'Then the way we act here will decide him,' said Danny Hislop. 'We're on exhibition.'

Guthrie's craggy, grey-bearded face looked at him. 'Pray,' he said, 'that we are on exhibition. And that when the time comes, someone out there has authority to declare the demonstration concluded.'

'Lymond?' said Danny Hislop. 'No, of course; he's spending the morning with Adashev. After we're dead, will they keep him, do you think, as a keepsake? Or do you think he suggested the whole splendid idea in the first place?'

No one answered him, for the arrows had started again

46

to arch through the windows and a call from Fergie behind told that the archers, protected now by a rampart of benches, had spread out to ring the whole house. Then the hackbut fire started again from the yard, and Plummer cursed and Alan Vassey, leaning out with his bow, fell back suddenly without a sound and was caught by his friend Ludovic d'Harcourt and lowered uselessly to the ground; the first of the eight men to die.

*

'And so,' said Alexei Adashev, 'you have small interest in us as a nation?'

'I had small interest in France,' Lymond said. 'I have none in Russia, save to study the minds of the men I have to serve, and the habits of those I must train to serve me.'

'The only man you must serve,' said Adashev, 'is the Sovereign Grand Prince Ivan Vasilievich.' With half a dozen of the Chosen Council he was sitting within the painted walls of his large timber house in the Kremlin, his ringed fingers holding the embossed standing-cup of clear liquid with which they had all been served. Richly but soberly dressed in cuffed hat and high-buttoned robe, he lacked the restless vitality of the princes: Kurbsky, Kurlyatev, Paletsky in their cut velvet and fur and glossy, insolent beards.

Instead, he turned his pock-marred face with its soft earth-brown beard towards Lymond and added, 'You have heard, no doubt, how the Tsar suffered as a motherless boy from the arrogance of the boyars, and how he took his revenge as a lad. All that is behind him. When the fire came seven years ago, the people said it was caused by his mother's family, the Glinsky, who had sprinkled the streets with human hearts soaked in water. Incited by the boyars hostile to the Glinsky, they demanded the execution of the Tsar's people: they hunted Yuri Glinsky, his uncle, and killed him in the Uspenski Cathedral, here in the Kremlin, where he had fled to the altar for sanctuary. Our Sovereign Prince put down that rising. Then he confessed the sins of his boyhood, and asked the forgiveness of the clergy; and granted forgiveness in turn to the princes and boyars who had crossed him. He spoke to his people, whom he called from all the towns of Muscovy two years later, and promised them, henceforth he would be their judge and their defender.'

Prince Kurbsky stirred. 'You should,' he remarked, 'quote our friend Peresvetov. *In whatever realm there is justice, there God abides and gives it great aid; and God's wrath is not visited on that realm.*'

'Ivashka Peresvetov,' said the princely voice of Kurlyatev, with equal suavity, 'is one of our best-known reformers. He has equally said, *There cannot be a ruler without terror. Like a steed under the rider without a bridle, so is a realm without terror.* The people agreed with him. The boyars less so. And you, Mr Crawford of Lymond?'

Viscovatu was there, but Lymond had not so far needed his services. Except for the long-installed merchants; the trading colonies of German and Flemish on the western edges of Russia, he was the first alien with whom they had thus been able to converse in their own language at first encounter. It was none of their business to show any awareness of the richness and style of his clothing, or the lack of any shade of the supplicant in his answers, his manner, his voice.

They had given him nothing to eat, but had refilled his cut over again with *berozevites*, the delicate drink drawn from the root of the birch tree. And since custom demanded it, they had drunk cup for cup with him themselves.

Only in Alexei Adashev, perhaps, the lightest sheen on the skin so far betrayed it. The princes, pressing a little now with the chilly, delicate probing, might have been empty of all things but malice. Lymond, with years of experience behind him, showed nothing he did not wish to show. He raised his silvery brows. 'Some respond to the goad,' he said, 'and some to the hayrack. The art of ruling is to know which is which. As the art of teaching is to know where to learn.'

'You think us backward,' said Andrei Kurbsky. 'Alas, what can we show to the contrary, except perhaps the small success of Astrakhan and Kazan?'

'I wish to learn from you,' Lymond said. 'There is nothing about the military art in the west that my officers are ignorant of. They do not know how to fight in the cold. They do not know how to speak to the mind of a Muscovite. I want the help and advice of every commander who has fought for the Tsar. And I want those who have never yet fought for the Tsar to join me in learning. You spoke of Peresvetov the reformer. He came to you from Lithuania, Wallachia, Bohemia. He had even fought on the side of the Turk. I want Prince Vishnevetsky.'

'The Cossacks?' Adashev said.

'Would you rather they fought with the Tartars?' Lymond said.

There was a little pause. Adashev, stirring himself, raised a finger and the tall-hatted servant moving forward filled Lymond's stemmed cup yet again, and that of his master and guests. Lymond raised his, savouring it, and then, tilting it, drank it straight off, the gem on his hard finger flaring blue with the movement. Kurbsky, smiling, and Adashev more slowly, did the same. 'And the boyars?' said Kurbsky.

'Leave the boyars to me,' Lymond said. 'They have had enough of the hayrack. I shall show them the scourge. When I have finished with the Streltsi the boyars will curtsey like girls when they pass in the street.'

*

By afternoon there were six of them left, but only five of them standing. Fergie Hoddim, his leg broken by hot flying metal, was dragging himself from window to window, his hackbut resting propped on the sill. Ludovic d'Harcourt, his shoulder pierced a long time ago by an arrow, had bled, moving about, till he fainted. Plummer and Guthrie were whole, though scarred as they all were with flying fragments and blistered into the bargain. The debris had come from the gaping holes in the side of the building, where they had survived several balls from a field-piece. The blisters had come from the inner doorway, held by Adam and one of his fellows, which had burst suddenly open and exposed them to a long, shuddering canopy of glistening, bubbling oil.

One man, Brown, had died under it. Adam, the skin sloughed off his arm, was fighting with his teeth sunk in the raw flesh which closed them, and the pallid skin dark round his eyes. Ludovic d'Harcourt lay beside him, the extent of his wound still unknown.

'More,' said Alec Guthrie.

Adam forced himself to look up. The men in the yard had been reinforced once already. Inside, they might have suffered; but the dying and the dead on the steps and at the foot of the windows told that St Mary's had inflicted the damage that, against odds, they had been taught how to do. But against fresh fodder, bigger guns, the frenzy of men who, failing their ruler, would strangle themselves over their cannon, there was no prospect now except death. 'Your godly and marvellous leader,' said Danny Hislop, rising like a cold smiling ghost at his elbow, 'has made a masterly ruin of this one. I have six arrows left, and there's nothing more we can do with the hackbuts. I have a suggestion. We have oil. We have tinder. We have bed sheets. And the houses of this quaintly old-fashioned city are constructed almost entirely of wood. . . .'

'But . . .' said Adam.

'There is,' said Fergie Hoddim plainly from the floor, 'a choice, *ipso facto*, of action. If we have merely been put to the test we can parley.'

'You're mad,' Plummer said. 'You still think this is a trial?' He stopped, arrow in hand. 'I wonder if Blacklock and d'Harcourt think it's a trial. Or Vassey or Brown, come to that. I hope it is. I hope they ring a bell soon. We're running out of people and stamina.'

Guthrie turned. He said, 'Do you want to surrender and risk it?'

Plummer hesitated. Danny Hislop answered for him. 'No,' he said through his teeth. 'Bloody hell, no. We don't surrender. If it's a test, we don't surrender. And if it's a slaughter, we give them as good as we get. I say, fire the arrows.'

'It's a city of wood,' Adam said. 'There are thirty thousand houses out there, full of men and women and children.'

'Fair enough,' said Danny Hislop. 'And a good proportion are trying to kill me. Excuse me while I protest.' And lighting the first fire arrow he waited, and on Guthrie's grim signal nocked, pulled, and loosed it to fly over the street with the others.

*

'You wish a house for your officers at Kitaigorod, and a military establishment also at Vorobiovo, where the Streltsi are already quartered. Should men and officers live then in two different suburbs?'

'Three,' said Lymond with flat-toned and lizard-eyed patience. 'I require a house for myself in the Kremlin.'

One of the princes said, hard-voiced and smiling, 'The Kremlin is for the Tsar and his court and his treasure.'

'Then it should have a lock,' Lymond said. 'And a key to turn in the lock.'

The Prince called Paletsky rose slowly to his feet. 'An iron door needs an iron lock,' he observed. 'Not a lock of quick gold cast over with diamonds. You make the demands of a conquering nation.'

'I thought I spoke to a conquering nation,' Lymond said. He rose, and Adashev and the rest of the Chosen rose with him. Outside, a noise had begun to intrude on their notice : a distant noise, as if many feet were hurrying, half in regular march, over the flat paths of logs which linked corner to more distant corner of the triangular sloping hill of the Kremlin. A voice called an order.

Lymond said, 'Don't you know yet what has happened while you lay under two hundred years of Tartar rule? Men have made such strides that you can hardly imagine them. Painting, science, writing, music and medicine, the rule of the sea and the stars, the working of metal, the making of ships and of engines . . . all the guidelines you once knew have vanished and new ones are being made. And it is with gold and with diamonds that the kings of the earth are acquiring them.'

Lymond looked at Alexei Adashev, and pitched his voice above the nearing hubbub of men. 'I come to sell the Tsar power. Without it, all the things I have mentioned are quite out of his reach and yours.'

The double doors, crashing open, screamed on their hinges. Men with axes, pinning them back, allowed other armed men to thrust into the room, islanding in silence the single robed figure with chains and rings and tall sable-trimmed hat, who stood alone on the threshold against the jostling backdrop of his soldiers.

'You have come to sell me despoilment and discord,' said the Tsar Ivan Vasilievich, and, raising a powerful hand heavy with rings, pointed at Lymond. 'Hang him.'

There was a long knife in Lymond's hand. It flashed there before the eyes of the Tsar, in whose city of Moscow no foreigner might walk abroad armed, and Andrei Kurbsky said sharply, 'Treason!' and flung himself from his knees. By the Tsar the halberdiers started to run, axe-blades glittering. But Ivan, grasping them, called harshly, 'Stop!'

For Lymond had not paused to bend his knee. Instead

51

he had plunged his hand deep in the long earth-brown hair of the man kneeling beside him, and dragging back his head, presented the thin knife, sliding red across the soft bearded throat of the Tsar's favourite. 'Let us discover,' said Lymond, 'who wishes to see Alexei Adashev dead.'

The princes froze. As if confronted with spells, the uplifted swords halted. Axes lowered; heads turned to the Tsar. The pale, china-blue eyes, rimmed with white, stared, speechlessly, disbelieving, while the hinged knuckles closed white on each imperial hand. 'May dogs defile your mother,' Ivan Vasilievich said, deep in his chest. 'Free my officer.'

With a grip whose cracking power they could hear, Lymond drew the Tsar's chief adviser to his feet, the knife steady throughout at his throat. Adashev, his hat fallen, his eyes slitted under creased brows, did not try to speak. Lymond said evenly, 'I have no quarrel with Adashev. He is my security for justice. Or is it Russian justice to hang out of hand those who come to do her a service?'

Under the dark sabled hat, a pulse beat in the Tsar's blood-darkened skin and his bearded lips moved, unconsciously, as the air whistled like an organ bladder, clapped from his lungs. He raised his clenched fist and extended it, fingers rigid, in Lymond's face. 'Twenty of my men lie out there, killed by scourings of sewers; the animals you bring me to sell their abominations for gold. I listened to you,' said Ivan, the breath tearing his chest, 'and twenty Russians have died. It burns my soul as with aloeswood.' And clenching his fist, he gave a cry which burst upon the low-ceilinged room. 'My people have died!'

Untouched, his hands pressing the blade to the body of Adashev, the foreigner answered unmoving. 'Twenty of your men would barely match three of my company. You should have sent more,' he said.

'Free my officer.' The Tsar disembowelled the air with a splayed and whistling hand. '*Free him!* If you touch this man I, Ivan, will knout you. I will roast your flayed back like dogs' meat on charcoal. You will be seethed in the cauldrons of pig-keepers and your half-strung bones made to dance for the bears. I will harness you to my horses and harrow you over the teeth of a flintbed until your body is milled flesh and bone meal and your face is a boll of raw silk ... *Free him!*'

'When you have heard me,' Lymond said. Behind him, slowly, Paletsky was moving, his hands open and ready. There was a sharp movement. Prince Kurbsky had stopped him, his hand falling hard on Paletsky, his eyes on the Tsar. No one else in the room stirred. *Let us discover,* Lymond had said, *who wishes to see Alexei Adashev dead.*

Francis Crawford did not turn round. But on the long, inflexible mouth there rested the faintest trace of a smile. Ivan said, 'Do strangers enter my city and hack down my Streltsi unpunished?'

'Twenty killed,' said a deep voice behind him. 'And as many more injured.' Sylvester, the Tsar's other adviser, had also entered.

'It is the privilege of your men to die for the Emperor,' Lymond said. 'It is the licence of mine to defend themselves.'

The black-robed figure of the monk stepped forward to the Tsar's side. 'My sovereign lord speaks of a killing. He does not speak of twenty men slaughtered by eight as an act of defence.'

'My sovereign lord,' said Lymond, 'does not know my officers in the execution of their orders. I will make three assertions. My men were attacked unprovoked by the Streltsi. They were outnumbered ten times by the Streltsi. And even now they have neither been taken alive nor surrendered.'

Behind him the princes said nothing. The halberdiers, standing uneasily, stared across from wall to wall of the room. The chief counsellor Adashev, his throat straining, swallowed and choked in the silence, and blood ran down, a bright thready stream, where his skin moved on the knife. The Tsar said, his neck and wide shoulders rigid, 'And did they act by your orders when they set fire to my city of Moscow?'

The moan ran round the room, invisible, from every throat, and movement followed: a recoil; a slow undulation of horror from men whose dreams still burned red in the night with the nightmare of seven years before, when Moscow flamed like a basket of coals. Lymond said, clearly, in Russian, 'They acted under my orders.'

The ring of men moved in on him sharply. The Tsar himself took a stride forward, and for a moment the hard fingers threatening Adashev's life tightened their grip on the dagger. The Emperor's wide nostrils stretched, and

53

he drew in bubbling air like a child who had been weeping. And in his voice, when he spoke, there was a sob. 'Alexei, forgive me. Forgive me, Alexei, but he must die.'

Lymond said, 'Alexei Adashev must die because my men are not milksops or cowards? Because they are trained as no other soldiers in Europe are trained? Because they are resourceful; because they obey orders? Yours had no skill to trap them – how should they have? They have never been taught. Were mine to wait like women to be overrun as the Tartar overran you, and die in their flower for nothing?'

The rolling voice of Sylvester cried out. 'Can eight men murder a city?'

'There is no limit to what we can do,' Lymond said, 'if you make us your enemy. There are no bounds to what we may achieve, if you call us your servants and friends. How widely spread is the fire?'

Sylvester answered. 'In two streets of Kitaigorod.'

'And where are my men?'

'There in the house. Those that are living.'

'Then, said Lymond, 'I will lead you to them, if you desire it. And we shall put this fire out, if you will protect us. When it is out, we shall require no protection, for the people will know us. They will see that we have your confidence; they will observe how you reward the services we perform for you: they will come to us to be fashioned as the men who today held off the Streltsi, the best of your troops. And they will thank their prince who provides them with such watchdogs, and the hunter who gives them such hounds. . . . Will my sovereign lord call Alexei Adashev?'

The Tsar stood very still. Only the big ringed hand, moving up and down jerkily, rasped on the jewelled brocade of the long over-robe. Then the hand fell to his side and he spoke deep in his throat. 'Alexei?'

Lymond's knife moved slowly down. For a moment the counsellor stayed where he was. Then he straightened, his eyes shut, his fingers laid over his throat while Lymond's iron grip held him. Then he sighed, open-mouthed, and unclosing his eyes, walked forward while Lymond's hand fell and Lymond's arms were seized, instantly, by Kurbsky. Francis Crawford looked down, once, at the alien grasp on his elbows and then stood still, contempt on his face, and watched the Tsar only.

Alexei Adashev reached his master, and the Emperor's two arms stretched out to grasp him. For a moment they stood, face to face; then Adashev spoke. 'Let him go free.'

The Tsar's bearded face stared at him without speaking. Then he said, 'You say so?'

Alexei Adashev slowly dropped his blood-spotted hand from his collar. 'I say so,' he said. 'For there is an effrontery which will bring us to maggots; or to conquest sweet as the magic well, which shall never want water.'

The Tsar listened. The Tsar put aside the counsellor and standing once more still in his place, spoke to Lymond. 'Franzei.'

It was the term given to all foreigners : to the Italians who had rebuilt the Kremlin : to the rare ambassadors who had been suffered to approach the sovereign lord. Prince Kurbsky released Lymond's arms, and slowly Lymond moved forward; paused; and knelt.

'You may kiss my hand,' Ivan said, deep in his throat.

Brazen and bright in the sunlight, Lymond's burnished head bent, and his lips brushed Ivan's outstretched hand.

'You may kiss my foot,' said the Tsar.

Unstirring, Lymond remained for a moment, head bent. Then, smoothly stooping, he kissed also Ivan's red slippered foot.

'Remain,' said the Emperor; and his voice thickened suddenly. He held out his hand. 'An axe.'

Adashev make to speak, and was still. It was the monk who took from an escort his silver, long-handled axe and placed it with care within the Tsar's heavy, imperious hand. Lymond, kneeling, did not look up.

Ivan Vasilievich lifted the axe with both arms. The sun sent a shaft like sea-dazzle to blaze on the silver, and lit the gathered silk robe of the still, kneeling man and the curved head and the pale, unprotected arch of the neck. Then the Tsar cried out and swung the blade down with all the strength of his powerful shoulders.

It bit through the skin of the floor, as into chickenskin, not an inch from Lymond's unmoving body. It had shuddered itself into stillness before Lymond stirred and in silence lifted his eyes to the mantled face of Ivan Vasilievich.

'You are forgiven,' said Ivan.

*

55

Through the black, clouded air and the glare of fire and the distant screaming of voices, four men of St Mary's saw their commander ride into the yard, and the bright helms of the Tsar's guard behind him. And Danny Hislop, with a handful of arrows, fitted one with exhausted care to his bow and, raising it, aimed straight at Lymond. Then Guthrie's hand leaned on his shoulder, but still he did not lower the barb.

It was in his hands still when Lymond came up the brick staircase, and when Plummer, in silence, cleared the door and opened it for Francis Crawford, every man on his feet held his sword still unsheathed in his grasp.

Lymond looked round at them all, and then, walking inside, said, 'Brown and Vassey?'

'Dead,' said Alec Guthrie. 'D'Harcourt and Hoddim are in the other room, wounded.'

The Indian silks, flecked with charcoal, were otherwise as fresh as in the morning : the seed pearls glimmered creamily. Lymond said, 'How many men came against you?'

'Forty, perhaps,' Plummer said. 'It was hard to see.'

'We were busy,' said Hislop.

Alec Guthrie said slowly, 'Who sent them? They were Streltsi.'

'The Tsar,' said Lymond. He opened the inner door, glancing at the wreck of the room and d'Harcourt, lying unconscious on one of the beds. On another, covered with rubbish, Hoddim was staring at him. Lymond turned back. 'He wanted to see if you would jump when he pricked you. The excessive zeal, I rather imagine, was the work of the boyars. Not everyone wants to see the Tsar with his own private army. Considering the odds, you seem to have achieved quite a massacre.'

'Do you mind?' Hislop said; and the impersonal blue eyes travelled to him.

'Politically speaking, it was a mistake. It makes it impossible for the Tsar to take his own people to task.'

Guthrie said suddenly, 'Will you tell me something? Did you know this was going to happen?'

'What are you asking me?' Lymond said. 'Did I know something of the sort was likely to happen? Yes, I did. I was under the impression that I had warned you. Did I know it was to happen this morning? No, I didn't : I have been informed only this moment. Did I have a fruitful morning drinking wine with the Council? Certainly, I did: and I have promised that those of you still surviving should come with me now, and as a gesture of forgiveness and goodwill, put out the fires which you started.'

'*And be damned to that!*' said Adam Blacklock into the silence.

'Because . . .?' said Alec Guthrie with patience.

'Because you are the new officers in charge of the Streltsi, as of this moment. The contract is for five years. For each of these five years the Tsar will house you, feed and clothe and equip you and pay you in gold or in kind the equal of four thousand roubles. If it was a trial,' Lymond said, 'you have apparently passed it. If it was an action, you have undoubtedly won it. If we have had losses, the fault is the nation's and that is what we are going to remedy. What happened this morning can never happen again. And whatever we think of the boyars, we cannot afford to sacrifice, at this moment, the goodwill of the city of Moscow.'

Plummer said, '*Four thousand roubles!*'

'Quite,' said Danny Hislop with a terrible brightness. 'It makes quite a difference, Maeve, doesn't it?'

CHAPTER FOUR

In October Philippa Somerville, a stickler for the more remote social graces, decided to write to her husband from Scotland.

It was to be a long, newsy letter, effective in spelling and conveying inexplicitly in its latter pages an explicit injunction from his mother to come home at once.

The fact that Francis Crawford's mother had made no such request and before she did so would bleed in her coffin like pie-meat was a matter of minor importance. So also was the truth that, having written the letter, Francis Crawford's child-bride had no idea in the world where to send it. For the one thing made clear to Philippa during her long stay that year at Midculter was that Lymond's return was needed and quickly, for the sake of Sybilla.

She never spoke of her son. It was noticeable, too, how seldom she allowed herself close to her grandson Kuzúm, now briskly tolerated by a concourse of violent black-headed cousins, and cared for in nurseries full of smiling, soft-handed women. Philippa, who had thought Kuzúm all her own but for the birth-pangs, saw with loving resignation the ties being loosed as his need for her now became less, and Kate saw more of the child now than she did.

But it was in pursuit of a straying Kuzúm that Philippa one day unlocked the door of a tower and climbing up, abruptly diverted, found herself in a round, airy room looking on the moat, with a low bed, and a chest, and a desk, and shelf upon shelf of worn papers and books.

They were not dusty, although the air smelt unused and the thin woollen stuff of the bedding felt damp to the touch. There was no fireplace and no means of heating. She took down a volume at random.

The round, unformed script on the fly-leaf said, *Francis Crawford of Lymond*. She stared at it; then put it down and picked up another. The writing in this one was older; the neat level hand she had seen once before, in Stamboul. This time it said only, *The Master of Culter*.

That dated it after the death of his father, when until the birth of Richard's son Kevin, the heir's rank and title were Lymond's. And all the books were his, too. She scanned them : some works in English; others in Latin and Greek, French, Italian and Spanish. . . . Prose and verse. The classics, pressed together with folios on the sciences, theology, history; bawdy epistles and dramas; books on war and philosophy; the great legends. Sheets and volumes and manuscripts of unprinted music. Erasmus and St Augustine, Cicero, Terence and Ptolemy, Froissart and Barbour and Dunbar; Machiavelli and Rabelais, Bude and Bellenden, Aristotle and Copernicus, Duns Scotus and Seneca.

Gathered over the years; added to on infrequent visits; the evidence of one man's eclectic taste. And if one studied it, the private labyrinth, book upon book, from which the child Francis Crawford had emerged, contained, formidable, decorative as his deliberate writing, as the Master of Culter. The Master of Culter who had been outlawed from Church and from State, accused once of murder and treason. Who had forced his way into Flaw Valleys and questioned her, a child of ten, while Kate begged for her, weeping. To whom she was married.

There were more books in an aumbry, set flush in the

wainscoting, and something else Philippa drew out and looked at. A lute, the strings long since gone or decayed, and a great splintered scar on the pearwood.

She touched it, compassionately, and was reminded of chipped and gouged timber she had noticed elsewhere, on the lowest panels of the nail-studded door, as if a boot had struck them, again and again. She shivered, as the bleak cold of the room struck through her lightly gowned body, and lifting the books, slid them back in their place.

A voice said, 'Take them, Philippa, if you have a fancy to read them. They were acquired with great pains, and it seems a pity to see them spoil now.' White-haired, blue-eyed; unblemished as fine fragile porcelain, the Dowager stood in the doorway and watched her, her face unclouded by anger or any kind of distress.

Philippa said plainly, 'I didn't mean to intrude. I thought Mr Crawford's room was downstairs.'

'It is,' said Sybilla. 'But before his father died, he slept here. And even after he moved, he liked to keep it. But it is cold.'

'I should like to read them,' said Philippa. She ran her hand softly along the limp leather bindings. 'I haven't Latin.'

'You could learn, if you want to,' said Sybilla. 'Wisdom is considered a durable asset. Did your governess address you like this?'

'She addressed Kate like that,' Philippa answered. 'And Kate said wisdom took many forms and she preferred the less expensive variety. We hadn't much money.'

'But a great deal of wisdom,' said Sybilla. Her glance fell on the lute and she fingered it, slowly, as Philippa had done. 'I'm glad the books are here for you. Some of the damage has been beyond me to mend.'

So began Philippa's second education, guided by the ancient priest who long before had first taught Sybilla's own two sons and her dead daughter. And, although no more was said, on that day was born her determination to write somehow to Mr Crawford her husband.

It was not an easy letter to frame. Kate had left, taking Kuzúm to Flaw Valleys with the Scots girl who, these past weeks, had tended him. It had relieved, subtly, the strain they all saw in Sybilla, and at first Philippa thought that she herself would be better, too, out of the way, but it was not so: in overseeing her work Sybilla, it seemed, found a pleasure remembered from the distant days of her own young family. So, without her mother's good sense and guidance, Philippa wrote her laborious letter to Francis Crawford, mentioning the weather, the harvest and what Kevin had done to Lucy and Lucy had done back. She referred, casually, to Kuzúm and then found, blowing her nose, that she had devoted four close-written pages to him. She added, hastily, an item of gossip about Jenny Fleming and then concluded with a paragraph which was intended to convey, skilfully, the unspoken need of his mother. She then signed it, *Your obedient servant,* PHILIPPA SOMERVILLE before she realized what she had said, and decided, on hasty reflection to leave it.

He could take it, if he noticed the wording at all, as an affirmation that Philippa Somerville, at any rate, would provide no impediment to his marriage plans. Assuming he wanted to marry. She read the letter through, looked up three words, and sealed and addressed it in French and Turkish and Latin, with all his various titles. Then she waited for Austin Grey to call, which he did every Tuesday, and put it into his care to be transmitted to London, and thence to a certain monastery in Volos, Greece, addressed to a wandering child of the road named Míkál. Whether it would reach him, and whether, receiving it, he would trouble to find Mr Crawford, was in the lap of the same gods who had taken her to Volos in the first place. About her other, personal intentions towards solving Mr Crawford's undoubted and most pressing problems, she said nothing whatever to anyone.

Doggedly embroiled in Latin and Greek, and reading her way privately through Aretino, she remained, helping Sybilla with her entertaining and twice, on Sybilla's shrewd insistence, making her appearance at the Edinburgh court of the Queen Dowager Mary of Lorraine. Since Lymond had induced her to marry him, she was to be seen, decreed Sybilla, to have the dignities of marriage. She was introduced therefore to the remotest members of Lymond's family in her extraordinary persona of Philippa Crawford of Lymond, Countess of Sevigny, and learned to keep a straight face while being so addressed.

Indeed, from the family tree she cajoled out of Richard, it seemed that only two senior members escaped the privilege of meeting the absent Lymond's well-educated bride. One of these was Sybilla's only surviving sister, a Semple from Ayrshire, who had taken Holy Orders thirty years before and was now Abbess of an opulent foundation in that county. The other was a great-uncle of Lymond's on his grandmother's side, about whom Philippa questioned her brother-in-law narrowly.

Richard, 3rd Baron Culter, was much amused. 'He's about a hundred and ten.'

'I don't see,' said Philippa, 'what's so funny. He's still your great-uncle. You mean he's senile?'

'I dare say he is,' Richard said. 'But I wouldn't know. We don't correspond.'

'I don't know who you do correspond with,' said Philippa acidly. 'It seems to me that you have no family feeling whatever for anyone outside the walls of this house.'

Richard agreed. 'You ought to know by now that everyone in Scotland is related to everyone else. It doesn't necessarily mean that we like one another.'

'And what's wrong with your great-uncle?' asked Philippa, who was not easily removed from a point.

Richard sighed. 'Nothing, apart from a brief lapse in judgement. He accepted English money from the late King Henry's Privy Council in return for some detailed information about King James's affairs, and was found out. He decided life would be safer and pleasanter if he made his home henceforward in England.'

'Dear me,' said Philippa after a pause. 'I'm sorry.'

'It happens in the best families,' said Richard cheerfully. Sobering a little under his sister-in-law's thoughtful brown eye, he said, 'It perhaps explains why my father was quite so hard on Francis. Although he always maintained his uncle was ill done by, and used to send him money, I believe, up to the time that he died. His name is Bailey. Leonard Bailey.'

'I know. Where does he stay?' Philippa asked.

But that Richard could not tell her. Sensibly relegating it therefore to the foot of her list of priorities, Philippa found occasion instead to visit her friend Agnes Herries and her seven children at Terregles, calling on her way back at the convent of SS Winning and Mary.

The Abbess, a tall pallid woman, turned out to be catastrophically lacking in her sister's nimbleness and delicacy both of body and wit. After keeping Philippa waiting for some considerable time, she sent for her and surveyed her without particular favour. 'To what do I owe the honour of this unheralded visit? Sybilla, I see, has not seen fit to accompany you.'

'She didn't know I was coming. Forgive me,' said Philippa humbly, her sharp brown eyes winsomely pleading. 'I should have known how busy a person of standing must be. We speak of you a great deal at Midculter.'

'I beg leave to doubt it,' the Abbess said, sitting down and indicating at last that Philippa also might take a chair at her desk. 'The Dowager Lady Culter seems to find it convenient to overlook the nearer members of her family. I doubt if she has been here in five years.'

Philippa did not doubt it at all, from Sybilla's rare references to her sister. She also knew, although she did not mention it, exactly how much in goods and endowments Lord Culter and his mother had paid and were paying annually into the foundation's treasury. She said, 'You knew Mr Crawford, I think, as a boy.'

'A gaudy child,' the Abbess said, 'with an insolent tongue. I have heard the tale of your marriage. You have come, I would gather, to question me?'

Proving, thought Philippa, paling, that one does not become an Abbess for nothing. She said, 'Then there is something to tell?'

The shrewd old eyes openly studied her. 'It is usual, I believe, for a husband's circumstances to be known to his bride before marriage?'

'Time was too short,' Philippa said.

'Then my sister has surely informed you?'

'She has said nothing,' Philippa said. 'And I have no right to question her. The marriage was purely a formal one, and will be dissolved shortly.'

'In that case,' said the Abbess, 'by what right are you questioning me? And why, indeed, should there be anything in your husband's life which is not all too blatantly public already?'

'Because,' said Philippa, 'when I returned to Midculter from Turkey, I didn't give a full account of what happened. There was a Frenchwoman as well on that journey, one who joined us in Lyons and stayed with us most of the time until we parted at Volos. Her name was Marthe.'

'I see,' said the Abbess of SS Winning and Mary.

'And,' said Philippa, 'she called herself Lymond's sister.'

There was a silence. Then, 'And did Francis accept that?' said the Abbess.

'He could do nothing else,' said Philippa bluntly. 'If they had been twins, they couldn't have looked more like each other.'

'And you said nothing of this to Sybilla?'

'No,' said Philippa. 'That is why I am here. It is two years, holy mother, since Mr Crawford left Scotland, and there is no sign so far that he intends to return. Lady Culter is not in good health. She depends on this son, and his absence is trying her badly. I think the root of the absence may be his meeting with Marthe.'

'Such revulsion over a by-blow? How did Marthe account for her birth, then?'

'She knew nothing,' Philippa said. 'Except that she had been brought up in Blois by a woman called the Dame de Doubtance.'

'Who died in the winter, leaving Francis a fortune? That I heard also,' the Abbess said. 'And what story do you think would comfort your husband's fears and bring him home to Midculter?'

She had known it was going to be difficult. She had not known how hurtful it could be as well. 'That his mother is all he thought her to be,' Philippa said.

True or not, it was the right answer to give Sybilla's own sister. The Abbess leaned back, and although she said, 'A child's view!' she was not displeased. She said, 'You realize that if his mother is chaste, he himself must then have been born outside marriage?'

'Yes,' said Philippa.

'And you think that knowing that, he will return all the sooner?'

'It won't be public,' said Philippa. 'And in other ways, I doubt if it would weigh with him. He has his own life.'

'And you? You do not object to the stigma?'

'You are what you are,' Philippa said. 'Birth can hardly change it. I want to see Lady Culter content. The rest is no business of mine.'

There followed a long pause. But before it was over she knew what the Abbess was going to say.

'It is true, of course. Perhaps you have heard of Gavin, Sybilla's late husband?'

Philippa nodded.

'After Richard was born, Sybilla ended the marriage.

63

In fact, if not by dissolution. Gavin would never divorce her. But the succession had to be secured. He made sure that there would be other children, and Sybilla recognized them in return for her privacy. Richard was born inside the marriage. The boy and the girl, Francis and his sister Eloise, were base born, of unknown mother or mothers in France, and Sybilla was there for each birth, and brought each child as her own back to Scotland. The pity was that she grew too fond, rearing them.'

'And Marthe?' said Philippa thinly.

The Abbess looked at her. 'The child of your husband's true mother, perhaps. I fear she had the happier part, being raised in her proper degree. . . . You are a girl of spirit.'

'Thank you,' said Philippa dimly.

'But you would be all the better, I think, for some wine. Then, because of what you have heard, I am going to place you on oath. This matter is the concern of one person only : your husband.'

'I know,' said Philippa. 'But I don't know how I'm going to tell him.'

*

Word of what was happening in Russia was slow to travel westwards to Europe. Hercules Tait learned it, in Venice, where he received a communication in educated handwriting which startled him somewhat and led him to cultivate assiduously his friend in the Council of Ten and thereafter to embark on a number of enjoyable letters.

The betting-shops were busy, as Mr Crawford would guess, about the fate of the Pope, Hercules Tait wrote. If age and disorderly living put an end to him, the French would lose a good ally. In England there was no other occupation at present but the cutting off of heads, since Mary Tudor became Queen and brought back the old Catholic religion. The rebels from all the uprisings were fleeing as usual to France or to Germany or to Venice. The Queen's rival William Courtenay was in prison again after fifteen years under duress, accused of trading cipher secrets engraved on the back of a guitar. . . .

The House of Commons, said Hercules Tait, had been begging the Queen not to proceed with her plan to marry Prince Philip of Spain, and had been violently rebuked by Queen Mary, saying she would consult with God on the matter and with nobody else; which greatly disturbed everybody. Even her friend Cardinal Pole had remarked that by the age she was, the Queen should content herself with the spouse who had always stood her in stead of a parent, he being God the Father. *It is doubtful however,* added Hercules Tait cheerfully, *whether this would produce an heir which the distrustful nature of her subjects would accept....*

Carried by many strange and subterranean hands, the letters from Venice passed all summer and autumn from Italy over land and sea into Moscow Other packets travelled the same route from different beginnings. In Brussels an anonymous banker wrote that the old Emperor Charles was better of his long sickness, had revised his will and tried on his armour, and by August had taken the field against France. To the Duke of Alva, negotiating the royal wedding with England, the Emperor had written: *For the love of God see to it that my son behaves in the right manner, for otherwise I tell you I had rather never have taken the matter in hand in the first place.*

From the Comté of Sevigny which belonged to Francis Crawford in France, Nicholas Applegarth wrote: *The small Queen Mary of Scotland is twelve and out of her minority: they speak of a marriage to the Dauphin within four years from now. The Queen Dowager of Scotland writes to her brothers in France that she fears her new Spanish neighbour, if the Queen of England's wedding takes place.... And in July: *Philip of Spain still delays his coming to England, and they say the Queen is in despair and the Emperor his father is furious. Marienburg and Binche have fallen both to the French and the Emperor declares that six days after the wedding Philip must cross to Brussels and join him with money and troops. The Prince, they say, is wont to be much sick at sea....*

From Malta, letters from a Knight of St John called de Seurre; and from Greece and Turkey long epistles, with ribbons, from a wandering poet whose name was Míkál: *Dragut Rais is leading the armada of Suleiman from Turkey to attack the Emperor's men in Florence and Corsica, so they say.*

And from a scholar of Guthrie's acquaintance in England named Bartholomew Lychpole: *The Queen has rati-*

fied the marriage with Prince Philip and called God to witness that she has not consented to marry from any carnal affection or desire, nor from any motive but her kingdom's honour and prosperity, and the repose and tranquillity of her subjects. All present, the letter added in its broad, angular writing, had tears in their eyes.

The Queen has decided not to execute William Courtenay, and he has been allowed out of prison. The Queen's half-sister the Lady Elizabeth has been released from the Tower, and the Stillyard merchants shot off cannon for joy when she passed, which displeased the Queen mightily.

And in early August: The Spanish marriage has taken place. The Prince has no English. The Queen speaks no Castilian, but understands it. The Spaniards he has brought with him are not impressed, and are heard to say openly that the Queen is a good creature, but rather older than they had been told, although if she dressed in their fashions she might not look so old and so flabby. At least, they conclude, the King of England (as he now styles himself) fully realizes that the marriage was concluded for no fleshly consideration, but in order to remedy the disorders of the kingdom and preserve the Low Countries.

Much was made at the wedding of the Lady Margaret Douglas, Countess of Lennox, than whom there are few closer to the Queen Mary. She acted as Mistress of the Robes and Purse Bearer as well as First Lady, and had with her a fair son of eight, whom they call Henry, Lord Darnley.

The letters moved backwards and forwards, but the secret of their destination was perfectly kept. Only the Countess of Lennox, cousin to Queen Mary, and mother of the fine son Lord Darnley, benefited from a hint dropped from the lips of Sir Thomas Wharton, who came by with Austin Grey one fine autumn morning, to pay the lady his manly respects.

A woman in her late thirties with King Henry's political cleverness; and King Henry's will; and King Henry's fair and untouched physical splendour, the Lady Margaret received the news at first coolly. 'Philippa Somerville has returned? A Northumberland family, I recall. With property adjoining Lord Allendale's.' Her voice had flattened a trifle. 'The girl is of some importance?'

'Not in herself,' Sir Thomas said mildly. 'Although the property, as you say, is fairly extensive. I was more concerned with her family connections. You know she's just spent a year with that Scots fellow Crawford of Lymond?'

'Ah!' said the Countess of Lennox. After a moment she said, 'No. Poor, misguided child. I had not heard of this. Where did this happen?'

Tom Wharton's voice, answering, clashed with Austin Grey's, attempting apparently to remonstrate. Tom Wharton won. 'In somewhat doubtful circumstances in the poorer parts of the Middle Sea, so I believe. It is said he went through a form of marriage with the girl. At least she claims to have papers.'

'She has papers,' said Austin Grey sharply. 'Tom, you know as well as I do this was a regular marriage. They went through it as a matter of form. But it was a marriage.'

'Well. She says it was a matter of form,' said Thomas Wharton. He flicked the young Marquis on the arm. 'Don't get so excited. Your friends will make fun of you.'

Margaret Douglas said slowly, 'Married? Francis Crawford is married to this farmer's daughter from Hexham?' Then without removing her fine eyes from Thomas Wharton, she added, 'Why?'

Far better than Austin Grey she knew from years of experience how to conceal surprise or dismay or excitement, but even so, the effort behind her very detachment told Tom Wharton all he wanted to know. He said, 'That we don't know. But Flaw Valleys is very close to the Scots Border. And he has used it already in actions against my father in England.'

'I remember,' said Margaret Douglas. 'Her father was Gideon Somerville. One of Lord Grey's staunchest lieutenants through the Scottish wars and between them. He served with the Queen for a while.'

'He is dead,' Tom Wharton said. 'There's only his widow now at Flaw Valleys, and his only child, Philippa. I tell you, I shouldn't like to see Flaw Valleys become the base for Francis Crawford's activities. And that is what may well become the outcome.'

'Tom, that's nonsense,' said Austin Grey. 'The man isn't even there. And she's going to have the marriage annulled.'

'How wise,' said Margaret Douglas. 'And where, then, is her importunate husband?'

'She says,' said Wharton, 'she left him in Greece. Volos, I think. She travelled back alone with his son.'

There was a moment's blank pause. Then the Countess of Lennox began, despite herself, to laugh. 'His *son*! How many foolish extravagances has he permitted himself, on this odd peregrination? By whom? Philippa?'

'The child is over two,' said Austin Grey. He was a little pale. 'In fact, Lady Lennox, Mr Crawford has disappeared and there is no reason to think that he will ever come back to Scotland. As Tom has said, the marriage is to be dissolved. I really think you need have no misgivings about it.'

'But,' said Lady Lennox, 'if he did come back, it might be quite serious. I think we should find out what is happening about the divorce. And whether in fact the child genuinely means to go through with it. How old is she? Fourteen?'

'Seventeen, Lady Lennox,' said Austin Grey.

He had displeased her. 'Indeed,' she said. And after a moment, 'Old enough, then, for Court. Sir Thomas, is she presentable? If her parents were in the Queen's household, she cannot be too rough in her ways.'

Thomas Wharton put his velvet-shod foot firmly on top of Austin Grey's toes, and kept it there. 'She would do at Court very nicely,' he said. 'She has an uncle somewhere in London. The Queen would remember the family.'

'Then,' said Lady Lennox, 'I shall get the Queen's permission tomorrow to invite her. And you shall take the summons with you, Lord Allendale, when next you go north to the Somervilles. I take it you would have no objection to showing this girl how to conduct herself in the city?'

And Austin Grey, flushing, confirmed shortly that he would be pleased to escort Mistress Philippa Somerville in any way the Countess might indicate.

CHAPTER FIVE

Philippa's letter, stained with food and sea water, arrived in the Kremlin in September and was laid by a servant on the Voevoda's carved desk in the palace granted to him and to his mistress by his sovereign prince, Ivan IV. It lay there, ranked with other papers and packets, neatly dated and docketed, awaiting the Voevoda's attention.

Crawford of Lymond, as demanded of his new office and title of Russian commander, was absent in the field with his officers; whether exercising or fighting, his household did not know.

Smoothly conducted by the Mistress's small, white-fleshed hands, the business of the luxurious house continued without cease. The Mistress's riches were unpacked; the carpets laid; the tapestries hung, the books and paintings displayed; the lute and harpsichord uncrated and placed in the new rooms designed and built to her orders so that the strict timber edifice, raised in a cleared space near the Nikólskaya Tower for some dead appanaged prince, had gathered wings and balconies and galleried gables linked with steepled porches and bridges and stairs, tooled and painted and fretted like a gingerbread mould.

Outside, Güzel's house was pure Russian. Inside, it was Venetian and Arab and Turkish, from the Murano glass and silk hangings to the silver incense burner and the blue and yellow tiles on the floor of the hot room where the lord of the house might strip off the stiff leather and steel of two weeks' campaigning and emerge, bathed and rested, in the fresh robes made for him from the velvets and damasks in her embroidery rooms.

Those who lived in the Kremlin, whose wives walked veiled to church and to weddings and, surrounded by slaves and by stewards, took part in public life not at all, watched the foreign princess secretly; defensively; consumed by an envious and frantic curiosity. Güzel, knowledgeable in the ways of both men and women and accustomed to ruling, steel within silk, the still greater establishment of the Stamboul harem, made no inexpedient advances but waited, allowing her visiting tradesmen and craftsmen to glimpse and be astounded by the tall Gothic splendours of her Nürnberg clock, and the fragile and unimaginable mystery of the Italian harpsichord.

On the day the Tsaritsa's chief lady in waiting called on her, Güzel's house was ablaze with wax lights and hung with the smells of jasmine and the almond and sugars of sweetmeats. She saw the kitchens and the serving rooms, and met Master Gorius Grossmeyer, Güzel's German physician. Two days later, Güzel received the first ceremonial visit from Anastasia herself and was able to present her with the silk robe, re-embroidered with crystals and bullion, which her woman had made for her new son Ivan, then four months old, and to invite her to consult with her doctor.

The following day, Güzel was received by Anastasia in the Golden Rooms at the palace of Terems, bringing some lengths of deep crimson velvet and a covered basket of sweet cakes, borne by her serving woman. There she met the whole household of women, including the widowed Tartar Queen Suunbeka and her son, brought as willing hostage to Moscow after the Tsar's victory over the Tartar stronghold of Kazan. She met too the wives of the princes, who soon visited her and were visited in their turn. But most of Güzel's time, from then onwards, was divided between the house she controlled and the palace.

Whether the Voevoda knew what was happening, and what place, indeed, he had in this intriguing establishment, was something that the curious ladies of the Terems were unable to discover. That the two were unmarried was ascertained at the beginning. So also was the certainty, though from what source no one knew, that it was Güzel who had brought to the Tsar this inestimable band of western trained soldiers, and that it was her resources which had furnished both the journey and the splendours of the residence which he shared.

The princes and boyars attached to the court, hearing the tale with a certain brooding interest from their wives, felt more than a spice of envy for the endowments which could call forth such favours. They were further gripped by what their wives could relay to them of Güzel's experiences in the seraglio of the Sultan Suleiman, and all she had learnt there and from Dragut her lover, of the Turkish army and naval command.

Güzel knew a great deal, and it was not hard to persuade her, now and then, to tell what she knew, about the Spahis and the Janissaries, and their numbers and leadership; about their weapons and practices; about the Sultan's advisers, and his policy towards the Tartars on Russia's borders and towards Russia herself.

From Güzel, indirectly, the Boyar Council learned as much, in a few weeks, as the princes learned about western customs direct from her favourite Crawford of Lymond, the foreigner they called Voevoda Frangike. But to questions about Güzel, the Voevoda had proved politely uncooperative, proceeding thence smoothly to intolerance: whether the Voevoda was thus defending his mistress, his

70

vanity or merely his right to possess a personal life was not entirely clear, either to his victims or to the men who were following him.

These, as it turned out, had little enough leisure to ponder it. Foiled over the house in the Kremlin, Lancelot Plummer exercised his talents as engineer and architect in designing a suitable home for himself and his fellow officers in Kitai-gorod, the merchant quarter of Moscow adjoining the swallowtail walls of the Kremlin, and walled itself in identical white-veined red brick. He made the building of brick : spacious and utilitarian, with room for their equipment and a disposition this time of steps, doors and windows which would make outside assault a very difficult proposition indeed. A chaste line of dog-tooth white stonework and a minor embellishment of the principal doorways was all he permitted of flourish.

The third building he made for St Mary's was at Voro-biovo, the country suburb south of the river, and had no flourishes within or without. It was here that their training ground was laid out, and where he and the others would work and live beside the rough wooden huts of the Streltsi, Ivan's only trained standing force, until the groundwork was done, and they had created the fighting arm which Russia needed.

Once it had begun, the swiftness of it surprised all of them; even those who remembered the start of the band of mercenaries known to western Europe as St Mary's. Some of it was directly due to the change, now unequivocally clear, in Lymond himself. The cleverness, the far-sighted-ness; the broadly imaginative grasp of basic essentials were there and identified, with mounting enjoyment, by Danny Hislop's bright watching eyes. But the remembered other side, so shrewdly guessed at by Danny, had disappeared as damascening melts in the heat, leaving only the iron. They were led, as was their due, by an active and distinguished commander. But any warmth, any camaraderie, any culti-vation of trifling pursuits and sharing of friendships and laughter must be engendered, they found, among the six men who were left, and the Muscovite soldiers to whom, by and by, they also gave office.

The Voevoda did not stand aside : he was involved on the contrary in the very fabric of all they were building. But to the members, old and new, of the company he had created, whom he worked, as he worked himself, with a disciplined and violent intensity, he showed a blank and courteous indifference. And nightly, when he could, he withdrew from their society to Güzel's civilized house, with its books and its music and its well-prepared food, bringing them in the morning the lists and orders he had prepared for their daily conference, and a group of boyars, to visit the training ground and watch his men as, with bow and axe and lance and handgun, on foot and on horse, they recovered the skills blunted in long weeks of travelling.

Addressed with the deference and charm he knew, to the touch of a hairspring, how to exercise, they would watch, studying the fine, the new points, and encouraged, would take lance themselves, to be allowed to achieve small success; to have their failures excused and explained to them.

Then, over a meal from their lavish kitchens, they would be shown the company's maps, the details checked and drawn in by Adam the artist from the dog-eared rolls stored in the armoury workshops with their carefree and contradictory inkings of coastline and rivers, added to by Adam himself, riding through the forests of birch, oak, fir and maple and the light rolling plains around Moscow; checking the cornfields, the marshes, the river systems between the Upper Volga and Oka; noting the bridges and windmills and huddled settlements doublestaked with tall poles to turn aside melting ice at the thaw; the occasional guard-post, sometimes ruined, sometimes re-built by Ivan, which he dismounted and examined; the wooden churches like clumps of sweet clover which he passed by, without looking back.

The results were impressive. So was their list of arms and munitions, compiled painstakingly with the help of the duma, and less meagre than they had feared. Ivan possessed brass Italian guns and pieces from Germany. There were brises, falcons, minions, sakers, culverins, double and royal basilisks and six great pieces with shot three feet high, as well as muskets, hackbuts and mortars, potguns for wild fire and bows for stone shot as well as the usual kind. There were the traditional hooked swords and pikes and ryvettes and iron maces, coats of mail and brigantines and steel targets and the characteristic spired helms. There were stocks and wheels for gun carriages and high mobile gun towers and all the appurtenances of siege and pioneer work, fashioned for them fifty years ago by engineers brought in from Germany.

Displaying the total Alec Guthrie conveyed, tactfully, a qualified satisfaction. It was not the moment to mention the fact that most of the weapons were of a certain antiquity, nor that it had become gradually clear that none of the Tsar's relatives, boyars, boyars' sons, courtiers, service princes, palace guards, merchants, burghers or frontiersmen knew what to do with them.

He did not discuss the other, private lists he and Lymond were compiling : of foundry and shot tower capacity, of raw material resources of iron and copper and salt and silver and potash : the plethora of timber and dressed leather; the disastrous scarcity of lead and corn powder and sulphur. They knew what stores of meat and fish, fresh, frozen and salted, the Tsar and his merchants kept in their warehouses, and what daily consumption of flour the Neglinnya corn mills could grind.

They had learned weights and coinage and were making costings for the best sources of army supplies : barrels, ladders and horsecarts; saddles of wood and Saphian leather; flax soap and mats from Novgorod; elkskins from Rostov; bows and arrows at five marks apiece from Smolensk; sledges costing a poltina each. They surveyed the supply of tall Argamaks, the Turcoman horses, crossed with Arab stock, whose long necks and fine legs made for great speed over the flat plains of the south, but who could not endure long riding over rough country. They found they could buy for three roubles the small, short-necked Pachmat horses of the Tartars, who were used to wooden saddles and stirrups and could live for a lifetime on sawdust.

Coinage was a matter for tact. There was no gold in Russia : for that they used Hungarian coins. The silver Novgorod rouble was worth twice the silver Moscow rouble, and that was worth sixteen shillings and eightpence English money, but less converted to sterling. And, as Fergie Hoddim complained with some bitterness, half the time the seller hardly knew how to set a price on his product, being accustomed to barter.

'Will I tell ye the price of a hatchet?' snarled Fergie at their once-daily assembly at supper, tearing apart a wild goose helped down with gobbets of rye bread and spirit. 'You try handing over an altine and they'll spit on your uppers. A tied bunch of sable skins drawn through the hole where the haft enters, that's the price of a hatchet. Forbye,' said Fergie austerely, 'if they're going to count they wee dengi in fifties, I wish they wouldna use their big mouths as pouches. I clapped one lad on the shoulders last Monday, and it was Thursday before he was able to pay me.'

Fergie, busy importing Permian yew and surveying Polish and Flemish cloth bales for his soldiers, disliked weighing in slotniks and poods and counting his journeys in versts instead of two-thirds of a mile. It disturbed him that the Russian calendar put the creation of the world at the 5,508th year B.C. and that it was therefore never the year that he thought it was. Apart from this, although he would not have admitted it, he was having the time of his life.

Ludovic d'Harcourt, their Christian hospitaller, was engaged on a different matter. Having mastered the Slavonic tongue quicker than any save Lymond, he was compiling his own register of Pomeschiks, those who had been given land on condition that they supplied one equipped horseman per obja of earth until death. He also, with discretion, interviewed the princes. Equipment, he found, consisted of food for one to two months: a bag three spans long with millet flour and up to eight pounds of dried powdered pork, along with a bag of salt mixed with pepper, if the man could afford it. Together with a hatchet, copper kettle and fire box, this made him self-supporting. D'Harcourt reported to base.

'All right,' Guthrie said. 'They put one man like that in the field, and he can live, after a fashion. But in God's name, what do they give him to fight with?'

'A pea-shooter,' said Danny. 'With terribly hard Russian peas.'

'Not exactly,' said d'Harcourt. 'The trouble is, they will overdo it. You'd expect a sword and a bow and a quiver. They've got lances and hatchets as well, and half a dozen knives and the kesteni, that stick with a spiked ball on a thong. They have the knives hanging on to their elbows, and their reins and whipthong looped on to their fingers, and so far as I can gather, expect to ride in to the attack with the bridle, the bow, the short sword, the javelin and the whip all in their hands at the same time.'

'With their kettle, their food and their tinder box

bumping along at their sides,' Danny said. 'I'm sure the enemy simply run off in droves; but my loving heart bleeds for their horses. The August Personage of Jade won't be at all pleased about that.' Danny Hislop was retraining the Streltsi, which was extremely hard work, and had mellowed his tongue not at all.

Adam Blacklock wished, not for the first time, that Lymond had seen fit to stay with them during this spell in the house at Kitaigorod, instead of abandoning them for his mistress. True, it was in the Kremlin that he was able to speak with the duma and the princes and engage their attention and support for what he was doing, and with d'Harcourt, make assessment of their varied ability and experience and the degree of their probable co-operation. To Vorobiovo he brought from the Kremlin Prince Kurbsky, who the previous winter had put down the rebellion at Arsk, fighting a running battle against the Votiaks, the heathen Finnish tribe driven north from Kazan by the Tartars.

A clever, ambitious man in his late twenties with a great deal of experience behind him, Kurbsky had not yet shown more than a guarded interest in what Lymond was doing, but he was prepared to talk of the wolf road to the north with its nomads and settlers and bring with him merchants who imported walrus tusks and seal oil and salmon, beluga and feathers and white foxes and snow larks and silver and sables at the fair at Lampozhnya, and could tell of the Samoyèdes, who worshipped the Slata Baba, the Golden Old Woman, and the people of Lucomoryae, who died in November and came to life again like the frogs in the following spring, and the races of Lapland, who know neither fruits nor apples, nor yet any benignity of either heaven or earth.

From them, the men of St Mary's learned of the northern frontiers of Russia, from which the tribes did not invade, but might revolt against paying tribute to church or to state; might ally with the enemy Tartars; might and did murder travellers and destroy the tenuous pathways of trade. And they learned of the snow and the cold, and the ways of travelling fast on a frozen network of rivers. They heard how to use snow to track and to assault the enemy, and how to defend themselves and their weapons from freezing.

They all attended these sessions. Among them, sometimes, were others: the beautiful boy called Venceslas who had suddenly appeared as Lymond's body-servant, and the elderly German physician called Gorius Grossmeyer, with his worn lambskin stomacher and his old Brunswick hat with the brass band pinned round it, who belonged to the Mistress's household and talked, in his ponderous way, good sense in medical terms.

On the western frontier, bordered by Lithuania, Livonia and Poland, the problems were different and entirely political. The most senior men of the Council, Adashev and the monk Sylvester and the secretary Viscovatu, came to Vorobiovo for these sessions, which were held strictly in private. Sigismund-August, King of Poland and Grand Duke of Lithuania, thirty-four years old and shakily lost in high living, wanted no war, and Livonia, under the declining feudal Order of Teutonic Knights, was the weakest of Ivan's neighbours. But the town of Pskov on Livonia's borders, reconquered forty-four years before by his father, was Russia's only station towards the western sea, other than the frozen coast of Ingermanland on the Gulf of Finland. It was a dream of the Tsar's, more than either of his chief ministers, to acquire part of the Baltic seaboard, and to recover the lands inhabited by Orthodox Russians and seized by his western neighbours when the Golden Horde held the whole of Russia in its grip.

So, vouchsafing no political opinions, Lymond with Guthrie's stolid presence beside him elicited the strength and the weakness of Ivan's westerly neighbours and then turned to the subject nearest Adashev's heart and Sylvester's too: the fending-off and eventual conquering of the children of Ahmed, the heretic remains of the great Golden Horde which had ruled for two hundred years: the war against the last of the Tartars.

Danny Hislop, temporarily seconded from wounding the feelings of the Streltsi, became their expert on Tartars. He visited the prisoners from Kazan and the renegades already working for Ivan: he found where the Tartar settlements were and in what numbers, and how they lived, camped, fought, ate and rode. He found the dangers were two. Across seven hundred miles of wild steppeland to the south-west of the Volga lay the Tartar Khanate of Crimea, vassals of Ottoman Turkey, who lived on raids into southern Lithuania and Muscovy, and sold jewellery, church gold and slaves into Egypt and Stamboul.

To the south-east lay the Horde of the Nogai, led by two brothers. 'Ismail likes Ivan, but Jusef breaks out in pustules at the thought of him,' Danny reported, sitting with his feet on the desk between Lymond and Guthrie. 'Luckily, Tartars don't much like other Tartars, and the ones who are sitting in Astrakhan at the mouth of the Volga are the least liked of all, especially by God's Key-bearer and Chamberlain, Ivan of Russia, who would like to possess the whole of the River Volga, including the mouth. There's a Khan called Yamgurchei in Astrakhan, and Ismail has offered to join his part of Nogai to the Russians to fling Yamagurchei out.'

'And hand the town over to Russia?' Guthrie asked.

'Not exactly. A former Khan called Derbysh is the current favourite. Everyone hopes that if he is brought back, he will show Ivan a proper gratitude. Two of the Kremlin princes, Pronsky-Shemyakin and Vyazemsky, went south in the spring to attack Yamgurchei with the help of the Nogai, and when they get back, if they get back, they are going to be the mascots of Muscovy. I'm tired of training,' Danny complained. 'Couldn't we plunder something, such as decadent idols with emerald eyes and a lot of clean, unspoiled village maidens?'

But instead, he was sent with Plummer to conduct a survey with Adam's maps of a proposed chain of fortified points to extend those already defending the hundred-mile zone about Moscow. He rode through Tver and Rzhev and Staritsa, Serpukhov, Kashire and Kolomna, Ryazan and Zaraisk and Kaluga; Mosaisk and Cheboksari and Sviajsk to the rumble of Plummer's unceasing voice, and the squeak of the clerk taking notes for him. At every second location Danny said monotonously, 'You can't do that,' and Plummer bridled and said, 'They built Sviajsk three years ago in four weeks. They felled the timber at Uglich and floated the logs down the Volga—'

'The cost. The cost, you fool!' Danny would scream.

'Four thousand five hundred roubles. From the foundations. My God,' Plummer would cry. 'Can't you get it into your head that it's a carpentry culture? Houses cost three roubles each. They buy them ready-made in the market from numbered stacks of standardized timbers, already tenoned and mortised. The buyer states the number of rooms, gets the logs loaded on carts and has them dragged out and built where he wants them. That's how the burned districts get replaced so quickly. Cheap wood, cheap labour and only one tool – the hatchet. Hence the uniform look of the Izbas.'

Lancelot Plummer had expected to undertake this survey with Adam, but had been foiled calmly in passing by Lymond. 'Ah, no. One aesthete and one philistine are what we require.' There could have been few philistines, thought Plummer acidly, as insistently common as Hislop.

Then they stopped making lists. For four days, Lymond was absent, in conference with the Chosen in some retreat in the Kremlin. When he returned, he carried between two boards the programme to which he had committed them.

He read it through to them in Kitaigorod all that evening, instead of returning as he usually did, straight from Vorobiovo to the Kremlin. In it were the provisions for all Fergie's supplies; the foundries to make Guthrie's new weapons, the forts for Plummer to build and the musters, district by district, of all the men owing horses, weapons and service, for d'Harcourt and Hislop to train.

They listened to him in silence, fired in spite of themselves by the scale of it. But for the sake of their pride they kept quiet, and only at the end did Guthrie move, and say growling, 'And so they agreed? Even the cost?'

The Voevoda Crawford of Lymond laid down the last page, picked up and tapped the stack on a desk to align it, and handed the bundle and boards to the boy Venceslas to bind and hold ready to carry. He looked at Guthrie. 'I have on record,' he said, 'the Tsar's public pronouncement that the only riches he cares for are peace with honour for Russia.'

'My God,' said Danny Hislop. 'He said that for effect, after the fall of Kazan.'

'No doubt,' said Lymond. 'But he said it. Peace and honour he shall certainly have, in due course. And those most deserving, no doubt, will be granted the riches.'

The letter from Philippa Somerville arrived at the end of the month when, in the field or out of it, they were working eighteen hours and more in every day and the messages from Rome and Venice and Brussels and London and Paris lay on Lymond's desk, waiting until he chose to step aside for an hour from the machine, and give them his due and orderly attention.

Even when he returned, he did not go at once to

Güzel's house, but was stopped, passing through the Nikólskaya Gate, and asked to call at Ivan Milkhailov Viscovatu's office. He went there on foot, dismissing his men and his horses, and found the secretary fondling the thick metal plate of his crucifix. 'My sovereign lord wishes to see you. Your riding dress will be excused. You may leave your weapons with me, Voevoda.'

His sheath, worked in the Turkish style, was inlaid with coloured enamels and had turquoises in it, set firm as apples. Lymond drew his sword and laid his dagger beside it. Then Viscovatu, darkly smiling, gave a clap of his hands, and the door opened on a file of tall headgear and ranked silver axes. The guard closed about them as Lymond with the secretary stepped into the open, and taking one of the wide boarded walks of the Kremlin, escorted both men to the west, behind the network of houses which backed the Uspensky Cathedral and the Church of the Robe of the Virgin and into the square containing the old church of St Saviour in the Wood, behind which lay the steps to the women's buildings, the Terems. And from that upper terrace, trodden almost daily by Güzel, was a doorway into the maze of connected pavilions which represented the Tsar's private apartments.

Ivan of Russia this time wore neither of his worked golden crowns, but merely a tall hat in velvet over a banded cap of black sable and an Ispahan gown in crimson and indigo, with long slit sleeves brushing his footstool. Adashev was with him and a handful of others, seated on a long bench hung with red fringed brocade. There was a table with books and an ikon hung with gold cloth in the room corner, before which an oil lamp glimmered scarlet. The lower walls were painted to simulate marble.

Lymond walked to the ikon, hat in hand, and crossing himself three times said aloud, 'O Lord, have mercy.' He then turned to the Tsar and made a reverence deeper yet.

Ivan's arms stiffened on the knobs of his chair. 'Hah!' he said on a shout. 'Protestant strumpet, you ape us?'

Lymond stood, deferential and barely tinged with reproachful surprise. 'Yes,' he said. 'The will of the Prince is the will of God. In the enlargement and tranquillity of his dominion, let us live quietly and peaceably in all goodness and purity, and follow him in all things.'

'The coronation service?' said the confessor Sylvester. 'The Voevoda is indeed a fountain of knowledge.'

The Tsar's voice, full of purpose, overruled his words without ever hearing them. 'Enlargement and tranquillity! Enlargement, Voevoda, yes: although I have not witnessed my domain increase itself by one pebble since you and your mess of ill-mannered dogs so used my city of Moscow that I came near having nothing to reign over but a city of carcass and ashes. You have brought no enlargement, and are thieving from us every tranquillity. My princes spit on you.'

'I cannot detect it,' said Lymond with diffidence. 'I should like to be excused from returning the courtesy.'

The Tsar did not speak. Only, stirring a hand, he signalled to the boyar standing nearest to Lymond. And the counsellor, lifting his heavy gloved hand, delivered two blows across the Voevoda's bland face which left it marked across, reddened and bleeding. Lymond said, without moving, 'I speak the truth. I always speak truly. What is your princes' complaint?'

The Tsar, his colour high, was breathing a little more thickly. 'Where,' he said, 'Where are the treasures of Astrakhan? Where are the carts, the slaves, the spices you stole from my captains? Exhausted from fighting—'

'They were perfectly fresh,' Lymond said. 'The Nogai did most of the fighting.'

'Box by box!' exclaimed the Tsar. 'By night and by day! Shall I tell you the merchandise which they lost from the boats, coming upstream on the Volga? What was taken between Kazan and Morum? What was stolen by land from Morum to this city – the Shemakha silk, the swords, the bows, the cotton wool, the walnuts, the ambergris and the musk which the new Khan Derbysh made free to my men for a pittance? Prince Vyazemsky tells me he found his own bow and dagger sheath empty. Prince Yuri Pronsky-Shemyakin declares the very camp fires were put out one by one with no warning. Are you a madman?' said the Tsar. 'For whom are you fighting? Are you a minion of Sigismund-Augustus and his master the Emperor Charles who wishes to see us a nation of peasants?'

'No,' said Lymond, his voice undisturbed. 'I am making you an army which can fight against Tartars. Your princes did well at Astrakhan, and Yamgurchei has been punished for breaking his oath of allegiance. But elated with their success, your army took no pains to protect themselves on the long journey northwards. They gorged themselves on sturgeon and kvas, and played tricks and were hearty. The Tartars stayed in their *yurts,* but they might well have done far more damage than we did. This your people must learn.'

'While you make yourselves rich?' Adashev said. 'You who already have tasted from us a generosity unprecedented?'

Standing still in his sashed tunic and splashed riding coat, Lymond showed neither insolence nor improper humility. 'The salt, the spices, the cloth and the personal goods of your distinguished princes have by this time been returned to await each in his palace,' Lymond replied. 'The other weapons and the three bags of silver, of which perhaps you have not yet been told, have been put to a purpose I considered would serve my sovereign lord better.'

'They are to be offered in expiation to our Most Holy Church?' said Sylvester with bitter derision.

'They have bought three Cossack leaders,' said Lymond calmly. 'And engaged the interest of several more.'

Adashev said, 'You have given arms to the Cossacks of the steppes? These are robbers; outlaws; stateless men without settlements who rove the Tula, the Putivl, the Severian Ukrainy and live off wild beasts and honey, fish and herbs and sweet roots. They raid the weirs of our fishermen, and sail their fast chaiki to rob and murder those who would pass peacefully down the Tanais to Azov.'

'They fight like Tartars,' said Lymond. 'You have used them before. Lithuania uses them still. Do you want them for you, or against you?'

'They are half Tartar,' said Sylvester with distaste.

'Then,' said Lymond, 'let us make them wholly Russian at heart.'

The pale eyes of the Tsar had not left him. Ivan allowed silence to fall, his beard on his chest; his long Byzantine face moist with choler; his long staff, gleaming steel at the tip, in his hand. At length, 'Approach,' he said to his foreign Voevoda. And as Lymond walked slowly close to his chair, the Tsar raised his thin stick like a cantilever until the metal point pressed hard into the leather of his chest. Holding it there, Ivan spoke softly. 'By my orders Andrei Shuisky was strangled by dog-handlers. My boyars rode over the importunate people of Novgorod. I bound the Pskovians when they made indecent complaint and had hot spirit poured on them, and fired it. Mishurin was skinned alive by the children of boyars, and for a passing error of boldness, I had the tongue of the boyar Afanasy Buturlin cut out here, where you are standing. I speak of these things with sorrow, for God has given me a nature which will brook insolence from none, high or low, My hand smites, although afterwards I may sorrow for it. . . .'

He let another long pause develop while his big-boned hand fondled the stick, its shod point grinding through the soft leather. Lymond said nothing, and the half-dozen men in the room held their breath. In the quietness the sound of feet passing up and down the stone steps came to them perfectly clearly, and muted voices, and in a while, the bell of one of the monasteries jangling from among its rooftops and trees. Ivan said, 'Twice you have been unwise. Twice you have been insolent. I demand that you lie down before me in terror.'

'I fear you,' said Lymond.

'You fear pain?' Ivan said.

'I fear, as any man would, the indignity of pain. I fear more to inflict on your highness the sufferings of a noble remorse, should you smite your jester too harshly. We are here to watch you deliver yourselves from the years of thraldom and oppression. There lies about us so much that is weighty,' said Lymond. 'Forgive us if sometimes we try in our poor way to be merry, and to lighten your burden. In his complaint, did Prince Vyazemsky remember to mention that on the occasion of every encampment he had in his tent the Khan Yamgurchei's five Tartar wives?'

The Tsar's eyes and mouth opened, and his hand became still on the staff-wood. 'You say?' he exclaimed.

'To remove his dagger and bow as we did, and even, be it said, his boots and his white linen breeches was therefore an exploit, I wished humbly to claim, of some merit?'

A rod between the two men, the staff remained still, but the ferrule had withdrawn, imperceptibly, from the glazed and burst skin of the jerkin. 'And the wives?' the Tsar said. 'You failed to steal off the wives? Was there no Cossack leader, no promising pioneer hot for pleasure to whom you could have presented them?'

'Alas,' said Lymond. 'None who has not heard already

whistled abroad the prince's liberal habit of life, and the unhappy reward of his ardours.'

'Ho!' said the Tsar Ivan, and repeated it, a good deal more loudly, suddenly dropping the point of the staff to the floor. His mouth open and working he stared into the unflinching blue eyes of the Voevoda; then lowering his head, he laid his cheek upon his two folded hands on the staff-end and began to breathe noisily, the saliva blowing rainbow-spotted into the air. 'Oh,' said Ivan. 'Oho. Oho. Oh. Oh.'

Gasping, he raised a blind hand and unclosed, shut and opened the fingers. 'Come nearer. Kneel. Let me see you.'

Lymond knelt. The Tsar lifted his head and unlooking, let the staff go. It fell unregarded, with a crack, bouncing on the thin carpet. Ivan leaned forward and, stretching both hands, gripped the bright hair on either side of his Voevoda's cool face, the thin skin lightly browned by the sun.

'You are not afraid,' said Ivan. He pulled one hand sharply away and Adashev, Viscovatu, Sylvester saw Lymond's lips tighten, but he did not call out or speak, as Ivan opened his palm and showed a feathering of snatched yellow hair. There was blood at the side of the Voevoda's brushed head. 'You are not afraid,' repeated the Tsar. 'You are not afraid of the boyars. You are not afraid of me, but for me. . . .

'I am twenty-six,' said the Tsar. He put out his hand, letting the lock fall from his palm, and gripped Lymond's shoulder. 'I confessed. I confessed to my rages, my sins against my people, and Dmitri my firstborn was taken from me, and my friends quarrelled and plotted about me when they thought I lay dying. I have no friends.'

'You have the men in this room,' Lymond said.

'The men in this room are afraid of me. All except you,' the Tsar said. 'They are afraid of the Tartar. They wish to send you to drive out the Tartar instead of defending the Grand Prince's honour before those swine-hating animals. Do you hear what the Poles say of me? That my ancestors licked the mare's milk off Tartar horsemanes while theirs were free princes. That a hen defends her chicks against the hawk and the eagle while I, a two-headed eagle, hide my cowardly head. They say that! And these councillors will not make war on them. Soon Livonia will send her ambassadors, suing for a renewal of this craven peace treaty, and these my councillors will readily grant it. . . .'

The Tsar withdrew his hand sharply and sat back. 'What would the Voevoda advise? What would you say to those dogs when they come?'

Lymond rose slowly to his feet and stood still, close to Ivan. 'What your councillors say. They are older and wiser than I am.'

The Tsar, flushing, dashed his closed hand on his knee. 'But if they are wrong?'

'If fresh facts arise, they will have changed their judgement by then.'

Sylvester's dry voice said, 'May one ask where these fresh facts might come from, that are so unaccounted for now in our reckoning? From the Voevoda?'

Ivan's eyes moved from Sylvester to Lymond. Lymond said, 'From the condition at that date of their army, and the condition of the one led by me. These are the only facts which concern me. Policy is a matter for you and the Tsar.'

'Perhaps,' said Alexei Adashev gently, 'the Tsar considers the Voevoda should have a share in our councils.'

Lymond said quickly, 'The Tsar has offered me the post of commander, and that I have accepted. Nothing else.' And his eyes followed Ivan as the Tsar rose, his shadow falling over the six men below him.

'The Tsar,' said Ivan, 'prizes honesty, and knows how to reward it. I dine in state, and cannot ask you to join me. But you will share none the less of my dinner, and those bold men you have caused to join you in my city of Moscow. Go in health to your house in Kitaigorod and these my officers will follow with that which will make you all merry.'

The hand stroking the auburn beard was held out and kneeling, Lymond kissed it, and was raised by it to stand before Ivan again. In a low voice, 'Lend me your honesty,' Ivan said; and meeting his eyes, Lymond bowed once again without speaking.

It was one o'clock on a still summer's night when Francis Crawford again entered the Kremlin, and, with torches and his boy Venceslas to guide him, picked his way past the Nikólskaya Tower to the palace he and Güzel shared behind it. He had opened the door of his chamber when he was stopped by the soft voice of Güzel's negro tirewoman Leila. So, dismissing Venceslas, he turned, and made his way instead to the musk-scented taper-lit room which his mistress had designed for her pleasure.

She was there, her hair unbound, dressed in light, soundless gauzes spread over the floor cushions on which she was resting, a little book stretched in leather unrolled with its strap loose in her hand. Beside her burned a claw-footed brazier, embossed with masks and harpies and sea monsters and swags of dully shining fruit. The red chipped eyes of the charcoal roused the uncut heavy stones she wore round her ankles, her wrists and her neck; the tasselled Greek earrings trembling against the smooth olive skin, the lips and eyes so finely brushed with oil and smooth pigments and tinting that she looked like a painting in gesso, the white highlights and ochre flesh tones overlaying the greenish brown undercoat, with the small mouth and the straight thin-boned nose and the long, clear-lidded archangel eyes. She said, 'Since we came to Moscow, I have never seen you look tired.'

Lymond closed the door and crossed the carpet towards her. 'I am not tired,' he said. 'I have been stabbed, fenced with, caressed and plucked like a chicken, and I have also drunk and eaten far more than I hope ever to be asked to again. But I am satisfied. As the Bishop of Arras remarked—'

'A good peace can only be made by a good war? It is peace then?' said Güzel. 'Ivan has admitted you to his Council?'

'Yes. He may not be aware of it yet, but he has,' Lymond said. 'I am far too dirty for your exquisite cushions.'

'You are,' said Güzel. 'Take off your coat and your jerkin.' She watched him. 'What have you been doing? Your shirt will have to go, too. If you look over there, there is a finished night robe I was going to give you. What have you been doing?'

'Baiting a boyar or two,' Lymond said. 'How did you know so much about the road to Astrakhan?' The robe she had shown him was fox-trimmed, and of Persian silk. Bare to the waist he allowed it to fall over his shoulders and subsided, with the oiled ease of total physical control, among the cushions beyond the low brazier.

'You are an animal,' the Mistress said. 'Barbarous Scot. You have no shame and no shyness. Who do you think nursed you in those days out of Volos?'

'Master Grossmeyer,' said Lymond. 'The sick do not interest you, unless with very good reason. Did you learn of the road to Astrakhan from Suunbeka or Ediger?'

'Suunbeka and her son have become Christian,' Güzel said. 'She has turned her back on the Tartars, her people.'

'She is none the less Yamgurchei's daughter as well as the captive widow of the last Khan of Kazan. I salute the persuasiveness of your doctor, your cook and your sewing women, not to mention your personal charms. The incident did all that was necessary.'

'The Tsar is lonely,' Güzel said calmly. 'Since his illness, he and his wife have lost confidence in Sylvester and Adashev. Anastasia is looking, too, for someone strong-willed who will steady him. There is a vein of unnatural violence.'

'In his brother. In his great-grandfather. But in himself I see nothing yet. There may be a good mind under all that loose-lipped emotion. But it is a gamble from moment to moment whether one is about to be embraced or garotted.'

'Can you control him?' Güzel asked. There was a tap on the door. Leila came in followed by Venceslas bearing a tray : he dispensed wine, which Lymond waved aside, and withdrew.

'I think so. We can do a great deal for him, if he will allow us. Whether I can also control the boyars at the same time is a matter which only the hangman will finally tell. . . . Güzel, I wish you to take back Venceslas.'

She looked up from her Sassinian goblet of wine. 'He is clumsy?'

'No. Like the elephant, a beast very docile and apt to be taught. But I prefer not to be served out of gratitude.'

'Now I,' Güzel said, 'think that the most intriguing form of service of all. I was sorry for him. In the manner of this most hoggish of nations, his father had drunk wife and children completely away. I redeemed Venceslas from the inn he was slaving for. Would you put him back? I thought tonight you were no friend to the winecup?'

The dense brown eyes were watching him as he lay on her cushions : his veiled lids and lit golden hair, and the polished brown skin between the open furs of his robe. He raised his eyebrows, studying the pattern of cut velvet under his fingers, and said, 'Do you want to hear of it? I joined the men of St Mary's at Plummer's brave piece of self-assertion in the Kitaigorod. We were followed there by six of the Tsar's courtiers and twenty-five serving men, together with a cart filled with silver vessels and platters of food, and two small carriages holding the drink. All, it was made clear, was to be consumed on the premises immediately, with the help of the visiting courtiers, and the silver vessels were ours to retain. We each received seven goblets of Burgundy and seven each of Rhenish wine, muscatel, white wine, Canary, Alicant and malmsey, twelve measures of hydromel and a quantity of food, among which I remember eight dishes of roast swan, eight of spiced crane, several of cocks dressed with ginger, boned fowls, blackcock stuffed in saffron, hazel-grouse cooked in cream, ducks with cucumber, geese with rice, hares with dumplings and turnips, elks' brains, cakes and pies of meat and of cheese, pancakes, fritters, jellies, creams and preserved walnuts, which I escorted myself half the way from Astrakhan.

'The meal,' said Lymond, 'was marked by a great deal of merriment and an embarrassment of toasts, the custom being for each proposer to stand in the centre and propose one by one the healths of each of the company and their respective lords or commanders, together with a number of other sentiments to do with health, fortune or victory. The proposer expresses the wish that not so much blood may remain in his enemies as he means to leave in his goblet. He then drinks, bareheaded, and turns the empty goblet upside down over his head. His listeners each time do likewise. The Russian has an exceeding capacity for liquor.'

'So?' said Güzel.

'So have we,' Lymond said. 'Adam succumbed, but the rest of us packed the six Muscovite gentlemen back into the cart and saw it safely back to the Kremlin. Alec Guthrie said it was the best night he'd had since he matriculated, and d'Harcourt embraced me. Even Danny Hislop glowed with a highly intellectual goodwill. The burning of SS Boris and Gleb has, I gather, now been forgiven me.'

His voice, lightly sardonic, lapsed into silence. For a moment Güzel did not speak either. Then she said. 'I understand. I shall take Venceslas to be my own servant.'

He looked up sharply then, his fringed eyes distended. 'What do you understand?'

The long Greco-Italian eyes smiled back at him. 'What

were you thinking of? Necromancy? I understand what is perfectly plain. That you are succeeding in what you have set out to do. And that of normal human impulses you experience nothing.'

He continued to stare at her, his hands lightly woven together. He said, 'All I can give you is Russia.'

The woman Güzel, courtesan and mistress to princes, smiled at him with parted, rose-tinted lips, her own white ringed hands lying loose in her lap. She said, 'It is a property of women, to know how to wait.'

Lymond said, 'If I have laid my traps as I hope, Vishnevetsky will make some move in your direction, or in mine. I want him to fight for us.'

Thoughtfully, Güzel stretched out and studied one hand and then returned it, slowly, to rest on the other. 'If you are content with Russia,' she said, 'then so am I. But you did not tell me you had taken an English girl-child to wife?'

'I told you. . . . Did I not?' Lymond said. 'It was the Somerville girl. It can be annulled. She has probably sent post-haste to the Papal Legate already.'

Güzel rose. She stooped and, lifting her wrought goblet, drank from it; then walking from the circle of tapers she lifted something white from the shadows and returned with it to the warmth of the light. She said, 'She says nothing of it. She has written you.'

The seal of the letter was broached. Without comment Lymond received it and unfolded the pages. There were several, covered in round schoolgirl script. He glanced at the first sentence, looked up to find Güzel standing, hands folded, watching him, and, rising himself, stood by the nearest group of branched lights, running his eyes down the pages.

The flush of wine had gone from his skin, and the amusement, the edge of interest and involvement had all vanished also. She knew what the letter contained: a young girl's chatter, of no weight or substance but evocative perhaps of a homeland vanished, and of a family and of friends. The girl had written in detail of the child, and had ended with the news which was clearly the purpose of the letter: that his mother was no longer young, and needed his presence. Güzel had made no attempt to conceal the letter from its recipient, and in such things the Mistress seldom made a mistake.

Lymond never finished the letter. He read half-way through and then, closing in into its folds, tossed it one-handed into the brazier where it lingered, the penned words for a moment bright-lit: *He is going to be tall.* Across the plume of new flame: 'Why should it matter?' he said. 'You can hardly imagine I pine for her.'

'Not when you leave half her letter unread. Does it offend you to read of the boy?' Güzel said. 'Or does it remind you too much of the other?' And met the gaze he turned on her, with serenity.

'A moment ago,' said Lymond with irony, 'you reminded me of my handicap. I have been cheated of the tender emotions. Including nostalgia.'

'Then play to me,' said Güzel calmly. 'There is the harpsichord. You compliment me on the life I have shaped which offers more than common refreshment for more than common employment. If there is nothing to fear, there is nothing to avoid.'

It was late. She was not as young as her protégé, and under the paint, the sills of her eyes were darkened with tiredness. But informed by experience, her instinct was quite unimpaired. She sank, cup in hand, in her cushions and sustained his level regard as he faced her, the light still and bright on the thready gold of his hair; over the mould of cheekbone and brow; about the strictly bracketed mouth.

Then he laughed, and, walking straight to the instrument, lifted the beautiful lid. He struck the spaced keys a few times to test them before, sitting, he brought them, ringing, to play.

When the noise had continued for some time the Chamberlain, who had no musical ear, called for a candle and knocked on Master Grossmeyer's door to invite him to share his wakefulness. 'God's mercy, a marvellous player,' said the Chamberlain, straining at loyalty. 'In twenty minutes, he fails to repeat himself.'

Huddled listening on the edge of his bed, Master Gorius Grossmeyer nodded two or three times. 'My scalpel, could you teach it to play, would give you just such a per-formance. The Tsar is fortunate.'

'The Tsar has no interest in music,' the Chamberlain said. 'And surely the Mistress's presence is fortunate enough for any ruler?'

Master Grossmeyer dragged off his coarse woollen hat and explored, scratching, the ruffled grey hair underneath.

'The Mistress,' he said, 'is a woman. But this is hardly a man, but an impervious and versatile engine. You have only to listen to hear it.'

'Does she hear it?' the Chamberlain asked.

Discretion, at three o'clock in the morning, is often a victim to slumber. 'She hears it,' Master Grossmeyer said grimly. 'She wished to be the eminence behind the Tsar's chair of state, and this she will be. She did not expect to see her chosen escort reach there before her, or to sleep alone in her bed while she did so. She is to be pitied.'

'I prefer to think,' the Chamberlain said, with a boldness he was later to wince over, 'that they deserve each other.'

Which was the conclusion, did they but know it, that the victorious and drink-happy men of St Mary's had, with tolerance, agreed on already that evening.

CHAPTER SIX

As a highly qualified Turkish-trained concubine from the harem of Suleiman the Magnificent, Philippa Somerville settled into English court life as a kite among chickens, and as a kite among kites into the Spanish court of the new King-consort Philip.

Never had summons to Court been more opportune. Returning stricken from the Convent of SS Winning and Mary she had alarmed Richard by a new gentleness in addressing them all, he said, as if they were dying. She had not told Sybilla where she had been, but, feeling those blue eyes studying her more than once, she had begun to fear that she might without thinking betray herself. And she had not, above all, penned another letter to her absent husband.

She had told Sybilla's sister the Abbess that Lymond would return if assured that his mother was blameless. Relating the whole matter, with difficulty, to herself in the same unlikely dilemma with Kate, she still stoutly believed it. What, with all her determination, she could not bring herself to do was put what she had learned in cold blood into a letter.

How did you inform a man, even a worldly and middle-aged man, that he was not the cadet of a fine Scottish family, but the nameless son of some woman in France? She lay awake toiling over the wording. She looked up a number of books, and assembled a number of apt quotations. She then concluded that whatever she wrote, she could not tolerate the thought that, on the blind and uncertain journey to Volos, it might be opened and read by eyes other than Mr Crawford's.

The safest course therefore was to wait. To wait until she had a reply, with address, to her first letter. Or to wait until somehow, from somewhere, the news of Lymond's whereabouts filtered through.

Then had come the offer of a Court position with Queen Mary. Kate had been astonished at her alacrity, accepting. 'The tedium will send you to drink in a week. Little glasses of holsum bolsum. Remember your cousins.'

'They had livers,' Philippa said calmly. 'I am a virgin with regular habits.'

Her mother Kate looked at her sourly. 'And what, pray, has London to offer that the great metropolis of Flaw Valleys has failed to supply of mad gaiety?'

'Austin Grey,' Philippa said. 'A Spanish nobleman, if I can find one, rented to the value of eight thousand crowns a year or thereby.' Reason, she might have added, to absent herself from the over-perceptive eye of the Dowager Lady Culter, and there to await further news of her husband. And opportunity, she might have said, to seek out the second of her elderly relatives who had been withheld so discreetly from her attention: Mr Leonard Bailey, her great-uncle by marriage.

So Philippa departed for London, with Fogge her maid, and a train of baggage which caused Kate's cook to jump up and down on the threshold. And so, prior to assuming her new post of lady in waiting, she arrived for training at the Sidney household in Penshurst.

This was Austin Grey's doing, with Tom Wharton as his willing accomplice. Austin, because his cousin was married to Sir Henry Sidney's best friend; Tom Wharton, because his wife's nephew, as he explained freely, was courting Sidney's sister Frances. And both because Jane Dormer, Sidney's sixteen-year-old niece, was already at Court and among the Queen's dearest companions.

Accustomed to the muddle of marriage alliances which joined English family to family in little but litigation, Philippa received the news philosophically, wondered who was paying whom and allowed herself a brief groan at the prospect of another girlish companion. The wide winter sky and soft country of Kent restored her natural optimism, a little overturned at the sight of the grey, Gothic splendours of Penshurst. The welcome she received from Sir Henry Sidney and his wife Mary not only redressed the balance, but added another dimension to what was already becoming a decidedly unorthodox life.

Witty, talkative, scholarly, Henry Sidney at twenty-five was an ornament to any society with his long-boned bearded face and thick brown hair and a degree of good sense and good taste which extended from his friendships to the Spanish black-work on his shirt. And he was a courtier, born and bred. His father had been tutor and household steward to the Queen's young brother Edward, and from the age of nine Henry had been the other boy's closest companion until he had died, a King in his arms.

Of his political sense and adroitness there could be no better proof than Sir Henry's present survival. Few of the late King Edward's near friends were also friends of his sister Queen Mary. More than that, Sir Henry's bride of three years was the daughter of Queen Mary's worst enemy. The Earl of Warwick was now dead, beheaded; but Lady Mary Sidney lived undisturbed with her husband, fair, stately and – Philippa found – cheerfully pregnant, and the Queen accepted their agreeable service, and did not molest them.

Like the Station Laudable of the prophets in Paradise, the gates of Penshurst opened to receive Philippa and she discovered a way of life with no parallel in Flaw Valleys or Malta or Turkey or Sir Richard Crawford's cordial and uncomplicated household in Scotland.

Below the tall timber roof of the hall there met poets and politicians, churchmen, navigators and merchant adventurers, scholars from Oxford and Cambridge; men who talked about hops and men who talked about ironworks. And it was in this company of men that Philippa, by Henry's decree, spent most of her time, or those parts of it which she felt Lady Mary could spare her. For to one trained under Kiaya Khátún, there could be little to learn in dress or deportment or manners, and the additional skills she possessed were of a kind better forgotten than exercised. But she read and sewed and chatted with her gentle hostess, and managed to recover, for Lady Mary's delight, her old skill at the lute and the virginals.

She enjoyed being praised for her playing, although she could not be prevented from pointing out, critically, her own errors of taste and execution after every performance. She enjoyed spending Madame Donati's despised money on gowns with shirred necks and cuffed oversleeves and fur and galloon in appropriate corners, although she protested mildly at the pronouncement that she must knot up her well-kept brown hair and cover it with a black gable headdress with lappets. 'I shall look,' she pointed out grimly, 'like a sentry-box.'

Henry Sidney, who was just discovering that his latest protégée was an original, sat on his wife's bed and laughed. 'Unbound hair is for maidens and brides on their wedding day. You are an old married woman.'

'She is just seventeen,' his wife intervened, blandly chiding. 'And surely you recall what Allendale told us. It was a marriage of propriety. Was it not?'

'A singular act,' said Sir Henry Sidney, 'of Anglo-Scottish co-operation. You have no idea what trouble your uncle and Austin and I have been put to to satisfy the Lord Chancellor that we are not corrupting his pure English corn with the malicious Scotch weeds of coccle. But you are having the marriage annulled?'

'Yes,' said Philippa. The papers would be in London, Kate had said, in a month.

'Perhaps the Papal Legate's first deed on his arrival?' Sidney said. 'Who should be called not Pole the Englishman but Pole the angel. I may not have told you, but I met your husband three years ago at Châteaubriant. I was with a dull English mission and he was distinguishing himself as a herald of the Queen Dowager of Scotland. Half the French court, male and female, were angling for his attentions, as I remember. Perhaps you should consider retaining him.'

'But if the marriage is dissolved,' Philippa said, 'I needn't wear black gable headdresses. Or should I have to go into mourning?'

Henry Sidney laughed again and got off his wife's bed. 'I should think your friend Mr Crawford will go into mourning,' he said. 'You are much too acute for your years. Poor Jane is going to be frightened into a fever.'

'It's just the novelty,' Philippa said. 'No affected phrase, but a mean and popular style. Do you think I should learn to speak Spanish?'

Sir Henry Sidney, knight, stared at her. 'I do,' he said. 'I am convinced that you must. I think you are exactly what the King's poor homesick nobles require to take their minds off the beer, the Pope, the prices, the climate and the women. Even when dressed like a sentry-box.'

Philippa Somerville lived at Penshurst for six weeks before taking her place at the Court. It was a strange interlude between the easy backwaters of Midculter and the chill reality whose shadow she felt even in that time, as she put it, of training and refitting : the stark reality of central office, where men strive with the management of human affairs.

From that interlude, out of much that was bright and shifting and sometimes unintelligible, two people made a deep impression on Philippa. One was Jane Dormer, her future companion, a fair and ethereal sixteen-year-old with a soft voice and an incredible perfection of deportment and manners. The other, visiting his motherless sons who were already part of the great scattered household of relatives, dependants, wards and pensioners of every degree, was Diccon Chancellor.

Philippa's first view of Chancellor was piecemeal through the segments of a man-high contraption of wood, advancing upon her card-table from the other end of the hall. Arrived before her, the object was placed firmly aside, revealing a short, stocky man in his thirties, with untrimmed black hair and a beard and round slaty eyes below a brow lined like a wrythen ribbed beaker. By his side, Sir Henry Sidney also came to a halt and addressed Philippa, one hand on the other man's shoulder.

'You've met his sons,' said Sir Henry. 'Richard Chancellor, who grew up here as a schoolboy and learned from Cabot all the tricks of the Seville hydrographical bureau, such as how to find the Great Cham of China in Moscow. Diccon, meet Philippa Somerville, an English lady within the years of innocence who knows more about the Levant than you do, and is at present disowning her husband.'

The confronting parties stared at one another. 'More than any masterful scorner I know,' Richard Chancellor said, 'Henry has to a wonder the art of suffocating conversation and then leaving others to bury it. Christopher tells me the Sultan of Turkey is shortly visiting Hexham.'

'Your son exaggerates, as does everyone under this roof,' Philippa said. 'Is the new quadrant for Moscow or China?'

'What years of innocence?' said Diccon Chancellor sourly to Sidney. He gave a passing stroke to the painted wood of his instrument and dropped into the nook of a settle, while Sidney came to rest on its arm. 'John Dee and I are about to take it to Cabot. Anticipate a long argument, and an abusive lecture on the variations of the magnetic needle and how to measure therefrom one's travels east or west on the earth's surface.' He flung up his hands. 'How do I know where I shall go with it? The Kingdom of Women? Barinth's Isle called Delicious? The land of the Cariai, who dry the bodies of princes on hurdles, and so reserve them, involved in the leaves of their forests. Ask my masters.'

'He means me,' said Sidney.

'I mean George Barnes and Tony Hussey and John Dimmock and Will Chester and Edmund Roberts and Will Garrard and all the other comfortable drapers and staplers and skinners and pewterers and haberdashers and grocers who sat back and thought up the Voyage to Cathay, under the direction of the right worshipful Master Sebastian Cabot Esquire, governor of the Mystery and Company of the Merchants Adventurer for the discovery of Regions, Dominions, Islands, and places unknown, in the year of our Lord God 1553. And expected me to sail east of Norway.'

'You asked to be pilot-general,' said Sidney calmly. 'They didn't know you wanted some riotous living. Think of all the free drink you've had as the first man to sail east of North Cape and arrive by the north route in Muscovy.'

'Think of Hugh Willoughby,' said Chancellor sharply. 'They picked him, too.'

Philippa looked at Sir Henry who obliged, undisturbed, with an explanation. 'Diccon's was the only one of three ships to get through. They reached the Lofotens, and then ran into heavy weather and fog, just past North Cape. When it lifted, the other two vessels had vanished, with Sir Hugh Willoughby, the captain-general, on one. Diccon waited seven days at Vardo, but they didn't come, then or later. Diccon, who doesn't like good-looking men, is inclined to blame Willoughby.'

'Bugg,' said Chancellor. 'His name was Bugg, till an ancestor changed it. I've nothing against him. He was well born; well connected; an excellent soldier and had a fine manner to parley with princes, and a lofty contempt for the sea. They didn't know it. They pulled the pole from the hop and dispatched him.'

Sir Henry's niece, walking past, sat down at the other end of Philippa's backgammon table and bent a grave look on Chancellor. 'He paid for the fault with his life,' Jane observed. 'And rendered his immortal soul to his Maker.'

'In December, I should accept it : a tragedy,' Diccon said. 'But in *August*?'

Sir Henry cleared his throat. 'When you,' he said to Philippa, 'were scaling forbidden royal trees and punching stable boys in the stomach, my Jane at six was reading the Office of Our Blessed Lady in Latin daily at Aylesbury, crossing occasionally with her governess to Ashridge to play, read and dance with the late child Prince Edward. We all fall silent when she speaks, except Diccon, who might as well have perished with Willoughby, for all we have heard about Russia.'

'I'm sick of Russia. Eden will tell you,' Chancellor said.

'I don't want to hear it in Latin,' Sir Henry said. 'My God, I've had enough Latin. I did you proud, anyway. *Vehementer pium institutum vestrum amplector, viri honestissimi* . . . "Prompted by your ardent affection for your native land, you are applying yourselves to the furtherance of a project which will, I trust, prove beneficial to the people of England and reflect also honour on our common country. I part with Chancellor for this reason : not because I am tired of him, or because I find his maintenance burdensome to me, but that the authority and position Chancellor so well deserves may be given him. While we commit a little money to the hazard of fortune, he commits his very life to the remorseless sea. With what toils will he not be broken? With what dangers and watchings will he not be harassed; with what anxieties will he not be devoured? While we shall remain in our ancestral homes, he will seek foreign and unknown realms; he will entrust his safety to barbarians and unknown tribes; he will even expose his life to the monsters of the deep," I said. I hope Jane is listening. And now what? Back wined and dined and hanging with furs from the Kremlin, you complain because a man has not the skill to get himself drowned in December. Now I look at you, you're getting fat.'

'He isn't,' said Jane. 'I hear the castle of Moscow is fine, and is set on a fair wooded hill.'

'There is a handful of churches and palaces, ringed about with high walls and rivers. The Tsar's home, the Kremlin, lies in the innermost ring, and the city outside it.'

'And is Russia rich?' added Philippa obediently. 'What nature of land is it?'

Diccon Chancellor spoke to her, but his eyes were on something beyond her. 'A land half-snatched by men from the hang-nails of winter, where heat and cold swing like a lodestone. For five months of the year the ice is an ell and more thick on her rivers. The poor may be smitten stiff in their cabins, and the sledges run into Moscow with the sitting dead grasping the harness. Of all the people of the earth, they have the hardest living.'

'They plant crops?'

'They are sunk in morasses and flooded with rivers : trees march through them like armies. They have no grains to export, nor jewels, nor spices nor any object of grace. They have walrus teeth and seal oil and sables, martens and grease beavers, hides and timber and tallow, salt and wax. They have no need of hives, for lakes of honey live in the trees. They say a man, slipping, lived in a pool for two days, and had to cling to a bear's fur to pull himself out.'

'They are a hardy nation?' Jane Dormer said.

'They are strong,' Chancellor said. 'Square, brawny men with short legs and big bellies, who do not repine. *I have nothing*, they say, *but it is God's and our Duke's Grace's.* They do not think, as we do, that what is ours is but God's and our own. They are content to scrape all their lives at the Tsar's princely pleasure.'

Philippa's brown eyes were wide open. 'Don't they rebel?' she said tartly.

'With what?' Chancellor said. 'They have only numbers. And without army, without navy, without order, without standing in Asia or Europe, where else can the Tsar find an income?'

'I read,' said Sidney, 'what you set down for Eden. *If they knew their strength, no man were able to make match with them; nor they that dwell near them should have any rest of them.* Fortunately, they don't know their own strength.'

'Unless you teach it them, trading,' said Chancellor.

It had the ring of a long-standing argument. Sir Henry

Sidney caught Philippa's bland eye and smiled. 'Diccon's dream is of travel and conquest. A new Caesar, a new Alexander who will reach further than India and bring back an empire without need for needles and hawks' bells and looking-glasses, and certainly without landing sheets and kerseys, and garnishes of indifferent pewter. But if you will go exploring, Diccon, you must allow those who dwell in the external light, by the essence of mechanical arts, to attempt to pay for the bottoms.'

'Without the inferior light,' Philippa said, 'which produces sensitive knowledge?'

'I exclude nothing,' said Sir Henry, 'except that Diccon will clamour to join the Worshipful Company of Drapers.'

'Why,' said Jane Dormer, 'may he not enlarge the Christian faith and dominion to the glory of God and the confusion of infidels comforted by the English merchants peaceably trading in Russia?'

'Especially,' said Philippa Somerville, 'if the Russians are taught to exterminate Tartars.'

The men looked at each other. Sir Henry Sidney got to his feet, and laying his hand on his hip, gazed down on them all with benignity. 'Thus,' he said, 'despite the late confused counsel of ministers, I am persuaded that in this schismatic world, those guided by lights external and lights inferior may well solve our problems in harness.'

Chancellor rose in his turn. 'I do not go,' he said, 'because I am tired of you, or because I find your entertainment burdensome, but because I am wrecked on the wit of your women. Mistress Somerville, I have to thank you on Nick and Christopher's behalf for your interest in them. Take heed at court. There are more monsters there than are born in the ocean.'

'*To laugh, to lie, to flatter, to face: Four ways in court to win men's grace.* Ascham will like her. I think I shall entrust her classical training to Ascham,' said Sir Henry. 'The voyage we are embarked on will demand the cunning and strength of the ancients before winter is over.'

*

On 30 November, the Sidneys' first child was born; a son named, with resignation, Philip after the current King-consort. Shortly afterwards Philippa, with serving-woman and escort rode the thirty-five miles north to

London to enter the bridal court of the middle-aged Queen, with the badger's nose and faded red hair and small, anchorite's body within the stiff, quarried case of her costume.

There were no eunuchs at the door of Westminster, or black pages, or cool fountains playing. Philippa made the same curtsey to her Queen as she had to Roxelana Sultan; but in a wainscoted room hung with tapestries, before a canopied chair of state embodying the royal arms of England and Spain, and surrounded, on stools, on cushions, on fringed velvet chairs, by extremely plain women.

All except one. Lady Margaret Douglas, Countess of Lennox, First Lady and Mistress of Robes to Queen Mary her cousin, was thirty-nine and still handsome despite ten years of child-bearing, and a lifetime during which she had found herself by turn heir to the throne, bastard, and maid of honour to three of her uncle's six wives.

She watched Philippa from her place by the Queen, her back straight, her eyes open, her hands still on the silver bone-lace of her kirtle, and the expression on her blonde, big-featured face showed nothing but faint, well-bred boredom. She said, 'The daughter of Gideon Somerville, who served your grace well in the north, and was once an officer of my own household. Now your grace has two Scots in your service.'

Philippa, who was wearing a great many jewels, rose from her curtsey and, with an effort equally invisible, refrained from replying.

'What child : no disclaimer?' said a strong, masculine voice. The Queen extended her hand, the broad wedding band sparkling on the unremarkable fingers. 'Lady Lennox is born of a Scot, and her lord is another : yet there beats no more true English heart here than hers.'

Philippa kissed the square hand and stepped backwards, her lips glazed with cold incense. She said, 'Forgive me, your grace. I believed her ladyship to be jesting. For I have no Scottish blood, and no marriage at all but on paper.' She did not look at Lady Lennox.

'It is a strange tale we have been told,' said the Queen. 'But your union was made, we understand, of necessity and without that blessing of divine and uxorious love with which God sometimes rewards selfless action. Does your husband worship as you do?'

Faultlessly groomed, Philippa's eyes lost focus slightly. She felt her sponsor, old Lady Dormer, shift slightly behind her, and cast her eyes downwards. 'The rites of Holy Church attended our marriage,' she said. 'We parted soon afterwards.'

'And the bastard boy whom you brought back to Scotland,' said Lady Lennox with interest. 'Is he being reared as a true son of the Church?' She leaned across to the Queen. 'The child is not, of course, Mistress Philippa's own.'

Philippa's face was perfectly winsome. 'The child is in England,' she answered, 'being taught his duty by my own mother.'

'And when your union is severed?' said Margaret Lennox.

'The child will remain at Flaw Valleys,' Philippa said.

The Queen's small mouth, the mouth of Catherine of Aragon, curled in a swift smile. 'So we have drawn one Scotsman whole to our kingdom,' she said. 'And I trust that one day you will give us many stout Englishmen from your true marriage bed. When you are rid of this marriage, we shall look to your fortunes.'

The cadence was one of dismissal. Philippa curtseyed, thinking of her true marriage bed not at all; but of the thin, bolstered figure before her with the broad Flemish features, worn with anxiety.

How goes my daughter's belly? had asked the Emperor Charles, who had been betrothed to this same Queen thirty years ago, sitting under his nightcap in the small Brussels house in the park, listening to the night-long ticking tread of his clocks. *Benedicta inter mulieres,* the new Papal Legate had said, *et benedictus fructus ventris tui.* If the Queen died childless, the Catholics said, her sister Elizabeth with French help would inherit the throne, and the kingdom return once more to heresy. If the Queen had a son, the Protestants said, it would prove no more than the conduit by which the rats of Rome might creep into the stronghold. And there had been a placard nailed to the door of the Palace, everyone whispered. *Shall we be such fools, noble English, as to think that our Queen will give birth to anything, except it be a marmot or a puppy?*

Many stout Englishmen would that uncompromising vessel of King Harry's majesty need.

On duty, Philippa was to sleep with Jane Dormer in the Queen's privy chambers. She had a modest chest taken there : the rest of her London clothes she had left at the Dormer lodging in the Savoy. She learned, with unqualified regret, of Queen Mary's habitual timetable, which from tomorrow henceforth she would share. The Queen rose at daybreak : she said Mass in private before plunging straight into business, which she transacted without pause till past midnight : she never touched food before two o'clock.

'Like her mother, the sainted Queen Catherine,' said Lady Dormer that afternoon, steering both girls firmly into the throng of the ante-chamber. '. . . So many well-bred young gentlemen ! . . . who rose at five, having wakened at midnight for the Matins of the Religious, and who fasted each Friday and Saturday and all Eves of our Blessed Lady. Who believed, poor Lady, that time lost which was spent dressing herself.'

'She was not permitted, dear grandmother,' Jane Dormer said, 'the joys which we celebrate.'

'That is so.' Arrested, Lady Dormer raised a delicate hand. 'The Cardinal Legate, restored to us after twenty years' banishment. The coming to this land of trouble of the greatest of princes on earth, to be spouse and son, as of old, to this Virgin . . .'

'With his disciples around him,' said Philippa. A man with black eyes and earrings smiled at her.

'. . . and the return of England, triumphant, to the See Apostolic upon the devoted petition of Parliament . . . Don Alfonso.'

'My Lady Dormer,' said the man with black eyes, smiling at Lady Dormer. 'May I assist you? You wish to pass to the royal apartments?'

On principle, Jane's formidable grandmother never spoke Spanish. 'There is no need, I thank you,' she said, her old eyes surveying, in one level stare, all the extravagances of Spanish high fashion. 'Mistress Jane is not yet due for her service, and Mistress Philippa is here to become acquainted with those more familiar at Court.' She turned to Philippa, and Philippa met the black eyes, her own well-drilled brown ones quite blank. 'Let me present Don Alfonso Derronda, secretary to the Prince of Melito. Mistress Philippa Crawford.'

The young Spanish gentleman, recovering from his bow to Jane Dormer, bestowed an even more convolute gesture on Philippa. He floated upright with his rosy lips open. 'But a coincidence!' he cried. 'Mistress Crawford! I have been required to present her to the Prince at the first opportunity.'

The hooded eyes studied him. 'The first opportunity has not yet occurred,' said Lady Dormer. 'When it does, I shall present her.' Through the chatter of high English voices and the flow of Spanish, halting and fluent, her voice sounded cold. Someone near broke into laughter and a string consort, playing unseen in the fretted room high in the screen, embarked on a galliard. The long room was too crowded for dancing, but the conversation, as if in sympathy, quickened and sparkled. A voice, recently heard, said to Don Alfonso, 'Let me present her. The Prince of Melito is standing just over there.'

Lady Lennox had appeared beside Philippa. In two more skilful minutes, she and Don Alfonso were pressing through the bright crowd, with Philippa captured between them. At the far end of the room, smiling, Lady Lennox came to a halt, her furred oversleeves swinging, and the young Spaniard laughed and lifted his eyebrows. 'I see no Don Ruy Gomez de Silva.'

Margaret Lennox allowed her eyes to rest first on the Spaniard and then on Philippa Somerville. 'Because he is changing his costume for cane-play, as you well know, Don Alfonso. You also know that my poor Lady Dormer dislikes him.'

'She thinks him a cynic,' Don Alfonso said.

'As he is,' said Lady Lennox.

'A realist,' said the young Spaniard. *'Upon the devoted petition of Parliament!* How impartial, one wonders, were the recent elections to Parliament, and is it not a co-incidence that barely a member inimical to Holy Church and the Queen's will was returned? Has this stiff-necked people, one asks oneself, really been led back so soon to the obedience of the Church? Last year they denied the Sacrament and married their clergy. This year, as they tell me, all their beliefs have been altered. Can it be true that, as Cotswold lions, the people of England follow the faith of their King : Judaism or Mahometism – it is all one to them? Does Parliament really represent the wish of the people?'

Lady Lennox did not wince, nor move as much as would stir the folds of black velvet laid under her jewel-sewn head-dress. She said, 'How can you doubt it? What else are we assisting their Majesties to celebrate?'

'The slicking down,' said Don Alfonso, 'of the thread of rebellion.'

Margaret Lennox laughed. 'Gloomy Spaniard! Will it stay down, do you think?'

'Perhaps,' said Don Alfonso. 'Or perhaps, looking again, we shall see not a single frayed thread, but a yawning black hell-hole of heresy. . . . If Mistress Crawford permits, might your humble servant take her to the cane-play?'

Philippa switched her obedient gaze to Lady Lennox, who smiled and laid a splendid ringed hand on her shoulder. 'Mistress Crawford, I am sure, would prefer to be called Mistress Philippa. Her marriage is soon to be null : perhaps Lady Dormer omitted to tell you. And yes, I am convinced that cane-play would appeal to her much more than the troubles of government. Although I do not suggest negligence in study. Master Elder, my son Darnley's tutor, has told me today that he would be happy, Mistress Philippa, to make you his pupil. A touch of the Latin tongue is advantageous in the household of princes.'

'How kind you are,' Philippa said. 'If my readings with Mr Ascham allow it, I should be privileged to study with Mr Elder as well.'

There was an elegant silence. Then Margaret Lennox smiled and touched the warm, scented surface of Philippa's cheek. 'I have offended you. Don't hold it against me. I am merely anxious to help. Don Alfonso, take good care of her. I suspect she is a mine of accomplishments.'

'So you are not afraid of her,' said Don Alfonso, after the Countess had gone. 'Although she is a formidable lady. You know, I suppose, that John Elder and Roger Ascham love each other as do God and the Devil?'

'Yes,' said Philippa.

'And if the Queen's Latin secretary will take you, then you must be a pupil of promise indeed.'

'My Latin is promising,' Philippa said, 'but my English not necessarily so.'

'Then we shall converse in Latin,' said her new conquest promptly. 'Although not in the hearing of Lady Lennox.'

Lady Lennox had half crossed the hall when a man she did not know, from the privy clerk's office, hurried after her and asked if she would repeat the name of the lady to whom she had been speaking. Lady Lennox did so, with courteous precision, and asked him his own, which was Bartholomew Lychpole.

CHAPTER SEVEN

The cane-play was an artistic disaster. To the thud of kettle-drum and fluting of trumpets the six quadrilles of riders wove through the long hall at Westminster and re-created with exquisite horsemanship the delicate tilting with reeds brought to Castile long before by the Arabs. The audience chattered.

Watching from the gallery, Philippa was pained, and said so. The bands of the Duke of Alva, Ruy Gomez de Silva and Don Diego de Acevedo moved forward, in a shimmer of tissue and a glow of deep-coloured velvets. 'It was worse the last time,' said Don Alfonso beside her. 'Last time your English friends laughed. They prefer something coarser, with blood in it. Have you distinguished King Philip?'

The shields glanced; the canes with their long streamers arched through the air. Protected by tapestried barriers, the Queen sat with her ladies, dressed at King Philip's expense, like a box of great nodding peonies. Jane, now on duty, looked grave in purple velvet banded with silver. On the other hand, Jane suited purple. Philippa said, 'Which is the King?'

'Opposite Ruy Gomez. In purple and silver, in the band led by Don Diego de Cordova,' said Ruy Gomez's secretary. Since he had discovered she also spoke Spanish, his black eyes, to her mild alarm, had outshone even his earrings.

'Oh,' said Philippa. Bearing the royal shield was the very high and mighty Prince Philip, sole heir to the realms and dominions of Spain, whose father had thrust upon him the titles of Naples and Sicily in time to call him King at his marriage. A widower, with a nine-year-old son, married to his aunt, twelve years older. A man of twenty-seven, small, bearded and colourless, with thick lips and a narrow, aquiline nose who was far, Philippa noted with regret, from being a natural-born athlete.

A cane, hurled a little awry, was deftly caught and retained by an anonymous English spectator in another part of the gallery. There was a small derisive cheer from his companions. The rider waited a moment, head upturned; then, as it was not thrown back, turned his horse into its pattern again. Another cane was passed to him. 'I am told,' Philippa said, 'that unlike Henri of France, King Philip doesn't care for pageants or field sports or chivalry.'

Don Alfonso raised his black eyebrows, sneezed, and apologized. 'It is the climate,' he said. 'We are sick with the rheum. First the rolling at sea; then the rain at the wedding. No, he dislikes physical games. His father writes him, *For the love of God, appear to be pleased, for there is nothing that could be of greater effect in the service of God, or against France.*' Another cane flew in the air. 'For what return? His favours would soften stones. He has given pensions of nearly sixty thousand gold crowns to the Queen's Council alone. He well knows how to pass over those fields of fleshly experience where your good Queen is not gifted : he treats her so deferentially as to appear her son, and the Prince heard him almost use love-talk last week. . . . For what? His coronation is delayed. They laugh at him. They write tasteless ballads and satires. You heard of the polled cat hung up dead like a priest, with a note like a singing-cake stuck in its paws?'

'Yes,' said Philippa. The King had lost his cane and someone had thrown him one from the gallery, slightly misaimed. He dropped it.

'And always the threat of rebellion. We daren't leave Spain for months because of it, and even then only with distinguished soldiers for servants, and our chests full of hackbuts. The English do not speak to us, except to pick quarrels. We are warned to stay in after dark for the robbers. We move among these people like animals, trying not to notice them, and they likewise with us. He was not going to a marriage feast, Philip said, but to a fight. As soon as his Highness was King of England, they said, we should be masters of France. And here we are. Decisions are taken, armies are directed by women without us, and so long as Parliament sits, we dare not leave England.' He sneezed, with violence. 'England : a Paradise inhabited by devils.'

Philippa said, 'You need bed and a hot drink and a little less fluent self-pity. Is Spain so wonderful?'

'Bed?' said Don Alfonso, and nearly captured her hand, before she slid it away. 'That, I do not deny, is a condition I greatly desire. Spain? It is wonderful, yes. For King Philip, his splendid Doña Isabel de Osario and their family. For me, I do not deny, a pretty face here and there. But in Spain our ladies do not kiss their friends on the lips in the streets, or dine with them unescorted, or show so much leg as they ride. When may I see you again?'

Below, on a ground strewn with half-broken rods, the cane-play was ending. The gallery had lost interest, although one or two canes were still being thrown: As Philippa watched, another sprang through the air and pricked King Philip's horse, sliding past before he could catch it. He reined in, looking upwards. 'Did you hear,' said Don Alfonso, 'of the baiting on the Bankside? A blind bear got loose, and bit a man on the leg. That is the kind of sport, they say, that we should provide for the English.'

'If you are sure,' Philippa said, 'that the man won't bite back.'

The following day, Philippa entered the service of Mary Tudor, this small, quick-spoken woman who prayed and worked with such alarming single-mindedness: who played the lute, through sheer force of practice, better than all of her ladies, yet had no eye for what would enhance her appearance: who hung her walls with gold-work on her tapestries, and her person with stiff, long-trained dresses paved with old-fashioned jewels. The jewels which her father's second wife Anne Boleyn had sent to wrest from her mother, and which her mentor the Countess of Salisbury had refused to give up. But Mary's mother had not lived long after that, and Lady Salisbury had been beheaded, and Mary to save her own life had signed the three articles King Henry demanded: that she submitted to her father the King. That she recognized him as the head of the Church in England. And that the marriage between the King and his first wife her mother was by God's law and man's law incestuous and unlawful, thus making a bastard of herself and a princess of her sister Elizabeth.

Small wonder, thought Philippa, that after the degradation, the poverty, the humiliation of that, one's first act on becoming Queen was to repeal one's father's unnatural laws, thus making oneself legitimate and bastardizing one's sister. And the second, to wear all one's rightful regalia and a pair of breeches if necessary, to show that, woman or not, here was the heir blessed by God under whom the kingdom would flourish.

Learning to know all the scattered buildings of Westminster, and of Wolsey's relinquished Whitehall; learning to recognize the officers of State and all their counterparts and double counterparts in King Philip's households of Spanish and Englishmen, Philippa began to see the reason for the obsessive hard work, in a woman who was only moderately clever, in one of the hardest offices on the world. The fluency in languages modern and classical which visiting ambassadors found so impressive. The aching need for success which showed itself in her fierce joy in gambling; in the cosseted throng of her cage-birds; in her njoyment of children; in the care – although, to be fair, her nature was to be thoughtful and careful to others – she took with the common people on her travels, stopping to speak with them, and anonymously to care for their troubles.

The desperate need she had for the bulwark of her religion.

Sitting sewing with Jane, or reading aloud, or playing, without much thought, on the lute or the virginals, Philippa's mind, like one of the Emperor's clocks, busied itself with the entrancing tangle of England.

The Queen's mother had been devout. But she had needed the support of her Church more than most – mother of five stillborn children in eight years; cast off for another after twenty-four years of marriage. Brought up in that household, naturally Mary Tudor would hold strong religious opinions, even had her own birthright not depended on it. Now, attempting to rule with no apprenticeship for ruling behind her, she needed it for support.

She had little enough, thought Philippa grimly, of the human kind. Jane Dormer was only sixteen; her grandmother too old to master the new political complexities; old Mistress Clarenceux too simple. Margaret Lennox, the oldest, the dearest, the most richly rewarded of all the Queen's circle, was also the Englishwoman with the nearest Catholic claim to the throne . . . was that why she had been given, Tom Wharton had told her, the whole three thousand marks yearly tax revenue from the wool trade, simply as a royal gift? The group of gentlemen who had quelled the rebellions and seen to it that Mary returned to the throne had had to be repaid with offices which they were not necessarily fitted for. Even Reginald Pole, Cardinal, royally born and man of integrity, had not supported the Queen in one thing: he had been against the marriage with Philip.

My lord and nephew, the King of England. When she first heard the Queen speak of her husband, Philippa had expected to catch in the deep, over-strong voice the slightest shadow, perhaps of defiance.

There was none. Perhaps there had never been. Perhaps in crushing the opposition to her marriage she had also argued into oblivion, to herself and to her prie-dieu, the personal reasons. The ponderous young man who had visited her daily, tastefully dressed; who gave a due meed of his time to being agreeable to those odd people, the English, and who then retired behind closed doors with Ruy Gomez and the Spanish lords of his court, was no one's soul-mate, except possibly the unknown Doña Isabel de Osario, mother of unspecified numbers of Spanish illegitimate children, and the predecessors of whom Don Alfonso was lyrical. The Emperor's exhortations to his son to please Mary Queen and to make her happy would hardly spring from cousinly kindness. No untoward personal emotions must upset the Imperial English alliance. More, a warm marriage bed might produce the son which would reconcile the English to their King and to his religion.

The Queen knew that, better than any. . . . But the pinched lips parted for him as they did for her love-birds; and the pale, shadowless eyes relaxed in the high-coloured face. At two, the Queen had been betrothed to the Dauphin of France, now King Henri. At nine, to the Emperor Charles, Philip's father. Yet again she had been sought by the Dauphin's father, Francis of France, twice married and twice widowed, with seven bastard children. She had been painted and inspected: ambassadors had surveyed her all her life, until her father proclaimed her a bastard herself. As a child, she had seen herself as an Empress, and as a grown woman had known herself to be no more than an ageing, emotional spinster, the bride of her God.

One could discuss none of this in the pure hearing of Jane, the dear and devout, herself almost the subject of a political marriage with Will Courtenay, the inconvenient Earl of Devonshire, to keep him out of Elizabeth's hands. One said it instead to Austin Grey, when he came to see her on her rare periods of leave at Lady Dormer's, and to escort her to the triumphs and tourneys or the celebration of the Feast of St Lucy, or the St Nicholas's going about, against orders, in the bright frosty glitter of a December evening in London.

Austin never required brisk handling, as Don Afonso did, by the end of the evening. He listened to her stream of speculation in silence, and didn't laugh at her at all, but seemed to regard her power of observation and analysis as something worth celebrating on their own.

Cut off in full spate, Philippa was apt to find it pleasant, but embarrassing. 'Oh, that's Kate for you,' she said the first time. 'All the Somervilles are fiends for dissecting their neighbours. We had you judged from the moment your nurse brought you to visit, and you cried when the cook's niece was sick. Tender-hearted.'

She thought, with contrition, that he flushed, but he had more than enough social ease to disguise it. 'If I were less tender-hearted, I might be tempted to wonder whether you saw in the Queen's marriage an echo of your own. What dreams are in your head, Philippa? Is it dreams which prevent the annulment from taking place?'

The round brown eyes which opened upon him were probably answer enough. 'My goodness,' said Philippa. 'You've never been in the hands of the Turks, or you wouldn't expect anyone to have much time for dreaming. Nor, I imagine, do you have any recollection of what Lymond is actually like. *My mother* can barely put up with him. We can't get an annulment because he hasn't written giving his formal consent. Which reminds me. Have you ever heard of a gentleman called Leonard Bailey?'

'No,' said the Marquis of Allendale on the faintest note of inquiry.

'Oh,' said Philippa. 'Well, if you do, I should be deeply obliged if you'd tell me. He's by way of being a relation by marriage.' And was thoughtless enough to giggle at his expression.

Roger Ascham, with whom she had begun her classical studies, was less tender-hearted in his reaction. 'There are one hundred and eighty thousand people in London. I know them all,' he said.

'Well, you write Latin letters for half of them,' said Philippa, unsubdued. She possessed, it would appear, a brain almost as quick for Latin as Madam Elizabeth's, and a great deal of rummaging about in the library of her nominal spouse had given her an advantage in some directions which the Queen's Latin secretary thought quite unethical. They read Virgil, Homer, Herodotus, Plato, Terence and endless pages of Xenophon together and wrangled about Philippa's analysis of King Philip's character, which Master Ascham claimed to understand completely after three years as the English Ambassador's secretary at Augsburg.

'It would never occur to the Emperor,' Ascham said, 'that his son is unpopular. He will give him everything, whether he can hold it or not; whether he has ever fought in anger or not. The Emperor is twisted with gout – a dying man, and no wonder. I remember the Golden Fleece banquet. He had his head in the glass five times as long as any of us, and never less than a quart of Rhenish wine at one time. And the boy's a tyro. Hates to stir himself : lies abed in the mornings; keeps his fine shape for wooing by diet, and none of your exercise. Have you seen him in the lists?' asked Master Ascham. 'I saw him joust genteelly at Augsburg. He hurt neither himself, his horse, his spear, nor the fellow he ran with.'

'*A stout stomach, pregnant-witted, and of a most gentle nature,*' Philippa quoted, with delicacy.

Ascham stiffened, his face going purple.

'I know. That mountebank Elder,' Philippa said.

'John Redshanks,' said Ascham thinly. 'An amateur cosmographer from some puny church in a place called Dumbarton. Who claims Henry Darnley to surpass the late King Edward – the Lady Elizabeth – the Grey children as a Latinist.'

'And me,' said Philippa.

Fastidiously, Roger Ascham laid down his quill. 'He does not presumably know of your existence, for which you should be thankful. Unless he is a friend of your husband's. In which case you would do well to deliver your husband a warning. No offers from that quarter will ever do good to anyone except the Lennoxes. I have heard them exhort the Queen to have her sister executed time without number. Fortunately, the Emperor's Ambassador has been as strong to dissuade her. The present talk is of marrying Madam Elizabeth to the Margrave of Baden, or any other small state lacking a coastline. They will be hard put to it to find a grate for that coal to burn in.'

'What cause have they to banish her?' Philippa said. 'I heard that her devotions were constant and her discretion alarmingly total. And when the child is born, she will be a further remove from the throne.'

'It is true,' Ascham said. 'A son will bring Burgundy and the Low Countries to England. If Don Carlos were to die, it might unite England wholly with Spain. But is there going to be a child?'

It was the sort of question asked by Jane, or by Austin, or by any of the plain gentlewomen surrounding the Queen. Philippa said, guardedly, 'There is a cradle. She speaks of it sometimes. And she is plumper, they say, and of a better colour than before.'

'She is happier,' Ascham said. 'But irregularity in her health there has always been. You have seen the bloodletting. You know of the medicines she takes. And if she has conceived, what chance will the child have? The hours of prayer on her knees, like her mother. The hours of studying papers, of committee with her ministers : this vast council of time-serving Privy Councillors, half of whom should be given provincial duties and sent back to their estates. Gardiner – Paget – Cecil – Petre . . . how can she know whom to trust, when during the last reign nearly all of them were against her?'

'She trusts you,' Philippa said. 'In spite of *the Roman beast and its dogmatic filth* in tail-rhymed stanzas, not to mention a few other injudicious pronouncements.'

'Do you suggest,' said Ascham with hauteur, 'that she should have appointed Elder? She took me because she had none better, as she should refuse retirement to William Petre. He has been there so long, he is a Council register in himself. While Princes come and vanish like swallows, the land needs some weight in the saddle. Only pray that she doesn't solicit safe birth for her heir by impossible largesse to the Pontiff. The banished friars are returning, I hear, and the Knights of St John are restored : soon the crown will give back its Church lands, and Reginald Pole will be Archbishop of Canterbury, if they make sure to ordain him beforehand.'

111

Philippa's brown eyes surveyed him. 'The Crown may give up its church lands, but I doubt if anyone else will be persuaded. The Earl of Bedford proclaimed that he cared more for his sweet Abbey of Woburn than for any fatherly counsel from Rome, and forthwith tugged off and cast down his rosary. The King was far from amused.'

'I saw him amused only once,' Roger Ascham said thoughtfully. 'At a Brussels procession. They had a bear playing the organ, with the keys tied to the tails of twenty cages of cats. It was extremely noisy. The Prince laughed himself into tears. I wonder if he will do the same if . . . no,' Master Ascham chided himself. 'It is bad luck to anticipate disaster. In any case, we have gossiped enough : our time is at an end for today. Collect your books. Do you know Bartholomew Lychpole?'

The secretariat was not large. Philippa said, 'The man in brown, who always wears spectacles?'

'Yes. He wanted to speak with you. Wait.' He bustled out.

Philippa was alone in the room when Master Lychpole arrived. She fastened her penner and then looked up to see him standing diffidently before her, the dim light grey in his lenses. 'Madame Crawford?' he said.

Used to another styling, Philippa did not at once respond to her married name. Then she said, 'Yes. And you are Master Lychpole?'

He nodded. He was not a young man, and he spoke in a low voice, as if anxious not to be heard in conversation with her. 'I wished to ask you the favour of a few words in private. On a personal matter.'

'Yes?' said Philippa, lifting her eyebrows.

Bartholomew Lychpole's voice had dropped half an octave. 'Your husband is Francis Crawford of Lymond?'

'Yes,' said Philippa in the same sweet, lying cadence she had learned in Stamboul.

'I am employed here,' said Bartholomew Lychpole, 'but I am a man of wide interests. I correspond. I hear many things. But I dare not say what I hear, you understand, or I should lose my employment. I am a poor man, and I dare not lose my employment. I beg you therefore . . .'

'You wish to tell me something about Mr Crawford, and you do not wish me to quote you. I understand,' Philippa said. 'Whatever you say will remain quite private with me. What do you want me to know?'

'I heard you were his wife,' Lychpole said. 'I don't take risks. I can't afford to take risks. But I thought you should know he is well.'

Philippa sat down very gently and looked at him. She said, 'I am glad to know that. You have heard from him recently?'

'Last week,' said Master Lychpole. 'Later, I dare say, than any message you have; even if the couriers managed to reach you. It's not like writing from Brussels. I thought it would please you just to know he was well.'

'Yes,' said Philippa. 'It will please his mother as well when I tell her. Where was he writing from?'

'Oh, the same place,' said Bartholomew Lychpole. 'He dates his letters always from there, although I hear he travels abroad in the country from week to week, on his master's business, whether it is attack or defence no one can tell me. This season, I wager he would prefer to be by your side in some good English rain. They say there can be a coldness well-nigh beyond mortal man's bearing, this month in Moscow.'

Philippa Somerville's eyes became exceedingly large. Lychpole said slowly after a moment, 'But of course they are prepared for the cold. You must not allow it to worry you.'

Lymond's titular wife drew a deep breath. 'It doesn't,' she said. 'I wasn't thinking of that. . . . I wonder if your post would reach him more quickly than mine.'

'You have a letter?' said Lychpole.

'I would give you one,' Philippa said. 'What direction do you have for him in Moscow?'

But there she came up against a politic silence. Whatever Bartholomew Lychpole's business, it was conducted in secrecy, and his correspondence was not sent direct, but entrusted to a series of messengers, the last of whom conveyed it to Lymond, wherever in Russia he might be.

For Lymond, it seemed, was in Russia. And the more Philippa thought of it, the likelier somehow did it appear. He had no wish to come home. He had no interest in old loyalties and ancient entanglements, and yet would take no steps, Philippa thought, to place himself in direct conflict with them.

What more likely than that he had stayed on the perimeter, half in, half out the known world, to build a new sphere of power with Kiaya Khátún, who worshipped power, beside him? And this well-meaning, inadequate man was no doubt in some form his spy.

Of all the peoples of the earth, they have the hardest living, Diccon Chancellor had said of the Muscovites. And Sydney had quoted. *If they knew their strength, no man were able to make match with them.*

Small wonder Lychpole was uneasy. Lymond's presence in Russia was more than an item of gossip: a matter of purely family concern. To reveal her knowledge of it would not only betray Lychpole's confidence. It would send all the statesmen of Europe to probe the occurrence: so many squirrels gutting a pine cone. It would force Russia to show her hand, perhaps, before she was ready, and put Lymond's own life at risk.

Or at more risk. Lymond had never shown any desire for security. Now, lodged at last in a land where his special gifts would be quite unsurpassed, he had an opportunity for dominion which he could expect nowhere else. Philippa had been aware, since the silence which succeeded her last letter, that she must write another, and in fairness set in it what she had learned from Sybilla's sister, the Abbess. The expedient by which she had hoped to hurry Lymond's return to his mother was likely, she now knew, to have the opposite effect. And to expect anything else to draw him from the brilliant prospect before him was childish.

She thanked Lychpole, and even gave him some of the coins in her purse towards his goodwill when her letter to Lymond should be written.

But she wrote first to Kate at Flaw Valleys, and not until after Christmas, when the endless Masses were over, and the playlets by Udall, and the masques of Venuses and Cupids, and the subdued but infinite bickering between Spaniards and Englishmen. Philippa, with her light hand on the lute and her hard-won suppleness for the dance, had been much in demand over Christmas, and had been in some degree thankful to see the exhausting Don Alfonso disappear with his superior to Brussels for a spell, although this left Allendale's quiet company, so undemanding that it troubled her conscience, the more she enjoyed it.

Then, after Christmas, her spare time was mortgaged by her mistress. The Queen was not well. Fatigue and wandering pains; an increasing number of the headaches

114

which always had plagued her were all added to the strain of the disturbed, warring court she ruled over, and the uneven, unpredictable course of King Philip's affections, and the interminable planning and plotting for the good of her people, with the barometer of their temper as odd and variable as her husband's. And all the time her courtiers watched her, assessing her bulk and her colour, her temper, her energy, her appetite, and counting each day of her pregnancy.

With the dignity of long, bitter solitude, the Queen never confided. Observant and sensible, Philippa simply deduced what was necessary and did it. Sometimes she was required to read; sometimes to sing; sometimes to take sides in some abstract discussion which was merely a treadmill on which an over-active mind could exhaust itself. She led the Queen to indulge her pleasure in instruction, and was lent books; and learned with genuine humility how her performance on the spinet could be improved. She undertook, for Shrovetide, to arrange a Turkish masque with the Master of Revels.

She was left little time for reflection. Don Alfonso had no sooner left than she was invited by Lady Lennox to her house, the old Percy manor, at Hackney, and there she met the child Henry Darnley and his tutor John Elder, who addressed her in Latin, inquiring how Master Ascham's young bride was faring.

Philippa, the silent repository of a great deal of Spanish gossip about Master Ascham's sweet Mag, also disliked being quizzed about it, and especially in Latin. She said, 'As well as your master, I hope,' and Elder bowed with a grimace. Lady Lennox's husband, of uncertain religious allegiance, was not much to the fore in this court of bouncing princely prelates, although the unseen influence of his plotting made itself felt from time to time. He suffered an ailment, they said, which made him nervous of solitude. It was the only reason Philippa in her tarter moments could think of for his adherence to the brilliant Margaret. Ruffled, Philippa lowered her gaze to John Redshanks's nine-year-old pupil and greeted him also in Latin.

There was a silence, during which the blue pebble eyes of Henry Lord Darnley stared sagging at Philippa. Then he sneered.

It was a very juvenile sneer, starting round the nose and disappearing under the eaves of the cheeks. 'I am afraid,

Madam,' said Lord Darnley in English, 'your Latin is not of the same order as mine.'

Taking her time, Philippa measured him from head to foot with her eye. She grinned. 'I should hope not!' she said; and, smiling at Elder, followed the house steward to Lady Lennox's chamber, where she behaved herself extremely well under trying circumstances. Only when she was about to leave did Lady Lennox introduce a new subject.

'You have not heard, I suppose, from your husband?'

'From Mr Crawford? No, Lady Lennox,' Philippa said. 'Nor do I expect any letters.'

Lady Lennox smiled, her back straight against a large walnut chair upholstered in ginger brocade, entwined with the arms of Stewart and Douglas. 'This churlish bridegroom!' she said. 'However fleeting the marriage, he owes it to you, one would think, at least to assure himself that you are well, and in no need. Indeed, it is more urgent than that. I am told that the annulment will depend on his communicating with you. He must assure them, as you have done, that the marriage was on paper only; and that further, he is willing to release you.' She smiled. 'Do you think he is? Or is it not possible that seeing you now, a privileged lady of the Queen's privy chamber, he might change his mind?'

A picture of Kiaya Khátún rose into Philippa's head, superimposed on a lengthy tally of other ladies, all remarkable for their beauty, brains and general complaisance as the mistresses of Francis Crawford of Lymond. Lifting her eyebrows, Philippa transformed a giggle, gravely, into a cough. 'No,' she said with regret.

It sounded bald, but there were pitfalls in qualifying it. She could mention his age, but it was possible that Lady Lennox was even older than he was. And even Ruy Gomez, one remembered, had married a child-bride of twelve. Further, it would be impolitic, Philippa felt, to refer to Kiaya Khátún. Philippa opened wide, disingenuous eyes on the Countess of Lennox, and the Countess of Lennox smiled back.

'And you?' she said teasingly. 'Are you so sure that this marriage was platonic? No man with his arts would give his name to someone he found distasteful, or would submit to a marriage service without a chaste embrace, at least, from the bride. Do you not find him pleasing?'

116

There was something between them, Kate had said. And looking at those smiling, violent eyes, Philippa suddenly knew what it was. She said levelly, 'I admire his cleverness. He, I think, admires my plain speaking. There is, I suppose, friendship between us. But, to answer your question, in all the years since I was a child of ten, there has never been a gesture of affection between us. There has been no occasion.'

The black eyes resting on her brown ones were calm. 'And when he came to Flaw Valleys,' Margaret Lennox said, 'of course it was to visit your mother.' She rose, and, pausing by Philippa's chair, lifted her clear-skinned face as she might lift a doll's, by the chin. 'Charming,' said Lady Lennox. 'A good, kind-hearted girl. We must find a husband worthy of you, from among all those eager escorts at Court. But first, by some means, we must find Mr Crawford and have you set free. Do you and your family use every means to discover him, and we shall also. He has obligations. He shall be reminded of them.'

Philippa began her letter to Kate in the palace that evening, and was found by Jane Dormer with her face swollen and her nose a brilliant red, in the first wave of homesickness she had felt since coming to London. Mistress Clarenceux, appealed to, made Philippa pack up her letter and belongings without further ado, and transferred her for four days of freedom to the Sidney's house at St Anthony's, Broad Street, where she realized for the first time how tired she was. Nursed by the staff of Sir Henry, she slept for the better part of twenty-four hours, and then resumed both her usual acute interest in her fellow human beings, and her half-begun note to her mother.

. . . in your rustic solitude, far from David's timbrels and Aaron's sweet sounding bells – how can you bear it? Outside Spain, there is nothing to touch us for living civilly, now gussets have reached us at last. True, our clothes are badly made, and our hair is dressed in the French style, instead of the way Spanish unmarried girls do it, which would suit us a great deal better. But our skins are good, and we are learning to dance properly, instead of all that prancing and trotting we used to do at Uncle Somerville's. Of course, our skirts ought to be longer. We show our ankles when we sit in a way thoroughly shocking, not to mention what licence occurs after all this sugared wine. As

117

you know, eating and drinking are our only distractions (we drink more beer than would fill the Valladolid river) as our conversation is exceedingly limited. Although, of course, there are no people on earth like the English for gossip.

As, dearest Kate, you can see. Would you like me to marry a Spaniard and worship the buttock-bone of Pentecost and the great toe of the Trinity, once I am divorced? Not that there is any prospect of annulment at present: Mr Crawford has not deigned to write. But I have heard, in the most roundabout way, that he is well and active, and no doubt making Hell hotter somewhere. Perhaps Sybilla will wish to be reassured. And I can confirm that, whatever he has done, he cannot have married.

I am at the Sidneys' in St Anthony's, very merry because their precious Russia Company is about to be granted its charter. The wool trade (did you know? do you care?) has declined in the last three or four years, and they want a new outlet. This lets them trade in any part of the world, and gives them a monopoly of Muscovy trade and all the north lands not before frequented by Englishmen. That is the practical element. The dream is to travel through to Bokhara, and open up a direct route to the Orient. They have their navigator in Diccon Chancellor. (You may commence worrying: he is a widower with two small sons.) And they have their genius in this old man Cabot, who can tell you more about the ways of the sea, sitting at his desk, than any man alive in the world. . . . Would you let me go overseas again, Kate dear? . . . I rather thought that you wouldn't.

I go back to Court in two days, and shall thereby miss Conception Day, and the Spanish procession round the Savoy. We are very stiff in our Poperies, but the Dormers are selflessly kind as well as devout. The Queen worships with a fervour which seems to disturb her nerves rather than calm them. But her outbursts of temper are quickly over: her intentions always good. She is afraid, more than anything, that King Philip will leave her before the baby is born.

I have nothing of news or of levity to tell you of that, for it doesn't bear speaking of. But the Cardinal, as ever, is confident, and working hard, as he says, for two births. To the Queen a son, and to Christendom that peace which is desired.

*He may be right. They can't fight for four months any-
way. But they say France has plenty of money and isn't
interested in peace, except to buy a delay. And that the
Emperor will never forgive what Henri did to his sister
last year, hacking the trees and statues at Binche with his
own sword, even though The Netherlands is exhausted with
a tax (did you know?) bigger than all the Peruvian
revenues.*

*Everyone is afraid that if there is a resumption of war,
Philip will drag us into it, even though the marriage contract said otherwise. At any rate, the Spaniards here are
longing to have an excuse to leave court and would
infinitely prefer, I rather think, to abandon us all safely
behind them. It might please you to know that Master
Ascham, on reflection, thinks the Sultan of Turkey to be a
good, merciful, just and liberal prince, and thinks that if
the Emperor Charles were as fair, he would have no trouble
with his subjects. It remains to see what trouble his subjects are going to have with his son.*

*Do you remember when all I did was make threatening
gestures at greenfly? You have seen all this, and so had
Gideon, and you chose distance and sanity, although there
could have been little enough safety when Henry was King.
Imagine what we have now, faced with the records of three
different reigns in seven years, each with differing policies
and attitudes to religion. And the statesmen from each
reign still here among us (those who have survived), each
struggling like an insect in gum with his history. Happy the
clever, political animals, such as Cecil, or Sir Henry or
even Winchester, I suppose, who hold only moderate pre-
judices, and can trim their sails lightly, man and boy,
through three reigns, and gain in comfort and status and
happiness.*

*Perhaps, when rulers have short lives, the state profits
best from devious men who can give it long service. A
matter of common sense, brains and experience, and not of
religion or ethics at all. Oh, Kate . . . your only error in
life was to make me a girl, instead of a man.*
. . . How is Kuzúm?

She completed the letter and sent it off later, with a
servant of Austin's. She did not add that the celebrations
attending the last stages of the framing of the Muscovy
charter had brought enough merchants to St Anthony's to

119

enable her to indulge her new interest in Russia. She met some of the company's agents: Lane, Price, bearded Killingworth, and the big man Rob Best, who broke a tasselled stool wrestling with Chancellor. She met old Mr Cabot and some of his coterie of cosmographers: Richard Eden and Thomas Digges and Clement Adams and Dr Record and Mr Chancellor's friend and instructor, John Dee. And she listened flatteringly to Sir George Barnes and Will Garrard, Lord Mayor elect, who had promoted Diccon's first trip to Russia, and were now planning the second.

'Diccon can do it,' said Garrard. 'Wyndham couldn't do it, poor devil. I couldn't do it. Don't want to. Snug in Southfleet and Dorney, counting my money like George, not in Mombasa, dying of the bloody flux. We'll fill the ships up with broadcloth, and maybe a little sugar to sweeten the Tsar. And send them off in the spring: April perhaps. The *Philip and Mary*. And Diccon will have the *Edward Bonaventure* again.'

'Back,' said Sir Henry, 'to the inferior and exterior lights, Mistress Philippa. Richard Chancellor, you have a gleam in your eye. You complain when we send you sailing north to the ice floes but you know very well that you would pay from your pocket to go there. How long will it take you?'

'From here to the Dwina? Two months by sea, I should reckon. The ships can land us and our cargo, and then sail back to England to winter. From the Dwina to Moscow I don't know. There is the cargo to carry, and a thousand miles of Rusland to cover. Last time we did it by horse sleigh. This time,' said Diccon casually, his spare frame supported on the upright of Philippa's armchair, 'this time, I thought I'd take Christopher.'

Philippa opened her mouth. 'As an apprentice?' Garrard said. 'The lad's surely too young.'

The black beard and clear charcoal eyes were both directed ominously upon Philippa. She shut her mouth. 'Nothing hardens like sea water,' said Chancellor.

'You mean,' said Philippa smartly, 'nothing pickles like brine.'

'I mean—'

'Did you know,' said Henry Sidney's smooth voice, interrupting, 'that Mr Garrard knows your Mr Bailey? I had forgotten to tell you.'

Her mind engaged in battle for the future of Diccon Chancellor's son, Philippa did not, for the moment, recollect possessing a Mr Bailey. 'I beg your pardon?' she said.

'Leonard Bailey. God confound you, Philippa; you made an eminent fuss about tracing him. The brother of Honoria Bailey, your husband's grandmother. You will observe that whatever you have forgotten, the relationship is engraved in my memory.'

But she had already remembered. Covering a genuine shock with a great deal of discreet and well-mannered acting, she learned that Leonard Bailey, whose sister had married a Scot from Midculter, Lanarkshire, was indeed a neighbour of Garrard's in Buckinghamshire.

'That was it, Henry . . . Mistress Philippa,' said Will Garrard cheerfully. 'You'll find old Lady Dormer knows him as well, shouldn't wonder. Of her generation, although it's a while now since all the tattle. A self-willed old gentleman, so I'm told, always complaining of poverty. And certainly, Gardington could do with some upkeep, although he must take quite a good sum in rents. . . . He's a relative of your husband's?'

'He cut himself off from the family,' Philippa said, her hesitation small but touching. 'I thought, since I was here – I thought perhaps I might effect a reconciliation.'

'Hum,' said Will Garrard. 'More likely to find yourself lending him money. If you don't mind my saying so. But perhaps he's improved. Age can mellow, they say.'

'They say wrong,' said Diccon Chancellor. 'I have known Mistress Philippa these two months, and I have aged while she has grown daily less mellow. Why else am I fleeing the country?'

CHAPTER EIGHT

As it proved, the distance between London and Gardington, Bucks., was greater than the sum of its miles, and certainly farther than anyone was prepared to let Philippa go, in spite of a certain amount of soliciting, before her presence was again required at court in the space of two days. Hogtied in any case by her own experienced conscience, Philippa marched back in due course to her mistress, declaiming sourly, 'Their willingness be the touchstone and trial of their fidelity,' and proceeded to subvert the lifestyle and philosophy of Sir Thomas Cawerden, Master of the Revels, under the guise of advising him on the coming masque of Turkish magistrates and torchbearers for Shrovetide.

Since no one, barring a few seamen, one or two merchants, and a member of the staff of the French Ambassador had ever beheld a Turk in their lives, she was given a free hand in the revels storehouse at the old Blackfriars Monastery, and held a minor festival of her own with tailors, painters and joiners among the bales of gold damask and green sarsanet and tinsel tawny brocade: the old masks and buskins and kirtles, and the old hanging cloths of velvet, satin and dornicks, thickly wrought with bright gold embroidery. The masque was a success, and old Lady Dormer, whose two brothers had been Knights of St John, declared that her arm had itched to cut down the infidels, and all for forty-nine pounds, fourteen shillings and twopence. Commended for both taste and economy, Philippa's stock rose higher at Court. Diccon Chancellor called on her, and agreed to teach her some Russian, but refused point blank to take her to Moscow. The Queen was ill, and had to be blooded again.

Serving, with iron good humour, this sick, harassed woman, hag-ridden by wearing compulsions, Philippa wondered what blind faith still encouraged her scrofulous subjects to apply to be touched for the Evil; what blind custom prompted Brussels's petition for cramp-rings of each new Easter's blessing. Thin-armed and drawn, the Queen had none of the glossy, bright-eyed complacency Philippa had admired in other expectant ladies at a similar stage. But like the listening thrush, the Queen's eye was bent, night and day, on the subtle murmurings of her own lax-muscled body: through the long, grinding prayers; through the dawn meetings of Council where she listened while the Bishop of Winchester chose the agenda, and sat upright through all the bitter discussions, and appended her name to the bills as they were drawn up and placed before Parliament.

In that way the Heresy Act had been carried, restoring the authority of the Bishops' Courts and making state prosecution for heresy a sudden reality. Before Shrove the Bishop of Gloucester had been snatched from his long imprisonment and burned, held by iron bands, stripped to the shroud, with a bag of gunpowder tied round his neck.

The day before, the Queen had gone to bed early and the palace had been full of the sound of raised voices. The day after, King Philip's chaplain had preached a long and calming sermon on tolerance, upbraiding the Bishops for cruelty. But the Act stood, and the Lord Chancellor, upheld by law and his own deep convictions, proceeded one by one to arraign and burn every heretic.

So far as Philippa could see, the claims of humanity had nothing to do with the consequent argument, which on the Chancellor's side had to do with the redeeming of souls, and on the side of the Emperor's Ambassador, not to mention King Philip ('Better not to reign at all than reign over heretics'), had to do with the angering of the Queen's already turbulent subjects, and the overthrow of all Spain's tedious, unremitting and unrewarding sacrifices to win over the whole nasty nation. The Ambassador talked to the Queen, harangued the Lord Chancellor and appeared in Parliament, begging them to direct the Bishops to banish, imprison, or conduct secret executions if they must, but at all costs to postpone the burnings. Parliament, which had not been elected in order to flout both the Queen and the Bishop of Winchester, refused to consider it, and the burnings proceeded. A small accident occurred, by night, to a spruce new image of St Thomas of Canterbury, and King Philip decided his presence was needed at Brussels. The Emperor's Ambassador, with some trouble, persuaded him otherwise.

The news of that small exchange reached Philippa by way of Alfonso Derronda, who had returned, full of fresh vigour, with his master. Since the Queen had not heard of it, Philippa did not mention it to Jane Dormer, or the quiet jokes of another kind, to do with the frightened King's quest for companionship.

'The baker's daughter is better in her gown than Queen Mary without her crown,' ran the limp couplet Don Alfonso quoted to her at the Lady Day joust, when Ruy Gomez and Sir George Howard, trimmed in white, were the challengers and ran twenty courses with the King and his company, in yellow and blue. 'Did you hear of the new plot at Cambridge? To make Courtenay King and marry him to Elizabeth? They say the Queen isn't pregnant, but means to pass off some child as her own. I wish she would,' said Don Alfonso cheerfully. 'It would be better than waiting.'

'Nonsense,' said Philippa crossly. 'Of course she is pregnant. If Philip runs off, what's more, she'll probably have a miscarriage.' The King was wearing ridiculous feathers in yellow and blue on his helmet, and they had resurrected her red Turkish robes for his attendants.

'Not *runs off*,' Don Alfonso chided her with extreme affability. He was wearing a new pair of earrings and a black braided coat, expensively furred to midcalf. 'We must all choose our words, including King Philip. If he goes, it must seem a necessary and seemly journey. On the other hand,' Don Alfonso said thoughtfully, 'the King may linger longer than we think. He is not perhaps the world's greatest administrator and the Duke of Alva is going to Brussels next month. I imagine King Philip would prefer to leave all the knottiest problems until after Alva has gone. If he does well, he will then get the credit. If he fails, then at least it won't be Alva who enlightens the Emperor. . . . So there is to be a child. Tell me, why does she endanger its future by allowing these burnings?'

More than a hundred staves had been broken. On the field, a messenger from the Queen hurried down for the second time to beg King Philip to have a care for his health. Philippa thought of the long hours of prayer and toil: how the exiled friars had been recalled, the Crown stripped of its church lands, poor though it was: the Queen's own laborious translations of Erasmus burned at her confessor's suggestion. 'I had rather lose ten crowns,' Mary Tudor had answered all remonstrances, 'than place my soul in peril.'

'On the contrary,' Philippa said. 'The burnings are her bargain with God. The recanted souls will save her child and her marriage.'

Don Alfonso, his eyes on the joust, gave an impatient click of the tongue. 'She is to be pitied.'

'No,' said Philippa with sudden extreme grimness. 'She is to be loved.'

The blue and yellow feathers twisted. King Philip was riding off early. 'By *him*?' asked Don Alfonso.

The week before Easter, the King and Queen moved to Hampton Court Palace, there to await the birth of the Queen's child. Before she moved with them, Philippa had a long talk with Robert Best, of the staff of the new Muscovy Company, who had been a fellow-pupil in Russian with Chancellor, until the demands of the forthcoming voyage forced Diccon to cancel the lessons. Immediately after that, she wrote the long-delayed letter to Lymond, and entrusted it to Bartholomew Lychpole, to be sent with his letters to Russia.

She wrote it this time without the aid of a dictionary, and without the nervousness which six months ago had made her so prolix. She had few points to make, and those were forthright.

She was well, Philippa wrote, and so were his family and son with the exception of Sybilla who, as she had already written, was stoical but much in need of his return. She herself was in London at court, where she was in need of nothing, but had been made aware that if their marriage was to be annulled, she must have a statement regarding both the reasons for the annulment and his consent, delivered either in writing or in person by himself. There was no haste for this, except in so far as he might wish to find himself free. Lastly, Philippa set out, without comment, the circumstances of her visit to Sybilla's sister the Abbess, and what she had learned there. *After the birth of Richard, Sybilla had no more children. You and your sister were born to your father in France, of mother or mothers unknown. . . .*

She ended: *This is an affair of yours on which I embarked perhaps childishly, since it seemed to me that, by ignoring it, you were doing yourself and your family a disservice. The results either way make no difference to me and should make no difference to you. Whatever your relationship with them, the people among whom you grew up are and should be the dearest to you. I am sure you know this without being told by a schoolgirl. It is only the love Kate and I have for Sybilla which makes me repeat it. Kate would join me in sending you our greeting and regard for your wellbeing. I remain, your friend,* PHILIPPA.

Then she retired with their Majesties to Hampton Court, Wolsey's red-brick kingdom down the river, which he had presented to his master King Henry, but too late to save his own head. And there, among its courts and galleries and gardens and offices, Easter came and April wore on, although the child which moved in the womb five months ago on Pole's arrival still delayed coming. The Emperor Charles, frail and twisted with gout, had entered on what seemed his last illness. Peace talks between Charles and France, promised for April, had yet again been delayed. On the Emperor's side the reason, said Don Alfonso, was exhaustion: the Low Countries had no money, and the soldiers were close to rebellion. Also they were waiting, as the whole world was waiting, for the Queen of England at last to give birth.

The French, on the other hand, were gay, fresh and well equipped with men and with money. The longer the talks were deferred, said Don Alfonso, the more opportunity France would have of discovering the enemy's plans. And there was the matter of the new Papal election. Marcellus II, so favoured by France, had died in the twenty-second day of his pontificate, killed by the rigours of celebration. Cardinal Pole contracted a fever, diplomatic or other; and the Cardinal of Lorraine hurried post-haste to Rome. The Queen took to her rooms.

By all the warring elements in her realm and outside it, the fact was immediately noted. Forty days before a confinement and forty days after, by royal and ancient custom, the Queens of England withdrew to their chambers and were attended only by women. By another inalienable and sensible custom, the enemies of the kingdom and its heirs – who were, it must be said, very often one and the same flesh – were either sent abroad, or kept under closest surveillance at the Palace.

So, towards the end of April, William Courtenay, Earl of Devonshire, was summoned to Court, and given royal leave to visit the Emperor and his sister the Queen Regent in Flanders, there to thank them in person for his final release from his recent restraint.

The day after Courtenay's departure from Court the Queen's sister Elizabeth arrived there, brought from her prison at Woodstock; as twenty-one years before Mary Tudor had been summoned to Greenwich for Elizabeth's birth, too shamingly soon after the wedding, to the Great Whore, Anne Boleyn, Henry's second, usurping Queen.

Madam Elizabeth entered Hampton Court by a little-used door, escorted by a handful of her own servants, and a detachment of soldiers led by Sir Henry Bedingfield. Philippa knew she was coming: one of the Dormer houses at Wing had entertained her overnight on the four-day journey from Woodstock, and Lady Lennox had mentioned, with brittle amusement, that Master Ascham would have two pupils now.

From Roger Ascham, Philippa already knew a good deal about this shrewd, scholarly, quick-witted girl whom he

126

had taught five years before in that merry household at Chelsea, and later at Cheshunt and Hatfield. The girl who at fifteen was already fluent in Italian, French, Latin and Greek; who was arrogantly proud of her likeness to her father, King Henry; and who had lost her mother to the block when she was three, and sworn Princess of Wales.

But lively though her curiosity might be, Philippa was too considerate to join the ladies who melted from the antechamber when the rattle of horse-hooves was heard, and hers was not one of the peering faces behind the mullioned windows. Pressed by her household officers, the Queen had at last decided upon the room for a nursery, and, once involved, had extended herself to see to each detail. Mistress Clarenceux had brought to her the gifts already arriving of clothes and of toys : she selected those to be kept, and gave orders for their storage, and made decisions about the infant clothes which her ladies, Jane and Philippa among them, had long since begun embroidering.

When her sister Elizabeth arrived, the Queen was in the nursery, with its dais holding the draped wooden cradle and its broken-backed legend, admirable only in piety : *The child whom thou to Mary, O Lord of Might has send, To England's joy, in health preserve, keep and defend.* The Queen stayed there all afternoon, with Jane and Philippa attending her, and Mistress Clarenceux massaged her fingers, when she complained of cold hands. Unwelcomed, Madam Elizabeth was received into the palace, and placed in the Duke of Alva's former apartments, close to those of King Philip, while in the Queen's rooms, the long evening passed.

It was an evening Philippa never quite forgot. The Queen left the nursery : her ladies returned. The Bishop of Winchester and Sir William Petre called and were given a long weighty audience. The King came for half an hour before supper, and was entertained by the Queen, while Philippa played on the virginals and listened, unashamed, to the conversation in Spanish.

'Sir Robert Rochester tells me Milady Elizabeth is safely installed,' the Queen's husband said. 'When will it be your pleasure to receive her?'

There was a little silence, which Philippa discreetly bridged with an unexpected coda to Jannequin. The Queen said, in her deep, uneven voice, 'My lord, I have no plans to receive her. She is here so that if I die in child-birth, she and her adherents will prove no threat to your Majesty's life.'

He was in a cajoling mood, Philippa saw. Instead of the sober, elegant dress he preferred, he had put on one of the puffed and slashed and gem-studded doublets which his wife and aunt publicly preferred. Stretching now from his chair, he took her square, powerful hand in his white one. 'God is good: you will not die. Instead you will give me and England a strong and beautiful prince, and it is fitting that all should rejoice. When the babe is born, show her your favour. It will please your people to show yourself magnanimous.'

'When the babe is born, I shall show her what kindness she has deserved in the meantime,' said the grim, broken voice. 'Meanwhile, she is to see no one and communicate with no one outside these walls.'

After supper he left. The Queen prayed late that night, and it was Jane, waiting to attend her undressing, who first heard the cry from the prie-dieu. When they reached her, she had fallen forward, clutching her stomach, and it was with some trouble, considering her smallness, that they carried her somehow to her bed. Before they got her there, Mistress Clarenceux had already sent pages flying to rouse the King and the Councillors, and to fetch her physicians.

There was no sleep for Philippa that night, and little rest next morning, attending to the needs of the anxious circle about the Queen, and the unceasing inquiries from the jostling anteroom. She was there herself when Sir Henry Sidney arrived, still wearing his cloak splashed with mud, and ignoring her smile and the voices upraised in greeting about him, picked out Arundel, the Master of the Household, and thrust forward to speak to him. 'The Queen?'

The Earl of Arundel looked at him sharply. 'Is well, thank God. What have you heard?'

'Is there a child?' Sidney said. 'I am told there is not.'

Arundel said, 'There is no child, as yet. Her Majesty was taken ill through the night, but it has been shown to be a mere defect in the environment of the body, caused by a colic. Why, is there a rumour in London?'

'No rumour,' said Henry Sidney. He looked tired, Philippa thought. A page, summoned by her nod, reached up and drew the wet cloak from Sidney's shoulders: as he took it away, Sir Henry turned to her and bowed, and gave his reply still staring into her face. 'Not a rumour. Word reached London at daybreak that, half an hour after midnight, the Queen had given birth to a male child with little pain and no danger. London is in festival, Lord Arundel : bells are ringing; shops are shut, and there are bonfires in the streets, with public tables spread with wine and meat for everyone. Word has travelled already abroad. I came here to do my office as courier.'

He finished speaking into silence, and in silence a harsh voice spoke behind him. 'They are premature,' said the Queen.

Turning, a pain in her chest, Philippa saw her standing with Jane in her doorway, the doctors behind her. 'They are premature, but perhaps it is fitting that an infant twice blessed should twice be celebrated. I am well, as you see, and England prospers within me. Give me your prayers, and you shall see a prince before the ash from these re-joicings is cold.'

A few days later, they heard that the Great Bell had been rung in Antwerp and English ships in the harbour had celebrated the news of a birth with volleys of shot, while the Queen Regent had sent a hundred crowns' drink money to the seamen. About the same time, a small crowd arrived at the court with three screaming children, suc-cessfully born a few days before to a woman, as they explained, of low stature and great age like the Queen, who was now strong and out of all danger. Philippa, her nerves beaten raw, was all for sending them packing, but Jane prevailed, and had them all brought to the Queen, who spoke to them, Philippa saw, with real tears in her eyes. She had been wrong. Jane still understood her mistress far better than Philippa did.

About that time, King Philip made his first official call on his wife's sister Elizabeth, but what transpired no one was able to discover. There followed two weeks of seclu-sion, after which her great-uncle William Howard was permitted to see Madam Elizabeth, and after him, several members of the Queen's Privy Council. It was believed that she was appealing to the Queen through her statesmen to release her from custody. It was certain that she was writing the Queen a great many letters. Philippa some-times saw them lying open on Queen Mary's desk, unmis-takable in Ascham's beautiful Italian writing, but she refrained with an effort from reading them. It was a surprise therefore to be called to the Countess of Lennox one day, and told that the lady Elizabeth had asked and been granted leave to resume her studies with Master Ascham, and that there were some books from the Cardinal's library which Philippa was to take to her.

'They are, as you might expect, exceedingly precious,' Lady Lennox said, smiling. 'I do not care to entrust them to ignorant hands. Also, you have sufficient knowledge of Master Ascham's methods to be able to discuss the books with Madam Elizabeth, and to note any others she may require. I am sure, as well, that you will be pleased one day to recall that you met the lady. If she marries abroad, she may well end her life a stranger to England.'

Unless, of course, the Queen's infant dies, Philippa thought. In which case the Lady Elizabeth, apparently so assiduous in her devotions, may well be the next Queen?

There was a guard outside Elizabeth's door, and more were waiting below in the gardens. Bedingfield escorted Philippa there himself, and on the threshold handed her over to William Howard, who took her into the small, wainscoted room hung with pictures, where a tall, thin-boned girl sat erect by the fire, dealing playing-cards with manicured, tapering fingers.

Howard fingers. What else of Anne Boleyn could be seen in her daughter? An olive complexion, adroitly lightened, as Philippa saw with the interest of an expert. Long hair, falling shoulder-length beneath the pearled arch of her headdress, which also looked coarser than its light colour would merit. Pale, shallow eyes, light and clear, which certainly did not come from black-haired Anne, and a small mouth the image of the pink, pursed lips in every portrait of King Henry her father. Except that the Queen would not admit that King Henry was Elizabeth's father, or that she could be her legitimate sister. Her voice was light, and chillingly clear; the expression on the mouth perfectly affable.

'Mistress Philippa. Place the books there. It was most courteous of you to call. I have so few visitors. Can you afford a moment to sit and take wine with Sir William and me?'

Philippa curtseyed and thanked her, sinking with ineffable grace into a rather hard brocade chair. Madam Elizabeth's eyes opened slightly. Wine was brought. 'So,' said Elizabeth. 'You also are learning the pleasures of Priscian's grammar, and savouring the style of Xenophon's Hippike, so vivid, so pure . . .'

'And whose views on education,' Philippa said, her lashes downcast, 'are strongly founded and quite without equal. Master Ascham is well,' Philippa said, 'and sends you his duty.'

'As well as some dutiful books. Or are those from the Cardinal? I am pleased,' said Elizabeth, 'to see Master Ascham safely returned from Brussels and comfortably installed with the Queen. I must demand a report on his travels.'

'He was disappointed,' said Philippa, 'to discover, when praising the sincere emotion of Cicero's lament for Hortensius, that Master Fugger was unable to lend him a copy as his library was always kept padlocked. Not a philologos, a lover of learning, but a bibliotaphos, a sepulchre for books. His disputations with Master Sturm have barely restored his confidence.'

The thin eyebrows lifted, and Elizabeth smiled, her long hands calmly crossed in her lap. Her servant had gone, and but for Howard, sipping his wine discreetly in the flickering firelight, they had the room to themselves. Elizabeth said, 'He would find more sincere emotion, perhaps, in the *pro Marcello,* but he is too wise, I am sure, to make witticisms about it.'

The delicacy of the hint was nothing short of enchanting. Philippa, limp with the backwash of liturgical emotion, saw opening before her the prospect of a practical conversation at last. 'You know,' she said, 'Pope Marcellus is dead, and they have appointed another?'

The pale blue eyes opposite moved to Sir William and back. 'Not Ferrara,' said Elizabeth. *'Quis demonium habet?* I heard twenty for the hundred were being laid in the banks on the Cardinal of Naples. Or has the huckstering spoiled him? I cannot believe the Sacred College has been prevented from carrying out the election as the Holy Ghost inspires.'

'I have heard it quoted,' said Philippa blandly, 'that the Emperor's Ambassador in Rome thinks that a little canvassing might be better than waiting until the Cardinals, out of pure exhaustion, agree on some devil who will be no good to anybody. At any rate Caraffa, the Cardinal of Naples, has been elected.'

Elizabeth rose. Lifting the tall, silver-gilt jug, arched and spired and nestling with cherubs, she poured more wine with her own hands for her great-uncle, Philippa and herself. Then, sitting, she raised the cup a little and drank. Then she said, 'A man rising eighty, and pro-French, to follow Marcellus!'

'Poor Marcellus,' said Philippa. 'The Imperialists say he is very well where he is, and this new one would not do badly there either. He will be known as Paul IV.'

'An austere and learned old man,' said Elizabeth thoughtfully. 'So perhaps Cardinal Pole will now be well enough to mediate for the peace?'

Philippa said, 'The Commissioners of France and the Empire are meeting near Gravelines this month, and the Cardinal is due to attend them.'

Elizabeth put down her cup and her lips, a little apart, showed, as was not usual, the small, shadowy teeth. 'Ah,' she said. 'Should they make peace, they must do as the doctors contrive, and pay Pole an annuity for each anniversary. Now my sister need only be brought to bed of her son, and they may even allow the right honourable and my very good lord the Earl of Devonshire home to offer me marriage. But perhaps even then, he would not accept it. I hear he is in fear of his life.'

A slight pause developed. 'Poor William Courtenay,' Philippa thought. Elizabeth said, 'Master Ascham has heard, no doubt, what has befallen his young friend, John Dee. A melancholy fate for a caster of horoscopes. I hear he had completed one for the Sidneys' son, sixty-two pages long. Saggitarius, I believe. I am Virgo.' She paused again. 'Do you know Dr Dee, Mistress Philippa?'

Philippa knew John Dee, Diccon Chancellor's friend; mathematician, geographer and astrologer, who had been arrested for treason after that last cheerful celebration of the Muscovy Company and thrown to the Star Chamber for questioning.

She also knew why he was charged. John Dee had been a visitor at Woodstock. He had cast Madam Elizabeth's horoscope, so they said. Worse, he had discussed with her the horoscopes he had already drawn up for the Queen and her husband. His lodgings had been searched, and some of Elizabeth's own staff arrested.

Philippa said, 'I have met him with Mr Chancellor. He used to bring his new instruments sometimes to Penshurst, and his mechanical insects, and find buttons for us, with a pendulum over a map. The servants were frightened. His intellect is so great that his manner sometimes seems mysterious.'

'Unlike the merry and widely esteemed Mr Chancellor,' Elizabeth said. 'Do you not find these geographers' matters tedious to listen to, with their cards and their globes and their plotting? They never see a sweet bay, or a stream, or a green flowering headland but it must be laid black on a paper: they trap the spheres in their springe like a woodman.'

'They are forbearing,' Philippa said, 'in their wisdom. I have read a little. Pliny and Ptolemy, Roger Bacon and David Morgan.'

'*Geographia*?' said Madam Elizabeth. 'I did not know Sir Henry had a manuscript. Or Dr Dee.'

'In Scotland,' Philippa said, growing, despite herself, faintly pink. 'I read most of them while staying in Scotland.'

'Ah, yes.' Madam Elizabeth was amiable. 'This Scottish husband of yours they tell me of, whom you are so anxious to cast off. Does your English spirit rebel against the poor gentleman's race? Or is he so obnoxious?'

Philippa put down her cup. She should have expected, of course, that this shrewd and cautious young woman would have acquainted herself with all the known facts about any visitor allowed by the Queen. She said, 'My marriage was one of convenience, made when Mr Crawford and I were held prisoner in each other's company in Turkey. I should prefer not to be tied yet to marriage with anyone, and he may well wish to marry elsewhere.' She began to feel that she could narrate this explanation to music.

Elizabeth cast a smiling half-glance at her great-uncle. She said, 'Ah. So his affections are fixed. And are you not jealous, Mistress Philippa? Or is he so old and ill-favoured that you are glad to be rid of him? What age is he: mine? Or perhaps nearer your mother's?'

'He is of my mother's years,' Philippa said.

'Well?' said Madam Elizabeth. 'And is he forthright and hairy, as I am told Scots are wont to be? A man happier with his sword or walking his fields, than in the chambers of princes?'

Philippa said dryly, 'I think, your grace, that you know him.'

'What! I?' said Elizabeth. 'Have I not shown that I know him so little, I depend on your eyes for a picture. Is he so like the man I have painted?'

And Philippa said, 'You have painted his opposite.'

There was a light and circumspect silence. Then Elizabeth sighed. 'It is as Dr Dee said. I have no sense of shadows, only of substance. Let us leave your smooth Mr Crawford to introduce himself, as one day perhaps he will, at my door. Is he in England now, Mistress Philippa?'

And Philippa, shaking her head, said, 'No, your grace. I left him in Greece, and have not heard of him since.'

'I see. I shall not ask,' Elizabeth said, 'if you have written to him. You know best yourself whether this Court would help his advancement, or would do quite the reverse. If you do not know, I suggest that you ask yourself the name of the person who sent you here today.'

There was a short silence while Philippa's mind made a single critical evaluation. Then she spoke. 'It was Lady Lennox,' she said.

'I see,' said the Lady Elizabeth. On the other side of the table, Master Howard had not moved, but Philippa had the feeling that the scent of triumph had come, like woodsmoke, and tinged the air of the room. 'Dear Meg. The old companion of my nursery days. I fear she would find me safer behind bars and a hanglock. Is she trusted in Scotland?'

'I hardly think so,' said Philippa bluntly. 'Or her husband.'

'Although the child-Queen's mother invited him north, did she not, to help her against her nobles when she wanted the regency? She has it now, so the Earl of Lennox's services are no longer wanted in Scotland. Which is as well.'

'Would he have left England?' Philippa asked. It seemed unlikely. Living was sweet under Queen Mary's favour: life in Scotland would never be half as opulent, even with all his attainted estates handed back.

'It was a pretty plot,' said Elizabeth lightly, and her pale eyes sparkled and her teeth, unregarded again, showed, small as a weasel's. 'Lennox was to go to Scotland at Mary of Guise's request, and once there was to suborn the nobles and declare the country for England, throwing out the

Queen Dowager and all her adherents and becoming, with the English Queen's blessing, her Lord Lieutenant and Governor in Scotland. He had the Privy Council's consent, I am told. He would have gone, except that she was given the Regency, as I said, and no longer needed that risky alliance. But I think he still hopes for it. Or at the very least, to have his lands all restored. He is bent on petty power and the return of old glories. My Lady Lennox is apt to aim higher. . . . Have you met the boy Darnley?'

'A small, scholarly encounter,' Philippa said. 'There was no meeting of souls.'

'No Lennox has one,' said Elizabeth with precision. 'The child is already sending copies of his Latin poems and translations to the Queen, and to his cousin Mary of Scotland. Largely written, I should imagine, by Master John Elder, or am I misjudging him? Perhaps he is precocious as well as unpleasant. But note well, Mistress Philippa. There are few women as subtle as the Countess of Lennox. I have enjoyed our meeting. But I should advise you, even if the opportunity presents itself, not to come near me again, and furthermore, to divorce your husband as quickly as possible. It is dangerous air for the wife of a soldier.'

A few minutes later, her brief visit had ended. Philippa returned to Court in a coma, which barely lifted as she became absorbed once again into the endless minutiae to do with the Queen's hourly health and wellbeing. From Don Alfonso, she knew that the King was in an agony of irritation over the birth which still kept him tied down in England : of irritation, and of fear. The Earl of Pembroke, sent to sound out the loyalty of the garrison leaders at Calais and Guisnes, had been recalled, so great was Philip's anxiety about his own safety in the event of a disastrous accouchement. Long since, the meetings of citizens had been forbidden in the commonroom of London ordinaries, and his attempts to stop the rising number of quarrels between Spaniards and Englishmen had only resulted in rousing his own nobles' resentment. Under pain of hanging, no man could raise the cry of Spain! for assistance. No swords were to be carried, and the first Spaniard to use a weapon was to have his hand cut off.

The precautions were probably wise. A clash involving five hundred of both races had taken place already and had been hushed up by the Privy Council, as Philippa well knew : only a handful had been killed, fortunately, and twenty-five injured. Don Alfonso and his friends, however, did not wish to be wise, or to be told to put up with any affront or persecution. They wanted to pick a quarrel, personally, with every native in sight, and then slay him.

The birth delayed. The Queen exhorted her bishops to do better in routing out heretics. There were more burnings, and riots at burnings. King Philip wrote and asked the Emperor, who was enjoying a spell of recovery, what to do about libellous placards. London was flooded with thousands of scurrilous pamphlets against religion and parliament, the Council, the Queen and the King, which the Lord Mayor assiduously collected. The Master of the Revels was arraigned, among others, for a share in the Cambridge plotting. The King's grandmother died.

It was the last straw. Joanna the Mad, mother of the Emperor Charles, sister of Catherine of Aragon, had been crazy for forty long years, and her passing, for which her grandson announced he felt a reasonable regret, had the simple effect of releasing twenty-five thousand ducats a year for the Spanish economy.

Unfortunately, it did not free that sum automatically for her own obsequies, or for the cost of Court mourning. The ceremony at St Paul's Cathedral alone, it appeared, would cost seven thousand ducats, and dress for the court over and above looked like requiring a fortune. The one cheering event Philippa was able to remember of that long dreary month was Don Alfonso's account of the English noblemen flocking to Philip to demand their black suits. 'And behaving,' said Philippa's confidant bitterly, 'as if their honour would be tarnished for ever if they didn't obtain them. When we have finished, I tell you, we shall have put more folk into mourning in this kingdom than has ever been seen before, or will be.'

King Philip retired with the colic. Ordered clothes must be paid for, and until more money arrived, he could not properly appear without mourning. It was little comfort to know that his father was in the same position exactly.

There was a wave of warm weather. The Queen, tempted out of doors, walked slowly about between the box hedges, leaning on the arms of her ladies. More ladies had come. The Queen's apartments at Hampton Court were a low rustle of feminine voices, and sweeping skirts, and unfolding needlework; weaving among the rumbling voices of the doctors, always on call, always in attendance; and the thin, high song of the cage-birds, answering the call of the blackbirds and thrushes and chaffinches, free in the gardens outside.

Next to her, day and night, the Queen kept Jane Dormer. And although Philippa took what she could from Jane's shoulders, it seemed to her that Jane, too, was most at ease at the Queen's side; tasting her food: sometimes, Philippa knew, sharing her bed when there were strange pains, or nightmares, or long waking hours of thinking and planning.

Philippa, too, felt the quality of this need, and subdued all her own impatience to serve it. She did so soberly, and with a conscience which pained her, for she had already taken the decision to desert this post she had taken so light-heartedly: for adventure; for freedom; out of some petty need, she now saw, to prove her adulthood by manipulating the affairs of her elders.

Before coming to London, she had viewed her life and that of her friends through the eyes of a child at Flaw Valleys, or a child pushed by circumstance on a stormy but magnificent journey through Europe. Now she was wiser. In this brief and dizzying apprenticeship, she had started to realize that, whatever his occupation, Lymond's life was lived on this level: the level on which the future of whole communities could be steered or reshaped, improved or jeopardized by a handful of people.

And the fascination of that, she was now aware, far surpassed anything else one could imagine. The search for the child, which she had thought so important, had been made at a cost which the death of one evil, powerful man, Graham Malett, had only just merited – the cost of months spent in limbo, far away from the world of affairs. She had once thought Lymond's life could be blighted by some accident of birth which had left his origins in some mystery. She knew that because of it he was unlikely to come home. But beyond that she could not imagine, now, that it would make any difference whatever to the career he elected to follow.

She knew now that Lymond had no need of her, or of Kuzúm, the child she had rescued. Her inclination and her duty lay here in London, with this small, unhappy, violent woman and the tragedy of her marriage. But before that, she had another duty: to Lymond's family who did not understand, as she did, and who saw themselves as spurned and discarded. And to her mother Kate, whom her marriage had so bewildered. Who had known Lymond first, as Margaret Lennox had so brutally pointed out, when she, a child of ten, had disliked and betrayed him.

So, for all these reasons, and quite unknown to any person at Court; to Jane or old Lady Dormer; to Henry Sidney her benefactor; to Diccon Chancellor, who would have put her in irons, or his son Christopher, who would have betrayed her with his approving exuberance, Philippa Somerville was going to Russia.

Her modest cloth bag was packed. Her letters to Kate and Sybilla were written. Her formal apology to the Queen was prepared and her arrangement was at last firmly made, with the reluctant Robert Best, to put her on one Will Whiskyn's hoy, lying between Tilbury and Gravesend, and thence smuggle her on board the *Edward Bonaventure*.

Two days before she was due at Tilbury, she obtained leave from the Queen to make a short visit. It was her excuse to leave Court but the visit, as it chanced, was genuine enough. Before leaving for Russia, Philippa had determined to pay her first and last call on Leonard Bailey, brother of the late Honoria Bailey and great-uncle of her husband Francis Crawford, at the manor of Gardington, Bucks.

She took with her one groom, lent her by Sir Henry Sidney, and her own maidservant Fogge. Through Sir Henry, she had received Garrard's directions on reaching the manor: from old Lady Dormer, she had learned a little more of this elderly man, whose sister had married into an eminent Scottish family and who, disillusioned, had left Scotland as a young man and settled, on a small English pension, to become a minor landowner of no great skill or resources, known largely for his liking for law and his constant embroilment in petty disputes.

It was not an appealing prospect, but Philippa, having sent off a letter announcing herself, made the journey with what stoicism she could muster, and found her virtue rewarded by a gift of a warm summer's day, which turned the Vale into a broad wooded meadow below the blue heights of the Chilterns, and drove free air through her lungs, stuffed with the sick intriguings of Court.

She found Gardington a modest white house with three gables and a central door flanked by crenellated bay windows, their casements open to the soft garden air. A thread of smoke rose from the tall, red-brick chimneys, and she could hear someone whistling in the big ivy-clad barn which adjoined the house on the left, but there was no sign of life from the house. Leaving her groom and her maid, Philippa dismounted and marching up to the door, rapped with the closing-ring.

No one answered. At the second series of knocks, a dog began barking, and, after a moment, was joined by another. The whistling in the barn stopped. Philippa waited, gave another unavailing bang on the door, and then walked to the barn, her bongrace jerking with the vehemence of her stride.

The whistler jumped to his feet, a lad in buff jacket and slops, his half-mended rake dropped on the floor. 'I,' said Philippa clearly, 'am Mistress Somerville from the Queen's Court at London. Mr Bailey expects me. Why does no one answer the door?'

The lad wiped his hands on his sides. 'He's out,' he said.

'His servants?' said Philippa.

'She's out, too,' said the lad. 'Jeff's took them to market.'

'I see,' said Philippa. 'And when will they return?'

'He said,' said the boy, 'he would be out for the day.' He looked up at the sky. 'Is it dinnertime?'

'Past, I should think,' Philippa said. She and Fogge and George the groom had shared some fruit and cheese from a basket, but there remained a certain emptiness of which she was not unaware.

'Oh,' said the boy. 'Then he's not to be back till tomorrow.'

'From *market*?' Philippa said.

The boy gazed at her with undisturbed amiability. 'No,' he explained patiently. 'If it's after dinner, he hasn't gone to the market. He's gone to stay with a friend.'

'And the housekeeper?' said Philippa.

'Off to see a sick mother,' the boy said triumphantly; and Philippa opened her purse, searched for and gave him a teston.

'Well done,' said Philippa cordially and left him, subsiding once more to the floor with his rake. She then walked straight back to the house and climbed through the open bay window.

The room inside was quite empty, except for a wainscot cupboard with an aumbry, a painted spruce table and one or two cheapish thrown chairs, although the cold fireplace had an overmantel of elaborate friezework, and the ceiling was also carried out in fine decorative plaster. There was a tapestry, discoloured with smoke, on one wall. Philippa left the room silently.

A narrow corridor, with more doors opening from it. A steep staircase, its banisters of carved and waxed oak. A shaft of daylight from the rear of the house, and the subdued clack of pewter or earthenware. Philippa, treading quietly, walked to the front door and opened it, and then made her way back to the sound.

The housekeeper of Gardington, a middle-aged lady with a pallid, ridged face, looked up when Philippa entered and opened her mouth. In the event, she neither screamed, fainted, nor dropped the bowl she was holding, although her hand gripped so hard that she cracked it, and, saving both pieces quickly, laid the two shells on the table and turned to face Philippa. 'And who's to pay for *that*?' she said harshly.

'I shall,' said Philippa coolly. 'And I'm sorry I shocked you so badly. But I seemed quite unable to make myself heard at the door, and very soon I shall have to return to the Palace—'

The woman interrupted. 'You weren't invited. How did you get in? You've broken the door!'

'The door is open,' said Philippa, with absolute truth. Her fine, plucked eyebrows rose to impossible heights.

'It couldn't be!'

'And besides,' said Philippa patiently, 'I have an appointment with Mr Bailey. If you would tell him I am here. Mistress Somerville from Hampton Court Palace.'

The woman stared at her, thinking. It was a crude weapon, but the only one Philippa could be sure of. She had used it also in her letter. Mistress Philippa Somerville, one of the Queen's ladies, was a friend of the family Crawford with which he had some connection, and wished the favour of an interview. She had not said what her relationship with the Crawfords might be, and she had not mentioned Lymond's name anywhere. The house-keeper said, 'He's not here.'

'I know,' Philippa said. 'He's staying with a friend, and you're visiting a sick mother. It is not an offence, of course, for a gentleman and his household to try to hide from one of the Queen's servants. It only gives rise to certain strange speculations at Court.'

The language was too formal, she thought, for the housekeeper. But it might be more to the weight of the person whose foot had made the floorboards cheak outside the door, just a moment before. And she had barely stopped speaking when the kitchen door was indeed thrown open with such passionate force that it gave way in one of its hinges and hung, like a hatch in a gale, framing the suffused face and gross, ill-clad figure of a tall man, powerful even in his late sixties, who turned his veined eyes and shouted at Philippa.

'And who's to pay for *that*?' Philippa said, cheeringly, to herself.

'Hide!' Leonard Bailey was repeating. 'You accuse me of hiding? Then what shall I accuse you of, Madam? Breaking and entering with intent to pilfer – take the candlestick, Dorcas! Move the cups to the shelf, there! How do we know where the woman is from . . . the Fleet, most likely, and wearing stolen clothes, and having lying letters writ for her by some renegade scholar!' He stopped, breathing heavily, and twisted his lips in a smile Philippa found less than becoming. 'The door was locked. How did you enter, if you aren't a thief? And if you are a lady of quality, where are your servants?'

'Outside,' said Philippa repressively. 'You would be able to see them if you were not bent, it seems, on conducting your business in kitchens.'

'Accomplices!' Bailey said. His face was still twisted.

'Friends,' said Philippa mildly. 'My groom is Sir Henry Sidney's, and wears his livery, if you will take the trouble to look. Why, Mr Bailey, I should dislike extremely calling unannounced at your house, if this is the treatment you mete to a family friend, who has written from Court to advise you of her visit. If it is my sex you take exception to, I cannot remedy that, although you seem to have no objections to sharing your house with a woman. If you resent bestowing hospitality, I have asked for none. If it

141

is the Queen you misprise, it would be as well not to make your feelings too plain.'

Harshly, the woman's voice spoke in her ear. 'Mr Bailey is a loyal subject of Her Majesty. None more loyal. It is lies and spite of you hear anything else.'

'Be quiet, woman!' said Bailey. He advanced unpleasantly close and stood, looking down at the bongrace. Philippa gazed at him with an outward serenity, and an inward gratitude that fruit and cheese were all that her stomach was saddled with. Then he said, 'Come!' and leaving the kitchen walked up the stairs.

Philippa stood where she was. 'My groom and—'

He did not turn round. 'Look after them, Dorcas!' he snapped, and, flinging open a door, strode into his study. Philippa followed.

The room was little more than a closet, surrounded by shelves, with a table-desk under the window, which this time was tight shut. The reason for caution was obvious, for in every available space in the room, on desk, floor, stool and all the lower shelves, were stacked ledgers and papers, held down, half of them, with rocks from the garden. On the other shelves, up to the ceiling, which was finely plastered like the one she had seen, was a dusty collection of book rolls and books which appeared to run into some hundreds and led Philippa, like a dog held by the nose, to walk staring up to the tightly packed spines. Mr Bailey, who had seated himself at his desk, rose and addressed her unpleasantly.

'Your stool is placed here. I shall have to lock up my library, I see. Or some palace cockscomb who has learned to read, and maybe to add, will be walking through locked doors to thieve it.'

'A bibliotaphos,' said Philippa dreamily. She took the stool by his peremptory finger.

The big, blunt-featured face, half shaven and threaded with veins, stared without apology at the sun-polished young one, with its delicate artifice almost invisible; its rich clothes bestowed with theatrical grace. 'You have your manners to seek,' he said. 'I wonder, mistress, that the Queen allows impertinent children to clutter her chambers. It is a sorry outlook for her nursery.' Taking his time, her great-uncle by marriage looked Philippa narrowly up and down, and then added, with heavy contempt, 'But you are not here on Queen's business, are you? No, or we should have heard many more or those piping threats, and a rattling of prison chains as well, I make no doubt. You are here on the affairs of that parcel of blustering rogues, the Crawfords of Culter.'

'Who married your sister,' Philippa said. With a training painfully learned, she avoided twisting her gloved hands together.

'Who made a fool of her,' said Bailey harshly. 'Married at seventeen, dead at eighteen, giving birth to the heir. The great 1st Baron Crawford of Culter. He seized her dowry; he took her, and bedded her, and never came near her again, from the moment he planted his son until the hour she gave life bearing him.

'That,' said Leonard Bailey, 'is how the 2nd Baron, Gavin, was born, and that is how he would have died, a half-orphan of brutal and vicious neglect, had I not been there to save him and care for him.'

Philippa felt very cold. The half-orphan, Gavin. Sybilla's husband. And the father – the putative father – of Richard and Lymond. She said, 'Did you take him to stay with you?' and then sat very still as he laughed.

'You don't know their history, do you? Whoever sent you on this little mission has kept the rarest morsel to themselves. No, I could not take Gavin with me, mistress, because I was a child of eight, and an orphan myself when Honoria died. I was already at Midculter, the Baroness's young brother, there on sufferance, there to be kicked and maltreated, and there to see them do the same to the baby when it was born. He saw it born, the great lord of Culter, then he barely waited to bury his wife before he was out of the castle. Out of the castle, leaving his son and his brother-in-law to the blows of the kitchen boys, to stinking food, to rags for their backs.'

Philippa said, steadying her voice, 'Were the family poor?'

He laughed, the black cloth hat shaking; the sun catching the silvery nap of his beard. 'Poor, madam? That dung-heap of rascals, respecting only the weathercock? They could have sold the Crown ten times over, and did. And did. No. He could have dressed us in velvets if he wished to, but the 1st Baron didn't like children. Didn't like Honoria, who knew too much of his lovenests. Resented her child, and loathed me, who reminded him of her, and who knew too much – damn me,' said

Leonard Bailey, his face sweating with anger remembered, 'what does a child of eight – ten – twelve not see and hear? He was away – at Court, in France; away for months. Away sometimes for years. But he heard. And we were told, sneering, by the men he had left to humiliate us. Gavin grew up as an animal grows, with no gentle company but what I could give him, and I knew little enough. But he grew handsome. And it was when the 1st Baron departed to France and stayed there that this woman laid hands on Gavin and married him.'

'Sybilla?' Philippa said. Her throat was dry.

'A Semple. Sybilla, yes, was her name. A shrewd family. They knew there was money. They had seen none of it spent on Gavin or me. But Gavin was nearly of age, and when he came into his inheritance, the wife got it all. When his father came back to Midculter the marriage was legal, the money was hers, and she had spent it as a riddle would spend it – Midculter rebuilt and refurnished, and filled with her clothes and her pictures, her statues and jewels fit for Solomon's temple. . . .'

'Was he angry?' said Philippa. Beautiful Midculter, with its painted roof and suites of fine tapestries. The jewel boxes in Sybilla's own solar. Lymond's wealth, now squandered also. . . .

The harsh voice was sliding and slow, and so was Bailey's glance. 'Have you seen a sow burst apart in a furnace? That was his anger. That was the day which repaid all the years of my wretchedness.'

Philippa said, 'What did he do?' from dry lips. She felt very empty.

'What could he do? Break the marriage? He tried to, but she would have none of it. Take back the money? But that was impossible. It had been spent, and the house was Gavin's as much as it was his. He could do nothing to Sybilla or Gavin, because, apart from all that, in his absence Sybilla had played her best card. She had given Gavin his heir, the boy Richard. No,' Bailey said; and despite the fierce smile on his face, the long quill in his thick hands bent and snapped as he stared grinning at Philippa. 'No: there was only one thing left for my lord to do in his rage, and he lost no time over it. I was flung penniless from the house. I, his dead wife's own brother; for thirty years his dearest relation. I was flung from the house and left to live as I may. There, Mistress Somerville,' said Leonard Bailey, and the glare in his eyes, fading, was replaced by the smile she was beginning to know, 'there are the Crawfords of Culter. There are your friends. There are the people who send you. You will not be surprised, perhaps, if you were not greeted in this house with roses, and if I now ask you to take your groom and your woman and your high-handed Court ways and remove yourself from my property.'

Philippa did not move. She said, 'I knew none of this.'

Its fury gone, the harsh voice was flat. 'I gave you leave, Madam.'

'I have no wish to stay,' Philippa said. 'Except for one thing. Where were Sybilla's next children born?'

Her fortitude no longer extended to stilling her hands. But it did force her, at least, to meet the long, speculative look he bestowed on her. He drew a slow breath. 'Ah,' said Leonard Bailey. 'So there lies the heart of the matter. The girl is dead, so – your interest is in the boy, Francis?'

'Yes,' Philippa said.

'And then,' Bailey said, on the same genteel note of inquiry, 'and then what is your interest?'

Philippa answered as steadily. 'That of a friend.'

'A friend. So. Then the boy himself has sent you to inquire? He has doubts, perhaps? Or is it a question of inheritance? Or knighthood? Or some prize for which legitimacy – ah, that precious thing, Mistress Philippa – legitimacy is essential?'

'No,' Philippa said. 'It is none of these.'

'Then why?' Bailey said. He was smiling again. He sat back in his hard-backed joined chair, the broken reed thrown on the papers, the coarse wisps of his hair escaped, in his emotion, from the thin greasy edge of the cap. 'I fear you will have to explain it. My time is limited. I cannot gratify your curiosity for no reasonable purpose.'

'He didn't send me,' Philippa said. 'He is not interested, nor are any members of his family except myself; and my interest is soon explained. Mr Francis Crawford and I have been married.'

His pleasure was a thing tangible to the sight: it spread from his shining broad hands to his mouth and his eyes; it emanated from him like an odour. 'Married!' said Master Bailey. 'With Sybilla Crawford's son for a husband! Then get you fast to a lawyer.'

'Why?' said Philippa bluntly.

'Why? Because your sons, Mistress, will have no more name than your husband has, and an inheritance of a kind no one can tell. I knew her ways,' Bailey said. 'I knew Sybilla Semple, and while I was there, at Midculter, I could keep her in check. But I was thrown out of Midculter, and when the 1st Baron went off, there was no one left, in Midculter or out of it, to restrain her.'

'Richard is Gavin's son,' Bailey said. 'But in the boy and the girl who came after him run the seeds of four, or six, or ten possible fathers. . . . Who could blame the dear woman? Rich, titled – there was only one flaw in the household, and that without remedy. It was too late by then to rear Gavin as he should have been reared in his youth. He was a rough man and a rude lover, but that was not poor Gavin's fault. Get a lawyer, mistress. Your children will be pretty, but nameless.'

'I don't believe you,' Philippa said. Sybilla, wise, witty and fragile, was the woman he was speaking of. And what he had said was untrue.

He was breathing hard still, with excitement, and the smile remained on his face. 'Naturally,' he said. 'It is not in your interests to believe me. And in her old age, I am told, the lady is most persuasive. Can you not imagine her in her youth? Such blue eyes : such golden-haired purity. Each man she met fell in love with her. But she was circumspect with her lovers. She chose wisely and enjoyed them in secret – in France, or behind some stranger's curtain in Scotland. And wherever the girl and the boy were begotten, the births both took place in France.'

'I don't believe it,' Philippa said, 'because the story I heard was quite different. I heard the second two children were not Sybilla's. I heard they were fathered by Gavin.'

'Then why come to me?' said Leonard Bailey. 'If that version pleases you then pray, mistress, believe it. But I'll warrant you it came from a Semple. And without a paper to prove it, at that.'

'And what proof do you have?' said Philippa.

He was enjoying it. He gave a laugh, his lips looped at the corners; the saliva winking between broken teeth. 'What a keen nose for facts ! How you long to hear me say, *None.* But I have proof, my mistress. First, her sweet children's colouring. Gavin was brown-haired, and so is Richard, his eldest. What of the second son, Francis?'

146

'It isn't proof,' Philippa said. 'His mother might have been fair.'

'You are right. It isn't proof. But it gives you pause to consider, does it not?'

'And in the second place?' Philippa said.

'In the second place, I have what no one else has. I have evidence, written evidence, that the children Francis and Eloise were Sybilla's.' He laughed again. 'Don't you wish you had scanned my shelves more closely? But they are not there, Mistress Philippa. The papers are where only I may find them. And there is only one way you will ever learn what is in them. If you send Francis Crawford here to me to ask me for them, with all the respect and duty that is my due as the creature's great-uncle. Tell him to come to me, Mistress, and beg for them. Then I might let him see what his true ancestry is.'

She could not move him. When at last she rounded on him, accusing him of the grossest misrepresentation and malice, he merely laughed again, and then, rising, took her by the arm and walked her out of the house. She made him stop on the threshold so that she could open her purse and fling down on the table the price of the cracked bowl for Dorcas. Then she marched down to the gate where George and Fogge waited, and mounted.

CHAPTER NINE

The road Philippa took then was not back to Hampton Court Palace, but to the city; and because she had confided in them, Fogge and George, her groom, rode with her to her appointment at Tilbury.

She made poor company. And they, after attempting to cheer her with conversation, lapsed into silence, glancing at her from time to time. Philippa, riding like one of Mr Dee's mechanical toys, heard and saw nothing but the strident voice of Leonard Bailey, overriding and destroying what she had already, with such trouble, accepted: the story of the untoward marriage, and the part played in it by the woman she knew, who had been Sybilla Semple.

In two days, she was to set sail for Russia. In three months or less she would be facing Lymond himself, already astonished and irritated by the responsibility of her presence, and would have to persuade him to come home to Scotland, and to Sybilla. And would have to tell him what Leonard Bailey had just told her . . . or would have to conceal it.

She could not tell him. Of that she was sure. And he would never learn it in Scotland, if in all the years of his life there had been no rumour: nothing that had come to the ears of his enemies, and used against him and Sybilla. Any misconduct there had been in Sybilla's life had taken place outside Scotland, Philippa propounded to herself, trying to face possibilities; trying to throttle the instinct to forget it all and do nothing. . . . Therefore if Lymond came home, who would tell him if she, Philippa, said nothing?

No one. No one, that is, unless Leonard Bailey, roused by her visit, decided to take a last, exquisite revenge. That was one risk she took, in saying nothing to Lymond. The other danger was subtler still. Suppose that, given the choice, Lymond would prefer to be the son of his mother, on any terms whatsoever, than to be the offspring of Gavin alone?

She knew too little about him. Kate would have advised her, but there was no time now to consult Kate. And even Kate could not see the circumstance, as she did, against a lifetime of war and diplomacy, education and statesmanship, in which this was merely a factor. To a cool-tempered man, a small factor. To an ambitious man, his emotional needs already sufficiently catered for, a factor of vanished importance. To Sybilla, life or death . . . which punishment was greater; which did she deserve? To Kate, what? There Philippa did not know either. She could plan nothing; understand nothing, until she met and weighed up whatever Francis Crawford had become.

The wages of meddling. If she had never seen Leonard Bailey: if she had resisted this one final impulse to take to Lymond in Russia this final and authenticated piece of equipment: his own blameless blood line. To Russia, with Rob Best and Diccon Chancellor, with Christopher and Killingworth and John Buckland, Diccon's sardonic sailing-master. To the sea, and bright adventure, away from the incense and whisperings. To the Dwina, where the white rose of Muscovy smoked on the bushes, and laced the wind with its cold scent. . . .

She was riding still, the tears still under her veiling, when the chance riders about them became suddenly many, and less than chance: and resolved themselves into a circle of men, armed and bearded, whose leader thrust aside George and Fogge, and riding up to her side said, 'Mistress Somerville? Do not be frightened. But it seems this rascal here has misled you. This is not the way to Hampton Court Palace.'

He was not young, but his voice carried every authority, and among the soldiers beside him, there was no friendly face. Philippa said, 'Who are you, sir? My escort is perfectly adequate. I am not going to Hampton Court Palace, but to some friends in the City.'

The man shook his helmeted head. 'In the City? No, mistress. The Queen has given leave for no one to visit the City. Your place is at Court, in the Palace.'

'But—' said Philippa; and then cut off her protest. George, his hand falling back from his sword, could do nothing against all these men; still less could one girl. They had been sent here to take her; they had been sent to bring her back to her duty.

Or worse. Who were they? Who had thought it important to find her?

It was then that Philippa saw the Lennox cipher on every cloak.

*

Philippa was ill, or so Lady Lennox was certain. Ill from her loving and onerous duties, and deserving of rest in the Countess's own fine apartments quite apart from the hubbub of Court, where she could sew, and read, and be quiet, and forget about the odd aberration which sent her wandering on some unspecified journey to London. 'It is for your health,' she insisted sweetly, on Philippa's every protest. 'The Queen understands. The child tarries still: there are more ladies at Court than any accouchement has need of, and the Duchess of Alba besides. Why fret? Are we so harsh in our care of you? Even if you returned, Philippa, the Queen would merely send you straight back to me.'

The prison was gilded: the jailers charming and quick with every dainty attention. But, of intention or not, it was a prison. And a man at arms stood before every door.

The *Edward Bonaventure* sailed, but without Philippa Somerville. And the week after she sailed, Jane Dormer came to take Philippa back to her duty.

She curtseyed to Lady Lennox, and put both hands on Philippa's shoulders. 'You are well. I am so glad to see you restored. It is your first season at Court: we were thoughtless to bear quite so hard on you. . . . Are you sure you wish to return?'

She herself looked less than well; her white skin sallow, and blue hollows between eye and cheekbone. Philippa, who for ten days had betrayed neither resentment nor anger, showed neither now, but kissed her cheek, and smiled, and went in her turn to curtsey to the Countess of Lennox, adding the necessary, neatly phrased thanks. Surprise and docility were all she had shown from the beginning, and docility was the essence of her leavetaking now. The Countess, smiling, touched the girl on the cheek. 'Charming. You do not know how you have brightened my household. I declare, I wish that Harry were older.'

Jane Dormer's fingers closed on her own, and Philippa smiled at the gentle reminder, and then again, agreeably, at the Countess of Lennox. Outside, and back in her own room, she did not smile at all, but unpacked, and ascertained her next duty, and swept upstairs and along corridors and across courtyards until she found Roger Ascham, and then the small office with Bartholomew Lychpole half-rising, startled inside it. She banged the door. 'The letter,' said Philippa. 'The letter to Mr Crawford. Did you send it?'

He stared at her, and then turning, laid down his pen and pulled a stool forward. 'Mistress Philippa! Sit, please. Yes, I sent it, these several weeks back. Has it gone astray? Or did you want to send others?'

Philippa said, 'Did anyone see it?'

He clasped his hands and stared at her, frowning. 'It went with my report. Mistress Philippa, no one must see these reports. No one knows of them. No one could have seen it.'

'Then who besides myself knows that Mr Crawford is in Russia?' Philippa said.

Master Lychpole rose to his feet, his hand pressing hard on the lectern. 'No one. No one, unless you have told them yourself. Why should you think so? Is it spoken of?

Do they know of my messages?' He gazed at her, his face drawn with anxiety.

'No,' said Philippa. Her voice flattened. 'No one speaks of you or your reports. It seemed to me that there might be a suspicion, a rumour, that Mr Crawford is now in Russia. I wondered if you had lost a letter, or had found your papers disturbed.'

'There are three clicket locks on that coffer,' said Lychpole. 'And I keep the key for each one round my neck. No one could read my papers without my being aware of it. And the letter goes by a safe messenger, and by now will be far out of reach. But what of its answer, or some message to you from your husband? News may come out of Russia as well. It is not a secret that will stay so for ever.'

'No. That is true,' Philippa said. 'I am worried, perhaps, for no reason . . . what is keeping Master Ascham so busy?'

'The letters,' said Bartholomew Lychpole. 'Forty-seven Latin letters to every prince in the known world announcing the Queen's happy delivery of a Prince. I tell you, they are right who say that if this birth fails, there will be trouble on a scale we have never yet known.'

For there was no prince or princess; only Ruy Gomez saying, *Life is short for such long expectations,* and, *When they saw her with a girth greater than Gutierre Lopez, they made an error, they say, in their adding.*

The Queen lay on her bed, her hair hidden under her cap, an embroidered robe over her shift of white satin, and prayers were said at her bedside, or readings of a devotional nature, or low talk and some discreet music. Sometimes the Queen rose for her meals, urged to the table by all her ladies, but her appetite had always been spare, and had increased little since the start of her pregnancy. She longed, it was easy to see, for hourly news of her kingdom, and to guess the mind of her King, but although he paid dutiful visits, and held her hand, and talked in slow, articulated Spanish and listened, patiently, while she answered in French, the exchanges were more formal, Philippa thought, than she had heard them before.

Then the mourning clothes arrived, and the money, and, released from diplomatic imprisonment, King Philip was able to appear in public at Whit. It was only then that Philippa learned from Don Alfonso how many of

Philip's attendant's had already gone to the Emperor at Brussels; and later, the reason. The peace talks at Marck had broken down, and the French and the Emperor Charles were preparing for war. 'So,' said her informant with his usual brightness, 'the King waits only for the birth to cross the Channel instantly. I tell you, a single hour's delay in this delivery seems to him like a thousand years.'

'And to the Queen?' Philippa had answered him tartly. So he did not tell her, as he might have done, that the Emperor had already written advising his son how to announce without undue fuss that his Queen was not pregnant. The Court thought it funny when the Polish Ambassador, come to condole with King Philip on the death of his saintly grandmother, droned onwards in unwitting Latin through every phase of his brief, not omitting those well-expressed paragraphs which congratulated Queen Mary of England on the birth of a beautiful Prince.

Philippa, more discreet in her way than Don Alfonso, did not relate that to Jane, or the hysterical laughter with which it was greeted. Or so said Sir Henry Sidney, who had been present, and who was interested in the Polish Ambassador for other reasons entirely. Learning this from Sir Henry much later, Philippa was momentarily puzzled. 'How does the Polish Ambassador affect the affairs of the Muscovy Company?'

'It's the other way round,' said Sir Henry. 'Poland is Russia's neighbour, you know, and one of her traditional enemies. The King of Poland is very anxious indeed that the Muscovy company should be forbidden to export any arms or military engines which could be used by the Russians against them.'

'And will you agree?' Philippa said. 'Will Barnes and Gresham agree?'

'The Privy Council will agree,' Sidney said. 'Or I think it extraordinarily likely. And loyal men that they are, how can England's brave haberdashers scruple to follow?'

In the middle of June, the Queen's pains began; the casements were shut, the doors barred, and her chambers locked against all save her doctors and women. The pains continued, but became intermittent. Jostled out by her superiors, Philippa did what she could, and tried to save Jane some of her unceasing duties, and sat in a corner and experienced grief, when she could do nothing else, for the middle-aged woman who lay rigid, praying aloud, behind the curtains of cloth-of-gold quilting, beneath the spangles and bone lace and crown of plumed feathers, and the flat counterpane, embroidered with roses in silk and gold twist, and the initials of Philip and Mary, intertwined.

She was asleep in her own room, exhausted, when Jane Dormer came to her in the morning, and kneeling by the low bed, touched her hand.

There was no need to speak. The question stood in Philippa's brown, waking eyes, and meeting them, Jane shook her head. 'The pains have gone, and the reason for them has shown itself. Not a birth, the doctors say, but the opposite. The Queen has restarted her courses.'

Philippa looked at Jane's white face. 'Not an imminent birth?'

'They say not. If the Queen presses them, no doubt they will say less firmly that it is unlikely. If she argues enough, they may even announce that the Queen's delivery has been *a little deferred*. But she is not pregnant. She is not pregnant, Philippa.' She was wet-eyed: within a shadow of an explosive outbreak of tears.

Philippa put an arm around her shoulders. 'Have you never suspected it? Think how simply such a thing happens. It begins with some unlucky accident of the flesh which this Queen is prone to, and because she needs and yearns for a pregnancy, she believes what the evidence tells her. She makes an ecstatic pronouncement in the joy at the Cardinal's return, and the pregnancy is irrevocably dated. I've seen a girl fearful of childbirth listen to her body the way the Queen has done, all those months. It's a curious music it plays, and if you study it long enough, you hear what you want.

'All along the Queen has been pushed: by the nation's eagerness, by the political need; by her own growing desire for her husband to stay at her side. Her household takes the steps for her: marks the weeks, prepares the nursery, makes the clothes; makes ready the celebrations, and she can hardly ignore them. She is part of it too: the miracle began within her; she cannot deny it. If she has doubts, their excitement reinfects her and she forgets them. Or, at times afraid, she may sometimes try to push it behind her; ignore the span slipping away until the reminders become quickly too many: until every eye is on her, and her food and her gait and her humour: until doctors are watching her day and night and false reports of the birth are flying already. . . .'

'You mean,' Jane said slowly, 'that she has known all along she was barren?'

'I mean,' Philippa said, 'that she believes that for the devout, all things are possible. And that for nine months she has prayed for a miracle.'

'Poor lady,' said Jane, and cried in Philippa's arms while, dry-eyed, Philippa stared into the new world she had discovered in London and begged, with a grimness unknown to the Marian shrines, to be vouchsafed the means to endure it, and even, one day, to mend it as it needed.

The Queen's doctors announced that an error of possibly two or three months had been made with Her Majesty's pregnancy, and that delivery was now likely to take place in August, or even September. Two gentlemen who indulged in ribald remarks as a consequence were sent to the Tower. And the King sent a note to his dear friend, Ruy Gomez de Silva: *Let me know what line I can take with the Queen about leaving her, and about religion. I see I must say something, but God help me.*

The Emperor Charles received a letter. The King his son and Ruy Gomez wished to leave England for Spain. King Philip desired above all to escape from the great and continual distress in which he found himself, but was intent on two things: to leave the Queen feeling convinced he would always continue to love her most dearly, and that he would come back shortly to remain with her – she showing that she would not consent to his departure either mentally or verbally otherwise. Also, to devise means of returning without trouble to England, so as not to have thrown away so much money, time, toil and repute.

There was another uprising in Warwickshire: Pembroke dealt with it.

Exhausted, the Queen's ladies continued to give her their care and their comfort. The Queen rose from her bed, and moved through her rooms slowly, undertaking no business. Then plans were announced to move the whole court briefly to Oatlands, four miles farther from London, and Philippa along with the others was plunged into lists and planning and packing. The Queen, sitting erect in her carved chair, a counterpane over her knees, issued the orders, and, when the time came, was placed in her closed litter and taken through the green summer park to her barge, and from there to her palace.

Hampton Court emptied, for cleansing. The ladies brought for the accouchement, unable to find rooms in the bijou restrictions of Oatlands, were advised quietly to withdraw and vanish. And a cradle, carried out and locked in a storeroom, lay on its side so that this time its poorly scanned legend had only the mice to be witness: *The child whom Thou to Mary, O Lord of Might has send* . . .

Ten days later, the King and Queen were back in Hampton Court, and the watchers and Ambassadors saw that the Queen no longer walked with her ladies alone, but had her statesmen for the first time around her, and was giving audiences once again, her manner affable; her face stiff; half-shorn, half-crumbled, like sandstone, and only the small, tightly-rimmed eyes liquid and suffering. Philippa heard then that the Emperor had sent a peremptory summons to Philip and that the Queen had agreed he should go.

He left for London in less than a fortnight, and the Queen, staying by his side at the last moment, unexpectedly shared his public farewells in the City, acclaimed in her open litter by the crowds who ran and shouted along the long road, and who had seemingly considered her dead. Then together, the Crown and the Court moved on down-river, to where Philip's ships waited at Greenwich.

And at Greenwich, the Queen summoned Philippa and at last gave her leave of absence. 'You have been my sweet servant, and you deserve rest from your labours. Your mother must lack you. Take your way home to the north, and comfort her, and on my good lord's return we shall see you.' And dismissing her, had given her a brooch and a chain; while from Lady Lennox there had emanated a kind smile and a message for her good lady mother.

Philippa retired to her room, wanly aghast. She did not want to go north. She could not face her own mother, and how could she avoid visiting Midculter, when all that she knew must be stamped on her face? And more than that, the ships would be returning from Russia. Not with Chancellor: that she did not expect. But the *Edward* and the *Philip and Mary* were to sail back to England to winter. And, since they might surely bear letters, Philippa wished to be there when they came.

She applied, as was her sensible habit, for aid to the Sidneys. Lady Mary did not inquire why it was inconvenient for Mistress Philippa to spend a month at her home in Flaw Valleys. She merely arranged, with the greatest good will, for Philippa to join them instead down at Penshurst. And two days later, sent her husband to Greenwich to escort her.

He arrived on a day of typical chaos. All the Court were still there, Spanish and English, for with King Philip to Brussels were going the Queen's principal ministers and almost the whole of her Council: a measure of safety, no less than a promise of willing and speedy return. And back in England, Philip was leaving his Queen yet another assurance: his German and Spanish infantry and Burgundian cavalry, his Chapel functionaries, his physicians and pages and his whole stable department were to remain behind him, patient pawns awaiting redemption; exiles in an unfriendly land.

Philippa was ready and thankful to leave. She welcomed Sir Henry as he stooped, spurs clinking, through the low door of her room, and he smiled and gave her a kiss and said 'It should have been Allendale. I was to bring you his respects. That's one young man, along with a number of others, who wish your divorce would speed, Philippa.'

So Austin had already said. She thought of him, smiling, and of all the warm farewells she had received today from her immediate circle. The kisses and gifts and affectionate raillery from all the men and women with whom she had brushed shoulders in the last ten months had both surprised Philippa and touched her. Don Alfonso, miming despair combined with exhausted relief, was going in the King's train to Brussels. Austin, she knew, would find more than one excuse to come to Penshurst. She said, 'I don't suppose they want it any more eagerly than I do. It seems to be delayed once again. They say now that nothing can be done until Mr Crawford sends his formal consent.'

'Sends,' Sir Henry Sidney repeated. He looked round and pushed the door shut; then pulling a stool forward for Philippa, went and perched himself on the window seat. 'Philippa, are you sure he won't come back to Scotland?'

'I am sure,' said Philippa. She would not be there to persuade Lymond. Her first two letters had brought no reply, and she had not sent a third, since Diccon Chancellor had sailed without her. She knew she would never commit now to paper what Leonard Bailey had told her. She knew that whatever excuse she had given, Margaret Lennox had placed her under restraint for one reason only : to prevent her from sailing to Russia.

How had she discovered her plan? Or was it merely a guess, based on the knowledge, somehow acquired, that Lymond was living in Russia? And why had she been prevented from sailing? Of all people, Margaret Lennox had no interest at all in her safety.

She had found no solution to that. Or to the choice she saw standing bleakly before her. Whether to sacrifice Sybilla's wellbeing to her son's peace of mind and safety in Russia. Or whether to persevere : to bring Lymond home to face what he already knew from the Abbess; or to be pursued and confronted by the outrage of his great-uncle's spite, needlessly destroying both himself and Sybilla?

Perhaps, Philippa thought flatly, they were wrong, all of them, in their view of him. Perhaps he would learn the truth, whatever it was, with perfect equanimity, indifferent to the lives of his parents and the accident of his own origin; occupied, sensibly, with his own future. If that were true, then for Sybilla's sake he should come home, for nothing could hurt him.

It had been a long silence. Coming to herself suddenly, Philippa looked up at Sir Henry and grinned, and said, 'Or I think I'm sure. Confidence, like Admiration, is the daughter of Ignorance. But so long as he writes, does it matter?'

'It matters now,' Sir Henry said. 'I am glad, Philippa, you are not going north. I would like you here when the ships come back from Muscovy. Because I think they may bring you word of your husband.'

The pause was perhaps a second too long, but she did not make a single mistake. 'From *Muscovy*!' said Philippa Somerville.

'You didn't know? He hasn't written you?' said Sir Henry quietly. And to the latter part of the question she answered with a truthful shake of the head.

'I wondered if perhaps he had. I have been in two minds whether to speak to you, Philippa. But if these ships bring letters for you, it is right that you should answer them fittingly. Mr Crawford, Philippa, is in service in Muscovy. His employment is honourable, but it is one which closely concerns this country and others in Europe. He is believed to be helping the Tsar to train and muster his armies. For that reason, no doubt, he has not written to you. And for that reason, his whereabouts have not been made known outside Russia so far.'

Philippa said briefly, 'Who told you?'

Henry Sidney said, 'That is why this door is closed, and why I must ask you not to repeat to anyone else what we are saying. Diccon Chancellor was told the news, before he sailed, by the Countess of Lennox.'

'Whom Mr Crawford had told?' inquired Philippa.

'She did not say, but I think it unlikely. She did appear, however, to be perfectly sure, although she took the trouble to swear Diccon to secrecy. Fortunately Diccon and I have known each other so long that in the matter of promises we are one soul and one flesh. But no one else at Court knows, or must know.'

Philippa said, 'I still don't see how she could have known. But since she did, why tell Mr Chancellor? He'll find out in Russia in any case. Or . . . I see. She wished to send Mr Crawford a message?'

'She wished Diccon to tell Mr Crawford to return,' said Sir Henry in the same clear, subdued voice. 'Mr Crawford was to be told that, unless he returned, there would be no annulment for you. He was to be told, that in the event of a war between England and France, your safety would be in question. He was to be told that if your marriage persisted, as it would unless he returned, Flaw Valleys would be seized to preserve it, and your mother obliged to remarry, at the Queen's instance. Diccon was told to use every means in his power to ensure that when he sails in the spring, he brings Mr Crawford back with him. And he has been told that if he fails, when he returns he will face an indictment for heresy. At worst, the stake. At best, ruin and banishment at the start of a brilliant career.'

'Then the Queen knows?' said Philippa, her heart plodding within her.

He shook his head. 'Only the Lennoxes. From what spite they do it, I don't know. Perhaps you can guess better than I. Perhaps they think truly they may do England a service. With all this secrecy, it seems unlikely. But Margaret Lennox is the Queen's cousin and what she threatens, she can carry out amply. She has threatened Diccon with death. She has told him this also. If Mr Crawford does not

158

leave Russia now, he will never leave it. He will be dead before the ship sails, by her agency.'

She did not speak. Nor could he possibly know the pressures of thought which for once had rendered her speechless. He said kindly, 'You are not to be frightened. These are serious threats, but he is a responsible man, Diccon, and so is your husband. They will return, I am sure, since they are forced to. But once back, these toils will be straightened.

'Meanwhile you must pray, as I do, that he comes.'

*

On 29 August, thirteen and a half months after his arrival, the very high and mighty Philip, by the grace of God King of England, France and Naples, and Prince of Spain, took barge at Greenwich to travel to Gravesend by water, and from thence on to Dover and Brussels. Before leaving, the King took leave of Queen Mary, who chose then to walk with him through all the chambers and galleries to the head of the stairs, where, in the face of the crowd, she bore herself with perfect and regal decorum, although visibly moved when the Spanish nobles bowed, saluting her hand, and, as was the custom in England, the King bestowed a kiss on each of her plain, weeping ladies.

Once in the barge, the King mounted the steps to be seen, and waved his bonnet back to the palace. The Queen stood at the river windows of her apartment until he had embarked and sailed out of sight, and then was overtaken by an unrestrained bout of violent sobbing. Later, as was her custom, she sought comfort in prayer.

'*Domine Jesu Christi, qui es verus sponsus animae meae, verus Rex et Dominus meus* . . . O Lord Jesus Christ, Who are the true husband of my soul, my true King and my master. Thou Who didst choose me for spouse and consort a man who, more than all others, in his own acts and in his guidance of mine, reproduced Thy image; Thy image whom thou didst send into the world in holiness and justice. I beseech Thee, by Thy most precious blood: *Assuage my grief!*'

PART 2

CHAPTER ONE

At Sweetnose, there was frost in the shrouds and a cold midsummer fog which forced the *Edward Bonaventure* to lie idle on the last stage of her journey to Russia, with the boom of the whirlpool in Chancellor's frustrated ears, and a flotilla of impertinent Lapps gathering under his poop, assembling for the midsummer fishing of belugas and walrus and salmon at Pechora.

He did not know until one of the grinning creatures climbed aboard, crucifix swinging, with a gift of fresh salted salmon, that Christopher had been off with them at half-tide to smear oatmeal butter on the Kamen Woronucha, the biggest rock by the whirlpool; and when the fog presently lifted, he viewed Christopher's crowing with fatherly disfavour, and mentioned to his sailing-master, John Buckland, that he should probably be burned as a heretic.

Buckland, a stolid Devonshire seaman, grinned without answering. Light-hearted by nature, with a questing, vigorous mind and a long apprenticeship in the exact arts, Diccon Chancellor was a good friend on shore. But at sea, launched on his adventure with the stars caught in his astrolabe, he carried, like a man drunk on small wine, an aroma of happiness.

It had been a fine trip, Chancellor thought, and better still since he had left the *Philip and Mary* to discharge her cargo and drop her agent at Vardo, and had been able to sail on alone, with his charts and his sightings, and Buckland, who knew what he wanted. Christopher had been all he had hoped. The new merchants had been no trouble, and three of them had been with him before, and knew what to expect; or were here because they liked the unexpected. Eleven reasonable men, barring the two Members' sons, Judde and Hawtrey, who had needed a little careful handling until Buckland got them interested in navigation. And Best had drummed some Russian into them as well.

'If we can keep the cook sober,' Chancellor said to the Master as, pitching slightly, the *Edward* stubbed her way round to Cross Island and headed for Foxnose across the wide gulf of the bay, 'we'll have sailed two thousand miles in a month. Then you can turn round and go back, while our troubles are only beginning. . . . D'you know why the Germans can't keep a navy afloat?'

And Buckland, who was in a state of some elation himself, grinned and said, 'Why? No oatmeal and butter?'

Richard Chancellor batted a derisory palm. 'No! The cooks burn them down to the waterline.'

They crossed the bar of the River Dwina on 23 June, and anchored off the village of Nenoksa, in the roadstead of St Nicholas, where the brine pipes ran in from the ocean. As before, the log cabins were plumed with the steam of salt boilings, and as before, there combined with the breath of violets and rosemary, drifting over the water, the fishy reek of the hot trenches swimming with blubber.

But this time, there was no need to send a party ashore, and to demand food and hostages. Men were aboard before they were content with the grip of the anchor, with gifts of eggs and butter and beef, and mutton from the white-faced black sheep they saw moving about the short grass. And in a matter of hours, Chancellor and his son and the members, agents and other employees of the Muscovy Company were within the log walls of St Nicholas Abbey and feasting upon mead instead of sour beer, and duck and goose and roast swan and pancakes instead of biscuit and salt pork and the never-ending diet of fish. The foolish loaves, fashioned like doughnuts and horseshoes, disappeared each with a powerful bite, and the regrettable fish-tasting bacon was devoured clean from the plate under the twenty pairs of calm, hooded eyes.

And the language came, creakingly, to the tongue again. Often as they had practised it, one forgot the abrupt, vehement cadences. Chancellor talked, haltingly, to the Abbot about his journey, about the weather here at St Nicholas, about the news from Kholmogory, the nearest trading town up the river; about, with difficulty, the health and affairs of the Tsar. It was only half-way through all this, applying to Sedgewick and Johnson and Edwards for the missing nouns and incompetent verbs and delinquent adjectives, that he realized what the Abbot, in turn, was trying to tell him. They had found Sir Hugh Willoughby.

He said, 'By your leave?' and fought off the chorusing voices of his companions, like a nest of competing and baritone birds, and the beautiful Russian of Robert Best, the most successful grammarian of them all, confident in delivery and despairing of understanding the tongue he had barely heard except from Chancellor before.

'By your leave, sir. Sir Hugh Willoughby and his two ships are safe?'

'My son, how could such news be?' said the Abbot. 'The ships are safe. You will find them here in the roads of St Nicholas, with their stores intact as on the day the storm divided you, two years ago. They were discovered last spring by the Lapps in Nokuyef Bay, on the Frozen Sea, at the mouth of the River Arzina, and word was brought to the Governor. They were drawn here with great pains, sailing from harbour to harbour, and when the sun rises, you will see their masts, over the bay.'

'But the men?' Chancellor said. 'Where are the men?' And this time no one spoke but the Abbot.

'The men were aboard, every one, from the least of the seamen to your lord, the Captain General himself. And dead, every one: frozen and dead, with ice for their shrouds.'

They took the pinnace next morning to where, lodged quietly at anchor, the *Bona Esperenza* and the *Bona Confidentia* lay, the flag of St George still flying in the clear Russian air. It was silent on board: their feet on the rungs of the ladders echoed through the crowded chambers, and a footfall on the deck above sounded out of place: hesitant and stealthy instead of light, uneven, purposeful; the footsteps of men at sea, about their business of sailing.

It was all as the Abbot had said. The cargo stood still in the holds; uncrated, so that the kerseys were white with mould and the copper spurs sweating and green. There were unwashed bowls where men had eaten at random, long after the rusted ovens were cold; and the surgeons' jars stood in rows clouded with dust, with their corroded blades and their books. The pilots' instruments were intact, and the charts, settled like cloth in the tube. And there was powder still, like cement, and slow matches stored by the cannon.

But in neither ship was there a rag or a blanket, or any item of clothing, from the Captain General's ceremonial doublets to the ship's store of blue watchet livery. Nor was there anywhere a ledge or a stool or a table, a door or a panel, a box or a crate or a chest which could be hauled out and burned. Only, emptied by the Muscovites, were the barrels which had held their food, and the makeshift bows and shafts they had used in their hunting. And one table and one chair, in Willoughby's cabin.

Willoughby was there too, that tall and fashionable man, with his long nose and high forehead and dark, pointed beard in a finely carpentered coffin, dust covered, which gave no offence. And by the coffin, laid there by the Russians, were the possessions of all his seamen, who had found graves less dramatic in Lapland. Chancellor did not touch the keys or the money, the knives or the rings or the crosses. Instead he walked to the desk, on which stood the hourglass, and the inkstand and the pen, still laid where Sir Hugh had replaced it when he wrote his last words in the log.

The log was there too. With hesitant fingers, Chancellor turned back the limp pages. *The Voyage Intended for the Discovery of Cathay,* Sir Hugh Willoughby had headed it; and below he had listed the souls in his charge on each ship. And below that, day by day, an account of their wanderings until, lost and despairing, with the *Confidentia* leaking and the inshore sea thickening to ice, he had run into the deep bay and stayed there. He had sent three search parties ashore, but found no human life in the darkness : the fishermen and hunters had long since left the north coast for the winter. And although it was only September, snow and hail came upon them, and severe frosts, which sealed them into their harbour.

They had had food for eighteen months, but heat and water were different matters. They lived, it seemed, through Christmas to January, and Sir Hugh himself was one of the last on board to die.

Chancellor took the log back with him to the *Edward*. To cross the sea in the sunlight; to step into the hot, reeking uproar of his own living ship, was a comfort whose poignancy brought tears to his eyes.

Then he set his men hard to work, for in a week's time the Governor of the Province would arrive, to escort them on the first stage of their thousand-mile journey to Moscow.

To Christopher, it was all fresh to his appetite, like food laid on a white cloth, tempting him with recondite colours and odours. And yet it was not so alien. No one spoke English. But who could speak English in Antwerp? There were trees outside, of a scrubby kind; and four little houses, and hens, which looked a bit smaller than London hens, but were still poultry; and sheep which looked about the same size as Norfolk sheep, although a different colour. And the church, although without pews and packed full of paintings and tapers and candles, had a cross on top, which everyone did reverence to.

During that strenuous week, he found time to explore the thick pine and birch woods and the small, straggling islands parting the Dwina's four mouths. He picked wild strawberries and saw the cinnamon rose spilling its single-starred blossom over acres of meadow; he walked along virgin white beaches, and ate blackcock, and bought snow larks, fat and sweet, for three kopeki a basket, and wished that his father or Rob Best were there to translate for him what people shouted at him, from the doors of their cabins, before they hurried inside with a swing of coarse cloth and stained deerskin waistcoat.

He helped them all unload the *Edward*. Under the carpenter's direction a log shelter was made, a primitive warehouse, to hold the Hampshire kerseys, the fine violet in grain, the London russets and tawnies and good lively greens; the barrels of pewter and the butts of Holland wine and the six hundredweights of sugar, which Christopher helped the purser to mark off and check. By the time the Governor came, the *Edward* was empty, and lying further east off the island of Jagro in a cloud of gnats, from which, provisioned and loaded, she would leave them to go back to England.

The Governor's name, alarmingly enough, was Prince Simeon Ivanovitch Milulinsky Punkoff, and with him came Fofan Makaroff, the Chief Magistrate of Kholmogory, together with three of his colleagues.

Chancellor knew them all. By then his Russian had regained its fluency: he introduced his son, and his own three countrymen from the previous voyage, and then one by one the agents and merchants who had not been here before.

This was his duty, no less than the long weeks of pilotage and the tasks in which lay his real interest: in defining and mapping this country of Russia, and discovering what had been unknown before. This journey to Moscow was his duty, and all the stately mummery at the Kremlin, where he must exchange regal gifts and regal greetings once more with the Tsar.

This was what, last time, Willoughby had been chosen to do and what he, with common sense only to guide him, had had to manage, somehow, alone. And manage so well, be it said, he thought with a twinge of self-congratulation, that at least he had been elected to carry out both tasks again. Through all this winter, he was to stay in Moscow, the figurehead of the new English traders now settling in Muscovy. And come the spring, with the cloth sold and the merchants well established, he would leave them there and, with Christopher, sail back with the new cargo to England, to tell the Company all he had learned, and to persuade the Company to send him once more, and untrammelled, to try for the route to Cathay.

But meantime, there were the lighters to load and a journey to get under way through which, like two threads, sometimes competing, would run his office as spokesman and ambassador, and the work of the merchants; the trading for which they had voyaged to Russia. Diccon Chancellor had no quarrel with commerce : it had paid for his ship and his voyage. But he was not, and never would be, a merchant.

Slow, ungainly, and not very comfortable, the great overland odyssey began on the broad River Dwina, with a long halt to load goods at Kholmogory, the first market town of size on the river. There they were to lose Dick Johnson, who was returning to England and who would see the new cargo safely north to the *Edward*.

Christopher found Kholmogory boring. There were a lot of meetings, and solemn pacings round warehouses full of stinking barrels of train-oil and crates of walrus tusks and heaps of glistening salt. Some of the Russians came and pulled at the pieces of cloth Mr Lane picked out from the *Edward*'s cargo, and then began offering roubles and altines with their fingers : Mr Lane packed the cloth away and just laughed.

There was nothing much to do in the town, which was very old, and stuck on an island in the Dwina. There were no brick buildings at all : only log houses with carved eaves and windows, and a ramshackle church made like a toy out of spills, and the ships in the river. The *Edward*'s cargo was in flat-bottomed river boats with their decks lined with bark and caulked with tarred moss, with a long, heavy rudder. They were like Gravesend barges, and had a mast and a sail each to use if there was a following wind, which there wasn't.

As it was, they would have to be towed all the way upstream, Christopher reckoned. He thought of the *Edward*. He wondered if Mr Johnson and the purser would remember to check off the marks before loading, and whether Mr Buckland would put oatmeal and butter on the Kamen Woronucha, and if they would see any whales. He rather wondered what Nicholas was doing at Penshurst, and then stopped wondering as Judde and Hawtrey came to find him and carry him off to someone's house to try caviare, which Hawtrey had just learned was an aphrodisiac.

Christopher asked someone later what an aphrodisiac was, and was convulsed with shame when the whole party exploded in laughter. Best patted him on the shoulder. 'Know-alls,' he said. 'You should hear George Killingworth when his poods are giving him trouble.'

They stayed an interminable time in Kholmogory. But at last there came a day when Dick Johnson set off north with the new cargo, and Christopher's father and his friends made their farewells and took to the boats, to be pulled south up the broad, dazzling reach of the Dwina. The magistrate Makaroff and Grigorjeff, his fellow merchant, came with them, while a light boat rode ahead to the *Peremines,* the towpath relay stations, to arrange for food and drink and new bargemen. Before them lay a sail of seven hundred miles. And after that, two weeks of riding to Moscow.

It took forty days, in clear summer heat, which blistered George Killingworth's tender, gold-bearded skin and turned the rest of them every shade from vermilion to russet. The bargemen sang as they pulled them past the short ochre scrub blocked with ice-tumbled boulders; past the queer fossil grove outside Yemza; past small wooden villages, and forests of elm and birch, oak and fir and fields of rich growing corn, fed by the river, while the hawks' bells trilled at the mast, and the streamers trembled like fast-moving water against the deep ocean-blue of the sky. At night they slept by the riverside.

Presently the Dwina turned into the single stream of the River Sukhona, shallow and stony where a canal had robbed it of water. In the lee of the tar sheds at Ustiug they transferred to flat-bottomed stroogs, and suffered a minor delay while Lane and Grey went to cast an eye over some hides and some tallow on Grigorjeff's recommendation. While the others were waiting, the cook drank himself senseless and fell into the river; they fished him out too late to save him. There passed a gloomy twenty-four hours, clogged with officialdom, which Makaroff spent largely in conclave. 'He's working hard,' said Henry Lane.

'He's hoping for a discount,' said Christopher's father mildly. 'I told you John Buckland refused point-blank to take that damned cook back on the *Edward*. I wish I'd never mentioned the Germans.'

'What about the Germans?' asked Christopher, mystified; but Makaroff came back at that moment, with all the arrangements completed, and very soon they had embarked on the stroogs and were making for Totma, and from there to their main halt on the way to the capital: the large and ancient city of Vologda, whose Namiestnik, Osep Grigorievich Nepeja, came to the river to welcome them.

They were very wet. The warmth had not yet abated, although they were now past the first week in September, but there had been a thunderstorm a few days after Totma, and Christopher, aware of new responsibilities on his shoulders, was glad that the bales were wrapped in sacking and cerecloth, and wished he were, too.

Nepeja was hospitable. A large man in middle years, with a square, curling beard, he had three or four words of English, from his previous meeting with Chancellor, whom he addressed, they noticed, as 'Ritzert'; and Christopher wondered if it were yet another legacy from the Tartars, this use of the simple first name which he had observed in quarters unexpectedly formal.

They were lodged by Nepeja's own house, an elaborate confection of wood with round and spired roofs and outside staircases all covered with awnings. Their own was plainer, with board beds attached to the wall in place of proper bedsteads; but compared to a wet night in the mud on the riverside, it was equal to any of the slope beds in red leather cases at Penshurst. Master Nepeja himself, in a long brocade robe with pearl collar, was richly dressed and possessed some elaborate horse harness and nice silverware, they noticed: there was no sign of a wife, if he had one. But there again, like the Moslems, the Russian wife kept to her terem, and was not exposed to the stares of the opposite sex. Christopher, who had found out what aphrodisiac meant, thought it a pity.

His father and Master Nepeja had an interminable meeting after dinner that first night, during which Christopher fell asleep, but was aware that the Namiestnik was being inquisitive about the exact names and histories of all the Englishmen in the party. He heard his father describing, floridly, George Killingworth's drapery business in London, and the eminence of Judde and Hawtrey's respective parents, and the experience of Richard Grey, who had captained the *Matthew Gonson* to the Levant twenty years before. He extolled Henry Lane's brains and trustworthiness and even mentioned, Christopher realized sleepily, that since his last visit John Sedgewick had become affianced to Sir George Barnes's grand-daughter.

It all seemed fairly irrelevant until Christopher realized suddenly that Nepeja was drawing up a report for the Tsar. No one lightly was allowed to enter the city of Moscow. And without the Tsar's agreement, no one was permitted to leave it.

The Namiestnik was now talking of conquests they had made at a place called Astrakhan, and how the Khan of the Crimean Tartars had sent an army to Tula that summer.

'To Tula!' his father had said sharply. 'Did they march on Moscow?'

Christopher sat up.

'No. There was a battle, but the Tartars retreated. They have gone back to the south. But in the spring, they say, the Tsar will send a pack of great hounds to rout this bear out of his hole.'

'Ah, yes,' Chancellor said. 'I hear the Tsar is following Sigismund's habit and reforming his army with mercenaries.'

'Where did you hear that?' said Nepeja.

'Or is that a sweeping assumption? I know of a Scot here in service with him,' said Christopher's father. 'I should prefer to think the Tsar free to turn his mind to matters other than martial. Trade, for instance.'

Osep Nepeja's sallow, thick-folded face was polite, and quite blank. 'The Grand Duke's army is purely for the purpose of defending his frontiers,' he said. 'There is a scattering, it is true, of service foreigners.'

171

'The man we know,' said Rob Best quite unexpectedly, 'is called Francis Crawford. Have you heard of him?'

The Namiestnik's thoughtful brown eyes turned on him. 'Yes. The gentleman with the eagle. His home is in Moscow.'

Suddenly, Christopher was perfectly awake. He said, 'A Scotsman called Crawford is—'

'Mistress Philippa's husband. We know,' said his father without turning round.

'Here in *Russia*?' Christopher said.

'Yes,' said his father, and this time looked at him with a quelling, slate-coloured eye.

'With an *eagle*?' said Christopher, failingly, under his breath, but this time no one answered him at all, and they had gone on to talk about taxes.

He got no further, either, when he questioned his father next day. Word had come through just before they left England that Mistress Philippa's husband had taken employment in Russia. It was none, said his father, of Christopher's business.

Christopher's romantic soul was disappointed. 'Doesn't he want to come home?' he inquired.

'You must ask him that if you meet him,' was all his father would say, rudely, in answer; and it was left to Christopher to try and squeeze more out of Rob Best. But Rob Best would not be informative either, except to say that he'd heard Tartars used eagles sometimes for deer hunts.

It sounded unlikely, but sustained Christopher in speculation for the four days it took to divide their goods and their party by half. Here in Vologda, in a warehouse hired for ten roubles till Easter, would remain the major part of their cargo, to be sold where prices were better and trading somewhat freer than in Moscow. And here, waiting in Vologda for permission to sell it would be Mr Grey as Company Agent, with Edwards, Hudson and Sedgewick to help him; and Judde and Hawtrey largely to hinder.

It was all fairly exciting, in spite of the time it took to separate the items for Moscow and transfer them from stroogs to telegas, which proved to be small narrow carts, of the kind you saw sometimes in Staffordshire, with four wheels, a pair of wood shafts and a box. The post horses alone, Mr Killingworth said, were going to cost over ten shillings.

Master Nepeja wanted to see what the cargo was like, and nearly everyone disappeared one morning into the warehouse and came back in different moods: Master Nepeja looked bland and Mr Grey very stiff, while Mr Killingworth was scarlet. Christopher heard afterwards that they had been offered twelve roubles for a piece of broadcloth and four altines, or two shillings, for a pound of Will Chester's precious refined sugar. They had refused and sold almost nothing. Christopher hoped, from the look on Mr Killingworth's face, that they would get better prices in Moscow.

Then the telegas were ready, including the butt of Holland and the cask of cane sugar which had been specially packed for the Tsar, and they began to assemble what was left of their party for Moscow: Christopher and his father as official royal envoy; Mr Lane and Mr Price to help Mr Killingworth as agent, and Mr Best to interpret. With them also came Master Nepeja and the two Kholmogory merchants.

Their departure, through shouting and chattering crowds, was extremely impressive: so was their return when, having stuck fast in the mud half-way to Nikolskoi, they had to send for help to the next Yam station at St Obnorski, and conduct half their load ignominiously back to the warehouse at Vologda, including the Tsar's sugar and Holland. As Nepeja carefully remarked, it was an unexpectedly warm autumn, and nothing could really be expected to travel until they had had the first touch of frost.

Cornfields passed: meadows, rivers, woods and pastureland and small wooden towns: Derevnia, Vochensko and Yaroslav on the Volga, where Diccon Chancellor invited his son to sniff the wind from Bokhara for musk, spices and ambergris.

He remembered Rostov, after that; and Peraslav, because of the fish, and Dubna because he had caught a cold by then, and the Outschak because he was bored and no one would speak to him because Mr Lane and Mr Killingworth were arguing over whether they should have sold the broadcloth at Vologda for whatever price it would fetch, and Mr Price thought they should have made their trading post right away at Kholmogory and bartered the cargo for furs where they were cheapest.

The effort to keep their voices down, in spite of the

173

thunder and squeak of thirty ill-made telegas squelching through mud like deep gruel, didn't do much for their tempers : his father had to remind them that until they presented the Queen's letter and had their privileges officially confirmed, they had no right to start trading anywhere. And that at the present rate of unrepeatable progress, they would barely reach the Tsar and get all their business completed before they had to start back to St Nicholas to meet the incoming *Edward* again.

They were still quarrelling when a rider, in a handsome furred hat, came spurring towards them and made a long announcement which Diccon Chancellor, his colour still heightened a little, translated anxiously. 'The representatives of the great Duke Ivan Vasilievich, by the grace of God great lord and Emperor of all Russia, are on their way now to greet us, and we are commanded to meet them at the Troitsa Monastery at Serghiev. . . . We've passed it. Haven't we?'

Nepeja had joined them, dismounting. 'It is ten versts behind us. We can be there very quickly. The carts can follow.'

Two years ago he would have thought, his brow ridged : What would Willoughby have done? This time Diccon Chancellor said immediately, and politely, 'I am in some difficulty. After your Tsar has generously agreed to receive us, we have no more than a matter of weeks in which to set up our trading stations, arrange for storehouses, offices and staff, meet merchants and visit commercial centres, sell our present cargo and arrange for another. And our journey has taken too long already.'

Master Nepeja bowed. 'I apologize for the weather. But the Troitsa is very near. One day will make little difference.'

'I will be frank with you,' Chancellor said. 'One day would make little difference, as you say. But if it were to stretch to a week, or two weeks, as has been known to happen, we may well have to return north before our work here is half completed. Who knows? – there may be further delay in Moscow. You say the Tsar is pressed with military concerns. It seems to me that, did he know all the facts, he would be concerned that this great opportunity for trade between our two countries should not be missed for the sake of a mere formality. I should like to proceed to Moscow as if we had never encountered his messenger, and

I would be in your debt if both you and the messenger would support me.'

A beautiful voice, speaking in English behind him, said, 'The messenger would have his heels broken, and the Sovereign Grand Prince would then send him limping on foot forty miles to the Troitsa as punishment. Master Nepeja would merely lose his province, I fancy. And you your pains : the Tsar is not noted for patience. It is really simpler to come with me as you are bidden.'

Diccon Chancellor turned, and the whole party with him.

Noiseless in the rain and the mud and the shifting trample of horses, a long train of glittering riders had moved in behind them and stood, double ranked and in perfect alignment, the rain chattering on the motionless spires of their helmets; their tawny felt cloaks drawn over the chain mail which curtained their faces.

At their head stood three mounted grooms, one of them with a great, ruffled bird hooded and chained to his crupper. And in front of these, sitting at ease in the saddle was the man who had spoken. A man, Christopher saw, with hair brighter than Killingworth's under his furred and jewelled cap : with fair skin hardened with weather and untold experience, despite the clear-lidded flower-blue eyes into which Diccon Chancellor was staring. A man whose clothes made motionless points of silver and flame beneath a buff coat paned and embroidered : whose reins rested in gloves stitched with gold wire and dark, anonymous stones. Christopher lifted his eyes.

'Ignore the dress,' said the gentleman pleasantly. 'It belongs to the Tsar. I have to hand it back to him on pain of fine, untorn and unstained, with the underwear. . . . Mr Chancellor?'

'Mr Crawford of Lymond and Sevigny?' said Diccon Chancellor.

The horseman smiled with his lips. 'Ah. You have heard about Slata Baba,' he said; and dismounting smoothly, threw his reins to the groom with the eagle, who moved up quietly to·take them. The bird sat erect, unstirring from the thin scarlet plumes on her hood to the yellow, powerful talons, their bright, scythe-edged claws hooked on a block at the crupper. Her master, still smiling, stood and ran his blue gaze over the six tired English figures before him, also dismounted and standing in their wet cloaks at Chancellor's shoulders. He bowed, and then smiled and bowed again to Nepeja and the two Kholmogory merchants. To Chancellor, he said, 'First, since you know who I am, may I deliver my message?'

'I am honoured,' said Chancellor. He spoke automatically, for to himself he was thinking : Philippa Somerville's husband. This – *this* is Philippa's husband. He dared not look at Robert Best's face, or Christopher's, beside him.

'Then I have to say,' said the other man mildly, 'that the great lord Ivan Vasilievich, by the grace of God Duke of Muscovy and Tsar of all Russia, has understood that you are come as Ambassador from his cousin Mary of England, and has sent me, his servant, to escort you to your residence, and to see that you are provided with every necessity. I am to ask whether you have been well on your journey?'

From a disadvantage of four inches and a quantity of stupefaction, Diccon Chancellor bowed. 'God give health to the Tsar. By the mercy of God and the favour of the Tsar, we have been well on our journey.'

It was the formula. The other man completed it. 'The great lord Ivan Vasilievich, Tsar of Russia, has sent you, Master Richard, an ambling nag with a saddle, together with other horses from his own stable for these your companions. Pray accept these and mount, while we have the honour of bringing you to lie at our monastery of Trinity St Sergius.'

His black beard lifting just a trifle, Diccon Chancellor stood his ground and did not glance at the string of horses approaching. 'I should prefer not to visit the Troitsa Monastery,' Chancellor said. 'As you perhaps heard. I do not wish to seem ungrateful, but my time is too short for formalities.'

The decorative person who was Mistress Philippa's husband made no effort to agree or to argue. 'It is the Tsar's order,' he said.

'The Tsar does not know the circumstances,' said Chancellor quietly. There was not a great deal of daylight left.

The horses had been brought up. The man Crawford put a gloved hand on the bridle of the first and finest, and held it waiting for Chancellor. 'He does not need to know them,' he said. 'He merely issues orders, and they are obeyed, fortunate man, as in England the Queen's desires are honoured by all her guests, invited and other.' His manner, irritatingly, was quite impeccably charming.

'Or you have your heels broken?' asked Diccon losing, suddenly, a thread of his patience. 'Or would your courier take the blame for all parties?'

And Francis Crawford of Lymond, undisturbed, replied. 'For failing to trace you before you reached the Troitsa Monastery, Sergei will be whipped with a flail, whatever misfortune later overtakes other parts of his anatomy. The Tsar is unlikely to offer me violence, and would never dream of inflicting it on the orators of his cousin. You have a choice. You may conform, or go back to England.'

Diccon Chancellor looked at him without humility. 'My apologies,' he said. 'I believed I was suggesting a sensible compromise.'

'In Russia,' said Lymond gently, 'there is no such thing as a sensible compromise. Besides, they have to clean all the silver. . . . Do mysteries appeal to you? They say there is a copper cauldron at the Troitsa, full of herbs and cooked food, which never empties.'

He was holding the new horse's stirrup. Chancellor hesitated one moment more; then, grasping the saddle, swung himself into place. 'I seem to have heard it,' he said. 'I hear the tomb of St Sergius can work miracles, and make barren wives pregnant.'

They were all changing horses. Lymond, mounting, paced up to Chancellor's side. 'The Troitsa Monastery,' he said, 'has an income of one hundred thousand roubles a year. They are the wealthiest merchants in Russia; and as their wealth increases, so the Tsar is able to borrow from them. The miracle of St Sergius and Russia,' Lymond said, 'is that they never need a sensible compromise. But don't tell Nepeja I told you.'

Christopher saw the monastery first, white and gold against the grey sky of evening. Then they crossed the dip of a stream and rode up under the tiered, undercut walls with their string-courses of pigeons, and below the canopied arch of its entrance, its painted walls whiskered with blunt, flying angels, their haloes like spinneys of sunflowers.

Beyond, in the mild, autumn air, stretched the towers, the churches, the cells of the lavra, lamps beginning already to glow under the trees, green and russet and bronze, of its gardens; and the blackrobed figures of some of its seven hundred monks moving, long-bearded and noiseless as shadows beneath. High above, fired like brands by the sunset, blazed the Dukhovskaya and Troitsa cupolas.

Dismounted, they walked between ranks of armed soldiers to the group of dark figures awaiting them. 'The monastery,' said Lymond agreeably, 'is likewise a garrison. It is also a centre of the Russian Orthodox faith, which holds that the Roman Catholic is a deserter from the Primitive Church. Anyone knowingly eating with a Roman must be purified thereafter with prayer. A Metropolitan has been known to take issue on the whole matter indeed with the Archbishop of Rome himself, accusing his Church of abuses, and himself of luring men to him by gluttony. . . . I take it that, as on the previous occasion, you are all dutiful subjects of the late King Edward and his father King Henry? The Tsar is an admirer of Henry of England.'

'We are,' said Diccon blandly.

'Then you will come to no harm if you conduct yourselves soberly. You may not, for example, introduce or play on a harp. You will observe the Archimandrite whose mitre is black and round, and who wears a black pallium with three ribbons waving in front, signifying that from his mouth and heart flow streams of the doctrine of faith and good works. Your compliments should be addressed to him : perhaps Master Grigorjeff would interpret.'

Christopher looked at his father and grinned. If Master Nepeja had been able to master six words of English in the entire month of their journey, it was still six more than Grigorjeff. But his father, far from sharing the joke, was giving Lymond all his attention. Then he glanced at Master Grigorjeff and smiled. 'But—'

He broke off, still smiling. Lymond said quickly, 'Ah. Forgive me. I see Master Grigorjeff does not speak English. Then if you will permit me, I shall act as translator. Unless you prefer to trust your own Russian? I am sure it is perfectly fluent.'

'But rusty,' said Diccon, still smiling. 'Please. There are subleties, I am sure, which it would be quite beyond me to convey.'

Through all the speeches and the excellent meal which followed, Christopher was still thrashing it out. It was not until later, when they were both in the chamber they were to share with Lane and Killingworth and Ned Price, that he said to his father, 'Do you like Mr Crawford?'

Diccon Chancellor, in the act of climbing heavily on to his bedboard, turned and said after a moment, 'He was helpful. Why, don't you?'

'He stopped you going to Moscow,' said Christopher.

'He was under orders,' said Diccon. 'When you're ready, you might blow out the tapers.'

'And he made Mr Grigorjeff look a bit silly. I wondered if there was some bad feeling between them. Pretending he could translate.'

'Ah,' said Diccon Chancellor. Harry Lane, already under his blanket, was grinning.

'What, *Ah*?' said Christopher, getting incensed.

'Ah,' said Chancellor, struggling down in his turn, 'but are you sure now he couldn't translate?'

Christopher sat up. A drop of wax, unregarded, fell on the arm of his shirt. 'You mean—'

'I mean,' said his father, 'that you should remember one paramount rule. Watch your tongue.' And he leaned over and blew out the taper.

CHAPTER TWO

They were in the monastery for three days and three nights, during which George Killingworth and his colleagues were in frequent session at long meetings held in and around the storehouses, and the contents of the telegas were subject to some picking and rummaging. Christopher, handed over to the monks for entertainment, ate rather well, and was conducted with some care through the buildings and along the fifty-foot walls with their twelve faceted watch-towers, and was shown the ten vaults with their immense nine-foot barrels of wine, beer and mead, filled by chute from above.

He had more time than he wanted to look at the Troitsa Cathedral, with its golden globes on tall, window-ribbed drums, and its thick white stucco, banded with stone fretted like lace. Inside, in the low trapeza, lay St Sergius's coffin in draped cloth of gold. Christopher had seen it manage no miracles, although he spent some time watching the constant movement of people chatting, eating and praying, and had drifted through to the high, narrow hall of the church, with the square painted panels of its inconostasis rising in tiers of gold to the ceiling. The light dazzled: from a dozen candles taller than himself, and the blazing wick of a hundred-pound kettle of wax. It set fire to the rubies, the sapphires, the gold of the rizas, the embossed shields of the ikons: the Virgin Platytera, the Virgin Hodigitia, the Virgin Blacherniotissa, and Andrei Ruble's three grave, almond-eyed angels seated at Abraham's table. It lit the chalices, the crosses, the incense burners, the royal doors to the sanctuary, and the canopied gold of the altar, with its circle of dark, singing figures. A ring of candles shone on the white beard and sparkling brocade of the abbot. He wore a slabbed medallion with a sad, sunken figure lost in its centre.

They were all around Christopher, the sombre figures, in picture and fresco. Profiled bodies, bowing in long, graceful rows, turned their faces to watch him. Here, the uplifted thumb-shapes of wings. There, the elderly, dome-headed Child within the engraved foil of its cover. The prostrate, holy figures, curved like an ark. The hyphen eyebrows and long, thin-boned noses and down-curved, patient mouths. The hunched shoulders and creased double fingers of benison; the robes veined in folds like body moulds made of thin leaves, rising on walls, pillars and ceiling: settling, dry and humble and melancholy, upon him. . . .

'They *will* use flax seed oil,' a voice said at his elbow. 'I have it on the best authority that varnish and candle soot together will soon turn every saint into an Ethiopian and the Virgin Platytera into a subject for prayerful speculation. Have you eaten yet?'

It was Mistress Philippa's powerful husband, with Makaroff at his shoulder.

'No sir,' said Christopher.

'Then come with us and rejoice,' said Mr Crawford of Lymond and Sevigny. 'You are going to Moscow to-morrow.'

They ate with the Abbot, and drank a great deal; and it was probably the vodka which loosened Diccon Chancellor's tongue; and exasperation because in three days he had never had more than a few hours of the man Crawford's company, and then as interpreter, with the monks crowding about him; or here with the abbot, or exchanging words, briefly, with Nepeja or Makaroff or his friend. At first, it seemed to Chancellor that he and Crawford were being kept apart by the Russians. Latterly, he had begun to wonder if he had been induced to think exactly that.

This was not a roistering, war-addled soldier boy, who had made promises to one girl too many, and had to marry her. For the first time, he understood and believed what Philippa had told Sir Henry Sidney. There was no relationship between them; no affinity, and no possible meeting of interests, he was sure, between the innocence on that side, and the experience on this. If Crawford had married her, it was for his own purpose, and for no other reason. That said, it seemed to Diccon, widower, father and man of considerable vision, that the least Francis Crawford could do was assure himself of the wellbeing of his wife, communicate with her, and, at the earliest moment, keep his promise to release her.

The fellow had not inquired how Philippa was. He had not mentioned her. He had asked almost nothing of events back in England : a policy understandable enough, perhaps, if one considered the fanaticism of the Queen, and the Russian view of Catholicism. If Ivan believed that England still followed the tenets of Henry VIII (why did the Tsar admire him? did he have his eye on the Troitsa?) then there was no need to disillusion him.

Crawford had spoken readily enough about Ivan Vasilievich. He was a great merchant : most of the tithes of the north came to him as furs and walrus tusks : his storehouses were full of goods for selling or barter. It ran in the blood : the brother of Zoe Paleologus, said Crawford cheerfully, had bartered his right to the throne of Byzantium – three times, to three different people.

On trade matters he was informative. He was also disposed to be searching in his own inquiries. Chancellor found himself answering questions about the objectives and standing of the Muscovy Company, the nature of its financial arrangements and the names of some of its two hundred-odd members. He did not require to be told what a joint-stock company was. 'I have a friend,' said Mr Crawford gently, 'who keeps me in a state of celestial enlightenment on legal matters. Seven peers then, and twenty knights, most of them members of the Privy Council or Household . . . it would suit such a panel, I imagine, to trade as a body, through paid employees such

as Mr Grey and Mr Killingworth here, rather than in-
dividually, as your merchant members in the other, regu-
lated companies must do. Seven aldermen . . . the Solicitor
General . . . the Attorney General . . . ten customs officers
. . . six holding office in the Mint . . . and Sebastian
Cabot as your permanent Governor. Mr Chancellor, your
company can hardly fail to be the most successful mer-
chandising venture in London. And who owns your ships?'

'The company do,' said Diccon Chancellor. The rest of
the table had fallen silent. He wondered, as he had wondered for three days, just how much English Grigorjeff
knew. Or Nepeja, for that matter. 'They were bought
and refitted with the six thousand pounds, initial raised
capital. The bulk of our members, Mr Crawford, are
merchants.'

'But the *Philip and Mary,* which you are hoping to see
in the spring, is a royal ship?'

'Chartered,' Chancellor said, 'by the company.'

'And the timber and hemp you are anxious to buy, Mr
Chancellor, will be used in the royal dockyards instead of
the masts and cable the Council used to purchase from
Danzig?'

Beside him, Chancellor could feel the faint, rising uneasiness of his three merchanting colleagues. George
Killingworth said, 'This is a small part of our cargo. Our
remit includes the purchase of large stores of wax—'

'Used,' Lymond said thoughtfully, 'by the English
Chancery alone at the rate of five thousand pounds in the
year for great seals, half-seals and writs. Or so my legal
confrère has told me. And you, Mr Chancellor, are here –
and most welcome too – receiving royal honours as a royal
ambassador from your mistress?'

Of course, it was true. Of course it suited the company
to obtain the Tsar's interest at the highest level of all,
by stressing that the negotiations had the direct support
of the Queen. Of course it suited the Queen to have free
diplomatic representation, without the expense of setting
up an embassy; and to have first claim on certain items
of cargo.

But the company had paid for these journeys. The
company had paid for the gifts he was about to present –
once they came from Vologda – to the Tsar. And the
company would have to pay for the Queen's continuing

interest, he suspected, by furnishing the Queen's dock-yards and perhaps even her Treasury on the longest possible credits. He said, 'I think it best to be plain. My presence here as ambassador is purely a formality, as I think you might guess. We are here, Mr Crawford, on a matter of trade. We have no political interest in Russia.'

'How improvident of you,' said Mistress Philippa's husband.

Behind the wide, cold eyes, the charming insolence, a woman might see, Chancellor thought, a life-long hunger for power; a litter of outworn romances. He said, 'What is your position, here in Russia?'

'I am a soldier,' said Lymond.

'Then you had some share in the successes last summer? I hear the Tsar has a much improved army,' said Chancellor.

'It is reasonably well organized,' said Mr Crawford with gravity. 'Osep tells me that you expected to find me in Russia?'

Diccon Chancellor, brows raised, looked along the table at Master Nepeja, who did not meet his eyes. 'I failed to realize,' he said, 'that you and he were on Christian-name terms. The title Voevoda surely means General?'

'I am known, as you seem to have heard, as the Voevoda Frangike. Christian names are common usage. But I do confess to an association, of course, with the Namiestnik of Vologda. Osep was merely showing discretion. The Tsar does not necessarily wish to advertise the composition of his army.'

'Unless he proposes to detain us permanently in Russia, I do not see how he can avoid it,' Chancellor said.

'You are perfectly correct,' Crawford said. '*Tout par raison, raison partout, partout raison.* There is no more point in secrecy. Especially if the fact is known in England already.'

It was a question. Restored to equanimity, Chancellor said, 'It is by no means widely known. I have, however, some messages to convey to you.'

The blue eyes opened wide. 'Then pray convey them,' said Lymond. 'I am sure our Russian friends will bear with us. . . . I take it you refer to my rib, my holy and innocent wife?'

Again the levity he, Diccon, found so misplaced. Press-ing his bearded lips together, Chancellor sought to pick out what could be said in public. 'You have had no letters from Mistress Philippa?'

'One, of no moment whatever. I imagine,' said Lymond, 'that she has found congenial company in Flaw Valleys, as I have in Moscow.'

'She is certainly surrounded by suitors,' said Chancellor. 'But at Hampton Court, not at Flaw Valleys. She is in the Queen's suite. Unlike you, therefore, she can expect little in the way of consolation until she is freed of her marriage. It is this I was to broach with you. We can speak of it later.'

'Good God,' said Lymond. 'Has she had a better offer? What does she want, a letter? I shall give you one to take back with you, releasing her from all formal connection with the kingly blood of the Billing. What is the reason for agitation, or would it be tactless to ask?'

Robert Best, six foot three and broad with it, laid down his goose leg and turned on the bench. 'It isn't a matter of tact,' he said bluntly. 'It's a matter of doing the right thing by the lady. Diccon, I didn't tell you. But she was ready to stow away on the *Edward*, to get to Russia and settle affairs with her husband.'

Diccon swung round and stared at his countryman, while Lymond leaned back, his hands loose before him and broke into genuine, uninhibited laughter. Chancellor said, 'Is that true?'

Rob Best nodded.

'You soft-headed idiot: and I suppose you planned to help her?'

'She thought better of it. At least she didn't turn up,' Rob Best said. 'She was worried in case Mr Crawford wasn't getting her letters.'

'Maybe she'll get on the *Edward* next time,' Lymond said. He was still sobbing faintly. 'Maybe she'll arrive in the spring. Or maybe she'll send her intended, thundering out his thrononicall threats.' He said something in Russian to Osep Nepeja, and Nepeja laughed. It was too idiomatic for Diccon, who caught only one word, 'Güzel'.

Chancellor said, 'I find the situation less comic than you do. Until now, I had no idea that Mistress Philippa knew that you were in Russia. I was told to open the matter of divorce by someone quite other, who did.'

'Told?' Lymond repeated. His face and his hands, very

still on the table, told Diccon nothing at all except that he had his attention.

'By the Countess of Lennox.'

'Ah,' said Lymond, on a long, noiseless sigh and stretched his back slowly, like an athlete, Diccon thought, kept too long indoors. 'And why should the Countess of Lennox be concerned with Philippa's marriage?'

'Because,' said Diccon Chancellor, 'Flaw Valleys is a manor of strategic importance placed on the English side of the Scots border. And because Philippa's mother is widowed, and could not hold it against you or your friends.'

The limpid gaze was full of encouragement. 'How exciting,' said Lymond. 'I had no idea that we had declared war on each other.' A thought illuminated the untrustworthy contours of his shadowless face. 'Or do you think the Countess of Lennox will come on the *Edward*?'

'We are not at war with Scotland,' said Chancellor curtly.

And I am no threat to Flaw Valleys so long as I remain safely in Russia, which I have every intention of doing. I cannot see, Mr Chancellor,' said Lymond agreeably, 'that my affairs constitute a serious problem, either to my bride's courting, or to the security of England, or to you. Meanwhile, we are imposing unimaginable tedium upon our kind hosts.'

And bowing, he turned to his neighbour, breaking into a murmur of Russian; nor did he speak English at any point for the rest of the meal.

On a sudden impulse, Diccon Chancellor crossed to the Troitsa Cathedral on his own late that evening, and lit a candle before the sparkling Trinity, and made a brief and private prayer to do with his ship and his sons. On the way back across the dark paths under the trees, he found his path barred by six armed men, one of whom addressed him in Russian, demanding that he should come with them quietly.

Unarmed and unescorted, attack was the last thing he had expected within the confines of the monastery. Diccon Chancellor ducked and ran, opening his mouth to shout as he did so, and was brought up like a galloping calf by the grip of men's arms round his shoulders, and the flat of a man's sweaty palm on his mouth.

He bit the flesh at his lips and almost tore himself free at that; then the men closed round him tighter than ever, and as he drew breath to call out once more, one drew a club and hit him, briefly and expertly, at the nape of the neck. He slid to the ground, into blackness.

He woke in bed, in a small, whitewashed room hung with dark, jewelled ikons, and two silver lamps whose glow touched the bright hair and calm face of the man kneeling beside him, a wrought metal dipper smelling of aqua-vite in his hands.

'My apologies,' Lymond said. There was no one else in the room.

Diccon Chancellor dug in one elbow, and sat up, with elaborate care. Speech eluded him.

Lymond held out the *koush*. 'But you shouldn't have tried to call out.'

Chancellor sipped, and the power of speech returned, quickly. 'In the dark, with six armed men at my back? What in hell's name are you playing at?'

'They were in my livery,' said Lymond mildly. 'Rumour said the Pilot General was observant. Since it failed, I can only say again, My apologies. I wanted to speak to you.'

Astonished fury invaded Chancellor's chest and made speech again a matter of will power. He said, 'So I had to be brought here unconscious?'

'A crudity,' said Lymond, 'that you would expect from the spawn of a naïve and barbarous régime. I am sorry I was unable to issue a written invitation. You are watched, and so am I. By the monks, the grooms, the merchants. Grigorjeff has fluent English, learned from a German trader, as Best learned his Russian from the Tartars of the Queen's stables. Makaroff has also more than you suspect although Nepeja, bless his patriotic heart, has no gift for languages. Only my soldiers are sentimentally loyal.'

'So even your masters don't trust you?' said Chancellor. He finished the aqua-vite, and bent to dip the ladle again in the wine pot while Lymond came to rest on the floor, his hands relaxed round his knees. The ends of his girdle, Chancellor saw, were worked with Ceylon pearls and bright, twisted silks, and his tunic was clasped with pale, bulbous stones, high in the collet.

'Why should they?' said Lymond. 'They don't trust anyone. When you get to Moscow you'll find that, as before, you will be confined strictly to your house, and allowed out by appointment, and firmly escorted. You will not be invited to Muscovite homes, and you will not be allowed to entertain on your own account. One reason is that, as a representative of royalty, your person is sacred and must be guarded from all untoward incidents.. Another is that, as representative of a western and civilized power, you should be allowed to see and describe only those things which reflect Russia's culture and power. And the last reason is that you yourself shall not infect the Russian, peasant or noble, with the enchantments of an evil religion, or the practices of other, corrupt peoples as regards food and justice and government, domestic freedom and taxes, clothes and climate and culture. Villages are emptying already round Moscow. The land cannot afford to lose all its people.'

'It is a corrupt rule then?' said Chancellor. He had forgotten the ache in his head.

For a while, Lymond was silent. Then he said, 'How can one answer that? Parliament consists of the Tsar, twenty boyars and twenty clergy also. The people are told of the Tsar's decisions after he has made them. He's never spoken to a peasant in his life, except to ride him down in the street as a boy. *The Empire is Majesty, and above that Majesty stands the Sovereign in his Empire, and the Sovereign is above the Empire.*

'A state of mind not exclusively the Grand Duke's. But, you know, with abuses wherever he looks, and no experience behind him, he has tried to do something. He's revised the law. He's put some restraints on the appointment of unpaid, single-term governors, who milk a province and run at the end of the year. He's thought of the Zemsky Sobor, the wider assemblies of gentry and boyars and church representatives. They still don't include peasants or merchants – and merchants, you already know, have no status at all outside Novgorod – but it's something. He's laid down clear rules for the landowners about raising an army. . . .'

'Yes?' said Diccon Chancellor, as the other man paused.

On Lymond's face, bare of all but the courtesy emotions, a touch of resignation appeared. 'You will discover it when you reach Moscow, so you may as well become used to it now. The Russian Army is my affair. I am supreme commander : Voevoda Bolshoia.'

Slowly, Richard Chancellor sat up, his eyes on the other

man's face. 'A foreigner? But what of the boyars? The princes?'

Francis Crawford smiled and rose, in the single, enviable movement of the remorselessly trained gymnast. 'One day, when I have given them Ochakov and they are loading their cargoes at Riga, someone will no doubt pass a sword through my decaying sinews. At present, they dare not.'

'Yet they watch you? You cannot speak to me openly?'

'The Tsar watches me,' Lymond said.

'It is the Tsar himself, then, who distrusts you? What future, what security can there be for you there?' Diccon said.

There was a short silence. The man to whom, out of all likelihood, that lively, normal young creature had allowed herself to be tied stood in thought by his bedside, the light showing no tremor on his still, hard-moulded face. Then Lymond said, 'You will see when you come to Moscow. It makes no difference to what I said there at table. I am staying in Russia. I want to know one thing only. Why does Margaret Lennox wish to force through a divorce?'

Margaret Lennox, noted the watching brain behind Chancellor's clear, blue-black eyes. He said, 'I mentioned a letter, purely because the Russians were present. Lady Lennox does not wish you to write releasing Mistress Philippa from her promise. She says that Holy Church will not grant a divorce on written evidence only. She says you must come to England.'

The lamp-lit face was merely attentively polite. 'Or . . . ?'

The threat to himself, Diccon Chancellor had long since decided, was the affair of Diccon Chancellor and no one else. He said, 'Or Flaw Valleys would have to be guarded in the only way possible.' He drew breath, but Lymond spoke first.

'Kate?' he said. 'If I don't return and Philippa can't remarry, then Kate must marry to make Flaw Valleys safe? Is that it?'

Diccon Chancellor stared at the other, fair face which was smiling.

He said, 'If Kate is Mistress Somerville's mother, then that is the threat. She shall be made to wed a loyal English citizen, for the sake of herself and her family.' And at something, a question, in Crawford's face, he elaborated. 'There is a boy, I believe: a lovechild who stays with her also?'

Lymond laughed. He laughed slowly and softly, turning away from the bed, and the sound of it, in the quiet night, made the hairs prick between Chancellor's flesh and his clothes. Then turning suddenly he lifted the dipper, presented it smiling to Chancellor, and, when he had done, tipped it twice down his throat.

'A lady of classical impulses,' said Lymond. 'The weaklings may hold to the Rule of Zosima: without women, how should we sharpen our wits?' He paused a moment, and said pleasantly, 'The child is not Kate's or Philippa's, but mine. A threat of such nicety deserves to be appreciated.'

'Why does the Countess of Lennox want you back?' Chancellor said.

'To play with,' said Lymond.

'Will you go?' Chancellor said.

Lymond smiled. Like a painting in gesso the lamplight caught the moment of pleasure: lit the ridged brows and gold feathered hair, the tips of the thick, open lashes; the sapphires glowing like oil on his doublet.

'Ask me in Moscow,' he said.

CHAPTER THREE

Four days later, through gentle country of yellowing birches and sunlit scarlet berries of rowan, they reached the joined wood walls and log bridges of Moscow, and passed between the izbas and churches to reach the inner city, ringed by its wall of rose brick, where Lymond conducted them to a modest, shingle-roofed house and introduced them to the two Pristafs, with their company of soldiers, who would be responsible for their lodging and food. Then he left them.

The following day, they received a summons from the Chief Secretary to bring him all their official missives for translation, and did so, finding Master Ivan Mikhailov Viscovatu prepared to be most cordial, and being conducted on their return to a larger house in a different district where they waited in total seclusion for almost a week, playing cards and trying to engage the Pristafs in frivolous conversation. Seven days after their arrival, they were advised by Master Viscovatu that the Tsar felt a desire to accommodate them in still greater comfort, and, with a great deal of bowing and baring of teeth, were escorted to a still larger house, hung with red serge, which had beds in it. Here they received daily eight hens and a portion of mead, together with an allowance of five and sixpence in cash, and a man to clean house and serve. Two days after that, the letters were returned, and they were warned that they would be called to the Tsar's presence in the morning. Christopher was sick.

'It's that drunken land-hog's unspeakable cooking,' said Best.

'No, it isn't. It's the detention and the silence,' Chancellor said. 'I give you leave to imagine what it was like the first time. We waited twelve days before he sent for us.'

'Cleaning the silver,' said George Killingworth, who had finished working on his boots and was brushing his beard, which was long, curling and golden and smelt of badly cooked rabbit. 'According to Crawford. D'you still think he's not to be relied on, Diccon? Maybe the Army thinks Englishmen ought to live in big houses.'

'I imagine the Army is far too busy consolidating its own position to have any charity left over for foreigners,' Chancellor said. 'No. The climate is different. Moscow is different. They've had another fire. They had one eight years ago. There wasn't a post left you could tie a horse to, and two years ago you could still see the mess. But this one has been cleared up, and the spaces between the houses are bigger, and there are water troughs and broom hooks at the street-ends. The buildings are better. There's more brick. More glass and less mica. Look at the studs on this door. Look at the work in that chest.'

Harry Lane said, 'But no beds. No chairs. No trenchers. No metalware for the table : beech cups and a case of wood spoons at your girdle. And the drink is God-awful.'

'Kvas,' said Chancellor reflectively. 'Described as water turned out of its wits, with a little mash added. Christopher . . .'

'Drink,' said Christopher aggressively, 'has no effect on me at all. You said so yourself. It was the stewed hare.'

'I said at Penshurst,' said his father calmly, 'that you could start drinking beer. English beer. Not mead sodden with hops and fermented in God knows what uncured receptacle. Tomorrow, God help us, we have to present our

190

credentials to the Tsar of this country and ask for his favour, remembering that the present we intended to give him is still in Vologda, and will stay in Vologda apparently until the ground freezes over. We shall be bidden to dine. After dinner, there is only one test of manhood, and none of us, surprising though it may seem, is looking forward to it. You are not coming.'

'But—' said Christopher.

'You heard your father,' said Killingworth. 'You can't hold enough liquor.'

'Can you?' said Christopher, goaded.

'No,' said George Killingworth, after a moment's reflection. 'But who else is going to help us to bed?'

So Christopher was not among the five men who rode out next morning, with a gaudy escort of boyars, and pressed their way to the gates of the Kremlin through the cleared market place with its closed shops and sealed taverns : cleared so that the people of Moscow, and the soldiers and the lower though valuable nobility, could suitably congregate, and impress with their numbers and vigour; and so that the people in turn could witness the honour done to their country by distant and powerful kingdoms.

Tricked out in new Russian gowns of branched velvet and gold, furred with sable and squirrel and ermine, and edged and faced with black beaver, Diccon Chancellor and his four English gentlemen rode through the ranks of packed faces, sweating slightly under the mild sun of early October, and over the rise, past the scaffolding of the Tsar's new Cathedral of St Basil, and dismounted at the Frolovskaya Tower, the ceremonial entrance to the Kremlin, where yet another company of soldiers awaited them at the bridge, in damascened helmets and coats of mail, with blue and silver tunics laid over them.

Their commander, a grey-bearded man with a face neither Slav nor Tartar, delivered a grave bow to Chancellor, and Chancellor saluted both him and the ikon over the gate, and crossed over the ditch into the Kremlin. The soldiers marched stiffly before him, and more of them stood at attention, lining the rising ground where he was to walk. (*Every soldier in Russia is a gentleman, and does nothing else.* Who had said that? It was true. These were not the inbred faces of high western culture, but neither were they the faces of peasants.)

Princes and elders, to greet and walk with him, robed in figured velvet on tissue, with twisted silk frogging and gold filigree chains, and tall seamed caps on their heads. The faces of others; monks, boyars' sons, servants, pressing between the ranks of the guard.

The palace square he remembered so well, with its lean churches hand-wrought like rizas above the dwarfed coloured forms of the people. The St Michael Archangel, with its clear fluted shells. The tulip-bed of the Blago-veschenski's golden towers; the tall painted hoods of the Uspenski and its thin-mortared ivory stones. And the winged golden crosses and cupolas crowding behind.

George Killingworth, beside him, had never seen it before, nor Henry Lane, nor Ned Price nor Rob Best, his broad shoulders laden with sables. The last time he had been here, he had carried with him the Tsar's reply to his King's letter, written in Russian and Dutch: *We, greatest Lord John Vasilievich, by the grace of God Emperor of all Russia . . . sent by your true servant Hugh Willoughby, the which in our domains hath not arrived . . . Whereas your servant Richard is come to us, we with Christian true assurance in no manner of wise will refuse his petition. . . .*

Well, Hugh Willoughby had arrived in the domains of Ivan Vasilievich: he was there now, on the *Esperanza,* floating under the banner of St George west of Nenoksa, with the log of that last, frozen voyage no longer where he had laid his handsome head by it, the pen gripped in the brittle, manicured fingers. Alas, Hugh Willoughby.

The stairs up to the terrace, with robed figures moving forward to greet him. The doorway to the Vestibule and the long room he remembered, with silent, deferential figures moving about. He heard George Killingworth, looming beside him, give a muffled snort in the midst of the tension, and knew he had caught sight of the wash of gold light from the walls, laden with burnished parcel-gilt on broad shelves : pitchers, ewers and basins, plates and salt cellars and tankards, flagons and standing cups, fat pineapple and thin knotted Gothic. Someone had cleaned the silver.

He must not let his mind wander. In unknown waters, you kept your lead going and sounded every half-glass. It was the second time that you sailed on the sandbar that bilged you. Then it would be alas, Diccon Chancellor.

The painted ante-room, with a silent revetment of sitting, gold-mantled Councillors and above them, the frescoes chosen by the priest Sylvester to edify and instruct his young Tsar : *The Wise Son is the Mother's and Father's Joy. The Fear of God is the Beginning of Wisdom. The Heart of the Tsar is in the Hand of God.*

Leading from that was the Chamber of God, which had once had golden frescoes under Tsar Vasily, but which Sylvester had caused to be covered with more vigorous stuff. The Ten Battles and Victories of Joshua, Chancellor remembered, and a number of prominent successes in Russian history, with the princes of the Rurik dynasty gazing inscrutably down from the vaults, and Christ Emmanuel where the lights were. At the doorway, recalling the previous occasion, he said, 'Do we wait?' and an English voice whose owner he could not see said, 'The lord Ivan Vasilievich is prepared to receive you.' Then the doors opened, and they were inside.

The figured vaults, prismatic with colour, chambered the room like a honeycomb, in which sat the Tsar's golden princes, like bees in the cell. And facing them across the empty, tapestried floor, the Tsar sat on his raised golden throne, foiled and jewelled as the ikon above his crowned head, the brocade of his gown seeded with pearls and plated with deep-moulded orphrey. His hair was more auburn than Chancellor had remembered : the nose long and slender; the eyes blue and cloudy under the brow prematurely lined. Chancellor swept off his hat, as did the four Englishmen with him, and the courtiers rose, in a flash of gold tissue, and bared their heads likewise.

Beside the Tsar, his brother Yuri did not rise; or the boy Tartar prince either. But Chancellor saw the Metropolitan stand, pulling the weight of his sakkos, and the Chief Secretary Viscovatu, who bowed to him gravely, and the richly dressed man with the soft, bearded face whom he remembered perhaps best of all : Alexei Adashev, the Tsar's closest adviser and once, with the priest Sylvester, his closest friend also.

He stood on the Tsar's left hand, beside the crystal trimmed *possoch*, and that meant that he still held high office : that of Chancellor perhaps. And behind him, among the guards matched in white velvet, was another man whom he recognized, and whom he had met for the first time over two weeks ago : the Voevoda Bolshoia. Mistress Philippa's husband, Crawford of Lymond, in court robes, bareheaded within the Tsar's circle, and holding him also in a chilly blue gaze. Diccon Chancellor bowed to the Tsar, and followed by his four friends, walked down the carpet until he came to the bench in its centre and pausing, made full western obeisance again.

'Great Master, and King of all the Russians,' said the Secretary Viscovatu to the Tsar. 'The Ambassador Ritzert strikes his forehead before thee, for thy great favour in receiving the message of his mistress of England.'

The letter from the Queen, in English, Greek, Polish and Italian, was read. Chancellor knew it by heart. *Philip and Marie, by the grace of God King and Queen of England, France, Naples, Jerusalem and Ireland, Defenders of the Faith, Princes of Spain and Sicily, Archdukes of Austrich, Dukes of Burgundy, Millaine and Brabant, Counts of Hapsburg, Flanders and Tyrol . . . Whereas by the consent and licence of our most dear and entirely beloved late brother King Edward VI, whose soul God pardon, sundry of our subjects, merchants of the City of London within these our realms of England did at their own proper costs and adventure furnish three ships to discover, search and find lands, islands, regions and territories before this adventure not known to be commonly haunted and frequented by seas . . .*

We thank you for your princely favour and goodness . . . abundant grace extended to the said Richard Chancellor and others our subject merchants . . . pray and request you to continue the same benevolence towards them and other our merchants and subjects which do or hereafter shall resort to your country . . .

It may please you at this our contemplation to assign and authorize such commissaries as you shall think meet to trade and confer with our well-beloved subjects and merchants, the said Richard Chancellor, George Killingworth and Richard Grey, bearers of these our letters . . . and to grant such other liberties and privileges unto the Governor, Consuls, assistants and Communaltie of the fellowship of the said Merchants . . .

It was translated fluently, as it should be, since it had been in the Secretary's hands for two days already for that purpose. But when the moment came for Chancellor to add his formal duty, and to refer, in language suitably rehearsed for a good hour to his mirror, the lordly gifts still awaiting transport from Vologda, the interpreter showed the same astonishing fluency. Chancellor, prepared

194

to speak in the painful spaced phrases of two years ago, found his thoughts caught before he had formed them, and had to bend his mind hard to its purpose, while avoiding the academic blue gaze under the ikon. The devil, he thought, take all missionaries.

But it was a comfort, all the same, when the Tsar spoke, and the same well-taught voice, speaking in English, translated without fear of mistake the grand prince's welcome, and his inquiry after the health of Queen Mary his cousin. Diccon Chancellor answered in English, and then it was time to walk to the steps, and look into the lean, bearded face below the arched brows, and hear the Emperor say, 'Give me your hand.'

The hand of Ivan Vasilievich, long-fingered and bony, held his. The fleshy lips, opening unexpectedly, said, 'Thou hast our tongue, I am told. Hast thou travelled well?'

'Through the mercy of God and your grace, quite well,' said Chancellor. He prayed that his grammar was less than ludicrous. 'God give your grace good health.'

His fingers were still in the Tsar's. 'Ritzert, thou wilt eat our bread and salt with us,' said the Sovereign Grand Prince, and with equal suddenness released him, his cloudy eyes sliding to where George Killingworth stood, Diccon knew, just behind him. 'Give me your hand . . .'

Diccon Chancellor moved back. And as he moved, caught somewhere the wraith of a smile between Francis Crawford and the Russian who had interpreted. His stomach, already taut, gave a faint and warning vibration as he glimpsed all the implications of that. Then Killingworth, Best, Price and Lane had all been invited to supper; they were all bowing in great heavings of damp fur and velvet, and behind them, the doors opened for a stalking, sideways withdrawal, and freedom.

'Christ,' said Harry Lane as they paced, handed from group to lordly robed group through the courtyard.

'Deacon Agapetus put it better,' Chancellor said. 'Though an Emperor in body is like other men, yet in power he is like God. Wait until you've lived through their supper. It will not remind you of Whitehall.'

'It's Oriental!' said Robert Best hoarsely. He smiled and bowed, elaborately, to a fresh group of boyars.

'. . . It's Tartar,' said Diccon Chancellor's supper partner that evening in the Granovitaya Palace, as the bread ritual was beginning (*Ivan Vasilievich, Emperor of Russia and*

195

Grand Duke of Muscovy doth reward thee with bread).
'The whole system of government is Tartar. The women,
shut away in the terems. The way their swords hang. The
post-horse system, the yams. Half their language is Tartar.
My God, they were subject to them for over two centuries.
The Grand Duke used to stand here every year and feed
the Great Khan's horse out of his bonnet as homage.
They tell you Tartars are born blind, like animals. But they
became Moslems before the Russians became Christians.
They were still struggling with Dasva, Striba, Simaergla
and Macosch in these parts long after the Golden Horde
had fought itself to a standstill.' The speaker, one Daniel
Hislop, stood up and sat down as another slice of bread
was ceremonially passed between Grand Prince and supper
guest. 'You needn't look haunted,' he added, not without
malice. 'No one near us speaks English. Yet.'

'You belong to the Army,' said Diccon. It was a foregone
conclusion. He had bowed to this short, clever-faced person
who wore his embroidered, ankle-length robe like a second-
best night-gown, and had betrayed no amazement, he
hoped, on being addressed in the accent of Scotland.
Daniel Hislop, without doubt, served under the Voevoda
Bolshoia.

Danny Hislop said, 'There are half a dozen of us with
Lymond, Mr Crawford.'

'Is he here?' said Chancellor, glancing round. Lit on its
three sides by windows, and from above by great hanging
lustres of bronze work, the big room was blazingly bright.
Light flowed from the white linen and massy gold plate
on the four long raised tables which lined it; from the long
jewelled *therliks* of the serving lords, over a hundred, now
moving among them with the dishes of young swan dressed
with sour milk : the first of seventy dishes, Chancellor
knew : baked meats and roast meats and broths, garnished
with garlic and salt in the Dutch fashion, which he would
be expected to sample with relish.

And light, above all, golden as sunrise upon the high
painted vaults of the hall, struck from the plate, the gold
and silver basins and goblets, ewers, flagons and jugs
wrought with beasts and fishes and flowers which stood
piled on tiered shelves round the massive middle pier of
the room. Beside it, two serving officers waited, napkin on
shoulders, each bearing a worked stand-cup, circled with

pearls, for the Tsar. A copper cistern of mead and sweet wine packed with snow, stood clouded beside them.

'. . . Are you impressed?' said Danny Hislop. 'We don't greatly care for western plate, as it happens, but we collect it to display to our visitors. He isn't here, and neither is Master Guthrie, whom you saw perhaps with the guard in the morning. Or I should not be having the pleasure of your company.'

'It seems,' said Chancellor, 'your sovereign lord trusts you.'

Danny's narrow eyes disappeared in a soundless laugh. 'I wondered what happened at the Troitsa,' he said. 'No. I am not valued enough to be spied on. Nor are Mr Crawford's four other senior officers, who are all here.' He raised his voice. 'Adam : Master Chancellor has been admiring the Golden Room frescoes.'

On George Killingworth's other side, a spare, brown-haired man in his thirties leaned forward, his colour a little high, and said agreeably, 'The devil rot you, my Daniel. Mr Chancellor said no such thing, I'm willing to wager.'

'Adam Blacklock,' said Hislop, introducing. 'Adam is artistic by nature, and even eloquent, if you encourage him, on the subject of the liberty of the artist. He likes the frescoes. He likes the vices and virtues on the voussoirs. Don't you, Adam?'

Some private baiting was going on, which Chancellor did not understand. He watched the next great vessel come in, and be presented, and cut up, and wasted. The Tsar, sitting alone in his high-backed ivory chair, was somehow different. Chancellor studied him, and realized that he was no longer wearing the Kazan tiara, but the crown of Constantine Monomachus, and that he had changed his robe of silver tissue for another, of scarlet sable-trimmed baldachine. Looking at the opposite table he saw, with disbelief, that all his courtiers had likewise exchanged their gowns of bright silver for others, edged and collared with snow-rafts of ermine. A tall figure, standing by his chair, made him look up, and he received Danny Hislop's ungentle foot on his ankle just as someone intoned, 'The Great Leader Ivan Vasilievich, Grand Duke, King and Lord of all Russia, extends his favour to Ritzert, and sends him meat from his own table.'

Diccon Chancellor hastily rose, as the dish was offered to him, and he took something and placed it on the flat round cakelike substance they gave you for platters. He bowed to the Tsar, and then on all sides to his Councillors, and sat carefully down. 'Do you like pickled cucumber?' said Danny Hislop. 'Or prunes. I'll pass them along.'

The sauce dishes were gold. The vinegar, salt and pepper vessels were gold. The dippers and small drinking pots at each cover were of gold, and some of them jewelled. All of them were quite dry. Diccon Chancellor toyed with his knife among the anonymous meat chopped up in saffron, and shook his head to the pickles. Danny smiled. 'Patience,' he said. 'In some things we are Muscovite. It will be wine, and not fermented mare's milk.'

'We?' said Chancellor.

'I am lavishly paid,' Danny said, 'to think in the first person plural. We are no mean acquisition, you know. Fergie Hoddim over there, with the moustache, God rest his razor, is our legal expert, the provider with snares in which apes are caught. Ludovic d'Harcourt learned his physics in Malta, and will defy any Montpellier man when it comes to hiring a leech. Lancelot Plummer, the beautiful gentleman in chastely sewn samite, is an engineer and architect unparalleled, who has built for our Voevoda Bolshoia a column for St Simeon Stylites to sit on.'

'I passed it, I think, on the way here.'

'Ah,' said Danny. 'The Kremlin Palace. You passed Mr Crawford's Kremlin residence. You have not yet seen the one Plummer has built at Vorobiovo but you certainly will. The rewards for expertise, as I have said, are enormous. We also fight.'

Chancellor said, 'The princes and boyars must envy you.'

He was understood. This curious, blunt-featured little man with the high pink brow under his seamed, stiffened cap said, 'The ruling powers in this enterprise leave nothing out of account. The princes led the army against the Crimean Khan Devlet Girey last summer and were extremely unlucky . . . Voevoda Sidorof killed and Ivan Sheremetev wounded, the hero of Kazan. He handed you the pork. Yes. It had all the marks of a rout,' said Danny blandly. 'But Devlet Girey received news that the Tsar was advancing with his army on Tula, and that was enough to put the Tartars to rout. They fled back to the Crimea and we captured some nice herds of ponies. Sixty thousand in fact. Only perhaps two hundred of them thoroughbred, but steppe ponies are useful. It almost consoled the widow of Voevoda Sidorof and the mistresses of Ivan Sheremetev.'

'You were with the Tsar's army?' said Chancellor.

'We were all with the Tsar's army,' said Hislop. 'It was sad to miss all the fighting. But we did rather better at Wyborg.'

'Against Gustavus Vasa of Sweden?' said Chancellor. Braced for an evening of stilted Russian conversation while plodding through uncongenial Russian food, he had expected nothing as fascinating as this.

'He felt,' said Danny sorrowfully, 'that we were encroaching on his possessions on the Gulf of Sweden. He hadn't heard, I am afraid, of the slight changes in the Tsar's defence forces. We laid siege to Wyborg and dealt fairly bracingly with the villages round it. There were so many prisoners that Swedish girls were going for a shilling.'

Chancellor said, 'The Tsar and his Council would be grateful.'

The lashless eyes opened. 'Oh, so were the princes,' said Danny. 'Everyone is grateful. Adashev. Sylvester. Viscovatu. Sheremetev. Prince Kurbsky, the other great hero of Kazan. We are to be permitted to mount an exploratory campaign against the Crimean Tartars next summer. With the Voevoda Bolshoia in command.'

'And that God-damned eagle,' said a distant voice, unexpectedly.

'Ludo doesn't like Slata Baba,' said Danny cheerfully. 'On Malta, they have no sense of drama. It is the double-headed eagle, my boy, which will demolish whole Tsardoms of blood-drinking Mussulmans.'

'I thought you didn't mind Tartars,' said the man pointed out as Ludovic d'Harcourt. A large man, Chancellor saw, with a round, cheerful face, freshly scrubbed.

'What I said,' replied Danny, 'was that I didn't mind the women of polygamous tribes, reared to please men upon the marriage couch or off it. Tartars are nasty, especially when raiding near my property. Stripping ikons for earrings; raping nuns; drinking from sacred goblets. They filled the monks' boots with live coals at one monastery, and made the poor bastards dance about frying. Tartars have rude impulses.'

He sounded disarmingly earnest. 'And the Russians?' Chancellor asked.

Shocked, the clever gaze turned on him. 'Pure with the pure, unsullied with the unsullied,' said Danny Hislop with simplicity. 'Inclined to shoot off their arrows at flying poultry and stripped peasant women, poor Sheremetev, but proud to march against the Ismaelite foe, singing divine liturgies.'

'And yourselves?' Chancellor said. 'The Swedish girls, sold for a shilling?'

'They went,' said Danny, 'to the very best homes. Holy Mother of God, he's elected to send round the wine.'

It arrived, in six-gallon basins of silver, and soon after that, the royal pledging began. Three times, Diccon Chancellor was sent malmsey, or mead, or Greek wine by the Sovereign Prince of all Russia, and in turn he watched as each of the Tsar's courtiers was called up by name to receive wine or meat. The feat of memory was beyond anything he had seen at court in Europe and its effect, he thought, was incalculable. It told the people that their Tsar knew and recognized them. It told the court, by the names unspoken, who might be out of favour. He waited, drinking as little as he might, and watching his colleagues from the edge of his eye do the same, until he was summoned to rise and go to the carved ivory chair.

The Tsar had changed again. On his head was a different diadem: on his shoulders a robe of dark blue and green velvet on a crimson silk ground, all wrought with gold and coloured silk pomegranates. The cup he held out was baroque mother-of-pearl set in silver.

'Ritzert,' he said. 'Thou hast come from a great sovereign to a great sovereign; thou hast made a great journey. After thou hast experienced our favour it shall be well with thee and thy countrymen. Drink, and drink well, and eat well even to thy heart's content, and then take thy rest, that thou mayest at length take my greetings back to thy mistress.'

This time no one translated, and Chancellor answered also in Russian, and drank, and on returning the cup found it pressed, as he had expected, into his hands. Holding his gift, and declaring, briefly, his gratitude, he bowed and backed from that disturbing, bright-eyed presence with the bony, hot hands.

The others got through the same ceremony with the smoothness of painful rehearsal, with the exception of George Killingworth, who had to wait while the Tsar called the Metropolitan to admire the colour and size of his beard, upon which the Metropolitan observed reverently, 'This is God's gift,' and blessed it. Clutching his goblet, Killingworth rejoined Chancellor in a hurry, his face red as a cockscomb above the flowing evidence of his Maker's generosity. Shortly after that, the Tsar watched the last man return to his bench, and tapped with his *possoch,* and spoke: 'You may depart.' The supper had lasted five hours.

It was dark outside. Escorted by nobles and lit by wavering torches, Diccon Chancellor and his three colleagues made their way, with dazed concentration, down the steep flights of stairs from the Granovitaya Palace, and across the shaved wooden paths to where their horses were waiting. The Secretary, Viscovatu, had said farewell outside the palace, and had told them that they would shortly be summoned to discuss their business with a panel of boyars and merchants. Meanwhile, with the help of their Pristafs, they were free to enjoy the city of Moscow, and to join the Tsar and his subjects in the entertainments of the season.

For their own safety, the Chief Secretary had added, he must request them to entertain no one in their own premises, without the protection of at least two Muscovites present. Until they found their own property, the house was theirs free of charge for their lodging. They would have a fixed allowance of bread, meat, hay and straw, wood for the kitchen and stoves, and salt, oil, pepper and onions each day, together with three sorts of mead and two kinds of beer. Meanwhile, said the Secretary, the Tsar was pleased to desire them to drink his health at their own board this evening, and was sending a cart with three barrels of wine for that purpose. . . .

'I can't,' said Ned Price.

'You'll have to,' said George Killingworth hazily. 'My God: If I can be tweaked for my Queen, you can spew for her.'

*

Francis Crawford of Lymond entered Moscow briskly just before midnight by the Elinschie gate, with a small company of men. A group of artisans, hurrying late with a lantern, bowed to the ground as the tasselled horses raced past and he lifted his whip in acknowledgement but did not pause until the Nikólskaya Tower of the Kremlin, nearest his house, where he dismounted and flung the reins to a groom. The captain of the barbican, hurrying forward, bowed and said, 'My lord . . . the sovereign prince Ivan Vasilievich desires your presence in his apartments.'

The Supreme Commander did not ignore him, nor was he scathing about the appearance and general alertness of the guard, which these days, certainly, was impeccable. He merely said, 'Advise his grace, if you will, that I am coming?' and, after a word with his men, walked off on foot towards the private staircase beside St Saviour, his servants and torchbearer following. He had unbuckled from his waist and left behind both his sword and his dagger.

He was challenged six times before he reached the Tsar's private chamber : by the hackbutters in the courtyard who waited there, matches lit and guns charged day and night; by the grooms who lay at every gate and door of the court; by the officers of the third chamber, where waited forty boyars' sons through every night : by the officers of the second chamber, where Alexei Adashev slept with three others. He replied to each challenge correctly, his veiled eyes assessing and automatically delivering judgements. Six months ago, after a banquet, the stairs and passages of the palace, half lit and stinking, would have been strewn with the weeping bodies of drunkards, while far out in the mud the grooms waited shivering for their masters to arrive and mount and ride home.

Adashev was asleep. Among the four men on duty, he recognized Lancelot Plummer, who bowed without speaking. He could not at once recall what was making the engineer peevish, but rightly assessed it as trivial. The guards on either side of the Tsar's door were expecting him : as he approached, they swung their silver halberds at the salute, and made way. He did not awake Adashev, but instead knocked himself; and when the Tsar's voice called 'Enter!' Lymond pushed open the carved double doors and went in.

The Tsar Ivan Vasilievich was in bed. The chamber priest, his office performed, was retreating, holding the crushed sprig of basil and the silver bowl of blessed water, sent each day by the abbots of the Tsar's scattered monasteries. As Lymond paused and bowed, the Tsar waved his hand, dismissing his household officers also. The door shut.

The Voevoda had come to know the room well. The walls hung with elaborate fabric and fish-scaled with dazzling ikons. The painted vaults. The silver shrine with its strange sculpted figures : the book of the gospels boarded with gold foil and jewels, and alive with the brooched forms of saints. The jewelled censer; the silver lamps and sconced tapers; the tall silver ewer and basin in which the Tsar washed his fingers clean of the handgrip of heretics. The Tsar's deep voice said, 'I wish to be told if you completed your errand.'

The bedcover was of fox fur and the bolster of drawn threadwork; the bed was new, with a canopy of changeable taffeta lined with sarsanet and tasselled with silk and gold. In it the Tsar sat in a loose gown and shirt over fine linen hose, his pocket ikon still in his hands. Lymond said, 'My errand was of no moment. But it is completed.'

'You obeyed me,' said the Grand Duke of Russia. 'I wonder how often you obey me? Your churl Blacklock is not obedient. Ivan Mikhailov Viscovatu has complained of him. You know the frescoes in the Golden Chamber are not painted according to the canonical rules. Near to the figure of Our Saviour a woman is shown, dancing nonchalantly, and the inscription on it is *Lechery and Jealousy*.'

Lymond gave no appearance of being disturbed. 'If Mr Blacklock appears to take Sylvester's part, it is purely on aesthetic grounds. Mr Blacklock is an excellent soldier.'

'The part of an excellent soldier,' said Ivan Vasilievich, 'is to obey orders and avoid matters which have no bearing on warfare. Such niceness of taste may lead him into strange pathways. Perhaps he will find he appreciates the art of Sigismund-Augustus better than ours, or the heretical painting of England.'

'Perhaps then,' said Lymond, 'you should have him followed, also.'

The bony fingers turning the ikon case became suddenly still. Lymond did not move. The Tsar stared at him, the trailing auburn hair concealing his lips, his arched brows drawn down over the large pale eyes staring at his commander. He said, 'You jest with me?' and the figured gold crumpled, like a walnut shell, under his fingers.

Lymond said, 'Your dagger is under your pillow.'

The bearded lips smiled. With a sudden movement, the Grand Prince cast away the crushed ikon and slid his hand searching under the pillow. When he sat up, the long blade of a dagger lay still and blue in his hands. The Tsar said, 'But you have a knife in your shirt-breast. Before I could move, you will kill me.'

'Then I should lose my life,' Lymond said. 'Alexei Adashev and your guards would cut me to pieces.'

'They would draw your ribs out with red heated pincers. They would sew you in a bearskin and set my hounds on you. They would drive a soaped stake . . .' The Tsar stopped, his flecked lips shining between the hairs of his beard. 'But your men are of the guard. They would save you. They would flee to the terems and take my son Ivan hostage.'

'Your cousin Vladimir would avenge you,' Lymond said. He drew off his gloves. The Tsar's knife, quivering, flashed as he turned the point outwards. Lymond said, 'If you will allow me?'

The Tsar made no reply. The knife quivered, and the room was filled with the sound of his breathing: harsh breathing, like the cries of a distant massed rookery. Lymond slid off his camelhair *honoratkey,* and letting it fall, pulled open the sashed tunic beneath it, and then the jewelled ties of his shirt. He said, 'I should prefer to keep on my boots and my breeches. But as you see, my lord, I carry no weapon in the breast of my shirt.'

The Tsar did not let fall either his eyes or his weapon. 'I know you,' he said.

Lymond suddenly smiled. Facing open-shirted the point of the dagger, his blue gaze alight, he made a sweeping, elaborate bow, and rose from it with an incredible flash of steel in his right hand: a flash that arched through the air and landed on the flat of its blade in the fox fur as Ivan's knife, in its turn, lunged straight for his Voevoda's heart.

Lymond leaped aside. He was not quite quick enough: the blade, as it passed him, drew a thin line through shirt and shoulder which pricked the cambric with red but drew not even a glance from Lymond himself. Standing still between door and window: 'You know me,' he said.

Pulled from the bed by the lunge, the Tsar of all the Russians stood panting and laughing by his pillows, and then, turning, picked up the little knife from the cover where Lymond had thrown it. 'Where was it? Your boot? Ah, Frangike Gavinovich.' He broke off. 'I sent for you because I wish to play chess. Come.'

'Like this?' said Lymond calmly. The embroidery on his shirt flashed with his breathing.

'Like this,' said the Tsar, and, crossing the room, he lifted from its chest the robe of dark blue and green velvet he had worn at the banquet and turned, holding it, to his Supreme Commander. For a moment, Lymond paused, and then, kneeling, he accepted it, and drew it round his shoulders. 'You are not obedient,' said the Tsar. 'You refused once to play chess with your sovereign lord. I remember it. You refused several times. An illness, you claimed. A mishap. A battle.'

There was a table, inlaid with onyx. Lymond opened the chessmen. 'I had not been told,' he said, 'that the duty of the Voevoda Bolshoia in Russia included the playing of chess.'

'You lie,' said the Tsar, pulling the cover once more over his knees, and propping the bolster comfortably in the small of his back. 'Why am I surrounded by liars and murderers and counterfeit officers of hearty complexion? You believed, being taught by the devil, that you would vanquish your lord, and that your lord, instructed by vainness, would kill you. . . .

'You are right. I shall kill you one day, but not until you teach me the abominable practices which allow you to win. Because I am weak, I shall claim to start with my white. Then we shall resume our quarrel about the true interpretation of St Ambrose. I shall send for the librarian from the Josef Volokolamsk to refute you. . . . It is your move.'

They played two games, while the stove burned low in the corner and the tapers flickered, and did not speak of St Ambrose, or indeed of anything else, as they sat in silence, matching each other, mind locked with mind in a game which was not a game, and a combat which was not a combat, but as dangerous in its intensity as the dangerous play they had engaged in already. The first game, a brief one, was won by Lymond. The second, against all precedent, was brought to stalemate by the Tsar.

He was joyous. He shouted, flinging over the table so that the onyx splintered on the tiled floor; and, striding to the door, called for food and wine, and light and his jesters. Sluggish with sleep, the *skomdrokhi* displeased him, and were kicked out while he cracked open a chicken, and swallowed mead served by Lymond himself. Lymond said, 'We didn't speak of St Ambrose.' His eyes were bright in the brilliant lamplight, but he had eaten and drunk very little.

The Tsar held out his hands for rosewater, and dried them on the fringed silken napkin Lymond brought over. 'What of the Englishmen?' he said.

Lymond replaced the ewer and basin and returning, took the tall-backed chair by the bed. The stove had been built up. The furred velvet robe, long since cast off, lay trailing over the arm of his chair. His skin was damp, but his face was not tired, or less than composed. He said, 'You have your Council's advice. Welcome them.'

The Tsar stirred irritably. 'They will break my monopolies.'

'Time will break your monopolies,' Lymond said. 'Best do it with good grace while you can.'

The pale eyes stared at him, the brow furrowed with weariness. 'The Queen of England is married to the Emperor's son. This English trade will harm the Baltic which are the Emperor's allies. The Emperor may send his armies to stiffen Lithuania and Livonia against me. These English may be here not to trade, but as spies.'

Lymond gazed up at the flushed face with its wet, shining beard. He said calmly, 'If I thought they were spies, I would kill them.'

'Are they?' said Ivan.

Lymond said, 'It is unlikely. If you will allow me to attend some of their meetings, I can assure myself of it. There is something else your grace should bear in mind. The people of England are unhappy with the prince their Queen has married. They may rise against him. It is almost certain that the Queen dare not offend her people by spoiling a trading adventure for the sake of her husband. The Emperor will not incite Lithuania and Livonia against you, if you do not give him cause by threatening his allies. He will be your friend for life, and so will England, if you continue your crusade against the Tartars.'

'So Adashev says,' said the Tsar. 'And it is plain. Turkey supports the Tartars. The fall of the Tartars is a blow against Turkey. And Turkey is the friend of the French and the enemy of the Emperor Charles. . . .' He drew back, and, with a half-closed fist, fetched Lymond a light blow on the shoulder. 'It is your career you think of, you dog. You yearn to wrest Turkish pearls and Tartar maidens from the Crimea next summer. . . . Rest content. I have said we shall march. And if these red English moujiks are true men, I shall give you something to take in your baggage. If England wishes me to fight the Emperor's battles, and be kind to her merchants, and give up my monopolies, she must do something in exchange. Give me arms.'

Lymond was silent.

The Tsar's beaked nose inhaled, with firm sonority. 'You persist in this obstinacy. You say she will not do it. I, who know women, say she will. The benefits are such that she will. When I have explained them, she will listen. You say there is no King in that country; that the people dislike her husband. So there is only a woman, a creature given by God to serve man and obey him. If you were a man, you would realize this.'

Lymond said, 'I serve your grace as a man.' His voice was level.

'I doubt it sometimes,' said Ivan Vasilievich. There was still some mead in the cup. He flung it, suddenly and pettishly, and it flooded over the white cambric of Lymond's shirt, splashing his face, and mixing with the blurred marks of blood from the scratch on his shoulder. 'I have offered you women. Why do you not take them?'

'I have a woman,' Lymond said. He had not moved to blot the thin streaks of wet on his skin. Only those who served under him would perhaps have recognized the look in his eyes.

'Of whom you are innocent,' the Tsar said. 'Innocent as a maiden. You resent being followed. You do not know how closely you are followed. I say again. Are you a man?'

Lymond took a long breath. Beneath his lips, his teeth were closed hard together, but his eyes were blue and open and lucid, and his limbs were composed. He said, 'My debt is to Güzel, who is satisfied.'

The other man nodded, galvanically, combing his beard with his fingers. 'She brought you here. It was her message which prepared us for your coming, and her money which conveyed you from Turkey. Does she feel she has received due reward?'

'She is content,' Lymond said briefly.

The Tsar continued to finger his beard. 'But if she felt less content, as time went on? Perhaps she might leave . . .

perhaps, being so deeply in her debt, you might feel you should leave with her. It comes to me,' said the Tsar, 'that it is this woman who is sapping your manhood. Perhaps the physic you need is quite simple – a fresh young princess from one of our rich princely families. I have one in mind; a gentle, pliable girl of seventeen or under, who has no brothers or cousins to inherit. Her father is old. When he dies, it will be my pleasure to leave the daughter her patrimony, and the title to her husband. She will teach you fleshly delights your Greek matron has never imagined. You may have sons, to become Voevoda in their turn. I will send your Güzel to a nunnery.'

'You are generous,' Lymond said. 'But I cannot accept. I am married already.'

There was a silence. Then the Tsar said, 'She is here? Your wife?'

'No. She is in England. The marriage was one of convenience, and will be annulled.' The pleasant, undisturbed voice did not alter in timbre. 'It has not been consummated.'

'Then it is true,' the Tsar said. His big hands lay loose on the fox fur, so deep was his interest and his curiosity. 'You are a virgin?'

Lymond's eyes dropped. For a moment, head bent, he appeared to be collecting his thoughts, or composing his answer, or even perhaps controlling an answer more natural to his temper. Then he looked up and said, 'No. The delights of the flesh do not interest me, but not because they have never done so. Rather the contrary.'

The pale eyes stared. Slowly the ridged forehead cleared. The Tsar bared his teeth in delight, and flung back his thick beard, and laughed. 'The pox. I shall send you my doctors.'

'A night with Venus and a month with Mercury?' said Lymond dryly. 'No. The sickness, whatever it is, is not subject to doctors, I fear.'

The Tsar fingered his lips. 'There is a soothsayer from Kola . . .'

'Nor a soothsayer,' said Lymond. 'I have had my fill of deadly harbingers.'

'You fear them, Frangike Gavinovich? Why? Whom have you consulted? What doom have they told?'

'I have met only one,' Lymond said. 'In France. A woman famed for her sayings. She prophesied that my father's two sons would never meet in this life again. She spoke the truth, I believe.'

'And,' said the Tsar, 'how many sons has your father?'

'Myself and another,' said Lymond. 'My older brother, who still lives in Scotland. You see, therefore, there is no need to follow me. I shall not be seduced from my post by the Englishmen or overcome with a yearning for the land of my fathers. Nor shall I give my mistress cause to regret that she and I have come to Russia, and stayed in Russia to serve you. Until you send me away, I shall serve you.'

Through and through, the pale eyes searched the other, unwavering gaze of flowerlike blue. 'You do not smile,' said the Tsar, 'when I give you my robe. When I have given you plate and jewels, rents and land, the handkerchief from my sash, you do not smile.'

Lymond stood up. 'My lord . . . I receive them, because you take pleasure in giving, but I do not serve you for gifts. I serve you for friendship. . . . And until that day comes when I cannot defeat you at chess, and you will no longer ask me to play with you.'

Ivan Vasilievich shouted. His laugh rang round the close, pictured room and drew chimes from the glass and the silver: he leaned forward among the heaped fur and struck Lymond's arms to his sides with the grip of two powerful hands. 'You will not leave me,' he said.

'No,' said Francis Crawford.

CHAPTER FOUR

The next day, Lymond flew Slata Baba, and Chancellor, mute on his horse, saw the eagle, a speck in the sun, plunge to her kill like a storm of Saracen arrows and then, opening her great ragged wings, soar three hundred feet to hang, bank, and dive yet again.

She killed in the air, wings backswept; muscled legs braced like forearms before her, and the hooked talons struck the crow or the grouse or the ptarmigan as knives into straw, crumpling bone and feathers and flesh into a broken cake of white and soft brown and scarlet. She killed on the ground and stood round-shouldered over her prey, held in the grip which could paralyze a man's hand, before stooping to tear with the open, hooked bill. Then she would rise again, the eight-foot spread of her great earth-brown pinions masking the sky. And bright and blue as the sky were Lymond's eyes, watching her.

She was flown at the hare hunt, which the Tsar led with his princes and boyars, and to which Chancellor and his friends were invited. Danny Hislop was not there, nor the artist called Blacklock. Riding between Lymond and the fresh-faced Knight of St John who did not like eagles, Chancellor asked after them. Ludovic d'Harcourt glanced at Lymond without answering. Lymond said, 'They are undergoing a course of correction. If in the event they are either correct or in the least chastened, I shall be surprised. You say you have hunted.'

'With Sir Henry. At Penshurst,' said Chancellor. The eagle had a ruby in its feathered hood, and its swivel and chain were of gold. He had told Christopher to stop staring at it.

Chacque automne autre fois oubliait en Ferrare, Avec quelques oiseaux le poids de la tiara. Yes. Well, this is different,' said Lymond.

Diccon Chancellor said, 'I see that.'

Lymond followed his gaze with perfect calm. 'She does her office well and busily, as a good hunter should. She is pagan, Slata Baba : the golden idol of the Samoyèdes, a people who eat one another, so I am told. You should visit the fair at Lampozhnya. They bring sledges of furs from Pechora which would drag down crosses, like that boisterous gown of black velvet. I intend to go to the Mezen at Lent. If you wish, you may come with me.'

Far to the north, the River Mezen flowed to the Lacus Cronicus, the Frozen Sea, farther than any Englishman had yet gone. Chancellor said, 'Your master trusts you?'

'Ask him,' Lancelot Plummer had said, nudging up to his horse when he had asked the same question, 'why he left the Emperor on the night of the banquet with blood on his shirt.' But Chancellor had not asked him and neither, he was quite sure, had Plummer.

'My master and I,' Lymond said, 'understand each other very well.'

Presently, the Tsar called Chancellor to his presence, and greeted him with his bare hand, and allowed him to present his son Christopher, who bowed as he had been taught, and tried not to look at the cloth-of-gold robe and the knives and daggers hilted with rubies, or the plated gold cap fringed with chained jewels. Around them rode the boyars in their furred brocades running with gold, on Turkish horses with necks curved each like a palm branch, coloured wolf grey, and the grey of lilac and starling, and red bay and gold-brown and russet. And between them thronged the grooms in black and gold and the dogs, pouring in spate like a brown mountain river over the sunlit field, towards the wide thicketed meadow where they were to hunt.

It was a preserve of hares, a simple cachement of animals as arbitrary as a byre or a dovecote or a warren of coneys, and the sub-boys of maple and sallow and blackthorn were man-made to furnish it. While Chancellor watched, the horsemen with the Tsar deployed themselves round the whole area, with men on foot, black and yellow, inter-leaving between them, and the dogs, hard-held, milling and tugging at the Tsar's side. He had been allotted two, with two men to hold them, and Lymond likewise. No one else, he noticed, was permitted hounds but a handful of princes appointed by the Tsar. Then Ivan Vasilievich cried aloud, and the mastiffs were released.

It was not a long business. Afterwards, they were allowed to change their dress at a tower five miles from Moscow where pavilions had been raised, and where the Tsar later received them seated on his ivory throne and talked in Russian to Chancellor, while kneeling men pre-sented them with confections of coriander and almonds and aniseed, and a pyramid of coloured sugar, on which Chancellor made no comment.

The marks of favour, so desirable for his business, were unexpected and plain. Merchants had been summoned, and his meetings with them and the Chief Secretary Visco-vatu were to begin in the Kremlin tomorrow. The Tsar's councillors Alexei Adashev and Sylvester and the staff of his Voevoda Bolshoia would lend their aid as became needful. With the Pristafs appointed to guide him, the Ambassador was now free to make what excursions he wished. The ships of the great lord Hugh Willoughby, whose death he regretted, were to be returned to the English intact, and might be sailed home in the spring, with the others. He hoped to have Master Ritzert's com-pany soon with his gerfalcons, to fly at crane and heron

211

and wild swan outside Moscow's posterns. He invited him and his son to a bear-baiting.

Chancellor answered it all. Christopher beside him, said nothing; nor did Lane or Killingworth or Price or Rob Best, seated sick-faced beside Lymond.

'I saw Willoughby once, in Scotland,' Lymond said. 'He held a fort there under the Protector, during the late King Henry's Rough Wooing. As the great-uncle of the Lady Jane Grey he would have needed all his social dexterity, had he lived to return. I imagine he must have died just about the time she was executed. If Christopher is going to be sick, I think you should make some excuse and remove him. Disgust is held to be the summit of weakness. As well as, in this case, an insult.'

They had driven the hares like sheep into the dogs. And when the slaughter was slowing, they had emptied sackloads of leverets into the arena, so that they loped and staggered and bumped, still blinded, into the mouths of the mastiffs. When the last dog was persuaded to leave, they counted three hundred bodies, of which the Tsar's dogs had killed seventy. The Tsar, bestowing favours so gracefully, was elated. Best said, under his breath, 'They are a nation of Goths. Rude, bloody and blind as the wild Irish.'

'They do not pursue the art quite as it is practised in France,' said the voice of Ludovic d'Harcourt softly. 'But then, few kings can claim to have killed seventy hares in a single day's hunting. *Un chasseur émérite.*'

'You are thinking of venery,' Lymond said. 'Whereby all men of worth may discover a gentleman from a yeoman, and a yeoman from a villein. This is something quite different, as I said. This is a demonstration by a ruler of his power and fitness to rule. I suggest you do not forget it.'

'I couldn't,' said Robert Best.

The following day, the business meetings began. Lymond did not attend, but Fergie Hoddim surprisingly did. It was not until his third intervention that Chancellor remembered *the provider of snares in which apes are caught,* and the Troitsa monastery, where Mr Crawford also had mentioned his legal confrère. Where Mr Crawford had refused point blank to do anything further about the affairs of his wife.

He had one winter in which to persuade him. He had

seldom met anyone who looked less amenable to persuasion. And yet, if Lymond did not return, he himself would go back, he had been told, to face an arraignment for heresy. And Lymond, Lady Lennox had said, would lose his life.

How? It was not the first time, looking round at his talking companions, that Diccon Chancellor wondered that. Who was Lady Lennox's agent? Not one of his seamen : they had sailed home to England, and when they returned would come no farther south than St Nicholas. Unless Lymond travelled a thousand miles north to bid them farewell, he would be out of their reach in Moscow. Therefore, it must be one of ten men : the six he had left at Vologda, and the four men, Killingworth, Price, Lane and Best, who were here at this table. Christopher, at least, could be left out of the reckoning.

Which of them had been paid to kill the Voevoda Bolshoia? Which, when Philippa's husband gave his last, bored refusal, would make sure that if he did not come home to England, he would not live to harm England in Russia? Who cared for England enough? Or who, perhaps, hated Lymond from long ago?

He looked at them all again, and found they were all looking at him, and that it had evidently been agreed, without his realizing it, that the Tsar should be approached with a request for stronger privileges than those so far mentioned verbally, and that Hoddim and he were to frame the letter, and Viscovatu to scan it. He nodded hastily and got hold of the inkhorn again and began to underline the headings they had already discussed. The leadline every half-glass. Or they would all follow Willoughby.

The Tsar's answer came promptly enough : if they would draw up a list of desired privileges, he would consider it. And that was already half done : they had discussed it long enough, God knew, among themselves. Permission to buy a house and build a warehouse at Kholmogory, where they could keep their books and store their goods prior to shipping. Permission to do the same at Vologda, where living was also cheaper than Moscow, and the opportunities for trade probably better, if the Novgorod merchants would come to them. Permission to set up a house in Moscow, where they must have the Tsar's goodwill and representation at Court.

Nothing, at this stage, could be said of the Tsar's monopolies, imposed at will on wax, silk or lead, cloth or pearls. No one might sell furs, corn or timber, fish or hay, sheep or poultry or wild fowl until the Tsar's warehouses were empty of all these goods, sent him as tribute. No one might sell anything if the Tsar wished to dispose of his stock — even spoiled stock he wished to sell cheaply. Permission . . .

Ivan Mikhailovich Viscovatu said, 'You make no mention of monopolies?'

The Russian merchants by now had left the discussion. George Killingworth said, 'We understand the Tsar reserves to himself certain items of trade. We have no wish to displease his highness.'

'His highness,' said the Chief Secretary, 'is sensible of your restraint. He wished me to tell you however that he is willing to reserve for your company his whole purchase of wax, which is usually sold to the merchants of Riga, Revel and Poland, Danzig, Lübeck and Hamburg. He will in due course inform you of the price.'

Diccon Chancellor bowed, and expressed his infinite pleasure, and so did Lane and Price and Killingworth and Best, preserving at all costs the decencies. But later that afternoon, in the privacy of their own serge-hung premises, George Killingworth swung Christopher off his feet, to his smiling astonishment, and dropping him, hurled his cap into a corner. 'The wax monopoly. It doesn't matter what price he charges. We can fix the selling-price at anything we choose. And who knows what else he will sell us! Perhaps the whole market. Perhaps the Hanseatic League will have to buy masts and pitch and cordage through us in future. . . .'

'Perhaps,' said Diccon Chancellor.

Ned Lane looked at him shrewdly. 'You think his merchants might object. The ones that matter : the monasteries. The Council members.'

Diccon Chancellor said, 'I think the Dutch and Polish and Flemish and German merchants would object, to no uncertain tune, and that if he pushes them too far, he might well find himself at war with the west before he is ready for it. I think there is no chance at all that the Tsar will do all his trading through us. . . . Not at present, at least. In fact, I ask myself why he has risked the surprising concessions he has so far allowed us. What does he want?'

George Killingworth had got hold of the vodka and was pouring it, expertly, into five wooden firkins. 'Trade,' he said. 'A route for imports and exports which none of the Baltic countries can interfere with. My God, he can hardly expect us to do it without some special sweetening. The sea's frozen half the year round : we can only get one fleet in and one fleet out at the best every year. And no one can say it's a convenient journey. We've lost two ships' crews already. We only arrived here safely both times because you and Cabot both know what you're doing.'

'Thank you,' said Chancellor. 'I still think he wants more than trade.'

George Killingworth put down the jug and picked up the firkin. He said, 'Maybe he does. But he hasn't said so. And even if he does, it's no business of ours. We are here to negotiate a trading agreement, that's all. If he wants anything else, the Privy Council will have to handle it.'

Ned Price said, 'But Diccon has called himself an ambassador, and is being received as an ambassador. The Tsar might well expect him to have powers to treat for the Queen.'

'He might,' said Robert Best unexpectedly. 'If the matter hadn't already been disposed of at the Troitsa Monastery.'

There was a brief silence while they stared at one another, recalling a provoking interrogation by the Voevoda Bolshoia, in the presence of Master Grigorjeff, who spoke more English than was apparent. Robert Best added, 'So they know the limitations of your powers fairly well. The question remains, as Diccon says, why is he pleasing us at the risk of offending the Emperor Charles? And I think I know who has the answer. Master Francis Crawford, the Voevoda Bolshoia.'

'Taking our part with the Tsar?' said Killingworth with vast scorn and drained off his vodka and spat. 'There goes a subtle, dissembling fox, who would barter his kin for a township.'

'No,' said Diccon Chancellor. 'I think I understand Rob. There goes a gentleman of doubtful attractions who is providing the Tsar with an army. We might question its quality but the Tsar may have no qualms.'

'Then he's a fool,' Killingworth said. 'Does he think one pack of vainglorious mercenaries will hold back Poland and Lithuania? I'd like to see them in action.'

'So should I,' said Chancellor thoughtfully.

Francis Crawford reached the same conclusion, on hearing Fergie Hoddim's report on the petition the Muscovy Company had been allowed to present to the Tsar.

'. . . complete freedom of trade, and special jurisdiction for all English settled in Russia. The English to decide their own quarrels, and the Tsar to settle all litiginous cases between subjects of England and Russia. A market twice yearly at Kholmogory, prices to be optional. Freedom from tolls—'

'What?' said Lymond.

'And he's offered them a wax monopoly,' Fergie said, eyes shining with legal mysticism. '*Proxime et immediate sequens*. And ye ken what the tolls are. A tenth of a dengi on all Turkish and Armenian imports. Two dengi a rouble on all goods weighed at the Emperor's beam. Toll-bars. River-dues. Storage-dues. Dues on the written contract if you sell an old nag. Dues on every God's pound of salt. . . . They send out fifty thousand pounds of wax a year, they reckon,' said Fergie. 'And they can get four pounds the hundred for it in England.'

'Maybe the Tsar will ask four pounds the hundred pounds for it in Russia,' said Lymond.

'No. It's fixed. Two pounds seventeen shillings and six-pence,' said Fergie with triumph.

The Voevoda's chilly blue eyes were open in thought. 'And what favours did the Tsar ask in return?'

'None,' said Fergie. 'Or none so far. Ye ken Viscovatu. He can eat without opening his mouth.'

'Then I think,' said Lymond, 'we had better have a show of strength. Tell Plummer to stop mourning over St Basil's and do something about the weather. There must be a use for engineers in the cosmos somewhere. Meanwhile, until the snow comes, we had better keep Master Chancellor and his party entertained.'

'Tartar women?' said Fergie helpfully. 'Danny Hislop . . .'

'Healthy physical exercise,' said Lymond tartly. 'Until the roads harden up and they can get on with their trading. They have to wait in Moscow anyway until the Tsar replies to their letter. And meanwhile we all want the Tsar's noble mind irrevocably set on war with the Tartars; none more so than Prince Vishnevetsky and his gallant Cossacks. War with Lithuania would be an unfortunate mistake. Not to mention the Poles. A haughty nation and a very insulting people upon advantage.'

'You've heard from Vishnevetsky?' said Fergie. He

missed the niceties of civilized law, but the nature of Russian intrigue almost made up for it.

'He's coming to see me in December,' said Lymond. 'Let's have our exercise in December. What a pity we couldn't induce a Tartar or two to set fire to us.'

'We could set fire to ourselves,' offered Fergie, with unthinking enthusiasm. 'Except then we'd have no one to fight with.'

'I shouldn't be too sure of that,' said Francis Crawford.

And thinking of the character of his leader, and the strong and divergent personalities of his colleagues in the company of St Mary's, Fergie Hoddim was inclined to agree.

Half-way through November, after the mildest autumn for three hundred years, the temperature in Moscow dropped thirty degrees. By the beginning of December, the days were bringing anything up to ten degrees of frost and the rivers became broad white highways along which moved eight hundred sledges daily, carrying corn and fish into the city. The winter ice market opened on the Moskva, outside the Kremlin, selling casks and earthenware pots and painted sledges and grain, and stiff-legged hogs and bullocks and poultry, frozen like boulders, and boys swooped and flashed on the crystalline ice, bones bound on their feet and iron-shod stakes in their hands, as staffs and as weapons. Tame bears danced, their teeth rubbed with vitriol, and wild ones crept closer to the villages. The rest of the Muscovy Company's wares set off by sledge at last from Vologda, and the sledge carrying the Tsar's wine and sugar overturned and was lost.

Diccon Chancellor, sick of hunting and hawking and eating and drinking and witnessing crude entertainments unrelieved by the presence of women, took George Killingworth off to the Kremlin to present his apologies to the Tsar through his Chief Secretary Viscovatu, and to ask, for the fifth time, whether his highness was graciously disposed to reply yet to the Company's humble petition. Master Viscovatu, faintly severe on the subject of the wine and the sugar, said an answer would certainly be supplied in due course, but that his highness was at present much occupied with affairs of war.

'*War!*' said George Killingworth, and broke off as Chancellor kicked him on the ankle.

'Yes. It is the Emperor's custom,' said Ivan Viscovatu, 'to

hold a Triumph in the fields outside Moscow shortly after the St Nicholas's Day banquet. It is the Tsar's desire that you and your fellows will honour the Tsar and his commanders with your presence. Afterwards, it is possible that the Tsar's time will be less circumscribed. I am sure you are anxious to visit trading centres other than Moscow.'

George Killingworth opened his mouth and shut it again, the golden beard drawn like a curtain. 'We are honoured,' said Chancellor, and got Killingworth out before he could say anything aloud about the Voevoda Bolshoia, whose fine touch would be detected behind every courteous sentence. They already knew that the Tsar was pleased with his army. It looked rather as if the Voevoda were pleased with it, too. It remained to be seen whether the Tartars would be pleased also. 'And every man in it a gentleman,' said Diccon Chancellor to himself, thoughtfully.

Later, when he understood what St Mary's was, he realized that any soldier in Europe might have told him what to expect on that clear, cold day when he and Christopher and his quartet of impatient merchants finally stood on a field of snow outside Moscow, and watched marching past a thousand-long column of hackbutters in blue stammel and velvet ranked five abreast, each with his gun on his left shoulder and with his right hand holding his match. On beautiful Turkish horses and jennets, the Tsar's boyars and nobles followed them in gold brocade, riding three by three. And lastly, there entered the Tsar in brilliant tissue, his scarlet cap hung with pearls and his high officials around him. At his right, grey furred and wholly calm, rode the Voevoda Bolshoia.

George Killingworth, as was his regrettable habit, spat.

Afterwards, they agreed it was a circus; a drama, a ritual dance; a precise entertainment designed and created by a clever and ruthless ringmaster. The silk pavilions; the flags, the rippling cloth which held back the crowds were all devices of western chivalry. The massed displays of drill and horsemanship were not. Only over the wide steppes of Russia was it necessary to move blocks of men by the thousand, riding hundreds of miles into battle; able to wheel and manoeuvre to distant, half-perceptible command.

It was a skill they had never possessed; just as they owned the endurance to sustain siege to the point where life ceased; where they ate rats and shoe leather and, sometimes, each other; but did not have the stamina or know-ledge or ability to mount the attack which would break the siege in the first instance.

To simulate these things, with wooden forts and mov-able towers, was only spectacular play-acting, just as the drill carried out on the pressed snow, on foot and on horse-back, by hackbutters and boyars alike, with brands and pennons and flashing silk cords, was to the eye merely a brave coloured pattern shifting like shaken mosaic on the glaring white sheet of the snow.

But even to the eye of a seaman or a clerk, or a mer-chant, it said something more. It spoke of brutal discipline. It told of a control based on skill, as well as on fear. And it showed a pride, in themselves and their training, which was reflected, in spite of himself, in the Tsar's austere, bearded face.

The last of the demonstration belonged to the gunners. Mounted on their long wooden platform, the hackbutters gave first their traditional display. Their target, sixty yards off, was a bank of pure ice, built six feet high and two thick, and stretching for a quarter of a mile before the chain of orderly, liveried men. The gunfire, rapping hard on the ears, seemed to be shot from the thin, glassy sky. Sound exploded around them like gorse-pods, striking their eyes and vibrating their finger-ends while the blue wall turned frosty and crumbled, and broken ice jumped like mirrors and cast long swathes hissing like salt to spangle the pale tender blue of the air.

The wall lay flat. Beside it, two earth-filled houses thirty feet deep faced the long row of cannon, gold baguettes beading the snow. A match flared, a flag lifted and fell, and the guns fired : brises, falcons, and minions; sakers, cul-verins and cannon, double and royal; and lastly in order of size, the great cannon : *Kazan*, a year old, and *Astrakhan*, cast only three months before, each over a thousand pounds' weight, with their black mouths more than a foot in diameter.

They fired the ordnance three times in all, from the least to the largest in order, and as the last round went off, the small-bellied pot guns shot wild fire into the smoke, rising in flashes of scarlet and gold among the reeking black clouds, as the fields shuddered to the mounting explosions. Where the houses had stood, there was nothing.

It was over. Unable to hear his own voice, Chancellor

obeyed the Tsar's summons to join him, and tried to express, in serviceable Russian, his ecstatic admiration for what he had seen.

'It is the might of Russia,' said Ivan Vasilievich. 'The Voevoda Bolshoia can answer your questions.'

'I have none,' said Chancellor. His ears ached. A young, bearded man in an incredible robe lined with white ermine smiled, and raised his eyebrows at Lymond.

'I have,' said Christopher under his breath.

The Voevoda, unhappily, had heard it. 'What is your interest? The guns?' Lymond said.

Christopher had gone scarlet. He said, 'Yes. No. I wondered how the men were trained.'

'Perhaps,' said Lymond, 'he would like to visit our training quarters at Vorobiovo. His father and friends might find it instructive indeed to accompany him. My own house is near by, and I should be honoured to offer you all hospitality.'

Diccon Chancellor said, 'We are only merchants and seamen. I am afraid we should not know how to appreciate what we saw. But Christopher would enjoy it.'

'Then let Christopher go,' Lymond said. 'Master Hislop will take him, and bring him back to my house, where you may take wine and await him in comfort. And, of course, your friends . . . ?'

But George Killingworth, mumbling into his golden beard, cravenly declined and so did Harry Lane and Ned Price. Only Best, who had so nearly smuggled the Voevoda's wife on to the *Edward Bonaventure* to join her soldier husband in Russia, accepted almost before he was asked. A marriage of convenience was what Philippa Somerville had called it. And Rob Best did not need any convincing that the Voevoda's domestic arrangements were very convenient indeed. He did not ask himself, as Diccon Chancellor did, why on earth the Voevoda should wish him to witness them.

CHAPTER FIVE

Lancelot Plummer, who had designed it, took Chancellor and Rob Best to Lymond's home at Vorobiovo, riding south through the snow, and across the broad links of the river, and up the white, wooded incline from which the Kremlin domes could be seen flashing golden against the dusky red snow-sky of sunset. Earlier that day, Christopher had gone to visit the Streltsi. D'Harcourt, riding briefly beside them, said, 'Danny is not perhaps the most maternal of guides, but he'll see the lad comes to no harm. On the other hand . . .'

He hesitated. They were riding together in the Voevoda's own massive carved sledge, drawn by matched and plumed horses, their harness whipped with silver and set largely with turquoises. Rob Best's mouth had been slightly open since they set out, but Chancellor's black-bearded face was unyielding. 'What?' he said.

'The boy is coming to join you?'

'Why not?' said Chancellor with some impatience. A tall brick wall had come into view, speckled with snow, with snow-laden trees like a painting behind it. The entrance was through a handsome tower of white stone, leaved and patterned with brick. The sledge drew up, was recognized, and allowed to pass through.

Plummer said, 'Ludo thinks our honoured leader is not to be trusted with children. You will realize this is nonsense. A harsh and holy life has our Mr Crawford, like the great and glorious St Antony. Ludo is only resentful because the Voevoda doesn't think much of his medicine. You must admit, Ludo, that Master Grossmeyer inspires a little more confidence.'

Ludovic d'Harcourt didn't reply. Chancellor said, 'But the Voevoda has a son of his own, I understood?' and was taken a little aback as they both turned and stared at him. Then d'Harcourt said, 'Yes. In England. He has a wife also. I gather they weigh equally on his conscience.'

They passed under a bower of branches, false-lit like a delicate woodcut by the riming of snow from the north. Bushes fled past them; beaded trusses of white; furred spokes of wood; and the veiled trees in the white distance almost hid the white-grey pile of a great house. Lights glimmered.

'All this is the Voevoda's?' Chancellor asked.

'It belongs, tax-free, to him and his mistress,' said Lancelot Plummer. 'So do the townships of his pomestie, his military fief. Also all the meadow and pastureland on both sides of the Moskva, and the rent of the bath stoves and bathing houses outside the walls of the city. His annual income is hard to keep track of but I imagine fifteen thousand roubles would safely cover it. . . . We designed the gardens on the lines of the Queen Dowager's at Binche, but had to take the statues inside in November because of the cold. We have marble rockeries and scented fountains, and flowers of silver and coral, with artificial showers and lightning. It would be a perfect showplace, if anyone ever came who could appreciate it.'

'Does the Tsar visit him?' Chancellor said.

'The Tsaritsa has been here,' said Plummer. The sledge was sweeping round to a halt before the dusky mass of a house, built like quartz, crystal on grey crystal, with the leaves and towers and cupolas of its rooftops like a worn flowerhead crowding the sky. A long, canopied staircase, cascading down the tiers of the building, ended in wrought copper gates between which stood the elegant, fair-haired person of their host. The grooms jumped from the sledge and drew the rugs to one side.

'Plummer wanted the sledge drawn by a team of white bears,' Lymond said, 'but I thought it seemed a touch precious.' He was wearing no jewels, but a caftan of oriental fabric so thickly embroidered that other richness was unthinkable. 'Plummer dresses me also,' added Lymond, with every appearance of candour. 'Sometimes I think he will put the weevils in jerkins and codpieces. Please be welcome, and come in from the cold.'

Chancellor got out and walked to the steps, with Best and the architect following. Looking back, he saw that d'Harcourt had remained in the sledge. He encountered the Voevoda's clever blue gaze. 'Our friend will stay and look out for Christopher,' said Francis Crawford. 'Then he can warn him against me and my habits, and we can feel relieved and secure all together. Are you tired of roast swan in garlic?'

'No,' said Diccon Chancellor in a superhuman access of courtesy.

'My God,' said Lymond, stopping and staring at him. 'In that case, I wish we had cooked it for you. Come along. Adam Blacklock is here, modestly reinstated, before you. I thought we should have a mildly cultural evening. I have not asked Mr Hoddim, who might expound too inconveniently on the laws of property, or Alec Guthrie, who is prone at times to be dismally moral. You are entering a

222

different world: a world of determined sybaritic experience. The bower of Majnún and Leylí.'

The reference struck no response from Diccon's navigational repertoire. Rob Best's mouth had opened again. Lymond looked from one to the other.

Into Lancelot Plummer's humourless eyes there came, without warning, a spark of undeniable entertainment. 'A pair of Persian lovers,' he offered.

'A pair of Persian lovers,' agreed Lymond, acknowledging the assistance. 'Do you have a mistress, Master Chancellor? It is an asset no man should deny himself. Without it, the cooking suffers abominably, and I dare not mention what goes amiss with the drainage.'

Chancellor laughed. He laughed for quite a long time because his sense of humour was touched, while his logical mathematician's brain was telling him that very likely he would be flung out of the house for it, if not banished altogether from this alarming country of Russia.

Lymond waited until he was nearly finished, and then, placing a hand on his shoulder, steered Chancellor up the remaining few steps, and along a gallery to the main double doors of the house. The light, flooding down from the sconces, gilded the bright feathered gold of his hair, and the cushioned silks of the caftan, and the faint lines round the relaxed mouth which were almost, but not quite, a smile. 'Well, thank God,' said Lymond. 'I thought you were going to go down on your knees. The occasion is expensive, but not so far meet for prayer.'

And so, with a degree of anticipation not far from horrified pleasure, Diccon Chancellor entered the country home of the Voevoda Bolshoia and his mistress, and did not look to see if there was a witch ball hung over the lintel.

It was like an evening at Penshurst.

If an evening at Penshurst could have been spiced, and scented and jewelled, and anointed, like King Raia Colambu, with oil of storax and benjamin, it would have bred handsome hours such as these, charged with good wine and light talk and music, enclosed with comfort, and incised all about with a curving, trephining wit.

The vulgarity he had expected was missing. The beautiful woman introduced by Francis Crawford as *The lady Güzel, your hostess and mistress of all you see about you,* spoke English as well as himself, with an accent part

Greek, part something else he could not identify. And recalling with compassion the pungent mind and honest gifts of Mistress Philippa, Diccon Chancellor recognized before him now, in the woman Güzel, the face and the mind and the power of a woman of destiny.

She dined with them, facing Lymond across a low, marbled table of malachite, with Plummer and Blacklock on one side, and on the other himself and the bearded young man in ermine, whom he had noticed while watching the Triumph. His name was Prince Dmitri Vishnevetsky, and he was governor of Cherkassy on the Lithuanian frontier, which made his presence in Moscow worth pondering.

He knew the Voevoda and his mistress fairly well, it was obvious, and called the Voevoda by his territorial name of Lymond, which his own men, out of habit, sometimes also used.

It suited him; Chancellor thought. Brief; impersonal; without title, or else, if you wished it, a title in itself. He tried to see him through Güzel's eyes. She had brought him to Russia, he had been told: had introduced him and his company to the Tsar; had established him in the position from which he had now risen to such eminence.

Of the eminence, there was no longer any doubt. Even had he not learned from Plummer of all the tangible marks of the Emperor's favour, it was only necessary to think of the display that afternoon; to hear the stories of the summer campaigning; to watch the people bow in the streets, as they did to the old princely families, when the Voevoda's train passed.

And for the rest, one need only look around one. Plummer had built for a king: or, being given the heart of a building, had worked it over to become a suitable setting for Russia's supreme commander. Outside, the groups of kokoshnik gables, the huddle of cones and pyramids and finials, the square stones set in thick mortar, with their black trim in scarlet sawtooth or zigzag embroidery round window and cornice and drums. And inside, the jarred doors with frames of worked stone; the gilded piers, the majolica floortiles. All the arts of Syria and the Orient, of Turkey and Venice, of France and Russia itself had been combined in the interior. They said they had flown from Stamboul as fugitives. If that were true, it was impossible to conceive how these treasures could have been smuggled out also, or how, in less than two years, so much that was perfect could have been chosen, or gifted, or brought in from the closed caravan routes that lay behind Astrakhan and Bokhara. Great God, look at the Baghdad robes she was wearing of Tyrian purple laden with birds and with panthers; and the earrings next to the smooth olive face with its large eyes and charcoal black hair; at her ring with the cameo head of a Negro, his neck encircled with diamonds.

The silk figured lampas which fell rustling over the door : the Flemish tapestry, mild and exquisite, clothing another room fitted with fine stools and carpets and bookshelves whose rolls and volumes Adam Blacklock's eyes had surveyed hungrily, his fingers smoothing the cover of the one he had borrowed, its boards laced and coloured with Persian cloisonné enamel.

The Turkish towels. The cushion covers, worked in pearled German falcons. The paintings, each with its curtain. The wrought silver fuming pots, faint with pastilles of musk and ambergris, jasmine and benzoin. The beds hung with chagrin silk and blonde lace, the lawn sheets fumed with lemon and violets. The silver. The ewers and basins; the clusters of cups; the bellied livery pots, parcel-gilt with fruit swags and strapwork. The tall Chinese jar hooped with gold, with fringes of great netted pearls hung about it. The glimmering fruit bowls and candelabra here on the table before him, and the crystal salt, and the wine jug, and the little trellised goblets on baluster stems, one of which he was emptying, and having refilled, and emptying again. . . .

Christopher came in, his eyes dilated from the darkness outside, with Ludovic d'Harcourt, the big, smiling Knight of St John. His manner, making his apologies, pleased his father in spite of himself : he did not stare at Güzel, but kissed her hand, and bowed to his host and the other men, and gave only a passing blink at the laden table where the youngest of the blue-shirted servants, a boy of perhaps less than Christopher's own age, was setting a fresh place for his son. The young manservant finished, and pulled back a stool, smiling, while Christopher, moving towards it, returned the smile warmly.

'His name is Venceslas,' said the Voevoda, whom nothing ever escaped. 'He is Polish, but speaks English very well. Sit and eat, while he serves you. You have some space to make up.'

Ludovic d'Harcourt left, closing the door ungently behind him. In spite of himself, Diccon glanced at his son, and then at the lad Venceslas serving him. The Polish boy was beautiful. Even if what the big knight had hinted was true, there was no need to concern himself unduly. The matter, he thought, was already adequately taken care of. Then they brought in the aromatic pie, which had small birds under its pastry, some stuffed with meat and some with eggs, and some fried in grape juice and limes, and the lambs stuffed with meat and ground pistachio nuts and cooked in sesame oil, and the sturgeon in broth, and the ground figs, cloves and mace, and the coloured jellies shaped like flowers and trees, and the golden spice plates with sugar plums and suckets wrapped in rolled aniseed leaves, and nougat and marzipan, and more spiced claret with honey, and Diccon Chancellor forgot everything else, looking at his son's scarlet face.

There was music later, when the table was drawn and they were seated at leisure, on cushions and long tasselled benches and tall chairs, watching the play of small flames in the brazier. Women played on the lute, and a boy sang, and accompanied himself on a curious eight-stringed lyre. Then Güzel herself took the lute, and played to them, singing in her true, mellow voice, but in a language Chancellor could not understand.

He had wondered at the beginning of this evening, what pleasure this handsome, wealthy woman had found in her creation. He knew now, looking at the powerful man they called Lymond. He had expected vulgarity; he had been afraid of embarrassing dalliance; he had been prepared to be disgusted or bored.

In the event, his host and hostess had barely exchanged a glance in the course of the evening : there was no call for it. Cool and assured, each wholly in command of all the civilized arts of giving pleasure, they wove and interwove their attentions, controlling the evening between them, guiding the talk; leading the laughter. Güzel was well read, as well as highly trained in all the womanly arts. She held Plummer in disputation and brought pen and paper so that Adam could dispose of some fanciful theory with a sweep of his long, artist's fingers.

But Lymond was more than well read. Somewhere, God

knew where, he had picked up a formal education and had bettered it. He was also well informed, to a degree Chancellor found disturbing. Political awareness one found in the Vatican, and at the courts of Henri of France, and the Emperor Charles, and in the unhappy government of England and the torn ducal palaces of Italy. One did not look for it here, in a soldier who lived by his sword, in a country so remote that the transmission of news was itself a feat worth remarking.

That kind of mind was not Güzel's creation. And that explosive combination of physical skill and intelligence, so dangerous in the world of affairs. Henry Sidney had it, but couched in a family setting which enabled him to stay in favour through two conflicting reigns. Ned Somerset had had it; and Warwick to a degree. And the de Guises in France : the Duke, the Cardinal, the Prior. Brains, hardihood, and looks.

Brains and hardihood were here in this man. And looks he had not observed before. Good hands, and a body agreeably marshalled. Hair strongly springing which was now yellow, but stranded with all the live colours between citrine and amber. An overbred face, with bone fitted to bone like the hilt to the tang of a blade; a gaze, wide and blue, and hard as the gaze of an idol. And the long, linear design of the mouth, with its hairline engraving of temper. . . .

What passion did this exquisite woman find there? The bower of Majnún and Leylí, Lymond had said; and Chancellor had long since recognized the unfair irony behind that expansive remark. Whatever took place between these two strong-willed and experienced people had nothing to do with cheap sentiment, or simple chapbook romance. He was glad that the Voevoda credited him, at least, with the wits to discover as much. And he knew why the girl Philippa never thought to speak of him except by his surname. He said to the artist, sitting beside him, 'What is Mr Crawford's Christian name?'

Adam Blacklock looked startled. He said, dropping his voice, 'Francis. Francis Crawford of Lymond and Sevigny. The Russians call him Frangike. . . . In St Mary's we prefer to use surnames.'

It was a warning, but one quite unnecessary. Diccon Chancellor could not imagine himself or anyone else addressing the Voevoda as a fellow human being. He smiled. 'You at least are back in favour,' he said.

Adam did not smile. 'Like God, he instructs with rebuke mixed with mercy. The issue was on a matter of principle,' he said.

'The Prince Vishnevetsky does not understand English,' said Lymond's voice from across the warm room. 'Can you bear to discuss the subject in Russian? Adam has been longing for sympathy.'

'I haven't asked for it,' said Adam Blacklock.

'No, you haven't, but it shows in your paintings. All those ikons in raw umber and egg yolk we're not supposed to be looking at,' Lymond said. 'Chancellor, did you know Ivan Mikhailovich Viscovatu was a painter? You should visit the ikon workshop in the armoury. When the fire destroyed half the work in the Kremlin, they brought in the best painters from Novgorod to replace all the saints in the iconostasis, and the finest ikons to copy their style from. Viscovatu's own work is not the best, but it has solid quality. Even Blacklock can be brought to admit it.'

Diccon said, 'What then is the matter of principle?'

'The Voevoda will tell you,' said Adam.

'Tancred is sensitive on the subject,' said Lymond. Christopher, his eyes shining like brass in the lamplight, was staring at him, Diccon suddenly noticed, like the eye of reason before the Divine Light. Lymond went on: '. . . but in fact the point is quite valid. Ikons are holy – you can't put them in the fire, you must bury them with full ecclesiastical honours when they're worn out. And they are painted according to a set of extremely strict rules laid down by the Church. It follows then that since most of the painting in Russia is commissioned by the Church – portraiture and sculpture are frowned on, and the Tsar is not interested in any other kind – there is no scope for the artist whatever. He cannot change his technique. He cannot experiment. He must approach every subject according to the versions in the Podlinki, the manuals of iconographic tradition, and obey the laws of the Church Council, the Stoglav. And the Stoglav holds that *he who shall paint an ikon out of his imagination shall suffer endless torment*. Have I presented your case fairly, Blacklock?'

'They've never seen an oil painting,' said Adam. 'They have plate from Germany and Persia and Italy, and fabric from China, and engineers and architects from Padua and Germany—'

'Thank you,' said Plummer.

'. . . but they've hardly seen anything later than Egyptian tomb portraits. No hellenistic painting, and hardly any classical sculpture. Russian art is frozen. It's been frozen for three hundred years, and men like Viscovatu are using force to keep it that way. Lifetimes are being wasted: all that skill and devotion squandered on nothing – on something which has already been done, and better, by painters now dead.'

There was a passionate silence. 'You see?' said Güzel gravely. 'All this frustration and ill will because no one has thought of separating art from religion. I wondered if Mr Blacklock had noticed my Egyptian portraits?'

Adam, caught off-balance, stared at her, and then in the direction of her amused glance. Chancellor turned his head also. There had been a sarcophagus, now he remembered, in one of the rooms they had passed through before supper. An old one, painted with lotus-flowers.

This was not a sarcophagus, but a statue perhaps nine inches high, delicately made, of a man's body with the head of an eagle. It was formed of pure gold. 'Thoth, the God of music and letters,' said Güzel, and Prince Vishnevetsky, rising, stood with the thing in his hands and looked at his hostess with interest.

'He said, 'What gave me the impression these coffins held spices?'

'Because I told you so,' said Güzel. Rising in her turn, she took the small statue from him and replaced it carefully on the inlaid chest from which he had taken it. 'You may ask the officers of the Tsar's Customs. Despite my protestations, they opened the next coffin sent me.'

'Then . . . ?' said Vishnevetsky. Carefully groomed, his hands loaded with rings, he looked what he was, a romantic leader from an old princely family, once Russian and now long settled in the Volynia, with behind him the ancient culture of Lithuania, where the palaces were garnished with books and paintings and sculpture, and the Italian court of Queen Bona had accustomed her nobles to luxury.

'They did not open the bodies,' said Güzel. 'The Egyptians also married their art to their religion. Below the skin, under the breastbone; within the cage of the pelvis, they left precious tokens, for the use of the dead. The comforts of this room were bought with gold which travelled to me from Egypt in a stronger casket than any smith could devise : a wrapping of dried skin and bone dust. Does it console you?' she said, smiling, to Adam.

He shrugged his shoulders and sat back, smiling in turn against his will as the interlude slackened his outrage. Prince Vishnevetsky said, to no one in particular, 'And who knows this man Viscovatu? He is Clerk of the Council, and a priest, and a painter. Is he a man, blessed in the eyes of the Almighty, who puts before all else the strict and terrible service of God?'

There was a decent silence. 'This is a man who detests Sylvester,' Lymond remarked.

Prince Vishnevetsky opened one dark eye.

'. . . and who complained to the Stoglav about Sylvester's new four-part commission for the Blagoveschensky Cathedral to such effect that the Council laid down the right to supervise the ethical content of any other work Sylvester might negotiate. Sylvester being priest of the Blagoveschensky and the Tsar's adviser and confessor.'

'I know,' said Vishnevetsky. 'So religion is merely an excuse?'

'It seems likely,' said Lymond.

Prince Dmitri Vishnevetsky glanced round. His gaze rested on the candlesticks and the silver-gilt brazier; on the crystal dishes of ginger, and orange in sugar; on the little sewn cushions of roses, pressed behind Güzel's velvet shoulders. 'And the Voevoda Bolshoia is afraid of Viscovatu?' he said.

'He controls the fate of the Muscovy Company,' Lymond said. 'Mr Chancellor and his friend Mr Killingworth would not be at all happy if the Tsar took against Catholics. And an attack on the Russian Orthodox religion would be taken as a Catholic attack. No one will pay the least heed to the grotesque inner springs of Blacklock's spiritual mechanism : they have never heard of the freedom of the artist and couldn't imagine what it meant anyway. They would merely recognize, and very readily recognize, that the heretic is hacking at one of the dearest roots of their foundation. Then they fling us all out and march into Lithuania.'

Güzel, smiling, said nothing. Christopher had shifted his position merely because he found he had cramp, but had still not taken his eyes from the lazy, lamplit face of his host. Plummer was looking at Adam Blacklock, and Adam, his lips tight, was gazing at the floor. Prince Vishnevetsky said gracefully, 'Really?'

'Really,' affirmed Lymond dryly. 'Who is more Catholic than the Emperor Charles? Neglect the Tartars; strike a blow at the Baltic countries and you strike a blow at the Emperor. If the Tsar pushes right through to the sea, he won't even need England, and her precious Frozen Sea route.'

Chancellor said, clearing his throat, 'You told us to act as if there had been no change of religion. The Tsar knows we have a Reformed Church.'

'The Tsar knows the late King Edward had a Reformed Church,' Lymond said. 'And he also knows that the present Queen Mary is the stoutest upholder of Roman Catholicism in Europe, because I told him myself. The device worked well enough for the first weeks, and, once confirmed in his plans for the Company, he is capable of ignoring unpleasant facts, so long as he feels they are not being subtly withheld from him. But a formal protest from the Council of the Hundred Chapters and the Metropolitan Makary would be a little hard to ignore. Thus the future of nations hangs on Blacklock's compulsion to paint St Theodore Tiron, legs astride, in a feathered bonnet, a smirk and a surcoat. Mr Chancellor does not believe it.'

'No one would believe it, put like that,' said Güzel.

'No one believes me anyway,' Lymond said. 'I am kept to be ornamental: a Cypriot sheep combed for my myrrh. In Stamboul it was simpler. There is no monkery in Islam.'

'And no profit either,' said Vishnevetsky.

It was almost over. Before they left, Güzel led them to see Plummer's masterpiece: the winter garden enclosed on the rooftop, and warmed with tall stoves in glazed tile. Here were rose trees in tubs, and plum and cherry trees and all kinds of flowers, and in the centre a pool with carp swimming, in dressed stone lined and bottomed in lead, and fed by a fountain with gargoyles.

Even this they hardly distinguished for the moment, because of the birds. These flew freely without cages among the flowering trees: doves and linnets, chaffinches and siskins, the rare white goldfinch, and vivid aliens Chancellor had heard nothing of. He saw peacocks.

Christopher was mute, but Best exclaimed aloud and so did Chancellor, turning to Plummer to praise it. Prince Vishnevetsky, by Güzel's side, surveyed it in silence, and then spoke reflectively. 'And does the Tsar sit content in the small white box of the Granovitaya Palace, his vain-glorious Bologna; his second Ferrara? Or have you not shown him this?'

Plummer's high-coloured, handsome face was smooth with food and wine and merited commendation. 'If he wishes, I may build him a palace with ten times the opulence of this one. Twenty times. He has only to ask me.

'Remembering,' said the Voevoda's cool voice, 'that the annual revenue of an architect is a round forty roubles in Russia. Building is your pleasure but soldiering, I would remind you and Blacklock, is your business and profit.'

Chancellor said, 'You said the Tsaritsa had been here. Perhaps she will persuade the Tsar to house his court more stylishly. Or even to purchase some secular paintings.'

Güzel smiled. A dove, its wings drenched with the sea-weed and roses of ambergis, flew to her shoulder, and he became aware that the thin, arching flutings he heard were not from some mysterious, unseen consort but from wings with silver flutes bound to their feathers. Güzel said, 'The Tsaritsa Anastasia is beautiful, and has borne him a living son, after the deaths of three children. I have a copy below of the ikon they made for him: the *Mernaya* of St John Climacus, which they make to the size of the newly born baby. It is seventeen inches long.' She paused smiling, and lifted the dove on her fingers, and threw it gently from her into the spray of the fountain: the sweet, wavering note of its music rose and vanished.

'She was chosen from fifteen hundred, as the Orientals choose, and has been a good wife to him, as Oriental wives are. But she will persuade him of nothing.'

'He despises women,' said Prince Vishnevetsky. Alas!' There will be no Diane de Poitiers, no Mary, Regent of Flanders, no Medici Queen, no child Queen or Dowager Regent of Scotland, no Tudor Queen ruling in Russia. In a hive of Queens, Russia holds the last masculine cell. The Athos of the world's monarchy. The Tsardom which does not admit the power of women.' He lifted the orange-tipped fingers of Güzel's small, perfect hand and looked at them. 'And that is dangerous.'

The dark, painted eyes returning his smile were profoundly decorous. 'A queen does not need to be crowned,' said Güzel, 'in order to rule.'

*

'They've got forty siege guns and fifty small cannon,' said Christopher, on their way down the stairs.

'Oh?' said his father.

'They've got six thousand horse and foot under training. You should see the stables. They've got a tilt-yard. They run at the ring, and they have the quintain and squills and trick riding and hippas. . . . They put me on a man's shoulders and we ran at another man on a man's shoulders and tried to knock the man off.'

'And did you?' said Diccon, when he had followed this.

'No. They have a steam room and when they're tired with exercise they lie there till they sweat, and then go and jump in the river.'

'And did you?' said Diccon.

'Yes,' said his son.

And looking at his bright eyes Diccon Chancellor apologized, silently, to the absent person of Ludovic d'Harcourt.

CHAPTER SIX

Güzel was downstairs, when Lymond returned from seeing them off. He found her in the room where they had been sitting, replacing in its box the blue and gold oblong of the child Ivan's *Mernaya*. She said, without looking round, 'Were you content?'

'Heliogabalus,' Lymond said, 'would have had the banquet spoons engraved with the lot of each guest. Ten pounds of gold or else ten pounds of lead. Ten flies or ten dromedaries. . . . It did, I think, all that was required.'

Güzel closed the box and moving back, leaned on the carved golden back of a chair. 'I have a feeling,' she said, 'that Master Best has marched off to rouse the rabble to storm the homes of the decadent.'

'He won't get far,' said Lymond peacefully. 'The rabble live in small villages separated by miles of unamenable forest, and have never been instructed in the art of storming, or even of resisting unfriendly invaders.'

'But you are teaching them,' Güzel said. 'From all those forts you and Plummer have created, you are teaching them.'

'The land must be defended,' Lymond said. He picked up the Persian book Adam had looked at, and stood, weighing it between his long fingers. 'Is that a bad thing?'

'Bad for the peasants, perhaps,' Güzel said. 'And Master Chancellor was taciturn. Or so I thought. He remained a great length of time in your writing room.'

'He was watching me write,' Lymond said. 'They are sending dispatches by post through to Danzig. I gave him a letter to France and a letter to Malta. And another, direct to Philippa Somerville, freeing her on my part from the formal contract of marriage.'

Her ringed hands, hanging laced from the chair back, made no movement at all. She said, 'I thought they demanded your presence.'

Francis Crawford looked up, with lucid blue eyes, from the book. 'Master Chancellor was good enough to say flatly that he realized the proposal was foolish. And that he would report to the English authorities that the only prospect of dissolving this marriage was to accept my written statement. He said he recognized that I had found my home and my life-work in Russia.'

Behind the calm, painted face there was still no discernable emotion. 'Perhaps then he will reassure the Tsar,' Güzel said.

Lymond shrugged. 'The Tsar will be reassured when the ships sail next summer without me. I have told him I am staying. I don't intend to labour the point.'

I have a word of advice, Diccon Chancellor had said. *Defer your public decision. Don't announce categorically that you are not leaving Russia. For if you do, I believe we carry on our ships someone paid to kill you.*

But Francis Crawford said nothing of that to the woman who had brought him to Russia, but drew the talk into minor cadenzas, and kissed her hand, and took his leave for the night.

It was late. Replacing the inkhorn and casing his papers, and marshalling his wide, impeccable desk, he made a decision of no importance, and instead of returning to his room sent his body-servant, one of the anonymous changing team who served his person, to warn the bath keeper that he was coming.

The baths in Güzel's house were Turkish in fashion. No one sweated at bath stoves, and, like the Streltsi, jumped naked into the river. The dressing-room was silk-hung, with Persian rugs on the floor, and low cushioned sofas lining the walls. The tepidarium and calidarium were in marble, with wall fountains and a stepped marble bath, from which the steam, with inspired ingenuity, rose straight to furnish the winter garden with warmth.

Above all, it was silent. The servant who disrobed his master; the masseur who oiled the scarred, highly trained body lying still on the marble after the bath, knew better than to comment on their work. The masseur's powerful hands moved kneading over the spider-white whip marks; the old wounds, gained in battle and out of it; the flourished white brand of the galleys. Strong and balanced and limber, the flesh warmed and eased to his moulding. What teemed within the still, arm-cradled head was the Voevoda's own affair: he looked asleep, but the masseur knew from bitter past experience that he was not.

Only afterwards, when he was standing barefoot in the dressing-room with the servant placing over his shoulders the short, furlined caftan he used as a nightgown, and binding round his waist the thin fringed silk of the girdle, did Lymond motion him suddenly to be still, and in the silence, cock his damp head, listening.

The servant waited, obedient. Far out in the mews, the man who tended the eagle was whistling. The calidarium boilers murmured. The iced fountain ran, distantly, like a song. Above them all, faintly, swooped the ctesiphon sound of thin fluting.

'It is the doves,' the servant said; and stopped, aghast at his own temerity.

'I know,' said Lymond; and catching sight of the man's ashen face, said curtly, 'Had I wanted a deaf-mute, I should have bought one.'

Colour crept back into the man's face and then left it. For the Voevoda, stirring the day garments he had discarded, had transferred to the waist of his caftan a small, glittering knife one could not have guessed that he carried, and then, unhurriedly placing each foot into the thin, curling slipper presented him, said, 'I am going up to the winter garden. If I do not call for you within the next five minutes, you may retire.'

The slippered feet made no sound. The furlined caftan,

calflength, did not drag on the steps. As Lymond mounted, the golden light from the sconces lit the fine coloured silks, full of pagan motifs: sirens and monsters and Alconosts, the birds with human heads who inhabit Paradise, where they delight the virtuous with their songs. He opened the door of the winter garden.

A dove fell like a flower at his feet.

They lay like orchids, veined and tender with wings queerly cloven, on the pool and the trees and the bushes, and on the blue Isnik tiles of the floor. As he stood, another flute-note cascaded, gentle as sallow, and bright feathers touched his slipper, and a drop of thick blood. Then the bird fell: a rare one, brought with long hardships from the islands of Java. 'How generous is your mistress,' said the light, mocking voice of Prince Dmitri Ivanovich Vishnevetsky, 'who said that as your guest I might hunt where I pleased.'

Half veiled by the blossom, he leaned against the opposite wall: a man strongly made with cleft chin and soft chestnut hair and moustache, and all the arts of a courtier. In his hands was a small Turkish bow; and across the spangled silk of his shirt hung a quiver. He smiled as he ceased speaking, and bending the bow, took aim, lightly, at a fluttering host of birds calling from the cherry tree over his head.

The Voevoda smiled. 'I am more generous still,' he said, and drew back his arm, the fingers brushing his girdle. A flick of silver, arching through the air, touched Vishnevetsky's bow with a click, and the Prince made a sound, cut off at once, as he stumbled off-balance, the sliced wood and hemp whipping about him: his arms flung involuntarily apart. Lymond's knife, its chased hilt gold in the lamplight, lay on the cracked tiles at his feet. Lymond said, 'I give you both weapon and quarry.'

Vishnevetsky bent, watching him, and picked up the knife. Then he unbuckled and laid down the quiver. 'You visit the birds,' he said. 'Then by all means, let us spare them. Crassus, they say, adored a marine eel which came to feed from his hand, decked with pearl collar and earrings. And when it died, he wore mourning. Let us spare the birds, if they are your passion. You have thrown your mistress often enough in my path.'

He moved as he spoke, between the thin, fruiting trees, treading the long, jade-pale stems of carnations. Lymond, empty-handed and calm, eased between the branches, never quite coming into view, while above the birds jostled still, shrilly piping, and displaced from a leaf, a plucking of white down rocked through the air to their feet. Lymond said, gently, 'I should test a Tartar Cossack, for courage and honesty. A Lithuanian prince I should have to accept, from what I know of him.'

Dmitri Vishnevetsky moved closer, but slowly. 'And what do I know of Scotland, a nation of tankard-bearers?'

Lymond said, 'I might say, perhaps, that in Scotland hospitality is sacred. It is also a country which has never been subdued by the enemy over its frontier, as you have never been able to subdue the Tartars.' There was a stand of tapers, ring upon ring on a wrought iron base just beside him. While still speaking he unhooked the snuffer and pressed out each light, one by one. Half the garden fell into darkness.

'We have such laws in Lithuania too,' said the Prince. 'But they apply only between gentlemen. So, your country being too mean to please you, it seems you have found the way to pomp and power, garlic to a gamecock, through the twelve modes of Cyrène. But I do not think I choose to find my life's work subject to a mercenary's whim.'

Lymond's eyes were wide and blue. 'Should I call for help?' he said.

Vishnevetsky put up an elegant hand and pressed a bough of white flowers out of his way. 'To put me out?' he said. 'Then the Cherkassy Cossacks would be denied to the Tsar and his army for ever. To defend you against my attack? The Voevoda's reputation would never recover. Besides, am I attacking you? I have trifled with your mistress's aviary, that is all. Surely the Tsar's supreme commander would not set the idle life of a bird against the favour of one who might be a powerful ally?'

'Subject to your whim?' Lymond said.

Vishnevetsky smiled. 'You take my point,' he said.

Lymond had stopped moving backwards. 'I wonder,' he said thoughtfully, 'what makes you think I can be influenced by personal violence?'

Prince Vishnevetsky had not stopped. 'I have no doubt of it,' he said cheerfully. 'I miscall you and your nation, and you stand behind bushes, a pretty mouset, and talk about shouting for help.'

Lymond stayed where he was. 'It seems reasonable,' he said. 'You have a knife and I haven't.'

'But you have another,' said the Prince. He had moved round the pool: a pillar, twined with some flowering shrub, was all that stood between him and the quarry Lymond had offered.

'No,' Lymond said. 'But keep your knife. I cannot throw an unarmed guest into my pool. It would offend my fine instincts. . . .' And he finished speaking, Vishnevetsky laughed and sprang.

The second candelabra was at Lymond's elbow. He lifted it like a tilting-pole and drove it, with all the power of his shoulders, at the Lithuanian's body.

The force struck the candles streaming asunder. Some fell. Some sprang like the spines of a hedgehog. But the edge of the ring, in a hissing, glutinous mass, struck the stuff of Vishnevetsky's bright quilted sleeve and set it alight as he ducked and hurled himself sideways, half overset by the weight of the blow.

The candelabra fell to the ground, in a crash of smashed tiles and rent foliage, and like napkins in a gale the remaining birds rose calling into the twilight. The last candles went out, and darkness fell on the garden.

Fragile terror filled the black air, with the buffeting of wings and the confused music of flutes. The air held all the life of the garden: the scent of blood and of jasmine, the stench of candlegrease and of singed and burned taffeta. From the ground below there was no sound after Vishnevetsky, thrusting his shoulder among the green leaves, had stifled the flames, and taking fresh grip on his knife stood waiting, somewhere, as his eyes widened in the dark. A siskin, crying, touched Lymond's cheek and beat wildly off, its heart pulsing. Lymond spoke.

> Seven Peters seven times
> Send Mary by her Son
> Send Bridget by her mantle
> Send God by his strength
> Between us and the faery host
> Between us and the demons of the air . . .

The voice wandered, tangled with flute music. '. . . Your birds are taking revenge.'

It was true, damn him. His ears clouded by bird-sounds, Vishnevetsky had to strain all his acute senses to hear and follow the other man, his arm smarting under the fragments of quilting. A fool not to foresee that. And a fool to underestimate a man at the pitch of his training. It had been necessary to teach humility to this ambitious alien, and to show to the woman Güzel the quality of the choice she had made. Honour now demanded a good deal more than humiliation. . . .

The knife was knocked from his hand.

It did not seem possible. He flung out his hands, whirling round, and struck the edge of a tub. There was nothing but flowers, and space, and blackness. He could not see: neither of them could see. He had made no sound which could have betrayed him. And yet his right arm had been found somehow and struck, so that the knife had fallen lost on the ground. A voice, distantly, said. 'Not alike are the inmates of the fire and the dwellers of the garden: the dwellers of the garden are they that are the achievers.'

He was mocking him, the dog, by revealing his own whereabouts. A bird blundered into him and rose with a whirr to the rooftop, leaving a draught of scent from its jasmine-soaked wings. But the flute wailing was less, and for the first time you could hear plainly the quiet spray of the fountain. The birds were quietening. Delayed by a second, Vishnevetsky's very competent brain followed suddenly a train of thought from that soft breeze of perfume. His tunic. His singed tunic must be signalling his presence as clearly as a drenching of ambergis. Raising his hands, he ripped down the fastenings and dropped the ruined cloth quietly to the ground. The warm air from the steam pipes touched the sweat on his brown, half-naked body. Then, struck by a better thought, he picked the taffeta up and moving noiselessly, one hand before him, found a little lemon tree and draped the tunic over one of its branches. Then, taking three steps back, he placed his fingers on the trunk and stood without moving, all his sharpened senses devoted to listening.

The birds were quiet. Once, high above, a leaf rustled and once, from across the pool, he heard the throaty sound of a dove, and the rasp of claws on the spars. But from below, nothing. Then the bark of the lemon tree shook under his fingers, and he sprang.

The Tsar's foreign mercenary was there. Vishnevetsky's

hands gripped a right arm and shoulder and held, while he kicked with the full force of his iron-shod boot.

He heard the other man's explosive grunt as it landed. But the Voevoda was already giving way before it. He did more. He used his rigid right arm as a fulcrum to swing his whole body against Vishnevetsky's. The Lithuanian felt the sudden increase of weight in his grasp, and before he could recover was hurled backwards, the other man on top of him, among the wooden borders and tubs of the garden. Something cracked hard against the ridge of his spine and he roared, just as the Voevoda's body landed with a crash half over him, winding them both. He kicked, and something caught his boot in both hands.

'Bears,' said Lymond, 'have weakest heads, as Lions have strongest. When forced to cast themselves down from any rocks, they cover their Heads with their Feet, and lie for a time Astonished.'

More bombast. It didn't worry Prince Vishnevetsky, who was beginning to get his opponent's measure. He grinned, and pulled his foot out of the boot. As he rolled away, he felt the other boot dragged off as well, against the full power of his kick. Vishnevetsky whirled and got to his feet.

'Now!' said Lymond cheerfully; and jumped at him.

While no kin to Milo of Crotan, who carried a calf daily to season his muscles, and continued to carry it while it developed through heifer to cow, Dmitri Vishnevetsky was a formidable professional, unfairly handicapped by the caprice of his adversary. Once at grips with him, feeling for the eyes with his fingers or the back of his neck with his strong knotted arm, the Governor of Cherkassy was able at length to employ all the arts he used so liberally with his Cossacks, and to thank his trainers who had fought in Spain and in Sweden and in Germany, and had taught him to counter the kind of nasty clip he got now, as they staggered together, and how to somersault out of trouble, taking his enemy if possible with him.

The Voevoda, it seemed, had been soundly taught also. Both men back-heeled expertly, and the first abrupt fall came when Vishnevetsky hooked the Voevoda's left leg on the inside, just below the calf, and the Scotsman gave way, so that they both fell with a crash, taking a trailing plant with them and upsetting the birds all over again.

The rest of the fight indeed, the Lithuanian seemed to remember, was implected with the lyre-like concerto of the birds, and their battering wings, and the crack of splintering pots and split tiles, or the deafening splash as some snapped bough or rocking statue cannoned into the pool.

At the time, he was hardly aware of it. His body ached, from the battering wood and porcelain and alabaster into which he slammed in the dark, cursing the blood and feathers which betrayed his bare feet, and the spray which made his hands slippery. Then he obtained the grip he wanted on the splendid Alconosts on the Voevoda's silk robe and he was able for the first time to throw him. He must have twisted and risen like the marine eel of the Lithuanian's taunt, because he came back through the spray while Vishnevetsky crouched, hands apart and panting, listening for him. The change in the sound of the water gave him his warning, but when he touched the Voevoda, his hands slid from bare, dripping skin. The Alconosts had been discarded. With no regret, Prince Vishnevetsky abandoned a finicky programme of leverage and settled down to some straightforward dirty fighting of a nastiness quite unparalleled.

He had not then seen the brand on Francis Crawford's bruised back. There is no foul trick in Europe or out of it which is not known to a chained galley slave. As the Lithuanian's teeth closed on his arm, Lymond drew a long, aching breath and used, in quick succession, the flat of his hand, his knee and his foot. Then, as Vishnevetsky's grip slackened, he began, very fast, all the unpleasant strokes. He stopped short of irreparable injury, and he collected some extremely painful cuffs and twists and punches himself. But he halted for nothing until, with the Lithuanian limp in his hands, he lifted him high over his head and cast him, with a flounce of water that reached to the ceiling, among the dashing carp in the swirling, invisible pond.

The Voevoda Bolshoia waited a moment, breathing quickly, until there was a movement in the lapping water and a dim blur in the whirling darkness, from which he judged that the Governor of Cherkassy had lifted his head and was sitting, sluggishly, at the foot of the pond. Then Lymond himself slipped into the stormy waves at the pool edge and, with a few long, lazy strokes, drove himself under and up from the cool, flowered water, until in turn he half sat, half lay, head thrown back, into the pool at the other man's side. 'You were saying?' he said.

Prince Dmitri Vishnevetsky moved his stiff lips. 'I was saying,' he said, 'that I believed my Cossacks would follow you.'

The Voevoda's eyes, unseen in the darkness, were wide and calm and smiling. 'I don't want them to follow me,' he said. 'They will follow you, as always. My hope is that you and I may find ourselves yokefellows. It seems to me our whims are well matched.'

There was a moment's silence. Then Vishnevetsky said gravely, 'I fear the winter garden has suffered.'

Somewhere at the side of the pool was a tinder box. Lymond made his way groping towards it, and found a candle, and turned in a moment, the golden flame high in his hand. Ghostly as ruined Atlantis about them hung the shreds of Güzel's winter garden. With equal gravity, the Voevoda looked at Vishnevetsky, his battered body supine in the water.

'Even doves,' Lymond said, 'sometimes quarrel.'

Prince Dmitri Vishnevetsky began to laugh. He was still laughing, holding his aching ribs, when Lymond pulled him out.

*

The Governor of Cherkassy was in bed and the house was totally silent when Lymond was free at last to walk down the stairs, the key of the winter garden in the pocket of his stained caftan, and make his way to his room.

The wall-sconces were burning low, their glow falling like waterlight on the fine tapestries hung throughout the long galleries which joined each wing of the great household. When, turning a corner, Lymond saw the loitering figure before him he thought at first it was a night-steward, tending the flame. Then he saw it was not, but the cloaked figure of a boy who slowed still further as he watched, and then stopping, looked over his shoulder as if he had heard Lymond's step.

But he had not, because at the sight of him he stood perfectly rigid, his dark eyes dilated, and remained staring, without speech, while Lymond in turn walked up and stopped. 'Venceslas?'

The boy took his hands away from his throat. 'My lord.'

Below the fine, curling hair, his face was as stiff as a sledge of shot hares : his eyes, on Lymond's face, were quite blank and darkly sleepless. He ran his hands up and down the cloak edge. Lymond said, 'What are you doing? It must be four hours to dawn.'

The fingers ran up and down, up and down. The cloak slipped and he caught it, his soft fingers trembling. 'My lady called me.'

Beneath the cloak, plain to see, had been the sheen of bare flesh. There was a pause of hardly perceptible length. Then the Voevoda's veiled eyes smiled. 'I think not,' he said. 'I think perhaps one of the Mistress's charming young sempstresses is waiting somewhere . . . or one of Leila's helpers? Am I right?'

The beautiful, clear face was grey-white as water-filled glass. 'Yes,' he said.

'And you wonder if you are to be whipped, or if I will bear with the frailty and unadvisedness of your youth. The answer is that I will not bear with it, but I shall not whip you either; nor shall your mistress. Go back to your room, and make no more assignations until you are a man. There will be time enough then. Too much time.'

The eyes were pools of darkness : the fingers ran up and down. 'Go!' said Lymond sharply; and the boy jumped, and clutched his cloak, and turning, ran down the gallery.

Lymond watched him go. Long after Venceslas had vanished he stood there unmoving, looking at nothing. Unlike those of the boy, his hands were quite still, their knuckles discoloured with bruising. His body was drying within the wet fur of the robe : his hair had sprung wet from its combing and his face, almost unmarked, was set in an expression of familiar indifference under which was something frighteningly different : the face of a man who once looked upon the dead body of an archer he did not love, called Robin Stewart. Then he turned to the door beside him, which was that of Güzel, and knocked.

The walls were thick, and she had heard nothing. When she called 'Enter' and he opened the door gently, she sat up in her lamplit drift of lace pillows, her black hair ribboned loose from her shoulders, her arched, henna-laced feet crossed like a nun's below the fine white Egypt robe, banded with coloured silk braiding. There was kohl on her eyes, and every fold of her body was scented, but she wore no jewels save a thread of gold which spanned her neck as if drawn by a quill, and ran between her breasts under the cuff of her robe. Held between cream and honey, the muted colour was exact from the undyed raw silk of the hangings to the sarsanet cover on which she was lying, woven in buff silk with spears and flowers and trees and Saracen horsemen. In all that lamplit mosaic within the dark warmth of the room, the only delicate accents were the darkness of her smoky black hair; and the stain on her lips.

Her cheeks had no flush of colour. The smooth olive of her skin did not change, nor did she move after her first sudden rising, except to lay her hands softly before her in her lap. Then she said, 'You have something to say to me? If you lock the door, we shall not be interrupted.'

He did as she asked, and when he looked up she was smiling. She said, 'Your hands. . . . Whose bones have thoughtlessly blemished them?'

Lymond spread his palms, smiling a little as he glanced down at the ruined caftan. 'Dmitri Vishnevetsky's. I have been removing the dross which bars his spiritual progress. I fear you must avoid the winter garden for the next few days.'

Straight-backed and wholly composed, she considered it. 'Poor Lancelot Plummer. And how is Vishnevetsky?'

'Wet,' said Lymond, 'but unimpaired, mark you, even in dignity. He has decreed that we are worthy of his Cherkassy Cossacks.'

'Ah,' said Güzel. 'The note called Coquetry and the note called True. Was it necessary to make your point with your fists?'

'Yes,' Lymond said. 'It was what he wished; and because he is a romantic, he is satisfied. The rewards of immaturity. Others do not have the same requital.'

A flicker of colour ran through her even skin, and was gone. She said, 'The mature are not incapable of making their wishes known. It is a matter of choice.'

'It is a matter of dignity,' Lymond said. 'And patience. And reticence.' He had moved half-way into the room and had come to rest on the arm of a couch, his hand laid like a fan upon the carved wood of the back. He said, 'Did you know that for the first hundred years after Mohammed, the King of Persia always kept a horse saddled for his return, and one of his daughters reserved for the Prophet? I wonder if the Prophet laughed, or wept for them.'

'They would be honoured,' Güzel said. She moved, giving a small sigh, and slipping her feet down the bed-skirts stood for a moment on the silk carpet, her linen robe straight as the robe of Osiris. She said, 'Life has many strands. You will take some wine?'

The swan-necked flagon with its silver chain stood beyond the circle of lamplight, where the paintings and the figured hangings and the diapered silver-gilt of the haunch pots reflected all the mosaic reds of the brazier. Flat-backed as a caryatid, her beautiful Greek face without expression, the mistress of all the Voevoda's great establishment laid her hand on the flask and found it taken from her, gently, by the Voevoda's hand from behind. Life has many strands,' said Francis Crawford, 'but with one lacking, it is a lame thing. I have been absent too long. I have come to ask forgiveness.'

Her hands dropped to her sides, she stared without turning at the brazier. She said, 'You have been absent too long. You are forgiven your debt.'

She could feel his warmth behind her, but he did nothing to touch her. He said, 'You must be more generous than that. You must say my debt is paid.'

'It is paid,' she said.

They were speaking in English. He was so close that she could see his hand leave the flask and rest on the table, the light from the silver lacing the bruised and capable fingers. He said, 'And what of your obligation?'

She turned then, to see his face. 'Mine?'

In the loose, glimmering play of the light his gaze was direct and blue and, for once unequivocal. 'You dragged out of Greece a sorry carcass, rotten with opium, and barred against every assault of the senses. You have destroyed the weak places and undermined, one by one, all the bastions. . . . They are all open, Güzel.'

'And my obligation?' she said with composure, while the thread round her throat ran with sudden, shimmering light.

'To walk through,' said Francis Crawford, and raising his hands to her shoulders bent and kissed her for the first time, softly, full on the lips.

Her lids fell closed. Her breath, issuing, made a short

245

sound, without words. Then her lessoned mouth opened and her body, trained and pliant as honeysuckle, joined its hard warmth to his. After a while, without speaking, he carried her to the lamplit pillows where she lay within the wick-black smoke of her hair, and putting up her fingers, threw back the abused, furlined folds of his night robe.

The fathomless eyes, searching up into his, possessed all the old secrets and mysteries, and had practised them. The concupiscent tongue, the soliciting fingers, the flexible body had owned many men, and had admitted few masters outwith her own implacable will.

But this time, her arts scarcely hid what her senses demanded. His hands wooed her, gleaning her body. And bringing to this his own long experience, every breath he took was a caress, designed only to please her. While her fingernails strayed and her lips changed beneath their long, unceasing engagement the jewel between her spired breasts jumped and jumped with her high, suppressed breathing until abruptly she found herself ultimately on that blind plateau from which there is no retreating. Her hands opened, stricken. Then, hard and sudden and sure, Lymond impacted the jewel between them.

Her needs over the years had become complex. Her passions, over the years, had found such force that one fulfilment could hardly assuage them. Couch to cushion to carpet became soft and desperate stations, moving from urging to torment to investment once again. And with an odd, detached insight, giving and withholding, exciting and loitering, he knew how to find her appetite, and force it into violence and withstand it without mercy, until she was aware of nothing in the whole moaning world but her famine. And then of nothing in the world but the exquisite act which occluded it. And towards dawn hunger, fed and fed, at last allowed her to lie dispossessed in dreaming calm, satisfied.

It was after that, when Leila had been sent from the locked door, that Güzel stirred from a half-sleeping haze to say, 'Do you never sleep? They say you don't.'

'And so they should.' Hands behind his head, Francis Crawford was gazing up at the tester, not at her. His hair, hazed by the sun from the window, was dry now and loose on the pillow. His lids were long and clear like the embroidered face on the cloth at her side, with its border of tall branching letters and its long figure, the mailed feet like willow leaves. He said, 'Commanders never slumber, nor share the common pursuits of the vulgar. In fact, I prefer to sleep alone. It is an indulgence you will have to permit me.'

She closed her eyes smiling, and then opened them, to study his face once again, fair and smooth and burnished like ivory, with no lax muscle in it. She said, 'I have brought you across many years for this night,' and watched his mind awake, and his mouth deepen a little at the corner. He did not look at her.

He said, 'Since Djerba?'

'Since long before Djerba. I had heard of you.'

He turned on his elbows in a sudden, swift movement and cast her one of the wide, blue looks she could not yet understand. 'I hope,' he said, 'that whatever you heard, you have not been disappointed.'

She smiled at him. 'I heard of your ability. I heard enough to know you could do what you are achieving in Russia today. As for the rest—'

'There has been no rest,' said Lymond, 'that I can remember.'

'. . . as for the rest, I think we have been to the same school, you and I; and to the same trade thereafter. Man has an animal appetite, or I would be nothing. I too have had my Margaret Lennox and my Agha Morat and my child-whore Joleta Reid Malett . . . more of each, and for longer. It has destroyed neither of us. And now nothing can hinder us.'

She could not see his eyes, but his lips were smiling. 'No,' he agreed. 'Excellent the recompense and goodly the resting-place. Now nothing can hinder us.'

He did not turn. For a moment, she lay without speaking and then, her thought turning again to the pleasure of the night, she lifted her hand, and ran its fingers, peacefully, down the suppleness of his skin. She remarked, 'Do you know what you said?'

He turned, his head in his chin. 'What did I say? When?'

'Last night.'

'I seem,' said Lymond, 'to remember saying a great many things last night. The manifest fool is known by every ninth word he says requiring verification. Was it ungallant?'

His mistress dropped her fingers and lay back in her

247

turn. Through the hangings, the snow-light touched kindly the black-browed face with its deep eyes and hard-boned, beautiful nose. 'You said, "I must apologize for the faint smell of fish." '

For a moment he looked at her, then he began to laugh softly. He buried his face in the pillow and went on laughing for quite a long time until it ran down, like a clock, and he said, 'I didn't think that you heard that.'

'Fish?' said Güzel.

He turned round, his fine skin flushed a little with laughter. 'The carp in the winter garden. I do apologize. Lover never came to his mistress in the state I did yesterday . . .

'. . . I can only say,' said Francis Crawford tolerantly from the high ravaged bed, 'that whoever slept with Dmitri Vishnevetsky fared much, much worse.'

CHAPTER SEVEN

I believe we carry on our ships someone paid to kill you.
So Diccon Chancellor had found himself saying to Lymond. And as he toiled through those dark months of winter, exercising a spurious authority and disentangling the assorted affairs of his drapers, Chancellor found himself no nearer discovering which of them he could trust.

What of the four whom on the surface he had learned to know so well in Moscow – statuesque, bearded Killingworth; burly Rob Best, Ned Price, the young, clever wits of Harry Lane? Or the two company sons, Judde and Hawtrey, who dashed back and forwards, overturning sledges, from Vologda; or Barnes's protégé Christopher Hudson, the first to get through with the delayed stock from Yaroslavl, and the man with the keenest nose for a bargain? It was Hudson who picked up sturgeons at seven altines each, which would cost nine marks for worse bought in Danzig. It was Hudson who reported that hemp was cheaper too, by two shillings and sixpence a hundred than in Danzig, and that George had been right to refuse twelve roubles for his cloth at Vologda, but should have jumped at the price for his sugar. As it was, Hudson had scraped up enough of the Tsar's spilled chest to make a small profit, and had even sold the empty cask seasoned with Holland, largely because of the crest on the bung.

Diccon thought Hudson was too keen to have much care for English politics. He thought the same of Richard Grey, who had gone back from Vologda to Kholmogory to arrange for the storage of their unsold goods and those ready for shipment in the spring, and to set up a counting-house, with invoices, ledgers and cipher books, helped at intervals by his two veterans, Sedgewick and Edwards.

What did any of them have to do with a petty feud two thousand miles behind them in London? For they had got their charter. It had come from the Tsar's *lordly house and castle in the Moskva,* grandly cased, with a small red seal depicting a naked and stunted Saint George demolishing a no doubt Roman Catholic dragon. The wording had a sycophantic English ring about it, largely because it had been drawn up with his tongue in his cheek by Fergie Hoddim, and retranslated twice since, gaining drama as it progressed :

Considering how needful merchandise is, which fur-nisheth men of all that which is convenient for their living and nourriture, for their clothing, trimming, the satisfying of their delights, and all other things convenient and profitable for them, in such sort as amity is thereby entered into, and planted to continue; and the enjoyers thereof be as men living in a golden world ...

It granted to all members of the Fellowship and successors for ever the right to buy and sell without tax or levy or safe conduct, to choose and discipline shippers and packers, weighers, brokers, measurers and wagoners; to govern and rule any Englishmen in Russia, and to deal with lawbreaking and complaints. It promised redress in case of injury, reparation for robbery; and enthusiasm for all the Company's pious practices : in every possible particular, it was unspeakably generous. On paper.

After enjoying his golden world for a week or so, George Killingworth fell into the habit of quoting it, with a coda entirely his own.

'Russians ! Vipers ! The cunning, wicked progeny of vipers !'

And Lane and Price and Best, holding him down, would talk him into a rational mood again. *Hold a daily meeting of agents and factors,* the Company instructions had said, *and have the secretary note the decisions in his books of*

249

proceedings. A weekly vetting of reckonings is to be made by the agents, and the ledgers are to be accurate monthly. All possible information is to be collected on customs, coins, weights, manners and wares so no harm may be done or dispute caused by ignorance. You shall avoid all quarrelling, fighting or vexation; abstain from all excess of drinking as much as may be, and in all use and behave yourselves as quiet merchants doeth . . .

'It's war!' shouted George Killingworth, and dented the committee table with his fist. 'They treat trading like warfare, and think every stratagem justified. If a lie will be swallowed, they'll use it. From the biggest to the smallest, they disbelieve what I say, and what they say themselves you would trust like the tongue of Beelzebub. What dishonesty will they not practise? Fraud and misrepresentation! They cheat me over the quality; they falsify the origin; they juggle with weight. What I buy is not what they deliver . . . look at that flax! They delay sales, and raise prices and argue. The more they swear and protest honesty, the greater the knavery.'

'It works the other way,' Harry Lane said ill-advisedly. 'Don't trust them if they agree too promptly, either.'

George Killingworth, who had just bought five hundredweight of flax yarn at eightpence farthing a pound, and who had since learned from the indefatigable Mr Hudson that hemp at Novgorod, had he waited, would have cost him one and a half roubles the bercovite compared with two and a half anywhere else, lifted his beard above the table edge and turned a snow-bloodied eye on Mr Lane. 'What's a pood?'

'Thirty-six pounds,' said Mr Lane, obediently.

'An areshine?'

'A Flanders ell.'

'A bercovite?'

Mr Lane was tactfully forgetful.

'You see?' said George Killingworth, and slammed shut the minute book. 'If you don't know your facts, you can't blame the Russians for taking advantage of you.'

There was silence, as they all digested this remarkable volte face. 'Anyway,' said Harry Lane, 'we're selling them cloth for three times what it's worth.'

George Killingworth looked at him coldly down the magnificent beard.

'That's different,' he stated. 'They need it.'

Chancellor conducted his battling merchants to Novgorod. He had been there before, but not as fast as this, travelling non-stop with their fleet of sledges, and changing horses in droves at the yams on the way. The first night they by-passed Klin and St Elias and drove ninety miles straight through to Tver, where they got food and fresh horses, and raced on their way, past Volochek and the deep-frozen Msta, to complete the six-hundred-verst journey in three remarkable days.

Two of Lymond's men were with them : Chancellor was not sure why, except that Lymond had ordered it. He had seen the Voevoda only once since receiving their charter; he was much out of Moscow, and only occasionally Christopher reported seeing the powerful sledge, with its team of six horses, flying up to the gates of the Kremlin, or out across the river ice and into the flat, snow-filled country, to guide his commanders and visit his strongholds and garrisons. In their one brief meeting, in the big merchants' hall near the Kremlin, Lymond had asked his plans, shaking the snow from his cloak, and on hearing them said, 'I see. A town of price, like Paradise.'

'Novgorod?' had asked Chancellor, faintly surprised.

'No. Ipswich, in fact. Who are you taking?'

George was going, and Rob Best. He thought he would take Christopher.

Lymond listened. 'You've been there before. The merchants carry much more weight than they do in the east. You'll find a good many Swedes and Livonians and Germans. The Germans are rarely sober in the daytime, but the Flemings may give you trouble. They have no privileges since they incurred the displeasure of the Tsar, and you're going to be milking off at Vologda all the Russian goods they used to be offered at Novgorod. By the same token, the Dutch have just paid thirty thousand roubles to have their Customs indemnity restored : and you're going to be odious to them as a toad. . . . I think you might find Fergie Hoddim useful. And Plummer. No, he would bore you to death. Danny Hislop, and he can tell you all the gossip.'

There was a note of private amusement in the pleasant, assured voice which Chancellor did not quite follow, but the unforthcoming demeanour of Mistress Philippa's husband had undergone no change since that surprising evening at Vorobiovo, and they completed their conversation on strictly impersonal lines, to Christopher's clear dis-appointment. Which was why Christopher accompanied his father to Novgorod, along with Mr Killingworth and Mr Best, in the large covered sledge provided by an indul-gent Muscovite government, with Mr Hoddim and Mr Hislop riding informatively alongside.

What happened at Novgorod was not entirely George Killingworth's fault, although Danny Hislop afterwards blamed his beard, which he claimed had a life of its own like Chang-kuo Lao's miraculous donkey, which could travel thousands of leagues a day, and then at rest could be folded like paper.

In the event they were not popular, as no pensioner of the Tsar was popular in this city which had once ruled from the Arctic to the Urals, until taken and planted by Musco-vites. It was still great in size, despite the fires which four-teen years before had destroyed the whole Slav quarter of the town, and the previous year had burned 1,500 izbas to the ground. It was still great in trade, forming the market for barter between the east and the trading routes to the west, and it employed a western mode of transaction, and a suavity missing in the oriental ambience of Moscow.

Primed with warnings; aware of the anomalies in the Company's position; reminded that on Chancellor's pre-vious visit petitions had been made to the Tsar denouncing the English as pirates and rovers, George Killingworth quartered the markets of Novgorod, and was overwhelmed with enchanting discoveries. Tallow, sold at sixteen shillings in England, could be bought at seven shillings the hundred-weight here. A piece of cloth worth six pounds, including transport, could sell here for seventeen roubles, or fourteen pounds at the lowest.

There was no competition. Flemish cloth travelled nine hundred miles overland to market at Novgorod : he could undercut it with ease. There was no product he could not buy cheaper or sell dearer, unhampered by taxes, while the peasant selling twenty geese for a rouble, or ten sheep, or two cows, or four sleighs, would have spent a quarter already on customs and tolls. 'My people are like my beard : the oftener shaved, the quicker it will grow,' had said the Tsar; and so the taxes flourished, and the usurers, extorting their furtive twenty per hundred in corners.

So it was perhaps inevitable that a scuffle should begin in the bazaar, among the Flemings, and that the Englishmen should be followed to the flax and hemp market and then to the warehouse for tallow by a growing crowd of angry, powerful-looking people in bedraggled skin and sheepskin coats and felt hats. There, Killingworth explained for the fifth time, to a group of booted officials, that he and his company possessed new duty-free privileges, and for the fifth time Chancellor produced and unrolled the creased document, and for the fifth time everyone waited while the customar sent for someone who could read.

Unfortunately, this time Killingworth's patience expired before the end of the long wait, exposed to the jeering, quarrelling crowd. Shaking off Chancellor, he simply strode into the warehouse, picked up a billet of wood and proceeded to make his own examination of the casks.

Rob Best made to follow, but Chancellor stopped him. 'Wait here, and hold the parchment. Christopher, go and fetch Hoddim and Hislop. Mr Killingworth will have to come out.'

The crowd were already pressing into the warehouse. Christopher saw his father begin to fight his way through the doorway to Killingworth's side and then, with a clap on the shoulder from Best, began to burrow his way in the opposite direction, swimming upstream like the idol Perun until he came to the building where he knew he would find the Voevoda's men.

They were doing some haggling of their own, but in a civilized way, at a table with a full jug of mead at their elbows. There was no question by this time of the Voevoda's authority in any of the principal cities under the Tsar. In theory, he could requisition what he wished, as his own price, for the use of the army. In practice, policed by Plummer and Hoddim, the bargains were struck if possible without antagonizing anyone. Now, Fergie Hoddim got to his feet as soon as Christopher was shown, gasping, into the room and reaching for his new fur coat said, 'Oh, aye. Is it spuilzie or wrangful detention?' while Danny Hislop, less philosophic, said, 'That bone-headed ox Killingworth?'

'In the wax and tallow warehouse,' said Christopher, wheezing.

'I've informed the Namiestnik. I've shown the document to every petty office-holder in Novgorod. They can't be in trouble,' said Hislop.

'They can't read,' said Christopher.

'They can read,' said Fergie, shoving papers into his

pouch and embarking on a hasty round of handshaking. Hislop had already gone to round up his men. 'They just dinna want to offend their well-furnished friends in the city. It's natural. Is it a case of litigation, d'you fancy, or just simple manual force?'

It was a case of both. By the time Christopher got himself on a horse, and with Hoddim and Hislop and twenty trained cavalry charged across the frozen snow of Novgorod to the warehouse, you could see the glare of its burning against the grey winter sky, and the trampled snow was overlaid like a lava-bed by a creeping carpet of mingled tallow and blood.

And Chancellor, Killingworth and Best were in prison.

'It was a grand case,' said Fergie dotingly afterwards, when they had been to Pskov and bought all the flax and felt and hemp and tallow and wax that four ships could hold, and Diccon Chancellor's black eye and Rob Best's bruises were turning yellow. 'Mind, in a decent country they would hae had you under Ejection and Intrusion, Molestation and Spuilzie, and a plea for dampnage and skaith sustained forbye. Man, they lost their warehouse.'

'It was a public market,' said George Killingworth, from sheer furious habit, through the scarf which shrouded the lower part of his face.

'Aye. But ye yere tellt not to go in by the customar. And then ye flung a cask at his heid.'

'Well, they were coming at him with hatchets,' said Chancellor mildly.

'Aye. It's the Lord's wonder ye werena killed,' said Fergie. 'I never heard of a fire more opportune. They tell me the flaxbox they found in the tallow was melted out of all recognition, which is just as well, because they're death on incendiarism. For theft now, they'd just put you to the pudkey, unless it was your second offence; and if ye had enough gold in your palm, maybe not even that. But traitors, church robbers, kidnappers, men who murder their masters and incendiarists – death. And not even an attorney. Man,' said Fergie, carried away. 'The crown must make a fortune. No costs to speak of, and for every simple arbitration, the roubles pouring out to the judge and the clerk and the notary, and the losing plaintiff to pay ten in the hundred of the sum in dispute to the Tsar. . . . D'ye know he owns all the *cabacks*, the drink-houses?'

'Yes,' said Rob Best.

'Leased at three thousand roubles a year, and the landlord daren't throw out a drunk or he'll be sued for spoiling his sovereign's income. . . .'

Chancellor let him run on, with the sledge. They had been saved, by Hislop's force and Fergie's jovial implacability in argument. Their right to trade had been proved. Their innocence in the matter of the fire had been, if not proved, at least left in doubt. Killingworth's mad disregard of the inspectors had been the only incontrovertible sin, and there had been a nasty possibility at first that the matter would be removed, as the law properly demanded, to the Tsar's courts as Moscow.

He did not want that, and neither did Killingworth. There must be no trouble between themselves and the Tsar. Nor – what would almost be worse – should the Tsar be moved on their behalf to punish the Novgorodians, and thereby end all hopes of peaceful trading with the city for good.

It was Fergie who had reduced the matter to a fine, to be paid on the spot; and it was Danny Hislop who, when the sum demanded proved to be stubbornly monstrous, suggested the common Russian alternative of duel by proxy.

They had argued all afternoon over that, choosing their champion, and then demanding Chancellor's. Chancellor had wanted to do it himself. He had been warned against this practice, which admitted any form of attack, and any weapon save the gun or the bow. Short and stocky in build, he was no match in weight for these thick-built men with the powerful shoulders and arms. But he was fit, and fast, and had learned a few tricks at sea he had found useful, before now, in dark streets in alien harbours, and he was tired of life as a draper's major-domo. But though he was vehement, and Christopher naïvely eager, and George Killingworth, in a dignified way, perfectly prepared to take issue on behalf of his rights, the matter was settled by Rob Best, who said simply, 'I'm the biggest,' and by Danny Hislop, who said immediately, 'Right. Best it is.'

Which was the intelligent choice. For no sooner did the Novgorodians see Robert Best issue, stripped to the waist, to defend his Company's rights in the courtroom, than they decided to cancel the fight and draw lots. Then, buffeted in the back by the swaying of half the citizens of Novgorod, held back neither by rail nor by bar, they had witnessed the name of the Company sealed in a round ball of wax, and the name of the Governor of Novgorod sealed in another.

Beside him, Chancellor knew, Fergie Hoddim was grinning. On his other side, Christopher had turned faintly green. Then the tallest man in the crowd was brought forward to hold the two balls high in the crown of his hat, while another stranger came forward on tiptoe, his arm stripped to the shoulder and stretching, picked out one moist lump of wax.

The judge broke the ball in his hands, and unfolded the stained scrap of paper.

It held the name of the Muscovy Company. They had carried their point, and the Company was held innocent of any malicious intentions towards the Governor and people of Novgorod.

The air had not been rent by cheering, and the thumping he received on his spine was not entirely that, Chancellor thought, of bonhomie, but no one knouted them either. Now, Moscow-bound with the sledges hissing in train through the snow, he said to Fergie Hoddim, 'What was grand about it from your point of view, Hoddim? No disputation; no subtle by-play between the opposing lawyers. Merely a display of animal force displaced by an accident of fortune.'

'Aye, well,' said Fergie, who with Hislop had joined Chancellor and his son in the heavy, roofed sledge for the homeward journey. 'It was the subtle by-play, ye might say, that got ye the accident of fortune, not to mention the happy outcome of the process, confirmed under the white wax, so to speak. As to disputations,' Fergie said, 'ye need look no further than Daniel Hislop.'

'You may be right,' agreed Danny Hislop, pink bull terrier to Fergie's lined bloodhound. 'I lack Mr Hoddim's profound faith in the powers of argument. I wanted to do something crude, like threaten somebody.'

'No, no,' said Mr Hoddim. 'Threats? Bribes? Remeid of law should be open to a'body, *proponi in publicum,* without recourse to perversion. Public justice is sacred.'

'What was in the second ball of wax?' asked Diccon Chancellor.

Fergie Hoddim looked astonished. 'The name of the Muscovy Company,' he said, affronted. 'A good lawyer leaves nothing to chance. The wax came from the store ye had just bought up yourselves, and at a better price, I may tell you, than if the Tsar had elected to commandeer it. Just so.'

Diccon Chancellor laughed suddenly. 'Just so,' he agreed. 'Mr Hoddim, don't you miss your compatriots? Rude of arts and ignorant of politics, they're too simple for you here.'

Above the long, glossy moustaches, the hooded eyes cast him a shrewd look. 'Simple, would you cry them? They knew just how far to go, to test your power and standing, and mine.'

'Not yours, my dear innocent: the Voevoda's,' Hislop said. His pale eyes gleamed at the Chancellors, father and son. 'You know he is a banner lord? Magnified, feared and beloved of all men. I hear you are considering a trip to the Lampozhnya Fair. I hope you will insist on his accompanying you. It will lengthen his life, I should think, by a couple of years.'

'I don't follow,' Chancellor said.

Turning from Christopher's open-eyed gaze, Hislop turned a bland eye on his father. 'A man of rare endowments, the Voevoda,' he said. 'But in the north he need exercise fewer of them, perhaps. We inferior beings would also welcome a respite.'

'Mr Crawford is a hard task-master?' Chancellor said. 'My son tells me that soon you will be able to put a hundred thousand well-furnished men into the field at forty days' notice. In a country of this size, with such problems of climate and communications, and a people totally undrilled, I should have thought it quite a feat.'

'Yes. Well,' said Danny. 'He has made sure there is one person we shall always fear more than the enemy. The atmosphere of lofty command can, however, be a trifle dispiriting. We do hope you will both go to Lampozhnya.'

Diccon Chancellor said suddenly, 'What keeps you here? Mr Hoddim evaded the question. You are highly paid, I expect. Perhaps your commander has passed on his passion for power. But there seems to be no camaraderie. I have never heard one of you call the other by his Christian name. And no one, except perhaps Mr Crawford, could call the life easy. When the fighting is over, what can you do with your leisure? Where do you go for civilized conversation? What sport can you pursue but the coarsest, within the harshest extremes of the climate? What entertainment is there : where can you find books, or listen to music, or enjoy the pleasures of the table, and visit the homes of your friends?'

The pale, clever eyes glittered again. 'Ah,' said Danny. 'You have a report to make to your superior.'

Chancellor made a sound of impatience. 'I have. But you may also credit me with the normal instincts of friendship.'

'And a nose, naturally, for the prevalent cult of Belial the Epicene,' Danny said. 'You have seen him at the house at Vorobiovo. I doubt if he is there, or at the Kremlin house more than two days a week, and sometimes not for a good many weeks at a time. It pains me to destroy the legend, but if he pursued a life of ease himself, I doubt if one of us would follow him.'

Chancellor said, 'You still haven't answered my question.'

'No. Why are we here, Fergie?' said Hislop.

The tall brow ridged. 'I'm damned if I know why you're here,' said Fergie candidly. Why am I ? The money's good, and some day I'll go home and spend it. I like fighting, and St Mary's does that better than anyone else now in Europe. And I have a mind for the law, and a country where jurisdiction is just beginning to shake itself free of abuses, and has a use, maybe, for a trained mind in doing it. I never thought about it, but I suppose that's why I'm here.'

'You're here because the land is virgin and you are an expert,' said Danny crisply. 'That's why we're all staying. Not only because we enjoy being superior soldiers. Plummer is spending all his spare time in a welter of bochki vaultings and wall systems. Guthrie visits a different lavra every week, unearthing ancient Greek scriptures like truffles. D'Harcourt is pursuing unfettered his God-given vocation to defend his sheep against the Mussulman wolf. And Blacklock, burning with artistic dedication, is teaching half the Ikonopisnaia Palata to oil-paint. . . .'

'Half the—'

'A slight exaggeration. Three pupils,' said Danny cheerfully.

'And you?' asked Diccon Chancellor.

'You are, I suppose, right,' said Danny Hislop. 'There's no conversation, except among ourselves : the princes aren't going to hob-nob with foreigners. There is no feminine company. The pleasures of the great outdoors are strictly limited unless you care for massacres or for fishing, which I do admit is prodigious. Given a fine day, you might find a group of ladies having a gentle swing on a wheel in the meadow, but you are more likely to come across gangs of boys kicking each other freely to death. The less said about the winter the better. And as you say, there are no entertainments, short of church and court ceremonial, caterwauling, trials of strength and the indifferent jests by the Tsar's team of paid buffoons.

'. . . I think I am here for the same reason as Mr Crawford,' said Danny reflectively. 'To enjoy a condition of absolute superiority. . . . Isn't that, after all, why you travel, Mr Chancellor? Why your friend Wyndham took combs and hatchets and nightcaps to the natives in Guinea: why Master Cabot returned so high-handed and generous from La Plata that he thought to bestow an island on his Genoese barber? Experts in a virgin land. What a world of confidence we may extract from it.'

'I think,' said Diccon Chancellor, 'you underrate both us and yourselves.'

'I know you think so,' said Danny Hislop. 'Wait, however. Wait until after Lampozhnya,'

It was then, Chancellor afterwards realized, that his decision was really taken to make the trip to Lampozhnya: the long, hard journey to the winter fair in the north, where men could see fire and ice on the same firebrand. And afterwards, also, he realized how much of that decision lay at the man Hislop's door.

Returned, he told Killingworth, and, in Lymond's absence, Alec Guthrie in the large house he and his fellows occupied when not out of Moscow. He had known Killingworth would easily be persuaded. He would take Christopher with him, and induce Richard Grey to leave the counting-house at Kholmogory. They needed train-oil, and furs of a fresh killing. Why wait for them to come to Kholmogory, when one could buy them at Lampozhnya, straight off the sledge? Lane and Killingworth had their charter and the protection of the Voevoda's establishment. They did not need his help to set up their warehouses and supervise the new house the Tsar was giving them at St Maxim's, next to the Romanov palace.

These were drapers' matters. He would travel north once again, conveying their cargo, calling on Hudson and Edwards and Sedgewick at Vologda; buying the Nassada and the two Doshniks perhaps on the way, which they would need on the Dwina in summer. He would renew his acquaintance with Nepeja.

Then, in February, he would come south to make his last call on the Tsar, and visit the merchants whose palms they had oiled so discreetly, and hold the final series of meetings with Lane and Price and Killingworth, and receive their reports and papers and the last of the cargo, ready to leave for St Nicholas while the snow still made travelling easy. And soon after that, the ships would be there.

He wondered if he should be sorry, in the spring, to leave this cold and savage and curious land. By then, perhaps not. But first, he had a country to explore for his nation; and a man, for himself.

Francis Crawford returned to Moscow just before Christmas: Chancellor saw him at the Play of the Fiery Furnace outside the Uspenski Cathedral, when the angel slid down from the roof in a cloud of irresponsible wildfire, and rescued the three children of Judah, slightly singed, from the circle of jumping Chaldeans.

He saw him again, after the Metropolitan's pageant, at the Christmas banquet given by the Tsar for his court and some three hundred guests. The display of plate and the cloth-of-gold gowns were the same, but this time there were singers, whose efforts he did not enjoy. The day afterwards, by invitation, he spent another evening with Lymond at his home at Vorobiovo.

It was as pleasant as before, and as unrevealing. The partnership between the Voevoda and his mistress seemed, as before, intelligent, skilful and courteous: Lymond expressed his satisfaction that Mr Chancellor wished to see something of the lands of the north. He said, as Güzel fingered her lute, 'I cannot leave Moscow until after the *Kreshenea,* the hallowing of the water. That is held at Epiphany, and we might set out the following day, if you wish. If you tell me what goods you are taking, I shall arrange for the sledges and post-horses. You will need no other escort. Who else will go with you?'

'I thought of Christopher,' Chancellor said.

'No,' said Lymond. 'It is not a journey for youths.'

Chancellor smiled. 'You need have no fears for Christopher. He will stand the cold better than we shall. He has already made the journey with us from St Nicholas, after all.'

The fair brows lifted. For a moment, Chancellor looked into a chasm of such chilly surprise that, experienced as he was, he felt his heart close with a blow.

'. . . No,' Lymond said, his face astonished, his tone one of utter finality.

Chancellor did not argue. And a moment later, Güzel changed the subject.

Later, after Chancellor had disappeared into the darkness : 'Your spring campaign?' Güzel said.

'Guthrie will finish the training. I shall be back in Moscow by then,' Lymond said.

She made no comment. Whatever his absences, they were his own affair, as was the conduct of her life her own in the interval. Only, when he was at home, he came to her when the day's work was over, and stayed with her through evening and night until she slept, brought to easement at last. When she woke, it was to find her bed her own, and herself her own woman again.

After a few weeks he had asked for, and received, the boy Venceslas as his servant again.

Chancellor had seen nothing. But not because there was nothing to see.

CHAPTER EIGHT

The morning before the Feast of Epiphany, the people of Moscow took chalk and marked their doors and windows with crosses, lest the devils conjured out of the water should fly next day into their homes.

At four o'clock on the morning of Epiphany the Tsar rose as usual, and as usual was attended on rising by Francis Crawford, waiting silently through the prostrate devotions (*Help me, O Lord my God; Lord comfort me, defend and keep me, a sinner, from doing evil . . .*). Later, crowned with the shapka monomach and bearing on his wide shoulders the burden of a robe woven of jewel-encased metal, he sent to ask after the health of his wife and met her, briefly, in the middle chambers to salute her before walking slowly, his fingers sunk in the Voevoda's steady shoulder, to meet his courtiers and lead the stately procession through the Sacred Vestibule and down the Red Staircase into the torchlit darkness of the Cathedral Square.

There he crossed the garlanded bridge erected over the

packed snow between the Granitovaya Palace and the Uspenski Cathedral, where the Metropolitan and his clergy awaited him, their breath white in the air; their shadows stepped down over the bright snowy ground, while light and incense and the deeply choired notes of the liturgy filled the tall painted spaces behind them, glimmering with their ranked enrichments of gold.

During the service, Lymond waited outside with all his officers and the Streltsi, drawn up in columns, their arms gilded, between the bridge and the people lining the square in the darkness. Distantly through the closed doors came the drone of the readings: the Athanasian Creed; the Ten Commandments; the chanting voice of the Metropolitan; the singing voice of a priest; the psalm, with its tenfold Alleluias. A chant began: six syllables repeated over and over by priests and congregation alike. Behind Lymond, Alec Guthrie said quietly, 'What's that?'

Lymond said, '*Lord have mercy on us.* The boys will answer thirty times, very fast, with the single word *Praise*. Listen.'

High-pitched and staccato, the sounds rattled dimly behind the towering walls, half drowned by the murmur of the crowds waiting outside. Behind the bell-tower there was an almost insensible lightening in the sky. It was approaching nine in the morning, and despite the faint clustered warmth of the square, the bones of the face ached with the cold. Ludovic d'Harcourt said, 'They say the Tsar's mother was Catholic. They say the priests are all quite unlearned and never preach, except for admonitions twice yearly against treason and rebellion and malice, and to remind about fasts and duties and vows. They say they do almost nothing but read the scriptures, and sing the liturgy, and administer the sacraments, and deck the ikons for church ceremonials. They barely know the Pater Noster, they say, or the Belief, or the Commandments. They say the priests are permitted to marry, and that abbots are drunken and slothful and worldly, and they talk of young boys in the nunneries. . . .'

Lymond said, his voice murmuring, 'You sound surprised. The abuses are those the late King Henry complained of in England. And in England, unless they have burned him, the Primate himself has entered the holy condition of matrimony. The difference is that here the monasteries still flourish, levying their own taxes, making

262

their own major investments, producing and storing their liquor. The Metropolitan's annual income is three thousand roubles while the Archbishops earn two and a half thousand and the bishops are worth a thousand apiece. By courtesy of the Tsar, it is a rich church in a destitute nation.'

'Living on superstition,' said Adam Blacklock. 'They have plenty of privileges, but what duties do they perform? The Troitsa will give hospitality to the Tsar and his courtiers, but the poor are barely allowed to enter its doors.'

'The Tsar has given sanction for church schools to be opened,' Guthrie said.

'The Tsar gave sanction for printing presses to publish the liturgies,' Adam said through his teeth. 'And what happened? The presses were burned overnight. By the clergy.'

'Has it been proved?' Lymond said.

'Have the new schools so much as opened their doors?' Adam shot back. 'And d'Harcourt is right. This sacred orthodoxy, on the distaff side, is hardly one generation old. Elena Glinskaya was a civilized woman brought up in Lithuania.'

'The Tsar's grandmother was an equally civilized woman, brought up as a ward of the Pope,' Lymond said. 'Unhappily, you are dealing with the only surviving independent Greek Orthodox state, and a culture wholly intolerant of gynarchy. They don't know what they are missing.... It is nearly time, gentlemen.'

Guthrie had already moved to give orders. When the bells rolled in the dark over their heads and the Cathedral doors burst open, casting golden light from end to end of the square, the Streltsi were already deployed and waiting, the horses saddled; the ornate, gilded sleigh standing awaiting the Tsar. Then the mile-long procession wound, singing, down the steps and set off through the Kremlin and downhill by the houses of Kitaigorod, to hold the *Kreshenea* of the River Moskva, and hallow the water.

The five Englishmen and one boy had already arrived, and stood, protected by soldiers, in the forefront of the jumping, hand-flapping crowd waiting there on the river-ice in the dark. People jumped because they were cold, and their torches, whirling sparks in the air, gave off stinking smoke and a flickering maniac light which touched the greased furs and the broken-backed hats and the broad, heavy faces, sallow with winters of thick, stove-heated air. There were children, and somewhere Chancellor glimpsed a grown man being carried. And women by the hundred: the discreet embargoes of the courtier did not seem to apply to the peasant. Hundreds of women, some with babies; most with some sort of vessel: an earthenware pot, or a pail of leather or wood clutched in their powerful arms.

Where the market was held, they had cut a square twenty-foot hole in the ice, lined and edged with white boards, and had set a staging behind it, on which the Metropolitan's tall gilded chair had been erected. Beside it, lit from within, was a small, spired pavilion of mica, with a chair and footstool inside for the Tsar, and the household guard, in white fur and velvet, standing around it. Beyond the guard were the Streltsi, forming a double line on the ice as far as the Beklemishevskaya Tower, at the south-east point of the red Kremlin wall, round which the procession was coming. Soon after the bells of the Kremlin rang out, the Englishmen could hear a rumour of noise from the city and presently, over the dark mass of heads on the ice, a moving river of fire as, led by tapers and lantern, the banners came, of St Michael and Our Lady, floating crimson and blue in the dark; and then the great silver-gilt cross, bright as drawn-wire on the tender tinged clouds farther east. Behind, in books of gold as transparent and thin as the mica, you could see marching the frames of the ikons.

By the time the processions had come: the hundred robed priests of Moscow, two by two with their copes and their shining panagias; the monks and abbots and friars; the six Bishops of Riazan, Tver, Torshok, Kolemska, Vladimir and Susdal; the four Archbishops of Smolensk, Kazan, Pskov and Vologda, and the Metropolitan Makary himself, led between two priests in his gemmed mitre and cloth-of-gold cope, with the double gilt crozier with its wrought cross in his hand, the sky behind them had paled and lightened to almond. And as the Tsar moved to his seat, with his courtiers sparkling about him, the sun showed its vermilion rim beyond the river; beyond the dark bulk of houses and wall, and behind the tall crowded towers of the Kremlin.

Beside him, Diccon Chancellor saw his son's face, and the grey, cold-drawn faces of Price and Killingworth, Best and Lane turn ruddy and shadowless, formal as a Book of Hours painting. Great as a city, the red sun rose higher.

The Tsar's gold sabled crown burst into flame like a coal, his shoulders suddenly dazzling, and as the Metropolitan stepped slowly forward, his sakkos with its flat plated orphreys flashed like a mirror in firelight. A prayer began, and a soft, close-grained chanting behind it.

Chancellor and the others were silent, feeling the cold air no longer. As the light grew, and the singing, and the domed censers swung to and fro, clouding the dim ice with frankincense, the peopled landscape before him grew in line and deepening pigment, like a painting redeemed from its shadowy burial and alight with Russian colours : yellow, brown and blood-red. And Russian detail : a sloping shoulder; a pursed mouth; a squat hand outspread. And behind, dormer roofs unevenly drawn through the tree-tops. The snow stood sherbet-pink on the roofs, and among the burning domes of the Kremlin, Chancellor thought he saw a hastening angel in sandals, its head bent; its knee-caps sharp under the lines of its robe. Christopher said, 'Father ! You're sleeping.'

The Devil was conjured out of the river. Salt was cast, and the cross dipped and shaken over the Tsar, who stood bareheaded to be thrice blessed, and kissed it. Then the Metropolitan, dipping his hand, cast the holy water in turn over the child Ivan and each of the princes, and Chancellor, roused and doubly alert, saw the Tsar stretch to draw someone else forward.

The fair hair was unmistakable, although at this distance he could not see the Voevoda's face. Killingworth grunted. It seemed to Chancellor that the Metropolitan hesitated, and someone else spoke : a tonsured figure with a long, square-collared robe frogged and slit at the sides. Visco-vatu. It was, he was sure, the Chief Clerk of the Council. Then the Tsar made an angry gesture, as if brushing some-thing aside, and Viscovatu bowed, and Chancellor saw the spray of water, fine as dust over Lymond's bent head.

Then it was over, and the Tsar withdrew to his tower of mica, and the Metropolitan to his throne and the guards, stepping back, let the people bring their young and their sick to the water.

The Tsar stayed only a short time afterwards, to see some Tartar men christened, and some boys jump naked into the water, and the first of the thousands fill their pots and their pails with the blessed water, to take home to worship. Afterwards, they would bring his horses to drink, and those of his chief courtiers, so that the virtues of the cold, hallowed river would be evenly spread. Some, given the icy draught on their sickbeds, would die of it. Some, thought Chancellor suddenly, overcome with a sense of inexplicable danger, would die of the hallowing, though they had not drunk the water. He said in Russian to the Pristaf, 'I wish to speak to the Voevoda Bolshoia.'

An uncommunicative man, the Pristaf was not un-friendly, but a stickler for orders. He said, 'You will see the Voevoda at the banquet.'

Chancellor said, 'We go to the banquet this evening. I wish to speak to the Voevoda Bolshoia now.'

The Pristaf looked over the heads of the crowd, to the vacant seats by the thronged edge of the pool. 'They have sleighs. They have gone. The Voevoda Bolshoia has gone with the Tsar.'

'Then we should have sleighs also,' said Chancellor sharply. 'Are the Tsar's guests treated like moujiks in Russia? Do we walk from the river?'

As until this moment he had been prepared to do exactly that, there was no sleigh already commanded for them, and it took the combined pressure of Robert Best's Russian and Killingworth's formidable beard to impress the Pristafs enough to discover one. Even so, they were not far behind the massive stepped sleigh of the Tsar, passing with its accompanying Streltsi between the prone ranks of his subjects. The Metropolitan was sitting with him, and his household staff, including Viscovatu, Chancellor saw, in the sledge running behind. The boyars followed, and the army officers on horseback, while the remaining Streltsi fell back, preparing to escort the re-forming procession on foot.

It was day. The torches had been put out, and the lanterns. The sun floating high above the bright golden clusters of cupolas lit the dazzling white stretch of the river, and the struggling crowd which filled it from bank to bank, hiding the sanctified chasm, and the long, richly robed file of churchmen moving slowly away, its banners held blowing and high.

Ahead, climbing the slope from the river, the Tsar's sledge moved slowly between the bobbing, morioned heads of the Streltsi, and the horsemen behind, talking among themselves, were allowing their mounts to find their own footing. Coming close, as the crowds thinned out Chancellor saw a group of faces he knew : Adashev and the Tsar's confessor Sylvester, with Prince Kurbsky and Sheremetev. Then Danny Hislop, with Blacklock and Plummer and the Knight of St John, Ludovic d'Harcourt. No sign of the eagle he hated so much : no sign of Lymond.

High on their left, the sky was cut off by the castellated red wall of the Kremlin, with the empty ditch at its foot. On their right, they passed a scattering of houses and small churches, bulbous as mushrooms. Ahead, almost on the crown of the hill, was the scaffolding of the new church of St Basil's, with the snow almost empty between it and the double rank of soldiers marking the Frolovskaya Gate into the Kremlin. Behind them, a trembling of bells told that one or two sleighs had freed themselves also from the ceremony and were running back home. As for the rest, the whole of Moscow, it seemed, was still on the river. And then, at last, Chancellor saw the Voevoda, riding one-handed beside the leading, slow-running sleigh, his head bent as the Tsar leaned over, speaking to him. Someone shouted.

It was unusual. In Russia cheering was rare. One showed respect for one's Tsar by sinking on the knees and knocking the forehead three times, with reverence, on the ground. To foreigners, you shouted, *'Carluke!'* an expression which had puzzled the Englishmen for days until, blandly, their tolmatch had translated it for them as 'Crane-legs'. Which, to the breeched and trousered Russians, is what they probably seemed.

But this was not a cry of contempt. It was a shout of pure horror, mixed with a sort of ragged disbelief, and, as it was repeated, Chancellor realized that it was a man's name which was being called in the thin air, and that the sound had come from the group of horsemen ahead. Then one of them wheeled, and disregarding all rule and order and, forgetting apparently even the presence of the Tsar in the sleigh just ahead, flung his horse over the snow to the white waste in from of St Basil's.

It was Adam Blacklock. Calling still, he pushed his horse up the slope, his horse's caulked feet throwing up the packed snow, and Chancellor saw he was riding straight to the only knot of people in the wide, scattered square : the group of officials round the *Lobnoye Mesto,* the stone tribune where the Tsar stood to address the gatherings of his people, and where criminals were executed, or put to the pudkey.

Some such thing was happening now. Chancellor could see two livid bodies strapped to the scaffold, and a cart which clearly held one or more, already cut down. Christopher, who had stood up, said abruptly, 'They've been flogged,' and sat down. Blacklock's flying horse, rearing, plunged into the group by the scaffold. They saw Blacklock dismount and heard his voice shouting; but already another horse was racing towards him over the snow as the procession reined, and the Tsar and princes and boyars looked, astonished, at the odd upheaval round the blood-stained snow on the tribune.

Lymond had left the Tsar's side to ride after Blacklock. He rode flat out, balancing the horse against the uneven, slippery snow and they saw him halt, far across the square, where Blacklock was yelling, held struggling in a swaying crowd of angry men. They heard the Voevoda's voice ring out, sharp and clear, and saw the men loosen their grip and drop back, reluctantly, from Adam Blacklock who stood, his cracked voice raised, saying something over and over.

Lymond raised his whip and cast it, with a whistling snap, full across the other man's face.

Adam stopped shouting. Cut in two by the red seam they saw his face stiffen, white as the ice, and heard that Lymond was speaking, sharply and clearly. The scourger and his officials stirred, and a moment later, began to cut down the remaining two flogged men. Another command, and, slowly, Adam Blacklock moved to his horse and put his foot in the stirrup. The Chief Secretary Viscovatu, bent over the Tsar in earnest conversation, straightened and moved round the royal sleigh, clearly to follow the Voevoda across to the tribune. At the same moment, the Tsar gave a sharp order and the Streltsi, with Danny Hislop riding with them, deployed and began to file on foot after the Chief Secretary's horse.

They met face to face within earshot: Viscovatu with Hislop and the Streltsi just behind him and the Voevoda, with Blacklock's reins in his grip. Lymond's face showed almost nothing: a mask of stone, Chancellor thought, to make worshippers tremble. And Blacklock, sitting unmoving beside him, with the blood coursing unchecked from that disfiguring wound, might have been dead already. Viscovatu said, 'Your officer is the prisoner of the Church, and you are to hand him into the Church's custody. It is the command of the Tsar.'

They saw Danny Hislop's horse stamp as his gloved hand crushed tight on the reins. But on Lymond's face there was no change; and Blacklock himself might not have heard. Lymond said, 'The Tsar's virtues are the salvation of his country; his wishes are my own; his commands are only to be obeyed. May I know the grounds for the complaint of the Church against Blacklock?'

'Is it unknown to the Voevoda?' said the Chief Secretary in surprise. 'He has corrupted the hearts of the faithful, and has caused them to flout the edicts of the Stoglav. The three he seduced to the path of the Devil are punished. The Holy Russian Church will decide what judgement his evil counsel deserves.'

For a moment, Lymond studied him without speaking. Then lifting his glove, he flung the reins of Blacklock's horse to the other man. Again, Hislop's horse moved, but neither Hislop nor the Streltsi said anything. 'It was unknown to me,' Lymond said. 'And I grieve for it. He is yours to punish as you think fit. Will the Tsar, who has heard the words of his secretary, hear the humble apologies of the Voevoda Bolshoia?'

He had raised his voice. 'Approach,' said the Tsar. He did not look at the Metropolitan, seated below him. But Lymond's hard blue gaze, approaching, was on the mitred, grey-bearded face of Makary before it moved to the stiff, beaked profile of his master.

Lymond said, 'Like your Tartar allies, this man is useful as well as a carrier of heresies. On men such as him, the success of your spring campaign in the Crimea might well rest. If the Church wishes to take his life, I bow to the Church's decision. If not, I ask that he be made to suffer today, not tomorrow or next week or next month, when the season is turning, and his skill and knowledge will be most needed. The hurt he has caused you, vile though it is, would be as a blessing compared to the infidel rule of the Tartars.'

Viscovatu had followed him. 'The Voevoda is over-modest,' he said. 'Without this one man, he cannot defend Moscow from the Khan Devlet Girey?'

Lymond did not look round. 'The Tsar knows how many men he has, and how many he needs.'

The pale, goitrous eyes looked at him from under the sable rim of the schapka. 'So you beg for his life?' the Tsar said.

Lymond's unemotional gaze did not alter. 'I beg for nothing save your highness's forgiveness. If the Church so decides, it may hang him from this tribune now.'

'What does the Church decide?' said the Tsar.

The voices, thin over the snow, came clearly to Chancellor. Beside him, Christopher was breathing heavily, and George Killingworth's face, above the vast golden beard, had turned an odd shade of red. Chancellor supposed he himself must be pale : he felt very cold. The other officers and the Streltsi had done nothing. It was, he supposed, part of the test. How loyal was the Voevoda; how loyal were his men; how strong was his grip on them? Strong enough, at least, to prevent them at this moment from taking wild action. And of the loyalty of the Voevoda, looking at that blood-streaked face and listening to Lymond's cool, implacable voice, the Tsar and the Metropolitan must have no permanent doubts.

The glittering form of the Metropolitan stirred, an old man, weary under the great uneven gems on the golden scaled robe, and the stole with its grotesque river pearls. He said, 'It is worthy of the offence that the decision be taken here, in the streets of the city?'

'Yes,' the Tsar said suddenly. 'I wish to hear what is in your heart. Half the case has been judged. The three ikon painters have suffered. This man did not outrage his faith, but corrupted another's. I do not see how his punishment can be less.'

Viscovatu's voice said softly, 'Your offending servants were flailed.'

In the sleigh with his father Christopher said, whispering, 'They were dead.'

'Not quite,' Chancellor said. 'But then, they were Russians, with Russian bodies. This man would die.'

The Metropolitan stirred again, clutching the crozier with its double gilt cross, looking neither at the Tsar nor the Chief Secretary. He was an old man, and cold, and although his power was great, the power of the Tsar was still greater. Finally, he raised his face, and looked, flatly and sternly, on the Voevoda and the artist, still and drawn and silent beyond him. 'His punishment also,' he said, 'is the flail. Let it be carried out.'

'Let it be carried out by me,' said Lymond.

There was a little silence. Then Viscovatu smiled. 'The Voevoda might be moved to be too lenient. A man is hanged by both hands at the pudkey, with weights attached to his feet. And the twenty-four lashes are from a wire flail.'

'In that case,' Lymond said, 'lenience hardly enters markedly into the matter. But you may send what observers you wish.'

Viscovatu looked at the Tsar, and then at the Metropolitan. 'There is the tribune. Why not settle the issue now?'

'Willingly,' said Lymond's crisp voice. 'Or tonight, if the Tsar would prefer.'

It was the solution. 'Tonight,' said the Metropolitan gratefully, shivering within the furs under his sakkos.

And: 'Tonight,' said the Tsar. 'After the banquet.' And raising his hand, caused the sleigh to drive off.

The second sleigh followed, and then the boyars, followed by the Streltsi, and the scourgers, and the cart with the three ikon painters, broken and bloody within it. They had taken Blacklock from his horse and tied him to Viscovatu's stirrup. The little procession turned into the Frolovskaya Gate and disappeared up the slope. Lymond, Chancellor saw, was again riding beside the Tsar's sleigh. Killingworth said, 'We're supposed to be going in there. Aren't we? For the banquet.'

'Yes,' said Chancellor. Christopher, beside him, said nothing at all.

Francis Crawford attended the Tsar's Twelfth Night banquet, and was even lightly voluble, seated among the noble guests and not far from the English party, who returned his graceful greeting but had no occasion to speak to him. Afterwards, they all issued by torchlight into the open space behind the terems, beside the church of St Saviour in the Wood, where a temporary post and crossbar had been erected, to which Adam Blacklock's hands had been strapped.

His body, stripped almost naked, showed a raw blueish white in the flambeaux, and the wound on his face was a black seam crossing its whiteness, from cheekbone to lip to chin, distorting its normal lean diffidence. The bright, hollow eyes were different, too, from the steady, observant gaze of the artist. They moved restlessly, following the movements of the torchbearers, of the servants and the boyars and courtiers as they passed and repassed in his view, wrapped in furs and enjoying the hazed after-warmth of the banquet. There was a great deal of talk, and some laughter.

He spoke only once, when he heard at last the step he was waiting for, and saw the flares close in and brighten, and the shadows of Lymond's coatless body, various as the blades of a fan, spring wheeling on the lit snow. Then Adam said, 'Once, when you had been flogged at the post by your own men, I helped to save you.'

He had been overheard. Someone uttered a swooping obscenity.

Unlike those of his audience, the Voevoda's voice was not thickened with drink, but neither did it reveal any minor key of concern or of pity. 'Once,' he said, 'you were Adam Blacklock. But I, sad to relate, was a different man.'

Chancellor watched the twenty-four strokes, which Christopher did not; and saw Lymond at the end toss the rod with its fine clotted wires to the officers waiting, and turn back to the Tsar, pulling down the plain, samite cuffs of his shirt. The drawn thread work, stitched and spooled down the edges was flecked black with haphazard blood. Then someone cut down the raw, senseless flesh on the scaffold, and lifted it, face down like a child, on to a sheet ready spread on the snow. The two men who carried it off were, Chancellor saw, Guthrie and Hislop.

The Tsar stood up. Bright-eyed in the firelight, he strode forward and gripped Lymond's shoulders. 'A strong arm! A strong arm for justice, and a strong arm to defend me from evil.'

He opened his hands, his face surprised. 'You are cold? A coat for the Voevoda!' And while it was brought, he said, 'I have that in my chamber will warm you. Let us see whose king will fall on the chessboard tonight!'

Lymond said, 'It is late, majesty.' They had put his coat, with its wide expensive edgings of fox round his shoulders.

The Tsar's voice was softly resonant in his chest. 'Do you refuse me?'

'My lord, you are the halter of the colt and the horse; the leash of the goshawk,' said Lymond. 'I am your servant. I refuse you nothing.'

That night, returned to his chambers, Chancellor called his servants to him and revoked every arrangement for his visit next day to Lampozhnya.

In Kitaigorod, the men of St Mary's did not go to bed, but waited all night without speaking outside the quiet room where Adam Blacklock was lying, in Dr Grossmeyer's pedestrian care.

In the Kremlin, Francis Crawford played chess; and lost.

CHAPTER NINE

Before Chancellor was awake, Lymond walked into his chamber next morning, bringing with him a baleful humour, dry and chill as the weather outside.

'Arise with mirth,' he said. 'And remember God. I have countermanded your orders. Springs of wine, milk and honey gush from the rocks, and love is born everywhere. Whether you wish it or not, you are travelling to Lampozhnya today.'

He was dressed for travel, in linen breeches and boots under a high-collared tunic, with a loose, widesleeved garment in wool gem-buttoned over it. Searching out the landscape of his face with the shrewd master mariner's eye, Chancellor noted the faint, spoiling traces of a night untroubled by sleep. No one but a European, Chancellor thought, could carry with him such an air of insolent decadence. Poor Philippa Somerville. He said, 'I ask myself how you knew I had cancelled my journey.'

Lymond said, 'Then I hope you answer yourself accurately. You are an Englishman, therefore you think like the canary, taught to repeat the song of the flute. I work for a different nation. I propose to guide and protect you, because it serves my own interests. You will not, like the ikon painter, be infected.'

'Did he die?' Chancellor said.

Lymond walked forward. With one fastidious finger he lifted the blankets and counterpane of the navigator's meagre bed and flung them back sharply, revealing, spread in anger, his sinewy body in its chaste white cotton nightgown. 'Thank God,' he said. 'I hate travelling with a man who wears lace in bed. Did you know that you may beat the Devil, but your whip must be drawn from a winding

273

sheet? So far as I know Blacklock lives, breathes, and is being sprinkled with aqua vite and marigold water. It does not affect your forthcoming journey.'

Diccon Chancellor stayed where he was, his eyes steady, his arms folded hard on his chest. 'You will excuse me,' he said. 'I do not go to Lampozhnya.'

None of the expected expressions, of anger, of annoyance, of impatience crossed Lymond's face. He said simply, 'If I order it, there is very little you can do about it. Your cargo is loaded, and the sledges are waiting below. You may travel dressed or in your nightshirt, as you please.'

Christopher had wakened. Chancellor saw his son's stiff, outraged face in the doorway and said slowly, 'I am in no position to resist you, of course. But you, in your turn – do you think this is a moment to abandon your officers?'

The handsome blue eyes opened. 'Do you think they burn to expel me? They don't. And if they did, they would have even less chance of it than you have. The bow and arrow, as they say, commands with a fine and delicate voice.'

Christopher said, 'It isn't the bow and arrow you shelter behind. It's the Tsar.'

Lymond turned. 'Ah,' he said. 'And you find that despicable? But you are wrong, you know. *Aut Caesar, aut nihil*. It is the Tsar who is sheltering behind me.'

An hour later, having kissed Christopher and shaken hands with his silent compatriots, Diccon Chancellor took his place in the sledge-train, and, escorted by a band of sixty fully armed cavalry from the barracks at Vorobiovo, swept out of the Neglinna Port and across the six-arched wooden bridge to turn north, along the Wolf Road, the great frozen highway to the sea. Ahead, enclosed in furs, Lymond rode with his captain, with Slata Baba on the sledge just behind him.

So, their estrangement complete, the two men, Lymond and Chancellor, entered a strange world of sleigh bells and silence. The sledges ran day and night, served by the post-stations, and Chancellor found that, supported by cushions, with the curtains drawn and bearskins heaped about him, he could sleep, and read his maps, and make his notes frozen-fingered in the daytime as he could not do two years before, shepherding his nervous merchants from post to unknown post from the Frozen Sea down to Moscow.

As far as Kholmogory their present journey was the

same, but infinitely faster, and with every care removed from his shoulders. Food appeared, or hospitality in fortress or village or monastery. Or failing all else, they carried tents, and the men would make windbreaks and shelter from the upturned sledges themselves.

The Streltsi were swift, obliging and cheerful. He grew used to the sound of Russian constantly spoken, and began to catch and understand the coarse, half-heard jokes, and enjoy their deep, throaty voices when they were permitted to sing. They were the élite of their corps, he began to realize; already stringently trained, and chosen to escort Voevoda Bolshoia. That they were afraid of him to a man took nothing, he saw, from their zest, or the sparkling tension which clothed them like frost. He had seen that once before, in a company under the Duc de Guise, about to go into battle. It was the sign of success; the fire and stamp of natural leadership.

He found it disturbing. And leaving Vologda behind him, with its lightly drunken, arguing oasis of confident English voices and futile English problems, he gave his mind and his eyes instead to the land, the mother of whiteness; to the falling snow, a host of dove-grey particles against the pale downy sky; a rush of white against the dark trees and bushes. To the sunlit snow, golden white against blue on the roofs of the villages, and the bright lime green and umber of the trunks of the thinning forests, their snow-white profiles lost to the vaster white space of the sky. The twin churches, for summer and winter, set like pine cones in the snow by the hamlets. The scrubbed wooden floors of the houses, the truss of foot-wiping hay by the threshold, the box of wood and barrel of water placed just inside.

There were no beasts to be seen but the wild ones : the hare in her milk-white coat, and the grey squirrel and the stoat with its snowy-tipped tail. In the woods there were wolves, and bears, and elks : they saw their prints, and the horses shied at the smell. But the stock, the small, runted cattle and lean hogs were killed and frozen, or sharing with their owners the unstable log izbas, built up so assiduously against the snow, which the thaw might so easily bring slipping to disaster again. Inside, the ikon; the wall-plank for bedding. The stove-room with its bundles of birch-slivers where twice weekly the steam bath was taken, for cleanliness and to ward off disease. A diet of roots and garlic and onions and cabbage and too much time to sleep, or to toil under the stinking tapers at your painstaking craft : the working of skins and furs, the shoemaking and woollen embroidery; the making of wooden bowls and stools and sledges and hanging cradles and chests, painted raspberry red, and yellow, and black; the shallow gingerbread moulds, with their cocks and their pigeons patterned in the white wood; the beehive tooled like a bear, with flight-entries formed in its muzzle. The harsh drink; the coarse clothes; the grey, crackling pile of hard fish, culled for soup with a hammer.

Poverty. Poverty in the presence of starving cold and great, earth-cracking heat, and life lived in the shadow of the wolf and the bear, and tribes more cruel and avaricious. For it was the land which was implacable, far more than its masters. An obja, tilled by one horse, could be rented for two or three roubles or its equal in labour, and a fee of perhaps half of the rotated crop of rye or of oats. In law, the peasant might be hanged, where the boyar was only whipped or imprisoned, but discrimination was less than he had expected; serfdom was almost unknown.

Yet where was the succour when the grain was struck cold in the ground, and had to be gathered and ripened on stovetops, and thawed in hot-houses, so that it might be ground? When the tinder-dry warehouses burned, and cities starved, and beggars, ragged and violent, roved the streets of Vologda, as he had seen them : *Give me and cut me; give me and kill me.*

How, if you were the Church, did you justify a single gold-collared ikon, with two thousand five hundred diamonds set upon its thick hammered surface? How, if you were the Tsar, did you vindicate your annual tribute, bartered for rich cloths and finer jewels for your treasure-house? How, if you were a man from a softer land, where debate was instructed and free, and all the scholars and books from antiquity were there to correct and advise you, could you accept in your turn such a tribute, and use it to clothe the body and house of your mistress?

But he kept his thoughts to himself, and barely saw the Voevoda, except to exchange the slimmest of commonplace courtesies, until the day before their arrival at Kholmogory, where they stopped to eat in a church by the flat, snowfilled ice of the Dwina.

It was a new church, wreathed with galleries, its steps

dropping from level to level in uneven flights, canopied and jointed like parings of apple. Above, the spires were leaved with fresh, gilded kokoshniks, and the onion domes with their tall, tangled crosses stood bright as an odd, untimely budding.

It was dark, even at noon, with the snow stretching white and stark to the violet slate of the sky. The frost, grown stronger and stronger, was an antagonist to be studied and countered, like a runagate thief with a knife. Stepping from the sledge, Chancellor pulled off his gloves and rubbed fresh snow on his nose and his fingers and his cheekbones, and beat out the stiff, frozen mass of his beard. The rank airless heat of the church by contrast sent the thawed nerves flaring and the skin of his face felt like tallow inflamed: he knew from experience that his nose was haplessly running. He dried it, and began to pull off the shaggy, snow-powdered coat from his shoulders. Lymond, appearing suddenly, said, 'They tell of a stallion which went for a trot one cold day in Slobodka and came back to its stable a gelding. They don't say what became of the rider. Are you all right?'

Chancellor nodded.

'I have three cases of frost-bite. The monks say we can remain for the night and I think we should do so. I shall send a man to warn the Governor of Kholmogory and your friend Grey to expect us tomorrow. Will your business take long?'

Speed, and always more speed; because there was a campaign in the south, in the spring. Chancellor wondered which of the soldiers had suffered, and if it was serious. Not, to do him justice, that the Voevoda had travelled as he had, cushioned and canopied, with the warmth and bulk of the horses between him and the searing air from the north. Free of the forests, he had watched Lymond fly Slata Baba at her proper prey, as the Turkestan hunters did; or the Tartars who killed wild horses with hawks, lured to seize mane and neck with their talons, and with wing and claw, to terrify and blind and exhaust.

In the same way, Slata Baba took deer, blinding with her powerful wings; sinking through eye and muscle and nerve with her razor-sharp talons, until the huntsman, with bow or spear, could ride to the kill. Diccon saw her swoop once, with her great, sooty brown pinions, and lift a calf from the ground, transfixed like rotten fruit, in passing.

He could tell the sound of her dive, with its swishing moan of twice-compressed air, and the tranquil flight, beating slow as the waves of the sea, and the silly, weak chirrup, which was the only song she possessed. Seen from behind, her golden-tipped ruff pricked in cold, or anger, or preening, she looked like a ringleted girl-child. Then the pretty wigged shoulders would swivel, and there was the tearing beak, hooked below the soul-piercing stare. To hold her, Lymond had his arm gloved to the elbow, and even he, Chancellor saw, turned his head when the bird came to land. Then she was chained to her travelling post, since no man's arm could bear the weight of a full-grown golden eagle, unsupported.

Hunting, he supposed, was Lymond's private pleasure : it gave them also fresh meat most days to cook. For the rest, the Voevoda had found business to do in each of the towns they had passed through; and when they were no longer near habitations, he would leave the train and disappear sometimes to follow some small beaten highway, taking no more than two or three of his men and using the light sleighs, which could take a man four hundred miles in three days drawn by a single fast horse, small and broad-chested and wild, with fox and wolf tails, grey and red and black, with frost decking its neck.

Sitting fidgeting under his bearskins, Chancellor watched him disappear on these explorations with increasing spasms of jealousy. With the winter's hard training he lacked, Lymond could steer his sledge by bodily balance like a canoeist, the reins in his left hand and a spiked staff in his right, sparingly used, to hold the rocking sleigh steady.

He also travelled with his feet strapped into artach, the slender pattens of wood nearly six palms in length which Chancellor had seen twice before, worn by Permians, but not like this, slicing free down the blue, hollow slopes, with the snow rising like steam in the sky. The Voevoda held a class once or twice, for his cavalry, and Chancellor, safely ensconced in his tent or his sledge or his chamber, heard the distant commands and the shouts and the laughter and experienced all the violent, pent-up emotions which would have better suited the temper of his absent son Christopher. It made him angrier because he knew that none of it was expected to interest him, and that both the business and private life of his host were being conducted, with every reason, outside his presumed sphere of attention.

Now, brief as ever, Lymond said, 'Will your business take long?' and Chancellor hardly heard him, because he was eyeing the strips of wood, long, snow-spattered and gleaming, which Lymond was carrying; and before he knew it, he said, 'I should like to try that.'

Lymond said, 'Would you?' The impersonal blue eyes, wet-lashed and narrowed with snow glare, surveyed Chancellor's face and then, briefly and clinically, his body. 'You would find it small trouble, I'm sure. On the other hand, if you break your neck, Robert Best will have my head cleft to my teeth for a murderer.'

'. . . So?' said Chancellor. The priest was approaching.

'So I think Aleksandre should teach you. My captain. He is an excellent performer. I shall arrange it.' And excising both him and the subject, Lymond walked forward, and engaged in the necessary business of organizing feeding and quarters for themselves and his men for the night.

It was a small church, with limited room for the few monks and for passing travellers. Across the yard, there were arcaded sheds where the horses and men both could shelter till nightfall, with wood fires and braziers for company. Inside, Chancellor was given a room, holding no more than a crucifix, a stool and a board for his blanket and bolster. There was no stove, and it was not until he had settled down after the slender evening meal they had shared with the monks in the commonroom that it struck him to wonder, fleetingly, if the men who were to sleep where they ate hadn't fared rather better.

Waking later, shivering under the pile of his sleigh rugs and coat, he was sure of it. He was still fully dressed. Putting his arms through the sleeves of his heaviest robe and taking his thickest rug with him, he opened the cell door and went to seek the commonroom stove, that great block, three feet by four feet of black searing iron, with winged angels and priests marching hot-foot for all time round its plating.

It was there, surrounded by sleeping heads resting on saddles. The centre board had been drawn, but even so, there was little enough room, on the benches or under them, for sixty men and their captain. Chancellor came in, treading carefully in the near-darkness. For the sake of warmth, he was prepared to lean against a wall until

morning, despite the smell and the raucous noises of ungainly slumber. Someone, stirring below his feet, said in a
whisper, 'My lord?'

It was the captain, Aleksandre, who was to instruct him
next day, he remembered, in the art of sliding with artach.
He answered, whispering also, 'I am cold.'

He had meant only to solicit help in finding a vacant
space in the dark, and was irritated when he saw that the
captain, rising, was about to give up to him his place on
the floor. He saw himself embarking on a hissing exchange
of self-denying courtesies when he was saved by Lymond's
voice speaking softly from somewhere beyond. 'Chancellor?
The chapel is warm.'

The captain subsided. Touching his shoulder, Diccon
Chancellor picked his way between the still bodies and
through an archway to the narrow passage from which
Lymond had spoken. The parvis was empty, but the low,
carved door to the chapel stood open, and he could see
the glow from the bronze lamps hung before the dark
pictures of the iconostasis, and the bending glimmer of a
circle of candles to the right of its doors. Somewhere, also,
he could feel the gentle warmth of a stove. Lymond's voice
said, 'If you close the doors, you will find it quite support-
able. I shall send someone to cut fuel for them tomorrow.'

He had resumed the place on the floor which he had
evidently chosen for himself, seated on a folded rug with
his head pressed back against the coarse cloth draping the
revetment, his legs stretched before him and his arms
loosely folded. Like Chancellor, he was still fully dressed,
with his sleeveless, furcaped coat spread about him.
Chancellor, dropping his rug on the wooden floor, lowered
himself against the opposite wall likewise. He was deeply
depressed. But for the frostbite, he would now, he supposed, be enjoying the relative comfort of Kholmogory
instead of being trapped in this mediaeval flickering gloom,
for what disagreeable purpose he could only guess. He sat,
breathing in dust and dead incense.

But Lymond, to his relief, did not attempt even a
standard exchange of civilities, far less a discourse or an
apologia. He merely remarked, in the same prosaic voice,
'The mortifying quality of cold,' and then abandoned
communication, leaving Chancellor wondering, for an unlikely moment, if he had read his mind. He waited, and
then, as nothing happened, spread his rug more comfort-

ably over the floor, and stretched himself full length to sleep.

To a healthy, vigorous man in his thirties pursuing an open air life with a clear conscience and an active mind, this presented no problem.

An hour passed, during which sleep surprisingly avoided him. Chancellor turned, twice, and settled down with a sigh, once more, for his night's rest. At the end of a further hour he was, to his annoyance, still fully awake.

So was Lymond. He discovered that, by a discreet glance, as he turned over yet again. The Voevoda was exactly as he had left him, his head resting against the wall, his body perfectly still, his face indistinguishable in the flickering candlelight. Only Chancellor could see the two points of flame, reflected in his dark, open eyes.

The next time he looked, the place was empty. Then the door behind him was pushed quietly open and Lymond came in, carrying in each hand a pewter tankard from which steam was rising. He pressed the door shut, waited a moment, and then having made sure Chancellor was still awake, moved forward and placed one of the beakers beside him. It smelt of hot mead, with something else added of a distinctly alcoholic nature.

'Drunk among the Scythian snows,' Lymond said. 'It is, sometimes, preferable to being sober.'

It was Candy wine. Chancellor sat up slowly. *To be drunk among the Scythian snows in their native purity and pleasantness* was what Richard Eden had written about Candy wines, in the Russian coda to his book he and Chancellor had worked on, before he left England. There was a copy in his baggage. He looked up.

'I have a copy, too,' Lymond said. 'Sent me from Danzig.' He took his place again by the opposite wall, and, resting his arms on his knees, cradled the tankard in his two ringless hands. Below his candlelit hair, his face was in shadow. 'It seemed a mischievous waste, to chain that observing brain to Moscow. In any case, no doubt Eden is planning to collaborate on a sequel.'

'That is why I am here?' Chancellor said. He did not believe it.

'You intended to come,' Lymond said. 'An irrelevant emotional crisis could not be allowed to prevent it. I am not saying it was unimportant. Only that it should not affect this experience.'

'Ah,' said Chancellor. 'Trade. The chief pillar to a flourishing Commonwealth.' He had taken a deep draught of the mixture and fire, human and reviving, again flowed through his veins. 'The Tsar commands that the Muscovy Company should see the best furs and buy the cheapest train-oil, and in all things be satisfied. Why, I wonder?'

'The Tsar's counsel is his own,' said Lymond. 'All I can tell you is that he is not responsible for your journey to Lampozhnya. And that I am beginning to be singularly weary of peddling.'

It struck, as it happened, a vibrating chord in Chancellor's present mood, but he did not say so. He said, 'It is a poor country. It needs trade, if only the Emperor would allow his people to benefit from it.'

Lymond said, 'It needs trade. It needs miners and metallurgists, architects, doctors and apothecaries. It needs good roads and schools and universities and first-class local government and a decent drainage and irrigation system and a stock improvement process and well-made bridges and a unified tax system. And security.'

'Beginning with security?' Chancellor said.

'Because it is needed most, yes. Because it will impress the Tsar most, yes. Because it will create the climate in which other reforms may be contemplated, yes.'

'And because the Voevoda Bolshoia, as a result, will be the most wealthy and powerful man in Russia?' Chancellor said. He had not intended to descend to personalities, and was not sure why he did so, except perhaps to keep an articulate and beguiling tongue at a defensible distance.

There was a moment's flash of total anger, abruptly destroyed. Lymond said, 'My dear Master Chancellor. You appear to have closed the conversation, don't you?'

Chancellor stared at him, his wits shocked awake. He said, 'How can you complain? It is the impression you give without stint.'

It looked as if he would receive no reply. Lymond put down his tankard and, stretching his legs, tilted back his bare head so that the light rested on his face and the length of his throat. His eyes were closed. 'I don't complain,' he said. 'I merely try to fill time with an exchange of views on a subject I supposed common to us both. You receive the impression that I am personally ambitious. I receive the impression that you are a draper. We may both be right. I had not expected to quarrel about it this evening.'

Chancellor said, without removing his eyes, 'I am paid by the Muscovy Company. And you are paid by the Tsar.'

Lymond looked at him. Astonishingly, the brittle, high-tempered face had altered again. 'And what do you see when you stand at the wheel,' he said, 'and face all the liberality of the ocean? A bolt of fine violet at eighteen pounds six shillings and sixpence the piece?'

In his turn, Chancellor was looking into his tankard. 'Cloth builds the vessel,' he said. 'And launches her; and pays for her crew.'

'But you do not travel by cloth,' Lymond said. 'But by sea card and compass and star. I say again. That is why you are here, on your way to Lampozhnya. That is why you have exhausted every merchant in Muscovy with your questions: about Sarai and Urgendj; about Bokhara, Samarkand and Otran. You will travel with trinket and parchment, but you will have no patience with huckstering. Your eyes are on the Ob and the Euxinium Sea: your heart, Master Chancellor, is on Cambalu.'

'You are pleased to be caustic,' Chancellor said. 'I am not a Mandeville. I am the servant of Sir Henry Sidney and Master Cabot. I have some aptitude for navigation and I have been trained for it, most rigorously. I am told where to go by the Company and I am taught how to go by John Dee and Dr Record and Digges. That is all.'

'Herbestein came here as an ambassador,' Lymond said. 'And left his writings, as Ibn-Fodhlan did six hundred years ago. Priests travel, dispatched by the Pope to make their conversions. Marco Polo became a trader of such wealth he was known as Il Milione. Pilgrims travel, and colonists, to escape persecution, and men sent by their monarchs to collect rarities: manuscripts or animals or evidence of natural phenomena. But there is always a reason, a primary reason to start with. But a man who faces such dangers as the unknown world still offers must have, within himself, another compulsion. An agitation, as Nicolas de Nicolay would put it. Why should it not be spoken of?'

'To fill an idle moment?' Chancellor said. He refused the lead.

'To learn,' Lymond said. 'We have cross-staffs and astrolabes at Vorobiovo. War means cannon, and cannon means a system of range-finding. Measurement is a basic science which we need for our forts and our buildings; map making is another, for our campaigns. Plummer and Black-lock are our experts : you know that; they have picked your brains often enough.'

'And you would pick my brains also?' Chancellor said. 'Or do you have something to offer me?' And again, before he could stop himself : 'An appointment if Adam Blacklock should die?'

But this time there was no answering anger. His arms folded, Lymond waited a moment, and then said without moving, 'I cannot discuss my disciplines with you. But it is all too recent, I gather, to make it possible to talk about anything else. It is a pity, because we may not meet after this expedition, and I understand perhaps better than you think.'

'From a cataclysmic encounter with Nicolas de Nicolay?' Chancellor said. He finished, obstinately, all that remained in his tankard.

The lines round Lymond's mouth deepened for a moment. 'His conversation, I agree, is entirely frivolous, but his mind is very admirable indeed. So are his charts. He became cosmographer to the King of France but he began, as I suppose you know, with a military career. Espionage and maps, I suppose, are natural bedfellows . . . John Elder, William Courtenay. . . . But that is by the way. Who else? De Villegagnon, who has gone to colonize Brazil, was a lawyer. I learned of Thevet from him and from Pierre Gilles, whom I met in Stamboul. Chesnau and Belon and Postel I heard of from d'Aramon, the French Ambassador to the Sublime Porte. Once, in Dieppe, I met Pierre Desceliers of the School of Hydrography, although not Ribault, who was in the Tower, I believe, at the time.

'Rotz, too, was already in England. It was just after all the Huguenots had rushed over from France to the court of Henry VIII. They say there were more than sixty French pilots and mariners in his service at that time. And Spain and Portugal were dividing the unknown sphere between them while schoolmen in the Low Countries were studying and talking and publishing treatises on cosmo-graphy and in England there was nothing, except a few Bristol seamen. The fishing fleet sailed out to Iceland and fished off the banks of unknown country far to the west, but no one saw their charts or cared about them.

'And then an English merchant living in Spain wrote to Henry VIII and suggested that Cathay might be reached by the route you have taken.'

'It is very different in England now,' Chancellor said.

'Tell me about it,' said Francis Crawford.

Later, Diccon Chancellor wondered how long he had been talking. He remembered beginning with John Dee, because he always began with John Dee, but then somehow much later he was arguing about Record's Pathway of Knowledge and describing what Cabot had told him about the La Plata voyage and diverging from that to give his opinion on Rotz's Differential Quadrant.

And later, also, he realized that what had occurred was not a monologue or an interrogation but an exchange, to more than a little degree, of ideas.

What they were discussing was not new to the Voevoda. He did know these men and had talked with them, and had read what they had written. Some of the questions he put had not occurred to Chancellor himself: much of the information he possessed about their ideas and their travels was novel. On a subject not his own, his experience and his interest together were enough to make, out of all expectation, a common ground between himself and Chancellor which had nothing to do with trading or warfare or, except indirectly, with Russia. He had said he understood something of the mind of a navigator, and this was true.

It was only when the little light they had started to fail that Chancellor realized that the night, once dreaded, was almost worn away without sleep; and that his body, neglected, was groaning with weariness. 'The time!' he said.

Channelled with sleeplessness, the Voevoda's eyes were clear still, and serene. 'Where there is no cockerel, the camel crows at dawn,' Lymond said. 'There is still time to sleep. Aleksandre will awake you. And you must forgive me. I did not mean to inflict a white night upon you.'

'It was, I think, worth the value of several dark ones,' Chancellor said. He hesitated, wiser than he had once been. 'Is it true what they say? That you mean to stay for your lifetime in Russia? Is it out of the question for you to return to your homeland?'

'It *is* out of the question,' Lymond said. 'But not because of ambition. Like King Lewis of Hungary, who was immaturely born, came of age too soon and was immaturely married, my age is out of joint with my phenomenal destiny. I shall not go back.'

'Do the thrones of Europe have no need for security?' Chancellor asked.

'No. I shall stay in Russia. I am too far away now from it all,' Lymond said. 'And if we are going to be metaphysical, I have no sea card, or compass, or star.'

In the silence that followed, sleep finally overcame Chancellor, and when he woke, the candles had guttered almost into darkness, and he heard by the bustle that a new, sunless dawn had arrived, and it must be time to bestir oneself. The Voevoda, he saw, had already gone.

Late that afternoon they ran into the scattered log town without walls called Kholmogory, and found Richard Grey snug in a large timber counting-house, pink cheeked and friendly and cheerful, and sporting a nascent grey beard thick as lichen. He was ready to travel. They spent a day loading and unloading chests and marking off invoices, and putting Killingworth's precious goods into storage; then, making rendezvous again with the Voevoda, they joined their depleted sledges to his, and set off east for Pinega and Mezen. Grey, Chancellor was exasperated to see, was inclined to be respectful to the Voevoda, about whom he had heard: his eyelids fluttered every time Lymond spoke English, and Diccon gathered that he had not yet brought himself to believe that the Tsar's Supreme Commander was not Russian. The only thing which seemed to worry him was Slata Baba.

Lymond, typically, exorcized his mistrust by flying the eagle at the first opportunity. After the first kill, a bloody one which brought her back to the lure, feet dripping and wings flapping like thunderclouds, Grey glowered, asked some belligerent questions and then surprised them, presently, by leashing her under direction, and putting her up later on, after a couple of hares. Then they had to stop, but a love affair, surprisingly, had been born, and he set himself the task of watching Slata Baba's crop for her castings as tenderly, said Chancellor uncharitably, as a capon with another man's egg.

Lymond grinned and then soared away, like the eagle, on his artach, which moved Chancellor to further complaint for, although he was learning, he had not yet attained the Voevoda's undoubted competence.

But Diccon Chancellor's sarcasm was a defence, for here,

outside all probability, had come upon him something unlooked for and rare; something he had experienced only a handful of times since Christopher's mother had died: which was the reason, although he would have told no one, for his adventuring.

They had left the horses behind. From Kholmogory to Lampozhnya their sledges were pulled by relays of reindeer, which could run post with an unloaded sleigh for two hundred miles in twenty-four hours without sleeping, and then, unyoked, return loose to their station. Who ran loose, herded by terriers. Who ran in herds of two hundred, each with its train of pack-sledges, made fast to one another. Reindeer blew like leaves across the white, blinding bowl of the landscape. The eye read them as script on a book-roll: the stretched neck, the tined bones of the antlers, the powerful, thick-pelted body; the long slurring stride with its snapping click as the cloven hooves met.

From solitary travellers in this icy white world of nearnight the party from Moscow had become part of a concourse of people: Lapps, Karelians, Russians, Tartars, sailing fleet as seal-boats across the glazed snows in their high-sided sledges; trawling the black ice of the sky with their thin, shrilling tongues and the crack of their whiplash.

Carriage had cost them four dengi a pood, and the cost of hire was ten altines per yoke for five hundred versts. Or so Grey reported. The information hung, like the frozen threads of his breathing, outside Chancellor's head, and his dazzled mind perfectly disregarded it.

They flew, hissing, through the surgical cold of the air, the scythed snow spinning like glass from the runners. Their guides, laughing and calling above the snort of the reins and the rolling of bells from their shoulder-harness, vied with the drivers of other dark teams. And soldiers and traders streamed torchlit over the snow, their furs blowing, their faces muffled with scarves, and tumbled out at the post stations among the trampled snow and fires and log cabins and the long wooden sheds, and the hide tents of the Finns and the Lapps, where the white steam from the breath of the deer rose like the fountains of Geyseir.

Then they would eat, their men and their sledges in orderly ranks round about them, while their fires hatched the clangorous darkness and strange faces came to their circle and sat, shapeless in skins, chewing shanks from their

287

generous cauldron, and talking in guttural voices. It was there that Chancellor for the first time saw the flat, slant-eyed face of the Samoyèdes, the queer Artaic tribe who roved the Arctic shores far to the east, and who worshipped the Golden Old Woman Slata Baba, who stood at the mouth of the Ob, with music issuing from the mouths of trumpets around her. Men said they were cannibals. The Voevoda's Slata Baba, hooded, sat on her perch in the covered sleigh, silent, and was not referred to by name.

Sometimes Lymond shared with Chancellor what he learned in these strange conversations: sometimes not. His Russian was perfect: the dry, astringent touch by which he directly controlled the violent and diverse men under his charge was by now very familiar to Chancellor. Travelling on his own, he had studied how it was done. In company with Richard Grey, he watched it being done at second hand, through the guides they had brought from Kholmogory: how Lymond addressed these queer, black-haired races directly, barely waiting for translation, and using the timbre and flexibility of his voice to convey his meaning. Chancellor had heard the same technique employed by an Italian priest among Arabs in Chios. He had tried it himself, among animals.

He saw that Lymond never visited the dark tents where the children were wailing, or where the women moved, muttering, indistinguishable from the squat, smooth-chinned men but for the coarse black locks of hair worn hanging between ear and jaw. The men came uninvited: Finns, Karelians, Samoyèdes or Russians, with a strip of fish or an axed hunk of meat, driven by a bald instinct for barter and a child-like curiosity, oddly combined. Lymond would not do business, or allow Grey to unpack the sledges before Lampozhnya, and Chancellor saw the reasoning in it. Their customers and their rivals continued to watch and visit them, and seldom went away empty-handed. And meanwhile both Lymond and the Company were gathering the information they needed to have.

Once, a low drumming made itself heard among the thin sounds spread out under the frozen crust of the stars: the cries and barking and warbling song: the coughing and squealing of livestock; and Chancellor asked what it was.

'The signal for massacre?' Lymond said; and then, relenting: 'The Samoyèdes are Shamanists, and worship Ukko as chief of the gods. The tribes are led by the Shamans, and the Shamans practise magic and medicine with the aid of their voices and drums. If you can manage an attack of the Marthambles, we could persuade one to say an incantation over you. You would then be anointed with infallible remedies – say, live earthworms mashed into alcohol.'

'I shall avoid succumbing to the Marthambles,' Chancellor said. 'Are their remedies all so alluring?'

'Take your pick,' Lymond said. 'For example, cornsilk and hot dough and live ants in warm oil for your joint pains. Celery water and goose fat massage for frost bite. That works, and you might as well make a note of it: the Company will have cases sooner or later. The voice and drum treatment is something again.'

'Faith?' said Richard Grey.

They were about to retire for the night. Lymond rose, as did his captain, a shadow behind him. 'I don't know. The Shaman will not come to me. He must invite me to his tent; and he has not done so yet.'

'Acquire an attack of the Marthambles,' said Chancellor.

'I have them,' said Lymond, 'every time I think of George Killingworth sitting confidently over a wine pot with Viscovatu. Do you still regret that you came?'

He spoke to Chancellor, and Chancellor, after a long moment, answered him truthfully. 'No,' he said.

'No,' Lymond said also. 'Verily, God hath eighteen thousand worlds; and verily, your world is one of them, and this its bright axle-tree.'

The odd phrase stayed with Chancellor, through Pinega and beyond where, ahead of soldiers and freight train, Lymond set him alone on a post sledge, and Aleksandre and Grey on two others, to swoop and race with him behind the galloping reins. Then, they hung, weightless as gulls, and dipped surfing through white spray like fulmars. They swept through the dark day and were running still when moonlight unveiled the snow and the Dancers shimmered, green and white, in the limitless spaces above and streamed over the snowfields towards them, cold as alchemists' fire.

On such a night, no one spoke. The four sledges soared through horizonless space, wreathed above and below with vapours of light, shot with trembling colour. Above the fear and his aching body and the pain of the pure and terrible air in his lungs Diccon Chancellor dwelled, with his heart on his wife and his sons, and his soul in a limbo far farther than that, and experienced happiness.

CHAPTER TEN

Lampozhensky Ostrov was an island, the southernmost and largest of a dozen in the wide frozen channel of the River Mezen, lying at the junction of a still smaller river, the Schuksa. And at the southern tip of the island lay the wooden town of Lampozhnya with its two churches, where twice yearly the Russian merchants brought their cloth and tin and copper for barter, and meal and bacon and butter, and salt and yeast and leather and oatmeal *tolokno*, and needles, and knives, and spoons, and hatchets.

In return, they bought furs. The sledges ran in from the east : from Pustozersk, with salmon and walrus and seal oil, with white foxes and feathers, with rattling bundles of yellowing tusks, two feet long and weighing up to twelve pounds apiece. Oil and hides and tusks and frozen fish came from Vaygach and Novaya Zemlya and the Kara Sea and Bolvanskiy Nos : trout and salmon, weighing three to a pood. Sables from Pechora, and white and dun fox, and the pelts of white wolves, and bearskins. From Siberia, red and black fox and the white fur of squirrels. lynx and ermine. Wolverine, marten and beaver. What once lived and breathed and hunted through forest and snowfield piled now in stalls, fifty small skins between boards, sold as a timber. Sold in deep carpeted piles, what once played with its young round the ice floes. Sold, the flayed skins whose flesh edged the piled shores every summer, while the hide covered fresh boats for its hunters.

At the fair, one said nothing as the snow fell, driving in on the pelts in their rough sheds, and the smell of the fresh kill rose sweet and metallic into the air. One watched Richard Grey barter, with his interpreters, keenly and well, and lent one's support as it was needed; and found the Voevoda at one's side or did not find him, as his several absences dictated. Man must eat, or he would starve. Man must be clothed, or he would die. And good hunters killed with economy : the promuschlenniks blinded the walrus with blowpipes or buckets of sand, and then moved in to slaughter with lances. The Dwina men clubbed them on summer icefields, pressing together in fright; weighting the rafts under the water. The Lapp, artist that he was, shot his seal through the nostrils to leave unblemished the pelt. In six hours, they could account for eight hundred.

Grey was pleased. Elkhides would fetch sixteen shillings the skin back in England, with the hair clipped beforehand to save shipping space. He could depend on nine pounds a ton for train-oil, in well hooped casks better than their own, from clean knotless timber, seasoned with water and trimmed with pitch at head and seams. And oil from the top of the seal fat at that, pure enough to oil fine wool for weaving. Everything was a bargain : white grouse feathers at five altines the pood; duck down at seven to eight altines. Salmon . . . he had never seen such salmon : fifteen thousand at least, given away each for a couple of dengi. Richard Grey, merchant adventurer, was happy.

Chancellor thought of something he had once read in one of Ned Lane's scribbled notebooks. *The princely ancient ornament of furs: they be for our climate wholesome and delicate: grave and comely; expressing dignity; comforting age. And of longer continuance and better with small cost to be preserved than these new silks, shags and rags, wherein a great part of the wealth of the land is hastily consumed.*

He repeated it to Lymond, in the rough hut with its three rooms which they shared, he and Grey and the Voevoda, while Aleksandre and his men were quartered more rudely elsewhere. And thought it odd, before he spoke, that of all the company, here or at Vologda or Moscow, Lymond was the only man who would understand him.

He said, 'You dream of a world where man kills like the eagle, for self-defence or survival. Discomfort without hope or betterment is not a great springboard.'

Chancellor said abruptly, 'Neither is luxury. It ends in the Gulf of Arzina.'

He had not meant to speak of Willoughby, and was thankful that Grey had left their evening meal early, and had gone out into the crowded, flickering darkness with his interpreter and an adequate bodyguard. Lymond, the soup bowl still in his hands, said, 'Was life at Robertsbridge so meagre?'

They had not spoken together in this way since that

night in the church outside Kholmogory. And even then, Lymond had not asked, and he had not talked, of his personal life.

Seated now like the other man, on the least luxurious of hide-covered crates, Chancellor looked across the stove at him and made a decision.

'The point is that I was, and am, a pensioner. I was schooled and brought up in the household because I had a head for mathematics and a mind to be interested in more than the household accounts. When Cabot came back from Spain I had already been studying navigation. I'd read Pedro de Medina and examined all the maps Sir William could get. I went to Cabot for instruction. He was seventy-three and Grand Pilot of England and I was twenty-eight. Three years later I sailed with Bodenham in the *Aucher* for Chios and Candia. We fought the Turks, and we brought home a cargo of wines. I studied; I worked for the Sidneys. Sir William died. My wife had died when Nicholas was born. The boys were being brought up as I had been, as part of the household. The Panningridge farm brings in something; but even if I had wanted to, I could hardly deprive them of that. When Sir Henry moved to Penshurst, I went with him.'

'And two years later, were proposed for the Muscovy voyage,' Lymond said.

Chancellor looked at him. 'I learned all there was to know about the route to this sea before Clinton had issued his orders to levy the seamen. I had every map; I had read every book; I had made every calculation. Other the Norman came to the Frozen Sea, seven centuries ago, and Cabot had the notes Alfred King of England made on it. You know about Herberstein. We had some other German accounts, and a Piedmontese map and information from ships at Vardo. Your Scottish herald called David had left notes of his visits for Denmark to Russia. Cabot and I went over them all.'

Lymond said, 'You were chosen then for the first voyage by Cabot?'

Chancellor said, 'Willoughby was chosen by Cabot. And I to serve under him.' It was not said pettishly: he was not a callow young man. But it was said.

Lymond said, 'He owed Willoughby a favour, I would fancy.'

Of course, it was true. It was through a relation of

Hugh Willoughby that Sebastian Cabot had been received at the start of his fortune into the court of Ferdinand, King of Aragon. But he, Chancellor, had had just enough pride, thank God, not to say so. He said, 'It doesn't matter. What matters is that I had my way to make in the world, and a faith to justify, and a debt to pay, so I strove to the uttermost limits to do my work, and I succeeded.'

Lymond said, 'You were navigator and he was Captain General. To sail the ship he had, as you had, a sailing master. To navigate the fleet, he had you. The storm which drove your ship and his two apart was hardly his fault.'

'We waited a week for him at Vardo,' said Chancellor. 'All he had to do was reach Vardo. It was agreed: so soon we lost touch, any of us. A common port, a fishing station, a harbour every boat used . . . it was full of Scotsmen, did I tell you that? And they told us if we went farther east we were crazy, for ships did not sail to the east. But Vardo was common to every ship. And he could not find it.'

'Why?' Lymond said.

Diccon Chancellor knew by heart the log of the *Bona Esperanza*: the contrary winds; the chartless wanderings. And how finally, they found the bight at the west side of Nokuyef Island, and, sailing up it, anchored off the mouth of the River Arzina. 'It was six weeks after they had left us, and they had arrived more or less where they had departed,' he finished. 'They thought perhaps they were in the Lofotens. Willoughby lived, it seemed, longer than any of them.'

It was very quiet. A serving-man moved in the inner room where he and Grey slept. And in the unheated part at the back they heard the eagle shift, rasping its talons. Lymond had long since laid his meat aside, and was sitting, hands clasped and head bent, his face half lit from the open door of the stove. He said dryly, 'A tribute to his superior nourishment. So. They had charts but they failed to read them. Their logging was faulty and their sightings must have been consistently bad. That is navigational, and none of it is Willoughby's fault. But having wasted six weeks and got himself frozen into the fjord at Arzina, the matter ceased to be nautical at all. It was Willoughby's job, and no one else's, to see that they survived. The sea

293

doesn't freeze without warning. And even when it has frozen, it is still possible to cut canals and warp a ship out of an inlet. And if that failed, they had lying under them food for eighteen months and the equal in ton-tight weight of eight hundred oaks and three hundred beech trees. Yet they froze ...

'He was not without resource in the field,' Lymond said. 'He had all the pewter in Fort Lauder cast into balls, as I remember, before they relieved him. I think the heart of the matter lies there. He was a man of the land, whom the sea mystified, and eventually frightened. And whatever his inventiveness at the end, it would hardly have mattered. He had probably lost his authority.'

Lymond lifted his hands from his knees, and, stretching his arm, collected the small pot which stood at his elbow, half a measure of mead still standing in it. He said, 'The sea demands a man who knows the sea and respects it. A man who is prepared to be lonely. There is no isolation like that of the helm in a storm, except the isolation when it is windless.'

Diccon Chancellor seized his drink, casually; slopping a little, in his firmness, on the straw floor. 'It was merely a point,' he said.

'It was two points,' Lymond said. 'And I have them both. It will be known as Sir Hugh Willoughby's expedition. There is nothing you or anyone else can do about it, and nothing you should. That was his epitaph. This is your beginning.'

He had risen, but not without courtesy. Chancellor rose slowly also. He said, 'To you it is no problem. I don't know whether I can sustain such isolation.'

There was a moment's pause. Then Lymond said, 'You have your sons.'

'And you your mistress. But only one man can stand at the helm.' Chancellor said abruptly, 'I don't want to go back.'

Lymond was studying him. He said, slowly, 'These young men in Moscow and Vologda are creating a business against high odds in an alien land, and are drunk with it, as they should be. They will never do anything as exhilarating probably again. But in five years – less – the excitement will be gone, the business will be routine, the complaints will be growing. There will be a little cheating; a little bickering; some slackness; some grasping for power.

The Merchants will stay. The pioneers, the men of isolation will move on.'

Chancellor said, 'Two years ago there was an ambassador in Moscow from the Siberian provinces. He said his father had been to see the Great Cham of Cathay, and that the city of Cambalu was all destroyed, by necromancy and magic. Kurbsky's father has been to Permia and Pechora. You were right. You were right in what you said there, that night. I want to go there. I want to go to the Ob and beyond it.'

Lymond was watching him still. He said, using words Chancellor knew well, *The people are tawny and the men are not bearded, nor differ in complexion from the women. On the way lieth the beautiful people, eating with knives of gold.* If it is destroyed, there will be no trade.'

'I wish to see it,' said Chancellor.

'If Henry Sidney is the man you say he is, you will see it,' Lymond said. 'If he and his merchants do not stake you to it, I will. But you must take the *Bonaventure* home first.'

Speech struck from him, Diccon Chancellor stared at the Voevoda Bolshoia of Russia, who had uttered those extraordinary words. Spoken crisply, as ever, with neither warmth nor any effusive emotion they were as incomprehensible as they were unexpected. He said, 'But there may be no trade.'

Lymond said, 'Then you will have to recoup by publishing a Commentary on Cathay. Richard Eden, I am sure, would be happy to collaborate. . . . I rather fancy Grey is expecting us. My offer stands, and you may wish to think about it. I needn't tell you that with the Company's backing you will be on slightly safer ground than with anyone serving the court of this Tsar, who may quite well be dead or deposed in a week. On the other hand, I should impose no obligations, except that of travelling as widely and as far as you can, and of returning to report on it. Write to me when you return to England, and tell me what you have decided. . . . And meanwhile, forget about it. Merchant adventurers should not only barter, but fraternize.'

They fraternized outside, round the roaring fires, sharing hard meat and horn cups of raw spirit in the thick of the smell and the noise and the buffeting, fur-bundled bodies. This time they mixed freely, in crammed huts and tents, where Lapps howled their songs to vie with the wolves and Lymond's soldiers found their way, free for the night, and no more than partially drunk because the Voevoda was there, and they feared him before God and the Devil.

Grey, when they found him, was not drunk either, but exceedingly cheerful, with his face almost concealed under another man's fur hat with ear flaps, and a battered stringed instrument in his arms. Lymond took it from him and tuned it, sitting on the table edge in a primitive drink hut, his hat pushed to the back of his head. His own soldiers, milling about him, made up perhaps half of the uproarious company : the rest were mainly incomers like themselves from Kholmogory. He struck up a Russian song, to which it was evident he knew all the words.

Chancellor caught some of them, but not all, because of the noise : what he did hear shattered his own belief that he was unshockable. The music was unwestern in cadence and not to his taste, but it hit exactly, he saw, the mood of the Russians. They howled at the end, begging for more, and when Lymond, his cup at his side, began playing again they joined in raggedly, and then in full force, stamping and shouting and pushing forward as more pressed in the low door and thrust in to watch. In a corner, Chancellor could see the man Aleksandre, a pot in one hand, trying the strength of his arm with a Russian, and getting the worst of it. A jug of liquor passed from hand to hand over their heads; the stove belched; the tallow smoked and sweating faces blossomed like water plants above the compressed turgid weed of their clothes. Transfixed, overwhelmed, his head throbbing in the intolerable heat, Diccon Chancellor grinned and endured it.

It lasted a long time, and Grey finally got impatient. 'There are Englishmen here who want a Christian song with a tune to it !'

Luckily, loud as he yelled, the shouting of others was louder and Lymond, his face bright as butter with sweat was too far away, too occupied and too mellow also, Chancellor suspected, to have heard him. He tightened his grip of Grey's arm and said, 'No, don't. Don't draw their attention.' The chorus roared to an end and he winced with the earsplitting pain of it. Before he could draw breath, the strings spoke again, among the clatter of drinking cups, and a voice sang, with neat economy:

> *Meum est propositum*
> *In taberna mori*
> *Vinum sit oppositum*
> *Morientis ori*
> *Ut dicant, cum venerint*
> *Angelorum chori*
> *Deus sit propitius*
> *Huic potatori*

Chancellor caught, as Grey did not, the solitary, far spark of irony as Lymond ceased, and turning back to his audience, took vociferous communion and launched into primitive song once again. The half-drunk army of the Voevoda Bolshoia had conceived that the Voevoda Bolshoia, drunk this night, was their brother. Chancellor knew that he was not, and was not.

The sleigh race was run later that night, when the moon was up, whitening the snowfields, and making plain the post a mile off up the islanding river, round which each team of man, sledge and reindeer was to turn.

Ten reindeer were yoked amid indescribable confusion. Chancellor, long since returned to his cabin, heard the noise from the inner room where he sat trying to make notes by candlelight. He knew more about the roads through Siberia than he had even hinted to Lymond. He had talked all day with interpreters, to men from the Kara Sea and beyond. So while Richard Grey snored in his blankets behind him, and the torches outside flickered dimly through the thick mica, he wrote until a hammering on the door made him shift back his stool and get up.

Grey turned over, snoring. The rest of the house sounded empty. The two men who served them were still outside then, as was Lymond. Chancellor walked through the outer room, which was Lymond's, and drew back the bolts of the door.

It was the lieutenant, Konstantin, respectfulness vying in his face with undisguised excitement. There had been a challenge, and the Voevoda was to take part with some of his men in a sleigh race. Did the Englishmen not wish to come and watch?

One Englishman was beyond watching, and Chancellor

said so, wondering if a common language made it imperative that he alone should put on his wet furs again and struggle out into the cold. As far as etiquette went, the bond was closer than that of nationality: the Voevoda was in some sort, he supposed, their escort and host. And earlier in the evening, he had proposed to go further than that, and become his personal sponsor.

He could not yet decide why, and asked to give his reply tonight, he would have refused. The man was too clever; too singular; too well endowed with all the obvious talents. He knew Lymond could use a sleigh well. He did not especially want to see him prove it.

Chancellor sighed and said, 'I'll come. Go ahead and I'll follow after. Who suggested the match? The Voevoda?'

His Russian must be getting much better. The lieutenant lifted a hand in acknowledgement and grinned. 'No. There was an argument. Only ten sledges are running, three of them driven by rather incapable soldiers to uphold the honour of the Tsar against the tribes of the north. The Pustozerskers challenged the Voevoda and he accepted. I fear he is angry.'

'Can no one else uphold the honour of the Tsar?' asked Chancellor rather sourly; and then remembered that Konstantin himself still had a hand bandaged from frostbite, and that Aleksandre had been today's casualty, in his stupid trial of strength in the drinking-hut. He added, 'I suppose the others are all too drunk. Never mind. Go on. I'll find you.'

Grey was too far gone to waken, and anyway wouldn't be interested. Neither, thought Chancellor, would be much use for guarding the hut, and the bales in the storeroom behind it. He wished he had asked Konstantin to send along two of his less incapable soldiers, or to find the two young men who served them. He could do that as soon as he saw him. Meanwhile, he walked through to cookroom and storehouse, to check that they were secure before he locked up and left.

All was in order. He had turned back, the candle still in his hand, when he realized that something was different. The heavy stock in the corner was empty. Slata Baba, the eagle was missing, and her chain, jesses, and swivel as well.

In the ensuing slow avalanche of enlightenment, Chancellor realized that he knew where the lure was, and her spare chain and hood. He got them, running, and thrust out into the crowds, locking the door with a wrench of his hand; pushing and belabouring without mercy to reach the hard-frozen snow of the river. The sledges were there: the canoe-shaped Lapp *pulkhas*, light as the skins which fashioned them, sharp of prow and square of stern, with no runners beneath them. Through the crowds he could see they were lined up already: the antlers moved as the reindeer heads tossed; the pitch torches flared from their sterns. He could not distinguish Lymond. But one of the drivers, lying back, appeared to have gone temporarily to sleep. And another, cursing cheerfully in Russian, had not yet succeeded in tying the cord round his feet.

He was still fumbling with the safety lashing when the captain of Lampozhnya, losing patience, gave the signal to start off the race. Nine whips cracked. Chancellor, flinging people aside, arrived shouting just as the last of the sledges slid past the start: Lymond, when he saw him at last, was out of earshot, far over the snow, his white coat and deep fur hat blending with it.

The fool with the ropes still had not succeeded in tying them. Chancellor pulled him out of the sledge and jumped in, glimpsing Konstantin's amazed face as he did so. He flung the lure on the floor and seizing reins, whip and stick, set off after the others.

He wasn't good enough. My God, until a week ago, he'd never raced a sledge. And although some of these were drunk – all the soldiers and at least one of the Lapps and Samoyèdes – the others were not; or were drivers of such infinite calibre that, drunk or asleep, they could fly like the spume in a gale. Then he thought, I don't have to beat them, or catch them. I only have to seize Crawford's attention.

The moon filled the sky like a casement: a celestial snowfield on which shadowy armies stood blurred in strange order, and viewed the black night below, brightly knotted with torches; and the long, chequered shape of the island, barred with snowlight and shadow and hazed with the smoke of its buildings.

All along the edge of the island, the sheds and houses and stables and huts of Lampozhnya cast their black shadows on the silver-grey stretch of the river. The packed snow was more slippery there. If you drove close to the houses, and the banks where groups of people were watching, black shapeless spools stuck in the snow, the moon-shadow flickered, barring your eyes, and although the sledge might run faster, you found it harder to see ahead, where your rivals fled, a scouring of snow and of sound in the silence.

For the noise had all dropped behind. Chancellor realized it suddenly, so preoccupied had he been with the deer and his balance; with acquiring the feel of the light swaying framework beneath him, and the touch of the stick which, too much or too little, could overturn him in a second. And moreover, he had been enclosed in a world of private noise of his own : the harsh, tearing sound of the runnerless skins underneath him : the rumble and click of the cloven hooves; the snorting breath from the massive, misshapen nostrils steaming visibly past him. He lifted his head, drawing shuddering through his scarf the pinching of air that must furnish him and shouted, long and carefully. He then realized that the thin sound which echoed scratching through the wastes of the night was all that the air would permit of a bellow; and that the aviary sounds he heard, twittering at the edge of his hearing were also bellows, from better lungs than his, and to as little effect.

He could go on shouting, and would, but it was unlikely to do much more than puzzle his reindeer. If he wanted Lymond's attention, he was going to have to catch up.

The slower sledges were sawing in front of him. He cracked his whip, passing one; and was nearly caught between the second and third as they veered blearily towards a collision. He saw, looking back, that the reindeer, with more sense than the drivers, had separated them. And looking ahead, that he had almost caught up with two others, but that the four flying sledges in front were farther off than they had ever been, and nearly at the spina, the turning-post of the race.

The animal pulling him, whip-cracking or not, had settled down to its gait, and although God knew it was as fast as he ever wanted to travel again, it was not fast enough. Diccon Chancellor, a decent and clear-thinking man, lifted the iron-shod stick in his hand, and jabbed the powerful, hairy beast in its haunches. The deer bucked and the sledge skidded, jumping and rocking; touched another and swung back once and then twice like a leadline; and finally shot forward, throwing him clean off his balance, and continued to race forward, as the reindeer took to its heels.

Chancellor lunged for the reins. His stick was gone. His ribs felt bruised on one side where he had fallen. He was aware of that not at all. His gaze was painfully ahead, at the dark huddle of sledges even now skimming up to the spina, a flash of white which was the Voevoda among them. He could never overtake them but sooner than he had hoped – in seconds – he would be face to face with them, and able to give Lymond his warning. A warning which now, half-way through the race began to seem faintly silly. A warning he might have killed himself just now in a feverish endeavour to give, when of course the whole notion was fantasy. Chancellor's mind, at last taking control over his imagination, caused his grip of the taut reins to slacken, although the deer, alarmed and resentful, still galloped on.

And in that moment, high, unseen above that vast yellow moon, Slata Baba swept hunting down.

They did not know until later how hungry she was: how for days her food had been stinted. Or how angry; thrown from an inexpert fist from the dark lee of a shed on the island to rise one, two, three hundred feet into the moonbright searing cold of the night and hang, looking down at the white, frozen river, and the animals which fled across it, thick, long-legged and ungainly, their rhizomed shadows flowing beside them.

Deer. Her prey and her quarry, which she alone of the hunting birds had the power to attack; whose blood she would taste and whose flesh she would tear until the beast stumbled and fell and her master would come with his knife and throw her her portion. She picked the victim she wanted among the bunched animals in the front of the concourse, banked a little, her wings half open and rigid, and then, her talons cupped, fell like a knife.

In the last moments of her fall Lymond saw her and, shouting, swept his stick in the air. Had she been aiming for his deer, he might have diverted her. But she was not. As the men racing beside him glanced round there was a long, echoing hoot, followed by a chain of high, panting squeals mixed with a hissing and something else, like the sound of a cloak thrown about by the wind. The antlered head of the deer next to Lymond's was invested with a demoniac presence, dark and vengeful as the Stymphalian Bird with wings, beak and claws of iron; piercing eye and brain with its spears; sucking out sense, air and life with the bat of its murderous pinions.

The deer screamed, tossing its head, bowed with the terrible weight and twisting, ran maddened straight across the course of the oncoming sledges. As it did so its own sledge overturned, throwing the Lapp it was carrying under the oncoming hooves. The sledge jumped, freed of its weight; cracking against the stamping legs round about it; throwing them off balance in turn while the reindeer, grunting and mewing, ran jarring directly into another beast's shoulder.

The shock of it dislodged the eagle. As its victim crashed back sinking, and the other deer, thrown off balance, skidded and fell, taking the turning sledge with it, Slata Baba flapped the eight-foot spread of her wings among the shying, scattering animals, the sharp, golden head jerking, and heard at last the voice of her master.

Driving one-handed, wildly tipping; jostled among the frantic bodies around him, Lymond had been calling from the start, his free arm high, his reins forcing the deer inwards, away from escape and towards the plunging centre of the still-moving morass of sledges and bodies. Three sledges broke from it and fled upriver, their drivers shouting, their reindeer crazily galloping. The eagle, baulked and malevolently angry, rose a little higher and considered the upraised arm she knew, without the lure to which she was accustomed. With deliberation, she took three, steady flaps of her towering wings; and flew straight at Lymond.

Chancellor saw it. He had cast the lure as Slata Baba made her first swoop; but he was too far behind; and with living flesh underneath her, the eagle ignored it, if she saw it at all. After that, he had found it hard enough merely to force the sledge closer to the wild, slithering concourse ahead. The *pulkha* trembled with the battle between himself and his terrified animal. Bearing his whole weight on the reins, he kept it running, wider and wider from the dark mass in front of him. He saw the three sledges break free and run straight ahead, out of control. He saw Slata Baba lift, pause and then suddenly fly towards Lymond, while Lymond's deer, flinching and swerving, turned against his one-handed grip and set on a new, panicked course sideways, towards Chancellor, alone far to its left. His own deer turned, against all the aching, ebbing strength of his arm and fled for the bank of the river as Slata Baba braked and closed on her landing-place.

The black talons, the muscular legs breeched with feathers, struck Lymond's head, and sinking down, closed on his shoulder and arm. A foot lifted, clogged with deer blood and flesh and a gouging of fur from his coat and he dropped the reins, speaking to her, his gloved left hand up and protecting his face while his right stayed outstretched, a path for her to walk down to her proper place, where the hooked, scissored beak might look outwards, and the slashing talons might settle six inches, a foot farther off from his head and his eyes.

With vindictive perversity, she stayed where she was. She flapped her wings once, bearing hard on his shoulder and then, leaving them loose in great eaves over her gold-ruffled hackles, she felt for and gripped the lower part of the thick of his arm with her free claw. As the sledge rocked and the deer careered blindly on, behind and parallel with Chancellor's, Lymond stayed very still, balancing, and bracing his gloved hand at his hip, held her steady. Chancellor, his left arm nearly dragged from its socket, picked up the lure with his other and flung it.

The eagle turned, glared and rose. Chancellor's deer gave a great swerve, pulling the reins out of his hand and sending the sledge slurring towards the high snowy bank of the river. He saw Slata Baba pin the chipped lure in the air, and Lymond's sledge turn on its side as his frightened deer bucked and stumbled, its feet trapped in the reins. He did not see Lymond thrown out because his own sleigh struck the bank at that moment, and crumpled, soft as the skin of a hare, and flung him straight into the glittering pile of ice blocks and snow and sheared glacial debris. There was a violent coloured explosion inside his head, and his mind ceased to function.

CHAPTER ELEVEN

He woke on Lymond's mattress, back in the hut, with Grey, unevenly flushed, kneeling on the floor by his pillow. Behind, his two aides moved purposefully backwards and forwards with steaming kettles and handfuls of cotton: he could see the backs of two soldiers pressed against the window, outside which there appeared to be a great many people, incomprehensively talking. His shoulder ached, and he felt very sore. He saw that the hand holding a cup under his nose for the second time belonged to the Voevoda, sitting with composure beside him.

Anger, deep, shaking and resentful swept over him, recalling all the resentment of the Troitsa. 'Only a bloody, arrogant bastard,' said Richard Chancellor, 'would choose a born killer to cut a bloody, arrogant figure with.'

The cup remained. Lymond said coolly, 'Who freed her?'

Grey said, 'I was asleep. I didn't see anybody. I was asleep until you woke me just now.'

Lymond repeated, without turning, what he had said. 'Who freed her?' He was still in his torn furs, spattered with deer blood. A scarlet handkerchief had been stuffed inside his coat, to one side of his neck.

Chancellor took the cup and sat up. His shoulder was wrenched, and his ribs hurt, and two fingers of his left hand were swollen and reddened. His head throbbed. He said, 'There was no one in the house when we came back from drinking. Grey fell asleep right away, and no one came in until the captain came and told us about the race. I found the eagle gone then, and the jesses and chain.'

Lymond said, 'I have sent someone to look for them, on the shore where we first saw the eagle. A faint hope. They will be safe in someone's cabin by now.'

Grey, willing but not yet quite awake, said, 'Would she not simply slip the thong from the swivel and fly out?'

Chancellor stared at him with equal dislike. 'And take her hood?' he suggested. 'Anyway, she had no jesses on her. No. Someone must have taken her when we were out drinking. Someone with a right to come in, or a key, or access to a key.'

'The two men behind us came in,' Lymond said. He was speaking in English, extremely clearly: it suddenly penetrated Chancellor's senses that he was in a towering rage: and that this harsh, level tone was a mark of the force he was at this moment using to control it. Lymond added, 'They say they were called out later by Konstantin, but locked and barred the front door behind them. Konstantin had a key. So had Aleksandre. Master Grey was

304

here alone before you, Chancellor, came. Any one of the soldiers may have stolen and replaced one of the keys. They will all be questioned, when they are sober enough to be frightened. Meantime the field, unfortunately, is extremely wide open.'

So were Grey's bloodshot eyes. He said incredulously, 'Seriously? Do you seriously think it would cross my mind to walk back there and free your damned bird? Someone stole it. Someone freed it. Someone maybe doesn't like you or it. Diccon was right. The fault for those deaths on the ice was three-quarters your own for having her with you.'

Lymond had stopped listening to him. He said, staring at Chancellor, 'The ironic thing is that I suspected that race from the start. I tested every inch of the reins and had a look at the shafts and the terrets. But it wasn't the sledge he had tampered with.'

So, against all appearances, he had taken seriously after all the warning Chancellor had been instructed to convey to him. Not excluding even Grey from his suspects. Too seriously to be perfectly rational on the subject, perhaps. Probably few people could be called rational, once they had been warned that their lives were in danger. Chancellor said, 'There are less devious ways, equally secret. Such as poison.'

'Except that I would have discovered it. Over the years,' Lymond said, 'a great many people have persuaded themselves that the world would be a brighter place if I were not in it. When I am given a warning, I never ignore it. Besides, this is the third attempt since Kholmogory.'

'The . . . ?' said Chancellor. Someone had brought hot water and, displacing Grey at his side, was unlacing his shirt prior to pulling it off. He wondered if he had put out his shoulder, and decided that he probably had, and someone had wrenched it back into place, none too gently. The door ratttled, and Grey went to open it.

The young Russian lieutenant Konstantin came in, his unbandaged hand holding a fragment of blue which he laid on the mattress. It was Slata Baba's hood.

'Where?' said Lymond.

'In the trampled snow between huts, a little upriver from where the eagle attacked you. There was nothing else there: it was the footsteps and sledge marks on the snow which guided us. It lay in the moonlight.'

'So careless?' said Chancellor.

'The spheres move,' Lymond said. He was still looking at Konstantin. 'Nothing else?'

Konstantin said, 'Only stains. Some small stains of fresh blood on the snow.'

Richard Grey, his face shocked, had said nothing since the conversation had taken this murderous turn. Now, hesitating, he offered, 'A lure? Some meat offered the eagle?' And then as no one answered, took confused thought himself. 'No. Not if they wished her to hunt.'

Lymond was still looking at Konstantin. 'Not meat,' he said. 'But flesh. We want a man who is bloody, as any novice handling Slata Baba would be bloody. Strip. Strip to the waist. Coat, waistcoat, tunic and shirt. Unwind your bandage.'

The lieutenant was white. He said, standing upright, 'I was here. I called the Boyar Chancellor. I would not have taken the eagle so far off in time.'

'You might have taken her there. You might have paid an accomplice to fly her,' Lymond said. 'Strip. And you, Master Grey. And every other man in this hut.'

Grey jumped to his feet.

'Do it,' Chancellor said. 'He is the Voevoda Bolshoia. Perhaps he will think I am stripped enough.'

The prick brought no recognition. Nor did the promptitude with which he was obeyed. Grey, the serving men and Konstantin were all without blemish, save for the dead flesh in Konstantin's fingers. Grey had begun to rewind the bandage for him when Lymond said, 'I want each of the soldiers stripped and examined, one by one. And Aleksandre brought here at once. Where is he?'

'Outside,' said the lieutenant. 'There is a Samoyèd Shaman with him who has been asking to see you. The tolmatch says that two of his tribe ran in the race.'

Lymond said briefly, 'That has been dealt with. The Tsar accepts the blame, and the Tsar will be generous.'

Konstantin said, 'He still wants to see you.'

'Later, then. Call in Aleksandre.'

He came in; a short and burly young man, the deftest and most intelligent of all the new Streltsi Danny Hislop had trained. He said, 'My lord—' and stopped against the unyielding wall of Lymond's face. Lymond said, 'We are endeavouring to reach the truth; always a tedious pro-

306

ceeding. You will humour us by baring the sprain you received in the tavern tonight.'

The lieutenant looked at nothing, and the captain did not glance at him, but flushed in an angry awareness of his audience. 'I, my lord?'

Lymond said dryly, 'You are not alone in your predicament. Every other man in this room has also obliged. Unwind the bandage.'

The fur coat came off, with stiff obedience. The narrow sleeve underneath was rolled up, with some trouble. The bandage, unwound, revealed a bloated patch, red and misshapen, on the upper part of the wrist. There was no doubt that it was a severe sprain, and painful.

'Now strip to the waist,' Lymond said.

He didn't do it. He had fallen, Chancellor conjectured, waiting and wondering, into some kind of daze, brought on by the lateness and the drink and the long and strenuous trials of the night. He saw Konstantin, with a glance at Lymond, reach out and touch Aleksandre on the arm. And he saw that Aleksandre, like a man frozen, still stood unmoving. Lymond said, '*Captain.*'

Aleksandre said, 'I have an old wound. It is not very pleasant to look on.'

Lymond continued, calmly, to hold his eyes. 'Konstantin. How many soldiers outside?'

'Four, my lord. I thought it as well. There is much drunkenness.'

'If they are sober,' said Lymond, 'bring them in. Then help the captain to undress.'

Diccon Chancellor saw, disbelieving, that Aleksandre's face had quite changed. For a long moment he stood glaring at Lymond; then as the door opened and his men began to come in, he dodged suddenly and ran head down, straight for the door. He fought so hard that they had to half stun him before they had him, arms spreadeagled, in front of the Voevoda, and Konstantin peeled of his tunic.

The shirtsleeve beneath was marked by a bloodstain. Konstantin ripped it off. Below, covered with scraps of rags, were three deep, livid punctures, as well as some patches of red, roughened skin stretching from shoulder to forearm of the limb with the sprain.

Slata Baba had left her own finger-prints. Lymond said, 'Who paid you to do this?'

Gripped by his bare arms, the captain spat on the floor. 'Son of a whore,' he said. 'Why should I tell you?'

Taking his time, Lymond studied him. 'Self-interest,' he said eventually. 'The question is not whether you die, but how you die. Tell me who paid you.'

Aleksandre smiled.

Konstantin struck him on the face. 'Speak!'

And Aleksandre laughed through bleeding lips. 'You teach well. You teach me how to withstand torture,' he said. 'I am not afraid. And meanwhile, you will wonder: who is it? Is it Prince Kurbsky who wishes ill to the Voevoda, that he may be the Tsar's undisputed Commander? Is it Dmitri Vishnevetsky who had decided to leave Lithuania and throw in his lot with the Tsar, given a suitable office? Is it the priest Sylvester who hates you because you flayed your officer for attacking his frescoes, or Chief Secretary Ivan Mikhailovich Viscovatu, who fears you are too close to the ear of the Tsar? After I am gone, you will live for a short while, I think, wondering. And then one of them will pay someone else to kill you, and they will do it.'

Chancellor saw, raw with shock, the eyes of the soldiers and Konstantin meet. Lymond studied Aleksandre. At length, 'It sounds well,' he said. 'I cowered, almost, to hear you. Save that rivers must break from their courses before a Russian dares lay hands on me. Or any man whose life depends on the favour of the Tsar. And if you doubt it, let me tell you this. If you do not tell me the name of the foreigner who thinks he can kill the Voevoda, I shall give you to the Tsar's courts for judgement. Who was it?'

Chancellor's mind's eye was awake, and witnessing the subtle, boundless range of the Tsar Ivan's judgements and its weapons: fire and ice, the knife, the axe and the stake; the cunning abuses by snow and by water; the execution by animal. He said, 'Judge and sentence and execute him here. You surely have powers.'

'He is tried,' Lymond said. 'And sentenced. And will be executed when he has told me what I want to know; but not before. Konstantin and any four men he chooses will be his persuaders. When he has spoken the name of the man who has paid him, Konstantin will report it to me, and I, if I am satisfied, will give the order which will award his body to death. Konstantin?'

'I understand, my lord.'

'Aleksandre?'

'I understand, my great lord,' said the captain, with hideous irony.

They were about to take him away when Lymond spoke to him unexpectedly. 'If you had attempted this solely for money, you would have been thankful to shorten your punishment. What grudge do you have, that is worth suffering for?'

For a long time, Aleksandre stood looking at him. Then he said, 'I am a Lithuanian. What I learned from you I would have used against you, in Lithuania.'

Lymond said, 'I see. But I am attacking the Tartars, not the Lithuanians.'

'I hear differently,' Aleksandre said. 'I hear the great Emperor Charles is dying, leaving one inadequate son tied to Mary of England. I think when the Emperor is dead, the Tsar will think it safe to make Lithuania and Livonia his own, and the Tartar war will be forgotten. And with the Voevoda Bolshoia dead, he will fail.'

The emotionless blue eyes stared and stared, mordant in their contempt, until at last, Aleksandre dropped his. 'With me or without me,' said Lymond; 'with the Tsar or without him, the army I am making will not fail, in anything it may set its hand to. Konstantin, you will have the truth from him by the morning. Take him away.'

Richard Grey moved and then stopped, as the small cortège marched out. Chancellor, hastily attended to by the two half-dressed servants, began to push himself off the mattress. From his makeshift seat, shoulders on the wall, Lymond surveyed him. 'Ah. The *lit de parade* is being vacated. Thank you. Which reminds me. I have another and pleasanter debt to pay off.'

Chancellor stood up rather carefully, his black-bearded face stolid. 'Having seen how the first fared, I had rather forget it.'

Lymond lifted his eyebrows. 'God hateth murder.'

Chancellor said. 'Punishment is one thing. Foul retribution is another. I can guess how Konstantin will try to drag the truth from that man.'

'I doubt if you can,' Lymond said. 'In some directions the Russian is peculiarly inventive. The Tsar, however, would have been more whimsical still. I take it you mean to sleep, or do you intend to hold wassail till morning?'

If Lymond was minded to be corrosive, Chancellor, blind

with weariness, was not minded to match him. He caught Greys eye and, stooping to gather up the stained remnants of his outdoor clothing, he dragged his feet to the door and, with the other man, entered with relief the warm, candlelit quiet of their own inner room. He glanced back once as they went, and saw that Lymond, alone, had already forgotten him, and was welcoming with what looked like elaborate courtesy the shapeless, skin-padded figure which must be the Samoyèd Shaman and his interpreter. From which he deduced, without pleasure, that the *lit de parade* had no particular importance for Lymond, who had merely wished to discuss the knottier points of the Tsar's compensation with the principal claimant in peace.

In that he was wrong. The two men entering the room might, to an onlooker, have seemed nervous. They were dressed in sewn tunics and breeches of deerskin, and both had the large head and broad olive face of the true Samoyèd, the eyes small and obliquely set; the chin smooth and beardless.

The younger and squatter of the two had pulled off his rough sleeveless fur and his hat, showing a crow's wing of coarse, straight black hair down his cheek. The older, wearing a long coat of rubbed and stained sables, and a deep, shapeless hat of the same, made no move to disrobe but walked forward, quietly, until he was standing before the Voevoda Bolshoia. And although his manner, like the other's, was alert and wary and to a degree diffident, there lay behind it something which was the reverse of diffidence, and which made it easy to look at him, and guess that here was the leader of his tribe. The door closed behind them as he stood and looked, without speaking, at Lymond.

For the first time since he had entered the hut, Lymond rose. He stood, his back to the wall, and said, 'On the river . . .' in English, and then, with an obvious effort, changed it to Russian. 'On the river this evening, you saw the power of Slata Baba and spoke to me. You offered me help.'

The older man spoke. His voice, deep and grating, curried the silence: Chancellor, hearing the sound but not the words, shivered as he drew the bearskin over his shoulder. The interpreter, in stilted Russian, said, 'We offer it still.'

There was an odd pause, during which the Voevoda was

certainly searching for words. Then he said, also in Russian, 'Then in the name of the respect I bear for your creed, and for the bird who carries in her the nobility of both your god and your race, I accept it.'

Then, since he could not stand any longer, nor find, groping, polysyllables of suitable majesty for any conceivable coda, the Voevoda Boshoia of Russia subsided, not without grace, on his bed and from there, quite unwittingly, to the floor.

*

The foreign party slept late the next morning. The last thing Chancellor had heard, before sleep entirely claimed him, was a subdued bustle of some sort in the next room, and the resumption of the deep voice he had heard earlier: the Samoyèdes were taking time, it appeared, over their argument. The voice rose and fell, changed and modulated almost like music: it was extraordinarily soothing. Chancellor thought, vaguely, that he must learn the language and then, even more vaguely, that it must be simple, to need no interpreter.

He wished the Voevoda well from the monologue and there entered his mind, like a foul taste, the thought of Aleksandre, and what at the moment was happening to him. Then the thick, undulating voice claimed his thoughts, and led him soon wholly to slumber.

When he finally stumbled into the outer room half-way through the next morning, Lymond was sitting fully dressed in clean clothes on his mattress with pen, ink and a litter of papers spread all around him. He looked, as Richard Grey looked, like cheese lightly set in the chissel. A linen pad showed discreetly above one rim of his high stiffened collar, and there was another dressing in the thick of his hair. Chancellor said, 'We may find it difficult to explain the quality of the ale in Lampozhnya.'

The look he received was wide, pure and cool as the ice. 'I am in no discomfort at all,' Lymond said, 'and so do not qualify, I fear, for the olive branch. Konstantin has just reported that the captain Aleksandre unfortunately failed to recover from questioning.'

Chancellor's bearded cheek jumped as his teeth came together. He said, 'So the next captain is Konstantin.'

'It was the inherent danger in the arrangement,' Lymond

said with a trace of regret. 'I come to thee, little water-mother, with head bowed and repentant. So such exquisite knowledge of the hellish squadrons of Lennox is denied us.' He paused. 'On another matter. You have heard of the Stroganovs?'

Richard Chancellor stared back at him and felt suddenly quite exhausted.

He had heard of the Stroganovs. On the journey north, the meeting between Lymond and Yakob Stroganov, whose father Onyka had established the forty-year-old saltworks at Solvychegodsk, had not escaped Chancellor. He knew, from hearsay, that the family traded with the Samoyèdes, far beyond the River Ob. He even knew that his brother, Gregory Anikiev Stroganov, had established some kind of trading-post on the River Kama in Permia, where dogs carried bales and drew sledges, and men ground roots for their bread, and the white rind of fir trees. He had not expected, in the short span of time now left him, to be able to meet them and question them.

Not until now, when he heard Lymond calmly arranging a meeting for their last day in Lampozhnya. And even then, he disbelieved it until next day he came in with Grey from their huckstering, and entering Lymond's room, saw the burly, grey-haired man in fine furs sitting at ease there, and was introduced to Gregory Stroganov.

Afterwards, he wondered at his surprise, for the Tartar *yurts* of the Siberian princes were spread far and wide beyond the Pechora, and although many, like Ediger, owed the Tsar allegiance and tribute and many others, quarrelling among themselves, were glad to call the Tsar brother, there were still tribes like the heathen Votiaken who found it more tempting to raid rich Russian settlements than to share the problematical benefits of a ruler so far away.

Successful settlers brought Ivan rich dividends in furs and in salt. It was in his interest to protect his Siberian frontiers. And Lymond was his Voevoda Bolshoia.

So one could understand this meeting, which had brought Gregory Stroganov from his Permian home, and had already lasted, from the look of the empty tankards and strewn, crumpled papers, a good part of the day. Its purpose so far as the English were concerned was not immediately clear. Then Lymond, bringing more vodka and discoursing, in amiable fashion, on the distinguished nature of the navigator Chancellor's career and on his interest in the world's unexplored quarters, led Stroganov to question Chancellor, politely, on his specific interests and allowed Chancellor, for thirty intense minutes, to ask all the questions whose answers he so burningly wanted to know. After that, by a means he witnessed with nothing but admiration, the talk turned insensibly to the discussion of iron.

Richard Grey, already intent, became avid. From Vologda to Moscow to Kholmogory had travelled the acrimonious letters, attempting to decide what course to follow about Russian iron. Their ore, smelted with charcoal, was less good than the Tula *uklad*, the Tartar steel they had found in small samples. None so far approached the quality of Persian forgers, who could make plates for light armour like silk, or the strength of a Turkish blade, which could cleave a skull to the brains like a mushroom. And yet London was desperate for cheap steel: had been in need of it for four years, since the Steelyard monopoly was abolished, and the price of German steel rose higher and higher. And here, to talk about iron, was one of the family who might know what was true and what fable of the tales they had heard of rich iron deposits, about copper and zinc, lead and tin lying far to the east.

Blandly, Gregory Stroganov told them what he knew: there was iron, in Karelia, Cargapolia, Ustug Thelesna, but imperfectly founded; there was silver and copper on the River Pechora, but little of it had so far made its way west. He said, 'For good steel, we should fire it as the Voevoda tells me you do, with stone coal. But our workmen are ignorant. We need metallurgists to find our ores and show us how best to mine them. Men come from Germany, from Italy, and then they leave us. We need ironfounders to teach us how to refine the metal, and forge it. Then we would have the best and cheapest steel in the world.'

Richard Grey said, 'Why shouldn't the Company do it?'

'Do what?' Chancellor said. 'Send founders and hammermen and refiners? We haven't got them. We have to conduct half our business at Robertsbridge in French as it is.'

'But not all of it,' said Grey. 'There are some ironmasters who would come. And what does Sir Henry Sidney expect for his steel – five or six pounds the firkin? We could freight it from Tula for four pounds, and make a profit if the quality were improved.'

He was deep in figures. Chancellor, the mathematician, left him to it, and in due course, having completed his business, Gregory Stroganov left, followed, after an ink-stained and well-lubricated interval, by Richard Grey, to close his affairs at Lampozhnya. Lymond, whose papers were already in order and cleared, offered the vodka jug once more, gravely, to Chancellor, who accepted it somewhat grimly. Lymond said, 'I doubt if Sir Henry's affairs will be seriously disturbed by an influx of steel gads from Muscovy.'

Diccon Chancellor took a long drink and stared at the other man. 'So the Voevoda Bolshoia wishes help to create foundries,' he said. 'To make steel with the strength of the Persians'. Because the Tsar is going to ask me to send him shiploads of armour and weapons, and I am going to refuse.'

'He is also going to ask you for an apothecary,' Lymond said. 'And we should like one of those. But I fear, as you say, that his hopes of munitions from England will return to him lame in both elbows. He will ask you for sulphur and lead and powder and saltpetre also. I hope you will be tactful.'

'Or we shall not be allowed to take our goods out of the country?' Chancellor said, descending to bluntness.

'I don't think you need fear that,' Lymond said. 'Unless you deal with him too curtly.'

Chancellor said, 'I am hardly likely to do that. But what undertaking can I possibly make? The last time a party of skilled German workmen was about to travel to Muscovy, Livonia stopped it with the Emperor Charles's backing. The Polish Ambassador has already been promised that no arms or military engineers will go to Russia. Sweden will feel the same. So will Cologne and Hamburg : England might find her own imports of weapons cut off. And Sigismund-August will continue to protest like clockwork, as you may well expect, against all such traffic to the Muscovites, *enemy to all liberty under the heavens.*'

Lymond, who had conducted the meeting sitting in comfort on his bed, closed his eyes and recited. '*Our enemy is thus instructed by intercourse and made acquainted with our most secret counsels. We seemed hitherto only to vanquish him in this, that he was rude of arts and ignorant of policies. If so be that this trade shall continue, what shall be unknown to him? The Muscovite made more*

314

*perfect in warlike affairs with engines of war and ships,
will slay and make bound all that shall withstand him,
which God defend.* The author is Sigismund-August, the
source is an excellent correspondent of mine in Venice. . . .
I think you may promise the Tsar what you like, for I do
not think for a moment that Mary Tudor will agree. The
Tsar needs munitions, but he needs trade and communication with the west even more. By now the Company
know this as well as I do. He may conceivably reduce your
privileges, but the Tsar will never totally sever the bond,
unless you anger him out of reason.'

Chancellor said, 'Why tell me this? Even with the Company's help, it will be a long time before your own cannon-
founders and forgers can supply all the arms that you
need.'

Lymond opened his eyes. 'I wasn't sure if you knew
which way the wind was blowing. By the time you have
your last interview with the Tsar, I shall be in the south
with the army. When he puts the matter before you, as he
is likely to do then, you will be ready to answer him softly.
I shall not be there to help matters if you don't.'

Chancellor said, 'Is he mad?' and received a long, half-
veiled look he did not understand.

Then Lymond said, 'No.'

There was a long and curious silence. Then Chancellor
said, as if following a long explanation which had never
been given, 'But that is why you are staying.'

'If the reasons for my staying,' said Lymond, 'could be
said to have any but negative qualities, that is one of
them.'

They left two days later, their business finished, their
compensation paid and their debts discharged by the
Voevoda himself; the God of Salaries, as he pointed out,
his symbol a deer.

Their last act before leaving Lampozhnya was to attend
the burial of one of the Christian Lapps of the sleigh race.
It took place not as Chancellor had expected in some
crypt or through some elaborate melting of ice, but consisted merely of a church service, followed by a procession
in thick falling snow to the belfry with its flaring log roof
and wide eaves.

Richard Chancellor walked there with Lymond beside
him, while the crowd wept and howled, and the candles
guttered and blew in the snow. In front, uncoffined, they

carried their dead, grey and hard on a board, in the sheep-skin tunic and cap, the crucifix and skin boots he was accustomed to wearing. And when they took him inside the belfry and lowered him stiff on his feet, Chancellor saw round him a leaning stack of dead and stony companions, staring out, head upon head at the living. And in the hand of each rigid monolith of humanity was clenched a scrap of birch bark for St Nicholas, affirming that this old wrinkled Lapp in his furs, that young Russian woman, this hairless baby, its half-made eyes open on nothing, had died devout and shriven in Christ.

'Even in Moscow,' Lymond said, 'they store them like billets all winter, until in the spring each man takes his friend, and buries him. Before, the ground is too hard. It is the crown of dead men to see the sun before they are buried. Or so they say. And each has new shoes on his feet because, they say, he hath a great journey to go.'

'I find no indignity there,' Chancellor said. The belfry blessed, the wood doors were closing. 'The soul has gone, and what is left is nothing but humbling. Although I should, like the Muscovites, prefer to see the sun before I am buried.'

'And I,' said Richard Grey in a voice of bottomless gloom, 'should merely like to see the sun.'

His conversation, all the way back to Kholmogory, was about the ninety-foot tar house he hoped to build in Kholmogory, in which eight workmen would spin hemp into cables and hawsers: two to turn wheels and two to wind up, at seven pounds per annum per spinner. By the time they reached Pinega, he had decided that three boys would be sufficient for spinning. By the time they reached Kholmogory, he had convinced himself that five Russians would do just as well, and would cost less than seven pounds together.

Chancellor was not listening and neither, he suspected, was Lymond, who spent the journey writing and reading in the big sleighs, and did not travel on artach at all. For Chancellor was now aware that, after Kholmogory, his way and Lymond's would part, and that he would not see Voevoda again. With half his troop, Lymond was leaving for Moscow, while Chancellor waited behind at Kholmogory, helping Grey load the furs into their warehouse, and making dispositions against the arrival of his small fleet from England.

Konstantin and half his company were to remain behind here to protect him, and to escort him when the time came to Moscow, to consult for the last time with Killingworth, and to speak for the last time with the Tsar.

But by the time he had arrived in Moscow, Lymond would have left on his campaign against the Crimean Tartars. And by the time Lymond came north from that, Chancellor would be at St Nicholas with Robert Best and his son, preparing to sail home to England.

To sail home to ruin, and possibly death. He had been told at all costs to bring Francis Crawford home with him, and this he had not done. He knew that, so far as high-powered soliciting could make it, Philippa's divorce from her spouse was secure. He knew that to bring Lymond home, even if it were possible, would involve extirpating a difficult and clever and dangerous man from his own chosen and brilliant setting, and throwing him instead into all the small, insidious intrigues which throttled the court of Queen Mary.

There was no place for him there or in Scotland, compared to the one he held in Russia. And although Diccon Chancellor once had thought, wistfully, of a land where likeminded friends might meet and might talk and might make new and astounding discoveries, free of fear, he knew that it was not to be found yet in England. And that if it were, and he brought Lymond to it, he might find that he had not brought to England the Francis Crawford who had talked in the church, or in the small wooden hut at Lampozhnya, but the man who had flailed Adam Blacklock, and who had had Aleksandre put to the torture. Who flew Slata Baba and lay with a corsair's late mistress and who had become what he was by unceasing servility to his Tsar.

So, for all these reasons, he said farewell to Lymond without asking again for his company; without begging; without referring at all to the threat under which he now lay himself. Only he said, 'You remember the message I brought you. Your wife and your wife's mother threatened. You made light of it when we met in the Troitsa. I have no reason to think you have changed your mind now. But when I return, I shall be asked for my answer.'

And Lymond, standing hat in one hand with his loaded sleigh waiting outside, said, 'Philippa will have her divorce.

Of that I am sure, and the danger to Kate will be gone. If you see them both, wish them both happy. As for Lady Lennox, you may give her my explicit refusal. . . . And when she has spoken to you, Master Chancellor, she will realize that she has the better part. You do not want me in England.'

Chancellor returned the blue stare. Then he said, 'There is a man in you I would want, but I think Muscovy has half consumed him. You will take care. Somewhere, here or Vologda or Moscow, is the man who bribed Aleksandre to kill you.'

'I shall take care,' Lymond said. 'If I am dead I cannot sponsor your travels. Except, clearly, in a direction you will never be called on to follow. I wish you God speed.'

And he left, swiftly, so that Grey, craning out of the window, lost his last, wistful glimpse of the eagle.

It was not until Chancellor entered the office and began going through all the papers awaiting him that he found among them a sealed packet from Danzig. It was addressed to himself and proved to contain several letters from London including one whose direction he could not read, because it was quite spoiled by sea water or weather. The seal was already broken, so he flattened it open and scanned it.

He knew by the first line what he was reading, and by the time that, without conscience, he had got to the last, he was troubled enough to fold it on hearing Grey's incoming footsteps, and to keep it inside his purse until later, he could ponder it, and decide how in God's name to treat it.

What he held was a letter from Philippa Somerville to Francis Crawford of Lymond, her husband. And what it contained was the unequivocal proof of his bastardy.

After the birth of Richard, Sybilla had no more children. . . . You and your sister were born to your father in France, of mother or mothers unknown. . . .

And swiftly as he had read it, he could still see the words of its ending. *This is an affair of yours on which I embarked perhaps childishly, since it seemed to me that by ignoring it, you were doing yourself and your folk a disservice. . . . The people among whom you grew up are your dearest charge, and ought to remain so. . . . I am sure you know this without being told by a schoolgirl. . . .*

Honest, sensible Philippa. Who was giving benevolent thought to the middle-aged man she was shackled to. And who had no notion of the public holocaust which might be touched off by the private one contained in these words.

He read it again that night and thought about it for several days before reaching a considered conclusion. Then he took Philippa's letter and placed a new wrapper, sealed and signed, over the old water-stained one. He did not send it to Lymond. Instead he put it among his own things in his sea chest, closed and ready to take back to England.

He was not sure for whose sake he did it. If he sent it to Lymond, he felt, without knowing why, that only the blameless would suffer. And the only time in his long deliberations when, for a moment, he wavered was when he remembered that clear, icy journey to Lampozhnya, and the sledges arching and hissing across the glittering axle tree of world.

For a few days, what he had felt was pure happiness. And what Lymond had known, he now saw, was freedom.

CHAPTER TWELVE

The spring engagement between the Muscovite army and the Crimean Tartars was witnessed in every absorbing detail by Robert Best, the burly London draper who had so nearly become the Company's champion with Danny Hislop and Fergie Hoddim at Novgorod.

He was there, invested in borrowed helmet and cuirass, when the Tsar and his nobles issued with ikons, trumpets and drums from the Kremlin and took their place, a bobbing procession, plumed and tasselled and surcoated in gold cloth and ermine, at the head of the troops drawn up in files in the market place, the banner of Joshua at his side.

The Tsar and his princes accompanied the army as far as Tula, and there remained, a bulwark protecting the capital from raid, recoil, or counter-attack. The rest of the army, led by its foreign commander, and under him all the officers of St Mary's, set off to cross the seven hundred miles of steppeland which lay between Moscow and the ravaging hosts of the Tartars of Krim. There, in the peninsula breasting the Euxinum Sea, lay the strongholds of the last fragment of the Golden Horde, and of its master, the Turk. From Perekov and Ochakov rode the Tartar armies, dressed and armed like the Turks, sometimes in hordes two hundred thousand strong, sometimes in small raiding companies, running about the list of the border, they say, as wild geese fly.

They lived by raiding. They swept into the small towns of Lithuania and up to the walls of Moscow itself, burning and stealing and seeking above all captives to drive south to Caffa and sell for shipment to Turkey or Egypt, the adults lashed to the saddle, the children in reed baskets like bakers' panniers. Or so Best had heard. And if a child fell ill on the way, they would dash out its brains on a tree, and leave it for the wolves.

The Golden Horde had gone, but Russia still bled from the Tartars. In the Tartar wars under the Grand Duke Dmitri, they said, the ground for thirteen miles was covered with dead. When the Khan of the Tartars took Moscow, the dead were redeemed for burial at eighty bodies a rouble. Kazan had been overthrown, Astrakhan was almost subjugated : only the Crimean Tartars remained, vassals of the Turks and supported by them, selling them their Christian children, and depending on their Janissaries to defend them from Lithuanian and Russian alike.

The Tsar, who had accorded the English Company the privilege of sending one observer, had made it clear that the hour had not come to send the full might of his army across the steppes south. This was a foray, a reconnaissance, a warning. But when the time came, a hundred thousand Russians would march rejoicing over the plains, and sweep the impious heathen into the sea.

George Killingworth, having no wish to find himself or his worsted on a stone stall in Caffa, thought it an excellent plan and without hesitation nominated Rob Best to be the Company's representative with the Voevoda. Rob Best himself was not at all sorry. Of them all, he had the least share in setting up this outpost. His role as the most fluent Russian speaker was to collect information and take it back in the summer to London. He would not be needed at St Nicholas until May or June at the earliest. The fact that the Robert Best who returned was not at all the same as the vigorous and uncomplicated man who set out was hardly the fault of either himself or the Company.

Considering the time of year, it was a campaign of astonishing celerity. They left Moscow at last on the far edge of the winter. Already the market was vacating the

Moskva and soon the breaking-up of the ice would be signalled, here and from river-forts everywhere, by the warning explosion of cannon. The rivers, rising swiftly, would bring down not only floes but logs and houses and cattle, and the streets of Moscow would be filled with labourers, axing ice and throwing it into the water.

A month later, and they could have travelled by water. Now, it was just possible to put their transport on runners, and, as the army advanced, Best was to see the runners give way to wheels over brushwood, and later to a flotilla of flat-bottomed river boats, with skin sails and leather thong ropes and a stone for an anchor, which waited with Cossacks to guide them.

By then, it was becoming clear how much of this army was composed of Cossacks. All round the south borders of Moscow ran the chain of Ukrainy – the Riazan, the Tula, the Putivl and Severian frontiers whose Cossack settlements, part Russian, part Tartar, defended the Tsar. Companies of these were with the army when it set out; later another, of Putivl Cossacks, joined them under the Diak Rzhevsky; and later still a band of Cossacks under their own captain who were not from the Ukrainy settlements, but from the free Cossacks, the bands who owned no masters but pioneered into the steppes, hunting and fishing in company with seine and net, and selling their catch in Kiev.

Violent and playful, they crowded the campfires at night in the stopping-places selected with such care, so that the grazing horses were protected by bluff or wood or marsh or barricade of telegas, and the pavilions of the commander and his officers were as strategically placed to control the hard-trained Russian companies lying between them. The men, as was their tradition, slept in the open, in shelters made of bent boughs covered with their own cloaks to protect themselves, their saddles and weapons. Their food, Best saw, was a departure from tradition: from the lump of dough mixed with water and pork meal, the Dutch-like dried fish and bacon, the onions and garlic carried or filched by each man for his food. The carts making up this pilgrimage contained not only hackbuts and cannon and slow-matches and powder, ladders and wheels and logs and the wherewithal to build shelters or stockades as needed. The Voevoda Bolshoia for the first time had brought food for his army, as well as for his officers.

Rob Best wondered, but could not find out, if the Tsar and his Chosen were aware of it. Fill a lazy man's belly; give a life of plenty to a man who has known nothing but the most extreme hardship, and will such a man fight? If he is sated, why should he throw himself upon the brown, harsh-fleeced sheep of the Tartars? Why should he risk his life to shorten a war and dispatch himself all the sooner back to home and bare platters?

Applied to, Danny Hislop merely said, 'My dear Best. It has been thought of. Everything has been thought of, by Wei-t'o, chief of the Thirty-two Heavenly Generals.'

And that was, Robert Best was prepared to believe, no more than the truth. He had watched the man Lymond leave for the north after the thrashing of Blacklock, and had waited, as predicted by Danny, for the slackening of the reins, a simple human reaction to the despotic personal rule of the winter; to the outrage of that scene at the Kremlin.

Instead he saw nothing except, possibly, a brighter glitter on the troops at Vorobievo; a still greater order and smoothness in the exercise of their professional duties. And at Kitaigorod, the officers too were active and silent.

Turned in upon itself in some curious way, the Company found no release in discussing Lymond either with Best or, so far as he could gather, among themselves. The act for which Adam Blacklock had been flogged was disobedience : disobedience to an order already given and already secretly flouted, which offended the nation upon whose bounty they were living, and placed at risk the employment and freedom of every one of his fellows. This much, briefly, Alec Guthrie was prevailed upon to convey.

Adam Blacklock himself had apparently neither sought nor avoided Lymond's company since his return : their relationship on the present campaign was uneventfully formal, as was indeed Lymond's relationship with all his staff : *in St Mary's we prefer to use surnames.* Thinner perhaps, Blacklock went about his duties, carrying the red scar of the whip on his face, but with no other visible trace of his punishment, and Hislop and Hoddim, d'Harcourt and Plummer and Guthrie performed their offices also with cold and steady distinction.

It was their training, Robert Best realized. In place of emotion, their leader had given them intellectual pride : a pride in themselves and their work not far short of arrogance. And pride, too, was what upheld this whole assorted army of untutored stock, and left them untouched by the flamboyant excesses of their Cossack allies, and made the Cossacks eye them sideways in the midst of their bluster : the hideous Cossacks, with the shaved heads and topknots under the tall sheepskin hats, the greasy moustaches, the shapeless skins tied round the waist, the breeches stuffed into the heavy sewn boots.

They were given food with moderation, and drink, with economy; and Lymond's casual, carrying voice cut into the obscenity round one camp fire and then another with a phrase, a story, a riddle that made them slap their knees and shout, belching with laughter. The aide at his side carried both a mace and a knout, and on the same round a man caught stealing another man's saddle was flogged on the spot, and a man who spoke lightly of the Tsar had his arm broken. At which, Robert Best noted, Russians and Cossacks alike rolled and laughed even more, their faces grinning at Lymond. A man born to lead men. A man of no gentleness, whose mistress had slept in the bed of the Turk.

East of Kanev they had their first clash with Tartars : a reconnaissance party routed and killed to a man, while the scouts moved to and fro, skilfully tracing the main body of Tartars. For two nights, no camp fires were allowed, and they ate food kept warm in straw while the enemy was located and their number assessed. Robert Best, forbidden under pain of expulsion to take part in the fighting, questioned Ludovic d'Harcourt, who was brief and not particularly explicit. 'It's a fairly large raiding party, based on a *yurt*, we think, within twenty miles' radius. Not Devlet Girey's advance troops from Ochakov. We don't want to lose men, and we want to make as deep an impression as possible, Voevoda's orders. So we are resorting to trickery.'

Deceit, the Tartars' traditional weapon. Once, by pretending to attack Russia in Lithuanian dress, a company of Tartars under the Circassian leader Tascovitz had induced the Russians to lay waste in revenge a great tract of Lithuanian land, and on their return triumphant, the Russians had been ambushed and killed to a man by the Tartars.

Lymond's method, Best afterwards learned, was simpler by far. A fast squadron of horse, in the tall hats and long dress of merchants, showed themselves briefly to the enemy's outposts, and then apparently taking fright, fled to the north, leaving their laden carts stranded behind them. In the carts, packed still in half-melted ice, was a sacrificial offering of part of the army's provisions: mutton, poultry; carcasses of stiff, watery beef. That night, deployed with muffled harness on either side of the Tartar encampment, the Voevoda's army swept in on the gorged and slumbering men and overran them with the loss of scarcely a man. No prisoners were taken.

Best saw the booty come back: the fence coats and hooked Persian swords; the cloaks of white felt which was so different from English cloth; which could keep armour from rusting and lock, piece and match dry in the Russian climate. And the droves of tough, short-necked horses which could live on roots and birch-bark and branches, with their wooden stirrups and saddles, and leaves for a horsecloth.

It has been thought of, Danny Hislop had said, when he had questioned the wisdom of lavishing food on this army. And Best realized that this had been thought of as well. That, at the turn of the season, the Tartar who quenched his thirst with fermented mares' milk and the blood cut warm from the veins of his horses; who thought horse-head as great a delicacy, they said, as boar's head in England, would be hungry from a long winter's deprivation, during which a man might travel four days and nights without food, and think it nothing out of the way. And that, given food, he would eat his fill and the worth of four days, as an insurance.

That night the fires burned brightly and food was plentiful and hot. And next day they crossed the steppes, riders and sumpter horses, like dancers, to the sound of trumpet and scawm and the thud of the little brass saddle drums until, mysteriously to Rob Best, the order came to draw up and stand, and they did so, under a clear, warming sky with the flag of St George reeling and clapping lazily over them, while another flag appeared far on the horizon, and another company of men, smaller it seemed than their own, came advancing over the melting snow of the grasslands towards them.

Best glanced at Daniel Hislop, mounted beside him. 'Baida. Prince Dmitri Ivanovich Vishnevetsky,' Hislop said. 'Starosta of Kanev and Cherkassy, with five thousand Cossacks. Our scouts encountered his yesterday evening.'

'I thought,' said Robert Best, 'that the Grand Duke of Lithuania was very far from a friend of the Tsar's?'

Danny Hislop glanced airily round him. Of them all, perhaps, he looked least like a hardened campaigner, although he wore, like his fellows, the furlined coat and chain mail over his padded silk tunic, and the shining spired helmet with its neck-curtain of rings. He said, 'On the other hand, news takes rather a long time to travel from Cherkassy to Vilna. I rather fancy that by the time the Grand Duke hears that his Starosta has been in action, it will be too late to do much about it. Or Prince Dmitri may simply mention a productive joint action with the Putivl Cossacks. I hope you note,' Hislop said, 'that we are going to endless discomfort in order to mollify the allies of Turkey. The Queen, poor thing, should be pleased.'

'The Queen?' said Robert Best, with fairly artistic confusion.

Danny Hislop surveyed him. 'Well, my God, that's why you are here; why else did you imagine? To keep our dear Voevoda company?'

'Well, he's got company now,' said Robert Best. Waves of song, half drowned by whooping and shouting, the banging of drums and the rumblings of thousands of soft, unshod hooves reached them from the streaming mass now advancing towards them. They heard a shouted command, and a single horse moved from the line as the rest slowed and stopped; a horse whose trappings were gilded leather glinting with jewellery, and whose high saddle was plated with deep beaten silver and dressed with a horse cloth, somewhat splashed, of silken fringed velvet.

The Starosta of Cherkassy, who during their last encounter had been thrown into the roof-garden pool at Vorobiovo, dismounted and striding forward met Lymond, also on foot, with his mighty gold-mantled arms widely spread. They kissed each other on both cheeks and stood, gripping hands, while the Song of Baida bellowed over their heads.

> *In the market place of the Khanate*
> *Baida drinks his mead*
> *And Baida drinks not a night or an hour*
> *Not a day or two . . .*

'Listen to them,' said the Prince, and pulled the fur hat from his tangled brown hair. 'I drink mead as a sick bear eats ants, in default of a better remedy.'

Lymond said, 'I cannot conceive you mean vodka?' and stood still as he was embraced again.

'A man of saintly perception! I hear you held a feast for our blood-drinking Besermani neighbours, which they attended in two parts, polled head on one side of the field and crossed legs on the other.'

'Rumour exaggerates,' said Lymond politely. Walking towards his own spreading pavilion, where Slata Baba sat hunched, her hooked bill exploring her mailes, he paused where Hislop and Best stood, politely erect by their horses. 'You met, I think, Richard Chancellor, the Master Pilot of the Muscovy Company. This is Robert Best, one of the Company's servants. If you will allow him to join us, he will, I am sure, be as impressed as my Tsar by the original of the legend. Hoddim? And Guthrie.'

The chosen joined the small procession.

> *And so he drinks and sways*
> *And looking at his valet, says*
> *'O youthful valet,*
> *Will you remain faithful to me?'*

The chorus rose and fell through the air. Vishnevetsky smiled, stopping beside Slata Baba. 'I do not see your Venceslas. Is this the eagle?'

'Venceslas does not go to war. This is the golden eagle. Perhaps you will hunt her with me later. Or have you had hunting enough?'

They were inside the tent. On the hide floor rugs had been laid, Turkish-style, and Lymond and his guest dropped to sit on a long woollen bolster, surrounded by cushions. On these, Guthrie, Hoddim and Best ranged themselves in silence, sliding the *shubas* from their shoulders. Vodka was brought. Prince Vishnevetsky, brightly knowing, waited until his beaker was full and, raising it, toasted his host before he answered. 'You observe we have prisoners.'

'I observe you have Tartar women,' said Lymond. 'So you found the *yurt*.'

'I found the *yurt*,' the Lithuanian said. 'It was fifteen miles to the south.'

The Turkish Sultan sends for Baida
And with flattery speaks to him.
'Baida, so young, so glorious
Become a loyal knight to me,
Take my daughter's hand
You will reign supreme throughout the land!'

Guthrie caught Hoddim's eye. Without speech, Best knew what he meant to convey. The *yurt* was the movable city, the heart of the nomadic horde. The Tartar tents, made of wattle and hide, were set on carts which spread over the steppe like a township, drawn by a thousand camels or more from pasture to pasture; set at night into streets swarming with women and children, chickens and cattle. By day the men hunted; shooting, fishing, hawking wild horses, raiding and stealing, for the Tartar had no money and no means of livelihood save barter, nor any art or science save war. And behind in the *yurt,* the women flayed the horsemeat and dried it, and sewed the sheepskins they wore, and milked the mares for the strong drink they lived on, while the old men taught the children to shoot, and denied them what food the *yurt* held, until they had hit the true mark.

From the *yurt* had come the menfolk that yesterday the Voevoda's army had slaughtered. Without their young men, it was unlikely the tribe would survive. And Vishnevetsky, neatly forestalling Lymond, had delivered the death blow. He said, 'They had made a few raids. You would have been amazed. There was gold in the wagons, and one of the Ataman's daughters was wearing sapphires.'

'Have you brought her?' Lymond asked.

'No. She was ill-favoured. You need not wonder long why their maidens wear linen over their mouths, and breeches to muffle their ankles, or why the Tartar would link with a man or a horse as soon as a boy or a woman. The wives are not all as your formidable Turkish beauty.'

'Greco-Italian,' Lymond said. 'But you have found some wenches worth keeping?'

'Oh Sultan! Your religion is cursed
And your daughter is a wretch.'
The Sultan summons his guards.
'Take Baida, and tie him securely,
And hang him on a hook by his ribs.'
Baida hangs not one night nor an hour
Nor a day or two.

The Lithuanian shrugged. 'My men are content. Like the butcher's hounds, they will eat anything.' He emptied the silver beaker and leaned back, a long limbed, vivid, malicious young man with a cleft chin and soft, chestnut moustache. 'Do you hear them throwing taunts at one another, your army and mine? How long since your men had a woman?'

> *Baida hangs and reflects,*
> *Thinking of his young valet*
> *And his jet-black horse.*

Target of the dancing black eyes, neither of Lymond's men offered anything. From his life in Turkey perhaps the Voevoda seemed more at ease than any save Vishnevetsky on the low, cushioned seat. Holding his cup on one knee, he studied it and not the Lithuanian, although his unsoftened face held somewhere the faint deepened grooves of amusement. His expedition to the north had brought about no change Best could see in the Tsar Ivan's favourite. He remained spare and sharp and deadly as the claws of his eagle. And as he did not at once reply, Dmitri Vishnevetsky added something, in a soft voice, to his question. 'And how long has the Voevoda remained uncomforted?'

Lymond smiled. He looked up, catching the eye of his servant, and then as the vodka was poured, turned the chilly blue eyes on Baida. 'I gather that I am about to be signally favoured. I take it the other problem has already been solved.'

Vishnevetsky gave a brief shout of laughter. 'You are right. There are fifty women between my five thousand: some will go hungry, and by God, we have none for your rutting pigs. My men have fought an action today. They need twelve hours' indulgence. Take your troops down the Dnieper, and we will catch you up before you are free of the ice floes.'

'And the women?' said Lymond.

> *'Oh young and faithful valet!*
> *Lend me a supple bow*
> *And a quiver of arrows*
> *For I see three pigeons,*
> *I'll kill them for the Sultan's daughter.'*
> *When he fired – he shot the Sultan,*
> *And the queen in the nape of the neck*
> *And the princess in the head.*

328

'They will be no problem,' Baida said.

Then the talk turned to Ochakov and how to so singe Devlet Girey and his horde that Moscow and Lithuania both might be spared his attacks in the summer.

They talked a long time, and ate, and Guthrie and Hoddim, when permitted, gave their cogent and less than subservient opinions, and Robert Best listened. And when the plan of campaign was completed, Lymond had the final word. 'We avoid the Turks, and we take no Turkish prisoners.'

'What?' Dmitri Vishnevetsky, as the song ran, had drunk deeply of liquor, but he was not so far confused as to let this stricture pass. 'Are you crazy? A kidnapped Pasha will fetch thirty thousand pieces of gold in ransom.'

Lymond said coolly, 'A kidnapped Pasha will be returned by the Tsar to the Sultan. I regret it as you do. But I gave this undertaking before I left Moscow.'

Vishnevetsky stood up, swaying slightly and smiling. 'As the Tsar's Tsaritsa, you give undertakings. The Tsar is not my master.'

The jibe made no impression. 'He pays me and my Cossacks,' Lymond said. He had not risen, nor were the small graven rings of his armour, each with its legend of faith, in the slightest disturbed. 'Who pays yours?'

The Lithuanian stood without moving. Then throwing back his smooth chin, he gave a great bellow. 'Why, my sickly Sigismund surely. My great king and his courtiers, who spend their time in dancing and masques, and not in war with the tartars. Who . . . what does Kurbsky say? Who stuff their gullets and bellies with costly buns and marzipans, pouring down wines as into leaky casks, and in their drunkenness promise not only to capture Moscow and Constantinople, but even if the Turk were in the sky, to drag him down with their enemies . . .'

Pleasantly, Lymond's voice took him up. '. . . who lie on their beds between thick down quilts, and get up barely alive and racked with drunken headaches, so timorous and exhausted by their wives that on news of invasion they shut themselves up in their fortresses, and put on armour and sit at table before their cups and tell tales to their drunken women: drinking from great full alabaster jugs . . .'

'. . . filled not with wine but with the very blood of

Christians. I came without the King's sanction,' said Vishnevetsky. 'You guessed as much.'

'And need the goodwill of Moscow,' said Lymond.

'When we have scoured Ochakov of its filth, I shall have it,' the Lithuanian said.

'And if you bring back Turkish prisoners,' Lymond said calmly, 'you will forfeit it. Your mother is of the blood of the Tsaritsa Anastasia and you are of the appanaged princes of Yaroslavl, but you will forfeit it. Be quite sure of that.'

The Prince Vishnevetsky regarded him with an attempt at a frown. 'As the Tsar himself was told on a famous occasion, the fulfilment of unwise promises, Voevoda, is not acceptable to God.'

'But,' said Lymond, 'we are not speaking of God. We are speaking of the Tsar of all Russia. And there was talk, what is more, about comfort . . . ?'

Best had forgotten the exchange about women. He saw the prince's handsome face break into laughter, and he stepped to the door of the tent and gave someone a command. Best did not see the girl when they brought her, for he was invited to leave while Guthrie and the rest made their dispositions for immediate marching, and shortly afterwards Baida also appeared from Lymond's tent and prepared his Cossacks, as the rest left, to make camp for the day with their booty.

The last thing Best heard, as he found his horse and prepared with the others to move, was the final stanza of that mocking, rollicking song :

> 'Take that, O Sultan!
> For chastising Baida.
> You should have known
> How to punish him.
> You should have cut off his head,
> And buried his body,
> Taken and ridden his jet-black horse
> And given your affection to the boy.'

That night they made their last camp on land before taking again to the Dnieper. Robert Best, healthily tired, snored his way through the night and did not hear the scuffle and cry from the principal tent, which brought the guard running, to halt as the Voevoda appeared in the

330

candlelit doorway, unhurt, unamused and fully dressed as they had seen him last. He surveyed them, commended their speed, and sent them for Ludovic d'Harcourt.

Off duty, the former Knight of St John was asleep reprehensibly in his small-clothes : by the time he had flung on tunic and breech hose and boots, Lymond was in no mood to be gracious. D'Harcourt received the unpleasant dressing-down he knew he deserved for lying unprepared in the land of the enemy, no matter how recently vanquished, and then was bidden to go into the tent and dispose of what he would find there.

What he found there was a dead Tartar girl, still clothed, but with her veil ripped back from her face. She lay among the cushions where Rob Best's powerful haunches had so lately rested, and she had been stabbed to the heart.

Rising from his knees, he looked round at Lymond, who had picked a finely chased knife from the floor and was carefully wiping it. From the turquoises on the hilt, d'Harcourt recognized it as the Voevoda's own.

'She tried to kill me,' Lymond said. 'Outraged maidenhood perhaps, but I doubt it. I rather think I have had a little gift from Prince Vishnevetsky. But I should not like anyone to lose confidence in me or in him. The less known about this episode the better, which is why I have sent for you. Mr Guthrie isn't interested in women, and neither is Plummer, for different reasons. Mr Hoddim's legal conscience would trouble him and poor Mr Blacklock is not yet strong enough, I feel, to make the thing plausible. So—'

'Mr Hislop?' said d'Harcourt woodenly.

The uncomfortable blue eyes opened fully on his. 'The sparrows know it, so why should it be hidden from me that Hislop has a Tartar wench at Kitaigorod? So you will roll her in the rug she is blemishing, and dispose of her how you will, provided that it is secretly, and sufficiently far from this tent. She is a murderess, and a heretic, an upholder of the faith you took vows to destroy. It appears therefore to be a task which befits you better than any other. Don't you agree?'

Ludovic d'Harcourt did not answer. But he did as he was told, and most efficiently, so that soon the Voevoda's tent was vacant and ordered once more, and the Voevoda was able to retire, as he preferred, without company; but with

the final verse of the Song of Baida remaining, freakishly
repeating itself in his mind.

> *You should have known*
> *How to punish him.*
> *You should have cut off his head,*
> *And buried his body,*
> *Taken and ridden his jet-black horse*
> *And given your affection to the boy.*

But of that, naturally, he said nothing at all to his
underlings.

CHAPTER THIRTEEN

The combined armies of the Voevoda Bolshoia and Prince
Dmitri Vishnevetsky sailed down the Dnieper, causing
damage to every major settlement on the way, and finally
raided the Tartar stronghold of Ochakov, lying in the
spring sunshine on the Euxinum Sea to the west of the
Crimean Peninsula. Using fire, using decoys, employing
the cannon concealed in their carts, they felled ramparts
and broke wooden walls, killed and looted, freed prisoners
and took them and confounded the violent defence of the
enemy with all these and one measure more – the touch of
flamboyant genius, the unexpected exploitation of the
obvious which was the mark of St Mary's. Into the streets
of Ochakov, where the children screamed and the scimi-
tars flashed through the swaying strings of dried fish, all
furred and buzzing with flies, Lymond released a double
cartload of swine, the abomination of the Mussulman, and
set the Streltsi firing their hackbuts over their heads.

The Khan of the Krim Tartars was not taken, and not
a tenth of his horde was lost in the raid : the numbers to
achieve that needed a different season and a different
campaign. But that night, in his round reeded house on the
steppes, Devlet Girey prostrated himself on his carpet, and
tears from his hollow eyes sank into his beard as he
mourned his dead, and promised vengeance, and considered, gnawing his lips, the new offence and the new
menace offered by Moscow.

Far to the north, on their way home, the combined
armies of Russian and Cossack raced across the fresh grass

of the steppes, hunting, singing and shouting in a clamour of wind-pipe, drum and brass while their banners flew reeling across the endless blue skies of the *Chernoziom*.

They were on the verge of the riches of spring, when deer and antelope would run to the bow, and wild boars frequent the thicket, and foxes and beavers. When the stork would come back and geese and heron, swan and pheasant and partridge would stand in the brush, when honey would spill through the trees and there would be pike and perch, tench, roach and carp free to take in the unfrozen rivers, and the birchwoods would smell fresh and sweet under the melting spring sun, and the nightingale sing.

Riding north, through the sharp wind and the light warming sun, the conquering armies felt the quivering change of the season. They rode bare-headed, thrusting off helmet and shuba, so that their mail tunics sparkled like river water and the ikons gave off great flashes, as if angel were speaking to angel, under the striding sword of St George.

The leaders hunted, Lymond with Slata Baba behind him, murmuring to her as he unstruck and drew off her hood, praising her with his voice as he fed her her bloody reward, watching her, head thrown back, as she stooped and struck and returned, perfectly manned, to stand behind him again with her half-mantled wings. 'For the first reason,' Lymond said to nobody in particular, 'is that hunting causeth a man to eschew the Seven Deadly Sins.'

Then at night they made camp and the races began, and the contests on horseback, and the gambling round the fires with the small dice, like the English, flipped over the thumb, as booty changed hands, and bedfellows. For they had free people among them, Russians and Cossacks who had been slaves to the Turks, and captive Tartars; a chief or two, with a flat face and a beard, and his black hair allowed to grow curling over his ears, unlike the polled heads of inferiors. These had earrings, which they would sell for a supper, and long, pleatless Hungarian coats, not unlike the Russians' own, but buttoned Tartar-style to the left. There were horses and camels, bales of silk and strange eastern spangles, as well as young Tartar girls by the score. There was plenty to gamble for.

Mesmerized, Robert Best watched it: watched how far licence was permitted, and when Lymond chose to send

333

round Guthrie, or Hoddim, or one of his newly trained captains and touch the wilder forces back into order again. Eating with the rest of St Mary's in their neat tent on one such night, he found Danny Hislop's pale eyes on him, gleaming. 'Not,' said Danny, 'the way in which the 13th Lord Grey of Wilton would care to arrange it. But you cannot expect an untaught people to be wrenched from their toys in a twelvemonth. It is not quite the Bacchanal that it looks.'

A shout, splitting the night, arose from that part of the camp where Prince Vishnevetsky's pavilion stood. His song, in quavering chorus, had accompanied them, fragmented, all the way from Ochakov.

> *In the market place of the Khanate*
> *Baida drinks his mead . . .*

'Isn't it?' said Robert Best.

'The Prince,' said Danny Hislop agreeably, 'is, you will accept, a law to himself. Like Caesar, a cock for all hens. Have you seen the Cossacks dancing?'

'Like witches' get on their hunkers,' said Fergie Hoddim. 'With all yon leg-jerking and spinning. It's not natural. They'll do themselves a disservice. And the lowping!'

'You should try it,' said Guthrie. 'You'll be getting as fat as a sty-pig, full of sour milk and malt, and d'Harcourt will have to discover a fast for you. I think we need some night marches.'

'Do you? So do I,' Lymond said from the door, and sat down without ceremony as servants closed around him, Best saw, swiftly bringing washing water and towel, beer and mead and vodka in snow-clouded flagons, and the first platters of meat. Lymond said, 'I think we shall allow them a day more of sport, and then begin some forced marches. Devlet Girey is unlikely to trouble Moscow, but other mischief is not slow to breed.'

Hislop said, 'You will disappoint your friend Baida.'

'My friend Baida is leaving us shortly anyway,' Lymond said. 'He is planning to build a fort on the island of Khortitsa, below the Dnieper cataracts, to be a base against the Turks and the Tartars this summer.'

'Oh?' said Lancelot Plummer.

'Without our interference, helpful or otherwise,' Lymond said. 'He has virtually committed himself to transferring allegiance from Sigismund-August to the Tsar, but his vanity on no account must be offended. Does anyone know how many women he actually has in his tent?'

'I rather doubt,' said Lancelot Plummer a shade self-consciously, 'if he is at present dealing with women.'

'The last time I passed his tent,' said Alec Guthrie sourly, 'there was a camel in it.'

A chorus of groans, accompanied by Danny Hislop's high cackle, derided him. Adam Blacklock's light, sharpened voice, from the doorway of the tent, cut clean across it. 'Voevoda!'

Almost before he had spoken the word Lymond was on his feet, staring at the man he had thrashed, with whom he had held none but formal conversation ever since.

Adam said, 'Vishnevetsky has Slata Baba.'

'And?' said Lymond.

'And he is flying her at the captives,' Adam said. 'Perhaps you suggested it.'

Before he had finished, Lymond was out of the tent with his weapons, and the others, rising, hurried to follow. Only Alec Guthrie, as he overtook Blacklock, struck his shoulder briefly and hard, as a bear might smack its thickheaded cub for correction. 'That is not for thinking,' said Guthrie. 'But for saying what you are thinking.'

The noise drew them, like an inhalement of steam, to the cockpit.

It was no more than the bare mound of a hillock, not far from the camp and beyond Baida's tent. Round it were gathered the Cossacks, their torches bright in a circle of fire, their shadows jerking and running before them. A little in front of them stood Dmitri Vishnevetsky, very drunk, with the golden eagle, hooded, weighing down his powerful arm. And thrusting past him, as he stood there, helplessly laughing, were two of his henchmen, not so drunk, and carrying something weakly moving between them, which they threw on the crown of the hill and cuffed into silence and then left, retreating a little, standing hands on their hips, waiting for their great leader Baida.

A Tartar captive. A Tartar child, perhaps eighteen months old, with a piece of raw meat tied to its sunken, bruised belly.

Baida pulled the tassel of Slata Baba's elegant hood, and flung her high, flags beating, into the air.

Lymond shot his eagle as she swept down: a high,

335

perfect shot with the little birch bow and the short, Turkish fork-headed arrow. He nocked again as she fell. Before she lodged on the ground he killed Baida's first henchman; he aimed and released the third arrow in the same sequence of deliberate movements, and the other henchman dropped, also shot through the heart. Then, as, screaming, the Cossacks surged up the hill, Lymond turned the fourth, cold shining arrow on Baida.

Everything stopped. Watching, his heart shaking his ribcage, Best heard the shouting diminish; saw the rush falter, watched Vishnevetsky, frowning, gather his resources and attempt, belatedly, to command himself, and the sudden, uncharitable turn of events. Through his nose, to Lymond, he said, 'Damn you!'

To Adam Blacklock, Lymond said, 'If the child is alive, save it. If the eagle is alive, kill it.' He had lowered the bow. But Baida he had never stopped watching.

Already kneeling at the top of the mound: 'She is dead,' said Adam Blacklock, with the Tartar child on his arm.

'How dare you?' said Lymond softly to Prince Vishnevetsky. 'How dare you teach my hunting fowl to turn rogue? Do I feed human flesh to your horse? Do I train your dog to pull the shaft from your leg as you stroke him at table? What do you offer me, to replace Slata Baba?'

There was a growl. Vishnevetsky shouted, 'You have killed my two men!'

'Forgive me. I thought they were your servants,' Lymond said. 'You have slaughtered, without leave and without courtesy, six months of my time. I am waiting to hear what amends you will make.'

Clear and savage and cold, the voice cut through all the confusion; the shouting dropped to a rumble, and already there was a move backwards from the low hill, leaving Vishnevetsky isolated with the Voevoda near the top. Best thought, He has only to pitch his voice so, and they believe it. They believe the lives of two half-trained moujiks are nothing compared to the life of this bird.

'If the fowl was your lapdog,' said Dmitri Vishnevetsky at last, 'I will get you another. Or this . . . ?' And, sobered now, he took the whip from his belt and, stretching it, hooked from the hands of an onlooker a cage, in which a terrified linnet chirped and fluttered and hopped. 'This might please your child, who does not go to war, rather better.'

Lymond said, 'I want payment in full.'

For a moment they stood face to face in the torchlight : the tall tousled man with the wide-striding boots and high colour, and the repressed and motionless foreigner, skin, clothes and hair bright and groomed and deadly as sharplings. The prince, staring at him, suddenly shrugged. 'I cannot manufacture an eagle.'

Lymond said, 'Take your bow.'

The other man had none with him. Before he could open his mouth, Alec Guthrie had leaned over, bow and quiver in hand, and was offering his. Frowning, Prince Vishnevetsky grasped it, while Guthrie took and held the small cage in its place.

'You have booty,' Lymond said. 'So have I. Whichever man of us clean kills that linnet, wins all the other may have in his tent. . . . Release it, Guthrie.'

Guthrie opened the cage.

The bird darted out while Vishnevetsky, still watching Lymond, grasped suddenly what was happening and, whirling, strung and nocked his first arrow. Lymond, holding back, had restrung and nocked his in rhythm. Both bows swung expertly upwards.

In its first beat, the bird had risen above the swirling blaze of the cressets. Rising, darting, hovering in the night, it fanned its desperate wings like a humming bird, sometimes flushed, like a fragment of cloud, by the fires down below, sometimes only a space, a dark scrap of sky against the stars of Aldebaran, whose flocks pasture the luminous grass of the night.

The arrows hissed into the air; and hissed; and hissed; and curving fell where the crowd, talking and shouting, were moving like weed to and fro, to let the archers take aim. But it was, as Best knew it would be, an arrow from Lymond's bow which pierced the fluttering fragment and brought it down, a morsel in someone's rough hand, and Baida's tent to which they all marched, laughing and singing, for the prize to be apportioned as had been agreed.

They walked past the flap of the tent, Lymond, Best and his officers, and the noise of the crowd was cut off. The silence inside, after the first moment, was quite as decisive. Within Baida's tent were no maidens, or valets, or camels. Shackled each to each, their rich clothes torn, their turbans

337

broochless, their dark eyes filled with a world of contempt, lay a group of kidnapped Turkish pashas.

Lymond lost his temper. With furious joy, exacerbated by the evening's aggravations, Dmitri Vishnevetsky also lost his. Lymond's words, of intent, even at the height of his anger, did not penetrate beyond the confines of the tent, but what he said turned Best's stomach, and the rolling voice of Vishnevetsky, replying, gladdened the hearts of the avid listeners crowded outside.

Even so, it was in a white heat of rage, the blood mantling his skin, that the Starosta of Kamev and Cherkassy saw wantonly freed five men who embodied thousands of roubles' worth of Turkish gold pieces, and saw them given horses, and food and weapons, and turned south out of his power. Indeed, when the first order was given, Baida lifted his arm, his head tilted, his eyes on the Voevoda's empty hands and bare head.

Then Lymond said, 'If you strike me, there will not be a man of your Cossacks alive to speak of it tomorrow.' And Best, for one, knew without doubt that he meant it, and that he could do it, and would.

Vishnevetsky knew it also. He said none the less, breathing hard, 'You would lose every Cossack in Russia.'

Lymond's cold voice remained steady. 'And what use would they be, to me or to Russia, once they knew that one of their leaders could strike me with impunity? If you have a private quarrel with me, pursue if off the field, privately. You cannot challenge me here and now without challenging the Tsar and his army.'

The black eyes glittered. 'I do challenge you.'

'With five thousand Cossacks?' said Lymond.

'With the army of Sigismund-August, King of Poland and Grand Duke of Lithuania,' said Dmitri Vishnevetsky, with fair clarity and a great deal of venom.

There was a short, weighty silence during which the unfortunate fatuity of this became expansively clear, and Lymond recovered his temper. He said dryly, at length, 'The Tartars, I am sure, would be delighted. I am not sure what we are disputing about. Did we not make a wager, and did I not win it?'

Prince Vishnevetsky grunted.

'Then your prisoners are mine, to do as I like with. I choose to set them free, because Russia is not yet prepared for full-scale war with the Sultan.'

His dignity salved, Baida's tone became again smoothly caustic. 'And this, of course, is what the Tsar sent Mr Best here to learn.'

'Mr Best is very well aware,' Lymond said, 'that we have neither the men nor the munitions so far to fight Suleiman the Magnificent. Our first objective is to drive out the Tartars. You claim to hate them. Help us.'

'Is it worth my while?' Baida said. Relaxed, he crossed to the chest where the vodka flasks stood and, splashing heavily, filled every cup on the board. 'What arms will England send you, if you make no effort to occupy Turkey's attention? And without arms, what hope have I of ever making a living from rich Turkish pashas? Tell me that?'

Lymond took the drink offered him, as did the rest, and saluted his host, and drank, sealing unspoken the reconcilement. 'What arms do Cossacks need?' he said. 'Except to make love and gamble. Please the Tsar, and you will be rich enough. Make your fort at Khortitsa, and we shall help you sweep round the Dnieper and send the Song of Baida clean through the steppelands and hills of the Krim.'

They left him, still drinking, presently, and went back to their tent more slowly than they had left it, through the quietening camp. Lymond, beside Adam Blacklock, said, 'Before you sleep. Take one of your men and see to the burial.'

'Of the eagle?' Adam said.

'Naturally,' said Lymond. 'And, if you can bear it, of the child.'

He had known, or guessed, Adam took it, all about those illegal Turkish captives. And despite Baida's crapulous efforts, he had saved the prince's face and the kidnapped pashas as well. Out of an unfortunate slaughter, a prize of exceptional sweetness. Adam said, 'Konstantin has already seen to it. The mother belongs to him. He is, more than ever, your dazzled and most humble acolyte.'

'They come in sets,' Lymond said. 'With two small *pi* drums and a set of stone chimes. You are going to tell me that you want to leave St Mary's.'

They had stopped outside his tent. 'Yes,' said Adam. 'Was it so obvious?'

'The lack of enthusiasm has been obvious. To leave before the campaign, I suppose, would have looked like pique, or like cowardice. So, you have discovered that your conscience will not let you put soldiering before other things. I wish you had found it out before.'

'I did not know it before,' Adam said. 'I can't stay. Plummer can use all his arts, and they will let him teach them, and follow him eagerly. I cannot stand silent.'

'No,' Lymond said. 'Then you are better away.'

Adam Blacklock said, 'There is one thing.'

'Yes?' A steaming horse was being led away from the Voevoda Bolshoia's tent, and there was the dark shadow of a man, standing waiting beside the guards.

'You refused me opium, I was told.'

'It is possible,' Lymond said, 'to bear pain without it. If I can do so, then I expect it of you. Is that all?'

'Ludovic d'Harcourt wishes also to leave,' Blacklock said.

The dark figure had come forward. Stained with travel; his beard uncombed, his face splashed with mud, he did not at first seem what he was : one of the Tsar's principal courtiers. Lymond greeted him, and in a few words provided for his comforts, and, before he let him go, opened and read by the torchlight the rolled dispatch he had brought in his pouch.

The questions he then asked the messenger were swift, brief and pointed, and the answers, as he turned back to Blacklock, had not, Adam saw, pleased him at all.

'D'Harcourt too?' Lymond said. 'Our evangelist. I wonder who else is pining for the role of Feodorit, the Enlightener of the Lapps? Whoever they are, if you will round them up, they had better all travel with me. I have been called back to Moscow. I shall be leaving the bulk of the army with Guthrie, and riding back to the Kremlin tomorrow.'

Without the army. A recall, therefore, direct by the Tsar. . . . 'Why?' said Adam.

'I have no idea. Perhaps the forces of winged retribution. The prophet Elijah being fed to the ravens. Like Baida, I have killed my three pigeons.'

'Two,' Adam said.

'Two died instead of Vishnevetsky. One died instead of my brother. Long ago. Attar, the Persian poet, saw the destiny of souls as a flight of birds across the seven valleys of Seeking, Love, Knowledge, Independence, Unity, Stupefaction and Annihilation, before at last being lost in the divine Ocean and thenceforth happy. A charming, if sterile, conceit. Next time, the bird may escape,' Lymond said. 'Happy pigeon. Next time, the archer may die.'

'Happy archer,' said Adam; and shut his lips, and went off.

*

As once before, the Chosen stood in support round Ivan Vasilievich when he received in audience his Voevoda Bolshoia, and the white-robed guard with their silver axes lined the coloured walls of the ante-room and did not salute him, since Supreme Commander to Ivan Vasilievich was as Ivan Vasilievich to Christ, our most merciful Tsar. And in the Golden Chamber, adorned with Sylvester's disputed frescoes : *The Baptism of Vladimir, The Destruction of the Idols, The Deeds of Vladimir Monomach,* stood all the familiar faces : Adashev and Kurbsky and Sheremetev, Palestsky and Kurlyatev, Vyazemsky and Pronsky-Shemyakin. And the small group of priests, including Sylvester himself and the Metropolitan Makary, his two fingers upraised in blessing as the Voevoda saluted the ikon and the Tsar.

So these two men, so close in age, so far apart in birth and training and temperament, confronted one another. Against the black gowns of his churchmen the Tsar's robes of brocatelle and cloth of gold and raised velvet knotted with silk glowed like enamel : the brooched *alkaben* over the *ferris,* the caftan over the *shepon,* and the *shepon* over the shirt with its collar, four fingers deep, of jewels and pearls. On his head, a deep kolpak concealed his short auburn hair, and his feet were in soft velvet shoes, the toes curled and jewelled.

Cap in hand, the Tsar's favourite knelt, in caftan and tunic, while Ivan Mikhailovich Viscovatu smiled and intoned. 'Great master, and King of all the Russians, the Voevoda Bolshoia strikes his forehead before thee, for thy great favour in receiving a gift.'

Behind Lymond were two of the changing band of Russians who travelled with him and served him. Each of them held a box wrapped in silk, and each box was passed in turn to the Chief Secretary Viscovatu, who handed them in turn to the Tsar. Ivan Vasilievich, without looking at his Supreme Commander, opened them.

The first held an ikon, dressed with an embossed silver mounting which hid nearly all but the calm tempera face with its arched brows and pouched, close-set eyes and long, reeded nose above the thin, drooping moustache. In the second box was a gold gospel cover, with its figures threaded and outlined with uneven pearls, and blue sapphires and crimson almandines set high in the filigree. For a long time the Tsar studied them, then, giving them to other hands, he looked at last at Lymond.

Lymond said, 'Wrested by the Tartar from a Christian altar, and now to be restored there by Christ's friend, the Tsar of all Russia.'

'Give me your hand,' Ivan said. And receiving it, held it, while Lymond stood by his footstool. 'Hast thou travelled well?'

'Through the mercy of God and your grace, very well,' Lymond said. 'God give your grace good health.'

Releasing him slowly, the Tsar laid his powerful hand again on the shaft of the sceptre of crystal and gold in his lap. 'They say,' he said, 'you bring me a victory.'

'They say kindly,' Lymond said. 'We have burned twelve Tartar settlements and raided Devlet Girey's town of Ochakov, killing many and releasing many Christian souls, with almost no loss and no harm to your servants. I bring you an army high in heart to defend you against all your enemies. I bring you the allegiance of Prince Dmitri Ivanovich Vishnevetsky, at present in Cherkassy, who is to build a fort below the cataracts of the Dnieper against the Perecop Horde, and who will join us, when we are prepared, to remove Devlet Girey and his host as your Highness removed the Khan of Kazan. The way to the Crimea is known to us, and its strength. In one year, if you will trust me, it shall be yours.'

He spoke, as he always spoke, in the clear, unequivocal cadences of the Slavonic tongue. And he listened, as he always listened, to the rumour, the voiceless burden of thought in the room.

An ear less finely tuned than his would have told that something was wrong. The silence when he had spoken confirmed it. Then the Tsar said, 'For what you have done, we know how to reward you. Receive now our token. As for the future, it is time for our plans for you to be made known.'

Adashev, the soft-spoken Councillor with the pleasant, pock-marked face carried the Tsar's gift to Lymond. It glinted in his hands: a necklet of pendant medallions linked with gold, openwork beads; each plaque bearing an image in cloisonné enamel, set with blue and green sapphires and garnets. He laid it over Lymond's bent head and over the caftan, where it sparkled, a major artefact, close to the sacred *barmi* of princes; an unwise, a violent token of favour. The Tsar Ivan Vasilievich said, 'It is our wish that you should travel to England.'

Lymond stood up. Because he knew Viscovatu was smiling; because he sensed the satisfaction on Kurbsky's face, he did so smoothly but his eyes, wide and cold, were scanning that big, raw-boned face with its jutting nose and soft, reddish beard; and saw that there was colour on the high cheekbones and a deeper furrow on the heavy, ridged brow. Lymond said, 'As close as the shadow and the stile are the Tsar's wishes, and his servant's deeds to fulfil those wishes. I am to travel with Chancellor?'

The Tsar, braced to counter resistance, was visibly solaced; the brow lighter; the deep-set eyes anxious instead of majestic. 'You were right,' Ivan said. 'The Muscovy merchants would accept no commissions. They would give no undertaking to carry our demand to their mistress : that if her people wish to stay here and trade, they must supply me with what my people must have : skilled artisans to teach us, and arms and munitions to defend ourselves from Antichrist and Mammon, the wolves on our borders.'

'They fear you mean to attack,' Lymond said. 'And that the Teutonic League, Livonia and Poland and Lithuania, the German princes and the Hanseatic trade, all dear to the Emperor Charles, would then suffer.'

The Tsar's hand was tight on his rod. 'I have told them,' he said. 'I have told them that if there is to be peace and not bloody war, if they desire calm seasons to trade in, they must see that my poor weakened country can defend herself against those who would run burning and scourging across her. I have told them that if we take arms against any man in aggression, it will be against the heathen, the Tartar. For how can I repeat in my prayers the words *I and the people given to me by Thee* if I do not save them from the ferocity of our age-long enemies?'

'They are obstinate,' Lymond agreed. He considered the matter, without undue haste. 'Chancellor is no politician. Robert Best, who returns with him, is little more than a draper. But Best has seen what our intentions are against the Tartar; he can report what we do with the resources under our hand, he can surely envisage what we might do, better armed. Why not let him support the case for you, and have the argument laid before the monarch of England by a Russian? Choose one of your councillors here to carry your prayer to Mary of England, and not a Scot, a former employee of France, a man whose countrymen are the foes of Charles and her traditional enemies. And while he is gone, I shall show you that without English armour, we may still take the Crimea.'

There was a little silence. Then the Tsar lifted his hand. Ivan Viscovatu said, 'A Russian Ambassador has already been appointed to sail with the English Pilot Ritzert. A merchant from Vologda who can answer well the questions the English may ask about trading, and who knows what privileges we require in England in our turn. This man is Osep Nepeja. But of martial matters, he cannot speak. And you will not ask us to entrust business of such delicacy to the two disaffected of your own company who, it seems, are also to be of the party. Only one man has the ability, the knowledge, the persuasiveness to carry weight in such a transaction. And that man, our wise and noble Tsar has rightly decreed, is yourself.'

The Tsar said, 'You will tell England that if we receive these arms, I shall declare war on Turkey.'

The sudden words fell on silenced air. Lymond drew a long, slow breath, standing still, the great collar of jewels steadily shining, his eyes holding, without mercy, those of the Tsar. 'And what arms,' he said, 'and what Commander will you ask for which could make such a war anything but the self-immolation of Russia?'

The Tsar sprang to his feet, arm outflung, and the heavy cross by his chair, rocking, crashed to the ground. He said softly, against the hissing groan of his courtiers, 'You give your sovereign monarch the lie?'

Lymond's voice was as soft. 'I have said that, with or without arms, I shall clear your land of the Tartar. I know Suleiman's strength. There is not a nation on earth, Christian or infidel, which could overthrow Turkey at this moment. Your Highness knows that. Your Highness had ordered, for this reason, that no Turkish prisoners should be taken.'

'I also know,' said the Tsar forcefully, 'that the campaign to Ochakov was a test. Was it not? It did damage –

of course, for you are the finest soldier in Russia. I tell you this. My Council cannot deny it. It showed the way for a greater attack later on. It did something else. It plumbed the depth of the Turk's displeasure, that his vassals should be so distressed. We shall know, by the end of the summer, what force of janissaries Sulieman will give Devlet Girey when next he makes his attack. What we do not know is how Turkey will answer Devlet Girey's overthrow.

'I say to Mary Tudor of England that I shall make war against Turkey. I say to you that whether or not we declare war, we may finish with war on our hands. You say that even with arms, we cannot prevail. I say that, with arms, we have English interest, we have the support of the Emperor Charles: we may have even the armies of the King of the Romans to help us, if by so doing he believes the Turk may be overthrown. . . . I say you underrate your powers as a commander. And I would ask you what will happen if, without guns and without armour or powder, we have to face the might of Suleiman's army. Then no friends would come to our aid. Then our enemies would stand by and laugh, while Russia died, and the heretic rabble exhausted itself.'

'You wish to provoke Turkey then?' Lymond said.

The Tsar was still standing, but in his shining eyes there glowed visions. 'When I have arms,' he said. 'When England sends me what I ask for. Then you shall strike a blow against the Tartar which will make Turkey rock. And even Sigismund-August will send his armies to march by our side. Baida has told me.'

'I see,' said Lymond. After a moment, he said, 'He did not say he had received the honour of an audience.'

'At Tula,' the Tsar said. 'The day after the army had left. He came to give me his loyal assurances.'

'And to suggest that I should go to England,' Lymond said.

'He said, and wisely, that only by threatening Turkey could we hope to attract English support. All the world knows the danger in that. You have just spoken of it. He said only you could persuade the English that such is our plan.'

Lymond said, 'Great as you are; great as your army is, you cannot declare war on Turkey. The English know this. You cannot use this argument with them.'

345

'So Baida said,' the Tsar answered. 'If you say so also, then it rests in your hands to find other means of persuasion. Only you have the knowledge, as Viscovatu says. Only you have the tongue. Only you have the trust of us all, absolutely and implicitly. I have ordered you to go to England. Now I, your Tsar, beg it of you. Sail to London, the home of this strange, married Queen, and speak to her in her own tongue, but with the heart of a Russian. Bring me what I want.'

There was no escape. No loophole; no answer, no argument; no excuse.

'Then of course, Lord, I shall go,' Lymond said.

*

It seemed as if Güzel already knew of the mandate. At least when Lymond greeted her in his house in the Kremlin after his audience, and conveyed to her its substance in five minutes' quiet conversation, she betrayed no alarm or surprise.

'If he gave you this audience in Council, it is because he does not mean his judgement to be shaken. And if you do so, he will hate you for it afterwards.'

'Yes. Oh, short of death, there is no quietus from this masterly errand,' Lymond said. 'I have made the Three Kneelings and I have made the Three Knockings, and, with this lord, there is nothing more to be done. It has taught me one thing. For exposing you to the conversation of Prince Dmitri Vishnevetsky, I had intended to bring you my apologies. Now—'

'Now?' Güzel said serenely.

'Now he may even be worth your passing attention. Even if I leave now on the *Edward,* I cannot expect to set out from England sooner than next year's spring sailing in May. The Tsar is obsessed. The army will be ten months – a year, maybe – without me.'

'What will they do?' Güzel said. 'Veil their beards, and sell their arrows for spindles?'

He laughed, briefly, holding open the door of her room for her to pass rustling through. 'It saddens me sometimes that you know so many Turkish expletives,' he said. 'I am not always in a mood for restraint.'

'Are you not?' Güzel said. He closed the door, and

they stood, looking at one another. Güzel said, 'Despite what you have said, you tried to see Ivan Vasilievich?'

'I am an open book,' said Lymond with weary irony. She sat; and crossing the room he seated himself, his face abstracted, opposite her, and leaned his head back among her silk cushions. 'I tried to see him, and was refused.'

Güzel said, 'It is for Russia. He yearns for you. He cannot sleep.'

'I know,' Lymond said; and she did not call him out of his silence.

Later, he looked up as if there had been no hiatus in their talk, and said, 'I shall go as soon as I have made all my arrangements with Guthrie. They tell me that Chancellor has gone north, but that the ships have not yet arrived at St Nicholas. I have four to six weeks, I imagine, to get there.'

'Osep Nepeja took his leave of the Tsar and went north in the last week of March,' Güzel said. 'You will find Makarov and Grigorjeff with him. I shall have what you need sent aboard.' She hesitated. 'They say you did not bring Slata Baba with you?'

'She is dead,' Lymond said. 'Having turned cannibal, alas, like her masters. One cannot, to be sure, love an eagle.'

'No,' Güzel said.

✾

Guthrie and the rest heard the news, when they came, with dumb disbelief verging on outrage. The Voevoda Bolshoia, his own temper under expert control, informed them concisely of the Tsar's motives for depriving them, so irresponsibly, of his own sterling company. He explained the situation, in fact, in terms so well argued and simple that his journey began to seem after all quite inevitable. So they dismissed their surprise and settled down to listen, writing furiously, to the orders and dispositions which followed in a day and a half of strenuous meetings, during which the lines were laid down for the army's development in his absence, and his authority until his return was invested in Alec Guthrie once more.

It was towards the end of the second day that Alec Guthrie, taking the Voevoda aside, told him that Hislop wished to sail for home also.

'God. It's a plague,' Lymond said. 'And the shapes of the Locusts were like unto Horses prepared unto Battle, and on their heads were as it were Crowns like gold, and their faces were as the faces of men. The girl, I suppose?'

Many of them had returned from Ochakov to find a change in their somewhat elastic domestic arrangements, to which the Voevoda so far had turned a blind eye. But Danny Hislop had returned to find his Tartar girl neither dead nor stolen, but without warning made off to her *yurt*. He had, at the time, made light of it: Guthrie had not even guessed Lymond was aware of the matter. 'Yes, the girl,' he said. 'He wanted to marry her.'

'And she thought, I suppose, that he would make her change her religion. As she probably would. An experience he should have had, for the good of his character, about ten years ago. Is he aiming, do you know, at the Order of St John of Jerusalem with d'Harcourt, or at Hans Eworth's studio with Blacklock?' And, as Guthrie hesitated: 'Ah, no. I see,' said Lymond. 'He wishes to salve his self-esteem by puncturing mine. And what urgent reason will you and Hoddim and Plummer now find for returning to England?'

Alec Guthrie did not trouble to reply. Instead, 'You may well find,' he said, 'that Hislop stays with you and comes back to Russia. He's the best we've had since Jerott Blyth.'

'In other words, humour him,' Lymond said. 'How dangerous it is when the shepherd cannot find the pastures, the leader of the expedition cannot tell the road, and the vicar knows not the will of God. How are you going to enjoy presiding over St Mary's, Guthrie, while I am away. . . . I have told them to pass all the dispatches from Europe into your hands, to keep for me. The last one from Lychpole had an enclosure missing: see if it can be traced. There should be no more after September: I have asked Brussels and Applegarth and Hercules Tait in Venice to write direct to me in the care of Lychpole in London. It may be that the success of the Muscovy mission depends rather more than they know on what is happening in Europe.'

'I am told,' Alec Guthrie said carefully, 'that the English have expressed some interest in your movements as well.'

'A heart-to-heart talk with Master Chancellor?' Lymond

said. 'The Lennoxes want me back, I imagine, to demonstrate their power to the Catholic faction and the monarch, using the Somervilles as a lever. Which will fail. I imagine the talkative Diccon has already mentioned my much-disputed divorce. The Lennoxes claim that without my presence, I cannot be disjoined from my child bride. I have enlisted the help of the Grand Prior of France and the Grand Master of the Order in Malta to prove them wrong. By the time I land at London, I should be free of Philippa Somerville and she of me, as the romantic phrase no doubt will incline. God knows who could conceive it had ever been otherwise.'

'Except on paper,' Guthrie said dryly.

'Except on paper. A stratagem,' Lymond said, 'I hope I am not going to have cause to regret.'

That night was his last with Güzel, and he gave it to her, minute by minute as his parting present, with all the sureness, the elegance, the strange and delicate reticences she had come to know and respect. And her gift to him was no less.

Next morning, dressed, he took leave of her in her chamber, where she stood clothed as if for a wedding in her robe of white Persian silk damask with bands of small winged creatures and animals, and the sleeves and hem inscribed in gold Kufic lettering: *In the name of God, the Merciful, the Gracious. There is no God but God.* Her hair, reeled with pearls, stranded her ears and hung at her white nape like ash buds. The glossy lids were open and clear; the scented lips smiling. She said, 'You gave me Russia. And now Russia is taking you away.'

'For a winter,' Lymond said. 'You said that nothing could hinder us.'

As a spring, brimming, swirling and waning, her smile ebbed and flowed with her thought. 'They say we deserve one another. I have no exhortations to give you. I understand what is happening. Perhaps I understand better than you do. You are not going to Scotland, so no vows will be broken.'

'And if I were?' Lymond said. 'You say I have given you Russia, but your gifts to me have been of a different order. The prize of your body. The companionship of your mind. The fruits of your experience. You have taught me hardihood and it is for me now to exercise it. Indeed, Güzel. . . .'

She looked up at him, with the familiar, fathomless eyes. 'I wonder,' said Francis Crawford, 'if it is not for this that I have been taught.'

She stirred. 'I have given you nothing. I have shown you what was there in you already, and you have been man enough to destroy what is weak and to foster what is strong until it is unassailable. There is only one country in the world now fit for your sovereignty, and that country is here.'

'I know it,' he said. He took her hand and bending his head, kissed and held it. 'Kiaya Khátún, your power is great.'

She smiled, a flashing spasm wide and queer as the Dancers on snow which began with her eyes and ended, trembling, in the fingers she closed hard over his, holding them warm, smooth and hidden as if in a glove.

Greater than the woman of Doubtance,' she said. '*Greater.*'

And slid her hands away to stand, stately and cool, while, hands light on her shoulders, he held her quite still for a long time, his gaze locked in hers, without speech. Then he kissed her lips and, without farewells, left.

The Tsar saw him at last, in his darkened room, while all round in the Kremlin the princes slept after dinner. He received his Voevoda Bolshoia alone, as he was once used to do; and from his bed, where he lay in his white jewelled shirt against the high duck-down pillows, a single candle in silver alight by the books at his side. He said, 'I do this for my people.'

Lymond knelt, formal and sober beside him. 'Little father.'

Ivan smiled, his beard and lashes damp in the candle-light. 'Who will play chess? I cannot sleep.'

Lymond said, 'The winter will pass. And a ruler with good counsellors, Solomon says, is like a city strengthened with towers. What has been built up cannot be destroyed in a season.'

'You say so?' said Ivan Vasilievich. 'But I smell fear. Why are you frightened?'

Lymond stood, his eyes steady, his hands still on the bed. 'Superstition.'

'The prophecy you once spoke of? That was a fate,

true or false, that lay waiting in Scotland. You will not die in London. Nor will your brother.'

'I have many fears,' Lymond said. 'But death is not one of them.'

'I fear it,' the Tsar said. 'When Mongui Khan died, the Emperor of the Tartars, there were slain three hundred thousand men, whom those who bore him to burial met on the way, to serve him in the other world. . . .'

On the coverlet, the large, square-nailed hands suddenly moved. Lymond rose, and, filling smorodina into the Tsar's golden pineapple cup, brought it to him. 'You need not ask,' he said. 'Although in this world I cannot promise to do the work of three hundred thousand. Meanwhile, what is your wish?'

The Tsar stared at him, his lips pursed, the veins standing red at his temples. The cup dropped, and rolled clanging over the wood of the floor. 'Stay!' said the Tsar. 'Stay! They ask too much. I will not have it. Stay!'

'The Tsar has spoken,' Lymond said steadily.

The man in the bed sat up, suddenly rigid. 'You want to go!'

Lymond did not move. 'I do not wish to stay, to be known as the man who can make the Tsar doubt his own wisdom. Little father, if I stay, you discredit me.'

The bony, silken-haired face looked flatly at his. 'You wish to go.'

Beside the books on the table, covered now with rich velvet, was the gospel Lymond had brought back from Ochakov. Slowly and carefully, Lymond crossed to the table, and, sliding the thick silver book from its shelter, laid it upon the Tsar's bed, and his own hands upon it, his eyes open and blank on the cloudy eyes opposite.

'More than my life, more than my soul, more than my hopes on earth or beyond it, I wish to stay in this place; I wish to be released from this journey.'

A wordless noise answered him. With a jerk, the Tsar laid his hands, without touching Lymond's, on the book also. 'Why did you not tell me?'

'You knew,' Lymond said. 'And because you are Tsar, you had to ignore what you knew. As, because you are Tsar, you will now hold by it.

'I fear. But I must face my fear. And when I return, I shall have conquered it. Nor is it of moment. A fragment

351

of a dead self, better buried. I shall bring your arms, if I can.'

'I know that,' said the Tsar. 'But how shall I sleep?'

'One will read to you,' Lymond said. 'See, what have you here? This perhaps?'

The book he drew from the others was in Latin, but the poems were noble; their rhythms subtle and varied: their cadences, in the light, practised voice, were beguiling and soft. Lymond read from it as if it were music; as the Shaman had done while his own heart had calmed and the blood from Slata Baba's sprawled and haemorrhaging lacerations had pulsed slower and slower, and stopped.

Now, as he read, the ragged breathing stilled on the pillows, the grasping fingers relaxed; the thick lids met in each shadowed socket. Lymond read on, and knew soon by the silence that the man on the bed, pitiful and tempestuous and tormented, and brought to the stark edge of greatness, was now at last sleeping in peace.

Before the Tsar wakened, his Voevoda Bolshoia had left Moscow.

The last man to see him was Alec Guthrie, waiting alone and unheralded at the Nikólskaya Gate as the brief cavalcade left the Kremlin: the sumpter horses and the servants; the compact group of armed men to protect them. He waited until Lymond came into view, and catching sight of him reined; then at a gesture approached and walked his horse with him. 'We shall do what we can. I hope your business speeds well.'

Lymond said, 'Alec.'

He was, Guthrie saw, staring frowning ahead. Guthrie said, 'Yes?'

'Güzel is on close terms with the Tsaritsa. Listen to what she tells you. It is most important that you do.'

'About the Tsar?' Guthrie said.

'Without me, I cannot tell how he will move. Between us all, we have steadied him. But if it goes wrong, it will be such a holocaust as you have never imagined. If that happens, you must leave, and take the rest with you. Güzel will tell you how.'

Alec Guthrie, a man not easily disturbed, found it necessary to deepen his voice in order to steady it. 'I cannot see such an extreme of danger developing in such a short time. But if it does, we shall see that Güzel comes safely to you.'

For the first time, his brows raised, Lymond glanced at him. 'I rather fancy it will be the other way round. Wild bears become meek for St Thekla.'

The grey-bearded face remained grim. 'You called me Alec just now,' Guthrie said. 'If you have dispensation to do the same, let me say it. Francis Crawford, I wish you away from this country; and if I had the hearing of a friend, and not that of the Voevoda Bolshoia, I would tell you never to come back.'

Abandoned by artifice, Lymond's face exposed, for an instant, his astonishment. 'Of course you may speak,' he said, 'At this moment . . . but why I cannot see why.'

'I know you cannot see why,' said Guthrie. 'You saw it when you fought Graham Malett. You saw it in France and in Malta. You saw it clearest of all at home among your own people.'

Lymond said sharply, 'That will do.' After a moment, he said pleasantly, 'Whatever motives of squalid self-interest you seem to be hinting at, there must be some credit accruing in heaven. You have served this Tsar, and so have I, for nearly two years through some pains and some peril.'

'With your brain,' Guthrie said.

Lymond glanced at him, with a touch of the familiar hauteur. 'Who expected a crusade: Ludovic d'Harcourt? Intelligence is the only indispensable commodity in life or in warfare. If you think otherwise, go live in a hut with a poet. The rest of us will do our best to defend you.'

'Man is not intellect only,' Guthrie said. 'Not until you reject all the claims of your body. Not until you have stamped out, little by little, all that is left of your soul.'

The emotive, squalling words, thin as a hare pipe, sank and were lost in the hearty, masculine noises: the chink of stirrup and buckle, the squeak of leather, and thunder of unshod, rapid hoof-beats around them. No one answered them. Lymond rode on as if he were alone, and did not trouble to speak any more.

Until the Neglinna Bridge, where the column slowed to clatter over the planks between the crowded wood houses and Guthrie, slowing in turn, reined aside and, waiting, prepared to be passed, ignored, by his commander. But the Voevoda reined suddenly also, and turned to him.

'We part here. I value your good wishes. I value the consideration that brought you to meet me. For two years and more St Mary's has been upheld by your staunchness, and so have I.'

He paused, and Guthrie, grimly watching, saw that he was choosing his words with some care. Lymond said, 'On the other matter . . . the terms of reference by which I live are my own, and those who dislike them must leave, as Blacklock and d'Harcourt have done. I have said the intellect is all that can matter. I haven't said it is easy — or painless . . . to rid oneself of all that is left.'

Guthrie said, 'You are destroying yourself. You are destroying all that makes common cause for your fellows.'

'Some of it,' said Lymond calmly. 'It is my parting gift to you all. You are free, and so am I. There are no bonds between us, except those of the intellect.'

'And the intellect,' said Alec Guthrie, 'will bring you back to us?'

'Self-interest,' Lymond said, 'will bring me back to you. And intellect, I trust, will maintain me.' The bridge was clear. The men were waiting for him on the other side. He gathered his horse and, for the last time on Russian soil, Alec Guthrie looked into the domineering, incongruous eyes which showed something of impatience and something of regret and something, blatant and wounding, of sharp self-derision.

'Abandon your quest,' said Francis Crawford. 'What you are looking for, dear Alec, is buried. And no leech in London is going to revive it.'

And wheeling, he turned his horse's head to the north, where a thousand miles off lay waiting the four ships for England.

PART III

CHAPTER ONE

On her sixth and last voyage through the Frozen Sea, the *Edward Bonaventure* drew away from the mouth of the Dwina, her sails brimmed with the sweet air of summer, her holds laden with furs and choice foods and delicate gifts, with a cargo worth twenty thousand pounds and three people of consequence to the pattern of her age : Richard Chancellor, Francis Crawford, and the Tsar of Muscovy's first Ambassador to the Queen of England, Osep Grigorievich Nepeja. It was 2 August, the month in which the small fleet of Hugh Willoughby had been scattered, and two of her ships later locked in the Arzina to die.

The season was advanced, but not impossibly so. The weather seemed settled. Oats and barley stood yellow round the four mouths of the Dwina, full of fat blackcock with their green shimmering bodies; the white strand of Rose Island burned the feet under the sun, and the fields of wild white briar exhausted the air with their scent. There were gnats.

Balancing at last on the forward deck, with the wind fresh on the cheek, Chancellor forgot those last anxious weeks in the heat of Kholmogory, waiting for the news that the *Edward* and the *Philip and Mary* had returned from their winter in London, bringing with them the extra crews to man Willoughby's two frozen ships. Now the small fleet sailed briskly beside him : the *Philip and Mary* with Howlet and Robins, the little *Bona Confidentia* and the *Bona Esperanza,* Willoughby's flagship, carrying a six-thousand-pound cargo and the two Kholmogory merchants, Makaroff and Grigorjeff, with eight of their friends.

All the ships had been scraped free of barnacles and checked and reloaded, to the satisfaction of himself, his masters and his pursers. Only he had made sure that the lightest cargo was carried by the two Arzina ships. One could not always see the harm done to the stoutest ship's timbers by a winter in ice.

It had been clear, when he came back from Lampozhnya, that the Russian merchants not only wished to barter their goods: they wished to trade direct on their own part in London. Ten of them, after discussion, had been chosen, and were to sail with their cargo to do so. It was only after his last round of visits in Moscow, including a formal audience with the Sovereign Grand Prince, hedged about with Viscovatu and Adashev, that Chancellor learned that, beside merchants, he was to carry an ambassador and his suite.

The reasons were plausible in the extreme. Goodwill should be exchanged. If direct trading was to take place, then reciprocal privileges would be required. The fact that with no seagoing ships Russia could make little use of them without the courtesy of the Muscovy Company was not one which anyone stressed.

The underlying motive was obvious also. He had been warned of it by Francis Crawford, but, ignoring the warning, had listened unmoved when the Tsar, addressing him kindly, had asked him to desire the sovereign princess his mistress to send him the materials of war through the Muscovy Company, and skilled men to operate and produce them.

Chancellor had listened, and he had spoken softly, but he had refused. Refused without prevaricating, as Lymond advised, because his business was navigation, not politics, and because trading, not politics, was the concern of the company which paid him. He had hoped that there, perhaps, it would end. The appointment of Osep Nepeja had enlightened him.

So his ships were to be full of Russians. And Robert Best, to his fury, had disappeared south with the army. And yet, waiting for the incoming vessels had tried Nepeja's patience even more than his own; and long before Best finally arrived with Blacklock and d'Harcourt, surprisingly, behind him Chancellor realized that the Tsar had picked the wrong man for his mission; that Nepeja was anxious about the effects on his trade of this sudden condition appertaining to arms; that perhaps in all Russia there was no man except the Tsar himself who could have placed his views with conviction before this alien sovereign.

It was therefore with a strange sense of foreknowledge that he received a crested packet at the end of July from the hands of a weary courier from Moscow, and learned that the Voevoda Bolshoia was on his way north to join him, together with his servants and Daniel Hislop as henchman. Christopher Chancellor, standing by his father when that message came, was shocked to see on his face an expression which had in it nothing of the disgust he had expected.

Adam Blacklock's reception of the news was even odder: he stood, blankly, staring at Chancellor and then said, his eyes brilliant, 'Thank Heaven.' And d'Harcourt, behind him, said, 'Amen to that,' very softly.

Christopher's angry 'Why?' was not answered, and remained unanswered after the lighters had come with the Voevoda's luggage and servants to be followed in due course by Lymond himself, self-contained and efficient and hard as Hislop behind him with the sun and the tempestuous ride by post-horse from Moscow. To Nepeja, he was charming, to Best, formal; to Blacklock and d'Harcourt, lightly abrasive. Chancellor introduced him to his sailing master, and Lymond shook Buckland by the hand and turned back to Chancellor.

'And so,' he said, 'I have to carry out your sordidous errands.'

'Not *my* errands,' Chancellor said. 'Those of Nicephorus your ruler, the pale death of the Saracens. How many did you impair?'

'Men or women?' said Lymond. 'Why in the name of the Muscovy Company, *refugium quorum in Deo est,* could you not have accepted the commission?'

'Because I have to come back to Russia,' said Chancellor bluntly.

'So you have,' said Voevoda Bolshoia. 'Bringing me and Nepeja. You will have gathered, I take it, what a merry bundle of fun *he* is. You have not yet discovered what happens to Russians at sea.'

'The same thing, I suppose, that happens to Englishmen,' Chancellor said. 'Scots, I take it, are immune.'

'To sarcasm, yes,' Lymond said. They had cleared a cabin for him below Chancellor's own, in the poop, next to the master's. Arriving there, he glanced round and then turned to the Englishman. 'What honours will the Lennoxes and their friends heap upon you?'

Chancellor was wise enough to hide the anger which filled him, and even, a little, to quench it. He said, after taking thought, 'They will lift the promised arraignment for heresy.'

Lymond said, 'You mentioned nothing of this until now.'

'It was my affair,' Chancellor said. 'I could hardly become a peddler of arms. I imagined the Tsar would give the commission to Nepeja.'

There was a short silence. Then Lymond said, 'For what it is worth, I believe you. It is not on your account I am sailing for England. . . . Did your sons know that you faced the stake if you came home without me?'

'No,' said Chancellor irritably. He added, 'No free man should be coerced by such means. However close to the Queen, this family must learn that such things do not lie in their power.'

'They lie in Gardiner's power,' Lymond said. 'Where would you have fled? France? She is an enemy of England, and you are not. Spain? Portugal? Brussels? Spain and her friends control the other highways of the world, and Spain is married to England. No. With Cheke in Strasburg, with Mercator at Duisburg; among John Dee's friends at Louvain; among the mathematicians and chart and instrument makers, where the newest books can be found from all the German and Swiss Universities; among all the scholarly Protestant exiles; among all the theorists who do not sail, and do not want to sail, and have no vessels even if that were their deepest desire, you would settle and live out your life. Perhaps that is what you want?'

'Perhaps that is what I should want,' Chancellor said. 'But I don't. Any more than you do.'

He had been wrong to read understanding into the Voevoda's face or his voice, or any of the softer emotions. 'But you do not know me,' Lymond said. 'Whereas I know you exceedingly well. You should be glad. I may well find it tedious; but you should have an extremely interesting journey.'

The interesting journey began smoothly enough, with the traversing of the great Bay of St Nicholas from Foxnose, which the Russians called Cape Kerets, to Sosnovets Island, its crowded timber crosses already robbed by foreign seamen for fuel. From Point Krasni, known as Cape St Grace, to the River Ponoy it was calm, although becoming colder, so that Adam's hands turned blue, holding the charcoal, and even below in the cabin he shared with Best and Hislop and d'Harcourt he had to huddle in his sheepskin to draw out his chart.

They were reasonably patient. But Hislop wanted to

read, and Best and d'Harcourt played interminable games with worn cards. When he felt he had monopolized the lantern long enough, Adam found there was always daylight enough somewhere on deck : the strange grey light which persisted most of the night, as the sun dipped, sootily red, into the west and, red and lightless, rose again almost at once. Past the River Ponoy, on the Lappian coast, they ran into thick fog.

For part of that night they were hove to, and Buckland did not go to bed. Neither did Lymond. Danny Hislop, lying awake long after the others, heard his quick step on the stairs to his cabin well towards morning, after a brisk, subdued exchange with someone who sounded like Chancellor.

Since they set sail, Lymond had spent most of his time on the quarter-deck, or in Chancellor's cabin, writing or talking. All the company with quarters in the stern castle had grown used to the murmur of voices, and the sight of Christopher Chancellor standing on deck alone, or walking by Buckland, or finding out Best or d'Harcourt, because he would not share his cabin with Lymond.

Danny Hislop had been there when the quartermaster, to keep his luff, had ordered the spritsail taken in and had seen Lymond calmly lay hands on the sheets to strike sail, and after, vault round to help pull on the mainsheet so that the helm could go down and the *Edward* come close to the wind. It was done with no fuss and an unthinking dexterity, so that Buckland turned and Chancellor said, 'You have sailed.'

'I have rowed,' Lymond said. 'It is not a fact of life with which I edify all my underlings. And three years ago I took a galley from Marseilles to Stamboul, for France. I have never handled a caravel. I know less, I imagine, than d'Harcourt does.'

'Surely not,' said Ludovic d'Harcourt. 'The Voevoda has been in Malta. I believe he has even fought for the Knights.'

'Was that—?' said Chancellor, and Lymond removed his eyes from d'Harcourt's whimsical ones.

'Where I met Nicolas de Nicolay? Yes it was; and also in Scotland. My stay on Malta was brief; and if you will follow d'Harcourt's tone, instead of his words, you will gather that I did not fight for the Knights, or if I did, it was purely for my own ends.'

'It has a likely ring about it,' said Chancellor gravely. 'And the exhibition just now?'

'Because I could sail the *Edward*, I think. I can use compass and astrolabe; I know what Plummer knows about the practical side of surveying. But I do not know how in God's name you are steering in these bloody waters.'

'Come to my cabin,' Chancellor said.

And so the sessions began which so riled Christopher and surprised Best and roused Danny Hislop's bright-bladed, excoriating curiosity. Lying now in the damp, foggy cabin, listening to those competent footsteps, he said aloud, 'You know, and I know, that without astronomy and the mechanical arts, and most especially without the most rigorous training in advanced mathematics, a navigator is only a seaman. Why, then, is Master Chancellor gulling the Voevoda, and why is the Voevoda ready to be gulled?'

Adam Blacklock, as he had suspected, was awake. 'Is he being gulled?' he said in a murmur, out of the darkness.

'You don't learn mathematics as a galley slave. He was a galley slave, I take it, and not merely the River Forth ferryman?'

'In his teens. He was on *travaux forcés* for two years. He is also a Bachelor of Arts of Paris University.'

There was a brief, overturned silence. Then Best's voice, joining in on the other side, said, 'What?'

'What indeed,' said Danny, recovering. 'A two-year test course for schoolboys in logic. Added, we all know, to a liberal self-education. Big words and Latin. But no mathematics.'

Adam said, 'He studied under Orontius Finaeus when he was fifteen.'

'You know all about him, don't you, Adam?' said d'Harcourt's voice thoughtfully. 'We find him, all of us, a subject for ceaseless conjecture. Do you realize that? Do you realize that since we've been here, none of us has thought of ourselves; of home and work and all the plans we were making? Is it a form of common subjection that holds us all together?'

'Speak for yourself,' said Danny Hislop. 'I'm held together by intellectual curiosity. So are we all. We were wonderfully specious at Novgorod – Best will remember – about our reasons for staying in Russia. No one gave the correct one. You can hate a man and stay in his company because of his sheer, God-given, irresistible powers to stimulate. We all liked fighting, and we liked talking about fighting. With Lymond you don't talk about fighting; you discuss the art of warfare, and then its philosophy, and then ten dozen other subjects all through the night, or for as long as he has patience to stay with you. I thought, God help me, that you were all trailing through Europe because you were enamoured of him. It wasn't that in the least.'

'We loved his mind,' said Adam Blacklock, with sudden terrible bitterness, and Robert Best drew in his breath. After a moment's silence, they realized that Blacklock had got to his feet, and an instant later, the door opened and closed behind him. Danny Hislop said, 'Daniel Hislop, you are a bloody fool.'

Robert Best said, 'I don't understand.'

In the dark, Danny was silent. Then he said, 'It's Adam's story. But it begins a long time ago, when he was in St Mary's in Scotland, and began to take drugs. He bore no grudge over that flogging, you know. It had to be done, and Lymond did it, sparing him as no one else could. And came straight from the Tsar and sat beside him till daylight afterwards, except when he was being sick. An unheroic and unpublicized scene.'

'Why sick?' Robert Best said.

'*A crise de nerfs*,' Danny said. 'Or, according to Guthrie, because the Voevoda had been playing chess.'

'And what,' said Robert Best, irritably sleepy, 'on earth has chess got to do with it?'

'Ask Alec Guthrie, next time you see him,' said Danny. 'But I hope you take the point *vis-à-vis* Adam. He is impelled by that wasteful fuel, love. That is why he is leaving. To stay would harm St Mary's, or the Voevoda, for whom living, as you have seen, is an exact science to be pursued with the brain.'

'And d'Harcourt and you?' Robert Best said.

'Ludo?' said Hislop. 'Why are you leaving? In case, perhaps, you came to like it too well?'

'I think he has too strong a hold over you,' d'Harcourt said. 'I think you might come to forget, too, that life is more than a science.'

'Then dispute it with him,' Danny said. 'He is not immutable. No man can be. I am here because I find in him a reason for thinking, and at present I want to think, and not, like Adam, to feel. . . . Does fog induce the confessional atmosphere? Ludo, devise us our penance.'

Robert Best said, 'None of you has spoken of Russia.'

'No,' said Danny. His voice, not without effort, came through the darkness, lightly jocular. 'And do you know why? Because, of all of us, only one man is thinking of Russia, and he is thinking of it to the exclusion of you and me and Ludo and poor Adam out there, which is why poor Adam is out there. . . . Lymond is thinking of Russia, and if Ivan Vasilievich were not three-quarters crazy, he should never, never, have allowed him to go.'

The next day, there was frost in the shrouds. Through the morning, the mist broke a little and the four ships could see one another as Chancellor took them ahead slowly, rounding the great bulk of the Kola Peninsula on their left, which would take them out to the wide, foggy expanse of the Frozen Sea itself, and their clear passage west. A wind rose and freshened, north by east as they came up to Cape Orlov, while the temperature dropped so that the straining sails sparkled with ice and the seamen, reducing sail as the short vessels blundered and pitched, found their hands ripped and raw with the sheets. Then, backing with a shriek north by west, the wind turned into their faces and blew a full gale.

The *Edward* fired off a cannon before she turned about, and making south-east, pennant streaming, led her three labouring vessels to the safety of Tri Ostrava Point, six miles to the south, where they anchored. Once secure, the conferences in the pilot's cabin went on, Chancellor writing this time to Buckland's dictation. *Three and a half leagues north of Cape Orlov Latitude 67°10', twenty-two fathoms. Big broken shells and stony sand on the tallow.* . . . Lymond, standing beside him, struck tinder quietly and lit the lantern.

Chancellor looked up. 'Christ, what time is it? I ought to go and see to the Russians.'

'I have,' Lymond said. 'They are Pskov green. There is nothing anyone but God the Great Navigator can do about it. . . . I suppose we are convinced that it is possible to get past North Cape at this time of year, in this weather?'

Buckland was staring down at his notes. 'It shouldn't

have broken so soon. When this blows itself out, we shall know better.'

Chancellor said, 'We have to try, because of the cargo.'

'Of course,' said Lymond. 'No cash, no Swiss. I merely make the point that I do not wish to spend the winter in a driftwood hut shooting barnacle geese and jumping through small hoops with Laplanders.'

Chancellor laughed. 'Eden. It was a figure of speech.'

'Then what about Herberstein?' Lymond said. 'He says Lappian hunters like to leave their wives with visiting merchants for safety, and if the wife is cheerful on his return, the hunter will give the merchant a gift. If you hadn't seen a Lapp lady, it would almost persuade you to merchanting. Ah, well. Take heart. At least, gentlemen, the gnats have all perished.'

The wind from the north blew for three days, and, when it finally changed, the weight of ice on the rigging held them stationary one day longer until it was shed, while a fair south wind blew maddeningly outside the anchorage. The following day, they called the shore parties on board and set sail again with a light north wind for Cape Orlov, which they had passed five days previously. It was Saturday, 15 August, and they were barely out of the Bay of St Nicholas.

And so there unrolled before them, although only one of them recognized it, the slow and terrible course they were to follow, without either the clear light of heaven or the curses of Malacoda, Alichino or Calcabrina; Ciriatto, Graffiacane or Rubicante.

Instead, lost in whiteness, enclosed in snow, whirled by storms and floating in sparkling mists, the flotilla moved; touching, swirling, floating haphazard as river ice from point to point, with the two ghost ships of Willoughby riding silently with them, who had been this way before, and had been lost in it, and were to be lost again, not to rise. And because death was a friend, the one man who was made to receive, like a tuning-fork, the whispering omens of fate did not recognize it, until too late.

It was not their navigator who failed them. From Orlov they set course for Gorodetsky Point, which they called Corpus Christi, where the abrupt grey cliffs, split and fissured, rose from the sea with misty snows on their crowns, and the soft russet landscapes of scrub trees and low Lapland cottages lay far behind them. They passed

Lumbovska Bay, and then thrust round the great headland at Sweetnose, where, fourteen months previously, Christopher had made his light-hearted offering of oatmeal and butter.

There, snow fell upon them with a gale out of the north, and Christopher worked with the others to clear it without mentioning the whirlpool; helping to melt frozen blocks with a candle; to fold and stow the deadweight, crackling sails; to take the soundings as they crept from anchorage to anchorage behind the small islands along the north Lappian coast; saying nothing as they passed Nokuyev Bay and the River Arzina where masters and mates, carpenters, cooks, pursers, coopers and surgeons, gunners, seamen and merchants, sixty-seven English souls strayed perhaps in that black howling air, and watched their living ships sail slowly by.

He had ceased to resent his father's companion. At anchor, or during the absence of parties ashore, seeking water and wood, the obscure discussions in Chancellor's cabin would continue, but at other times Lymond became without argument one of the team which ran the ship as Buckland liked to have it; safe and clean, with rules for prayer and rules against fire; regulating the course by signal of his three fellow vessels, and conferring with their captains daily. He had time to spare for Christopher, and showed him once, between squalls, where great patches of ambergris were lurching on the steep seas, and at another time whales, pursued and tormented by threshers, the plunging dolphins nicknamed by Nepeja *kossatka* from the twisting scythe-tails which betrayed them.

Of intention, the Russians were no longer separate, but joined with Best and the men of St Mary's for as much of the day as was possible, talking Russian among themselves, and sleeping and gambling, or playing long, inconclusive games of chance or of chess. It was Danny, instructed by Lymond, who browbeat them up on to deck and tried to teach them, in the white sparkling cold, some simple truths about the forces of wind and of water, but they listened, livid and uncomprehending, and fled as soon as might be to the dark creaking squalor below.

Fear was their great enemy. Buckland was everywhere, and Chancellor, when he could leave his deck also, below decks, working with and talking to seamen, for this time they had no minister with them. Often they found Lymond had been there before them. Buckland, walking up from the waist of the ship, remarked on it to his pilot.

'Handling men is his profession,' Chancellor said. 'You should be thankful for it. You've seen what he is doing up here.'

'I've seen him take sightings for you. I take it you trust him to do it. I've found something he won't do.'

'What?' said Chancellor.

'Take over the bloody gerfalcon. I thought he knew all about birds. He had an eagle, they tell me.'

'And he killed it, they tell me,' Chancellor said. 'Why doesn't Nepeja look after it? It's his master's royal gift to Queen Mary.' Six timbers of sables they carried, from the Emperor to the monarchs of England. Twenty entire sables, exceeding beautiful, with teeth, ears and claws. Four living sables, with chains and with collars. Thirty lynx furs, large and beautiful, and six great skins, very rich and rare, worn only by the Emperor for worthiness. And a large and fair white gerfalcon for the wild swan, crane, geese and other great fowls, with a drum of silver, the hoops gilt, for a lure for the hawk.

'Because,' said John Buckland wearily, 'he spends all his time vomiting. In Russian.'

'I've noticed that,' Chancellor said. 'Give him an interest. Give him the sables to feed. My God, you don't want any harm to befall the Emperor's presents?'

His sailing master grunted, without responding to the cursory irony. The gifts, for all they were discussing them, occupied the bulk of their thoughts not at all. All they hoped for, all they were striving to do, was to bring these four ships somehow to London.

They rounded Cape Teriberskiy, which the sailors called Sourbeer, and passed the Kildin islands, where the reindeer graze in herds all through summer; and the mouth of the River Kola, empty now of its crowded boats of a few weeks before, when was held the great St Peter's Day Mart, and watched by customars from Denmark and Muscovy, English cloth would change hands for salmon and cod, oil and furs. Robert Best wondered aloud if John Brooke was earning his salary at the new English station on Vardo.

They were making for Vardo. One of the three little islands, two miles off the north coast of Finland, Vardo had a castle, church and garrison and was the most easterly of the King of Denmark's possessions. The natives lived only by fishing, and raising a small store of fish-fed cattle, but boats of all nationalities put into its bight, and John Brooke, the Muscovy Company's new agent, would be there with news and letters and fresh stores and goods perhaps to be loaded.

Also, there would be news of the *Searchthrift,* the pinnace dropped by the *Edward* on her April journey back to the Dwina. Chancellor knew Buckland was tired of questions about the *Searchthrift,* so he had stopped asking, but not before he had heard in detail all Buckland could tell him. Stephen Burrough was in charge of the pinnace, and Richard Johnson was sailing with him. And they were on a voyage dear to Diccon Chancellor's heart : a voyage of pure exploration : to go farther east than any of them yet had been, and, passing Vaygach and Novaya Zemlya, to sail past the mouth of the Ob. They said the way past was land-barred, but he didn't believe it. He believed the coast sloped south-east to Cathay, and the *Searchthrift* might find it, not Richard Chancellor.

They said old Master Cabot had boarded the ship at Gravesend, and had given alms to the poor, and prayed for them, and then swept them off with a great concourse of men and women to the sign of the *Christopher* and given Burroughs and his company a great banquet, at which the old man had danced himself half the night, as lusty as any young seaman there, in his black cap and his long, forked white beard.

He must be well into his eighties. Chancellor knew the sign of the *Christopher*. It didn't matter if Burroughs found the way to Cathay. He was a good man. Not a mathematician, but a good man, whom Dee had taught well. Not like the man he had found here, whose first name he could not even use, and whose mind was like the star over their heads.

They struggled, sluggish with ice, towards Vardo. The Ribatsky Peninsula, across whose narrow neck you could drag your ship if, for example, you were sailing a pinnace, but which otherwise you must laboriously round. The sounding, Christopher said, was like the scurf of a scalded head : his spirits must therefore be rising. They anchored in thirty-three fathoms and rode out yet another storm in a bay west of Point Khegore, with a group of Norwegian boats including a big one from Trondheim. He remembered afterwards thinking longingly of Trondheim, and wishing to God they were round the North Cape and so far safely home.

Then Buckland came back to tell him the peninsula was seething with Russians and Danes and Lapps with fish to barter, and even some Dutch. They had nothing to sell, but they went on shore, and had some strong Dutch beer over a stove in a worm-eaten log shed, and borrowed someone's ovens to make a good batch of bread. Two of the Russians refused to get up and had to be carried by main force back to the ship. They were still thirty miles south-east of Vardo.

Then the Varanger Fjord, which the sailors had named Dommeshaff, because of the little round hill on it, five hundred feet high. There was a monastery, on the south shore, founded twenty years ago to convert the Lapps. They turned their backs on it, and on Lapland, and sailed north-west to Vardo.

They reached it with the wind in their favour. So, instead of the haven it might have been, it became a place for garbled talk and quick loading: Brooke had gone to Bergen, they said, with the captain, and they had to glean what news they could from his deputy. The *Searchthrift* had been at sea all during May and June, and had left Vardo again after a brief stay in July: the captain's deputy did not know where they were going. The snow blew like burst flock on the shutters and Buckland, getting to his feet with the meal hardly over, said he ought to be getting back, and dragged Chancellor and the rest with him.

He was right. The days were shortening; the cold had not lifted, and would never lift now. And the bays and inlets and fjords which were shallow would begin to fill with a thick, shining gruel of ice, against which their arms would crack, rowing the pinnace; into which their ships would sail, and never move afterwards. While the bays which were not shallow would give them no holding, but would let them rock and spin past on the wind like the keys of an ash tree, to seed their profitless souls on a reef. So they sailed, knowing they must now trust only to God and their pilot.

And Chancellor did not let them down. A quiet man with a quick sense of humour, he stamped no menacing mark on his company. Only the observant eye, the lively brain, the pure, canalized flair of the mathematician had made him what Henry Sidney always said he was : the supreme man of his time on the sea.

He took the *Edward* on compass and chart out of Vardo, and sailed her on instruments, on instinct, on geometry for a month while the wind drove the fleet on bare poles from one point of the compass to the next; into and out of the sight of land; in quarters where he had no charts and no books of reference, and could only trust to his work, to his tables, to his and Dee's calculations. And where Willoughby's pilot, lost and weary and desperate, had fallen at last uncaring on land, and had dragged himself and his two ships towards it, regardless of where and what it was, or what fate it might bring, Chancellor kept to the sea, marshalling his ships through darkness and mist by every means Buckland and the rest could devise : by drum and beacon, by cannon and trumpet. And they kept together, and sailed round North Cape, and at length, in the last days of October, started south down the high crumbling coastline of Finmark.

Forty miles west-south-west of the Cape, in the sound of the island of Ingoy, the wind dropped for a day. For a few brief hours of daylight the tired, patched ships, heavy with seawater floated together, and men stood on the decks under the bearded ice of the rigging, unshaven and hollow eyed, and called to one another : greetings, and messages, and obscene, rueful jokes. They tried for fish in the flat, gelidous waters and came up with glistening netfuls of cod : a matter for weeping when the milch cows and sheep are long since slaughtered and eaten, the eggs and cheese finished, the onion and garlic rotten, the butter rancid, the bread moulded and hard as the bacon and peas. They ate them half raw, because there was neither water nor wood to spare for their cooking, and thought them finer than saffron cakes and white bread, or oysters wooed down with claret. Then, that night, the gales sprang up again, from the north and the west, and the last struggle began.

They had to cape south-west, past the reefs and islands and cliffs of west Norway, driven by a wind which turned them always inwards, against the threatening land. The problem was how to win sea-room; to avoid steering too far west into the empty white Arctic; to keep far enough from the coast to deny the quick-veering wind which would hurl them on to the rocks. Chancellor did it by standing day and night on the quarterdeck over the helmsman, his eyes red, his lashes and beard coated with frost, with a line round his waist as the *Edward* pitched and rolled, her timbers shrieking, her sides thudding with the crash and hiss of the waves while above in the darkness there floated the long, chorded voice of the wind which you listened to, for it spoke its own language, to the sea and to the men who sailed on it. And at one shoulder, through it all, stood Buckland his sailing master and friend, relieving him when he could; transmitting into painful, deliberate action all Chancellor's ceaseless, precise orders. And on the other, like a rock, Francis Crawford.

So they passed round the shoulder of Norway: past Soroya and Senieno; past the teeth of the Lofoten Islands; white spray like knives against the staring snow ranges beyond; for a hundred miles and fifty miles more rock after rock, cliff after cliff, until they heard, above the thunder of their own passage, the rolling voice at Moskenesoy of the Maelstrom, which could swallow trees and toss them out, limp as hemp stalks; whose roar could shake the door rings on cottages ten miles from its brink.

Because they knew precisely where they were and were expecting this; because Chancellor had given the right instructions and Buckland, using his sails like a sculptor, had carried them out, they weathered it and pitched past, changing the helmsman over and over because of the weight of the whipstaff, dragging a ship foul-bottomed and battered, laden with ice and with bilge water which moved over her keel like a boulder, pushing her shuddering into the waves.

Past Vaeroy and Rost, with open water before him again, and daylight to see by for a while, Chancellor untied his lashing with frozen fingers and got back to his cabin where Lymond, waiting to relieve him, had fallen asleep on the edge of the straw mattress which had been Christopher's, before this small shack on the poop quarterdeck had become the workbench and altar and parliament of the Muscovy fleet.

Francis Crawford was asleep, for once dreamlessly, in the clothes he had worn for three months, with dirt grained in his hands and dulling the salt-tangled hair over his eyes. Unable to shave, he had joined them all in the uniform anonymity of a barberless beard : even fur-hatted on deck, he could be picked out from the rest by the bright glittering gold, which concealed the marks of undernourishment and fatigue, as Chancellor's clinging black hair emphasized his.

He bent now over the Voevoda and, touching him, said, 'A penny for the turnspit. You are needed.' And as Lymond opened his eyes, 'I have news for you. We are going to winter at Trondheim.'

He was roused into automatic movement at once, swinging round from the mattress, and reaching for the matted sheepskin, soaked still from its last wearing. He said, 'Weather ahead?'

In the doorway, Chancellor shouted, 'John!' into the wind and then returned, Buckland on his heels.

'Weather ahead. The wind is veering again. And the beakhead has broken again, and one of the spars. The sails will hardly mend one more time : the forecourse and maintop are in tatters.'

Buckland said, 'We're more than half-way home, with by far the worst of it behind us.'

Lymond said, 'But with the weather worsening, and this bloody wind heading us off. We haven't got time to wander about. Or if we have, the other three haven't. The *Esperanza* springs her planks if you cough.'

'That's the point,' Chancellor said. 'We have 160 tons under us. The *Bona Confidentia* is a cork and the *Esperanza* little more, and low in the water. Even if we could make the crossing, they can't.'

'Have they said so?' said Buckland.

'They won't say so,' said Chancellor.

Lymond said, 'How good are your charts?'

'Good enough. It's a dirty entrance. I shall have to con them in.'

It was his supreme domain, and there was no argument. Only Buckland said, after a moment's silence, 'It means spending the winter in harbour. Once in, we shan't get out until the spring. If you have contrary winds, you might not be back in London till May, or back in the Dwina till summer or autumn. You won't get a cargo from Muscovy next year at all.'

'If we don't do this,' Chancellor said, 'we may not get a cargo from Russia this year, never mind next. Some of the cargo will keep through the winter. We save that, and the ships, and the men.'

He took his decision a thousand miles north of London, on the edge of November, with a gale coming from the west bringing weather that they had not had, even yet. He confirmed it later that morning, when by flag and cannon shot he drew the fleet towards him and took aboard the captain of the *Esperanza* and the *Confidentia,* but not Howlet, of the *Philip and Mary,* whose boat was half stoved in making the attempt, and who had to be picked up by pinnace. It was only then they learned what damage the small ships had suffered, and it was realized beyond all doubt that these could not hope to reach London.

There was time for that, and a quick consultation over Chancellor's charts; then they parted. Over the noise of the wind, presently, the men on the quarterdeck of the *Edward Bonaventure* could hear singing, reaching fitfully into the growing storm from the ships round about them. Chancellor listened to it, his face stiff and salted, his bloodshot eyes and ridged brow turned to the weather. 'You can ask your ships to do too much,' he said. 'And your men.'

They reached the entrance to Trondheim Fjord with the tide and a full gale from the west, which brought the sea green round the poop and over the worn and cracked pavisades of the four weary ships. They skimmed rocking before it into the cannonading spray of reef, rock and island, carried under bare poles as fast as four bladders, and as capricious; caught and swirled by the currents; turned by the waves and pushed and pulled by the wind.

The entrance to the fjord was dirty. A lordly hand, gay with malice, had dusted the sea with black rocks and brought mountain heads, gritty with reefs, to its surface. Quicker than the eye could run on a chart, the ships poured and swirled through the great throats of water, and the less able died first.

The *Bona Confidentia* struck at full speed. She exploded as if the reef had blown up beneath her, with men, planks and spars spurted into the sky like math from a scythe blade, seen small and distinct, between the wall of one sky-reaching wave and the next.

The *Bona Esperanza* turned, shearing her sides, took water and turned again; half struck and turned again into the wind, her mizzenmast down and her rigging fallen, tangled with men. Then the current took her and she fled jerking, like a disabled creature, dragging her dying trap with her. The *Philip and Mary* disappeared in her wake.

Chancellor pulled the *Edward* out of the fjord. He did it

conning the ship minute by minute, with the helmsman's head raised by his foot and the whole crew working to him as his lips, his eyes, his ears, his finger-ends. He drove her between the islands as he had once envied another man in his element, swift and hard and firm on the reins, winning point by point from the winds, giving and winning again; reading the spume and the breakers and lifting his ship like a child round and over them. And he held it until he had brought her outside Froya; and outside Froya, the wind moved to the north, and let him turn aside from the haven which was no haven, and whose entrance they knew the *Edward* could never brook twice.

He consulted nobody; but divined his course and gave his directions; and the *Edward,* swinging slowly, brought her beam to the storm and, limping, began the long journey homewards, alone.

He wept that night, but not again; and held prayers for the dead in the morning, his voice hoarse and steady above the roar of the wind. He had fifty men and a tired ship to bring home in seas which turned the sun green and mantled the moon and the stars through the night. There was no rest, nor was it time yet for speaking.

CHAPTER TWO

On 8 November 1556, with her casks empty and her sails in tatters; with two of her crew washed overboard and one dead from the flux, the *Edward Bonaventure* sighted land and was able, slowly, to make towards it. A day later, it was possible positively to identify it as a major north-eastern headland in Scotland, by name Kinnairds Head. The wind was in the north-west, and had held steadily there for a day. Hoping for harbour, but praying for any inlet or bay where their anchors would hold and their shattered ship would have peace from the wind, they staggered on. Late in the evening of 10 November, a Tuesday, the wind started to gust and also to back, increasing in power, and Chancellor, using the Lindesay rutter and chart, sailed slowly up to the broad, rocky coastline, bare of trees and broken with low bights and sand dunes, and felt his way into the nearest small bay which gave promise of shelter.

They had time, before the light went, to see the outline of a fairsized keep on the skyline, and a modest handful of bothies. They had time, also, to note the position of the reefs behind and beside them, and to take up their position in clear waters, with every piece of ground tackle down that they had. The holding, Christopher reported, was good.

Then they went below, to the strange rocking creak of a ship swinging at anchor, and set their watches, and chewed their salt meat for the last time to stay them till morning, when the pinnace would steer her way through the rocks to the shore, and they would feel the earth swaying under their feet, and drink sweet water again, and tear bloody meat at a fireside . . . and see a new face . . . and listen to a tongue that they knew . . . and handle a girl . . .

'The ship is sleeping already,' Chancellor said. Too tired to eat, he had come in after the others and sat down fully dressed as he was. On one of the mattresses John Buckland was already stretched out, his face a landscape of bone-peaks and hollows, and Lymond had dropped on the sea chest behind him, his elbow on the chart table.

Under the hand, with its unhealed blisters and callouses, his eyes could not be looked at. Chancellor said, 'You will have to shave off your beard. I can't tell what you're thinking.'

'About beer,' Lymond said, without moving.

'No,' said Chancellor. After a moment he said, 'We couldn't have done it without your men. Blacklock and Hislop and d'Harcourt. I've been to see them. They're sleeping.'

'I know,' Lymond said. He took down his hand and let both arms rest on the chart table. In the candlelight his blue eyes looked dazed. He said, 'I can listen.'

And Richard Chancellor, bowing his head, rested his arms on the same table and sobbed.

A long time later, moving softly past Buckland, Lymond brought him aqua vite, and he found it at his elbow when, sniffing, he stirred at last to find a kerchief and put his wet face to rights. The candle had been moved, too, away from the table and was where it threw no light on his face, or on Lymond, leaning back against the wall. Lymond said, 'You are allowed this much for every ship you go to Gehenna with, and bring back again.'

'I lost three ships,' Chancellor said. 'And eighty-five souls.'

'I stopped counting,' Lymond said, 'after I had seen the first hundred or so of my soldiers dispatched to their earthly rest through me. You lead, therefore you kill.'

Chancellor said, presently, 'We are in Scotland.'

'And that, as perhaps you know, is *my* weakness,' Lymond said. 'I shall not be among the volunteers for your shore party.'

In the chest on which Lymond was sitting, there was a letter, forgotten until this moment. Chancellor said, 'Does it matter who you are, or where you come from? You don't need to know that Jenkinson is a Northampton man; just that he knows the world, and the secret of crossing it. The Burroughs are Bristol seamen; Bourne is a Gravesend gunner, Adams a schoolmaster, Eden a Treasury official...'

Lymond said, 'You are going to ask me to meet John Dee again. What use would it be? My God, in three months I still haven't learned enough to understand half your arguments.'

'That isn't true,' Chancellor said. 'You have a... you have the right sort of mind. You know enough already to conceive ideas and discuss them. You only need to be guided.'

'I know,' Lyomnd said. 'You want me to feast amazed upon the Table of Ephimerides, and you will take the credit, as Henry Sidney does for you. But there is only one Richard Chancellor. And although I should like to join your unofficial academy of the geographical sciences, I have only one winter in England. I should have liked to have met Sidney.'

Chancellor said, obstinately, 'It is Dee you must meet.' After a moment, he added, 'It was you who told me Sir Henry had gone to Ireland?'

In the shadows, he could see Lymond's eyes studying his. Then Lymond said, 'People write to me.'

Chancellor said slowly. 'As they do to Dee. He is ambitious for England. Letters come to him... from Antwerp and Worms, Rome and Paris and Amsterdam, Vienna, Seville and Genoa. And he is young; younger than I am. He is only twenty-nine.'

Lymond did not speak. Chancellor said, 'How old are you?'

'The same,' Lymond said. 'I imagine... no. I have had

a birthday, I suppose, in the last day or two.' He rose, and crossing to the candle, brought it back and planted it straight on the table, so that on either side of it, Chancellor's face and his own were clearly and strictly illumined. Lymond said, 'I have misled you. I have never met Dee, but I have been corresponding with him.'

'Not about navigation,' Chancellor said.

'No.'

Chancellor said, 'You have burned the letters.'

'I have burned them, yes. I have told him I shall take no part in the thing he wishes me to meddle with. But we exchange news.'

Chancellor said, 'You should take him your dreams.'

He meant it literally. He saw realization dawning on Lymond's face; in his eyes deep-scoured like his own, he knew, in the candlelight, with a blurring of indigo underneath, on the thin eggshell rim of the bone. Lymond said, 'Have I been talking?'

'We all have, in nightmares. But yours have not been about the sea.'

'You think Dr Dee cures opium eaters?' Lymond said. And then, as Chancellor's face changed, he smiled and said, 'It was three years ago. But the effects are tiresome. I sleep alone when I can.' He paused, and then said gently, 'Your son will be John Dee's next pupil. You cannot face marriage again?'

Richard Chancellor drew in a short breath, and let it carefully out, without stirring the candle. He said, 'I have only met one girl to match Eleanor. And you are married to her.'

Lymond slid his hands off the table. On his shadowless face rested, openly, an astonishment so unexpected, so vivid that Chancellor himself was taken aback and said quickly, almost in anger, 'I'm sorry. But she is a remarkable girl.'

'She is a remarkable girl,' Lymond repeated. He looked startled still. 'She must be Christopher's age.'

'She must be about Christopher's age,' Chancellor agreed flatly; and Lymond suddenly shook his head, and pressing one hand, like a masseur, over the bones of his face, took it away, smiling.

'No. I am sorry. You have the wrong impression entirely. If you are serious, there are no two people, I can imagine who would suit each other better. I think of her as a child because I knew her as a child. But she is old for her age.'

Chancellor said, 'She is concerned for your future.'

'She is concerned for her dog and her cat,' Lymond said. 'It is a Somerville failing. Tell her *your* dreams. She would help you realize them. Burroughs won't get to the Ob; not on a pinnace. But the charts he'll bring back will set you on your course. When you have corrected the compass bearing. . . . Does Dr Dee object to corrections?'

He did not expect a serious answer, and Chancellor did not give him one. Lymond answered his smile with another. 'No. What is his motto? *Nothing is useful unless it is honest.*'

'Some of these tables are yours,' Chancellor said. 'He is going to want to see you about them. And the cross-staff Plummer made, and the drawings. . . . Something has to come out of this voyage.'

'Something comes out of every voyage,' said the other man sharply. 'Out of every bloody fruitless endeavour. All the striving after the unknowable. The unattainable, the search for Athor, the creative force, rolled into a circle. You with your quest; I with my cart-ridden Emperor; Sir Thomas, sitting before the fire, his bowels burning before him. We add something. If we didn't add something, there would be no object in it. . . . I had better stop talking,' said Lymond; and stopped.

Chancellor smiled. He watched the other man drop to his pallet, then, pulling forward his own, blew out the candle and walked for the last time to the door. He had to save it from crashing wide open : the *Edward* was facing into the wind, and the wind was rising again. He checked the lanterns at topmast and stern and calling to the watch, was answered promptly. He turned back in, and closed the door.

Everything creaked. It was not like the sound of a sea-going ship, nor like the motion. The *Edward* danced, as the short waves came in from the North Sea, and were blown back again by the wind. The noise in the rigging sidled and swooped, and the waves thudded, like a solid blow on the thighs. 'I wish,' said Lymond, 'it would try a major key sometimes.'

'Wind,' Chancellor said, 'is a melancholy creature.'

He fell asleep first.

It was no one's fault that the watch slept. Or if there was a fault, it belonged to the wind and the sea, which had fought them for three months without respite, and now was to conquer.

The *Edward* snapped her first cable at three in the morning, when the wind, rising to towering heights, sent its first gust from the north; and even then, as she jerked, her load of dog-weary men barely stirred in their sleep. Then the second cable gave way; and the third.

At that, Lymond woke. He called Buckland's name and was driving out of the door, the sailing master on his heels while Chancellor, felled by sleep, was still rousing.

A wall of black air, thick as a blockhouse, struck them out of the north and rammed them, suffocating as a quilt, against the low starboard rail while the sea crashed down after it, like an axe on their shoulders and backs. Then Lymond had gone, leaping, crashing, colliding to get to the helm and Buckland, gasping, cannoned off after him. And Chancellor, stumbling at last on to the howling darkness of the quarterdeck, saw.

The *Edward* was running free. Pushed and thrust and buffeted by the changing, violent wind she had burst her worn shackles and was lurching, beam to the wind, through the ghostly white surf of the bay while the sea raced and the stars reeled above her and the jagged coast, black on black, went spinning past, offering itself and withdrawing, a wanton and merciless lottery.

The ship had roused. Before Buckland had arrived, gasping, to find Lymond dragging the whipstaff there was shouting, and dark figures holding against the tilt of the sea-swirling decks, and then the bos'n's whistle, cutting across as Buckland began to relay his orders, Chancellor talking quickly beside him, straining his eyes, trying to get his bearings, trying to remember what they had seen last night; what they had gleaned from the chart. Lymond, abandoning the weight of the helm to a seaman, found his own men at his side and sent d'Harcourt to make a sea-anchor and Blacklock down to the Russians and then, sliding and hurtling, made with Hislop for the lee rigging. He was up it, already calling directions, when she struck.

The heads of the reef stoved her sides, as a line of pikes impaling a cavalry charge. The men still on the main deck below died where they were thrown as the granite thrust through planks, beams and standards and the white ballast poured like chain-cable, followed one by one by the blundering weight of her guns. The mainmast came down, sweeping the sloping deck clean with its rigging; snatching at Lymond as he jumped free, to be met and dragged clear by d'Harcourt's powerful arm. Lymond shouted against the wind, 'Get Nepeja into the pinnace!' as a wave struck, and sent them both staggering. Then he broke away and began to pull himself up the towering waterfall of the deck, marshalling with his voice the dim figures which remained struggling about him, black against the dim, rushing spume. Blacklock's voice, suddenly clear, said, 'I've got the Russians. The pinnace has jammed.'

They were half a mile from the shore and the reef, almost wholly submerged, offered no foothold 'The small boat. We stay,' Lymond said.

They dropped the small boat over the lee side five minutes later, and formed a staggering barrier, shoulder to shoulder as the blundering form of Osep Nepeja was dropped into its bows, followed by his six semi-conscious fellow countrymen. Then the good oarsmen followed, with Robert Best, and Christopher and Diccon Chancellor, because he knew the rocks, and the safety of the Muscovite Ambassador to England had been placed in his hands.

Chancellor boarded last of all, and the *Edward* lurched and settled as he laid hands on the rope, her timbers squealing plainly through the thud and the crash of the waves, and the new resonant sounds of water pouring, from all around them, under their feet. Chancellor stopped, his hair clawed from his scalp by the wind, horror and despair on his face, staring at Lymond.

Lymond said, 'We will launch the pinnace. Go quickly,' because the ship was breaking beneath them, and the five of them were holding back, by main force, the screaming men who had not found a place in the boat. Richard Chancellor looked at them all. Then he said to Lymond, 'I have lost you before I have found you,' and turning quickly, jumped into the boat, and cast off.

Adam Blacklock was sent to fetch Chancellor's box, and what he could collect of the ship's papers while Buckland directed the repair on the pinnace. How long they had, no one knew: the wind, gusting in the dark, was kicking the ship round the reef, and probably only the reef itself was staunching its gougings. When the wind sucked her off, she would sink, giving them to the storm, and the cold winter sea, and, half a mile off, the shore with its black, spray-dashed rocks. And of them all, only Buckland and the men of St Mary's could swim.

Only Lymond did not at once turn to help with the pinnace. He sent Blacklock on his errand and stayed alone where he was, braced by the shards of the mast, watching the spray rise and fall in the dark, and the pattern of white, disclosed and hidden again, which was the wake of the small boat, plying west and dipping its oars. And achieving his errand, Adam came to his side also and said, 'What is it? They should be all right.'

It was hard to hear in the wind. Lymond said, 'They are safe,' and Adam saw with a shock that his face, under the short, blowing hair was withdrawn and perfectly calm.

Adam Blacklock said, 'You think we are lost.'

'Perhaps,' Lymond said. 'There was a prophecy once. . . . I think it is going to be fulfilled. And not before time.'

He looked at Adam, and from the flash of white in the dimness, Adam realized he was smiling. 'You are going to live anyway. Someone has to do Chancellor's maps.'

He had turned to go, thrusting Blacklock before him, when the shout came through the thunderous spray. They heard it, down in the waist where the pinnace was ready to launch. But high on the wrecked fo'c'sle with Lymond, Adam saw it: saw Chancellor's boat stop only half-way to shore, between the long white breakers piling on one another, with marbled white water their fabric, and starring the black air with a sudden bloom of white spray where they snagged, there and there and there on a rock. Standing in the boat was a dark figure shouting, and struggling about it were others, clutching, clawing, trying to pull the man down.

Lymond said, '*Oh, Christ in heaven,*' and didn't wait. They glimpsed, as they ran, the black figure fall from the boat, and then the struggling mass heel and tumble into the pale spume around him. The last thing they saw was the whale shape of Chancellor's boat, upside down, lifted on the waves like the bellowing kit, tormented by dolphins.

A moment later, Buckland got the pinnace into the water and they were aboard, and seizing the oars while the last of the *Edward*'s crew thudded over the gunwale beside them. Then they in turn struck through the waves, towards the overturned boat, and the black specks which were men's heads, dead or alive, in the sea.

The tide was against them, and the wind, pushing them south. You could see why it had taken the other boat so long to make such small headway, hampered with passengers as they were. Even with all the force of practised oarsmen, sparing themselves nothing, progress was killingly slow; the consequences of it unbearable. Blacklock, watching Lymond, saw him miss a stroke once, his hand hard on the bench, and then resume, without speaking, in rhythm. The temptation was just that; to plunge overboard and cut through the waves to the rescue. Forfeiting the power of fifteen men for the leverage strength of just one. So they waited, all of them, until they saw the boat heaving and lurching beside them, and then, catching Buckland's eye, Lymond shipped his oars in one shining sweep and was overboard. The three St Mary's men followed.

It was a slow and desolate harvest, garnered in darkness and danger, and in a cold which turned warm flesh to glass. What you touched might be fur-lined *shuba* or sheets of strong, red-brown seaweed, chequering the long, streaming shore waves like mosaic. It might be a head, fronded with waving black hair and beard, or the soft, weeded face of a rock, overcome by white needle-clusters of spray which rose, and veined it, and vanished. And always the sea strode and surged and split over their heads; rocks threatened them in low, metal-grey ranges jutting into the ocean like gun batteries; on every side danger exploded, in the sudden ghost-like burst of a spray-palace, rising, changing, vanishing in the dark.

The first two men Adam Blacklock touched were quite dead, and he ceased the effort of dragging them back to the boat; feeling was leaving his body, and he had to save his strength for the living. Then he heard Ludovic d'Harcourt call and saw he had a man in his arms and another was swimming feebly beside him. He struck through the wall of black waves, blind and deaf and desperate, and got to him in time to support one of them. The pinnace was near, the arms were stretching over the side, to pull the half drowned men in. Then Lymond's voice came, sharply, from the overturned boat, and both Adam and d'Harcourt turned and fought their way to him.

He had Nepeja. Inert as a stranded walrus, the Ambassador lay on the sliding belly of the overturned boat and beside him, groaning through clenched teeth with the effort, was Robert Best the Englishman, half in and half out of icy water, holding him firm and secure. As d'Harcourt gripped Best, Hislop appeared out of the darkness and helped Lymond steady the Russian. Lymond spoke to him.

Nepeja groaned. Best said, gasping, 'He's been unconscious mostly. The Russian lads have all gone. We tried to get them up on the boat. . . .'

'Chancellor,' Lymond said. 'Chancellor and the boy. *Where is Chancellor?*'

Best said, 'Christopher slid off the boat.'

'And—?'

'His father went after him.'

'Where? When?'

'Ten minutes ago. God knows. God knows,' said Robert Best, and started retchingly to sob. 'On that side.'

The pinnace was feeling its way towards them. Without speaking, Lymond took Blacklock's shoulder and thrust him, in his place, to share with Hislop the shuddering weight of the Ambassador. Then he turned, with a flash of wrist and pale skin and sliding, shimmering water, and went, with the wind and the tide and the current, into the darkness.

Under guidance, Best swam to the pinnace. But it took Blacklock and Danny Hislop five long minutes and all their remaining strength to lever the Russian up and into the long, rocking boat, even after she manoeuvred alongside, standing off again and again to avoid collision with the other, derelict hull. Then Buckland said, 'Get in. We're going for shore.'

Hislop said, 'Chancellor.'

Buckland's voice, worn with shouting, embodied a tired authority, over-riding all weaker inclinations. He said, 'If he has been in the water this long, he is dead. If I don't get these men to dry land within the next few minutes, they will be dead, too. And you. Get in.'

His eyes shone in the darkness. Adam, gasping and shuddering at Hislop's side, realized why. A faint, ruddy light far off on the surf of the shore showed that someone was lighting a beacon. Someone grasped hold of his arm and tried to heave him aboard. He resisted. Ludovic d'Harcourt's voice said, 'The Voevoda is out there. Give us oars and help us overturn the small boat.'

The weight of the small boat was the weight of a shot tower, filled to the skyline with lead. Adam, heaving, thought his heart would crack; knew that Best and Chancellor and the few seamen who could swim could never have done this, beset by drowning, struggling men. When it was over, dancing, half filled with water, it rose above his eyes, blacking the stars, and looked no more possible to scale and enter than the bright gates of Paradise. Hislop caught him as he collapsed, still looking up, and manhandled him up to Buckland, over the gunwales of the pinnace.

The light from the shore was brighter by then; a real bonfire, rising smoking and crackling into the blustering air, with small figures dark round about it. Fisherfolk, from small cottages inland. There was a dark track, as if made by a snail; a boat was being launched. John Buckland said, 'I must go. You're certain?' And the two men, burly d'Harcourt and Hislop, gripping his oar, unable to speak, looked from the small boat and nodded. Then the pinnace lifted away and, rowing, d'Harcourt started to call.

Lymond heard him, an almost indistinguishable sound, flat as a gull's cry above the crash of the waves on the rocks round about him, and the noise of the surf, like seething fat hissing and the bodiless buffet and thunder of the uneven wind, with its thin solo voices winding and weaving around it.

He had always been a strong swimmer. Even after weeks of short commons, and the remorseless, unremitting strain of the voyage, he was still probably the best of them all, except perhaps Ludovic d'Harcourt, whose Order owed its strength to the sea. And since he had also an excellent brain he used it, to draw certain deductions.

Christopher had slid from the overturned boat. He had slid without being seen, or his father would have caught him. And since he had not stayed near the boat, or shouted to attract their attention, he must have been nearly or wholly unconscious and at the mercy therefore of wind and of tide.

So his father would also argue. Therefore one must swim with the pull of the sea, away from the shore and away from the ship, where one might find, as a very slim chance, the body of Christopher, floating unconscious, or awake now and somehow struggling far out here in the dark.

Or more likely, one might meet with his father, still swimming strongly, intent on nothing but finding and saving his son.

Having calculated so far, nothing remained but to apply the physical laws relating to motion and force. To deal with the violent swinging and constant belabouring of high, powerful waves, their tops sliced into spume by the wind. To avoid, if one could, the invisible reefs. The broken ridge dimly revealed, coursed like a dog by the waves, cheek to cheek with savage affection. The rock which stood ahead in the foam as you were pitched head-long and fighting down the shell of a cataract.

There was not all that much time, for his shoulders were very tired, and his body losing its skill as it chilled. He was, however, as methodical as it was possible to be, and the fire on the beach helped: now very large. He hoped Buckland had had the sense to take the pinnace in and get Nepeja and the rest round its warmth. He believed someone would come out again, looking for him and for Chancellor, and he hoped he would have strength left to shout when they did. He tried to watch the sea all the time, in the faint rosy glow from the fire and thought, the farther outwards he went, the better chance he might have of seeing a swimmer, or two, silhouetted between himself and the shore. On the other hand, a floating man had no more substance than a rock, or a tumbled patch of torn seaweed. It meant, in cold blood, visiting every half-hidden stone in the bay, and he was swimming as if disabled already.

What he wanted was very near. It was typical of the monstrous, egregious, laughable irony which dominated his life that with every dragging lift of his arms, he should be saying over and over, *'Not yet.'*

Hislop and d'Harcourt got to him soon after that in the small boat, and pulled him in. He did not give them much help, and they took in a good deal of sea. D'Harcourt, breathing hard, let him be where he was and snatched the oars again. Behind him Hislop, who had been shuddering violently, suddenly let his oar slip altogether. Water swirled round their legs. D'Harcourt said, 'Her planks have sprung. Can you see to Hislop?'

He didn't say, 'We shall have to turn back.' For a long

time now, the boat had been making more water than they could bale. And Danny, he knew, had now collapsed.

Lymond said, 'He's unconscious. I'll bale you out so far as I can. Send the pinnace.'

'For you? I can't leave you!'

'You can't take me. She'd sink. I haven't finished,' said Lymond. The wind on his wet body was throwing it into convulsions, like the sea, as he set about baling. He paid no attention at all to d'Harcourt's expostulations. Only when d'Harcourt, stammering at him, tried to turn the boat, with the three of them still aboard, and row against the tide towards the shore, did Lymond put one hand on the gunwale and without wasting breath or temper or time, lift himself overboard.

D'Harcourt stayed, shouting for a while, and rowing raggedly after him, until the boat began to settle low in the water and he realized that if he stayed, he would sink. He baled and rowed for a long time, single-handed, and in the end it did sink, but within sight of the shore, and there were men running through the firelit crocheting surf to drag him out, and Hislop.

Robert Best was among them, seizing d'Harcourt's shirt and shaking him so that his wet head rolled to and fro, and shouting in his face, 'Did you find them?'

His voice was rusty with seawater. He said, 'Send the pinnace.'

'Buckland's gone with a fishing boat. There's another out there already. *Ludo!*'

D'Harcourt opened his eyes. 'Lymond is still there. There.' He rolled on one elbow and pointed. He added, 'Nothing else.'

Robert Best said, overtaken with anger, 'You could have—' and stopped, because it was wholly unfair. The boat had sunk. And the Voevoda was his own powerful law. He helped the other man to his feet, and laid him with Hislop near the fire, where the others were. The sailors from the pinnace were now helping to keep it going, and lying in its warmth, the others were beginning to recover. He and Buckland had moved no one yet, although the men and women who had come to their help were readily hospitable, and had brought sacking and bannocks and a cauldron of soup and a dipper.

They said 'Sir Alexander' was coming; and somebody else. He supposed they were the local lairds; one of them belonging perhaps to the castle he could see, now pricked with lamplight, on the south shoulder of the gentle small rise up above him. Apart from that, and the scattering of bothies well up the shore, there was no sign of civilized life.

They were lucky to have as much. It was a pretty bay, half-moon in shape, with white grainy sand rising to thick sweet grass, still very green. Below, were the slabby rocks, sloping down to the sea, ochre and charcoal in the fire-light, with their black feet in the spray. And the roar of the water. Sometimes, as the waves shifted, he saw the queer cabalistic shape of the *Edward,* like a black thorn-bush caught on a nail. The *Edward Bonaventure,* with her cargo. With her six timbers of sables, from the Emperor to the monarchs of England. Twenty entire sables, exceeding beautiful, with teeth, ears and claws. With four once-living sables, with chains and with collars. With thirty lynx furs, large and beautiful, and six great skins, very rich and rare, worn only by the Emperor for worthiness. And a large and fair white gerfalcon, upon which the wild swan, crane, geese and other great fowls might look down as she floated dead on the Bay of Pitsligo, with her drum of silver, the hoops gilt.

Francis Crawford had decided, quite sensibly, to give up, just before the fishing boat found him, there being a point beyond which in any philosophy, fruitless endeavour served no valid purpose. The white-hot wires by which he was operating had turned long ago into fodders of lead. His limbs, barely stirring, answered him rarely and he knew that none of his senses could be relied on, any more than a wrestler's, who had been punched, continuously, on head and body for a very long time. The final point, the deciding factor was that if he found Chancellor in the next thirty seconds he could do nothing about it, except possibly drag him down to his death. And if Chancellor had to die, let him do it ignorant of this small fiasco, at least.

So, characteristic of an impervious and versatile engine, the '*Not yet*' became, with logic, '*Now.*'

The lantern found him, because his hair was so bright. The Buchan man in the prow of the big, solid boat said, 'There's a loonie there. Bring her round, then.'

They hung over the side, fascinated, while the rowers, swearing, got to work on their oars. 'It's a Russ, for sure. Is he deid?'

'Aye, he's deid,' said the owner. 'But he's got rings on his fingers.'

'Then bring him in,' said the owner's uncle, impatiently. 'See's the lantern, Aikie. Are we far fae the ship?'

'Na. But the sailing-maister's in Martin's boatie. He'll see us.'

'Never a bit. Or tell him we're saving the cargo. If she lifts off the rocks, it's tint onyway. . . . He's no deid.' It was the voice of regret. A moment later he said, 'Jesus, did he hear what I said?'

The owner, who had skinned his fingers landing their catch, looked at him without sympathy. 'I dinna ken. Ye'll hae tae wait and find out. And then you'll hae tae set to and mend it. Them that burns their arse has tae sit on the blister.'

There was no possibility, hearing that, that he had arrived either in Paradise or Purgatory, or regions less monotonous. Returning as an act of obedience, as Timothy to Paul, Francis Crawford said, without opening his eyes, 'I am very deaf in both ears.'

'It's no a Russ!' Aikie said

'I hear it's no a Russ,' said the owner's uncle. 'My lord. But for my sister's son here ye'd be droont.'

'On the other hand,' Lymond said, keeping to a misty but obstinate point, 'the Courts of Admiralty are extremely strict about stolen cargo.'

There was a long pause, occasioned by shock on the part of his audience and extreme inertia on the part of the swimmer. Then Lymond said, 'But for one consideration, I shall see to it that no questions are asked.'

For his pains, he was swamped by a full wave of white water, and it was some time before they baled out and set themselves once more to rights, with an exhibition of colourful cursing in the direction of the bemused oarsmen who had neglected their duties. Then the owner, who had evidently achieved some serious thinking, said, 'And fin ye say, no questions asked, fa might ye be?'

'A Crawford of Culter,' Lymond said. 'And able to do what I say.'

'And fit are we to do?' asked the owner's uncle. Impelled by sudden optimism, he helped the stranger to sit up.

'Search for two men,' Lymond said 'And bring me them both, or their bodies. Before you unload that cargo.'

'And if we dinna find them?' said the owner, a realist.

'Then I'd advise you,' said Lymond, 'to leave the cargo alone. You won't fox the master.'

'Na,' said the owner's uncle, pulling his lip, He stared at the Crawford of Culter, who had lost a brief, if inevitable, battle, and was now, for the moment, no longer with them. 'He's dwined away. Ye mith pit him back far ye got him.'

Aikie said, 'Fat's her cargo?'

The owner said, 'Fae the Emperor o' Muscovy. They'll watch it like gleds.'

His uncle said, 'Culter's namely. Could he dee it?'

'Keep the Admiralty off? Like enough It winna hurt us tae claa his back an' dee as he wants us. Twa men. Russes likely. And never a mile fae a coo's tail likely, the callants. . . . There's Martin's boat.'

'Then wave your bluidy lantern!' his uncle yelled.

So Buckland brought Lymond back, in the boat owned by the opportune Martin, and Robert Best on one side and Adam Blacklock, cursorily restored on the other, stood in the surf and helped haul it in. Lymond was virtually conscious and walked, with Buckland's support, as far as the fire. D'Harcourt got up on one elbow and Adam could sense, on the other side of the blaze, that Osep Nepeja was stirring and also about to turn and struggle on to his feet He stood between both of them and Lymond, and waited until Buckland had laid him full length on the sand, and wrapped sacking round the shredded cloth on his shoulders.

His eyes were shut, which meant very little, except that he did not intend to be sociable.

'Soup,' said Buckland. Adam followed him to the cauldron, stopping on the way to speak to Nepeja. Solid, bearded and hatless, after weeks of hunger and desperation, when he saw his compatriots drown and went from day to day, more than them all in fear of his life he sat now, his hands on the great silver crucifix which had hung from the day he was born at his neck, and prayed to his God, two thousand miles off in Russia. It had been a Russian, mad with panic, who had overturned the *Edward*'s small boat. And the man hurt most perhaps by what had then happened was this man, surviving.

So Adam spoke to him reassuringly in his serviceable Russian, and saw him sit down, and went to Buckland and said, 'A man Fraser has offered us hospitality, and Forbes of the castle up there. They seem well-meaning and responsible : horses are coming, and carts for those who can't walk. They have room for the seamen.'

There were nineteen men on the beach, out of fifty. Or out of a hundred and thirty-five, if you cared to count the four ships

Buckland said, 'Who—?' and broke off, with the steaming ladle still held in his hand. And Adam understood. Of the seven men of birth who were left, who was to lead them? Robert Best, interpreter for the Muscovy Company, or John Buckland, their hired sailing master? The Ambassador, dumb without his interpreters? The three men, once of St Mary's? Or . . .

Buckland looked back, and Adam with him to where Francis Crawford still lay in the brilliant glow of the fire, his lashes parted; and the seawater bright on his skin.

'The Voevoda,' said Buckland firmly, and prepared to march with the soup to his patient.

Adam's hand on his ladle-arm stopped him.

'Yes,' said Adam. 'The Voevoda. But for the mercy of God, not just now.'

*

Although the fishing boats searched, for their own venal reasons, for quite a fair length of time, no man that night or any other laid hands on Richard Chancellor, Grand Pilot of the Muscovy Fleet, or his beloved son Christopher.

Long before then, they had moved out of the bay, at first tangled kindly together, and later alone, out of sight of each other, but with the same broad and harmonious current bearing them east.

Over the lightening sea lay the path Chancellor had discovered, and the door he had opened, expending on it a sovereign order of courage in an element exacting of courage, for he sailed from home, and not towards it.

We commit a little money to the hazard of fortune; he commits his life. Wherefore, Sidney had said, *you are to favour and love the man departing thus from us.*

The way he had found opened for him, and his long-studied seas with dignity gave him his bier. And in the morning, he was accorded the crown of dead men, to see the sun before they are buried, and he set out with shoes on his feet as do the Muscovites, for he had a long way to go.

CHAPTER THREE

The *Edward* touched her rock and settled on it, frail as a fly, and the filament of intelligence, from London to Brussels to Fontainebleau, trembled and marked it.

Within three days, the news was in Edinburgh, where, freshly back from the North, the Queen Dowager, Regent of Scotland, sat with her lords and examined it. Then, since one English ship was not an invasion and the ambassador of any reigning monarch should not, unseen, be offended, she made her dispositions and sent her heralds north to the Earl Marischal of Scotland in his castle of Dunnottar, to convey the noble refugee to her court. Then, of certain subtle intent, she dispatched a courier west, to Midculter.

Four days after the wreck, accordingly, Sybilla Lady Culter received word from her Queen that Francis Crawford her son was in Scotland and, for the first time in her long life fainted, before the courier's eyes. And Kate Somerville, who was staying with her, swept up the royal dispatch and read it, sitting by the Dowager's bed, long after the courier had gone and the excitement had died away, and then sat pale faced, with her sight quite detached from her brain until the exquisite little woman on the bed stirred and opened her eyes, and a moment later, summoned a smile. Then Philippa's mother, abandoned equally by her unaccountable young, fell forward, eyes-streaming, and hugged her.

The tidings reached London on 1 December, and were brought to Philippa forthwith by Jane Dormer, entering their own room and clasping her hands. 'Mr Crawford is back.'

To Philippa, who had been reading Bartholomew Lychpole's correspondence for weeks, this was not the news it might appear, but a franchise at last to display the satisfaction she felt at his coming. She said, 'I must write to his mother. Where is he? St Anthony's?' And then, taking time to read Jane's transparent face, she said baldly, 'What?'

Because Philippa knew the men of the Muscovy Company, it was hard at first to conceive the scale of the disaster; the fact that every ship had been lost, and every life, save for a handful of men on a beach in the north-east of Scotland. And Diccon. And Christopher. She stood by the window while Jane told her and then said with flat efficiency, 'Will you go to Penshurst, or shall I?'

Alone and sick on a diet of promises, with war rushing towards her, and her sister, sweetly recalcitrant, in the city, the Queen was in no mood to permit her women to leave her. It was Philippa therefore who fell ill with an unexplained fever and retiring from court, rode thirty miles through icy roads to tell Mary Sidney that her dear Diccon Chancellor was dead, and to break the news to his younger son Nicholas. She missed therefore the brief appearance in London of Robert Best and John Buckland, brutally altered, during which they attended meeting after meeting, answering the endless, harassed questions of the Muscovy merchants and set out north again in the second week of December in superior company, and armed with two documents. One, drawn up by the Muscovy Company, was a public instrument for registration in the books of the Lords of Council and Session in Edinburgh; the other (*rycht excellent, rycht heich and mychtie princesse our dearest sister*) was from the Queen of England to Marie de Guise, Dowager Queen and Regent of Scotland. Both referred to the merchant ship called *Edward Bonaventure* of one hundred and sixty tons' burden, thrown shattered and broken by storm on the Scottish coast next to or near the shore called Buchan Ness while making for London, and which so perished and sank that part of its goods had been lost, floating in the sea, and part thrown into the hands of the inhabitants from the coast at Buchan Ness and other adjacent coastal places belonging to the Serene Queen of Scotland and by them unjustly seized and detained.

The Company, legal in Latin, begged by these present instruments of administration that Queen, Council and officials of Scotland would have these goods returned to their owners, and recommended the party of six, including Robert Best and John Buckland, through which their request was conveyed.

The Queen, requesting letters of safe conduct for the same little party in Scotland, dwelt longer upon matters proper to kingdoms, such as the *person of good estimation sent from the Duke of Muscovy in embassy with certain gifts and jewels to be presented to us.* These goods, jewels and letters she asked to have restored, along with those of his fellow survivors, reasonable reward being given to those who recovered them. Her dearest sister would also, she begged, succour the Ambassador during his stay in her country, and also those loving subjects of England now coming north to see to his business and to conduct him thither to England.

Thus the news came to London and spread. Spread to King Philip at Brussels. Spread to the Hanse towns, and Sweden and Poland. The last to hear it was Russia. The first to hear it was the man for whose sake, because of a prophecy, Francis Crawford was committed to his deliberate and industrious exile.

Richard Crawford, 3rd Baron Culter, was at Dunnottar Castle, sixty miles south of Pitsligo, when the news came of the *Edward,* sent by Alexander Fraser, 7th Laird of Philorth, the biggest landowner of the Pitsligo area, and the Earl Marischal's kinsman by marriage.

It arrived late on Wednesday, 11 November, the day after the shipwreck, and the two men read it together; both moderate, middle aged and agreeable : William Keith, 4th Earl Marischal of Scotland and its wealthiest citizen, and Richard Crawford of Midculter, Lanarkshire, whose well-run lands provided him and his widowed mother and young, growing family with a living of comfort and grace, and whose steadfast and unpublicized services to his Queen and to his country had not gone through the years without recognition, though never with the traumas of love or hate, fear or envy which had surrounded the life of his brother.

William Keith read the message, in the Upper Hall of the strongest castle in Scotland, and then, because his secretary was in Aberdeen and the script was too small for his spectacles, he handed the page to his guest who had toiled for two months with macers, clerks, Justice Deputes and aggrieved plaintiffs over the aftermath of the Queen Dowager's Justice Courts up in Elgin, and who, thankfully, had been about to take his leave and ride back to Edinburgh. And so Richard saw the unmistakable writing, clear and even, and straight, line after line, as if ruled by the thread of the mistar. And at the foot of the page, without flourish, the signature : FRANCIS CRAWFORD OF LYMOND AND SEVIGNY.

Nor, making his quick dispositions; taking directions of

the tired courier, discussing with the Earl Marischal the steps necessary to warn the Queen Regent in Edinburgh or brushing aside, with grim heartiness, the Earl Marischal's views on the folly of setting out on a sixty-mile ride without sleep on a wild night in November, did the 3rd Baron Culter dream of the degree of cold, considered thought which had forced the dispatch of that letter.

Instead, smiling, he left his host, and climbed the steep cliff-face path with his servants, and, looking back, saluted the rock of Dunnottar, glossing the sea as it rose from its coarse russet crust, appled with primaeval pebbles. Then he set off, buffeted by the unruly wind under a sky like a pod of grey whales, slowly moving, outlined in apricot.

It was after five of the clock and lamplight showed, here and there, a pale yellow. To the west, you could see a salting of rain, shaken over the marshlands, and a shallow pool by the roadside was full of blurred, running wavelets, fine as bird claws. Soon it would be dark, and all the sea would be dulled by the hammer marks of the rain. He nodded to his men, smiling still, and wondered if he would ever meet his only brother without this groundless turmoil in mind and in body, which was not fear for himself but fear, he knew, for all those dearest to him. And further wondered why, in the midst of relief and thanksgiving, he should have such misgivings at all.

*

For a man who did not wish to be in Scotland to stay in Scotland, and to advertise his presence there, mystified Adam Blacklock, until he thought it through, and realized why Lymond had written the letter which Alec Fraser, as red as a Rosehearty onion, had dispatched with such elation to his son's guid-brother, the Marischal. Best and Buckland had to go south, to report the loss and set in train all the processes which would extract both their goods and their Muscovite passenger from this alien country of Scotland. Englishmen both, it was something they alone were able to do.

Conversely, someone in authority must remain with the Ambassador, to be his interpreter to his hosts, his guide and his protector; to safeguard what was left of the pitiful cargo. Since they had been swept into the tall keep of Pitsligo and from there, against John Forbes's voluble protestations, to the ampler hospitality of the manor of Philorth, the bay had been thick as peasemeal with rowboats; large and small, well manned or driven past reef and through breaker by one dedicated pair of stout Buchan arms.

What was left of the cargo of the *Edward Bonaventure* was transferring itself, swiftly and effectively, into the pockets of Buchan, and Alec Fraser 7th Laird of Philorth, four miles to the south-west of Pitsligo and forty from Aberdeen, of which city his wife's father was Provost, was doing little to stop it.

Nor was Lymond, but for, Adam suspected, quite different reasons. Whatever strange bargains had been struck out there in the dark and the wind, fishing boats had quartered the bay long after the fire on the shore had died down and the last exhausted man from the *Edward* was sleeping. By dawn half of the *Edward*'s cargo had gone, farther than any Pitsligo fisherman would locate it. And the rest had been worked for.

That act of Lymond's alone would have marked him. His name was known, his authority obvious; soon they would discover his station. To abandon his charge and disappear like a tinker over the Border; to be found lurking under an alias would discredit his mission and turn Nepeja's despair to hysterical fury. Only now, in the peace of dry land, was there leisure to study how storm and sea and mistrust of the unknown land had changed Osep Nepeja, the wealthy Vologda merchant, with the pearl-collared dress and the fine house and the invisible, obedient wife. His colleagues Grigorjeff and Makaroff had disappeared, with eight of their fellows, on the foundered *Confidentia.* Two days before, he had seen seven other Russians die and all his wealth sink into the cold Scottish waters. The Muscovites who served him now were Lymond's servants, but for two whom the Voevoda had kept at his side. Accustomed to Lymond and accustomed, as well, to unquestioned obedience the men had settled first, and, though quieter than usual and frankly wolvish at mealtimes, they showed no permanent harm save exhaustion.

Nepeja was different. Through all the rescue he had prayed, his voice rising and falling, his hands working on the great silver crucifix, his forehead beating the sand. Now, in the little stone room given him in Alec Fraser's brave manor, he took to his bed and only clambered out of it to peer at the weather, and rub his hands at the fire and attack Lymond, whenever he opened the door, with questions and anxieties, accusations and complaints.

It was understandable enough. He had been told he was coming to London; he had expected to arrive, richly dressed and primed with gifts, with his merchandise in chest and barrel behind him. What was he to understand, knowing nothing of the sea, of a nation which, far from achieving these things, cast him naked on the shores of a different country and made of him, it seemed, not an ambassador but a beggar?

And to all these outbursts, Lymond was patient. Patient as he was not the night before, wandering half-slept up and down their big room, Robert Best had stopped and said, stupidly, 'I am the only one left. All the freighting of those bloody cargoes. The lists and the invoices, the account books and ciphers, the notes and charts and letters of privilege. All the stuff that we bought in Pskov and Novgorod and Moscow and Lampozhnya; the furs we worried about, the tallow we thought had too great a foot, the honey we haggled over . . . even Brook's cargo we took on at Vardo . . . all of them gone. The seamen gone to the bottom, with all they could teach of the coast. The new compass, the new astrolabe, the man the Tsar knows and trusts, lost and gone. Lost and lost and lost and lost . . . and no one to tell of it. No one knows it but me. *My God, I'm the only one left!* . . .'

And his voice, rising and rising, had snapped like a stalk, for Lymond, standing cold-eyed before him, had struck him full on the face. And then, with a thrust of both hands had made him collapse on the floor, where he sat, his face livid, staring up at the Voevoda Bolshoia who said, 'You are an adult Englishman, I believe. Then act like one,' and walked away.

But Best did not break down again. Nor did anyone else.

So, in private and derisive challenge to the unmannerly fates, Lymond wrote the letter the Laird of Philorth was to dispatch, notifying the world of the end of the third Muscovy voyage, and in the same temper signed it. And thus on the second dawn after the wreck, riding on an uneven road through a night black with wind and arched with a glittering frenzy of stars came Richard Crawford of Culter, and saw the forty-foot grey castle of Philorth, with its new keep and round tower rising from its green mound, and the white running light of its stream, spilling through the short marshy grass to the dunes and between the rocks to be lost in the sea.

What made him look to the sea, he never afterwards knew, unless his eye was drawn by that trickle of sweet running water, and the noise it made in the silence of sunrise, against the spaced hiss of the waves and the wind sound, never wholly expended, as of a man whistling absently now and then, high and low, soft and loud, through his teeth with a muffled orchestration behind it like kettledrums dried out by distance.

He looked to the beach and saw, far off, a man standing there; and without knowing why, stopped his servants, turned his horse and, alone, set out towards him.

The grass was bright yellow-green and caulked underfoot with brown mud, from other horses and Philorth's black cattle. Behind it the rain-wet beach was the colour of pastry, with the sea beyond, white against grey, and a paler grey sky flat and heavy above.

It had been, until now, a mild autumn. There were still, here and there, the tall white heads of angelica, and starry fool's parsley, as well as club rush and deer's grass and the wide leaves of plantain. There was, somewhere, a small budding of gorse and he had seen, coming, a single harebell and some soiled, green-eyed daisies. The wind still blew, sending light leapfrogging through the short grass, and the bearded dune grasses ahead stood combed, like a fine Arab's mane. But it was not the wind of two nights ago, bemusing the nostrils with its uneven force, exposing the thin pain of face nerves, the icy ache of cheek flesh and the flanks of the nose, the aching seizure, like cramp, in the fingers. A crow passed, planing, like a still, triangular rag and he thought, suddenly, that the man on the beach had moved also, and vanished.

Then he saw, rounding a bluff, that this was not so. He was still there, far across the grainy dark peach-coloured sand, resting in a coign of dune and grey rock, his hands round his knees, his face quite still, turned to the sea. An oyster-catcher, which had risen, piping, settled again at the water's edge in a flash of black and scarlet and white and began its angular walk. Richard, dismounting, tied his reins to a gorse bush and walked also, across the heavy sand, to that unreal figure.

Half-way there, a touch of his normal common sense returned to him and he slowed down, wondering what exchange of courtesies he was going to offer a vagabond, an Abram man, or an idiot. Then the man turned his head and Richard saw that he was none of these things. That the frieze cloak he wore was rich, and fell back from the silk of a high-collared tunic; that his hair, flicked by the wind, was yellow as mustard and the shadowless face, faintly engraved upon and tired as cered linen, was indeed that of Francis his brother.

Lymond did not move. His head lifted, watching, showed no conventional welcome; his brows, cloudily drawn, suggested the weight of something so firmly extinguished that nothing was left, in thought or expression, save a curious air, part of resignation, part of defiance which had to do, perhaps, with his stillness. Only the edge of his cloak stirred tardily, with his inaudible breathing. His parted lips closing, Richard Crawford came to a halt and stood, looking down at his brother.

'There is not a soul but over it is a keeper,' Lymond said. 'Welcome, *brother.*'

You cannot embrace a seated man whose long sleek hands, broken with callouses, remain strictly clasped round his knees, and whose two open eyes are discs of smooth blue enamel. Richard stood where he was and said simply, 'Thank God you're back. And safe.' And then, moved moved beyond pride, dropped on one knee.

Lymond's face warned him off. The repudiation, though he did not move, was as stark as if he had jumped to his feet, coldly incredulous. Shocked, Richard said abruptly, 'Are you ill?'

With care, Lymond changed his position. It was not a retreat, but the space between them undoubtedly widened. It made it possible for Richard to move in his turn, and finding a stock of grey rock, to sit on it, with a stone from the beach to employ him. He had picked it up before he found it was fractured; an eggshell guillotined by its fellows, to show a quartz yolk of glistening olive.

'I must apologize,' Lymond said. 'One is afflicted with a certain enjambment of silence. Before our miscarriage at sea, we were accustomed to living like cormorants.'

'Is that why you are here?' Richard said.

'That is why I am here. The nest is rather full, with a great deal of bill-snapping. It is a little like Ramadan. At the appearance of the first star nothing but gluttony, drunkenness and lust. Brechin will be rotten with pox.'

'I was at Dunnottar. Did you know?' Richard said.

'No. I had, perhaps, a premonition,' Lymond said. 'The wonderful celerity of hasting nature. And here you are.'

He was, of course, very tired still and looked it; the voyage, wreck apart, would tax any man's endurance. But that didn't account for quite everything. Richard said bluntly, 'I thought I should be welcome.'

'I have fallen out of the habit of talking to brothers,' Lymond said. 'Is the Earl Marischal sending a courier to Edinburgh?'

'Yes. And a party north, some time today. They will see the two men you mention on their way south to London, and arrange to conduct the Ambassador by easy stages to Edinburgh. The Queen Dowager will wish to see him. In any case, there will be some legal formalities to do with the wreck and the cargo. Is there a guard on her?'

'On the *Edward*? Of a sort,' Lymond said. 'Most of it has probably gone. And *pace* the Muscovy Company, it would be a benign gesture not to pursue it too heartily. The fishermen gave up a good deal of their time on the night of the wreck at my instance, looking for Chancellor.'

He had heard the name before. 'The new English pilot. A pity that,' Richard said.

Lymond's fair brows shot up, in a way suddenly and sharply familiar. 'He died in tender years, but ripe in grace. And conducted to heaven these his sailors, being drawn to enjoy these celestial waters which God hath granted to the faithful. At least we don't have to bury them.'

The edge, suddenly, was back, with all the hurtfulness he remembered so well. Richard said, 'I hear you killed Graham Malett.'

Lymond opened his lips before he spoke. 'Eventually,' he said.

'And saved one of the two boys he had taken. Don't you want to know how your son is?' said Richard.

'Since Moscow is in the same planet as Philippa, I know how my son is,' Lymond said. 'At least, she sent me a letter. If he were dead, I imagine she would have mentioned it in the first sentence.'

Richard stared at his brother. 'Philippa's mother has him, at Flaw Valleys. They're at Midculter on a visit, just now.

He is all that any man would want his son to be. My God, Francis, you gave a year of your life towards finding him. He has the exact Crawford colouring.'

'Egg mimicry,' said Lymond. 'How many more of yours have you hatched?' He had loosened his hands and was delving his long, ruined fingers through the sand of the beach, scattered with immaculate shells and small sharp stones of all colours. Lower down, nearer the sea, lay the shining thick satin scarves and maypole confusion of seaweed ribbons : bright green; strong sage yellow; with great bronchial branches of tube and artery, five feet long. Beyond that, the profiled waves, bearded like trolls, came riding black to the shore.

'I have another son,' Richard said. 'Three children in all. Mariotta is well. Sybilla is not.'

Lymond said, 'Did Philippa get her divorce?'

There was a little pause. Then Richard said, 'That was crude, for you.'

'But as you will find,' said Lymond softly, addressing the sand, 'I am a very crude man. Did she get her divorce?'

The hammer strokes of fear, soft and regular as he had felt them at Dunnottar, began to beat in Richard's chest. Now, he schooled his pleasant brown face and guarded his eyes as Lymond no longer needed to do, and said, in a voice of which he was not ashamed, 'Don't you know?'

'Moscow and Philippa being, although on the same planet, some small distance apart, the most recent news,' Lymond said, 'has escaped me. The Lennoxes were trying to interfere, I rather gathered.'

'You will have to look higher than that,' Richard said. 'The culprit for the moment is Pope Paul IV. There is a test case on foot in the Vatican.'

'Oh, Christ,' Lymond said, with mild irritation. After a moment, he added, 'All right. You may as well tell me.'

'I don't know how much you know,' said Richard. Resentment, fear, desperation seemed to shadow all they said. He pushed them aside, looking out at the grey moving sea with its looping of foam; the even, grey sky curtained by hanging dark vapours of storm-air. He said, 'There is a truce in being, signed nine months ago, between the King of France and the Emperor Charles. It is supposed to last for five years, but it may be broken already, for all I know. Already France has formed a defensive league with the

Duke of Ferrara and the new Pope, Pope Paul, the Caraffa, who is eighty years old and loathes Spaniards.'

'The scum of the earth,' Lymond said. '. . . the spawn of Jews and Moors, now the masters of Italy, who have been known only as its cooks . . . ?'

'So he has said,' Richard agreed. 'France is ready for war. Or at least, the de Guises want it, if the Constable does not. And if France wants to invade Naples and take back the old Angevin inheritance, she could hardly have a better opening than now, with a Pope strongly antagonistic to Spain, and the Empire ruled not by Charles, but this sluggish, inexperienced Prince. . . .'

'So the Emperor has abdicated?' Lymond said. 'And left Spain and the Netherlands and Sicily and Spain to the noble Philip, Queen Mary's husband? Then I should guess he has not been back to England.'

Richard shook his head. 'The Emperor left in the autumn, after putting off the abdication for a year. Philip is in Brussels, supposedly bound by the truce, facing the Pope's little league with King Henri and consulting the theologians, they say, on how to wage a defensive war against the Pope. In fact, he's done rather more. The Duke of Alva is outside Rome already, with twelve thousand foot and sixteen hundred horse and twelve artillery pieces, and the city is waiting in panic.'

'Defended by?'

'Monluc and your friend Piero Strozzi. The truce is a farce. The French army is ready. They have been withdrawing troops from Scotland all autumn. Senarpont, they say, is gathering men at Boulogne to attack Calais and your other old compère Lord Grey of Wilton.'

'And England?' Lymond said.

'Waiting, as ever, for Philip to come. He has promised, I hear, to cross over at Lent. Spain wants the Queen of England to crown him, and declare war on France if the French won't observe the peace. The Queen, they say, has decided that if the truce is broken and the Low Countries attacked, she will stand by the old treaty Henry VIII made with the Emperor. That is, she will supply horse and foot without actually engaging in war.'

'An honourable, if lunatic, proposition,' Lymond said. 'And if she does, will her people follow her? What of the religion?'

'Pole is Archbishop of Canterbury. The burnings go on.

Mostly of theologians or people of humble position: the rest were given early warning to fly off to Geneva or Strasburg; some had gone there long before. The bishops have sent a hundred or two to the stake. At the same time, thirteen hundred Lutherans and Anabaptists have been cremated in Holland. . . . There was a plot against the Queen in the spring, but it was betrayed months beforehand. To rob the Treasury and establish Elizabeth as Queen, married to William Courtenay. In which case, she would have been a widow by this time.'

Lymond said sharply, 'Courtenay is dead?'

'Yes,' said Richard slowly. 'The only male claimant to the throne. He died in September in Padua.'

'I see,' Lymond said. He was looking out to sea, where a gull was soaring with white, knuckled wings, but his eyes did not see it. 'And the lady Elizabeth?'

'Is at Hatfield. There was a fuss in the summer, over some seditious papers found in her house. Some of her staff were arrested, and her household has been organized and staffed by the Queen. Since then it has been quiet. Since the hopes of a child heir have vanished, the marriage plans for Madam Elizabeth have been fairly constant, of course. The current one is to link her with Philip's cousin, the Duke of Savoy. They suggested the Archduke Ferdinand, but the French Ambassador said that if they went ahead with it, they would marry the child Mary Queen of Scots to Courtenay.'

'Before or after his death?' said Lymond with unexpected savagery. He added, 'You realize you have told me nothing about my lisping child-bride and her tedious divorce?'

'Oh. Yes,' said Richard. 'One of the objects of the truce was to allow the ransoming of prisoners of war. After haggling for months, the Constable of France got his son back, to find that, while in prison, he had fallen in love with a lady and married her.'

'It happens,' Lymond said. 'More frequently in prison than out.'

'Quite. Except that the Constable had been at great pains to affiance the young man to the King of France's illegitimate daughter, with all the honours and recognition that implied.'

'Did it?' asked Lymond.

'If your father is the King of France,' Richard said. 'So

there arises the matter of a divorce. The marriage between the young lady and the Constable's son has not been consummated.'

'So they say,' Lymond said. 'Do you believe Philippa?'

For a moment, Richard was silent. Then he said, 'Naturally. So does her mother.'

'I thought you would believe her,' Lymond said. 'Yes? Well? You had got to "consummated".'

'So it is to be placed before a public convocation of cardinals, and on the current mood of the Pope will depend the outcome of their marriage and yours. . . . Why do you *do* that?' said Richard. 'You know we believe Philippa.'

'Perhaps I envy her,' Lymond said. 'No one believes me.'

'Not even Kiaya Khátún?' Richard said.

Lymond's eyes, surprised and informed with pure malice, swung back from mid-ocean contemplation. 'And what do you know about that? You astonish me, Richard.'

'Only that you took her to Russia. Or so Philippa says.'

'It was the other way about. But of course you are right. Kiaya Khátún is of the happy family circle.'

'No! No,' said Lymond soothingly. 'All but the ceremony. We hope to have the four children legitimized.'

For a moment, with sinking heart, Richard believed him. Then he saw the look on Lymond's face, and found he could bear it even less. He got to his feet, stiff and unslept, with all the weariness of the night suddenly upon him. 'At least,' he said, 'you are back.'

And if he had been looking at his brother's face then, which he was not, he would have seen worn into the bones a burden identical to his own, which rested a moment and then was as swiftly banished. Lymond, rising also, stood for a moment, contemplating the brightening sky. From nondescript grey, the shell-rim of each turning wave had sharpened into a deep peacock green : the distant sea, tweeded and slubbed with frantic white, lay brown on the horizon. Lymond said, 'While Best is away, I shall have to be Nepeja's interpreter and act with the Queen as his principal. I have no hopes of private exchanges. Nor, with the life I lead, would it be suitable. When you go back, I should like you to tell them.'

Face to face, they were the same height : one middle-aged and heavily built; the other light to the point of attenuation. 'Tell whom?' said Richard harshly.

'Oh, *God!*' said Lymond explosively; and then, drawing breath, set himself to take hold again. 'Look. It's my fault. You're falling asleep as you stand. But give me a moment. Sit down on that bloody rock for a minute, and let me try to explain. And listen to me as if I weren't related. Can you make some sort of frenetic endeavour, and pretend to do that? Because in the only sense that matters, Richard, it's true.'

He stopped as Richard reseated himself, a hand on his shoulder, and stood looking down at him crookedly, as he used to do long ago, but with different eyes, and a face differently blocked. He said, 'You rode sixty miles through the night for a brother who doesn't exist. I haven't been here for four years. I have been growing and changing, somewhere else, with different people, speaking a different language. The old ties are gone: my family wouldn't recognize me: what in God's name do you think I could find to say to them? And the new ties are only on paper: the divorce is a formality as the marriage was. And for all he knows of me, the boy could be anyone's son; perhaps . . . it doesn't matter. Do you know how he was saved?'

'Not in detail. By a chess game, Philippa said.'

'Do you know how the other one died?' Lymond said. Richard shook his head.

Lymond took his hand away. 'By the deaf-mutes, at the same game,' he said. 'I don't want to see this child. If you can't understand that, I can't help it. I don't want to see anyone at Midculter; it would serve no purpose and the second parting would only be worse. I am part of this embassy. I have a share in it. I have to go to London with the Ambassador and aid him in all he has to do, and carry out other duties, for which I am entirely responsible to the Tsar. When I have done so, I shall sail back with Nepeja to Muscovy. And after that, I am not coming back.'

Richard, his face white with fatigue was staring at him as if, indeed, they were not related. 'You are going back to that woman in Russia?'

'To Güzel, yes. And to St Mary's.'

Bitterly scathing, 'Is there any of St Mary's left?' Richard said.

'Hislop will come back with me. It is more than St Mary's. We are the nucleus of the Tsar's army.'

404

'So you are important?'

'My life is there,' Lymond said.

'A big fish in a little pool. What you wanted,' Richard said.

If he was moved suddenly to laughter, he did not show it. 'Or, *If you have made your bed well, well may you lie on it,*' Lymond said. 'The Buchan version is even apter. . . . Richard, I am not not worth anyone's heartache.'

'I know that,' Richard said. 'But she does not.'

*

'She will have to learn,' Lymond said.

It was full day when they returned to the castle, and Alec Fraser (my wife's Da is the Provost), voluble with excitement, led the 3rd Baron Culter into the Great Hall the party shared, off the Ambassador's room, the 3rd Baron's brother modestly following.

They all rose; but Adam Blacklock first of all, to greet the man he remembered well from his early days at St Mary's in Scotland, when the first great struggle began between the two leaders who hated each other: Lymond and Gabriel, Sir Graham Reid Malett. So he shook Richard's hand, and noted the distress on his face and the serene and arrogant calm of the Voevoda's, smiling behind him. And noted, too the quick turn of Culter's head as the Russian flowed from man to man about him; the domestic language they all used: Yeroffia to Lymond; Lymond to Simeon and Phoma to discover if the Ambassador would receive them. Ludicrously, Lord Culter had not expected his brother to be familiar with Russian. Certainly, he had not looked for the deference which surrounded Lymond on every side; and not only, Adam was aware, from the Russians. To d'Harcourt and Hislop and himself, he was the Voevoda Bolshoia. But, obviously, Lymond had not told his brother.

The two men, talking, disappeared with Alec Fraser into the Ambassador's room, and the door shut behind them.

Danny Hislop, who had slept for thirty-six hours, on and off, with a sporadic remission for eating, stretched himself and said, 'So that nice man is Belial's family.'

'Do you think,' d'Harcourt said critically, 'he has enjoyed the reunion?'

'Do you think,' Danny Hislop said even more critically, 'either of them has enjoyed the reunion? I know that smile. Cooled in snake blood.'

'In which case,' said Blacklock with foreboding, 'we are due for a hell of a journey to Edinburgh.'

'Via Aberdeen,' Hislop said. 'My wife's Da's the Provost.'

They left Philorth the next day, on the Earl Marischal's horses, with Nepeja in borrowed clothes bringing up the rear of the little procession, the 3rd Baron Culter beside him.

Lymond was not in borrowed clothes, because alone of all their possessions, his had been loaded into the pinnace. For that, and for Chancellor's chest, now on its way safely to London, he had Adam Blacklock to thank.

Riding beside him now, at the head of the company, Adam found occasion to ask the question he had been longing to put, ever since they rode through the arched gate of Philorth and left the grey manor behind, and the yellow green grass, and the beach upon which the long breakers moved in dark pleatings, under a clear, light blue sky white with cloud.

The sun was low. It struck the grass like green fur, with a sparkle; the hills were half-dried velvet and the thin coloured leaves of the trees glittered in the long shadows and orient light: autumn trees, their branches combed by the gale and moving overhead in veil upon veil of chestnut and auburn and yellow, of flame and chrome and veridian; the large coin of the poplar paper-yellow against the fine hazy mist of the birch; the sprays hanging, nebula upon nebula, coarse grained and fine as bright flour, swaying over the riders as they made their way south in the clear, mellow air.

And as they rode, they were partnered with music, voices and lute, just and sweet in sonorous harmony, from a cheerful cluster of pilgrims who joined them, riding in company. The music, light and merry, accompanied them. The leaves, in notes and chords and cadenzas soared overhead, and the yellow sun shone upon them through the long dancing nets of the trees.

'That prophecy,' Adam Blacklock said then to Lymond. 'I can guess. It was that you and your brother should meet once again.'

He could not see Lymond's face, but his voice was perfectly clear. 'No. In fact it wasn't,' he said.

Adam was shocked, as well as disappointed. 'Oh. So,' he said, 'it didn't come true?'

'I'm afraid,' Lymond said with infinite calmness, 'I'm rather afraid that it did. . . . Do you really enjoy poor motet singing?'

Adam stared at him, his eyes open, words of informed protest hanging, unsaid and smug on his lips.

Lymond did not, however, wait for an answer. 'There are times,' he said, 'when I can tolerate Robert Carver, and times when I find him quite incredibly banal. I wish you well of him.' And touching his spurs to his horse, he drew it out of the column and into a sudden full gallop which took him far ahead, and through the distant dazzle of trees, and out of sight of the whole trotting convoy.

Danny Hislop touched his horse to ride, busily, beside Adam's. 'He remembered an appointment?'

'He remembered something you have forgotten,' Adam said. 'That this is his country.'

CHAPTER FOUR

Fortunately or unfortunately, the effects of shock and exhaustion do not last for ever. By the time the train of Osep Grigorievich Nepeja, Envoy and Nuntio to the great lord and Emperor of all Russia, had creaked into Edinburgh, a full choral rendering of *O bóne Jesu* with John Fethy playing would have found the Voevoda once again quite impervious, as he was to the whims and vagaries of his Ambassador Osep.

Restored, by time and by deference, to more sanguine good spirits, Osep Nepeja sat on his horse, full bearded, bluff as Magog and stared about him, uttering questions. All, on this first excursion abroad, was bewildering. The diminutive scale of the country with its crowded, changing topography moved him to much benevolent jesting : he said nothing, the St Mary's men noticed, of the good wainscot bed with a quilt he had been given at Philorth, or the painted ceilings and carved freestone fireplaces, the tapestry cloths and armed chairs and cushions, the decent tableware of glass and china and pewter in the same laird's house.

The number of cottages amazed him with their roofs of thatch instead of wood shingle. More than that, the number of buildings everywhere constructed of stone. Lacking Plummer, it was left to Adam to explain how Russia's condensing damps and deep frosts were no problem in Scotland; to display the solid charms of the abbeys they stayed in and the French graces of the great royal homes with their carved walls and picturesque gardens; their fountains and chapels, their beautiful ceilings. He explained, with unwonted enthusiasm, the schooling provided by church and by tutor, referred with pride to the three universities, no less, of St Andrews, Glasgow and Aberdeen, and pointed out, in Aberdeen, the only granite cathedral in the known world. He then remembered, somewhat belatedly, the well known antipathy of the Russian Orthodox Church for the church of his fathers, and cast round for rescue by Culter. It was not until Culter left them, to ride south on business to Edinburgh, that the rôle of guide was taken over and executed, without quarter, by Lymond.

He was not concerned, it soon appeared, with the superior blessings of climate or culture; he did not offer, as Adam had vaguely envisaged, to immerse their visitor in a total full day's performance of Davie Lyndesay's *Three Estates*. He was curt with Osep's complaint that, in Scotland, one ate at eleven in the morning and then failed to retire, as in Muscovy, for one's afternoon of restorative slumber. He answered instead questions about weights and coinage and taxes, trying to instil into the merchant's head the matters he had begun to learn long ago in Vologda and, with his pitiful English, had forgotten. He explained briefly, and with great clarity, the workings of the burghs of barony through which they were passing, the function of the professional guilds, and from there, the operation of church, law and parliament, illustrating the lectures from their surroundings and their company as they progressed. He pointed out, uncompromisingly, the uses of good communication, including paved roads in town and in country and the lessons of husbandry : how the hogs were fed; the sheep and poultry of better quality; the beef better flavoured and firm. He then applied all he had related, item by item, to the future welfare of Russia.

Riding on Nepeja's other side, Danny Hislop saw with fascination a hearty, devious, half-educated Russian Governor becoming, under his eyes, a harassed and rebellious graduate. And catching the gaze of his fellows, shrugged with mock anguish, and grinned.

They were met, by the Queen Dowager's command, at the estuary crossing at Queensferry, and from there taken by her lords into the city of Edinburgh.

Separated by three files from his mentor and able, at last, to unbutton his normal thought possesses, Osep Nepeja's first words on standing on the hill of Corstorphine and beholding, far over the marsh, the end-rock and castle of Edinburgh, bore witness to a long and weary journey, of which this was by no means the end. 'Do we climb it on ropes?' he remarked. 'Or do they take up the horses in buckets?'

They were given a house in the High Street, the steep cobbled main street of Edinburgh, which led down to the Queen's home at Holyrood, and up to the heights of the castle. Riding up from the West Bow to reach it, Nepeja saw a thoroughfare lined with tall grey stone houses, each with its turnpike stair; its flight of steps from first floor to street. And since, shoulder to shoulder, they admitted no entrance between them, you found your way through them by pends, arched tunnels pierced in the stonework which led through to green sloping gardens, their limits washed by a broad lake. The Ambassador stood a long time the first evening, on the lawn hedged with brambles, still red and green and black on the bush, and among the late roses, tall and leggy, with blooms like soggy brown vegetables. In Moscow, the snow would have lain three feet thick, this last month. And Lymond did not disturb him.

For their lodging, their food and their servants, they were indebted to the Queen Dowager of Scotland, and the following morning her officers came to call on the Tsar of Muscovy's noble ambassador, to receive his thanks, and to inquire his further wishes. And also, by shrewd and courteous questioning, to obtain what information they could about this curious embassy, to take back to their mistress and regent. Two days after that, Robert Best and John Buckland arrived back from London with four

Englishmen and a number of documents. They also brought money, the Ambassador was pleased to discover, and instructions to comfort, aid, assist and relieve him and his, and to conduct him forthwith south to London.

It was just before Christmas, the rites of which the Muscovite Ambassador celebrated privately with his servants, after his own fashion. Immediately afterwards, primed with all the necessary legal and political advice, the Queen Dowager of Scotland invited the Muscovite Ambassador to court.

It is doubtful whether, despite Adam's incorrigible salesmanship, Osep Nepeja appreciated any of the draughty splendours of Holyrood Palace; its music, paintings and furnishings, its trumpeters and heralds, its painted friezes and wainscoting and long suites of tapestries on subjects of which Viscovatu would not have approved. Boiling unseen within the ranks of the newly clothed Muscovite party was the battle which had raged ever since Master Hussey had arrived from Paternoster Row and the quiet legal ambience of Doctors' Commons to supervise, as he thought, the proper disposal of the wreck of the *Edward Bonaventure* and all that remained of her cargo.

Firstly, there appeared to be, according to the news from Pitsligo, very little wreck and no cargo to dispose of. And secondly, the Muscovite Ambassador Osep Nepeja was not prepared to leave Scotland until he, personally, had received back the merchandise, crates and possessions which he had intended to barter in London. In vain, Lewis, Roberts and Gilpin, Hussey's associates, tried to persuade him that the matter could be left in their hands : that no quirk of Scots law would escape Master Hussey or public notary Lewis; that no sharp dealing would be tolerated by George Gilpin, the resident secretary in Antwerp of the Society of English Merchants or by Edmund Roberts, a leading London merchant and charter member of the Muscovy Company. Nepeja simply announced that, until the pilfered cargo was recovered, he was staying in Scotland.

The argument raged for the better part of twenty-four hours, and Lymond took no part in it whatever, thereby reserving, as Danny Hislop cynically remarked, all the undoubted respect and awe which he already inspired in poor Osep. Only, on the day of the royal reception, the

Voevoda Bolshoia drew Roberts and Lewis aside and said agreeably, 'You represent the Muscovy Company. May I ask what reception the Company intends to give Master Nepeja in London?'

'Oh, you need have no doubts of that,' Roberts said, expansively. 'The best. No expense will be spared. Your friend Nepeja, Crawford, is about to find himself esteemed like a king. And yourself, of course,' he added comfortably, for he and his colleagues, after the closest questioning of Buckland and Best, were resigned to the fact that the Tsar had sent not only a trading Ambassador but an envoy of another kind, whose business the State would negotiate. 'The Company,' said Edmund Roberts, 'wishes the Tsar to understand the importance English merchants attach to the growing bond between our two nations.'

'And the enjoyers thereof to be as men living in a golden world,' Lymond said. 'I merely wished to point out that the Muscovites are not the most trusting of races. If you wish him amenable, I am afraid you must allow Nepeja to do as he wishes in Scotland.'

Irritating, as it turned out, but true. Warned in advance, the Queen Dowager, Regent of Scotland, gave audience therefore to the Ambassador of the noble King Ivan of Russia, and returned him gentle answers, and hope of speedy restitution of the goods, clothing, jewels and letters lost or pilfered from the English ship *Edward,* for which purpose she intended to send north her Commissioners, with a Herald of Arms, to Pitsligo, there to command by Proclamation and other edicts that all persons, no degree excepted, with any part of the spoiled goods should restore them.

Nepeja, with Best as his interpreter, answered suitably, if without particular reverence. No one was wearing silver tissue, nor were the cupboards laden with white and gilt plate. The Court was handsomely dressed and more than adequately jewelled, but he found it hard to reconcile these bluff men with their chains and furred gowns with a nation which would permit a woman to order them; a group of foreigners to fight and rule in their midst. The Queen was a child, the Voevoda had told him, affianced to the young heir of France, and being brought up in that Kingdom. And until she came of age her mother, a Frenchwoman, was ruling in Scotland, advised by Frenchmen and protected by Frenchmen, as well as by

411

Scots. 'Are the boyars powerful?' he had asked the Voevoda, and the Voevoda had said, 'Yes. But they are divided. And the kingdom is under a strong rule, and a moderately wise one. If war breaks out between England and France it will be another matter.'

'This country will side with France against England?' Nepeja had said. 'The English then are its Tartars?'

And the Voevoda had been amused, but had said, 'Not every Scotsman wants to fight France's quarrel. But there is a long history of coercion between the countries on the two sides of our border. The crowns of England and Scotland are both Catholic, but the refugees of Queen Mary's persecution find harbour with the Queen Dowager in Scotland. She is tolerant, and far sighted in a number of ways. Don't underrate her.'

One listened and if one was wise, replied nothing to the Voevoda. For one found little to admire in such a nation, where the groom taking your bridle would exchange the time of day to your face, and the porter, the ferryman, the very peasant walking the fields would expect without shame to address you. Nor where the ruler was of that sex which no proper man could underrate.

The exchange therefore was brief: the welcome and answer between monarch and ambassador concluded and Master Osep Nepeja given permission, if he so pleased, to stay in the realm of Scotland while these matters of restitution were being pursued. He kissed the Queen's hand. So, too, did Messrs Buckland and Best, Hussey, Gilpin, Lewis and Roberts. Last, with equal deference, came Mr Crawford of Lymond and Sevigny, presently in the employment of the Russian Tsar, and companion to Master Nepeja on his momentous embassy. As he took her hand, the Queen Dowager said, 'If the Ambassador permits, we should like to have private words with this gentleman.'

The Ambassador, his eyes sharp beneath untrimmed brows, gave, through Mr Best, his willing agreement. The group of Englishmen bowed, and Master Nepeja; they backed, and the door closed behind them.

'Now, Mr Crawford,' said Mary of Guise.

He could not have expected to leave Scotland without this confrontation. Four years before, in this city, he had refused to lead his company of St Mary's as an instrument of the Queen Dowager's. Since then, she had tried to

412

form a standing army of her own, and had failed. Now, whatever she guessed, she must know, from the suave, visiting lords who had called on him, who had entertained Buckland and Best, and chatted to Hislop and Blacklock and d'Harcourt, that the nucleus of St Mary's at least was now in the employment of the Tsar. So now she gazed at the presentable, unpredictable Scotsman before her and said, 'We hear you favour Muscovy with your advice and your presence. Before your brief sojourn is over, we were curious to learn what gross defects in its people, its form or its management you had found in this country to spurn.'

It was a game, and these were its opening moves. 'Your grace,' Lymond said. 'What defect has France, that so many of her noblest sons stand at your side? They advise you out of their wisdom, I the Tsar out of my humility.'

The large, pale eyes studied him from the stiff head-dress; her skirts, spread widely about her, did not disguise the strong, big-boned frame of the de Guises, the most powerful family in France. She said, 'Out of long-standing alliance and amity, France supports this nation, and defends it. We have no such commitments to Muscovy. On whose behalf do you support its Tsar?'

'On my own,' Lymond said. 'I am a soldier of fortune.'

'But you are in English company, and supporting an English adventure.'

'Your grace may rest assured,' Lymond said. 'My loyalty, as with all mercenaries, is towards the sovereign who pays me. I am not paid by England.'

'And the Tsar is so munificent?' Mary of Guise observed.

For this audience he had dressed soberly, neither in the long robes of the Russian merchant nor the tunic and breeches of the Russian soldier. Like any of her courtiers, he wore a formal close-buttoned doublet and cloak, the high stiffened collar opening in front to show a shirt lightly decorated; his long, sombre hose neatly shod, with no extravagance anywhere, except the extravagance inherent in his colouring and style. 'Or,' said Mary of Guise, 'is it power you seek, Mr Crawford? For I cannot, I fear, commend your frankness. Do you still say your only duty to the Tsar is that of adviser?'

413

No trace of alarm showed in the chilly blue eyes. 'It is what the terms of my embassy say.'

'In public, yes. But since we are not on the borders of Russia and our trade, our Church and our people are not threatened by this barbarous race, might you not have been candid with us, Mr Crawford? I am told that you are not either leader of the company of St Mary's or a clerk of the English tongue to Ivan of Russia, but his general, the Supreme Commander of all his armies?'

'It is not a closely kept secret,' Lymond said pleasantly. 'It seemed irrelevant to your grace's Court.'

Round the Queen were her Council; the men who severally had called on him; colleagues of his brother Culter, lifelong friends of his mother, Sybilla. The blandness they all recognized. And the courtesy. And the arrogance. The feelings of the Queen's ladies, who had not seen him before, were something again. The Queen said, 'And irrelevant, it seems, to your brother Midculter, who was not made aware of it. For a man who has attained such high honours so young, you have been slow to announce your good fortune to your queen and to your family. Are we to understand that your new allegiance now conflicts with theirs?'

Invisibly, Francis Crawford's patience had come to an end. He said, 'Your grace : if you know that I am Voevoda Bolshoia of Russia, you also know why I am here.'

The Queen's erect shoulders moved, within their wide, stiffened sleeves. 'I have heard certain rumours. But knowing the Baltic alliances of our dear brother of Spain, I can hardly countenance them.'

'My mission,' Lymond said, 'is to serve Russia as best I can. I can only repeat. I am not paid by England, or by the Queen's husband Philip.'

'Your mission will fail,' the Queen said. 'And if war should break out while you are in England, what then?'

'I am an envoy of the Tsar,' Lymond said, 'Not of Scotland.'

'So, to the outward eye, it would seem,' said Mary of Guise. 'But I, because I am a woman, know that you are not only Scottish bred and bear the gift of a French Comté, but you have a kindness for us and our daughter which has been manifest over many years and does live, I believe, somewhere still. Mr Crawford, you have not been open with me, but I shall bare my heart and my

414

mind before you. Where your conscience may take you, or your fortune, in England or Scotland or Russia, will you take our fee and serve us?'

He was an enviable prize; and he knew it. She was only the latest in a long, long line of men and women who had come to him, smiling, with offers. 'Your grace is too kind,' Lymond said. 'But I fear my time and my conscience have already been purchased.'

And at last, she had received an answer she could not gracefully turn. For a long moment she stared at Mr Crawford of Lymond, Count of Sevigny; and then, turning the light eyes to her Chamberlain, she gave the nod which signified instant dismissal. To Lymond, 'Then, you may leave, sir,' she said, and did not again offer her hand. And as he bowed, smiling, and turned to go, there was more than one man among those about her who would willingly have spun him round and disfigured that worldly, impervious face.

*

The Muscovite Ambassador stayed a month longer in Scotland, and, held by a certain doomed fascination, the three officers of St Mary's stayed with him, acting as his equerries; forming, in the rare leisure moments of John Buckland and Robert Best, a strange brotherhood which had grown without warning : the closeness of a group of men who have lived and faced danger together, and suffered a loss.

Danny Hislop had always intended to stay. Now Ludovic d'Harcourt as well deferred and then dismissed his plans to travel to London and make a new career for himself either there or in France, and Adam, for reasons so fragile he would have admitted them to nobody, had tacitly decided the same. While Nepeja was in England, they would stay with him. 'Otherwise, poor Osep,' said Danny Hislop, 'as the likeness of the Ass bearing books, poor Osep will finish in Bedlam. What will you do, Ludo, if he gets another eagle? They have them in Scotland.'

But since the journey to Pitsligo from St Nicholas, Ludovic d'Harcourt was no longer so easy to bait on the subject of Lymond. And the process of self-questioning, observed by Danny's bright, ironic gaze, had begun even sooner than that, on the night Lymond had shot Slata

Baba. Now, staring critically at d'Harcourt without waiting for him to answer, Danny said, 'You just admire him because he can swim better than you can. You realize you are joining the choir?'

Ludovic flushed and Adam said, 'Danny, be quiet.'

'Don't interfere with my subject,' Danny said smartly. 'I'm not in St. Mary's because I like it. I am embarked spellbound on a study of devil-worship. Tell me, what is going to happen when the sweet Philippa comes inside his range?'

'Nothing,' said Robert Best shortly. 'She is at the English court with Queen Mary. I was told all about her before I came up.'

'And?' said Danny encouragingly.

'And nothing. She has work that she likes, and a mind of her own, and a group of excellent friends, with one or two who want to be more. She isn't troubled about the divorce. But the moment it comes, she will marry.'

'And then he will be . . . available,' said Ludovic d'Harcourt thoughtfully.

'For Güzel?' Danny said. 'No, how silly. Availability has been nothing if not the keynote these two years or more. For somebody's wealthy widow? She need not trust her delicate health to the long journey to Russia. Someone should suggest it to the Voevoda. A mistress in Moscow, and a bonny wee wife with a mutch and a full belly in England. Which reminds me—'

'The new ladies have arrived,' said Adam grimly. 'Guaranteed of clean stock, and inured to Russian practices. Osep has announced himself suited.'

'For the time being,' said Danny, open-eyed. 'That's ten since Pitsligo. Do you think it is a subversive attempt at colonization, or the long Russian nights that ought to be setting in about now in Vologda?'

'We shall have to wait till the spring,' Adam said, 'to find out.'

Lymond was in Pitsligo. In spite of his efforts there, or perhaps because of them, little was found of the thousand pounds' worth of goods reckoned to be taken from the wreck of the *Edward,* although he and the Commissioners made exhaustive inquiries, and January was spent in laborious sittings, attended by Nepeja in Edinburgh, during which innumerable witnesses travelled backwards and forwards from Buchan, and innumerable lawyers made speeches, comprehensible and quite otherwise. By the end of the month even the Ambassador's will was worn down. And by the beginning of February, he had agreed with grumbling reluctance at last, to sign a document giving Lewis, Roberts and Buckland full powers as his legal administrators to pursue the cause of his lost possessions in Scotland, and had notified his willingness to proceed on his way south.

If the bells of St Giles did not ring, there was a certain sense of release in the city and Best and Buckland and Gilpin, with the way open before them to London, became, even in Nepeja's presence, dangerously hilarious. Nepeja, who had just received his congé and a four-hundred-pound gold chain from the Dowager, merely sat in his beard and smiled grimly.

No further summons from Court came for Lymond. But on 13 February, the eve of their departure from Edinburgh, he received one final visit from Richard his brother.

They had not met since the first journey south from Pitsligo and now, in the slender privacy of a small room high in the Ambassador's lodging, neither showed any wish to break into fluent reconciliation, or indeed, unnecessary speech of any kind. Richard, dressed for court, made no attempt to sit down. He said, 'Since I hear you are leaving, I have come to put certain matters before you. They are important. If I were a different manner of person, no doubt I should do more than this; I should plead, and I should cajole. I mean you to understand that if I cannot do that, it is not because I don't think them worthy. I wish you to listen to them and I will accept the answer you give me. I should only warn you, Francis, that on these matters, I will not brook lightness or insolence.'

Half-dressed; straying about a strewn room and arrested, as so often before, in the act of abandonment, Francis Crawford drew a long breath of monumental patience and said, 'No, but Christ, you invite it. Let me do your work for you. You want me to stay here in Scotland. The answer is, no. You want me to visit Sybilla. The answer is, no. The Queen Dowager is anxious, through you, to lay hands on St Mary's. The answer is, no. Failing that, she would like me to spy for her in England. The answer is, no.'

If it had been reeled off with defiance, Richard could

417

perhaps have tolerated it. Instead, delivered with restraint and with clarity, it was the voice of the Voevoda Bolshoia, unquestioned master of armies, giving his considered decisions. And although these were what he had promised to hear and accept, the cavalier judgements, in cold blood, on all the principles and people he held dearest stopped his voice, in a sort of nerve-storm of grief and resentment. And when he could speak: 'You *are* a bastard,' he said.

He was nearly killed, then. He half recognized the look on Lymond's face, and thought it an attack of plain anger. In any case, he was occupied in finding words for something which had to be said, and by the time he was speaking, Lymond was standing with his back to the wall, far away from him and resigned, apparently, to hearing him out. Richard said, 'There have been so many misunderstandings in the past. What you did, often, was done for good reason. I know I am simple. I know you are devious. But, oh God, if there is any good reason for what you are doing now; any excuse; any unknown factor or subtle circumstance you are afraid I can't grasp, for the mercy of God, this time, tell me.'

'What shall I tell you?' Lymond said. As on the beach, the movement of his dress betrayed, if one cared to look for it, the depth of his breathing; otherwise, back to the wall, he did not stir. 'Graham Malett made a tool of St Mary's which would have wrecked Scotland. I do not want the Queen Dowager to have that power. I cannot spy for Scotland with any plausibility: I shall be watched. I cannot spy with any moral sanction either: I am trusted and liberally paid by the Tsar, and it is in his interest that trade between England and Russia should proceed without interruption, and that his first officer should not, if possible, be beheaded for espionage. I have told you why I do not want to see my son.'

He had come to a concise halt.

'And Sybilla?' Richard said.

Lymond was drawing long breaths now, his hands forced back rigid behind him, driven into the lime of the wall. 'That is as far as I go,' he said flatly. 'I have never in my life subjected you to this kind of inquisition about your purpose, your doings or your relationships. I have answered you fairly enough.'

Richard stood where he was, surveying the clever, imperious face of his only brother. 'Yes, you have,' he said at last. 'You have said that, whatever happens, you want to wield the glory and power of St Mary's, and that if this means exile from Scotland, it does not matter to you. And you will not face Sybilla because alone of all of us, she does not know you are venal. She still thinks you care for Scotland and for us, and are prepared to think both more important than riches; for our sake to govern your ambition; for the boy's sake to master your emotions. And when she sees you—'

'She will know she was wrong,' Lymond said.

Richard walked over to him. It was not a long way but he walked slowly, as if he were tired, and halted, eventually, face to face with his younger brother. He said, 'Change your mind. It is the last chance in life you may have.'

Spoken soberly, with all the honesty of which he was capable, it was neither threat nor impassioned appeal but a simple plea, simply put. To which Lymond, looking him in the eyes, shook his head.

And Richard's temper, so steadfastly held, without warning escaped his control. Even had he known what was coming, Lymond had no chance at all where he stood. Richard's right arm came up and struck him, as Lymond had in the past inflicted so many blows, but with the clenched fist, not the flat of his hand, and with a violence that drove Francis Crawford sideways into the wall and then pitching away from it. Richard hit him once again, with the same extreme force on the chin, and watched as, quite unable to stop himself, his brother was flung spreadeagled against chest and chair, wall and, finally, floor.

He lay without moving. At that point, Lord Culter felt no strong compulsion to discover how bad were his injuries. He stood, breathing hard, for a moment and for a moment longer looked down, cradling his knuckles. Then he gazed round and picked up his hat, and found his gloves, and prepared, still short of breath, for departure.

From the door, he glanced back, once, at the unresponsive wreck of the room. 'Then God damn your soul!' he said, and walked through it.

CHAPTER FIVE

Deliciously, for the rest of the household, it was Yeroffia who found his master some five minutes later, returning to help with the packing. Being Russian and not of any repressive Western persuasion, he strode down round the newel-post bellowing, and shortly had Phoma, Adam, Hislop and Nepeja himself in the embattled bedchamber. Lymond, the marks of the blows already thickened and dark on his face, was lying exactly where he had fallen, between the stretcher rails of a stool and an overturned chair, with his head hard against the uncompromising carved doors of a press cupboard.

Osep Nepeja, Slavonian words of alarm and concern issuing from his beard, stood looking at him with a certain solid and undeniable satisfaction. Adam said, *'Christ!'* and Danny Hislop, wriggling past said, 'No. Lord Culter, I do declare,' and, dropping to his knees, found the Voevoda's wrist, and then his pulse. He sat back on his heels. 'Cease to mourn. The voice of David will sound again in the land, although you might find a leech to confirm it. He has had an ungodly crack on the head.'

He got up. 'What shall we do with him? We have him at our mercy. Think of all the browbeaten Streltsi at Vorobiovo who would like to take their revenge at this moment. We could hire out his carcass for *money!'*

'There is a Russian proverb,' Nepeja said. *'Beat your shuba, and it will be warmer; beat your wife and she shall be sweeter.'*

There was a brief silence, while his hearers considered the analogy. 'Beat your brother and he shall be deader?' at length Danny said.

'He will be, if you leave him there,' Ludovic d'Harcourt said, suddenly arriving. 'His skull may be fractured, you idiots. Look out. Let me.' And taking charge, in a Christian way, he supervised the lifting of the Voevoda Bolshoia and his transfer, sensibly, to the bed. Then he got everyone out of the room, keeping Danny.

Danny stood, his hands dangling unhelpfully. 'Well?' he said. 'Adam is your man, you know, for sensitive nursing.'

D'Harcourt, his hands pressing through Lymond's hair, said, 'But just think how he is going to enjoy finding you watching him when he wakes up. It isn't fractured. My God, he must be a good man with his fists.'

'Lymond?' said Danny sweetly.

'Lord Culter. I assume,' Ludovic said. 'At least, he was the last person up the stairs before Yeroffia. What did they quarrel about?'

'Can you remember,' Daniel Hislop said, 'how many times you have wanted to do that in the last two or three years, and the occasion each time?'

'Once a day,' d'Harcourt said. 'Sometimes twice. And for as many different reasons.'

'As you say,' Danny agreed. He dipped a cloth in cold water and squeezed it. 'He can make you want to knock him down, if he feels like it, by simply saying "good morning". He possibly said simply "good morning" to Lord Culter. The difference was that being his brother, Culter hit him. Will he travel tomorrow?'

They both gazed, united in fascination, at the insensible and manhandled person of the sacrosanct Voevoda Bolshoia. 'I doubt it,' said Ludovic d'Harcourt.

But he did. He stirred some time after that conversation, and if his awakening took rather less time than was obvious, the effect was to cheat Danny Hislop's expectant ears of whatever uncouth revelations he was hoping for. Without warning, his eyes closed, Lymond said, 'Hislop?'

'Yes sir?' said Danny, jumping. Then he said sympathetically, 'How are you, sir?'

'Well enough to guess which vulture would be present,' said Lymond pleasantly. 'I wish to know the exact time.'

'Three by the clock, sir,' said Danny. 'I'll change the cloth. You must have a—'

'Leave it,' said Lymond. He opened his eyes. 'If you are here, where are Blacklock and d'Harcourt?'

'Downstairs. I don't know,' said Danny. 'Sir.'

'You have forgotten, in your excited interest in my colourful family affairs, that you were to meet the Queen Dowager's harbingers at three?'

There was a slight pause. Then Hislop said, with an edge, 'D'Harcourt will have—' and was interrupted with impolite flatness.

'D'Harcourt has news to spread, and will be spreading it, while Blacklock no doubt is wringing his hands at an apothecary's to find a leech who knows the bottom layer from the buffy coat. What the merchants are saying and doing, I can imagine. Is it really necessary to remind you all that the great adult world must continue, no matter what childish by-play may occur? Get hold of d'Harcourt and get to that meeting. And send Phoma, while you're at it, to me.'

Danny got up. 'Yes, sir.'

The open blue eyes travelled up in the general direction of Daniel Hislop's face. 'And Hislop?' said Lymond softly. 'Don't sound so aggrieved. There are no rewards, celestial or mundane, for the best display of pure, bloody inquisitiveness.'

Which drove Ludovic d'Harcourt to a deduction, five minutes later, as Daniel Hislop marched into his room. 'Let me make a guess. He is awake.'

'He's awake. The honeymoon,' said Danny, 'is over. Come on. We've a meeting to go to.'

*

So on the following day, Sunday 14 February, the cavalcade of Osep Nepeja, his friends, colleagues, English supporters and servants set out from Edinburgh, lavishly escorted, on its fourteen-day journey to London. And straight-backed, wan of face and suavely vitriolic in temper, the Tsar's friend Mr Crawford rode with them. Since the marks on his face, tenderly discoloured, were so obvious, he made no effort to disguise them, and to the solicitous inquiries of the lairds of Corstophine, Craigmillar and Restalrig, of Innerleithen, Elphinstone and Niddrie Marshal, of Herdmanstoun, Wauchton, Bass, Langton, Blackadder, Wedderburn, Swinton and Blanerne merely made delicate reference to the brawny fists of Master Nepaja's ladies of solace. The three escorting courtiers, Home, Coldingham and Morton, the son of his old adversary Sir George Douglas, presumably were better informed, but if so, they maintained a discreet silence. Whatever Lymond might be suffering, there was nothing wrong with his tongue, or his sword-arm. And in four days they were off Scottish soil, and in Berwick.

By then the bruises were fading, although the eye of a connoisseur such as Thomas, 1st Baron Wharton, could distinguish them. Stepping out from under the flag of St

George to welcome, as Governor of Berwick and General Warden of all the Marches, the first arrival in England of his Muscovite Majesty's embassy, Lord Wharton's gaze fell and remained on the embassy's sole damaged member. But Lymond, when his turn came to be greeted, was the first, briefly, to refer to it. 'May we exchange our beaten refugees for your singed ones?'

And Lord Wharton, who knew all about Lymond from both English and Scottish sources and was not a master of riposte in any case, grunted and ushered them in through the gates and up to the castle of Berwick on the banks of the broad and beautiful Tweed.

They were given a banquet that afternoon, attended by the Mayor and officials of Berwick and the lords of all the surrounding countryside whose roads the new snow was not blocking. Best, on English ground and with English food on the table before him, talked himself hoarse answering questions and interpreting Nepeja. Lymond, who might have helped, was placed some distance off, with a purpose he soon came to realize. On one side of him sat the well-dressed, confident person of Sir Thomas Wharton, the Warden's middle-aged son. Privy Councillor, master of the henchmen, parliamentarian and former steward of Mary Tudor's own household, Tom Wharton had gone far since the days when hunting down Crawford of Lymond had become a national pastime.

And on Lymond's other side was a dark and fragile young man he had never met before, but who was now introduced, with inexplicable enthusiasm, as Austin Grey, 14th Marquis of Allendale.

A moment later, and the object of the manoeuvre was obvious. 'He knows your wife,' Tom Wharton said. 'We both do.'

There was no guilt-filled hiatus whatever. 'The one I married in Stamboul?' Lymond said kindly. 'How is she?'

Tom Wharton bellowed and said, 'Have you got others?' but Austin Grey did not smile. He said, 'She is well, and extremely happy in the Queen's service. Her grace depends on her a great deal.'

The stark blue eyes turned on the long-lashed dark ones, which did not flinch. 'I am not proposing to take her back to Russia,' Lymond said. 'Except perhaps to bottle the soft fruit in season. She cannot possibly excel the other members of my household in anything else, I am afraid.'

Austin Grey was rather pale. He said, 'She is still your wife.'

Tom Wharton was grinning. 'Don't be simple, my child. He has a magnificent mistress. I want all the details.'

'Perhaps after the food?' Lymond said. 'I hear you are married yourself, and breeding more Whartons?'

'A bantling. Philip,' Tom Wharton said. 'They're all called Philip. My wife's in London; her brother's just died. I'm coming south – so is Grey – for the burial. You'll meet Anne, and all the Sidneys. They're kinsfolk. Great wailings over that fellow Chancellor.'

Lymond said, 'I thought Henry Sidney was in Ireland.'

'They come back and forth. My God, the Brussels couriers all look like bricked-up greyhounds. You know there's war afoot?'

'So I am told,' Lymond said. 'Is the Duke of Alva in Rome?'

'Not quite yet. They had a try at a truce. Two chairs, a table and a little bell in a tent on an island. It finished last month. That old bastard the Pope!'

'Wharton!' said Austin Grey sharply.

'Yes, well : he's not religious. You're not religious?' said Tom Wharton to Lymond. 'The last Pope didn't live through the installation ceremonies, and this one is waging wars in his coffin and loving it. Got the Jews harnessed to artillery pieces and dragging them to the bastions of Rome. Promises he'll make one of the French children King of Naples and the other Duke of Milan if the French King sends an army to help him. Says he'll call on the Turks if he has to. It'll be war.'

'And the Queen of England approves of her husband making war on the Pope?'

'If you'll believe that, you'll believe anything,' Wharton said. 'But who's going to stop him? He's coming to England in Lent. And then the fun will begin. He'll want English help.'

'Will he get it?' said Lymond.

But Tom Wharton was not quite drunk enough to go on. 'Ah,' he said. 'Time will tell. The Council doesn't babble its business in England, you know. You have to be under the table to know what goes on in England. Austin could tell you, but he's a nice, discreet boy. Your little wife could tell you, and a lot more than I could, I fancy. The secrets of that bedchamber would be well worth knowing, if you were a man of affairs. I say that woman will never breed. Not in her forties, not in her thirties, not any time. Nor will her sister. Men mistaken for women. Like the widow of Binche. Not what a proper man fancies. Now—'

'I have a message for you,' said Austin Grey directly to Lymond.

With some regret, having brought his other companion to simmering point, Lymond turned back to the youth. Austin Grey of Allendale, a diffident man of quiet and obstinate purpose, lifted his chin a trifle and looked into the cold face of authority, faintly marked, faintly impatient, which had surprised and shaken him so profoundly. He said, 'It is from Philippa's mother.'

'Mistress Somerville,' Lymond said. Someone, in the centre of the room, was rendering an English folk song, with indifferent success. Against the noise, he added, 'From my home in Midculter?'

'No. Here in Berwick,' Allendale said. 'She heard you were coming. She has taken rooms at an Ordinary.'

'With the child,' Lymond said. His voice was amused; his face chiselled with fine contradictory lines; of irony, entertainment, even, possibly, of a scathing anger which might have been stronger than any of the rest. 'Whom she wishes to transfer to my keeping. Along with my loving wife Philippa?'

'She said,' Allendale said levelly, 'that you were certain to suppose she had demands to make on you. I was therefore to give you this letter.'

Without speaking, Lymond received it. He read it then and there, in such a way that even Tom Wharton peering beside him could see nothing. It began without preamble; without his first name which she, of the vanishing handful of those closest to him, had earned the right to employ.

From what Richard has said, and more from what he has not said, I know what you wish us to understand about your intentions. I will not speak here, or at any time, about my personal wishes or anyone else's. I am mentioning the name of Kuzúm only to assure you that it will not be referred to again.

All I wish to put to you is that here, on neutral ground, it is necessary for us both, as her elders and, I hope, her well-wishers, to make what arrangements are needful for the future of Philippa.

I have heard the circumstances of the marriage, and I

understand your desire to give her a standing after what she had done on behalf of you and the child. Since a legal step was taken, and matters of law and finance are now involved, simple consultation of some kind seems necessary. Should you agree to this, Austin will bring you to where I am staying this evening. If he brings me your refusal, I shall try to understand, and at least you may be sure there is no possible ill will between us. . . .

There were no conventional greetings. Only her own Christian name, KATE.

Across the table, watching the Voevoda read his letter, Edmund Roberts was reminded of something. 'My God, I nearly forgot, Crawford!'

Lymond looked up.

'I've got a letter for you as well. Remember Chancellor's chest?'

'Yes,' Lymond said. To Grey's watching face he said shortly, 'I shall go. Perhaps you would take me.'

Roberts raised his voice a little. 'Buckland took it to London. Well, they found a letter in it. A sealed letter, addressed to you. It must have come straight to Kholmogory. Buckland brought it back, and then left it with half his clothes here in Berwick. He told me to find it and give it to you. Have you time after the dinner?'

'I am going out,' Lymond said. 'I shall call for it on my way. Do you leave in the morning?'

Roberts and Lewis, having seen the Ambassador safely in England, were to return to Scotland forthwith, to their sorrow, to throw themselves yet once again into the contentious legal fray. The talk, begun in this vein, became general. And later, when the meal had long finished but the convivial uproar was reaching its height, Edmund Roberts joined Lymond and Allendale when they made their excuses to Wharton, and set off down the steps of the castle to obey that formal summons from Kate.

Outside, there had been a fresh fall of snow and the house lamps laid their squares of light, sparkling, on the still virgin coat of the roadway, flat as white worsted. Lips of snow hung from the rooftops: with soft, unseen collisions, pills and tablets and showers of snow fell from thatch and bracket and shutter and settled like footpads behind them.

The air, cold and sweet, had no trace in it of the black air of Lampozhnya, which suffocated a man with its ice,

426

and left his eyelashes hoar, and his breath like silver sarsanet on his neck-furs. Three men maudlin drunk back at the castle had known it like that, and one man treading here in the white, silent street, immune to the thin, meaningless chatter of the two others walking beside him.

Lymond and the Marquis of Allendale climbed the stairs of the lodging Edmund Roberts shared with his fellows, and stood in the empty parlour while Roberts found and brought out the letter which Buckland had mentioned. 'There you are. It's never been opened. You'll likely have all the news in it already, in ten other ways. But you might as well have it.' He paused. 'What beats all of us, is why Diccon never gave it you in the first place.'

'He must have forgotten,' Lymond said. It had been put in fresh wrappers and sealed, as Roberts said. He wondered if it was Chancellor's seal, and held it out to the candle to see, just before he put the letter away.

The seal was Chancellor's. And dim under the wrapper, he could see the original cover, much over-written. Beneath it all, his own name and direction were here and there dimly visible. The handwriting, he recognized in a moment, was Philippa's.

Lymond looked up. 'Do you mind if I glance at this? It has to do with the meeting I'm going to.'

Roberts, jovial and relaxed with good food and malmsey, made him free of the candle. 'I'll be sorry to lose your company. We had some good chats, back in Edinburgh. You know a good lot about iron, for a man who says he's a soldier. I told the Company that you're interested. Henry Sidney will tell you. Have you finished?'

'Yes,' said Lymond. Yes . . . thank you.'

It was, if you considered it, a remarkably legible letter, in view of the tour it had made. From Philippa's round hand in London by some means on shipboard to Emden, and from there to Bremen and Hamburg, Lübeck and Rostock, Stettin and Danzig, Königsberg and Memel, Riga and Novgorod, Tver and Moscow. From Moscow to Kholmogory. And there, it must have been read by Richard Chancellor, who had resealed it and put it into his chest where it remained, through the wreck at Pitsligo and after, to finish here, in an anonymous parlour in an English garrison town, being read by the man it was written to.

And it was obvious, now, why Chancellor had not handed it over. The misguided schoolgirl you married had written carefully to inform you that you were born out of wedlock : an idea by no means new; one so well-supported that already one was more than half-way towards accepting it. So, as Richard had so coincidentally said, one was a bastard. But . . .

He read it through twice, trying to memorize it, for he supposed it was important. *After the birth of Richard, Sybilla had no more children . . . You and your sister were born to your father in France; of mother or mothers unknown. . . .*

He did not look again at the ending : . . . *since it seemed to me that by ignoring it, you were doing yourself and your folk a disservice. . . . The people among whom you grew up are your dearest . . .* but lifted the paper, and holding them into the flame, let the whole thing take fire and burn down to ashes.

'I told you. You knew it already,' Roberts said.

'No. It was news,' Lymond said.

And Austin Grey, looking at him with those attentive dark eyes said unexpectedly, 'Bad news? I am sorry.'

Lymond put a picturesque hand on his shoulder. 'Don't be so sensitive,' he said, faintly chiding. 'It makes everyday commerce most trying. It was a letter from my dear wife. . . . I have just remembered where we are going. Do you suppose she shows her mail to her mother?'

Austin said, 'You will know better than I do.'

'But I don't,' Lymond said. 'I didn't know she could write, until recently. She spent most of her time in the cradle. And if Kate knows what she wrote in that letter, you have no idea what an intriguing meeting this is going to be. You will have your divorce by next Friday. . . . You are passionately in love with the lady, I take it?'

Austin said, 'I think Mr Roberts probably wants to go to bed.'

'No, he doesn't. He's enjoying the conversation,' Lymond said. 'But we shall respect your finer feelings if you insist on it.' And, smiling, he did indeed exchange all the necessary courtesies which placed them, five minutes later, outside in the still, snowy street.

'The inn is there,' Allendale said, and pointed. 'You have only to ask for Mistress Somerville.'

Lymond made no move to go. 'I can be a great deal ruder than this,' he said. 'You really must stand and fight. You won't safeguard the Somervilles by running.'

He did stand then, very straight and slender against the dark snow, with no fear on his face. 'I don't need to fight,' said Austin Grey. 'You haven't become what you are without intelligence. You know the world, and you know Philippa's mother. You won't harm either of them.' He hesitated, and then said, 'I am not perhaps as easily upset as I look. I think I can protect them, if I have to.'

'Can you?' Lymond said. 'I am going to call on Philippa, when we get to London. What will you do if I take her straight to my lodging and rape her?'

Austin was very white. 'Kill you,' he said, 'if I can.'

'But she is my wife,' Lymond said.

'Not—'

'Yes!' said Lymond softly. 'Before God and man. And for that, my dear Marquis, you would hang. If, of course, she told you about it in the first place.'

Allendale's hand was on his sword. He took if off again and drew a long breath. His body was trembling. He said, in a low voice, 'This is uncivil.'

'Yes, but it's quicker than question and answer,' Lymond said. 'And we know where we stand. I'm delighted, in fact, to have met you. You may have her first, when the Pope and I have both finished.' And he walked off, smiling, into the inn, leaving Austin Grey standing where he was, very still in the snow.

He brought the same bright, deadly mood to the meeting with Philippa's mother, and Kate Somerville, that small, wise friend of long ago who knew him better than anyone, stood in her small crowded bedchamber and watched him come in, fair and smiling and elegant with his face marred and marring shadows, too, in his eyes and about his temples and mouth which had never been there before.

He saw the woman she had always been, buttoned purposefully into a gown which, on equal purpose, would not be her best, with her brown hair accommodated hopefully in a rather nice cap but coming down, and her brown eyes, frowning, on the marks on his face. He said, 'Richard, you will have heard. It probably did him a lot of good, because he wanted to do it so badly. I received your unaddressed, badly spelt note with all the poly-syllables.'

'Yes. Well,' said Kate. 'I don't know what you want to be called.'

'Home, like the cattle?' said Lymond. 'No. No, that is

what we are all trying to avoid talking about. I don't object to being called by my Christian name, on purely social occasions. The Russian version was Frangike. Rather scented, I thought. Or alternatively, like a new brand of onion.'

'I don't suppose you meant to get drunk,' Kate said flatly, 'but you are, rather. Would you like to sit down over there?'

He took the chair she indicated, on one side of the fire, by the bed. 'But you must sit down as well.'

Kate Somerville stood, her lips shut, and looked at him. 'I don't know that I want to. Are we going to have a sensible discussion?' she said.

'Well, you are sensible,' Lymond said. 'And I am not unconscious, yet. The trouble appears to be with the subject. I am here, on legal advice, as your son-in-law.'

'I'm not going to sit down,' Kate said, in some desperation, in view of the fact that her limbs would hardly uphold her.

The beautiful, intolerant blue eyes surveyed her. 'It is perfectly safe to sit down with sons-in-law. Not with prospective fiancés. I have just asked Austin Grey what he would do if I carried Philippa off and then ravished her.'

He stared at Kate.

Kate licked her lips and surmised. 'Kill you?' she said. Her voice, she found, was not totally reliable.

'Yes. That's satisfactory, isn't it? I thought perhaps she was in love with Diccon Chancellor.'

He never said what he meant. He never said what he meant. . . . All through their encounters, their clashes, their crossing of swords she had known that and learned a little to deal with it, and to translate, if only to herself, what lay under the stream of hurtful, facile words. And, suddenly, this time she felt panic, a seizure of fear so unexpected that she stared at him, quite unseeing, listening to the tone of the words. And then she saw what was behind it, and sat down.

'I think everyone was,' said Kate Somerville.

Lymond said abruptly, 'What about the divorce?'

Kate said, 'Lady Lennox is blocking it. The grounds, as you may have heard, are the test case of the Constable's son.'

'Why is she opposing it?' Lymond said. 'She knows the situation?'

Her confidence mildly restored, Kate threw him a look of withering irony. 'You mean is Philippa moaning and plucking off daisy petals? I am sorry to dispel the fancy. Philippa thinks of you, as she thinks of me, as a rather run-down institution for indigent imbeciles.'

'That was the impression I got,' Lymond said. 'So why ... ?'

'Because Lady Lennox wants to hurt you through her. At least, that is my reading,' Kate Somerville said. 'You have Laurence Hussey with you just now, haven't you?'

'Wills, wives and wrecks?' Lymond said. 'Yes; he's been concerned in the *Edward*. What else – ah. Boyar Angus has just died at Tantallon Castle.'

'I wish,' said Kate, 'you were just a little more sober. ... The Earl of Angus is dead, Lady Lennox's father. There arises the matter of the inheritance. All those rich lands, and Tantallon Castle, one of the strongest in Scotland.'

'The laird of Craigmillar is in it,' said Lymond comfortably. 'He told me the other day. Holding it for the Queen. But Margaret Lennox, of course, will lay claim to the lands and the Earldom, and Master Hussey, being a civil law practitioner and a member of Doctors' Commons, will no doubt be asked to pursue it. ... He seems a harmless enough little man. What has Philippa done?' said Lymond.

'Passed on to your family a Lennox plot to control Scotland,' said Kate bluntly.

Lymond's eyes studied hers. 'Who in turn, in their simple, loyal way, have passed it on to the Queen Dowager. Who will therefore take great pleasure in squashing any claim whatever from the Lennox family to the Earldom of Angus.'

'You aren't drunk,' said Kate.

'No. I have had a severe blow on the head, and a great deal of provocation. But Kate, Philippa can only be harmed if Master Hussey discovers what the Queen Dowager knows about the Lennox plot, and how she knows it. Who would tell Hussey?'

'Maitland of Lethington,' Kate Somerville said.

'Who is close to the Queen, and loves the Lennoxes? And then Mary Tudor is told that her young lady in waiting has been passing State secrets to Scotland. How very careless of Margaret. Lennox secrets are usually very

431

large and costive and never pass anything anywhere, like English bowels in hot weather. Where did Philippa hear this?'

'From the lady Elizabeth,' said Kate shortly.

After a while, he let out his breath slowly and began, equally slowly, to shake his head without speaking. Kate said, 'Well?'

Francis Crawford got up and lifting his cloak, tossed it on her bed. Then, edging round furniture, he worked his way across the small room thoughtfully and stood looking at his mother-in-law, with a sober expression for once. 'What do you know?' he said at length.

Kate said, her eyes very large, 'I find your rudeness abominable and your politeness obnoxious but my goodness, Francis Crawford, what terrifies me more than a jungle of tigers is the moment when you look worried. I know only what Richard has guessed, and if Richard has guessed it, then you have been over-relaxing with your secrets also. What is your interest in Elizabeth and the late William Courtenay, Earl of Devonshire?'

There was a pause. 'Academic,' said Lymond.

'I don't believe you,' said Kate. 'There is something to connect Philippa with the Queen's sister. Now there is something, academic or not, which connects you to Elizabeth too. It only needs a shred of evidence to send you both to the headsman for spying. And Elizabeth with you.'

'Perhaps I should go back to Russia,' Lymond said. But she did not smile, and after a moment he said, half to himself, 'How she must hate me.'

Kate said quietly, 'Margaret Lennox?' and he nodded, his back to the wall. 'I suppose she is older than me by . . . oh, about the same as the difference between Philippa's age and mine. I was sixteen. Seventeen, perhaps. She has never forgiven me. And now she wants Elizabeth out of the way. For that, of course, leaves the child Queen of Scots as the next heir to England and Scotland. And if anything happens to her . . .'

'Margaret Lennox,' said Philippa's mother.

'Or the boy. Darnley. It must seem very tempting to get rid of me as well. But she won't do it.'

Kate said, 'How can you be sure?'

Lymond said, 'If I were unsure, I shouldn't be going to London.'

'And Philippa?'

'The divorce,' Lymond said. 'The divorce, somehow, as quickly as possible. And get her into church with young Tristram Trusty.'

'There are quite a lot of young Tristram Trusties,' said Kate. 'One of them Spanish.'

'Well, if she can stomach it; that,' said Lymond without compunction, 'would without doubt be safest of all. In any case, leave the other side of it to me. I shall see they don't touch her. What about money?'

'Well, she has all yours, if that's what you mean,' said her mother. 'The entire possessions of the Donatis and another fortune waiting to be picked up, I gather, in France. From a witch?'

'Not a witch,' said Lymond. He made his way back again and picked up his cloak. 'She can keep it. I have enough in Russia to do several lifetimes over. . . . They told me that if I didn't come back, they would force you to marry?'

In the plain, sensible face, the brown eyes were derisive. 'Is that why you came back?' said Kate Somerville.

'No. I knew you could handle it.'

'Thank you,' said Kate. 'I thought perhaps you had had one of Philippa's persuasive letters.'

He stood with the cloak in his hands, quite still, looking at her. At length : 'I had two,' he said.

Kate said, 'I'm glad. She wanted you to know how things were. She told Richard she would be writing.'

Lymond said, 'Kate. Do you know what you are saying?'

Kate said sharply, 'Of course I know what I am saying. Philippa has been worried sick, and so has Richard and so have I. Now we have you back, at least for a visit. You're here, and still nothing happens. It's a thousand times worse for her.'

Lymond said, 'You promised—'

'Not to talk about it. I'm breaking my promise.'

'Because,' Lymond said carefully, 'of what Philippa wrote in her letters?'

'Because the person who brings you up matters,' snapped Kate. 'And it's time you thought less of your emotional feather bed and more of other people's. And when you look like that, I know exactly how your odious father came to be detested. Stop !'

'To hear more?' said Lymond. 'Goodbye, Kate.'

'No,' Kate said. 'Wait. There is someone out in the

passage to see you.' She grabbed his arm and he stopped, his face hard with animosity.

'Who? The child, on its hindquarters, begging?'

'No . . .' said Kate, and fell back as he wrenched his arm from her grasp and, swinging from her, pulled the door open.

Outside, standing very straight and patiently against the opposite wall was a small person in a long, hooded cloak worked with fur, with jewels on her lightly clasped fingers and more, gleaming through the chain at her throat. Her hair, unlike Kate's, was dressed with shining and perfect elaboration below a fragile French hood and its colour, once so blonde, had turned the pure porcelain white which suits only a fair, finegrained skin, and makes the depth of blue eyes still more striking.

Small and silent and elegant she waited, and did not move as the door was pulled open, although the hem of her skirt, had you looked closely, was trembling and her eyes, hollow with vigils, were unnaturally dark.

So, as Lymond strode out and stopped, rigid and white by the doorpost, Sybilla set eyes on Francis, the son of her heart; and so Francis Crawford, after four years of unharnessed power, came face to face at last with his mother.

And Kate, falling upon the door and looking up at her self-contained relative by marriage, saw his face torn apart and left, raw as a wound without features; only pain and shock and despair and appalled recognition, all the more terrible for being perfectly voiceless.

There was time to comprehend it, and to see a reflection of it begin to break in Sybilla's paper-white face. There was time for Kate to cling to the door and realize, with a sickening ache in her heart, the size and scale of the mistake she had made. Then Lymond drew a long, unsteady breath and moved. Without a word or a glance, he thrust between Kate and his mother, and walked to the end of the passage. For a moment, his back to them, he paused. Then with his fist he struck the door open and vanished. A moment later, they heard his step on the stair, and the main door opening, with an ostler's voice wishing him a good night. Had they looked out of the window, they might even have seen him walk off through the snow, his bare head bright and dark by turns under the lamps.

But they did not see it, for Kate was on her knees on the cold flags of the public inn passage, crying, and Sybilla was standing beside her, on the same forlorn spot, and unseeing, stroking her hair.

The girl Osep Nepeja did not want was coming downstairs as Francis Crawford came into their lodging, and she drew aside on the landing, since she saw it was the head one, the one who paid and never came near them. Who likely, they said, wasn't able.

But Lymond greeted her, smiling, and smiling gripped her and walked her into his room and kicked the door shut.

Half-way through the night she said, 'What's the matter?' but he didn't answer.

And Osep's friend drew a long, lonely sigh, there in the darkness; for he had been thoroughly able, and she had thought that perhaps he had liked her. But it was the old story. Some bought a drug for their troubles; and some bought a body. She waited until she thought he was sleeping, and left him, with her money, and a few extra coins as a keepsake.

CHAPTER SIX

With their funds, their possessions, their lives threatened by the forthcoming war, the merchants of London decided as a measure of trust, a measure of pride and a measure of long-headed commerce to give to Osep Grigorievich Nepeja the finest reception ever received by foreign envoy to the capital city of England. And the Crown, for intricate reasons of its own, elected to support them.

Come in stately progress; escorted from county to county by sheriffs, the Ambassador's party was met within twelve miles of London by a company of eighty Muscovite merchants riding in velvet coats and gold chains. By them he was taken to spend the last night of his journey in the house of one of their number, where he was given gold, velvet and silk to make a riding coat for his processional entry. The following day, after an apprehensive night, he was received by an even larger number of representatives of the Muscovy Company with even more horses and liveried servants, and taken fox-hunting.

To a man accustomed to hunting bear and seeing three hundred hares slaughtered in one afternoon, it may have seemed a strenuous and not over-productive occupation.

But after two weeks of travelling through the rich English countryside and being entertained in commodious English mansions, Osep Nepeja was not the voluble traveller he once had been. He kept his mouth shut, except for smiling, and allowed himself to be led among the fields and commons of the northern suburbs of London, witnessing hawking and archery, and admiring the manors and gardens of the wealthy and the religious houses, ruined or privately bestowed, which gave to the countryside so much of the general appearance of his own suffering land under the Tartars.

Then, after sufficient time had been wasted, he was led to meet the Queen's representative the Right Honourable Viscount Montague with three hundred knights, squires, gentlemen and yeomen, all warmly and expensively dressed, and attended a brief open-air ceremony where he received from four richly dressed merchants a large gelding finely trapped, with a footcloth of Orient crimson velvet enriched with gold laces. Mounted on this, he was taken to Smithfield, the first limits of the liberties of the City of London.

There, translated by Robert Best, the City welcomed him in the person of Sir Thomas Offley, Lord Mayor of London, with his Aldermen all in scarlet, and the procession of Entry formed up. It was, considering the penurious state of the Ambassador and the months of privation which had preceded it, a praiseworthy production. Dressed in his own style (by the Company) in a gown of tissue, embroidered with jewels and pearls, and with a long stiff cap, also jewelled, set upon his massive brow, the Muscovite Ambassador rode between the Lord Mayor and Anthony Browne, Viscount Montague, with his servants in golden robes following. Behind them, brightly dressed, came the servants and apprentices of both English parties : ahead, in spectacular ranks, rode the knights and merchants, with the other Muscovite guest and his three companions discreetly among them.

From Buckland and Best, the Muscovy Company knew who Lymond was, and had a very good idea what he was doing there. To their relief, discreetly approached, he had proved last night to be a man of good sense and reason. Nepeja was the Ambassador. Mr Crawford's rôle, out of the public eye, should appear quite subsidiary. The Company, used to refugees of their own through several reigns, found nothing unusual in dealing with a foreign-born Russian, and in the ease of communication a positive blessing. Riding as it happened beside Sir William Chester, Alderman and merchant, Lymond talked about sugar all the way through Aldersgate and Cheapside and Lombard Street and into the opening of Fenchurch Street, while the London crowds, shouting and struggling, packed the network of streets all about them, and hung out of windows and dropped things, on occasion, on their heads.

No one fell to their knees and abased their brows to the Queen's representative, or to the Voevoda Bolshoia, or to the first Ambassador of the lordly Prince Ivan, Tsar of all the Russians, but Master Nepeja had grown used to that. In spite of its money, it was an unruly and barbarous nation. But what would you expect, under the ignorant rule of a woman?

Lodged under the eaves of the extravagant Fenchurch Street mansion which was to house Nepeja during his sojourn in London, Blacklock, d'Harcourt and Hislop were not the only men of his party that night to throw themselves on their beds with groans of relief and exhaustion. Prone, with his hands over his face, Danny Hislop said, 'My God. Do you realize there is going to be two months of it? Who is Master John Dimmock?'

'A lion-hunter,' said Ludovic d'Harcourt, his eyes closed. 'The man with the biggest house and the most money and a penchant for entertaining Russian Governors. I approve of the house. Did you see Nepeja's rooms?'

'Yes. It isn't all Dimmock's. Rob says the Queen supplied the bed and the hangings and the furniture. They've got some silver out of the Jewel-house as well. Rob says there's a guard with pikes round the house twenty-four hours a day and they can't sleep at night in case the old man draws a thread in the hangings. The Voevoda's room is almost as good.'

'Do you think he will notice?' Danny said. 'I sometimes feel if I placed myself nude on the floor between the Voevoda and one of his meetings, he wouldn't even walk round me.'

'Dedication is the word,' said Ludovic d'Harcourt. 'He has more patience with Nepeja than I have.'

'Power is the word,' said Danny Hislop. 'If you control a large slice of Russia and are anticipating controlling the rest of it, that is how you behave.'

'I think there's something else,' Adam said. 'I think something happened at Berwick.'

'We know what happened,' Danny said agreeably. 'He celebrated his return to English soil by hiring in one of—'

'Not that,' Adam said. 'Or before that. I suppose being pushed in the face by your brother may be said to loosen the family ties.'

'Adam!' said Danny. 'You mustn't drop out of the choir. We have too much to do. What *do* we have to do?'

'Wait about for three weeks,' d'Harcourt said. 'To-morrow's the first day of March: King Philip hasn't set out yet from Brussels. And the Queen won't receive Nepeja officially until King Philip arrives. The Privy Council won't go near him either. He'll have to kick his heels, and content himself with long talks with the merchants.'

'In this house? What about us?' Danny said.

D'Harcourt said, 'I thought you were tired of the baubles of ceremony? Lymond won't be received anywhere either; not until Nepeja is formally recognized. That means he can't do his business. The Muscovy Company can talk about arms as much as they like but they can't promise anything: only the Queen and Council can provide or withhold all the licences. All he can do is clear the air with the merchants by telling them what the Tsar wants and why. And Nepeja can do the same, on the trade side. My guess is that all our time will be spent with the Muscovy Company. Remember, all their records have been destroyed, and Chancellor's eye-witness account. They know all Best can tell them. They're bound to want our help as well.'

Adam said, 'In full, deathless detail? How George Killingworth's beard conquered Novgorod?'

'What happened to the Emperor's sugar?' d'Harcourt said.

'Who got carried out of the Emperor's banquets?' Danny said. 'You know, it's a funny thing, comparing England and Russia—'

'*No!*' howled Adam and d'Harcourt together.

'No. We've had a lot of that. I was only going to say,' Danny said, 'how chastely agreeable it is to sit next to a woman again.'

Which only went to show, as the other two, exchanging

438

glances agreed, that the sweet panacea of England was lancing the carbuncles of Russia already.

*

With Best and Nepeja, Gilpin and Hussey, Lymond and his three officers, it took the Muscovy Company three days to work through the obvious agenda : the progress on the wreck; the social news about the company's officers still remaining in Russia : word of his son Richard for Sir Andrew Judde, of Richard Grey for his wife and daughter, of Charles Hudson for Sir George Barnes's grand-daughter; of Thomas Hawtrey for William, his brother.

For the Company, it became slowly clear to all the outsiders, was one close-knit in friendship as well as commerce, and linked by inter-marriage as well as by kinship of blood. And wealthy as these men were who inflicted on them, with such disarming apologies, long aching forenoons recalling the price of train oil and the terms of long, vanished documents, they were, many of them, Londoners of the first generation and merchants of the first generation, who had come to the city in their youth, and stayed, showing industry and initiative and imagination, and had prospered.

They commanded respect. In spite of their boredom, the three officers of St Mary's found themselves spending long hours, willingly, round the table; combining with Best and Nepeja in an attempt to define markets and explain officialdom; detailing the concessions made by the Tsar and interpreting those demanded in return by Nepeja. Lymond, mercifully, seemed equally ready to offer help and to exercise restraint through all the discussions which had nothing to do with munitions – that aspect, it could only be guessed, was being negotiated through firmly closed doors. On occasion, he relieved Best as interpreter, and it was noticeable then how their progress improved, as he steered Nepeja, and clarified for him.

Nepeja was already dependent on him. As time went on the three cynical pairs of eyes from St Mary's could see that the merchants also, little by little, were beginning to lean on his advice. They had Buckland's notes of the probable lading of the three vanished ships. They knew now the total losses, including the fragments being recovered from Pitsligo, hardly worth the total cost of the rescue. And, facing reality, they included in these the pinnace *Searchthrift*, sent out to Vardo with the *Edward*, and never heard of since the *Edward*'s last call there. So there came the day when Sir George Barnes threw his quill on the paper before him and said, 'Gentlemen, we have lost six thousand pounds in two years. What is this Russian trade worth to us?'

It was an argument which would be thrashed out in the end, with the Company's powerful Government members, and far from the Muscovite Ambassador's hearing. No one had to be told that war might be coming; that to buy and refit and victual a fresh fleet of ships the Company would have to raise capital by calling once again on its members. It was Lymond who said, 'But it seems to me that your trade with Russia on both sides is perfectly secure, whatever happens in the Narrow Seas or the Baltic. This indeed is your lifeline, and perhaps Russia's. Your object should be to improve your ships, and foster any research which will improve your navigation. And then to look beyond Russia.'

'Chancellor is dead,' Garrard said.

'There are others,' Lymond said.

'Burroughs. Vanished on *Searchthrift*. Wyndham's dead, and so is Pinteado. Roger Bodenham's too old, and settled in Spain. No one at Penshurst, and Sir Henry's off with his map-drawing secretary and his tract-writing chaplain to write the topography of Ireland. Buckland—?'

'No,' Lymond said. 'I am told there is a man called Tony Jenkinson.'

Garrard said, 'You hear a great deal in Russia. Or – you were friendly with Chancellor?'

'We talked a little about this,' said Lymond. 'Could Jenkinson take a fleet of four ships to St Nicholas?'

'Perhaps,' Garrard said. 'If Buckland and the rest of you advised him. The charts would have to be redrawn.'

'Adam here could help with that,' Lymond said. 'As for the rest, we can supply what we know for a rutter, whether Jenkinson is the man to use it or not. Who could meet us and draw the notes up?'

There was a short silence, during which d'Harcourt met Adam's eye and Adam in turn avoided looking at Danny. Then Sir George Barnes said with a sigh, 'There really only is one man. But he's living quietly. I suspect . . . I think

I had better find out if he can see you. But he's the man. By the name of John Dee.'

The meeting broke up soon afterwards.

'We deceived you there,' Danny said to Ludovic d'Harcourt, watching all the black gowns and fur collars sweeping down the oak stairs. 'You thought we were interested in trading with Russia.'

'I did,' said d'Harcourt obediently.

'And we're not,' Danny said. 'We want an excuse to call on a caster of horoscopes and a heretic. Maybe he wants his future read? I hear it's all done with a crystal of coal.'

'In that case,' said his colleague briefly, 'I hope they keep sousing the damned thing with water.'

*

On foot and unattended, with the blessing of the Muscovy Company, Francis Crawford of Lymond next morning walked to the market in Gracechurch Street, and turning north, crossed the cobbles of Bishopsgate to the house in Threadneedle Street of John Dee.

It was not easy to find, being one of a group of houses belonging to a former religious foundation and occupying, with its gardens and courtyards, the triangle between Broad and Threadneedle Streets. The servant who opened the door was of the kind one might expect to find in a scholarly bachelor's household, and the room she took him to, dark and crowded, was as sluttish as herself, with a vague smell of sulphur and horseradish. The dust lay on the woodwork like rock flour. There she left, and Lymond waited.

It was very quiet. Outside it had begun to rain: the creak of it against the small, obscured panes of the windows was the only sound in the room once the maid's footsteps had receded and vanished; louder than all the far-off London noises: the chatter, the cries and the barking, the rumble and squeak of cart wheels; the perpetual landslide of horses' hooves between the leaning canyons of wood and plaster and stone. In the room itself there was nothing to see: it was a parlour for receiving unwanted guests and held not even a book which would have identified the interests of the occupier. Lymond glanced round once and then stood perfectly still with his back to a rent table, his cloak thrown beside him, his face serene, as the silence stretched on.

There was no sound of movement to break it. Only a voice, suddenly, light and dry, which spoke from the shadows. It said, 'You are observant. But there is no need to defend your mind against me.' And a tall man, moving from the dark inner doorway where he had been standing stepped into the room. A lean man with a long nose and high, ruddy cheekbones, who wore a dusty gown over his black, shabby doublet, and a black cap on his light, glossy hair; whose eyes were ageless but whose hands, loose at his sides, were capable and broad-fingered and young. He came to a halt a pace away from Francis Crawford and said, 'I have certain foibles, which you must forgive me. Perhaps you think this meeting unimportant. It is not. I am John Dee.'

Lymond said, 'We have met, at Rheims.'

The pupils in the large eyes moved back and forth, studying him. 'You heard my lectures on Euclid? Ah. You were in France with the Scottish Queen Dowager, and it was fashionable. What did you learn from them?'

'That you find lecturing tiresome,' Lymond said.

'So you find me patronizing,' the other man said. 'And I am rightly reminded that you are the master of armies. Shall we proceed on a basis of mutual respect until we find out whether we may endure something closer? Come. My study is warmer.' And moving ahead of his guest, he walked along a dark passage and standing aside, opened a door. Lymond entered.

The dazzle of light inside was so great that at first he shielded his eyes, blinded after the shadows. Then, dropping his hand, he traced the cause, and, angry as he was, his lips relaxed.

Mirrors lined the walls of John Dee's sanctuary. Mirrors subtly aligned and invisibly misshapen, placed on frieze and wainscoting and ceiling so that every aspect of the crowded room was repeated to cheating infinity: the piled books and crossed scrolls, the racks of instruments and shelves of pots, jars and alembics, the pinned maps and charts, the iron clock and the magnifying glass, the great Mercator globe on the floor, and the bunches of dried herbs, slowly swinging from the beamed ceiling. It was less a study than a workshop, with standish and quills competing with auger and handsaw and file: sawdust and filings were gathered everywhere and only the mirrors opposite the door, wilfully distorting, had been kept deliberately clean.

Lymond studied himself, by turns squat and undulating, and suddenly laughed. 'I am duly deflated. May I look?' And finding his way across, examined them. He said, 'You are severe with your visitors, Master Dee. You know why I am here?'

John Dee shut the door. 'Because Courtenay is dead,' he replied. 'Or does the merchants' business come first? I may not taint Master Dimmock's house, as perhaps you have gathered, since the recent unpleasantness. I have been acquitted of treason and absolved, with reluctance, from the charges of heresy: they sent poor Philpot through to examine me, and he became quite upset. *Master Dee, you are too young in divinity to teach me in the matter of my faith, though ye be more learned in other things.* You are right. I lack intellectual humility. A good thing to be without. But Cheke is broken and Eden dismissed and the Merchant Adventurers being scanned, one by one, for their faith. If I am to pursue my work I must do it quietly, living on horoscopes for frightened men and avaricious women. And my advice to the Muscovy Company is not publicly proffered. They mean to send out another adventure?'

'They have four ships fitting, and the cargo already half gathered. We need charts. Better ones, including what was learned on this voyage.'

'We?' John Dee said. He lifted some books and revealed a stool, on which Lymond sat himself. 'You are sailing with them to Russia? Scotland offered you no blandishments?'

'I am sailing to Russia,' Lymond said. 'Even if the Queen of England changes her religion and dissolves her marriage tomorrow.'

'Or dies?' said John Dee.

'Or dies. You have been gathering information for one purpose, I for another. We began to correspond because we appear to use the same sources. That is all.'

'It is more than that,' Dee said. 'You helped me pass letters between Madam Elizabeth and William Courtenay. She is entitled to think of you as not unsympathetic. She hoped you would be more.'

Lymond said, 'I thought they had purged her household. Are you still able to exchange messages?'

'My cousin Blanche is still there. They don't know the relationship with James Parry either. My good lady Elizabeth's grace knows you are here. When Buckland and Best first arrived in London she was at Somerset Place with a lavish retinue of two hundred in red and black velvet, much admired by the populace. The business was to offer her marriage with Philip's cousin, the Duke of Savoy, any heir to be educated and brought up in England, while the Duke and his wife live abroad. With Philip returning, the Queen's anxiety to see her sister abroad is quite intense.'

'And King Philip?' Lymond said.

'Would further the marriage. After all,' John Dee said, 'he is not likely to stay in England long. He has a war to pursue. And Brussels is a gay court, with King Ruy Gomez reigning. However, the Duke of Savoy was refused, which upset the Queen considerably. It is said she was hardly dissuaded from calling parliament and debarring the lady Elizabeth from the succession formally as a bastard. She certainly turned her out of London forthwith and back to Hatfield.'

'An over-vehement refusal perhaps?' Lymond said.

'My lady Elizabeth? You haven't met her, have you?' said Dee. 'She informed her sister that her afflictions were such as to rid her of any wish for a husband, but rather to induce her to desire nothing but death. I am told the Queen wept at the time, but not afterwards. The Privy Council don't want the Queen's sister abroad, and neither do the people. With no heir as yet, and the conflict over religion and over King Philip's demands, the Queen dare not go too far against public opinion. As she always does, my lady had judged it exactly.'

'You have great hopes of her,' Lymond said quietly.

Dee sat at his desk, an hour glass turning and turning between his big palms. 'I have great hopes of this nation and someone must lead it. I look to whatever will serve. You cannot be unaware that that is why I have been writing to you. What in Russia can compare with the prospects which lie before England? You will have power and wealth, but what are these to a scholar? You will end your life an oasis in a desert of ignorance. You have thought of all that?'

'Obviously,' Lymond said.

'Therefore there are other considerations. . . .' John Dee broke off, exasperation on the lean, bearded face. 'We

444

cannot talk. You are behind bulwarks and entrenchments massive enough to protect a city from capture. The mistake is mine, to have angered you. Where did you have experience of this before?'

The effect of the mirrors was prismatic. Wherever Lymond looked he could see himself, his hair, his hands, his body, and the bright repeated blaze of the candles, over and over. 'In France,' he said. 'I know when my mind is being attacked.'

'Do you think I stand here as your enemy?' said Master Dee. 'Mr Crawford was your horoscope drawn up in France?'

'No,' said Lymond curtly; and then in the blaze of the mirrors saw a picture long since sunk from his conscious mind: of the house called Doubtance in the Rue de Papegaults, Blois, and a strange and feverish awakening with a woman bending over him. . . . *What was the date and hour of your birth?* He said, 'It may have been done, once. With what results, I don't know.'

'If it were to be done again,' John Dee said, 'what could you fear? What would you lose?'

'My privacy,' Lymond said. 'And would that speed our business?'

Dee sighed. 'No,' he said. 'You are right. Let us persevere. The Courtenay matter. There must be letters. Many of them appear, as you know, to concern the problems of navigation in which he was interested, but it is not difficult to read behind the lines. He died in Padua, and from what I can learn, all his papers were sealed in a casket and locked up by the Bailiff for safety. Rumour has it that Peter Vannes the English Ambassador has been told to get them and bring them with him to London. He has certainly left for London.'

'That much I have heard,' Lymond said. 'With a thousand Venetian crowns and the commendation of the Council of Ten, Ayes 19, Noes 0, Neutral 0. And he left with the casket. Whether he arrives with the casket is another matter. I think you should leave it to me. Lychpole should have letters for me from Hercules Tait.'

'Lychpole has no letters for you,' John Dee said. 'It is one of the small mysteries I was hoping you would resolve.'

Lymond stared at him thoughtfully. 'Yes. That certainly calls for attention,' he said. 'So does another small matter. How does Philippa Somerville happen to be on visiting terms with the lady Elizabeth?'

John Dee's pale lashes blinked, once. 'It was brought about, I believe, by the Lennox family,' he said. 'The pretext was the sending of some volumes from Ascham. I believe Madam Elizabeth warned the young lady.'

'She may have done. She also embroiled the young lady in a matter with which the young lady had nothing to do. I really do not relish the idea,' Lymond said, 'of being the medium through which Margaret Lennox and Elizabeth Tudor are assailing each other. And still less do I like the rôle of stalking-horse allotted to Philippa. If you will convey as much to the proper quarters you will do both of us a service.'

'But it brought you to England,' John Dee said. 'That, or the threat to Richard Chancellor?'

'I didn't know about Chancellor,' said Lymond shortly. 'I came here on a mission for the Tsar because the Tsar left me no option. Both now and on subsequent journeys I shall willingly give what help I can to Chancellor's successor, which is the other reason why I am here.'

'To be sure,' Dee said. 'The housewifely purpose of trade.'

'Slightly higher than that,' said Lymond pleasantly. 'So that the fleet shall in good order and conduct sail, pass and travail together in one flote, ging and conserve of society, to be kept indissolubly and not to be severed. You have the makings of a school of cosmography, financed directly or indirectly by the Muscovy Company, which presumably is what the more speculative minds among you have always intended. Charting information Buckland can no doubt supply partly from memory, and we shall help him. On the navigational side, you know what you discussed with Chancellor and what tests you wanted him to carry out. He did use the Tables and instruments. We made some new ones for him in Russia. He also used the paradoxal compass. If you wish, I can tell you a little of that.'

The shining globe of Mercator was standing, ruffed with papers, on the uncarpeted floor. John Dee, sinking slowly, sat on his hunkers before it, and with his big hands began to turn it, slowly, gazing on the uneven marks as they passed. He said, 'He explained it to you?'

'He explained how one might use it to get something

close to great circle sailing. A class with one ill-informed student. But he used it to lay a course coming home, and there were some notes taken which were rescued with my chests – these.'

He carried the packet at his belt. He withdrew it now and laid it on Dee's desk. Dee, rising slowly took them and said, 'I thought we should hear nothing . . .'

Lymond said, 'I think they will ask you to approve the appointment of Jenkinson.'

Dee said, 'This is not Diccon's writing.' He looked up. 'It is not the comprehension of a student, either. Chancellor knew I favoured Jenkinson after himself.'

'Yes. He told me,' said Lymond. And as Dee went on staring at him he said, 'I said that you clearly found lecturing tedious. Not that you were less than a brilliant teacher. On the same note of guarded ambivalence. . . .'

'You are a mathematician,' John Dee said.

'I am a musician,' said Lymond. 'Or was. I believe the cast of mind is the same. Orontius opened another door, but I have never been through it, except with books, until Chancellor taught me to assemble what I knew. It doesn't matter, except to explain that there might be some profit in conference, with yourself, Digges – anyone else who might care to know how his thought was developing. I should like to see these journeys extended, and bettered. If you like, Chancellor deserves that sort of monument.'

Dee did not answer. He stood, looking at the stained packet held tight in his hands, then turned abruptly and went out of the room, leaving Lymond alone, with the globe and the clock and the mirrors.

When he returned, he bore a pair of beakers in one capable hand, and in the other a large flask unstoppered. 'I wish to drink,' said John Dee. 'You will come back to this house and meet the men you have been told about, and we shall hear what you have to say, and question you, and in turn you will hear what is happening in our world. I wish to drink to celebrate another proof of something I hold to be true : that what is mathematical is divine, and what is divine is mathematical, and that a transfusion of both creates the flame which is known as beauty.'

He poured the wine and handed it, patches of wet standing unashamedly under his eyes. Lymond said, 'I believe I should like prior warning of that statement, or a little more leisure. I think neither of us, in spite of the logical spirit, has displayed a great deal of percipience this morning.'

'I do not ask,' said Dee. 'You note I do not ask – but I would swear, by all I have learned, that you are Scorpio.'

'With the sting in the tail?' Lymond said. 'You are probably right.'

'Then since you have given me this mark of confidence,' said John Dee, refilling his glass, 'I shall ask you for another. I am bidden to dinner, where I am welcome and my affairs are well known. I have been asked to bring my guest with me. The house is not far – you see it across the yard there, and the postern by which we shall enter. It belongs to the Sidneys, and the bidding is from Lady Mary. What is your answer?'

It promised interest, and it seemed, then, innocuous enough. So his answer was in the affirmative.

*

Master Dee had, it appeared, a gown of superior appearance with a velvet cap, which he placed on top of the other, collecting at the same time a number of manuscripts which he tucked under one arm before taking Lymond with the other to lead him out of the house in Threadneedle Street and across the crowded courtyard with its pump, its straw and its barrels to the gardens and the low back entrance to the Sidneys' big gabled house in Broad Street, once part of the religious foundation of St Anthony's.

There they were obviously expected. A pretty maid in a blue cloth gown and an apron led them through kitchen and passage and up the twisting steps of a carved wooden staircase to a long room lit on one side by bright latticed windows and decorated from ceiling to the low panelled wainscoting by a design of floral and geometric paintings, done in white and dark green and rose to blend with the tapestry on the long table and the velvet upholstery of the cushions and tall chairs and stools.

The salt was on the table, and the covers set with covered bowls and gilt standing cups, all with the porcupine crest or the bear and ragged staff of the Dudleys. And Lady Mary herself, a soft, fair-skinned woman with a light voice, came forward smiling and said, 'You are just in time. I am being taken to task by my kitchen. Come to table. And this is Mr Crawford? Or do I call you M. le Comte de Sevigny, since there are no Spaniards present?'

Lymond smiled at Sir Henry Sidney's wife and made, automatically, the right impression in the right kind of way while he glanced at the rest of the company. There were no more than a dozen all told. Some of them, he guessed, were members of the Sidney household; companion, secretary, chaplain. The others, handsomely dressed, must be either relatives or close friends : the Sidneys were far too wise to expose Dee or himself to risk or discomfort.

Then he saw that he was wrong, and that there were in the room two people who were neither kinsfolk of the house nor inclined to be well disposed to himself, whether called Crawford or Sevigny.

One, standing by the window with his hands firmly clasped behind his well-cut doublet, was Austin Grey, Marquis of Allendale, whom he had last left standing trembling in the snow outside the inn where he had met . . . where he had spoken to Kate when in Berwick.

And the other was his wife, Philippa Somerville.

CHAPTER SEVEN

'I hope,' Lady Mary was saying, 'you do not object to surprises? Philippa could not call on the Muscovy Ambassador and she is so dear to her mistress that she is seldom free for those of us who wish to see more of her. Austin Grey I believe you have already met?'

Bowing, Austin Grey failed to offer his hand. Lymond turned smoothly to Philippa.

It was, of course, the girl he had left at Volos, remarkably tidied, in a square necked gown with a great many chains and medallions, and a brimless black beret and crespin, which was a little alarming when one remembered the brown hair, in Kate's fashion, sticking to her neck and her cheeks. But she now had the best excuse, naturally, for indulging in all the fashions forbidden to the well-brought up single girl. He smiled at her suddenly, on this thought, because she was staring at him with Kate's eyes, starkly distended, and because he was aware of how much he had changed, and of the two thousand miles of age and culture and experience which divided them now; and took her hand, and said, 'I may hold you to your marriage if you continue to make such impressive improvements. Does that terrify you as it should?'

'It doesn't bear thinking about,' Philippa said briefly. It had to be brief, because she could feel Austin's protective anxiety like a feather mattress beside her and her breath had leaked away somewhere into the recesses of her buckram-lined bodice.

She had had a cup of wine before this particular meeting. She had come indeed fortified in every direction, and prepared for a full spectrum of Mr Crawfords, ranging from a rather nauseating opium addict she had once observed with her mother in Newcastle to a gentleman like the Duke of Alva, who would browbeat her one moment and try to pinch her the next.

There was also the little matter of her interference. At intervals of roughly two hours over the preceding three months, Philippa Somerville had wished she had never been seized with the idea of investigating Mr Crawford's past history, and that, having done so, she had never, never written that letter and given it to Lychpole to send him.

On the other hand, it had been a reasonable letter, placing the whole matter in quite a proper perspective, and to a rational human being, these days, bastardy was no slur and at least it had given him, she thought, no reason to think less of his mother. Or so she believed until Austin had come back with the news of what had happened at Berwick.

And Austin must have been mistaken. That was her first thought when the door opened and John Dee came in, and then the man one remembered so well, in the saddle, talking to Kate at Flaw Valleys, at the whipping-post at St Mary's; rolling over and over with Graham Malett before the high altar at St Giles and again, confronting Graham Reid Malett in Stamboul in the chess game where Kuzúm was nearly lost, and the other child died. And who, without touching her, had shared a bed with her in Stamboul, on the night forced upon them by malice, which had resulted in his prosaic offer of temporary marriage.

Since then, he had grown in authority. Used to assessing those in authority around her, she could feel the strength of his presence; the concealed blaze of nervous energy, lightly controlled. In everything he was sharper and brighter and harder than she had remembered and the shock when he smiled was such that she was sure, staring back at him, that Austin had misconstrued what happened at Berwick. And then realized that, of course, her letters had probably never come near to reaching him.

He said something, and she said, 'It doesn't bear thinking about,' and then, as he was turning away she said, 'Did you get my letters?'

She was sure of his answer. She was still happily sure of it as he stopped, and the faint smile left his lips to be replaced slowly by a delightful one, full of open-eyed candour. 'Yes,' Lymond said. 'The first *and* the second. What infinite trouble you took with them. If there was a third, it must, I'm afraid, have eluded me. Unless you sent it direct to my mother?'

And he turned to the table leaving her, silent, to find her place opposite him.

Through the first part of that meal Austin held her hand, and she needed it. She drank her wine and had it refilled, smoothly, by Lady Mary's expert men servants as the conversation flowed easily all about her. They were asking questions, naturally, about Russia and as the answers caught her attention her hand slid out of Austin's and her composure came back; sufficiently at least to allow her to catch the talk when it veered in her direction, and finally to ask a question or two herself.

Lymond neither avoided her nor singled her out in the course of it. Because it was an informed and intelligent gathering, the conversation was never monopolized, and moved lightly among matters concerning them all for which the Russian parallel became only the springboard: the philosophy of government, the use of power, the place of religion and education, the exploitation of natural resources. They discussed the strategic problems of moving large armies across empty steppeland, where none could live off the country and the violent changes of climate made communication a hazardous thing at the best.

Master Dee propounded his theories on the use of the burning-glass and tried to impress on the tapestry, until halted by his dinner partner, a design for a new form of traction. The question of health arose, and they pondered, with fascination, the treatment employed by the Samoyèdes. Dr Dee said to Philippa, in an uncompromising aside, 'I also have been attacked as a marauder. It is because of the letters?'

It was not a subject she intended being questioned about. 'Yes,' Philippa said.

'You touched on something personal. An odd flaw in an overwise rational being. If you will take my advice, peace may be restored by referring to Richard Chancellor. There was some friendship, I would collect. At least it will place you on neutral ground. . . . I don't suppose you happen to know the date and time of his birth?'

'Mr Chancellor's?' Phillipa said. 'No, I'm afraid that I don't.' And restored to combat raised her voice at last directly for Lymond's attention. 'Did you have a physician, Mr Crawford?'

He glanced at her. 'They are hard to come by. I am hoping the company will send one with the next voyage. There was an elderly German, Grossmeyer, attached to my household, and he taught some of my staff. Also we had Ludovic d'Harcourt, whom you haven't met so far, who was trained in the Hospital in Birgu.'

'A Knight of Malta?' Lady Mary observed, covering with fine social ease the two words *my household*. 'Philippa, you must have old Lady Dormer to meet him.' She smiled at Lymond. 'Jane's grandmother. Two of her brothers were knights, and she has Commander Felizes staying with her at present.'

'Mr Crawford knows Malta well,' Philippa said. 'And Tripoli. Which reminds me. How is Kiaya Khátún? Robert Best came back perfectly dazzled.'

'Exactly as she was in Stamboul,' Lymond said. 'Well-behaved.'

'Can a man have several wives also in Russia?' Philippa said.

'Not concurrently. He can however,' said Lymond pleasantly, 'keep his legitimate wife under lock and key without comment as long as he pleases, and beat her as often as she offends him. To signify which, on the eve of marriage he sends her a small box containing whip,

452

needles, thread, silk, linen and shears, and she sends him in return a shirt and handkerchiefs of her own making.'

'A hair shirt?' Philippa said. 'Or does remorse play no part in this amiable society?'

Lymond viewed her with calmness. 'We may lack some polish,' he said. 'But distrust the society which displays overmuch dangerous charm. *Chi te carezza piu che far' no'sude—*'

'. . . *o che gabbato t'ha, o che gabbar' te voule.* I am sure,' said Philippa, 'that not even the Russians could deceive the commander of St Mary's and the Tsar's own private envoy to England. Perhaps you think of yourself now as Russian? *Chi beve bianco,* they say—'

With extreme swiftness, Lymond interrupted her. 'They may, but not in this company. Lord Allendale, you require to keep your fiancée in order.'

The murmur of laughter increased. Lady Mary said, 'I declare you both out of order. Philippa can hardly be betrothed when she is married.'

Austin Grey had flushed deeply and then become rather pale. He said, 'Marriage does not seem to impede Mr Crawford.'

'So just is God. He is a man,' said Mary Sidney, 'and treads the world while we sit at home with our sewing silks. What of Russia do you enjoy, Mr Crawford? There is music? One hears that, as the Turk, the Russian is skilful at chess?'

Beside Austin, Philippa's hand had closed very hard on her wine cup. In face and hands, voice, mood and posture, Lymond, considering, showed no ruffled nerve. He said, 'There are some marching songs which would amuse you. But their music is to our ears disagreeable, and the Church does not favour it. Every Lent, wagon-loads of dulcimers and rebecs are taken over the Moskva and burnt. The virginals in my own house were the first ever seen, I believe, inside Russia. But you are right about chess. They play in the fields and on the stoves. It suits the Muscovite mind. The trading company would do well to remember it !'

'Whom do you play with?' Philippa said abruptly. 'Or is it a game confined only to menfolk?'

There was laughter, which she had expected, and Lymond's glance, which she summoned the courage to meet. But it was a look quite free of overtones, of mildly simulated reproof. 'My opponent in fact was usually the Tsar Ivan. A matter of some diplomatic strain. One must not win too many games, and, on the other hand, one must not lose too many either.'

'Tell us,' said Lady Mary. 'What is he truly like? One has heard such tales, of dogs hurled from the battlements, of wild exploits riding down peasants, of childish dabbling in the blood of dead animals. We have so many Englishmen there now. Is he to be trusted?'

Lymond said, 'My advice to the Muscovy Company has been to establish their trading post there. They are in more danger from the Tartars at present than they ever will be from the Tsar. And that danger will be, I hope, short lived.'

There was a small silence. Then Lady Mary said, 'Robert Best has told us, you should know, your position with the Tsar's army.'

Lymond said, 'So long as it is not public knowledge, no harm is done. I am making no claims to hold the whole of Muscovy secure single-handed. But I have tried in some measure to contain the threat of the Tartars. There are other complications on the borders, but I shall not bore you with these.'

'But you are here,' Philippa said. 'Can Muscovy spare you?'

Lymond's blue eyes dwelled on her with chilly amusement. 'In the nature of things, there are a number of gentlemen filling the void, I imagine, with some assiduity. Have you ever heard of Baida?'

No one had.

'An extremely mettlesome leader of Cossacks, who has become a legend already in the Ukraine. There are many songs his men sing about him. You were asking about music. This is an example of it.'

'Play,' Lady Mary said. 'There are virginals. Play and sing it to us. Or the harpsichord.'

He rose with ease and perched at the harpsichord, one hand on the keys. 'It's only a marching song. But this version is interesting.' And he sang lightly, picking out the notes one-handed, an expurgated version of the song which had roared round the camp, on the night Prince Vishnevetsky had joined him.

In the market place of the Khanate,
Baida drinks his mead
And Baida drinks not a night or an hour
Not a day or two . . .

He did not make it too long, and they left the table and moved round him as he played, and made agreeable sounds as he finished. Philippa said, 'Who did you say Baida was?'

'I didn't,' said Lymond. 'In fact, his name is Dmitri Vishnevetsky.'

He did not expect it, clearly, to convey anything. And, indeed, only on Philippa's face did any enlightenment show. But Lymond saw it, and before she had drawn breath to speak, he forestalled her. 'But anything Rob Best told you about that,' he said agreeably, 'I should advise you to keep to yourself. Have you heard this new piece of music from France? M. de Roubay's musicians are playing it in Edinburgh.' And he turned and played properly and then rose and gave up his seat, and would not be persuaded to play again, but became part of the audience while Lady Mary herself played an estampie, to be followed by one of her cousins.

Philippa, with loving care, favoured them last of all with a furious piece which fell short of the surprising technical skill of her husband, but far exceeded it in violent expression. He congratulated her winningly. 'Music. The Medicine of the Soul.'

'Aristotle,' said Philippa impatiently. 'But yours isn't music. It's numerology.'

'Numerology,' said Mary Sidney, 'is the basis of all great music. Or so – don't you? – Master Dee holds. But before we discover an argument, I suggest, Philippa, that you take the opposing army away and attack it in private. You did wish to see Mr Crawford, didn't you?'

She did not. But, she remembered with exasperation, it was necessary. Lymond was looking at her with raised brows and the rest of them, damn them, were smiling. 'Yes, of course,' Philippa said. 'If you will excuse us?'

'Go to Sir Henry's room,' Lady Mary called after her. 'And if you use weapons, be sure to call witnesses.'

The laughter followed them both along the dark passage.

*

Lymond shut the door and said, 'Be a good girl and keep it short.' Against the dark panelling the clear, colourless skin and fair hair looked deceptively delicate, like a tutor she had once had who turned out to be a practising gelder.

The room, littered with cases and boxes, had obviously never been used since Sir Henry had left the previous summer to become Vice Treasurer and General Governor of all the King's and Queen's Revenues in Ireland. There were two white Irish rugs on the floor and a little slope field bed which still filled the room, with a cloth counterpoint lined with fustian and a leather lute case lying on it. Philippa squeezed her way irritably between a flat Flanders chest and a magnificent joined chair, with its seat lozenged in cream silk wrought with gold porcupines, and perched herself at last, with infinite if Turkish grace, on the windowsill.

A large curtained object decorating the wall on her left provoked her to investigate with one finger : the painting beneath was of St Jerome, notable for his involvement with the lady Paula and her daughter Eustochion, and disarmingly naked. Philippa whipped back her hand and said with irritation to the St Jerome still standing immobile with his back to the wall : 'I can barely see you, never mind confound you with eloquence. Come and sit on the porcupines.'

'And sing? Prick-song?' Lymond suggested.

Philippa was silent. Then she said, 'I don't suppose either of us has had a particularly rollicking morning. I was stupid, and everyone else seems to have suffered for it. When did you get the letter?'

'It doesn't matter,' Lymond said. 'The damage is done, and at least we are less ignorant, if not noticeably wiser than before. Now you *have* involved the rest of us, I suggest you step back and let us struggle on in our own puerile way. That apart, where do we stand? I assume Tristram Trusty has passed on my talk with your mother?'

'And your memorable talk with himself,' Philippa said. 'I can quite imagine what you would have done in his place.'

'I doubt it,' said Lymond dryly. 'But I shall speed the divorce all I can. What else?'

'This,' said Philippa, hauling papers out of the service-

456

able bag at her girdle. 'They're yours.' And she held them out.

Slack-lidded, Lymond did not at once move. 'Today, you are full of surprises. What are they?'

'Reports,' Philippa said. 'From de Seurre and Nicholas Applegarth and Hercules Tait. Didn't you wonder why Bartholomew Lychpole had no letters waiting to pass on to you? He didn't have them because I intercepted them. Here they are.'

'Now,' said Lymond slowly, 'you *have* astonished me.' He moved forward thoughtfully and taking the papers she offered him, stood turning them over. 'These have been opened.'

'I opened them,' Philippa said. 'Didn't you wonder either how my letters reached you? Lychpole came and told me he was in correspondence with you. He's not very discreet. Or very clever.'

She had his full attention now. He was watching her face, the blue eyes dainty as metal embroidery. He said, 'Do I have it clear? Bartholomew Lychpole informed you unasked that if you wished to write to me, you could do so through him. He also informed you that I was leaving Russia and that all the dispatches from Europe would therefore be coming to him. And because you thought him untrustworthy, you decided to intercept them? How could you do that?'

'I am studying with Ascham,' Philippa said. 'The Queen's Latin secretary.'

'I noticed you capped all my best quotations,' said Lymond absently. He turned, and, finding the porcupine chair in his way, laid the dogeared packet for the moment on the seat, and sat himself on the arm of it. 'And on the strength of Lychpole's tender concern for your marriage vows, you decided to stop all the traffic between us?'

'I've read all your books as well,' said Philippa, getting the confession over quickly while he was unlikely to dwell on it. 'It sounds feeble, doesn't it? But there was more to it than that. Lady Lennox also knew that you were in Russia. And I didn't tell her.'

'So?' Lymond said.

'So I feel,' Philippa said, 'that Bartholomew Lychpole may be a little more than just careless.'

'In which case,' Lymond said, 'Lady Lennox has seen

all the letters Lychpole has sent me already, including the two written by you. Why did you open these?'

Philippa, who had gone red, said flatly, 'They might have been important. You were a long time on the voyage.'

'So you knew I was coming,' Lymond said. 'And Chancellor. What a tense winter you've had. All the same, it's a pity you opened them. Now we shall never know whether the Lennoxes reached them before you did. Were they important?' And picking them up, he began to leaf lightly through them. 'Christ, what a gossip.'

'Espionage is gossip,' Philippa said. 'Is that the series about our octogenarian Pope's wars against the Imperialists?'

'He fights Charles because he is an octogenarian,' Lymond said. 'He was born when Italy was free: a well-tuned instrument of four strings, Naples, Milan, Venice and the States of the Church. He has waited for this all his life, a priest, a linguist and a scholar. Now he sits there with his three scandalous nephews, drinking his repulsive mangiaguerra and scheming how to recover Naples and Milan and keep Venice Ayes 0, Noes 0, Neutral 19. Helped, I gather, by Piero Strozzi's Germans, Protestant to a man.'

'And by the French,' Philippa said.

'Yes. Well, de Guise is supposed to have a remote claim on Naples through Renée of Lorraine. Hence the secret treaty between France and the Pope to recover Naples, and the Pope's fury when the Constable pushed through the truce two months later. So our old man goes to work, and five months after that, manages a new secret treaty between himself and France – here it is. The Pope to create a new batch of French Cardinals, just in case. Each side to provide twelve thousand foot, five hundred men at arms and five hundred light horse. The crown of Naples to go to King Henri's younger son, and land to the Papal Territory and the three nephews' estates. Also, the French King is to invite the Sultan Suleiman to attack Calabria . . .

'How the Pope adores Charles. *That schismatic and heretical Emperor . . . . We will deprive him of the Empire, of his realms and of his existence as a human being and a Christian . . . that devilish soul of Charles, in that filthy body . . . the most vile and abject nation in the world . . . gnawing the vitals and drinking the blood of*

458

the poor . . . diabolical, soulless, thirsty for the blood of Christians . . . born to destroy the world. . . . If the enemy crosses my frontier by so much as the distance of this tooth-pick, a sentence so tremendous it will darken the sun. . . . And a bit in Italian, which is just as well. What sentence? Perpetual residence in Naples?'

'I understand Italian,' Philippa said. 'The threat, if you read on, is to release the Emperor's subjects from their oath of allegiance, and confer the kingdoms on those who shall obtain them. And the justice of God, he says, will cause even the Turk to come and inherit them.'

'I see,' Lymond said. *'We love the King of France and will make use of him, as we would even of the Turk, for the need of the See Apostolic.* But the King of France doesn't want to fight, yet. The Duke of Alva crosses into Papal territory on some small excuse, and Strozzi and all the French ministers are hanging on to the pontiff's coat tails to persuade him not to give Philip cause to start a full-scale war. For now Charles has abdicated and King Philip is running the Empire – I see his character has not escaped blessing, either.'

'Little beast, begotten of that diabolical father?' Philippa said.

'You *do* know Italian. *An inexperienced youth, having by the grace of God become master of so many kingdoms, his first exploit is to take up arms against the See Apostolic to give proof of himself . . . . That accursed silly boy; would to God he had never been born, nor yet that iniquitous father of his: rebels to God; a treacherous race, without faith. . . . Rely upon it, the powder is prepared and the guns shotted and that if ignited, everything will be consumed in all directions.* A fair estimate. And note of a letter from Queen Mary of England to her husband King Philip, congratulating him on the Duke of Alva's success, and suggesting that since all is going well, he should come back to England. . . . Oh God, the asinine woman,' Lymond said.

Philippa Somerville was silent.

'But she pays you. The point is taken. Ah, here is Venice. *We love the Seignory, both as Pope and as man.* Offered half Naples to intervene on the Pope's side, the Seignory declines, and hopes that matters will adjust without their help – Ayes 100. The Pope is angry : *To-morrow or the next day we shall depart this life and you will remain, and in the ruins will remember this poor old man, and lament not having chosen in time to provide against our downfall. . . .'*

'His Serenity the Doge,' Philippa said, 'has accommodated His Holiness with three tons of coarse cannon powder. You *have* reached the bit about Courtenay?'

'Through the thumb-marks and liquor stains, barely,' said Lymond. 'Perhaps I failed to mention—'

'That you don't like your correspondence read?' Philippa said. 'But you did tell Kate that you had no interest in Elizabeth or the Earl of Devonshire. That wasn't true.'

'That wasn't true,' Lymond acknowledged, still reading.

'Hercules Tait says that Courtenay died after fourteen days' fever in Padua, and that Vannes, the English Ambassador, got the chief Magistrate of Padua to lock up all Courtenay's papers until the Queen wrote to say what she wanted.'

'Luckily,' Lymond said, 'Hercules Tait, who wrote the report, has a friend in the Council. So the following day, without Vannes being aware of it, the Bailiff of Padua was asked to send Courtenay's papers secretly to the Chiefs of the Ten back at Venice, where the box was opened by a carpenter and the contents all read. A number of letters, marked with a cross, were taken out of the bundle and the rest put back into their linen cover, stitched, replaced and nailed into the casket, which was sent back to Padua, apparently intact. From there, presently, Peter Vannes was allowed to collect it, and is at this moment on his way home to hand it, with the letters, to the Queen. Unfortunately,' said Lymond reflecting, 'Tait doesn't know which letters were abstracted, and he says he is watched and may not be able to get the casket from Vannes.'

'Why does it matter?' Philippa said. She looked again at the report in her hand, which included none of these extremely interesting facts.

Lymond shrugged, 'Courtenay was the sole male heir, several times removed, to the throne of England, if Queen Mary dies childless. There have always been plots to marry him to the lady Elizabeth. He was supposedly involved in the scheme to rob the Treasury last year – they put his secretary Walker in prison. Ruy Gomez and his friends were only recently suspected of trying to kill him

460

— even the merchants can tell you all about that. So his correspondence is highly inflammable.'

'And who is liable to be burnt?' Philippa said.

'I am,' Lymond said placidly. 'And more important, John Dee. And more important still, the Queen's sister Elizabeth. But not until Vannes arrives with the casket.'

In silence, they stared at one another: sardonic blue gaze into clear, vigorous brown. 'And I,' said Philippa at last, 'am about to be suspected as a junior unpaid courier scurrying about between you all?'

'It is no doubt Lady Lennox's hope,' Lymond said. 'As I told your mother, I shall do what I can to thwart it. She said you had been to Hatfield only once. Is that true?'

'Yes. Mr Elder asked me to go once again, but I made some excuse,' Philippa said. 'Madam Elizabeth did warn me, to do her credit.'

'I am not sure that she deserves any,' Lymond said. 'But if you took her nothing but books, nothing can be proved against you. And if Margaret Lennox did read your letters, she will know that it was not the last sprig of the white rose which had engaged your attention. . . . What a pity that we rushed into marriage. Your reputation has never been questioned, and you acquired all my ill-wishers instead. . . . The Pope, it says here, is angry with France for not coming to help him more quickly. He has not therefore hastened to present the French with all their new cardinals, or the Constable's son with his divorce, which is still being strongly debated. To wit: *can the Pope separate a marriage contracted per verba da praesenti, but which,* and the rest of it.'

'. . . but which has not been consummated. Don't be diffident,' Philippa said. 'The theologians say no, and the canonists disagree, quoting Leo I who in letter 92 to Rusticus, Bishop of Narbonne, says that *matrimonium per verba de praesenti* is not marriage, *nisi accedat copula carnalis.*'

'And you understand Latin as well,' Lymond said. 'As I remember?'

'Well enough to note the implications and observe them,' Philippa said. 'Although it removes a certain zest from court life. I should like you to read the papers from Brussels.'

'You would?' he said. He put down the papers. 'How long is it since you were home at Flaw Valleys?'

461

'Two years,' said Philippa.

'Are you by any chance . . .' said Lymond.

'. . . baiting you?' Philippa said. 'Only when you are inclined to be magisterial.'

'Oh, good God,' Lymond said. 'Kate must be out of her mind.'

'And thank heaven you aren't my father?' said Philippa.

'Roughly,' said Lymond, and began to laugh, and then stopped. 'Look. I must go. Is there anything else?'

Philippa said, 'You called Mary Tudor asinine : I want you to read these reports. They begin two years ago when King Philip left her to join his father in Brussels for a stay, so he said, of two months. Read them. Read how often she begged him to return, and how often he promised, and how often he disappointed her. Read about all the gossip that began to reach us from Brussels : about the tournaments and weddings and masked assignments attended by the King and his most intimate servants. . . .'

'Ruy Gomez?' said Lymond.

'Yes. King Roy,' said Philippa. 'I know his secretary.'

'Not,' said Lymond, 'the Spanish Tristram Trusty?'

'Spanish, yes,' Philippa said. 'Trusty, no. You know the saying. Germans woo like lions, Italians like foxes, Spaniards like friars and French like stinging bees. I don't know why they left Scotsmen out. And Greco-Venetians. The only one I know about Greece is the old one. *Chi fida in Grego, sara intrego.*'

Lymond said, 'When you tell me about your Spaniard, I shall tell you about my Greek. Attend to what we are discussing. So what did the Queen do about it all?'

'She took his picture down and kicked it out of the Privy Chamber,' Philippa said. 'She wept. She wrote to the Emperor, begging him to let Philip return, and sent Paget to implore him to hurry, *because of the Queen's age, which does not admit of delay.* King Philip told her, through Paget, that if he did not return to her the following month, she was not to consider him a trustworthy King.

'So, for the fourth or fifth time, arrangements were made for the dear man's arrival; and for the fourth or fifth time he cancelled it : because of illness, he said. She sent three couriers to Brussels, one after the other, and when after nine days not one of them had returned, she was nearly crazy with worry and suspicion. But he didn't come anyway, because of the Abdication. The Emperor Charles was retiring to his Spanish monastery, having given his son all his kingdoms. They say he turned back at the gates of his palace, crying. But by the middle of September, all his luggage was on board ship for Spain, except his bed and his clocks; and in October the Queen was again told that Philip was coming. I can tell you,' said Philippa feelingly, 'nothing was thought of, nothing expected save this blessed return of the King.'

'Whom Maximilian described as *not a prince of much ability, nor with counsellors of great experience and prudence, and no money.* Then he put off his coming till Lent,' Lymond said. 'Why? Oh, I suppose the trouble with His Holiness.'

'Ruy Gomez was here last month,' Philippa said. 'And you won't find what happened in these papers. He brought a letter from the King to the Queen, dwelling on the Pope's misdemeanours and explaining why it was necessary to fight. Paget, but not the Queen, was to be asked to engineer a break between England and France.'

Lymond said, 'Your Spanish Trusty again? The French are putting it about that the Queen has promised to pay for ten thousand foot and two thousand horse, on condition that Philip crosses to England.'

'She has promised him three hundred thousand gold crowns,' Philippa said. 'Apart from that, she hasn't committed herself and won't, I think, until he arrives. She isn't well. But she observes all the canonical hours. She prays day and night.'

'And has just sent the Inquisition to purge the University of Cambridge,' Lymond said, 'with coffins tied to the stake, and dead men tried for heresy. All for her husband, who is about to make war on the Head of the Catholic Church. While time is moving on : for the Pope, who must have Naples before death finally claims him; for Mary Tudor, with the gates closing between her and her unborn children; and the husband who comes and comes, and has not come yet. . . .' He looked up. 'You are right, of course. She is far from asinine. This Queen is tragic.'

'You see that. Now then,' Philippa said, in an apparent non sequitur which was the very essence of cunning : 'will you play for me? Properly?'

He didn't answer at once, but at least he didn't dissemble. 'I'm sorry to disappoint you,' he said. 'But although it might be proper, it wouldn't be in the least different. Perhaps it's the Russian climate.'

She had thought of something else. 'The prophecy may be true then, may it not?' Philippa said. 'That your father's two sons would never meet in this life again?' Since it seems—'

'Since it seems that Richard is not my brother. Even by opening my letters,' Lymond said, 'I don't see how you knew about that.'

'About the Dame de Doubtance? You've forgotten. I was in Lyons on the day that you saw her,' Philippa said. 'So was Güzel. Do you like Russia better than Scotland?'

Sitting deep in the chair, Lymond had a faint smile in his eyes. 'I am not being kept in Russia by evil enchantments. If that is what you mean to imply.'

'I meant to imply that Güzel helped us all to escape from Turkey. And that perhaps there was a price to be paid for it?'

'If it helps to think so, I have no objection,' said Lymond. 'In fact, there is an infinite range of reasons, among which that plays only a fractional part. All I want is in Russia. I have been taught to face reality: an excellent thing.'

'Music, the Medicine of the Soul, And chess,' Philippa said.

Lymond's gaze, faintly hostile, was level. 'And chess,' he agreed.'

'But you can't face the facts in my letter?' She was sitting, rigid, on the windowsill, neat from her caul to her velvet slippers, and her hands folded like a child's in her lap. The brown eyes were stubbornly challenging.

'Lymond rose, with charm quite as lethal. 'Oh no,' he said. 'The *chasse à cor et à cri* is quite finished. I am going back to the others. Or your chivalrous Marquis will worry.'

'Why?' Philippa said. 'Because Sybilla deceived you? Or would you feel differently if it were your father she had deceived?'

Half-way to the door, he turned quite deliberately and faced her. 'No, Philippa,' he said. 'Listen to me, for I shan't say this again. It is the end of the matter. Why you began it, I can't conceive. It has done nothing but harm, and to pursue will only cause more. Finally, it is really no possible business of yours. You kept these reports out of the wrong hands. That I do appreciate. And if you will drive it now from your mind, we shall manage very well together in the short interval of marriage which I trust, remains to us.' And he smiled, turning already.

Philippa said, 'And if that isn't being damned magisterial, I don't know what is. It's my business because I love your family and you love your own, stately, self-perpetuated miseries. I have found a great-uncle of yours called Leonard Bailey in Buckinghamshire, at a manor called Gardington. He says Gavin Crawford is not your father, and he has papers to prove it. If you go there, he will show them to you. Or so he says. If you will take my advice, you will go. If you don't, it's because, for all Russia has done for you, you haven't got the backbone.'

There was a catastrophic silence. Then Lymond, speaking very softly, said, 'Don't be childish. What else have you done?'

'Faced up to reality,' Philippa said. She had got off her windowsill and was standing facing him, her hands at her sides. 'I knew you would be angry. I do this for my own private entertainment.'

'You don't know what you're doing,' Lymond said. 'You're performing a play, in a schoolroom, for an excited audience of one. I said *what else have you done*?'

Below the long, taffeta bodice, Philippa's interior had begun to ravel with cramp pains. She said hardily, 'Nothing, so far. I didn't know another permutation in breeding was possible.'

There was another brief pause. Then Lymond said pleasantly, 'I would strike a man who was stupid enough to say that to me. Were you followed to Gardington?' His face, carrying little colour at any time, had the sallow bleakness which a sharp change of wind can effect; his responses, far from automatic, were made under a pressure exactingly contained.

Bent on her purpose, Philippa received his question without understanding. She said, 'No,' and then remembered : the group of horsemen so opportunely placed on the road coming back from Gardington and the civil confinement which followed. 'That is,' she said, with her spine staring like a plucked fowl's, 'I may have been. I was met by the Lennoxes.'

Lymond drew a long breath and said. 'Ah. I wonder which version they'll publish. Unless they find another permutation, as you call it, to offer?'

Philippa said, 'I'm not the Voevoda Bolshoia of Russia, so I make mistakes. I make diabolical mistakes. But I'm the only one trying to help. You don't know what Bailey is like. I was prepared to be hurt, and I got hurt. You weren't prepared to do anything. Not even to go to Sybilla directly and ask her for the truth.'

'Which would have proved my devotion to my family,' Lymond said. 'What did she tell *you*?'

To her inner self, Philippa Somerville said, *I am not going to be sick*. To Lymond, she said, 'I didn't ask. I don't care what you are going to say. I don't care. I don't care. These things have got to be said. Everyone is frightened to speak to you.'

'But I allow no one – no one at all, to speak to me like this,' Lymond said. 'Come here.' And as she hesitated, he said in the same, pleasant voice, 'I don't need to strike you. Words will do just as well.'

She came towards him, between the furniture, with her neat beret and jewellery and fine satin skirts and took her place in front of him, her mouth firm, her round brown eyes open. She said, 'You despise Mary Tudor. You are offered love and won't accept it except on your own terms. That isn't magic. It's the word you've just mentioned – it's childish.'

He waited until she had finished, and for a moment indeed he did not speak at all. Then he said, dropping the words with lucid, passionless economy into the stillness, 'Of all the homes I have known, yours has been a shining model of wisdom and kindness and honesty. For what you and your mother have done in the past, for me and for the child, I owe you a profound debt of honour. You have that claim on me. So has your mother. But if you press it too far; if you will accept no appeal and continue to press it, over and over; if you move into my life, both of you, and take your stance there and feel obliged to command and instruct me in how I should or should not behave, you will destroy our relationship. I shall walk away from you both; I shall deny you both; I shall repudiate all you have done for me. It will all be as if it had never happened . . . I don't know what you fear for me, but that you should fear. For I cannot afford it.'

She was unbecomingly crying. She said, 'How do you find what will hurt?' because she knew his temper and was braced for it, whereas he had employed a lance she had never dreamed of, against a place which had no defences.

He said. '*This matter is mine, and not yours or Kate's, I never want to hear you speak of it again. Do you hear me?*'

And Philippa said sobbing, 'Yes. But I won't do it.'

'Yes, you will,' Lymond said. 'My God, do you think I said all that because I can't make you? Be quiet and get out of my life. Or I shall send Bailey's papers to Richard.'

Then she cried protesting aloud and Austin Grey, waiting anxiously and restlessly at the end of the passage outside heard the sound, and other sounds of Philippa in distress, and drawing his sword, blundered along the narrow corridor and flung open the door. Philippa choked. Lymond, his face perfectly stark, said, 'Oh, God in heaven, Tristram Trusty . . .' and moved quickly back as the sword flashed towards him. Philippa yelped.

It held the stuff of both climates: the tragic and the childish. Lymond was quite unarmed. The room, crowded with bric-à-brac, was no more fit for a tournament than a woodshed. As Austin Grey came pursuing towards him, Lymond slid back between stool and box and bed until, glancing sideways, he was able to snatch up a baton, left stuck under the buckle of a round leather chest. He used it, parrying, just as Austin's first sword-stroke descended and said breathlessly, 'What in hell are you doing here? It isn't your quarrel!'

Philippa, joining her voice to his, said wetly, 'Stop it!'

'She says, Stop it,' said Lymond.

The sword, flashing wickedly, slid past his shoulder. His face grim, his dark eyes unexpectedly savage: 'Someone has to teach you a lesson,' said Austin Grey.

'Oh, Christ,' said Lymond with exasperation, and finding the field bed behind him, somersaulted to freedom behind it.

Philippa said sharply, 'Stop! Austin, stop it!'

But Austin, slithering over the bed, paid no attention. The sword cracked on the baton, and cracked again; then as Lymond ducked, the blade bit into the square maple table and then lifted, flashing again. Philippa hauled open the door. 'Mr Crawford!'

'What, battling down the staircase?' said Lymond, and laughed. 'No, thank you. Allendale, don't be a fool. Put up.'

Austin said, 'She came here to help you.' He cut, across the width of the porcupine chair, and splinters flew from it.

'She helps everybody,' Lymond said. He heeled round the bedpost within an inch of the sword and, ripping the silk off the face of St Jerome, threw it bunched over the blade rising behind him. 'Wait until you are wed. She'll do your breathing for you.' Austin shook off the cloth.

Philippa said, 'That isn't true!'

'No,' Lymond said. 'He's breathing the way you want him already. Gallant, sensitive, and kind to his mother.' He flung himself sideways and laughed. A large box, fallen on its side, revealed itself as Sir Henry's quilted black velvet close stool. The pewter pot, rolling out, was scooped up and appropriated, in a second, as a bizarre shield by Lymond. Austin's sword clanged on it; and again; the blade sliced, spraying, through the candlestick stand on a desk and Lymond, tapping and dodging, met a stool and was nearly sent staggering. Austin's sword, unimpeded for once, slashed down and cut the baton cleanly in half.

Philippa said, 'That's enough. He didn't harm me. You must stop now, Austin.'

Austin did not respond.

Philippa, lifting her skirts, plunged from the wall and thrust her way to the scene of the action. 'Austin. You are fighting an *unarmed man* with a *sword*.'

Austin pushed her out of the way and, taking a sudden stride forward, nearly managed to pin his opponent between the window and the bed, dodging the lute which Lymond flung at him as he did so. 'It will perhaps teach him,' he said, breathing hard, 'not to force his presumptuous manners on women.'

'Oh, don't be a fool, Tristram Trusty,' said Lymond. And making three precise movements: a step by the stool, a feint by the chair and a swinging stride by the bed, kicked Austin Grey's sword neatly clean out of his hand.

It fell beside Philippa. She picked it up before Austin could turn, jammed it hard behind Sir Henry's desk, and hurtling forward flung her arms from behind round her protector. Like the jaws of a crocodile, two capable feminine hands closed on Austin Grey's arms over the elbow, rendering him for the moment totally helpless. And a capable feminine voice, directed past Austin Grey's ear to his opponent, said, '*Hit him.*'

Lymond, already balanced on the upswing to hurl himself forward, dropped his arm and said, with dawning reproof, 'I was going to.'

'I know,' said Philippa. 'And it'll take half an hour and end with an audience. Hit him.'

Under her hands, Austin Grey suddenly struggled.

'*Hit him!*' said Philippa sharply. 'It's the only way he can stop now, with honour.'

Which was not only perceptive, but practical. So Lymond hit him.

The Marquis of Allendale fell very neatly and was caught and lowered to the ground, quite insensible, by Francis Crawford and his wife.

Lymond was laughing, with not quite enough breath to do it with. Straightening from Austin Grey's body, he was gurgling still with breathlessness and hilarity : he sat on a box for a while, with his hands nearly touching the floor and his tangled head drooping between them, gasping at intervals. Philippa said, 'Now, I'll stay with him. You go along to the others and take your leave.'

Lymond pulled his head up. 'As if nothing had happened.'

'Well. Nobody knows,' Philippa said. Poor Austin was moaning a little.

'Except you and me,' Lymond said rising abruptly. He walked to the door. 'You were going to give me a promise.'

From where she knelt by her knight, Philippa looked up at the other man, graceful, facile and worldly. 'You are thinking of someone else,' she said bluntly. 'I don't change from minute to minute. I don't change at all.'

'I don't think you have changed since you were ten years old,' Lymond said. 'How fortunate we all are, in some ways.'

He made his farewells with perfect courtesy and left by the door into Broad Street. Back in Fenchurch Street, shocked by his looks, Adam Blacklock was rash enough to address the Voevoda, and was treated to the kind of response, white-hot, venomous and unforgiveable, which he had largely spared Philippa Somerville.

The holocaust in his head by that time was on its most staggering scale : was there a scale for headaches? Perhaps Master John Dee could plot them. Except that Master Dee would certainly want his date, time and place of birth, and Master Dee was not going to get them.

A commanding resolution. Margaret Lennox presumably had them in detail already.

There did come a time, eventually, where thought was quite impossible. Francis Crawford read for a little, then, since he knew very well what was coming, locked his door and lay, face downwards waiting, upon the high pillared bed.

He did not welcome it. But in its own way, sometimes, it was better than thought.

CHAPTER EIGHT

On Thursday 25 March, twelve months to the day since he took leave of the Tsar his master, Osep Grigorievich Nepeja, the first Muscovite Ambassador to England, was summoned to Westminister to present himself before the King and Queen, and to make his formal Oration.

The State barge, in which he left the Three Cranes wharf in the Vintry, was decked with streamers and flowers and gilding and flew the flag of St George for both England and Muscovy, and carried the arms of both countries. With him travelled Lord Montague and a large number of merchants from the Muscovy Company, as well as ten City Aldermen and his own far-travelled escort, which included the Voevoda and three men from St Mary's. On the jetty at Whitehall he was met by six lords in velvet, with trumpeters, and by them conducted up the Watergate stairs to the long gallery, and from there to the Great Chamber, hung with brilliant blue baldachine and spread with one of Wolsey's damascene carpets.

There he was saluted by Nicholas Heath, Archbishop of York, the Lord Chancellor; William Paget, Baron de

Beaudessert as Keeper of the Seals, William Paulet, Marquis of Wiltshire, the Lord High Treasurer; and William Howard, Baron of Effingham, the Lord High Admiral, the last two being Charter Members of the Muscovy Company.

The intent on both sides was to impress. Nepeja, dressed by the Muscovy Company, whose members comprised half the Government wore a gown paned with gold wire and sewn jewels like acorns, with a tall jewelled hat on his great bearded head. The Voevoda with his three colleagues following was as refined as a charming shell cameo in thick silk brocade sewn with white sapphires and cloudy star rubies. Across his shoulders he wore, as Danny Hislop's dazzled eyes registered, the Tsar's great *barmi* of pendant medallions.

Treading between the double line of brilliant courtiers, brittle as the Queen Dowager's iron flowers at Binche, Danny wondered how much it impressed the middle-aged Governor of a trading town in frozen, Tartar-torn Muscovy. The broad river, so like the Moskva, but lined with great houses and long garden walls, pierced by handsome gateways and jetties. And behind it, instead of the uniform ranks of the izbas, the whole crowded panorama of London with its church spires and towers and the tiered rows of its houses in wood, brick and plaster with their random gables and windows, deep-carved and gilded; the booths and taverns and gardens; the palaces of bishops and kings and the town houses of merchants and nobles in every extravagance of texture and period. Gothic and classical : the black and white of timber and plaster beside brick, moulded or carved in all colours from silver to red to yellow to the kiln-burnt ripeness of mulberry.

The tall chimney stacks, crusted and twisted and diapered. The tiers of glittering glass from tower windows, square headed and mullioned and transomed, and the tailored grey cupolas, capping them. Trefoiled friezes and curling leaf ornament; swag mouldings and roundels in terra-cotta of pure Italian work. Running patterns of plasterwork, such as those which clad the walls of this building, with trailing flowers and mythological monsters : arches of flint and brick chequered, like the one standing outside in King Street. Square Gothic gatehouses, with their feet in the river, such as that which led into the Palace. The tennis courts. The tilt yards. The twenty stone piers of the Bridge.

And what did he make of the Presence Chamber, thought Danny, with its ranks of high leaded lights and great gold compartmented ceiling? And below it, the hangings of gold tissue with the emblems of England and Spain entwined in raised purple velvet, and the frieze of antique work, picked out in gold.

The dais was at the end of the room, under a heavy fringed canopy. And there, the Queen and her consort sat, unmoving, on tall gilded thrones.

Queen Mary looked ill. Dressed as if for a wedding, with her neck thickly ringed with large pearls within her rigid winged collar, and her gemmed skirts unwieldy as curtains, she breathed from her stillness a kind of violent impatience. She was suffering, it appeared, from the rheum and a toothache. And Philip, it was said, from something worse, which he had brought uncured from Brussels, having failed these many weeks to make a recovery.

But he gave no appearance of restlessness. Elegantly disposed, with his thin acquiline nose and stubborn, fair-bearded jaw he was wearing the dress sent him by his bride for their wedding day, of cloth of gold with English roses and pomegranates, all picked out in gold beads and seed pearls. On each sleeve Danny, counting discreetly, identified nine table diamonds, and his white plumed bonnet had a little chain and a medallion with diamonds and rubies.

The long-deferred, long-wanted reunion had taken place at Greenwich, four days before. At every stage of his return, from Calais to Dover, from Dover to Canterbury, from Canterbury to Greenwich King Philip had found two of the Queen's gentlemen waiting, one of whom had ridden off forthwith to take the Queen news of his arrival at Greenwich, each London church sang the Te Deum by order of the Bishop of London, and the church bells rang all the time, while in the palace down river the King and Queen walked to their closet, and heard their first Mass on their knees there together.

They had stayed two days at Greenwich before passing upstream to Tower Wharf with the Court, where they were met by the Lord Mayor, aldermen and sheriffs and all the Crafts in their liveries for the ceremonial ride through the City. King Philip pardoned the prisoners in the Tower in passing, and the noise of bells and trumpets and guns shooting off from the Tower was only surpassed in horror by the noise of the waits on the leads of St Peter's in Cheap, whom Danny had joined, with Ludovic d'Harcourt, to gain his first, unprejudiced view of King Philip.

The shopkeepers were glad to see the King present, and the Privy Council, with their palms itching, it was said. But the people gazed at the Spaniards, as Danny was gazing now at the Spanish lords grouped round the throne, and heard without enthusiasm King Philip's publicized statements instinct (in translation) with goodness and clemency. He wished to enjoy his states, he said, rather than to increase them. And more than anything, because of its cost, its toil and its perils, was he opposed to the waging of war.

Danny recalled retailing that to the Voevoda, and the Voevoda listening with sympathy. In fact, Lymond had quoted him Elder :

> O noble Prince, sole hope of Caesar's side
> By God appointed all the world to guide
> But chiefly London doth her love vouchsafe
> Rejoicing that her Philip is come safe.

He could do it with his face as bland as a bishop's. He was perfectly serious now, standing behind Nepeja and his nine Russians in cloth of gold and red damask, listening to the start of the Oration. Nepeja's voice began with a tremble, and then settled down to its normal vibrating sonority. The Tsar's letter, somewhat marred with sea water, had already been delivered : *The most high and mighty Ivan Vasilievich, Emperor of all Russia, sends from the port of St Nicholas in Russia his right honourable Ambassador surnamed Osep Nepeja, his high officer in the town and country of Vologda to King Philip and Queen Mary; with letters, presents and gifts as a manifest argument and token of mutual amity and friendship to be made and continued for the commodity and benefit of both the realms and people.*

Rob Best, threadily, was translating to English, and someone Danny couldn't see into Spanish. Perhaps the Count of Feria. The beloved, Ruy Gomez had gone to Spain, to fetch money and troops and supplies and without him, it was a wonder that the King went on breathing. But the other lords were all standing round him, and somewhere must be the Jesuit, thirty-seven years old, it was said, and suing for the hand of Jane Dormer. Moved by a quest for knowledge, Danny was scanning the languid cloaked forms when it came to him, as a fly to the nose of a a salmon, that he had nearly missed something much more important. The Somerville girl must be there somewhere

A tall, regal woman : the Countess of Lennox. A small one, Madame Clarenceux. A young one, with fair hair drawn sleekly back in a caul : Jane Dormer, he suspected. And another, perhaps a year younger, of no very great height, but straight-spined, with the fine, straying grace of one of the lesser carnivores. Her dress was modest; her unchildlike face shadowed by a winged cap of sheer stiffened white, with a gemmed tassel worth a small fortune laid quivering against one pure cheek. Danny Hislop said, 'Christ!' although under his breath, and saw Adam turn, and then follow the line of his gaze to Mistress Philippa Somerville, newly of Lymond and Sevigny.

She was looking at Lymond, gravely but with a question somewhere, it seemed, in the fine-drawn line of her brows. Hislop saw the Voevoda counter the stare with another one, perfectly soulless. Then as the girl continued to look at him, Lymond's mouth relaxed for a moment, into something which was not more than resignation but showed some advance, at least, on its habitual arrogance. Under his breath : '*Majnún and Leylí,*' said Danny Hislop to Adam.'

Then the girl looked away, but not before someone else, he noted, had absorbed the small tableau. The Countess of Lennox, it seemed, was interested in Francis Crawford, and Francis Crawford's wife Philippa. Indeed, her splendid eyes, scanning him, made Daniel Hislop mildly glad, for once, not to be the object of a woman's attention. He was so intrigued that he barely heard the Oration end, and its two translations, and the Queen's reply, and the handing over of the two timbers of sables : eighty fine skins of full growth with long, glossy black hair, spared with some pain from the Company's Storehouse. For the six timbers of sables, the twenty entire sables, exceeding beautiful and the six great skins, worn only by the Emperor for worthiness had never reached London, but swam waterlogged through some deep northern waters, and made mysteries for the inquisitive seal. The Embassy advanced, one by one, to kiss the Sovereign's hand and be greeted.

The procession re-formed when it was over, and as processions do, took some time to retire from the chamber, and nobly escorted, traverse the Great Chamber and then the long gallery which led back to the Thames. In the gallery, Lady Lennox touched Lymond's arm.

'Mr Crawford? You can spare an old friend a few minutes. It will be ten at least before your Russian friends are allowed to embark.'

He did not appear, to the three men behind him, to hesitate. 'I should be honoured,' he said. 'A friend is a friend, old or young, in these troublous times.' And drawing Hislop's attention, lightly, with a touch on the shoulder, Lymond moved softly out of line and followed the august woman sweeping tight-lipped before him.

She found a small chamber through the next doorway, and walking in, turned swirling to face him. He said, 'Is the door to be closed? I am uncertain.'

She was wearing the large brooch which had been one of her wedding presents from the Queen twelve years before, showing the History of Our Saviour Healing the Man with the Palsy. And she was on her own ground at last, fortified by royal wealth and favour and the victory of her religion. Margaret Lennox said, 'What, my dear Francis? Do you think my reputation could be harmed by a man who is soliciting a divorce from his wife on the grounds that he cannot bed her? I am afraid, my dear, your affairs do not speed. A public congregation of Cardinals called specially over the Constable's matter has proved disinclined to give dispensation. *Quos Deus conjunxit*, they say, *homo non separet.*'

'I wonder,' said Lymond mildly, 'if you erect mazes because you enjoy twining. When King Philip declares war, France will at once come to the aid of the Pope, who will then allow the divorce of the Constable's son to proceed without hindrance. Mine will follow.'

'But if England and France are at war,' Margaret said, 'will not Scotland declare war on us also? And until the divorce is made final, think of the plight of poor Philippa, tied to a Scotsman.'

'An absent Scotsman,' said Francis Crawford. He had closed the door and was standing just inside it, the gold *barmi* glistening in the dimness. 'I shall be in Russia, I trust, by that time. And I have had legal papers drawn up, abjuring all claim to Flaw Valleys.'

'But if you leave,' Margaret said, 'your divorce cannot

475

go through. And what will the child's lovers do then? Repeat the sad history which Mr Bailey tells of your mother?'

'Am I supposed to be devastated?' Lymond said. 'I doubt, I truly doubt, if you have time to discover what does and what does not interest me. I take it that you are threatening Philippa?'

'Your Philippa has been a trifle indiscreet,' said Margaret Lennox. 'A childish error of judgment, but it has done me a disservice in Scotland at a time when I wish the Queen Regent's favour. I think it would be only fair if Philippa's husband so conducted his affairs that this favour was restored to me. I want my inheritance of Angus.'

'Will, wives and wrecks,' Lymond said. 'I beg your pardon. The story goes that you sent your priest to Tantallon Castle where your father breathed his last in his arms, thus allowing Sir John to adjust the testamentary documents at his pleasure. I thought you were using the title of Countess of Angus.'

'I am using it because it is mine,' Margaret said. 'Tantallon is mine. All my father's possessions in Scotland are mine.'

'Then how inconvenient,' Lymond said, 'that you are married to an outlaw and attainted traitor from Scotland. May I advise you about a divorce?'

They gazed at one another. Lymond added, reproachfully, 'I shall have to swim to the Vintry.'

'You take it lightly,' said Lady Lennox. 'Perhaps you take it lightly from disregard for the girl. But the sentence for treason in this country is execution. And that applies not only to Philippa Somerville, but to her mother.' She walked forward slowly, her back to the small latticed window, until she stood immediately before him, blocking the light. She said, 'I have evidence of her conspiracy. I have only to take it to the Queen. And I shall, unless you help me win my inheritance.'

'From the Queen Dowager? With my notable lack of prowess?' Lymond said.

'And you shall hold Tantallon for me,' Margaret Lennox said. 'And, in time, put my son Darnley on the throne.'

There was the briefest of silences. Then Lymond, stretching out his gloved hands, raised her ringed one and brushed it with the lightest and most sardonic of kisses. 'Margaret. I always misjudge you. Tudor and Douglas you will always be, but Lennox never. We are ignoring the fact that Scotland already has a Queen, betrothed to the Dauphin of France?'

'We are remembering the fact that war changes many things,' Margaret said. 'The Scots are not eager to go to war for the sake of the French, however the Queen Regent may coax them. If they refuse, the French marriage may never take place. Then Mary, Queen of Scots, must needs seek a husband. And my son is eleven.'

'While she is only fourteen. My felicitations,' said Francis Crawford. 'You will be the young Queen's goodmother. I must encourage you to see Kate Somerville, if she isn't beheaded, and exchange notes on the experience. I am sure you will succeed but it must, I am afraid, be without assistance from me. I am going back with Nepeja to Russia.'

'And the Somervilles?' said Margaret harshly.

He raised his eyebrows. 'Did it not occur to you,' he said, 'that your convictions about my nature and my habits might now be a trifle outdated? I am not sixteen. I am the Voevoda Bolshoia of Russia, my dear Lady Lennox, and what you do with or to the Somervilles is a matter for your own conscience and undoubted ability, as the Race of Japhet is a matter for mine. And if you fail, send your Darnley to Russia. I might find a princess for him to marry. If she will take him. . . .'

'Such as your woman; the woman who keeps you? What is she, this fine whore from Turkey?' She had clasped her two hands hard together, unable to believe, as yet, that he had refused her.

Lymond smiled. 'What she is not, despite all you have said, is frustrated. I am not on offer. I extend to you and Matthew my deepest regrets.'

He stretched his hands to the door, and she pulled her fingers apart. 'You would send your wife and your wife's mother to the headsman? I mean this. I mean this, Francis. If you sail back to Russia, you will arrive there to find your union dissolved by a higher authority than the Pope.'

He stared at her, and for the first time the wide blue eyes were faintly troubled. 'Do you suppose that the fine whore from Turkey will expect me to marry her? You almost persuade me to stay here. In any case, why be so impetuous? Your inheritance of Angus may come to you in all the pride of its grease without any inducement but your obvious merits. There are six weeks to pass before the fleet sails. Let us enjoy them, each in our own petty way, and see what the Grand Joculator will bring us. You have forgotten to mention, by the way, what you proposed to do with my son.'

And that, in the end, was what dismayed her : that he could outguess and anticipate even the secret ways of her venom. She set her jaw and staring at him said, 'I would take him into my kitchens.'

'Yes. That was what Graham Malett said,' Lymond remarked. 'Except that he added something about his bed also. So then I shall admit you to a secret. I killed my son. The child at Flaw Valleys is the son of Graham Malett and his sister Joleta.'

*

He missed the barge going back to the Vintry and the Ambassador, expansive with satisfaction and relief, worried about it at intervals all the way back to Fenchurch Street and upbraided him the moment he arrived, which he did shortly afterwards. Lymond handled him a little like a blast bloomery with an order for toasting-forks, and Hislop and d'Harcourt had to retire hastily, exploding and also regretfully aware that whatever passed between the Voevoda and the Queen's stately cousin, it was not going to be vouchsafed to them.

Two days after that, by arrangement, two members of the Queen's Privy Council arrived at Fenchurch Street to open private negotiations at last with the Ambassador, and to begin discussions more secret still with the Voevoda Bolshoia, Mr Crawford. One of these, Sir William Petre, the Queen's Principal Secretary, was a member also of the Muscovy Company and the other, Thomas Thirleby, Bishop of Ely, likewise a negotiator of long experience through several reigns.

The talks with Nepeja, covering ground already well explored by the merchants, lasted more than a fortnight in all, and were not quite so straightforward as either Sir William or the Bishop had been led to expect. The gravity, wisdom and stately behaviour noted and commended so

478

far in the Ambassador were replaced, as the discussions went on, by a certain querulousness.

He was a single foreigner in an alien land, whose tongue he still found incomprehensible. Makaroff and Grigorjeff should now have been at his side, and eight other merchants from the ill-fated *Bona Esperanza* guiding him; supporting him. lending weight to his arguments, helping him to detect sharp dealing and bad faith among these arrogant Englishmen. Left on his own, Osep Nepeja made sure that at least he should be no easy victim of guile.

With concealed exasperation, the Company officers noted it.

The trading concessions, it was true, were not quite so boundless as those granted them by the Tsar, but were reasonable enough considering that English ships would be carrying Russian cargo, and that the Russian cargo must therefore necessarily be limited. There was no limit on the number of trading posts the Tsar might set up, in London or outside of it; although it was highly unlikely, considering the Russian economy and their dependence again on English bottoms, that the Tsar would find it worth while to have any.

All this had been thrashed out already, in long sessions with the Company at which Lymond and his colleagues had sometimes assisted, and other invisible sessions, between the Company and the Queen's Privy Councillors, at which they had not. It seemed to the merchants now, excusing themselves to an impatient Bishop and a resigned Principal Secretary, that the Ambassador's recalcitrance was due in part to his distrust of the separate talks which were also proceeding, in English, between the two Privy Councillors and Mr Crawford on another subject entirely.

Osep Nepeja resented the confounding of commerce with politics. He had told Robert Best, privately, that King Philip had led him aside on the day of the Oration and had asked him his views on the provision of materials of war between his nation and Russia.

'And what did you say?' had said Robert Best, who was as fascinated as anyone by the spectacle of Russian rebellion.

'I said,' answered Master Nepeja, 'that such matters lay outside my commission, and I did not understand them. Would that I could be sure that the Voevoda will reply so, when consulted on matters of trade.'

Best, in the interest of all parties, reported this later to Lymond. 'He thinks you're parcelling up Russia in English between you.'

Lymond was not in a tolerant mood. 'Then if he can learn English in time, tell him that he is welcome to sit in on our discussions. But I am damned if I am going to conduct a major negotiation with an interpreter perched at my elbow. The terms of this treaty were made clear long ago by the merchants. All he has to do, for God's sake, let them rewrite it all in long words.'

The second treaty, they all knew, was a different matter. Long before this, Lymond had delivered to the Privy Council, with the greatest circumspection on both sides, his formal note indicating the Tsar's wish to discuss with her Majesty's Council the provision of certain skilled men and materials outwith the normal channels of commerce. Long before, he had placed the same note before the leading members of the Muscovy Company with a single question. If the Privy Council gave him licence to proceed, were the Company prepared to supply such items as he required and give them space on their ships, assuming a reasonable percentage of profit?

To this, the Company had agreed. Conditions had never been mentioned. A withdrawal of the Company's privileges in Russia had never been threatened or even hinted at by Lymond. But the possibility was there, in the very fact that the Tsar had sent this man to negotiate. It was small wonder, the Company recognized wryly, that Osep Nepeja, merchant of Vologda, was uneasy.

So the official negotiators set out, most anxiously primed by the Company and bearing with them also, on the other side of the balance, all the concerted warnings of their fellows on the subject of the Crown's present outlay and embarrassments, both fiscal and political; and the Crown's commitments, apprehensions and expectations in all those areas which this inconvenient demand from the Tsar of Russia might affect.

Because of the secrecy of the matter, only Sir William Petre and the Bishop of Ely came to the house in Fenchurch Street for these talks, with a scrivener, who entered with them, and their servants, who waited below. And in the room where the Tsar's envoy Mr Crawford greeted them was permitted only one other person : the owner of the house, Master John Dimmock. For although *lion-*

hunter had been Ludovic d'Harcourt's epithet for their host, he was much more than that. Now in his sixties, and older by ten years than the other two members of the commission, John Dimmock had spent the better part of the two previous reigns as royal agent on the Continent, with the care of buying provisions and levying soldiers. And the provisions he had been buying were the munitions of war. If the Queen's Council were to decree that the Tsar should have what he asked for, Master John Dimmock was the man who would supply it. The house in Fenchurch Street had not been lightly chosen.

Nor were Petre of Oxford and Thirleby of Cambridge, both practised in civil and canon law; both experienced in negotiations at home and in embassies overseas also since the reign of King Henry. The French had complained of Sir William Petre during the haggling over Boulogne six years ago : *We had gained the last two hundred thousand crowns without hostages, had it not been for that man who said nothing.*

He said nothing now, listening to the man Crawford embark on his preamble. He had found him cordial, which was to be expected, and also a man of address, which he had been warned about. The exposition was brief and also lucid : it dealt with the geography of Russia and the nature of her government, with her income and her natural resources, and with the measures now being taken to lead the whole country forward to that prosperity which its states had once enjoyed before the incursion of the Tartars. It described explicitly the present threat to the nation's security, and the steps the Voevoda Bolshoia had taken to counter them. It then proceeded to make the two obvious points on which the Russian case rested : that in order to trade successfully, Russia must have stability. And that in pushing the Tartars from her borders, she would be performing a service for the whole of Christendom, and particularly for those countries opposed to Turkey, who held the Tartars in vassalage.

Petre, who had a pain in his stomach, wished it was time to eat. However, so far, so good. Behind him he could hear the scrivener's pen squeaking, and he hoped he had put down, and accurately, all the facts and figures Crawford had just given them. It was unusual, to say the least of it, to be quite so frank. Whether it was naïveté or the exact opposite, he was not quite yet sure. It was certainly an extremely large army, and well organized, so far as one could gather. Thirleby, beside him, said, 'You are to be commended, Mr Crawford, on what you and the Tsar before you have achieved already. Two of your Tartar settlements have been disbanded, I gather, and you have already launched attacks on the third.'

'It is the third which concerns us,' Lymond said. 'It is so placed, as I have said, that it is difficult for an army of any size to overwhelm it. On the other hand these Tartars can, and do, send raids up to and into Moscow itself. May I remind you also that they dwell on the borders of Turkey. Even if we exterminate the Crimean Tartars, Turkey is always a threat. More so now, when her attention is no longer occupied with the Persian wars. A Russia overrun by Turks, as Hungary was, is not something, I imagine, that England would favour, however great the distance between us.'

The Bishop said, 'The Queen's grace would indeed be desolate were such a thing to happen. Although, to be selfish, it would be pleasing to see Turkey occupied in something other than aiding our enemies the French.'

'You must weigh that,' Lymond said, 'against the disadvantages should Turkey obtain a foothold in the Baltic.' He did not pause, Petre noticed, to register the hit but proceeded in the same conversational tone. 'I am under no illusions about your own difficulties here. Poland and Sweden have already lodged formal objections against any proposal to supply us with arms. The Tsar has made no secret in the past of his wish to win back the land on the west of his borders. There has already been fighting in Sweden. If Russia obtained a firmer hold on the Baltic through conquest, the Hanseatic towns would have cause to protest: Antwerp would be rightly disturbed.'

Sir William Petre removed his hand from the front of his doublet. 'And so should we,' he said dryly. 'There would be no need for shipments from St Nicholas Bay if Russia were to begin trading directly through the Baltic.'

'And this trade with Russia is important to you,' Lymond said. 'As, of course, it is to the Tsar. It is five years since the wool trade began to decline. We all know how the new discoveries have taken shipping away from the Baltic, and how your markets there are being affected also by war. Russia has given you a new outlet for trade and a new use for your ships since the fishing fleet dwindled. The Company will increase its fleet as it prospers, and hence the number of ships and trained seamen which the Queen may call on at need. The Navy, I am told, would not be displeased at the prospect. Already the Company is providing cheap cable and timber; it is patient in the matter of loans; it is financing exploration which may open Cathay before you, with promise of treasure far exceeding that of New Spain. And further, at this . . . confused station in the nation's affairs, the success of the leading merchants in London would continue to support and uphold the Crown at a time when goodwill is perhaps as precious as money.'

'I wonder,' said Sir William Petre, 'if I understand you aright. You desire the Queen's grace, notwithstanding the protests of her neighbours, to provide you with the wherewithal to make war, or we forfeit our trade with you and have our explorations curtailed by the Tsar? It seems, whether he knows it or not, that your Tsar has the Golden Horde within his gates once again, throwing aside peace and prosperity for a mirage. If that is the case, sir, we have nothing more to say to one another.' And he laid his hand on his papers.

Outside the door something clinked, as it might be a dish on a tray. Lymond said, 'You must tell me, of course, if you wish to renounce your trading agreement, and we can at least avoid wasting your time or mine any longer. Mr Dimmock, is that your intention?'

The door opened and the smell of food entered the room. Mr Dimmock, remembering without surprise that he had informed Mr Crawford only yesterday of Sir William's poor stomach and its need of constant replenishment, said, 'It is not the Company's intention, sir, but in these matters we must be ruled, as you know, by higher policy.'

'Then,' said Lymond, 'perhaps, after a break for refreshment, we should consider what those matters of higher policy are.'

It was remarkable, Sir William thought, truly remarkable what a difference to the temper a morsel of food could bring about. He remembered the other day attending a long and devoted conference between the Queen and her Cardinal Pole, while still awaiting the Bull to confirm him in possession of all his monastery lands. The Queen had forgiven him, he now believed, the service he had performed for her father in suppressing the monasteries. It had left him with a good thirty-six thousand acres in Devonshire alone. But he still felt the knife in his stomach when he thought of the dangers.

Thirleby, on the other hand, had changed coat quite as often and appeared to feel nothing at all. His only great disappointment had been to miss the Lord Chancellorship when Gardiner died. The Queen had suggested it but King Philip, he knew, had objected. He wondered if the Tsar's envoy knew that. He was extremely surprised to discover how much the fellow did know. It was usual for an envoy from one of the less worldly quarters of Europe to state his case and then reiterate it against all opposition, with whatever weight of threat or financial blandishment could be added, until one side or the other began to concede, and an adjusted agreement was somehow thrashed out. It always took a long time.

He did not think this was going to take a long time, because this fellow not only knew what he wanted: he had thought through the English objections. Disconcerting. Agreeable, even, since argument was one's business. He thought of the patient hours with Nepeja and fully understood, even more than the Company, precisely why the Tsar of Russia had entrusted this errand to this man.

After the break, it was the English objections they began with. Petre let the Bishop take the lead, while he gazed around at the books. He thought he saw a *De republica*, but it couldn't be. Pole had once spent two thousand gold pieces trying to trace that in Poland. He behaved, as he often did, as if he were not listening.

'Since you speak of Sweden,' said the Bishop of Ely, 'you may well know the consequences of your fighting there last year. The harvest suffered. No Swedish corn has come to Brussels and bread has failed, so that no armies can be mustered. No men may gather anywhere until the new harvest is reaped, and wheat meal sold last winter, sir, at forty-six shillings the quarter, so that our women laid their newborn babes in the streets, unable to nurture them while you were sailing at your ease upon this embassy.'

'I beg to say,' said Lymond, 'that I cannot recall standing in so many cornfields: perhaps some other conflicts took place in Holland and Brittany as well. Your point, however, is taken. And at this moment the Tsar should be receiving an ambassador from Sweden in his turn, suing for peace between our nations. Provided Russia is strong and firm, as she showed herself to be last summer, this peace will continue, and your corn will be safe. Meanwhile Sweden may upbraid you, but she cannot march upon you.'

'She can, however, cancel her commercial treaties,' Dimmock said.

'It is unlikely, because they are to her advantage. But she may do so,' agreed Lymond. 'It is for you to decide how severe a blow this could be. It was a risk you also took, I imagine, when you launched your present trading agreement with Russia. It may reassure everyone to remember that Lithuania has no standing army and is unlikely to resort to force, particularly when it would mean depleting her Russian frontiers.'

It was time to interfere. 'On the other hand,' said Sir William Petre, 'it may encourage an alliance between Poland and Lithuania and Livonia, and Livonia belongs to the order of Teutonic Knights which have long been the special concern of the Emperor, and therefore of King Philip.'

'Except,' said Lymond, 'that thirty years ago the Order's Master repudiated the Pope and turned Lutheran. And I am told that both Poland and Lithuania are being pushed by the Czech Brethren towards Protestantism, while the Lithuanian lords have come to think Calvinism fashionable. It is not a fever which the Queen presumably would like to see spread. In fact, my Tsar extracted an undertaking three years ago from Livonia that they would make no alliance with Poland, and he is at present in a position to enforce it. He is not a friend, as you may know, to the Roman Church, but neither will he allow other faiths to spread within his borders.'

'You have said that Russia is making a peace, on her own terms, with Sweden,' Petre said. 'You have said that, given arms, she can secure herself from attack from the Tartars and from the group of countries inclined to Protestantism on the west. You have not told us what the Tsar's own ambitions are towards these last two groups. Do you expect us to believe that, given the chance, he will not force a way through Livonia into the Baltic? Or do you wish us to believe that, given the chance, he will send his armies, suitably fortified, into Turkey?'

One did not judge by question and answer. One judged by the tone of the voice and the speed of the breathing; by the unexpected move of a foot or the flick of an eyelid. Petre knew he was watched, and he watched in turn, and saw nothing but an excellent mind operating with perfect serenity. Lymond said, 'Under no circumstances whatever, while I am Voevoda Bolshoia, will Russia send an army to Turkey. If you will think of what I have already told you, you will see that this is impossible, and if I were to promise it, I should be quite unworthy of my position, or else stupidly deceitful. We shall drive out the Tartars, and we shall destroy Turkish prestige and the supporting armies they send at the same time. But that is all I can promise. That, and the fact that we shall resist any invasion by Turkey to the last stone and the last man.

'On the West, my answer is as plain as I can make it. These lands belonged to the Tsar. Their loss has meant the loss of an outlet which we sorely need. I cannot pretend that the Tsar has forgotten this, but he sees daily, with the return of your ships, how this loss may be repaired, or partly compensated for, by this new link by the north with your country. I am therefore empowered to give you, and therefore the three nations of Poland, Lithuania and Livonia, a guarantee. My tenure of office in Russia is to last for five years: I hope longer. But I shall promise you, here and now, that for these five years I shall not send an army or permit an army to be sent against any one of these three countries, provided that in their turn they make no move to attack me or the Tsar.'

There was a brief silence. Then Petre said, 'Can you make such a promise? I have Master Chancellor's report on this man. He is a fickle ruler, Mr Crawford. Were he to change his mind, I would not give a fig for your contract, for five years or indeed for five minutes.'

'But,' said Lymond, 'I have the army.'

'So long as you live,' the Bishop said bluntly.

Lymond smiled. 'It is another risk you must weigh in the balance. I can only say that, fully trained and appointed, this army under its junta will be capable, with or without me, of keeping its undertaking. And that you must consider that the life of the Tsar, in that country, is exposed to quite as much danger as mine.'

'And after five years?' John Dimmock said heavily.

'After five years,' Lymond said, 'we should offend no one, because we should be self-supporting, and need no country's help. You find it profitable to trade with us now, when we are underdeveloped and backward. You will find it ten times as profitable, whatever other outlets we have, when we are thriving. You fear, perhaps, the rise of a new power in the east, where you already have troubles enough with the competing claims of the Empire and France, of the Pope and the German states and Turkey. I can only say that these will change: that the Emperor has abdicated and that the fate of the Empire is not at the moment secure: that Suleiman is old and Turkey may not always remain the power; that she has been the secular power of the Pope is also in question. Affairs change; power shifts. You cannot stop it happening. And I should like you to believe that if you exercise your veto, and keep Muscovy in the backwater where she has fallen, it will not serve your immediate ends, and it may bring about an explosion out of her ignorance and poverty and resentment which your descendants will have cause to regret.'

The Bishop of Ely was unmoved by the thought of his descendants. 'Should we send hackbuts and teachers to the Gold Coast, so that the natives may greet us in Latin when we go to buy pepper?'

It was a mistake. Lymond looked at Sir William Petre and Sir William heaved a brief sigh and said, 'As I am sure Mr Crawford is aware, we sent shiploads of pikes and armour to the Gold Coast with Wyndham, only five years ago. It was less a matter of education, it must be said, than of securing our trade there against other competition.'

'In spite of the complaints of Portugal,' Lymond said. 'Perhaps, Sir William, we have covered sufficient ground for one day. There is the list of men and materials which my Tsar would wish you to send him. The profit to the Muscovy Company will be comparable to the profit they would be prepared to accept on the highest grade of their cloth. I propose that a thousand pounds of corn powder should yield the same profit as one piece of double-grain velvet; and that the same amount of serpentine powder should equate to one piece of a pile and a half, the rates for the rest to be settled between us. I am at your disposal at any time : perhaps your secretary would advise me when you wish to continue the discussion.'

It was the kind of list Petre had expected, if a little more specific than he had hoped : 3,500 hackbuts; 1,000 pistolets; 500 lb matches; 100,000 lb saltpetre; 3,000 corselets; 2,000 morions; 3,000 iron caps; 8,000 lances; 9,000 lb corn powder; 60 cwt sulphur; 52 fodders of lead. And the trained men one would also expect : ironfounders and engineers and gunners, physicians and apothecaries, printers, mathematicians; shipwrights.

Petre took the list and rose, Thirleby with him. 'As you say, we shall place this before our colleagues and return. You are assiduous, Mr Crawford, in the service of your master.' He bent an inquiring gaze, not ill-humoured, on the other man, twenty years younger, now standing before him with Mr Dimmock. 'Your own country of Scotland then holds no attraction for you? I thought perhaps you were bent on repeating the great alliance between Scotland and Russia and Denmark, which was to result in the crushing of Sweden.'

Lymond did not smile in return, nor turn the matter as Petre expected. 'I have had offers from that quarter, certainly,' Lymond said. 'But, so far. I have not been tempted.'

With an effort which contorted his stomach again, Sir William Petre refrained from looking at the Bishop. But outside on his horse, riding through the streets with his thirty velvet-dressed followers, he looked at Thirleby all right, and said with feeling, '*My God!*'

'Yes. It was a threat,' the Bishop said, 'to make all other threats pale into insignificance. The question is, how far does he mean it?'

*

Behind them, Daniel Hislop put his head round Lymond's door and said, 'Yes, my lord? You wanted to see me, my lord?'

'Come in and shut the door and stop being vivacious,' Lymond said, without looking at him. Dimmock had gone. His papers, scattered over the table, had been gathered together and he was putting them away in his cabinet : Danny caught sight of glassware and licked his lips, audibly. 'No,' Lymond said.

'But it went well?' said Danny.

'Well for whom?' Lymond said. 'It went according to plan. I want your report on the Vannes affair, please.'

He had shut the cabinet door, and locked it. Instead of sitting again, he stayed by the cabinet, tossing the key a little, idly, in his hand. He looked perfectly fresh, which was more than Petre and Thirleby had done. A clever bastard. Danny said, 'Unless Peter Vannes lands off the south coast in a rowing boat, we'll know as soon as he sets foot in England. I have men at Dover and Canterbury and Gravesend and Greenwich. And if it's humanly possible, they'll get his papers from him. It cost me a fortune. That is, it cost you a fortune. But if the Queen gets those papers and finds you've been corresponding with her sister and Courtenay, I suppose it will cost you your neck. It's a pity we couldn't take action earlier. We might have had Vannes waylaid in Venice or after.'

'I am hoping,' Lymond said, 'that Hercules Tait has done precisely that. He was under orders to do so, if anything happened to Courtenay. The double precautions are simply because it has become doubly important. It now seems that Mistress Somerville has implicated herself.'

'With Courtenay? Deceased?' Danny said.

'With the lady Elizabeth. Alive,' Lymond said. 'Through the Lennoxes' efforts. They are merely attempting to control my movements : a popular occupation.'

'They want you out of the country?' Danny said, speculating generously. And as Lymond threw the key, with a sudden sharp gesture, on his bed, Danny said, 'I simply love having secrets from Adam and Ludo, but I *am* risking my fair neck in the Cause. You are supposed to supply me with some basic information, if not to inspire me. Actually, I should love to be inspired. Why don't we like the Lennoxes?'

'Because they talk too much,' Lymond said. 'What are Blacklock and d' Harcourt doing?'

'Blacklock, Adam, is drawing maps,' Danny said. 'Having been offered the position of cartographer with the Muscovy Company at twenty pounds per annum when you have departed, and having accepted with alacrity. D'Harcourt, Ludo, has got a new woman at Smithfield. Neither of them is likely to burst in on us.'

'And you?' Lymond said. He did not, to Danny's regret, address him is *Hislop, Daniel*.

'I,' said Danny, 'am risking my neck for Philippa Somerville. I suppose. When your divorce comes along, may I court her?'

'You will have to discuss the matter,' Lymond said, 'with a number of other gentlemen, including one Austin Grey who may even fight you. As a reward for . . . what is your principal characteristic, would you say?'

'Treacherousness,' said Danny, gloriously.

'That,' said Lymond pleasantly, 'is everyone's principal characteristic. As a reward for bloody persistence, you may know that the Lennoxes have threatened Philippa if I leave the country. They may do it, it seems in two ways. One is by implicating her in my downfall, which is what you are contriving to prevent. The other is by accusing her of trading information to Scotland, which I hope the Queen Dowager is contriving to prevent. There is an inheritance which Margaret Lennox wants very badly. The Queen, I trust, is going to offer her a Chancery suit provided she exculpates Philippa in writing from any suspicion of treachery.'

'But I thought,' Danny said, 'that you and the Queen Dowager of Scotland were no longer on visiting terms? Have you written to her?'

'No,' Lymond said.

'Then——' said Danny, and cut it off, because he knew now where Lymond had written. There was only one person in Scotland who both knew Philippa Somerville and stood well enough with the Queen Dowager to persuade her to take part in the stratagem, and that was Lymond's elder brother, Lord Culter. Who at Edinburgh had knocked Lymond clean out of his senses.

Daniel Hislop, in whose being a mad curiosity flourished at the expense of his undoubted acumen, said simply, 'Christ! What did you say?'

Francis Crawford turned, and looked at him; and Danny's smile became suddenly very pretty, if a trifle rigid. 'I doubt,' said Lymond dryly, 'if it would inspire you.'

*

Sir William Petre took occasion to call on Cardinal Pole and ask him if he had discovered the Cicero he was looking for: Cardinal Pole, who shared his interest in rare books, admitted that he had not. Several days after that, Sir William and the Bishop called again to hold soothing talks with the Muscovite Ambassador Osep Nepeja, and to pass directly from there to another part of the house, where they continued their rather more interesting discussions with the Tsar's other envoy, Mr Crawford.

The grounds for negotiation this time were slightly more practical, and had to do with the very real obstacles in the way of supplying either men or material of the kind the Tsar wanted in these ominous days of impending war. While making this perfectly clear, it had to be admitted that, first, the current truce between France and the Empire was still, officially, unbroken, and that, secondly, although there was talk of war, informed opinion stated that war could not possibly occur until after the harvest, or June at the earliest. Which argued that since England – of course – was neither at war nor about to go to war, the lowering of her own stocks of weapons and powder was undesirable, but not completely out of the question, provided they could be replenished.

But that, of course, was a different story. For gunpowder and sulphur, as Mr Crawford surely knew, were imported to England from Antwerp. And the Low Countries, of course, were conserving every ounce of munitions against the feared counterattack by the French in the summer. Permission would never be given by King Philip's advisers in Brussels.

Discussion, becoming speculative, lingered round the possibility that the Tsar, supplied with hackbuts and morions and lances, would feel that England had responded sufficiently. This was countered, quite as delicately, by the assurance that the Tsar would understand all England's problems: none better. But that the less secure her frontiers, the less security Russia could offer her traders. Which left Sir William Petre and Mr John Dimmock with the prospect of explaining to their fellow members of the Muscovy Company why their privileges were being curtailed. Not because of the whim of the Grand Duke of Muscovy. But because King Philip needed the powder for his forthcoming war on the Pope. . . .

'Unless,' Lymond said at this point, 'the Council cared

491

to leave this particular aspect in Mr Dimmock's most able hands?'

Murmuring, Sir William expressed the opinion that the conference might well break up for further individual discussions. Through the years until his son's marriage, the Emperor Charles had made many attempts to prevent the export from the Low Countries to England of war materials needed for his own continuing wars. And for the further excellent reason that the English, having bought his supplies, were not above reselling them to the French to use promptly in battle against him.

Through the years, also, the English had found many ways of circumventing this embargo, and none better than Master John Dimmock. Curious transactions took place between the owners of different warehouses : solid citizens of Amsterdam bought sulphur from solid citizens of Antwerp and resold it; and, mysteriously, hired ships from Antwerp were to be found unloading barrels of gunpowder at Harwich. The captain and searchers at Gravelines were rarely sober for work, so often were they sought out and banqueted, and each New Year's Day, the captain received twelve ells of black velvet and his customars eight ells apiece of black cloth to encourage them to leave their gates open.

But that, of course, was before the fortunes of England were linked to those of the Empire through the marriage of the Queen to the Emperor's son. As Lymond, bidding them all farewell, assured them that he fully understood. At the same time, he pointed out that he believed the Court was moving to Greenwich for Passion Week, and that if a cargo was to be collected, the time remaining for discussion was not therefore very great. . . .

Sir William Petre and the Bishop of Ely did not speak to each other on this occasion, when riding home. The book on the shelves, Sir William had taken occasion to check, *was* the *De republica* of Cicero. Mr Crawford had noticed his interest, and, taking it down, had let him look at it. 'A fine copy, I think. I bought it from a man called Pierre Gilles for fifteen hundred gold pieces,' Lymond said. 'Or was it a thousand? I really cannot remember.'

'Well?' said Danny Hislop, poking his head round the door again afterwards.

'Well enough,' Lymond had answered. 'I give them three days.'

They came back in two, with the regretful refusal of her Majesty of England to license the sale to the Tsar of all Russia, through the Muscovy Company, of the arms and munitions of war he had requested, together with the services of known men of skill.

'The Queen,' Sir William said, looking at the ceiling, 'is sensible of the goodwill of her cousin the Tsar, and would like nothing better than to help him in his present desire for the munitions of war. But the needs of her country, and in particular of her dear husband Prince Philip, at present preclude it.'

He looked at Lymond. There was something faintly inquiring about the look. Meeting it formally, Lymond said, 'It is a matter of regret to me also. And, I am sure, to the Muscovy Company.'

'Ah. Yes,' said Sir William. 'The Muscovy Company has been much in our minds.' There was a short pause, which no one filled. Then Sir William said, 'In Master Dimmock, as you may know, the Company has an energetic and able member who has already proved in the past his ability to conjure men and munitions from the air. It may be that he could do so again. If it were possible for such a thing to be done, without depleting the Queen's stocks in the Tower and without, of course, distressing her royal spouse and those of his advisers by bringing the matter unnecessarily to their attention, the Council, I must tell you, would feel they had no cause to complain.'

'I see,' Lymond said. He looked to his left. 'Master Dimmock. Is it possible to supply the items on the Tsar's list on those terms?'

Nothing of this, clearly, was novel to Master Dimmock, but he preserved the fiction nobly. 'I see no reason why not,' he said.

'And in reasonable secrecy?' the Bishop of Ely inquired. 'You understand; none of this arrangement is directly the Council's concern, and none of it, therefore, may be set out by the Council in writing. You supply these goods, if you supply them, from your own sources and at your own risk. If King Philip's advisers discover it, we shall not be able to contravene any veto he will impose.'

'I think,' said Master Dimmock, 'that we can promise to take all reasonable precautions. Mr Crawford, if you wish to proceed, then the Muscovy Company will help you.'

'I was sure you would,' said Lymond gravely.

It was over. Master Dimmock served them all with his very best wine, to celebrate the occasion, and Sir William went off with the *De republica* packed in his box, and the prospect of a thousand gold pieces' profit to be made from the Cardinal. After they had gone, Lymond stood for a while, looking at the empty place where the Cicero had rested on his book-laden shelves, and then locked his papers away and, banging the door, ran downstairs to call on Nepeja.

There, rejoicing had already broken out: the room seemed to contain half the two hundred members of the Muscovy Company and the wine had been round three times already. Master Nepeja's business had also prospered at last, and on the desk by the window lay the last draft of the league and articles of amity concluded between the kingdoms of England and Russia, ready to be copied and confirmed under the Great Seal of England. He was free to see to his merchanting and to sail.

He was just sober enough to rise to his feet when Lymond came into the room, and then, after the first frowning moments, to realize what Lymond was saying. The second part of the treaty was in operation also. The Privy Council had acceded, in secret, to the Tsar's other demands.

The implications of that were beyond Osep Nepeja's interest or understanding. The talks were over, and without prejudicing his or anyone's trade. He flung his arms round the unexcited person of the Voevoda Bolshoia and scavenged him like a bass broom with his beard. The Voevoda surprisingly did not give way more than a steel fence before him, although he did exchange the greeting, smiling, in the Russian fashion. The sound of his round Russian speech, after two hoarse weeks of Rob Best, made tears spring to the Ambassador's eyes and he blew his nose, belching. Lymond left as soon as he could.

'Well?' said Danny at supper. There was no news of Peter Vannes and his casket from Venice. There had been no further threats from the Lennoxes: no communication from the Queen. No word from Philippa, who was preparing with the rest to leave London for a week on the 15th. King Philip's married sister the Duchess of of Parma and his widowed cousin the Duchess of Lorraine had arrived at Westminster and were to stay at Greenwich for Easter as well: in order, it was said, to persuade the lady Elizabeth to marry the Duke of Savoy. Since everyone knew that the pretty Duchess of Lorraine was not one of Queen Mary's favourites, a gloomy Easter was anticipated.

Danny said, 'Well?' and as Lymond did not respond, he tried again. 'Sir? Now the ships can be loaded, the Company is talking of sailing for Russia by the end of April, or early May at the latest. What if Vannes hasn't arrived when you sail?'

'An interesting thought,' Lymond said. He was not, Danny thought, looking quite so carefree as on previous occasions; or perhaps had merely less patience than usual for the bastards of Bishops. Lymond went on, 'I am not, if that is your point, contemplating taking Mistress Philippa with me to Russia, much as you would adore to witness the consequences.'

'What, then?' Danny said. 'He may be held up indefinitely.'

'Somehow,' Lymond said, 'I don't think so. I think Peter Vannes will arrive, with papers or without them, before the Ambassador and I leave for Russia.'

'And me,' Danny said. He gazed at his commander's occupied eyes. 'Why? Why should you think so? A premonition? Mr Dee's crystal ball?' He flinched as Lymond looked at him at last. 'I'm just persistent by habit,' said Danny.

But Lymond, changing his mind, had decided to answer him. 'For one inadequate reason,' he said. 'Today, the English Privy Council agreed to all the Tsar's demands for skilled men and armaments.

'I know. Mind, voice, study, power and will, Is only set to love thee, Philip, still. Hooray,' Danny Hislop said.

'Hooray,' Lymond agreed. His face, older than his years, was not accommodating and his eyes, too brightly coloured for a man, were perfectly bleak. 'Except that when these talks started, I had no hopes of this concession, and there was no reason why it should ever have been granted. Why did they grant it? Why? Why? *Why?*

To which, if the Voevoda Bolshoia did not know, Danny Hislop could venture no answer.

CHAPTER NINE

In April, Sir Henry Sidney returned to London to obtain money and arms to make a second incursion against the Scottish colonizers in Ulster. On his way to Whitehall he called at Penshurst to see his two small children Philip and Margaret, and to learn from his wife the latest news of the Court. When he left, he took Nicholas Chancellor with him.

After what he had learned from his wife, his reception by Heath and Petre and the rest was no great surprise : it seemed that the supply of arms was at present even shorter than the surplus of money. Bearing this discovery with him, more in rueful admiration than anger, Sir Henry descended one bright Monday in April on the London home of old Lady Dormer, and demanded an introduction to Philippa Somerville's husband.

It was the sole invitation in that macabre three weeks of celebration that Lymond accepted with any willingness. Received at Court and released from his ambassadorial duties, Osep Grigorievich Nepeja was free at last to plunge over the beard into the revelries arranged by the Muscovy Company, feasting and banqueting in other men's homes, and seeing without stint the unrivalled wonders of London.

Muscovite Ambassadors, outwith the control of their Tsars, were not encouraged to view the marvels of other lands and comment upon them. But after weeks endured chained to the conference table, Master Nepeja was unable to resist it. He was shown all over Whitehall and Westminster. He saw St Paul's Cathedral, the Tower and the Guildhall of London. He viewed, as the Spaniards had all done before him, the Round Table of the enchanted King Arthur, with the names of the twelve knights still written where they used to sit round it.

The Lord Mayor gave him a banquet, with five Knights Aldermen and five other Aldermen and many notable merchants of the Muscovy Company. Master Nepeja attended it in a gown of rich tissue, his undergown being of purple velvet embroidered, and the edge of his hat set with pearls and other fine jewels, while his horse trappings were crimson velvet embroidered with gold, and his bridle gorgeously sewn. Those who lined the streets and admired him were not to know that the horse was a present, or that the rich cloth of tissue, the cloth of gold raised with crimson velvet, the crimson and purple velvet in grain, the crimson damask and the damask purpled of which his clothes and those of his nine servants were cut, were all gifts sent to his rooms by Her Majesty.

Nor, from a distance, did they as yet show much signs of soiling. Master Nepeja hoped, when the time came to hand them back to their donor, that she would take the length of wear into her reckoning.

Francis Crawford, with clothes of his own and money to supplement them, did the same polite rounds without enthusiasm, in between arranging, with great efficiency, for the four ships now loading in London to be suitably freighted with his special cargo. It was there that he came across Tony Jenkinson conferring with John Buckland his Master, and Buckland introduced the two men.

Jenkinson showed him over the *Primrose,* his flagship. At two hundred and forty tons, she was a third as big again as the *Edward Bonaventure;* and the *John Evangelist,* the *Anne* and the *Trinity* were all larger than the little *Esperanza* and *Confidentia,* and even than the *Philip and Mary.* And Jenkinson, too, who was to succeed Richard Chancellor; who was to try the overland route to Cathay which had been Richard Chancellor's dream, and whom Richard Chancellor had commended, proved to be young and dark haired and vigorous, with the kind of driving curiosity which had already taken him to Germany and the Low Countries, the Alps and Italy, Piedmont and France, Spain and Portugal, Rhodes, Malta and the Levant, Sicily, Cyprus and Candia, Greece and Turkey, Galilee and Jerusalem, Algiers, Bona and Tripoli.

They should have met long since, he and Lymond. Jenkinson had been conferring for weeks with Best and Buckland and with the other three men from St Mary's: in several sessions at the house of John Dee they had barely missed one another. It was not all entirely by accident. Lymond did not greatly wish to meet Tony Jenkinson, and although, once introduced, the younger man's enthusiasm overbore any restraint on his part – did Mr Crawford know that they had been in the Levant at exactly the same time? how strange that he and his

friends had not met in Aleppo! was it true that Dragu
Rais's mistress was now living in Moscow? – Lymon
left before long. It was coincidence that the first perso:
he met on entering Lady Dormer's parlour by invitatio:
next morning should again be Jenkinson, and the second
Richard Chancellor's younger son Nicholas.

There was no doubt who he was, even before Lad
Dormer led him forward to introduce him: he was th
image of Christopher. And he was staring at Mr Craw
ford as his brother had looked at the Voevoda Bolshoia
one night long ago, in Güzel's beautiful house in Voro
biovo. Nicholas said, 'I am told, sir, that you swam afte
my father,'

There was no escape from the tasteless situation. Besid
him was his hostess, old Lady Dormer; beyond her Jenkin
son; and behind him Ludovic d'Harcourt, whom he ha(
also been asked to bring. Lymond said, 'We all did &
great deal of swimming, and some of us were lucky.'

He paused, and the voice of his child-bride said prosaically, 'If you are wondering who enlightened him,]
did. Robert Best told us the story. Nicholas, Emma i:
asking for you.'

'But——' said Nicholas uncertainly.

'Emma is asking for you,' said Philippa firmly. 'You
can come back at suppertime.' And to Mr Crawford, a:
the boy disappeared, Philippa said, 'It is really not easy
to receive someone's thanks, but you must make the effort.
Is this the man who doesn't like eagles?'

Ludovic d'Harcourt, smiling, took her hand. 'What . . .?
Robert Best?' Lymond said.

'No. John Buckland,' said Philippa. She grinned back
at Ludovic d'Harcourt. 'It was you who buried the Tartar
girl?'

'Philippa . . .' said Lady Dormer with a perfect and
natural kindliness. 'I think the gentleman would prefer
to enter and sit. Where is Henry . . .? Ah, there you are.
Mr Crawford, Henry; and Mr d'Harcourt. This, gentlemen, is my dear Jane's uncle, Henry Sidney.'

Courtier, soldier, patron of the arts and sciences, con-
queror in single combat of James Mack O'Neil and Vice
Treasurer and General Governor of all the King's and
Queen's Revenues in Ireland, Sir Henry Sidney rose to
his feet from behind a red velvet chair with silk tassels

and said, 'I beg your pardon. I am delighted to meet you. Aunt Jane, I've dropped an eye on your beautiful floor.'

'Then pick it up!' commanded old Lady Dormer. 'I will not have my maids tormented by your wandering eyes. Mr Crawford, you will help him.'

Mr Crawford, exquisite in a high-collared jerkin with hand-ruffs, dropped neatly on his hunkers at the other man's side and said, 'One of Master Dee's contrivances, do I gather? Is this what you are looking for?'

Sir Henry received the round painted glass with relief. 'He gets them from France. It's not worth my life to mislay them. Now.'

'Over here,' Philippa said. Standing just inside the porch of the room, she had her arm round a great feathered owl. Four times life-size at least, it reached as high as the neat, stiffened pads at her shoulders. The great dish of its face, lacking an eye, gazed at the company soulfully.

'My . . . stars,' said Ludovic d'Harcourt. Sir Henry fitted the eye in its place.

'Now,' said Philippa, and stepping aside, let the owl go. There was a rumbling sound, and the owl started to move. It advanced upon them across Lady Dormer's small Turkey rugs; it lifted its wings. Its eyes, headily beginning to spin, gave off intermittent beams of red and mysterious light. Its beak opened, and a strident call, earsplitting and monotonous, attacked the eardrums of everyone in the room. Lymond, on his feet, slid a table out of its way: Jenkinson, jumping, removed a cushion. The call wavered and sank; the revolving light halted, the wings dropped to rest. The owl, creaking, came to a sudden sharp halt, and one of its eyeballs fell out.

'Damn!' said Henry Sidney, dissatisfied. 'I beg your pardon, Aunt Jane. Now where did it roll to?'

They played with it until they were called in to dinner, by which time the shadow of Richard Chancellor had temporarily vanished, even though Nicholas took his place at the board and was kept talking, briskly, by Philippa, while Lady Dormer steered Jenkinson and d'Harcourt to share their reminiscences of Malta. Henry Sidney leaned back while his wine was being poured and said to Lymond, 'I met a friend of yours in Ireland, a man called Phelim O'LiamRoe. You won't remember me in France, during the Northampton embassy. It was six years ago. You were rather occupied, I gather, in chastising the Lennoxes.'

'You know the story, then,' Lymond said.

'I know why the Lennox family dislike you quite so much, yes. I am glad you came back from Russia,' said Henry Sidney. 'Whatever befalls, I am sure you will handle it capably. But I was afraid for Mistress Philippa.' He paused. 'I have often wondered if Diccon Chancellor told you of the threat to his own life.'

'The heresy charge?' Lymond said. 'No. Or not until we were already on the way home. He warned me of my own danger if I stayed on in Russia. In fact, if we must speak of it, he saved me from one attempt on my life. But you know him better than I do.'

It was difficult to continue against a resistance so adamant. Henry Sidney said, 'The sledge races: I know. I have had it all at second hand from Rob Best. Did you ever discover who paid your captain to kill you? It is a matter which troubles me. The English colony over there is very small. A man who would murder a fellow countryman for money is a danger to the whole Muscovy Company.'

'And you wish him disvisored. Yes, I know who it was,' Lymond said. 'And I promise you justice, once I have proof of it.'

Henry Sidney could read nothing in his profile; nothing in the hands dealing with his knife and his food. Sidney said, 'Will you not tell me of your suspicions? Or at least Best and Jenkinson and Buckland, before you arrive back in Russia? It is Jenkinson and Best and Killingworth who will have to act for the Company, and bring the assassin to justice. Unless . . .' He ceased speaking, his lips pursed.

'Unless either Best or Killingworth is the culprit. Or Richard Grey, your other agent, who was with us at Lampozhnya.' Lymond's voice was perfectly calm. 'If I told you, could you speak of him to your fellow members without betraying yourself? Perhaps you could. But I prefer to be certain. If it reassures you, I believe that he is quite harmless to all except me.'

'Then you will be careful,' Sidney said. 'From what Will Petre tells me, the Tsar cannot afford to lose you. Perhaps you have heard that they have refused my whole order of gunpowder?'

500

'Perhaps,' said Lymond, 'you don't know the right people.'

'Or read the right books,' Sidney said. He turned and, stretching out his arm, lifted something from a table against the window behind him, and laid it beside Lymond's plate. 'I bought it back for you.'

It was the Cicero. For a moment, Lymond sat without touching it, then he lifted his eyes, for the first time, directly to Sidney's. He said, 'But I did not find him.'

'Open it,' Sidney said.

Inside the front cover, two lines of quotation had been added, below Lymond's own name and the name of Pierre Gilles, the first owner. They had nothing to do with the Cicero. One was from Robert Thorne's letter to King Henry VIII: *There is no land uninhabitable or sea unnavigable.* And the other was merely a phrase: *They made the whole world to hang in the air.*

'But you tried,' Sidney said. 'I now wish to speak about owls, and this excellent theory of John Dee's, that a mirror propelled into space at a speed greater than light should be able to reveal all history to us by reflection. M. d'Harcourt, do you favour the prospect of all your lightest actions being subjected to the scrutiny of your grandchildren? I have begun to shed all my vices already. Philippa, when he returns from Spain, you will have to watch your conduct with Don Alfonso.'

'I have to watch it already,' said Philippa gloomily. 'Don Alfonso is the first thing any mirror would pick out; like a cake with periwinkles on it. Have you noticed my hat?'

'I have noticed,' said Henry kindly, 'that you are wearing a sock with a tassel in scarlet. I thought it better not to refer to it. Spanish?'

'Spanish,' said Philippa.

'The Count of Feria,' said Lady Dormer, 'has given my dear Jane a diamond.'

The company murmured its approbation. 'And there you have it,' said Philippa, turning her brown eyes owl-like to Lymond. 'Jane Dormer gets diamonds and I receive socks.'

He turned and looked at her, his face perfectly blank. Then he said, 'Where are you wearing the other one?'

Her eyes, staring at his, were equally expressionless. 'I keep my dowry in it,' she said.

He studied the smart little cap below which, for once, she had allowed her brown hair to hang loose. 'Forgive my scepticism,' he said, 'but is it big enough?'

'My head,' said Philippa, 'does not require a large hat. And a Somerville cranium brings its own dowry. Moscow does not have a monopoly of females with compounding assets.'

'No. The world is full of them,' Lymond said. 'But not usually borne in the head. Robert Best is as good as a play, isn't he? What else has he told you?'

'Why?' said Philippa. 'Shall I be shocked?' She reflected. '*Could* I be shocked?'

'After Suleiman's harem? I should think it unlikely,' Lymond said. 'I was simply afraid you would explain it all too clearly to poor Robert Best. Your wedding night, sweet Philippa, is going to be a revelation to someone.'

'When I wriggle up from the bottom of the bed? Do they do that in—'

'Lady Dormer,' said Lymond, 'is listening to you.'

'She is watching me. She is listening to M. d'Harcourt. Why do you call him M. d'Harcourt? You called Jerott Jerott.'

'I called Jerott a great deal worse than that. His name is Ludovic. You will like him. He doesn't like eagles.'

'Slata Baba? Did you call her Slata or Baba?' Philippa said. 'Or was she exempt, since she couldn't presume on acquaintance?'

Francis Crawford turned to her and laid down his knife. 'Philippa Somerville,' he said. 'Will you kindly take a new sight for your cannon? You see me beaten quite flat to the groundsilling. Try Mr Jenkinson. He may understand Persian love-poetry.'

'With internal rhymes?' Philippa said. 'What about the most copious and elegant language in the world, the Sclavonian tongue? Or is Baida the only man to have ballads sung for him? No odes to the Voevoda Bolshoia?'

'Incantations,' Lymond said. 'Wisdom in the form of counterfeit pearls of dried fish eyes, to accompany the votive offerings.'

'Travelling about in a wheeled cult-vehicle known as St Mary's, to the sound of imprecations. . . . Do I frighten you?' said Philippa.

'Yes,' Lymond said.

'That's odd. I don't frighten Austin Grey. The Lion in Affrik and the Bear in Sarmatia are fierce, but—'

'. . . but translated into a Contrary Heaven, are of less strength and courage. It is not necessary, Mistress Somerville, for the heaven to be quite so contrary. Are you looking forward to Greenwich?'

'No,' Philippa said. 'The Queen has a cold. She isn't appearing in public.'

'And King Philip is arranging to go hunting with the Duchesses of Lorraine and Parma?' Lymond said. 'How is Cardinal Pole treating the delicate problem of King Philip's threats to His Holiness?'

Philippa glanced at Lady Dormer and smiled, while diplomatically lowering her voice. 'As Papal Legate, he publicly failed to give King Philip the formal welcome which was his due. In private, he called on him later to apologize.'

'And the Queen?' Lymond said.

For a moment, Philippa was silent. Then she said, 'The Queen has written to Rome, expressing great regret at the rupture between His Holiness and the King her consort, especially as she had done so much to return England to its devotion to the Church. And she excused herself for giving King Philip her help, as she couldn't do otherwise.'

Lymond said, 'They talk of war when the harvest is in.'

The chatter all round the table covered their words. Lady Dormer, assuming them launched on a battle of words, had not attempted to separate them. Philippa said, 'Sooner than that.'

Lymond gave his attention to the meal. 'Can you tell me?'

She said, 'There is a plot afoot, among the English rebels in France. The English Council know all the circumstances. If . . . the threatened event occurs, the blame will fall on France, whether the King was truly implicated or not. And if that happens, it may move English popular feeling at last towards war.'

'Against the Pope?' Lymond said.

'Against the French. It is the same thing,' said Philippa. 'I am not looking forward to Greenwich. And my advice to anyone with a shipload of munitions would be to sail. To sail quickly, before you are stopped.'

'I shall be gone in three weeks,' Lymond said.

'And I before that,' said Henry Sidney, catching it. 'Aunt Jane, I have an errand. May I steal some of your guests to befriend me?'

His journey was only to Blackfriars, a few minutes down-river from Lady Dormer's. His errand was merely to talk to a man about hangings. And because the place of his appointment was the Office of the Revels and Masques, Mistress Philippa begged to go with him, on a matter, he understood, to do with feathers.

Sir Henry had hoped to have a few minutes' quiet conversation with Mr Crawford. Mr Crawford, perhaps, had hoped the same. But in the event, five of Lady Dormer's dinner guests took leave of her presently and embarked for Blackfriars: Sir Henry and Mr Crawford, Philippa Somerville and Ludovic d'Harcourt and the boy Nicholas Chancellor who had never, he said, been in the Storehouse of the Revels. And since it was a sunny, sparkling day and the company was both gay and congenial, Sir Henry smiled and let affairs take their course.

It was a short journey, and more fateful than any one of them knew. A journey inevitable from the day Francis Crawford was born, and set firm in his stars where already old eyes had distinguished it and younger eyes, also far-seeing, had chosen to ignore and defy it.

Of its significance he himself had no inkling when he set out, relaxed by the company a trifle more than was usually possible; his quilted shirt sleeves white in the sun under his sleeveless green jerkin; his sunlit head sheathed in his high, elegant collar. The two barges rocked at the steps, their four oarsmen waiting, and Philippa's maligned scarlet sock unbent and flew like an ensign in battle as she took her place under the bow hood and settled down, confidentially, beside Lymond. 'I wanted to speak to you.'

He eyed her warily, in the way she had learned to mistrust. 'You aren't devoted to feathers?'

'I can take them,' said Philippa, 'or leave them. I wanted to speak about Lady Lennox and the Angus inheritance. Queen Mary has had a letter from the Queen Dowager of Scotland.'

'Yes?' Lymond said. Sir Henry had stepped into the other barge and Nicholas had followed suit. Ludovic d'Harcourt was still to come.

'The Scottish Queen Dowager says that she has given favourable audience to Dr Laurence Hussey, appointed by the Privy Council at our Queen Mary's insistence to break ground for Lady Lennox's claim to the Angus castles and property in Scotland. And that she has now opened justice to him and given express command that the Chancellery shall be patent to Lady Margaret. That means she is to be permitted a Chancery suit on the matter.'

'I know,' Lymond said. 'In fact, I have, back at Fenchurch Street, a packet I received from the French Ambassador yesterday. It contains a statement sent by Lady Lennox to Scotland, clearing you of all implication in any untoward passage of information between the two countries. I assume you know of the bargain because you are in ceaseless communication with your mother?'

'Yes,' Philippa said; and shook the sock free of her shoulder. Kate *had* told her of that particular bargain. Kate had told her also of the letter from Lymond to Lord Culter, invoking him by his full name and addressing him nowhere as *brother*. Of what had happened at their last meeting, or at Berwick, there had been no mention either : merely the outline of Philippa's present predicament, and the further outline of how Lord Culter, if he so pleased, could help her. And Lymond had signed, omitting pointless civilities, with his surnames.

She did not know, for Kate did not tell her, that there was no answering letter from Richard Crawford. Only the required document, forwarded by the French Ambassador the day before, and a small parcel with Culter's seal on it. And even had she seen what the parcel contained, which was merely a trinket, a crested rose-bush with a single black rose set in silver, she would have been none the wiser.

But Lymond, who did know what it meant, raised his eyebrows at the girl and said, 'So that at least is happily concluded. Was that all you wanted to tell me? I think d'Harcourt is about to step in.'

And Philippa said, 'Oh. I shall tell you later. It's about Michael Surian, the new Ambassador from Venice to England. He came to Court on the 5th . . .Mr d'Harcourt, Sir Henry is calling you.'

'No, I think he's calling you,' Ludovic d'Harcourt said. 'He says if you'll cross to his barge, we can take this one home down river afterwards.' And taking Philippa's place: 'I wanted to talk to you,' Ludovic d'Harcourt said to Lymond.

'About feathers,' said Lymond, his shoulders restfully propped on the cushions. They had begun to move: the grey river wall of the Savoy Palace, green with weed, slid off behind them.

The barge was really too small for d'Harcourt. He stretched his legs, and then folded them under him; then, bumping his cap on the hood, he felt for and straightened it, smoothing the wild, tightly curled hair. He said, 'I hope you'll forgive me. But I heard what you and Sir Henry were discussing at table. You think you know who attacked you in Russia.'

'Well?' said Lymond. He looked, if anything, bored.

The fresh face beside him was grim. 'I know you don't trust me,' d'Harcourt said. 'Probably you don't trust any of us. Since the day we joined you, you've kept us all at our distance, and I don't say I blame you. You talked to Sir Henry as if your killer was bound to be one of the Muscovy Company in Russia.'

'Well?' said Lymond again.

'While you know as well as I do,' said d'Harcourt, 'that it might be one of us.'

'And is it?' said Lymond.

The backs of the rowers, in Sir Henry's bright livery, moved backwards and forwards. Below them swept the rushing noise of the water, and against that, the creak of timber, the grunts of the oarsmen, the faint sounds, of splashing and calling, of talking and hammering, and the loud, raucous cries of the gulls, floating across the whole sparkling river. Two voices, speaking quietly under the muffling hood, were as private as in a stone room in the Tower. Half turning, Ludovic d'Harcourt looked into blue, cold eyes resting upon his, fully open, and he sustained them, though he reddened more than a little, and said, 'It could be. I thought you said that you knew.'

'You think I suspect you?' Lymond said.

Ludovic d'Harcourt looked down. 'You would think that after Malta a man could stomach anything. It isn't so. I couldn't whip a man as you whipped Adam Blacklock. I couldn't cosset that bird, and feed it and fly it as you did, or ignore what you could ignore in the man you called master. I couldn't call men to me across Europe and then gamble their lives as you did, when the

Streltsi attacked us in our first days in Moscow. I couldn't speak to fellow human beings as you do, or deal out unmoved such violent punishments. And I made no secret of it, so that if you suspect me, it is not without cause. Only—'

'You have had a change of heart?' Lymond said dryly.

He sat, a big man, with his hands dangling between his knees, and said, 'It is easy to mock. But you cared for that bloody eagle, and yet you killed it, for a Tartar baby that turned out to be dead already. And at sea . . . there is no disguise that will serve a man on the sea.'

'So? What are you saying?' Lymond said.

'That I want to go back with you to Russia,' said Ludovic d'Harcourt bluntly. 'I shall serve you to the best of my ability. You will be safe from me and I shall protect you against any man wishing to harm you. And if you fear any danger to that girl, I beg you, take her back with you. She is worth . . . I have never encountered her like.'

'Ye Gods : another,' said Lymond staring at him. 'I must introduce you to her excellent, widowed mother, also *multum in parvo* : if you can stomach the Somervilles you can probably even contrive to endure my behaviour without sickening. Do I understand that, in your humble Christian fashion, you are indicating that I should look for the culprit in St Mary's? Now I come to think of it, Fergie Hoddim now and then had a very odd look in his eye.'

And as d'Harcourt shifted uncontrollably, Lymond sat up and added unexpectedly, 'I know. It is easy to mock, and not so easy to make a confession of ill will. As it happens, suspicion lies somewhere else, with a man who had access to my correspondence. But if you are concerned about Philippa Somerville, then you can engage your courts of higher authority in all our interests. Because if anything threatens my liberty in the three weeks now left before sailing, Philippa will also be implicated. And far from being allowed to sail with us to Russia, she may not live to sail anywhere at all.'

Philippa thought, when they stepped out at the River Fleet watergate, that poor Mr d'Harcourt had been receiving a lecture, so subdued and concerned did he look. But Mr Crawford, on the other hand, sparkled, paralysingly bright and sharp as an icicle; and it was only listening to him, with the inner divining ear which the Somervilles bent upon everybody, that Philippa noted that the easiness she had felt for a moment had gone. With a sign and a flip of her sock-hat, Philippa set herself to restore him.

Since the Dissolution, the handsome buildings and gardens of Blackfriars Monastery had been put to many and impious uses. In its heyday, the Emperor Charles V had stayed there more than thirty years before on his State Visit, and a gallery had been built over the Fleet to join it to the Palace of Bridewell, where lived all his accompanying courtiers.

Now, the grass was as green and the apple trees still fruited in summer, but the great hall held an hourglass instead of the tall clocks of Nüremberg, and instead of warming the short Flemish frame of the Emperor, who had wept, last year, turning back to the gates of his palace, the gaping fireplace served to heat the glue-pots and size-pans; to boil the water for sponging and to dry the clay and the paste, the painted boards and the strange moulded figures which the office of the Queen's Revels and Masques had to furnish.

At the door they met Philip Gunter, the sober merchant from Cornhill who supplied Sir Henry with most of his bedding and hangings and who, delivering buckram and bells to the Office, had remained there to speak to Sir Henry. It was, Philippa said, a matter of choosing a tapestry. The two men disappeared and Philippa, aping faintly the custodian of King Arthur's Round Table, led Mr Crawford, Mr d'Harcourt and Nicholas through the door and into the hall of the Revels.

At first, dazzled by the sun, the gloom seemed unrelieved and the smell of horse hoofs and flax oil unbearable. Then it could be seen that sun, of a sort, was entering through the high rows of dim churchly windows, and that the vast fire at one end, spitting coal dust and wood smoke and frying jewels of rosin was barred by the untoward assembly of manifold objects for drying.

On either side of the fire were the benches: long, rough benches with butts of thread on them, and cutting and paring knives, and shears, and pins and bodkins and thimbles, and coils of wire and black chalk and rolls of tinfoil. And paper and ink, and fine pens of swans' quills, and powder for dusting. And nails and cering candles and rubbing brushes. And on shelves over the tables, painters' pots of red lead and yellow ochre and vermilion, and saffron and sap green and dragon red, and a row of wood headblocks for hats, on which some treasonable hand had sketched royal likenesses.

Gum arabic over there. Beside the fire, buckets of glue, thick as cloth at the edges, and painters' paste of thick flour and white wine, reeking gently. And against the wall, stacks of pasteboard with cut buckram long as bolsters leaning beside them, and the painters crawling between on the rushes : Dick and George, the Bosum brothers. Philippa introduced them. John, the property maker. The twenty tailors, crosslegged among the bales of new cloth sent straight from the Queen's own royal wardrobe : 25 yards of red velvet; 15 yards of carnation velvet; 9 yards of purple gold sarsanet, 25 yards of yellow, 49 yards of red, 33 yards of white and 4 of silver. Philippa admired them, and the Yeoman of the Revels, John Holt, called her by name.

'They know you,' said Ludovic d'Harcourt.

'She is the model,' said Lymond, 'for their dragons. What are they preparing for? War with the French?'

Philippa smiled at John Holt. 'A St Mark's Day Masque for the Duchesses. Allmaynes, Pilgrims and Irishmen, with their Incidents. Right, Master Holt?'

'Right, Mistress Philippa,' said the Yeoman. He turned, grinning, to the two men and the boy. 'I don't know how we'd have managed with those Turks, but for Mistress Philippa.'

'Mistress Philippa is excellent at managing Turks,' Lymond said. 'Allmaynes . . . Yes. Irishmen . . . I believe so. But pilgrims? Mistress Philippa, could you manage pilgrims?'

She looked up at him, her brown eyes astonished. 'I start with the Whifflers,' said Philippa, 'and work my way up.'

'Whifflers?' said Ludovic d'Harcourt.

'They march in front of the pilgrimage,' offered Nicholas eagerly. 'And clear the way with wood wands. The wands striking the air make a—'

'Whiffle,' said Philippa gently.

'To make people buffle,' said Lymond, even more gently. 'Unlike hufflers.'

'Who take umbrage too readily,' said Philippa, frowning

at him. She said to Master Holt, 'I arranged with Master Becher the milliner to leave me his drakes' necks.'

'They're there,' Mistress Philippa.' They followed him across to the store racks. Nearing the tall wooden erections, Nicholas saw for the first time how many there were. What seemed at first a thick screen of shelving was in fact a type of rough scaffolding filling a good half of the great hall, and halting just before the clear firelit space where the men worked. Between the long racks the carpenters had left passages, so that moving along and reading all the crabbed labels, you could identify the baskets and hampers and chests; and the mysterious bales wrapped in cloth and the other, towering objects muffled in ticking, whose nature you couldn't even guess at, not on a quick visit, with grown-ups all around you.

'*Drakes' necks?*' Lymond said. He lifted a basket of brass bells in passing and shook it, so that all the tailors looked up. Master Holt, walking heavily in front, hoped the young people weren't going to be any trouble. 'For the pilgrims, the Germans or the Irishmen? What will Mr Becher's ducks do?'

'For a harem,' Philippa said. 'Like Vladimir, who converted your Russia to Christianity. He had, I am reliably told, three thousand five hundred concubines.'

'I should think,' Lymond said, 'Christianity was his only hope of survival.'

Nicholas cried, 'Look! A dragon?'

It was indeed, painted green and red, with a plated mouth and a flax-box beside it. Ludovic d'Harcourt, suddenly entering into the spirit of the thing, picked the box up. 'Gentlemen!' said Master Holt, smiling anxiously. 'Gentlemen, please! The stuff are the Queen's, and strongly inflammable. . . .' Ludovic d'Harcourt tossed the flax-box to Lymond, who tossed it to Nicholas, who gave it to Philippa. She handed it, apologetically, to Master Holt. The procession moved on.

The labels were enchanting. *Cats, to fur a garment,* read Nicholas. *Masks of Covetous Men with Long Noses. A coat for the Ape. Furred Heads for Savage Men.* And bales and bales of cloth of gold and cloth of silver and velvet. Hangings from the King's old timber Houses, to cut down for masques. Crates of old masquing garments for men. Crates of ditto for women. *Antique Head Trimmed About with Changeable and Red Sarsanet . . .*

'Who does that remind you of?' said Lymond.

'*Ox Legs for Satyrs.* Who does that remind you of?' Philippa said. 'Wigs,' said Ludovic d'Harcourt, embarked, oblivious, on a tour of his own. 'Canvas shirts of mail. A pottle of aqua vite to burn in a masque . . . empty.'

'A pity,' said Lymond. 'My God. Hay, for the Stuffing of Deaths.'

They all came to a halt. '*Medioxes, stuffed with Hay, Half Death, Half Man,*' Philippa read.

'Now I do know who that reminds me of,' said Lymond feelingly. 'How much farther, for heaven's sake, to your butchered drakes' necks?'

'Here,' said Philippa. They had reached a tall stand filled with parcels of feathers: red and white plumes for angels' wings, pheasants' tails, peacocks' plumes, cranes' feathers trimmed over with spangles. The Yeoman, delving, pulled out a shimmering bundle and shook out a fur made, indeed, of drakes's necks. Nicholas had found a stand full of wooden swords, hatchets, targets and staves, and, seizing a sword and a shield, had attacked Lymond and d'Harcourt. And nothing loth, his two elders, who happened to be among the best fighting men then in Christendom and had not touched a weapon in anger for ten months, lifted a sword each in turn and set to, delicately.

Master Holt, turning, said, 'Gentlemen! The stands are not stable!' but this time was ignored.

They were certainly not very stable. As the boy, laughing, prodded and dodged, the two men moved like wraiths after, swords clacking, and turned on the tall posts like maypoles: a lion's head of paste and silk feathers, dislodged, dropped from above on a shelf full of lanthorns. 'Gentlemen!' the Yeoman said again.

'Yes, *gentlemen,*' said Philippa impatiently, and seizing a stout wooden heading axe, let it fall on the next person who passed.

It was Lymond. He dropped to his knees, his hands covering the nape of his neck, his skin flushed with laughter. Philippa, lowering the axe, said. 'I have never in the whole of my life seen you laugh before.'

He looked up at the red sock, still gasping. 'Now that,' he said, 'is ridiculous. Although, now you mention it. I didn't laugh last time it happened. Hit d'Harcourt on the head and see if he laughs.'

511

But d'Harcourt had put back his sword and had found something else meanwhile to look at. 'Plays,' he called 'Books and books of manuscripts. Listen to this.'

He didn't read very well, but it was enough to expose the lapses in the playwright's inspiration. Crowding round him they found some Udall, and Philippa, clad in her drakes' necks, declaimed a sentence or two. Lymond, finding a ready-made balcony on some high shelf, perched himself on it, gesticulating, and recited some more. The stand rocked.

'My God,' said Ludovic d'Harcourt, echoing the Yeoman of the Revels, for other reasons entirely. 'Listen to this. *Love and Life, by William Baldwyn.* A Comedy concerning the Way to Life. There be in it of sundry personages 62, and the play is three hours long. I bring in a young man whom I name Lamuel, who hath a servant called Lob. These two will attempt the world to seek their fortune. They meet with Lust, Luck and Love. Lust promiseth them Lechery—'

'I don't believe it,' Lymond said.

'Be quiet,' said Philippa. 'Go on, Ludo.'

'They follow Luck and through Lechery be lost, then through Luck they recover. Luck bringeth them to Lordship, from which through . . . I can't go on,' said d'Harcourt, painfully. 'It says all the players' names begin with *L.*'

'And so they do,' said Philippa, reading. 'Leonard Lustyguts an Epicure. Lame Lazar a Spittleman. Liegerdemayn an Old Courtier; Lammarkin, a Lance knight; Little-lookedfor, Death; Layies Lechery a Sumtuous Hore. . . . But the play is missing.'

'They never did it,' Nicholas Chancellor said. He, too, was flushed with pleasure, in this unforeseen romp in the Revels. 'It was all full of *L*s.'

'I can guess,' Philippa said. There was a wig box beside her. She hauled off the sock and jammed on her head a long flaxen wig, with a headpiece of spangled white sarsanet. *'I'm Lechery, a Luscious Hore . . .'*

'Wait,' said Lymond. His jerkin off, he was rummaging shirt-sleeved through the stands: a moment later, he emerged with a long Turkey gown which he tossed to d'Harcourt. 'Come on, Hospitaller. You're Lame Lazar. Nicholas, you can be Luck. And' – as Nicholas caught the red cloth cloak tossed him – 'and I, of course, shall be

512

Lamuel the Lewd.' A satin doublet of hideous orange
engulfed him for a moment, and then he pulled it down,
and began to tramp, without progressing, before Philippa.
'Now go on.'

'I've forgotten. . . . No, I haven't,' said Philippa. Long
Sunday evenings of nonsensical charades with Kate and
Gideon paraded before her, and evenings spent devising
songs, and poems, and doggerel, with Ls or without. . . .
She drew breath and started, haltingly, making it up as
she went.

> 'I'm Lechery a Luscious Hore
> A Lady Loose who Lists to Lower
> Her Limbs upon a Lance Knight's Lap
> His Lips to Buss and Cheeks to Clap. . . .'

'Very good. Not enough Ls in the last line,' said
Lymond critically.

'Then you do better,' said Philippa, incensed.

'Gentlemen !' said the Yeoman.

> 'And I, Limp Lamuel Longing Sigh,
> Beside Light Lechery to Lie
> Lo Here I Learn my Lesson Lewd
> And Love and Lounge in Lassitude.'

'What in God's name is going on?' said Sir Henry
Sidney's voice, from behind stacks of shelving.

'Go on,' said Philippa. 'The Lazar.'

'I can't,' said Ludovic d'Harcourt, clutching his gold
gown about him.

'Why not? Go on,' said Philippa.

'I can't think of any words,' said d'Harcourt apologetically.

'Never mind,' said Lymond. 'Say after me :

> 'Which I, Lame Lazar List to Cure,
> But Light beneath the Lady's Lure
> And Lift my Crutch with Leprous Glee,
> And Leap upon the Lady's Knee . . .Nicholas?'

'You do mine,' said Nicholas, glowing.

'No, I'll do it,' said Philippa, feeling her oats. She
thought.

> *'But I, dear Luck, will Lead you all.*
> *On Lilied Lawns of Light to Loll* ('Bravo!' said Lymond.)
> *Where Lute and Lyre will Lilt their Lay* ('Oh, *bravo*!')
> *And Lull sweet Lovers at their Play!'* said Philippa
triumphantly.

'That's really very good,' said Sir Henry. 'Is there more?'

'Yes : Death,' said Lymond. 'Where are the Medioxes? Philippa?'

'Up there. I'll get them,' Philippa said. Hampered by drakes' necks, she clambered on to a middle shelf and from there made her way upwards.

'Gentlemen!' called Lymond warningly.

She called back, 'It's all right,' and tossed him the death's head, which he put on, while she perched where she was, observing approvingly.

'Right?' said Lymond.

> *'Till Little-lookedfor Death appeared*
> *And Loathsome on the Lovers Leered*
> *And Laughter's Lodge was Let to Fear*
> *And Love to Lugworms Fell . . .'*

'You've changed the metre,' said Philippa.

'I reserve the right,' said Lymond, 'to change the metre. Don't interrupt.

> *'Ah, Lamuel, lest your Life be Light*
> *Lament not for your Lost Delight*
> *Beshrew Loose Ladies in the Night*
> *Or . . .'*

'Let me do it,' said Philippa.

Lymond said, looking up, 'That is robbery.'

'I don't care. Let me do it. You got all the last verse.'

'All right,' said Lymond generously. 'It has to rhyme with *fell*.'

And from her high perch, happily, Philippa declaimed.

> *'Ah, Lamuel, lest your Life be Light*
> *Lament not for your Lost Delight*
> *Beshrew Loose Ladies in the Night*
> OR LANGUISH LOCKED IN L!!!'

There was a roar of applause, from friends, tailors and Yeoman, and Philippa fell off the stand.

And, since the stand was not stable, it toppled with her, and striking the next stand, toppled that, which falling sideways, pushed a row of stands, with majestic slowness towards that part of the room where the paint and glue pots were standing. Chests opened. Hampers yawned. Cloth, clothes, bells, masks, heads, hay, swords, wigs and feathers erupted crashing upon floor and tables, while painters fled and tailors rose yelling and the explosions, continuing, dwindled; leaving nothing but silence, and the trickling of saffron, vermilion, yellow ochre, sap green and red lead, as they spread on the floor of the Revels.

'Philippa?' said Henry Sidney.

'She's knocked herself out. She's all right,' Lymond said. 'So's Nicholas. Look. I think d'Harcourt has broken an arm.'

The dust hung in the hall like a tapestry. Picking his way over the rubble, oblivious of the noise of men's voices returning, Sir Henry found and knelt by the wigged bundle which was Sumtuous Lechery, and felt her pulse anxiously. She had had, as Lymond said, a crack on the crown and was quite unconscious. Otherwise, miraculously, she seemed to be unharmed.

D'Harcourt had been less lucky. By the time Sidney got there, Nicholas was helping Lymond pull him from under a chest : his left arm was undoubtedly broken, and he had had a bad blow on the head. Sidney said, 'There are beds in the offices. I shouldn't like to move him until he's been looked at and had the arm set. Nicholas, find the Yeoman and tell him one gentleman is hurt and will he go to the nearest apothecary's for a bonesetter. Mr Crawford . . .'

'I shall stay with him,' Lymond said. His shirt torn and his hand and cheek grazed, he had taken no other harm and was intent, with some success, on making d'Harcourt more comfortable.

'No,' Sidney said. 'If you don't mind my saying so. I know these people here. I shall see that your friend gets the best service possible, and I shall have him taken to Fenchurch Street as soon as he is able to travel. But I think Mistress Philippa should be in the care of Lady Dormer. These are kind men, but rough. . . . Nicholas would help you carry her, and the barge will take you straight to the gate.'

Lymond rose and stood, frowning.

'Truly,' Sir Henry said. 'You can do no more for him here. Trust me with him.'

And after a moment more, 'Yes, of course,' Lymond said; and stretching, looked for the first time about him. 'Oh, Jesus Christ. I shall have to go down and unload the *Primrose*.'

'It was a notable play,' said Henry Sidney. 'And worth any cost in my book. Provided your officer here bears you no resentment, I think the other victims may soon be propitiated.'

'That,' said Lymond, 'is precisely why I dislike leaving you. I must exact the promise, please, of an accounting.'

'I promise,' said Sidney. 'On the other hand, you still have to make your peace with Mistress Philippa.' He glanced, smiling, towards the flaxen wig and Lymond, his lips twitching, surveyed it as well. Sidney added gently, 'The men who fight under you are fortunate.'

Lymond turned and looked at him, and then smiled; and for all there were only two years between them, Sidney felt his maturity of a sudden drop away. 'But life,' Lymond said, 'is not quite like this in Russia.'

Philippa was still unconscious when he disentangled her from the cluster of Medioxes and, pulling off the wig, lifted her in his arms while Nicholas, climbing before him, pioneered their footing out of the shambles.

Outside, the sun was still shining, and the oarsmen waiting, patiently, to take Sir Henry back to the Savoy. Lymond explained, briefly, and climbed into the barge, Nicholas helping. Nicholas, in spite of the unfortunate outcome, was still full as a millstream with bubbles : he giggled all the way to Lady Dormer's, in between droning verse and applying, frequently, for the lines he had failed to remember. Lymond settled with Philippa's head on his arm, and was disposed to smile, sometimes, too.

Whiffle. She was a quick-witted child. From Kate, of course. He stirred back the brown hair which had caught in her lashes. And that was Kate's too. What did she take from Gideon? Honesty. That both her parents had. And courage. Riding through the night once, into unknown country, to find him, and pay some sort of debt she thought she owed to him, or her parents. And, of course, following him for the sake of the child. In spite of a good deal of uncivilized behaviour, he recalled clearly, on his part.

Courage from both parents, too. You would go far to find a woman braver than Kate. And music – from Gideon? Yes. Both studied and felt – that furious display on the harpsichord at Lady Mary's, defiant though it had been, had been more than plain pyrotechnics. But then, she was no longer ten, and had put to use the years of study and practice. How old, then, was she?

The year he fought his brother, they had met. The year of Pinkie, or the spring just after. Which made her . . . nearly twenty.

He was aware of deep surprise. But of course, the mind which had comprehended and discussed with him all the intricacies of the present blunderings of nations was not, could not be a child's. The loving spirit which could serve Queen Mary, seeing clearly all her weakness, had nothing immature about it, or the wit which Ascham had found worthy to teach.

Unlike Kate, this girl had broken from her setting. All that Kate was, she now had. And standing on Kate's shoulders, something more, still growing; blossoming and yet to fruit.

All that he was not. He looked at her. The long, brown hair; the pure skin of youth; the closed brown eyes, their lashes artfully stained; the obstinate chin; the definite nose, its nostrils curled. The lips, lightly tinted, and the corners deepened, even sleeping, with the remembrance of sardonic joy. . . . The soft, severe lips.

And deep within him, missing its accustomed tread, his heart paused, and gave one single stroke, as if on an anvil. 'We're there, sir,' Nicholas said.

The air hurt his skin. His nerves, unsheathed, left him over-sensitized and defenceless, as sometimes happened : exposed raw to the touch of his clothes, as if his flesh had been stripped off with acid. He remained perfectly still.

'. . .Sir?' Nicholas said.

So Francis Crawford moved and, bending, took the weight of the straight shoulders and the crumpled skirts and the supple hands and the fall of long, ruffled hair. It was not a child's body, any more.

He carried Philippa from the boat and through the

517

garden of the Savoy, without moving his hands. Somewhere he stopped, because Nicholas was speaking to him : it seemed that Lady Dormer was out, with her women, and the house was empty except for the kitchen maids. Nicholas offered to go find them and the physician they favoured. He agreed, and found himself inside the house, with an excited kitchenmaid beside him, showing him to Mistress Philippa's chamber. She was still in his arms, and had not wakened.

The maid seemed to have gone. He lowered Philippa on her bed and took his hands away, without touching her again. Then he simply stood, watching her face. Once she sighed, and he moved backwards, unthinking, and came to rest half-way to the door as she fell silent again. Shortly after that, she moved her head once or twice : she was not far from waking. He stood, with his back to the door, until Lady Dormer arrived. Then he went downstairs, and stood at the window.

Almost immediately, it seemed, Lady Dormer was beside him. Mistress Philippa had wakened : she was well, except for a headache. She sent him her apologies and had also uttered, on waking, some words in Turkish which Lady Dormer was thankful to say she was unable to translate. Lady Dormer did not recommend visitors just at present, but perhaps Mr Crawford would send to ask how she was in the morning.

He said something, and became aware that he was expected to leave. He felt like a dog, he thought, whose master had died. He left the house, but did not remember the journey to Fenchurch Street.

The next thing he did remember was Ludovic d'Harcourt's voice behind him saying, 'Are you all right? You've been standing there for two hours.' And it was probably true : he was in his own room with the lamps unlit and the door left half-open behind him. The light from the passage, coming through, fell on d'Harcourt's big form, and the broad scarf which cradled his arm.

Francis Crawford said, 'I . . . beg your pardon. Pantokrator brooding in the dome. Come in and sit down, and tell me how you feel.' He walked to the nearest lamp and picked up the tinder, his hands shaking. He threw it down.

'Let me,' d'Harcourt said, and, using the fingers of his immobile arm, lit the lamp. He said, 'Are you hurt?'

'No,' said Lymond. 'It's delayed shock, I suppose.' The stroke of his pulses, unremitting, gave back the accelerated beat of his heart. With a profound effort, he gripped himself, and steadied his breathing. 'But what happened at Blackfriars? Your arm and your head?'

After five minutes, d'Harcourt said, 'You should go to bed. I've been perfectly looked after : it's a clean break, and I feel the ache, but nothing more. I enjoyed the revel. If you'll forgive me, why in God's name don't you—' He broke off.

'Do it more often?' Lymond said. He looked as if he wanted to laugh, but hadn't the energy.

'Go to bed,' d'Harcourt said abruptly, and left him.

At some point during the night, Lymond went downstairs and sat in the dark before John Dimmock's harpsichord. He played, when he did begin, very softly, and it reached no further than the room where his three disciples of St Mary's were fast asleep. D'Harcourt did not wake up. Danny Hislop who was not musical did, and, rolling over, stuffed his ears with the blankets. But Adam lay for a long time listening, his eyes wide in the dark to music which, without opium and without alcohol, Lymond had never allowed within his hearing before.

He could not guess at the echoes which lay under the music. *Man has an animal appetite, or I would be nothing. I, too have had my Margaret Lennox and my Agha Morat and my child-whore Joleta Reid Malett . . . more of each, and for longer. It has destroyed neither of us. And now nothing can hinder us.*

He was asleep before Lymond closed the lid quietly and quietly returned to his room. It was daylight before he seemed to have time to go to bed, so he stayed dressed, and watched the sun rise, clean and virginal and bright from the east.

Soon, men would be around him and he must stop thinking, since there was nothing to think about. And allow the event, which was not an event, to sink forgotten to the recesses of d'Harcourt's questioning mind, and fade, unmarked, from the recollection of Lady Dormer or Nicholas. He remembered, with sudden, meticulous clarity, the woman he had bedded at Berwick and how, when he could bear it no longer, she had left him alone.

Too late, too late, too late; it had happened.

CHAPTER TEN

So England, resting upon her truce as upon a springboard of nettles, passed the dwindling days of her peace in attending to the departing comforts of Osep Nepeja, the first Muscovite Ambassador to London, and the fleet in which he would sail two weeks hence lay at the wharfside in the City, and discreetly completed its cargo.

For Nepeja, the two weeks were to pass in a welter of dedicated and unrestricted indulgence. Never before, so they said, had any ambassador been received in this country with the honours heaped upon himself. He passed, in his purple damask and his gold and red velvet, from table to merrymaking to seldom untenanted bed, drinking heartily, belching frequently and retaining, by a Muscovite miracle, a sort of regal and unsteady dignity which bore him through the most unlooked-for occasions.

He made the most of it, for he had their measure, this sordid nation gaping after wealth. Which after four centuries of kings could produce no monarch but this small, middle-aged woman, whose Secretary of State, whom he had been at such pains to please, turned out to be the son of a tanner.

In Russia, a man knew to whom he was speaking : boyar or peasant. Unless, by taking orders, a moujik turned into a clerk, a man in Russia kept his station, and his son after him through the generations. With this nation of madmen, where were you? They laughed at the stake, and boasted of relatives hanged : if you had no kinsmen quartered that you knew of, it was because you were not a gentleman, they remarked. They might well go to war, the other ambassadors said with resignation, for not other reason than a sheer love of novelty. And the Queen claimed she was poor, but where in Russia would you find such ostentation in living : the palaces of Whitehall and Westminster, Nonesuch, Chelsea and Oatlands, Richmond and Greenwich. And the clothes . . .

He had discovered that he was expected to retain the Queen's gift of his clothes; that, in England, an ambassador's perquisites were his own, and did not have to be handed back to his monarch. In this matter, and the freedom these traders possessed, unhindered by royal monopolies, Muscovy had perhaps something to learn.

On the other hand, he had found many particulars in which, however little the English might think so, the two countries were not so unlike. One of the Tsar's greatest difficulties, everyone knew, was to find land with which to reward princely service : in England, the dissolution of the monasteries had served this very purpose and the reconstitution of a few of them by this new Queen had not, so far as he could see, altered the circumstance by a whit.

These Englishmen claimed to despise a régime which dared not maintain a printing press. But what of their own, pouring forth scurrilous and seditious leaflets? Could they claim that no one had tried to suppress these? Why, they had even caught and brought home one of their scholars, for the crime of producing such print overseas.

They claimed to shrink from the Tsar's rough chastisements, but what of their own burnings? They had no cause to sneer when they heard of Muscovite coffins exhumed and dragged by a team of pigs to the scaffold. Worse happened in England. In England the heir to the throne, the Queen's sister, was watched and suspected as Vladimir always had been, but the Muscovites had been cleverer. Prince Vladimir was already elected future Regent and guardian of the child Ivan in the event of the Tsar's sudden death : he was satisfied and the country was quiet. They pretended here to be surprised that so great a monarch could not overthrow a few Tartars, but what success was the lord Henry having in Ireland? Why, if the Queen called herself monarch of France, was she content with owning two fortresses only?

He had come to this country with an open mind. The Voevoda had told him so, and the Voevoda had shown him those things from which he thought Muscovy should benefit. But, in time, a man grew tired of foreign ways, and foreign food, and the incessant chirrup and yowl of uncouth foreign tongues, and Osep Nepeja felt he owed England nothing, and himself a small rest from his labours, with his journey done and his treaty concluded and the prospect before him of the long hardship of the *Primrose*'s homeward voyage.

So he did not seek to have the incessant pressure of instruction renewed, and went his own way, merely mentioning his surprise and disapproval to Robert Best over the undignified and expensive accident in the Office of Revels and Masques. The following day, the big Anglo-French man, Master Ludovic, making light of his broken arm, had gone back up river to call on the young woman the Voevoda had married and had taken her an armful of spring bluebells gathered, so Master Daniel suggested sardonically, from the woods and fields outside Smithfield. The young woman, then recovered, had joined the Court and removed herself for Easter to Greenwich.

The Voevoda, as Master Daniel had also pointed out, had neither sent flowers to the young woman nor visited her, although he had dispatched a messenger the following morning to inquire how she was. Master Daniel, who found this inadequate, was properly caustic. The Voevoda himself had not accompanied Master Nepeja to any of his engagements that day, but had elected to spend it in contemplation, sitting deep in thought (or slumber? or post-revels exhaustion?) at the big desk in his room.

Danny Hislop, already staggered by intimations of unheard-of levity, made the most of the Voevoda's changed plans for his day and put the reason down also to lassitude. He perceived his blunder the following morning when he was called to the same desk with d'Harcourt, to hear the outcome of the Voevoda's day of silent retreat. It was, as he might have guessed, alarming and it did, as he might have guessed, entail a monstrous amount of work for Masters Hislop and d'Harcourt thus putting an end, as Danny expressed it, to his nice fineness and breathing desire towards effeminate and superfluous pleasures, not to mention Ludo's visits to Smithfield.

The matter, as they might have guessed, was inevitably the business of Russia.

Through all the banquets and the routine engagements the Voevoda's work for the Tsar had continued, and since the treaty had been concluded, and they were free to engage men and seek expert advice, Lymond had been fully occupied. Now, with the help of Hislop and d'Harcourt all that he had already done in this field was drawn together and intensified, so that in the short time still remaining in London his self-imposed task should be completed.

The Tsar had wanted men from every profession to advise him. This was not possible. But from those men who came forward, Lymond chose the likeliest, with the help of Dimmock and his colleagues. And in those trades where no men could be hired, he sought the best man he could find, and picked his brains mercilessly. He gathered books. John Dee, unearthing from his mountainous desk the plans, rejected, for a National Library, found for him the standard works, and men who, briefly, could explain or annotate them, however crudely. He sought advice on buildings and transport; on roads and law-giving; on finance and farming. He commissioned books and papers; he found those members of the Muscovy Company who were on the Privy Council and questioned them. He did what it was Nepeja's place to do and what, unlearned and unable to communicate, the Ambassador had never contemplated.

And on top of that, with all the standing and authority he possessed, he set himself to force through the annulment of his marriage.

Of that, Danny Hislop was not made aware. Hislop only knew that leisure, always short, was now quite circumscribed. That as the ships were loaded and the lists came in of all the armour and the weapons Dimmock found for them, he and d'Harcourt were set to make lists in their turn; to work out where and how to use this windfall; where to store it; how to allocate it; whom to train.

They sat with Lymond at his desk and worked, as they had done at the beginning in Russia, but this time not for the army alone. They saw illumined before them area by area the other regions in which Muscovy was backward or vulnerable and, together, discussed the solutions. Adam Blacklock, now a paid employee of the Muscovy Company, found himself being drawn in spite of himself to watch the solid weight of informed power moving slowly, as in a forge, against the obstinate and primaeval mass which was the present condition of Russia.

On a task such as this, Lymond was always easy to work with. The caustic disciplines and the violence were for the field, not for the study. There he was quiet, carrying other minds with him; his own thinking heavily concentrated and naturally lucid in exposition : he was not, as Philippa had once called him, magisterial. On the other hand, he did not invite to work with him any but those who were capable of it.

After a week of it, broken certainly by many interviews

and absences, Danny Hislop rose at the end of a day's work, yawned uncontrollably twenty times, stretched himself, and said, 'What in God's name, dear Ludo, made you decide to abandon the life of fourscore winters and sail back to Russia? Not only will you have to work like a coining-wedge: you will have to fight Tartars *as well*.' And gazing at Lymond, who was standing reading a paper, Danny said, 'You realize we haven't had any food? We know you don't mind dissolving to a rat-trap of brass wire like the Bishop of Sisteron, but Ludo needs food to make his sore arm get well.'

'I am thinning you down for the *Primrose*,' said Lymond, still reading. 'Have we missed a meal?'

'We have missed two meals,' said Danny Hislop with precision. 'And God knows how many drinks. I haven't been working at all well. Hislops need lubrication.' And thank God, for his stomach was rumbling, the Voevoda gave the order for food and wine to be brought, and, when he caught Adam glaring at him, Danny merely glared back. It was his hard luck, as he told the Voevoda later, that while Ludo, helped occasionally by Adam, was merely putting Russia to rights, he, Danny, was also organizing all the rigorous arrangements to make sure that Ambassador Peter Vannes did not arrive at the English Court with a bundle of dangerous papers under his arm.

Vannes had not yet arrived. It seemed possible, despite the Voevoda's conviction, that he never would, before Lymond and Danny and Lodo had to set sail for Russia. In which case, to preserve Mistress Philippa from unpleasant repercussions, someone else should be deputed to help stop those papers arriving. Adam Blacklock, for example.

But Lymond was still adamant: he wished neither Blacklock or d'Harcourt to be told of the matter, and he was not prepared to be chivvied about it.

Danny did not pursue it. Ludo d'Harcourt, returned dazzled from Blackfriars, had given him hope that, against all expectation, the Voevoda was about to become human.

That had proved a fallacy, as d'Harcourt had also discovered. The damage at Blackfriars had been generously, even royally, made good. But after it, the Voevoda had withdrawn behind a barrier as distinct as it was deliberate. There was no more playacting.

And Adam Blacklock, whose business was charts, and who had no right to be eavesdropping when Best and Buckland called and brought Jenkinson with them, or when Ludo and Danny, undressing, exchanged some terrible reminiscence of Novgorod or Ochakov, noticed it too, and noticed more than that.

It was only by accident that, calling at the Voevoda's room late one evening, Adam saw by the half-empty cup standing among the books on his table that Lymond had been drinking as he worked.

The flask was put away and he was not unsteady on his feet or in any way affected that Adam could see : he was long past the time when he could not judge, to the thousandth part of a litre, just how far he wished to go, and then stop. But it was now so far from his habit that it gave Adam pause.

He mentioned it, stupidly, to the others. 'He doesn't want to go back to Russia?' Danny speculated, horrified.

'Don't be an ass,' said Ludo impatiently. 'You can see he is counting the days.'

And althought d'Harcourt was not usually, Adam thought, the most perspicacious member of the small party, in this instance he believed he was right. For Francis Crawford, the days of his life left in London could not possibly pass soon enough.

*

The bluebells Ludo had given her died before Philippa got down to Greenwich, but she took the tulips Sir Henry Sidney brought her, grown from the bulbs she had given him, begged by the French Ambassador from his colleagues in Turkey and Venice. And Austin, calling at Greenwich, had brought her sweetmeats and had been too distressed to examine the lump on her head.

Except when she combed her hair, she had forgotten about it. Recollection of the incident itself still made her want to laugh at inconvenient moments, and, in respect of its effect on Mr Crawford, gave her much satisfaction. He was improving. He was making, indeed, unforeseen strides. She only hoped that Kiaya Khátún would not undo the good work when she got him.

She was kept busy at Greenwich, for the Queen's cold made all the extra Masses a trial, and her toothache refused to yield to treatment. So when the festivities began, the Queen remained indoors out of public view while King Philip took his sister and cousin to fire off hackbuts and hunt in the sunshine. Or so they claimed. From the Queen's lonely irritability, Philippa doubted if she believed it. And thought, privately, that it was less a matter of dalliance than a family conclave, from which his wife's emotional ear had been excluded. King Philip's affliction, they said, still troubled him on occasion. About its nature, no one had been quite specific.

She worked hard, too, in order to free Jane to see her Count of Feria. Don Gomez was well born and wealthy and eighteen years older than Jane Dormer. He was also a Jesuit, which meant that he believed that consummate prudence, allied with moderate saintliness, was better than greater saintliness and mere prudence, which made it interesting to conjecture whether the betrothal, when it came, was likely to be protracted or short. The difference in age, Philippa supposed would be overcome, Jane being very mature for her years, although she could not imagine the Count of Feria in a bright orange coat and a death's head. She made up her mind to find out how old Mr Crawford was.

It was the Queen, concerned about Philippa's situation, who told her that further representations were being made from all quarters about her divorce, and Austin at last began to look cheerful, and a number of other young men, who had become her regular escorts, began to be a little less manageable as the rumour went round. While extremely tired of her condition, half maid and half matron like the Medioxes, Philippa was aware that the matter was still far from simple.

Cardinal Pole, the Papal Legate and supreme authority on such matters was still at his palace in Canterbury, suspended in space between his recalcitrant monarch and his even more obdurate Pope. It was said that the Pope intended to revoke the Cardinal's Legation, to deprive him of the means of doing injury to God and to himself, as he put it. The French, who had still not broken the truce in order to come to the Pope's aid, were now wholly out of favour, and the Constable's son still awaited his divorce.

His Holiness, who had borne the fatigues of Holy Week with incredible vigour, filled the air with thunderous grievances: Flemings and Spaniards took root like weeds, unlike the French, who flew off and would not remain were they tied and bound. All Italy, he warned the Venetian Ambassador, would be dispatched and Venice remain as the salad. But England, he bellowed, would remain at peace despite Philip, since the English were not quite so easy to cook, and the King of France possessed Scotland, a scourge for the English, who, being almost savages and poor, would go joyfully for gain into England. . . . *Would to God,* said the Pope, referring to the unwell King Philip, *would to God that misguided youth would do as he ought: he has excited the great he-goats who might bite him in earnest.*

And in the Pontiff's gracious reply to Queen Mary's letter of appeal and contrition: *We would willingly separate the Queen's cause from her — we know not whether to call him husband, cousin or nephew — and to have her as a daughter. She should not allow herself to be induced to do aught to our detriment, or that of the French King, or we will spare neither relatives nor friends, but include in our maledictions and anathemas all who shall desert the cause of God.*

And King Philip, who never now discussed matters of religion, save to urge less severity in order not to upset the Queen's people, weathered a stormy interview with his Queen with his usual cold-blooded calm, and laid before her the results of his consultations with scholars, universities and theologians on the propriety of disarming this frantic Prince, the Vicar of Rome. *It is lawful for a vassal,* said the scholars, *and even more for a son, to anticipate the attack which he sees is being prepared against him by his spiritual father and by his Prince.*

Thus the princes of Christendom, rising from their knees to hurry to their writing-desks, that Easter.

Overwhelmed with debt, surrounded by inexpert and detested commanders, with his provinces mortgaged and his revenues alienated King Philip awaited the return of Ruy Gomez with money, and a response to the humble message Ruy Gomez had borne to his father the Emperor, begging him to leave his retirement in Spain: *The success of my enterprise will depend on it . . . I am sure that if the world hears he has done as I ask, my enemies will take an entirely different view of the situation and will reconsider their plans. . . . Beg him to send me his opinion about the war, and where I had better attack and open the campaign to gain the greatest advantages. . . .* And while waiting, King Philip issued a letter to the nobles of England. In it, he declared that His Holiness the Pope, having seized an unjust pretext to break with him, had invaded the Kingdom of Naples, having concluded a league with the King of France and the Duke of Ferrara, and having called the Turkish fleet to assist him.

He himself, declared King Philip, had decided to raise a powerful army to create a diversion in France this summer, and, this being the first campaign in which he had taken part, he was anxious that it should go well. Since he was unable to finance it wholly from his own resources and those of Spain, he requested the bishops, the leading nobles and the high officers of State of England 'as you are animated by the greatest zeal for our service and the general good of the Spanish kingdom', to lend him as much money as they possibly could. And, promising ample security for repayment at the earliest possible date, he signed it, as it was written, in Spanish.

The air was not filled with the murmur of Englishmen, obediently counting their gold. And Philippa, traitorously, had cause to be glad that the four ships now lying above London Bridge were already freighted with their cargo of arms, destined for another country entirely.

They were due to sail on 3 May; and on 19 April the Court returned to Whitehall Palace in London. On the same day, the Muscovite Ambassador went to Westminster Abbey to hear Mass, and later to the Lord Abbot's for dinner. Afterwards, he was invited to tour the reopened monastery and to inspect St Edward's new shrine. Then, escorted by the Aldermen of the City and the merchants of the Muscovite Company in splendid array, he rode into the park and back to the city. He wore his cloth of gold with raised crimson velvet, and the Voevoda Bolshoia was not with him.

On 22 April, the Queen gave a farewell banquet in Westminster for the two Duchesses of Lorraine and Parma, on the eve of their long-awaited departure. Philippa was there, but not the Muscovite Ambassador.

Ludovic d'Harcourt sent her a note and later called, by appointment, to see how she was. He himself, his cloak covering the empty sleeve of his doublet, was well on the mend. The Voevoda Bolshoia did not call, or send

528

her a note. Philippa, accustomed by now to the minimal courtesies, recalled that with Mr Crawford the proffering of even the minimal courtesies was dependent on the current state of his nerves. She took, since there was no other course, a philosophic view of the matter.

On 23 April, the Feast of St George, the Crown held a chapter at Whitehall of the Most Noble Order of the Garter, the premier English order of knighthood, and combined with it, in a stroke of inspiration allied to economy, the ceremonial leavetaking of Osep Nepeja, the Muscovite Ambassador.

After the ceremony, which included a procession by King Philip and his knights in red velvet through the Hall and round the court by the Hall, viewed by the Queen from a window, the Muscovite Ambassador was received in audience upstairs in the Queen's presence chamber in an audience attended by both Philippa Somerville and the Voevoda Bolshoia.

The whole Court was there. The room was filled with noblemen, Spanish and English, and their ladies; with Aldermen and Muscovite merchants, conducted hence by the Earl of Shrewsbury in loyal support of the Ambassador. With the ten Knights of the Garter, including Sir William Petre, sweating under the weight of his robes, and Henry Sidney, accompanying his brother-in-law Sussex, newly invested as a Knight of the Order. With Austin Grey, Marquis of Allendale, whose uncle, Lord Grey of Wilton, had also today been elected *in absentia*.

It was an occasion for extravagant costume. The Heralds' tabards outglittered the rich coats of the Royal Guard, ranked with their halberds; the courtiers crowded the spaces amongst them, bright as chattering fountains in sunlight. Philippa, entering gravely as the Queen, to the sound of trumpets, moved to her Chair of Estate saw that the merchants, in a frenzy of optimism, had fitted out Master Nepeja with a new garment, jewelled and embroidered and more splendid than any he had exhibited yet. She thought, but could not believe, that there were earrings lost somewhere on each side of the box-cut brown beard.

She had spent a great deal, it had to be admitted, on her own dress, which had a jewelled petticoat, quite impracticable, and a train of white gauze, lightly wired, cut to fall from her shoulders. Philippa added to it all the

accessories it demanded, which were a straight back, a
severe hairline and a scowl, and sailed into the room to
take her place, standing, by the Queen's chair. Since she
had a point to make, she made it a positive one.

Nepeja, naturally, was waiting in mid-floor with his
sponsors. Last time, it had taken her some searching to
disentangle the supercilious face of Mr Crawford, and
even then, all she had received, tardily, was the concession
of a raised pair of eyebrows. This time, she cast one
stately glance round the packed and perfume-soaked room
and saw him, instantly, although he was not even looking at her.

He was not where she had expected him to be, and far
from being conspicuous. In front of him, she now saw
was the cheerful bulk of Ludovic d'Harcourt, smiling at
her, and the short man with the fluffy hair, whom she
had been told was called Daniel Hislop, and Adam
Blacklock, familiar from long ago, with the thin pink
scar like a pen mark running across his lean face, which
no one had been able to explain to her.

But she saw them all afterwards. What had drawn her
eye was the sensation of being looked at; which was odd
because she was used to the considering stares of the
Court, as they weighed up your rings and your semp-
stress and your behaviour, and the look in the Queen's
eye as she addressed you. But where the gaze was which
had attracted her she could not now tell. Mr Crawford's
eyes were downcast, and she could see, even at this distance, the graze he had received at the Revels and
Masques, standing out against the rest of his profile.

She stared at him for a while, with her eyebrows raised
and then realized that Lady Lennox was looking at her
and let her eyes wander. Master Nepeja, echoed by Robert
Best, was making a long oration in Russian thanking her
gracious Majesty for her hospitality and for all the loving
kindness shown to himself and his master by the Queen's
gentle subjects. He began, she noted, with some over
confidence and then lost his way half-way through and
had to be guided back to his page by Rob Best. Then
the Queen replied, and the reply was duly translated.
After that, one by one, the Embassy stepped up to the
dais, to kiss hands and take formal leave.

And then, of course, Mr Crawford had to emerge, and
walking forward knelt, while the Queen's short-sighted

eyes, frowning, looked down on him. Philippa could not hear what was said. But she saw him rise and step back bowing, first to the Queen and then to King Philip, and then incline his head, smiling faintly, to Petre and one or two other Councillors. Then, just as he stepped aside, he turned his head and sent the same smile, shared, between Lady Lennox and herself.

Recognition at last. Philippa grinned, despite all her resolutions, and he caught it, backing deftly into his place. Then, seeing she still had his eyes, she smiled again, but he had stopped looking and was listening, head bent, to something Rob Best was whispering. Then it was time to assist the Queen rise and walk, with the whole company following, to the chapel for Evensong. The Muscovite Ambassador was led before the entire Order to take his stately seat with the Duke of Norfolk, higher in order of ranks than all the lords of England and Spain and above all the other exalted personages then of the company. Afterwards, eschewing the reception upstairs, he was escorted to his barge to return downstream to his lodging.

Philippa Somerville, staging a brief and spurious moment of giddiness, handed her duties briskly to Jane Dormer and, chastised by her train, raced down to the landing-stage after him.

The Ambassador was there, surrounded by his merchants, his nine Russians and his aldermen, but the Voevoda Bolshoia had vanished. Ludo d'Harcourt, applied to, searched the landing-stage also. 'He was here a moment ago. Has he gone back to the Palace?'

No one knew. At least, when the barge departed ten minutes later, he was not in it; and it had to be concluded that he had decided to make his own way back to Fenchurch Street. Which, indeed, proved to be the case. Long after the Knights of the Garter had laid their robes thankfully back in their coffers, and the Court, equally thankful, had retired to the chambers it happened to favour that evening, Francis Crawford strolled into Master Dimmock's fine mansion and appeared surprised and even faintly displeased to find himself waylaid on the stairs by d'Harcourt.

D'Harcourt, forced to deliver his message on the landing, was made aware of precisely how lame his embassy was. 'I deeply regret,' Lymond said, 'and even had you approached me in the morning, I should equally deeply regret, that I have no leisure at present for calling on ladies. If *you* have, then perhaps you would convey as much.'

'She says then, Will you write,' said d'Harcourt, with difficulty. Doors creaked audibly, but the Voevoda remained on the landing.

'What about?' said the Voevoda, eyebrows raised, watching him. 'My dear d'Harcourt, I thought you were pursuing the lady. Do you really mean to act as her errand-boy?'

Ludovic d'Harcourt, keeping his temper under extreme provocation, made one last attempt for Mistress Philippa. 'She said, if you wouldn't write, I was to give you a message. She says, *What about Gardington?*'

'And what does she mean by that?' Lymond said. In the torchlight, his eyes were hard and arrogant : the Voevoda Bolshoia interrogating.

Ludovic d'Harcourt threw open his arms. 'How should I know? She didn't say. I'm only her errand-boy.'

He suffered, for an undue length of time, Lymond's considering gaze. Then the Voevoda said, 'I see. An angry piece of flesh, and soon displeased. Then you may retire gladdened by the assurance that your loving office is ended. Is there anything else?'

It was the kind of treatment which above all d'Harcourt disliked. He turned on his heel and walked off, and Lymond, standing, watched him quite out of sight before, at last, he let himself into his room and striking tinder, lit one stand of candles. Then he walked to his aumbry and stood before it a few moments longer before, with a sudden flare of distaste and impatience, he turned the key and flung open the door.

He did not drink any more than he had become accustomed to drinking. But he did not answer, either, when Ludovic d'Harcourt, penitent, returned to tap on his door.

On 25 April, there was held at Court the Masque of the Allmaynes, the Pilgrims and the Irishmen. It was most successful, although it was noted that the Pilgrims' robes were decorated with a most unusual linear design in yellow ochre, sap green and dragon red. Mistress Philippa was complimented on the effects of her feathers.

On 26 April Master Peter Vannes, Dean of Salisbury

and late English Ambassador to the Doge of Venice, crossed from Calais to Dover with his secretary, his servant, his four stirrupmen, his men at arms and a prisoner. In the baggage, nailed down as he had received it from the Bailiff of Padua, was a box containing all the personal correspondence of the late William Courtenay, Earl of Devonshire, sometime claimant to the monarchy of England. An idle man, waiting about the harbour at Dover, witnessed the arrival and, travelling post, set out to cover the seventy-two miles from Dover to Fenchurch Street, London.

On the same day, 26 April, there arrived off the town of Scarborough on the north-east coast of England two French ships, on their way to land French troops in Scotland. They also carried an English rebel named Thomas Stafford and a hundred soldiers, part French and part English refugees. Stafford, a nephew of Cardinal Pole's and a grandson of the late Duke of Buckingham, landed on the coast with his friends, and, seizing Scarborough Castle, proclaimed himself King. The local militia, who had been warned long ago to expect precisely such an attack, were awaiting him quietly and moving in under the leadership of his other uncle the 5th Earl of Westmorland, captured Stafford and rounded up almost all the invaders.

On Wednesday, 28 April, before the news of Peter Vannes's landing or the news of the Scarborough invasion reached London, and ignorant therefore of both events, Francis Crawford of Lymond cancelled his engagements and, releasing his staff for the day, set off alone and fast out of London, to ride forty miles to the manor of Gardington, Bucks., there to call on his great-uncle, Leonard Bailey.

It was raining. He passed some carts making their way to the city, with milk, and farm produce, and kegs and parcels done up in sacking; and one of two vagabonds, and the odd man in a good coat, with servants and runners, coming up early from his house in the country. But few, as yet, bound outwards from London as he was.

Lymond had ridden a few miles therefore before he became aware of the drumming of hoofbeats behind him, travelling as fast as his own over the mud and stones of the highway. Without pausing, he threw a glance over his shoulder, and saw the rider was hooded and cloaked, and was waving to him. An instant later, and he recognized Philippa.

For a long and critical moment, it appeared to Philippa that he had not observed her and that she was going to have to put two fingers between her teeth, regrettably, and whistle him over. Then he brought his weight to bear on the powerful horse, and slowed it down and wheeling, rode back towards her.

Her hood bounding: 'Ludo told me,' called Philippa, trotting likewise to meet him. 'You were going to Gardington?'

He looked underslept. He came to rest beside her, his gaze wry but not unduly harsh. Only Philippa recognized the aura of resistance surrounding him, like the kindly, masterful, obdurate resistance Lady Dormer displayed when brought face to face with a lapse in good breeding. But Philippa, through the months, had learned how to deal with Lady Dormer. So she greeted him again. 'Khúsh Geldi. Are you going to Gardington?'

And he said, 'Yes. And are you going to protect me?'

'You need a witness,' said Philippa. 'Unwanted, unasked, unwelcome as ever, here I am.'

'Again,' said Lymond.

If she had not been expecting it, it might have hurt; although he had not spoken sharply. 'Yes, again,' Philippa said. 'Has it ever occurred to you that if you sometimes invited me somewhere, I shouldn't always have to keep standing in doorways being glared at?'

He said, 'I hadn't thought of it as a social occasion.' Then after a moment he said, 'I can hardly glare at you, when you have taken all this trouble to follow me. You think I shall need a witness?'

'With Bailey,' said Philippa grimly, 'you need a full suit of armour. He was born, like Genghis Khan, in a Rat Year. I think this is one occasion when you will have to forget your finer feelings and let the populace in. I shall try, I promise you, not to humiliate you.'

'You could hardly do that,' Lymond said, and his horse, shaking its head in the rain, moved restively under him. 'You know more about my sordid parentage than I do. Leonard Bailey being what he is, do you think it likely that I would allow a royal lady-in-waiting to go with me?'

She raised her eyebrows. Thinned and glossy and perfect, they arched over her dense brown eyes, invisibly cultivated: the rain had brought fresh colour, naturally to her young skin. She said, 'Well, how nice. I seem to have the moral ascendancy this time. Dear Mr Crawford, I have been there already. Alone. And on your behalf. It is for you to repay the obligation. Trencher chippings, please, for the dutiful sow.'

'Oh, Christ!' said Lymond, and gave a gasp of laughter, and then stopped, looking down at his gloves. After a moment, he said dryly, 'So, having disposed of my finer feelings and my obligations, there seems to be only one objection you haven't thought of. With an annulment pending, it would be quite ludicrous for you and me to spend a day and a night unescorted.'

'Oh,' said Philippa.

'Checkmate,' Lymond said. She could feel his eyes on her, filled no doubt with ungenerous triumph. 'Stalemate. Goodbye, Philippa. *Allaha ismarladik!* And let my Lord, when he divorces me, give me in your place wives better than you: submissive, faithful, obedient, penitent, adorers, fasters, widows and virgins. . . .'

'Speaking of virgins,' Philippa said.

His horse moved again. 'No,' said Lymond.

'Speaking of virgins, there can be fewer acts more directly prejudicial to a divorce on the grounds of non-consummation than sharing a double bed in the Sultan of Turkey's seraglio. If you remember,' Philippa said.

And stared at him owlishly for that, she knew well, was a tricky matter. Not because of what happened between them, which had been precisely nothing. But of what Mr Crawford had experienced that night, the night the child Khaireddin had been killed.

But he had forgotten, for after a moment's thought he said only, 'So you are intending to rely on medical evidence to dissolve the holy union between us. *Ubi tres medici, duo athei?*'

'And *vituperato sia chi mal pensa,*' said Philippa blandly. 'Could we, do you suppose, begin riding on? It is really rather wet.'

But he did not move his horse. 'I have one move left to play,' Lymond said. 'Do you want me to see this man Bailey?'

'Yes,' said Philippa warily.

535

'Then I will see him,' said Lymond sweetly. 'But only if you go back to London.'

She had thought of that, too. She kept her brown eyes fixed open upon him, and allowed her mind, lushly, to fill with the injustice of it all. Her nose grew pink. 'Then,' said Philippa simply, 'I shall cry.' And, to order, her eyes filled and spilled over with the first of two surfing tears.

With Austin, it had always been most effective. Mr Crawford, on the other hand, neither offered his kerchief nor words of chastened apology. Instead he drew his horse sharply from her and, without a word, wheeled and rode forcefully off.

After a moment's sinking comprehension, Philippa gathered her own reins likewise and stubbornly set off at top speed behind him.

There followed a long and unpleasant hour's riding. The rain continued to fall in heavy, irregular showers. Mud flew against Philippa like snow, from the hooves of her own mare, and the riders and carts splashing by. She was never close enough to catch the mud from Mr Crawford's big horse. He had very quickly vanished from sight, and but for the chance that she knew his destination and was still convinced that he intended to go there, she would have had no idea which road to follow.

As it was, she rode on grimly, accepting what punishment the elements chose to inflict on her, until she emerged from a small, noisy wood to see the road winding empty before her, and a single horseman waiting silent beside it, his long cloak sleek as satin with wet.

Philippa Somerville slowed her horse to a trot, and, pulling off her right glove, held her hand high and flat, white palm outwards as she paced forward to Lymond and stopped. 'Never again,' Philippa said. 'Never, never again.'

He sat still, breathing deeply as yet from the ride, with his face brushed and ridged with wet light from the rain. 'No,' he said. 'I don't deserve that. I think.'

Philippa looked down and then up again, her cheeks red with mortification. 'It works with Austin,' she said.

His lips tightened, and Philippa sat, empty and braced for the stinging attack she deserved. 'It works with me, too,' he said. 'But perhaps not quite in the same way.'

There was another brief pause. Then he said, 'I can hardly let you ride back on your own. Do you always get your own way by—'

'Persistence,' Philippa said, 'is the secret. *So many buls do compass me That be full strong of head. Yea, buls so fat as though they had In Basan field been fed.* I haven't had my breakfast.'

He lifted his eyebrows, but not quite in the same way as before, insolently, in the presence chamber at Whitehall. 'Then you are going to be very hungry, aren't you?' he said. 'Because on my journeys there are no halts before dinner. For bulls or heifers.'

But that worried her not at all, for she had got what she wanted despite him. Although, as she knew very well, she could never have caught him had he not stopped, from regard for her safety. For he did not want her. Of that, there was, loweringly, no possible doubt.

They had forty miles to cover to Gardington : a longer journey than any she would normally ride in one day; but she was light and active and determined and did not hold him back as they galloped, changing horses at post stations as they went; or, if she did, he concealed it. For the rest, it was a strange day which remained in her memory, for it was so different from her experience of him hitherto.

The quick, vituperative exchanges which she had found so challenging and exasperating and, sometimes, hurtful did not appear; and when she thought of the purpose of this journey she accepted that, today at least, his mind would be removed far from banter. He did talk, however, when there was breath at a ford or a ferry, or when he commanded a meal for them both, or half an hour's rest and shelter at an inn. It was none of it personal conversation and began, so far as she could afterwards remember, with a book she had just read by Leonard Digges about prognosticating the weather from the sky. It appeared he had read Digges's last book and they discussed it; and then went on to talk about Roger Bacon.

It was only gradually that she came to realize how steadily he was controlling the conversation : how, whenever it became less than detached, he steered the subject elsewhere or exchanged it skilfully for another. It was noticeable simply because there seemed, Philippa concluded, to be so few dull topics in the world, and even when he thought he had found one, it would suddenly burst into life, full of new aspects and intriguing possibilities as they discussed it, and then he would switch subjects again. She wished, looking at his face, that he would yield, and let the talk drift, as he would with some of his friends. But the strains of today were already quite bad enough, without forcing unnecessary demands on him.

Twice, they did stray briefly from the impersonal. She remembered querying, in surprise, a quotation from Sir Thomas Aquinas and he smiled and said, 'Forgive me, but I *have* read some books since I left my library at Midculter Castle.'

It was the first break in the wall with which he had surrounded himself. It was also surprising that he remembered what she had told him. She pursued it, indirectly, through the subject they were discussing at the moment. 'If I were a man, I think I should choose to follow Cabot and Burroughs and . . . Jenkinson. I should want to explore.'

They were indoors at that point, resting and sharing a hearty, overcooked meal which she was too absorbed to eat and Lymond, she supposed, too apprehensive. He said, watching the ale in his tankard, 'You avoid Chancellor's name.'

'I thought it was in the rules,' Philippa said. 'No emotive topics in case we exhaust ourselves before reaching Master Bailey. I know you offered to finance Diccon Chancellor. There was a letter to Nicholas in his papers. If I become the first lady merchant in Cambalu—'

'I couldn't afford it,' Lymond said. 'Nor could Cambalu. And I have a feeling you would need more than three doctors, even if all of them happened to be atheists. Of course, these explorations are important : perhaps the most attractive prospect the world holds today for any one of imagination and stamina.'

'But not so important as what you are doing for Russia?' Philippa said.

'I don't know,' Lymond said. 'I only know that I believe it must be done, as Chancellor's work had to be done.'

'I tried to join you,' Philippa said. 'It was stupid, of course. But there is a saying about people who write letters to other people who do not trouble to answer them.'

'*Chi scrire a chi non responde O egli e matto, o egli ha di bisogno.* . . . Who writes to one who doesn't reply, Is either a fool, or in need. . . . Was that in one of my books?' Lymond said.

'I,' said Philippa forbiddingly, 'have read some works other than the primary textbooks in the inadequate library at Midculter. Did you *read* my first letter?'

'Yes,' he said; and looked up as she put her palm over the top of his tankard.

She said, 'There is nothing wrong. But you are going to need your wits.'

'Ah, yes,' he said. 'So I am. . . . I read half of it.'

'And stopped at the maternal outpourings. I was mad,' said Philippa gloomily. 'Kuzúm was the last person you wanted to hear about: any fool could have told that. And even more so if . . .' She paused, rather pale. 'Can I have one, little, creeping excursion into sentiment?'

And knew by his body, if not by his face, that he had divined already what she was going to say, and that the fear, the cold and brutal misgivings she had carried about with her for two days were true. Lymond said, 'Margaret Lennox has told you of a conversation we had about Kuzúm's identity.'

Philippa nodded, her straying hands firmly gripped in her lap. 'She says that Kuzúm is Joleta's child. The son of Joleta Malett and her brother. And that Khaireddin, who died, was your son.'

'That was what I told her,' Lymond said. 'She believes it. And you must pretend to believe it. So long as she thought Kuzúm mine, Lady Lennox would be a threat to his safety.'

There was a brief silence during which Philippa Somerville fought and won a battle to keep her eyes dry. Lymond said, 'I give you my word. It was a lie.'

Philippa looked at him. 'And I don't believe *that*,' she said.

But this time, he did not give way. 'Kuzúm is who he is. As everyone keeps insisting, parentage doesn't matter. Love him for what he is: let your mother continue to love him. The death of the other child is my affair.'

'And you run your affairs so efficiently,' said Philippa, with sudden acidity. And then ashamed, she said. 'Will you have a son by Güzel?'

'With my heritage?' said Lymond, and stood up. 'I have my sons by peasant women and prostitutes, not by my mistress. If you are still anxious to reach Gardington and witness all my family secrets exposed, to the last

539

ludicrous dregs, I think we should leave and get on with our journey.'

Which she did, silently, for she understood she had made an error of judgment. And from then until late afternoon he hardly spoke to Philippa until, in a small hamlet within about fifteen minutes of their destination, he dropped speed unexpectedly and, for the first time in a long while, turned to her. 'Are you very tired?'

'No. Yes,' said Philippa truthfully. He back ached. Her wet clothes, now the rain had gone off, encased her limbs, moist and warm as papier mâché. She sneezed.

'Oh, *God*!' Lymond said. It had such an unheard-of ring of feeling that she turned immediately, but he had swung himself abruptly from his horse and taking his own reins and hers had instantly resumed talking quite normally. 'I apologize. It suddenly seemed to me that I have forced you to ride forty miles through filthy weather on an errand of impeccable charity, from which you will probably receive no reward but a fever. It was unchristian to be bad-tempered as well.'

Philippa gazed at him, and then at the inn courtyard towards which he was leading her. '*You* have forced *me*,' she repeated thoughtfully. 'Oh, well. I don't mind helping you to feel guilty if you must. On the other hand, I should point out that of all our various encounters, today is the only time you have favoured me with two civil words in sequence. I find it quite worrying.'

But the attempt to find safety in badinage did not bring the intended response. He went ahead of her into the inn to bespeak some refreshment while an ostler helped her dismount, and when at last she joined him, alone by the fire in the rush-strewn inn parlour, he was sitting quite still in a settle, his ringless hands clasped white together between his long, mud-splashed boots, and his burnished head bent brooding over them. She stood still, watching him until she heard the bustle of servants behind, and then, moving forward, said calmly. 'What can be done for these headaches?'

He rose immediately, and then glanced from her to the door as it opened, and a maid came in, with a tray of hot punch, and cold meat, and a loaf of new bread on a platter. 'Short of execution,' Lymond said, 'I think the problem is insoluble,' and smiled, and sat when Philippa sat and the maid, her burden deposited, had left them alone. Then, since Philippa continued to study him, he said, 'I am sorry it seems to be so obvious.'

'No. It isn't obvious,' Philippa said. 'But it won't help much with Mr Bailey if you have both a blinding headache *and* an excess of hot punch.' She paused and said abruptly, 'I shouldn't have come. You were right. You have enough to contend with already.'

'I think,' Lymond said, 'I can probably deal with Master Bailey and Mistress Somerville in one day, without succumbing altogether. If you give me a moment, I can probably even manage some frivolous conversation. And the hot punch is for you, not for me.'

So she disengaged for the moment. But later : 'Why did you change your mind?' Philippa said. 'And come to see Bailey?'

It was a bad question, on an excursion where emotional matters were barred. For without emotion, his answer was chilling. 'Because, I think, of something you said. One should be able to face anything. I have learned to play chess again. I have learned to listen to music, and to play it. I have learned to buy self-indulgence and enjoy it. I have learned to take a line of logic and follow it through, whatever the consequences. I should be able to withstand the revelation that I am a bastard, and my mother a whore.'

Philippa swallowed, and put her hands under the table. She said firmly, 'So long as you allow yourself that kind of self-indulgence, you can expect to have headaches. If you can face anything, then face up to the one basic fact in all this. You told Mìkál once, in Thessalonika, that you have never loved anyone. That was a lie. You feel for Sybilla quite as much as she has always felt for you.'

He had risen, his face too well trained to betray anything : after a moment's thought, he walked to the window and stood there. Philippa said, bluntly, to his back, 'If I were you, it would matter to me very much to prove that she was my mother. So much, that I shouldn't even attempt to find out the truth, if I thought I might learn she wasn't. I shouldn't want to be Gavin's son, either.'

'I don't think,' said Lymond, 'you could be.' He sounded politely amused.

'I don't know,' Philippa said. 'Heredity is an odd thing. Look at—' and then broke off.

'Don't,' Lymond said. He had turned round, his eyes

very bright. 'Don't, wise Philippa. The damage is spread too widely as it is.'

'But,' said Philippa, 'even if you accept bastardy, you are left to wonder why Sybilla didn't confess to you, since you have always been so very close. And from that, to surmise that the facts of your birth must be such that Sybilla knew they would destroy even your love for her. And that is why, at first, you wouldn't make any inquiries or allow them. But now . . .'

'Wise Philippa,' said Lymond again. Standing very still, with his back to the window he offered no resistance to what she was saying, but simply remained, his eyes dwelling on her as she sat bolt upright in the firelight, her wet, combed hair glowing chestnut where it fell forward over the darkened brocade of her gown. He said, 'Tell me, then, why I come now to Gardington?'

She drew a long breath and released it again, her eyes open and honest on his. 'Because, as you say, absence has hardened you. There are things you can face now which you couldn't face in Stamboul. And because, I think, at last, the bond with Sybilla is being shared with another. Before, all your mind and all your emotions were contained in your feeling for her. Now it is different. Now you have Güzel's love also.'

He had been holding his breath. He released it all at once, leaving his fair-skinned face for a moment as drained as his lungs, and then, after a pause, inhaled again with a long, vagrant column of air, caught as on the teeth of a ratchet with snatches of shock, and of laughter and of a sort of tearing, choked self-derision. 'Wise Philippa,' Lymond said. 'Wise, wise Philippa. . . . Do you know: after all, I do not think I can manage both Master Bailey and Mistress Somerville . . .?'

And when, looking at him, she said sharply, 'Sit down!' he did drop, abruptly, on to a stool by the window and remained there, his head in his hands, while Philippa found his unused cup and poured into it the last of the punch. Then kneeling beside him, she said, 'It will be worse if you don't go. Do you want me to stay here and wait for you?'

But instead of answering her he said, 'Philippa, will you go away? Out of the room. . . . Anywhere, just for five minutes. I shall come to you.'

And so, leaving the cup beside him, slowly she did.

He did not come in five minutes, but in ten; and then, although still extremely white, he had assumed again, flawlessly, the supreme self-possession of the Voevoda Bolshoia. He said, 'Poor Philippa : it must be worse than the Masque of the Pilgrims and the Irishmen. There are no more hands to be held. But I think, if you can bear it, you should come with me after all into Gardington. After that masterly exposition, you deserve to see how it all ends. . . . I have taken two rooms here for us overnight. Unless, of course, Master Bailey offers us hospitality for the night. He is, after all, my great-uncle.'

'And mine. By marriage,' said Philippa in the same tone exactly. 'But if he does, I shall look under the bed for the bombard.'

*

On the same day, Wednesday 28 April, Peter Vannes, the former English Ambassador to Venice, reached the town of Sittingbourne on his journey from Dover to London, and at about the same time the idle onlooker from Dover, riding untrammelled at fullest possible speed, arrived at John Dimmock's house in Fenchurch Street, London, where he found and had hurried words with Daniel Hislop.

Danny, with a catastrophe on his hands and no Voevoda to deal with it, made his excuses to Dimmock and his fellows of St Mary's, threw a saddle on the swiftest horse in Master Dimmock's stable, and set off for Sittingbourne as fast as he could go, making rendezvous with certain highly paid rogues on the way there. The idle man from Dover he sent, with a fresh horse, north-west to Gardington, in an effort to trace and bring back the Voevoda Bolshoia as fast as possible. The far from idle man, who had travelled seventy-two miles in an extremely short time, set out in good faith, but being overcome with sleep after sunset, made the mistake of hitching his horse and retiring, rolled in his cloak, for ten minutes' rest by the roadside. He slept for eight hours.

At the same time, Danny Hislop's absence was barely noticed by the household at Fenchurch Street, since something had happened which set all the merchants conferring. News had reached London of Thomas Stafford's attempt to capture Scarborough Castle, and, helped by

all the Spaniards at Westminster, the tale was not long
in spreading.

Long ago, Thomas Stafford's vainglorious plans had
been discovered by the English Ambassador to the French
Court, and long ago, King Philip had been made aware
of them. But from Brussels, King Philip's advisers were
writing him daily: *Your Majesty's affairs will benefit
greatly if the English can be made to declare war on the
French.* . . .

In all England, therefore, no one had lifted a finger
to stop Thomas Stafford from leaving France, nor to
prevent Thomas Stafford from landing and declaring
Mary Tudor an unrightful and unworthy Queen. Stafford
had come from his refuge in France, with French ships
and French gold and French soldiers. However Henri of
France might deny it, the sluggish citizens of this unfriendly country could place only one interpretation on
that.

'The French have spared us the trouble of breaking
the truce. Now you will see,' said Philip of Spain to his
Councillors. 'At last . . . at last we have this nation of
Englishmen ready for war.'

CHAPTER ELEVEN

Once before, the old man at Gardington had got the
notion that someone would rob him, and all the able boys
in the neighbourhood, and one or two lads from the
smithies, and some pikemen from the town had come out
to lend him a hand, with their bows and long staves
and cheap swords and sharp-headed pikes, to protect
Leonard Bailey and his property.

That time no one had come, and the pay had been as
you would expect from the twisted old miser, but the
woman Dorcas had made them all a rabbit broth with
bran bread to dip in it, and if you went about it the right
way, she would serve spitted urchins. So when the old
man called them round next time, when the great-nephew
from overseas was coming to steal the old fellow's books
and cut the old fellow's throat in his bed, by his way of
it, the idle stout arms in the district came again with
their bills, and got their potage, and hung about in the
544

arn and garden and kitchen, waiting for the rogue to
rrive since news had arrived from a groom at the 'Chicken'
hat he was coming. There was a lady with him, they
aid.

Since the rain had come on again, Leonard Bailey's
enchmen were mostly in the barn when his great-
ephew finally came to the gate, in a great cloak and a
eathered hat with a jewel, and a young hooded lady
with fold after fold of blue velvet skirts hanging down
y the fringe of her horsecloth. Twelve pairs of admiring
yes rested on Philippa Somerville, and then the leader,
collecting himself, ran to the gate with his fellows and
presenting a pike at the gentleman's chest said, 'Stand!'

'That,' said Lymond with some acerbity, 'is what I
am trying to do. Take my horse, you!' And dismounting,
e threw the reins and a gold piece together. Philippa,
iting her lip, waited for him and was swung down in
er turn. The gate was crowded with faces.

'*Well?*' said Lymond.

The spokesman, who had tried the gold in his teeth
and then made it vanish, in one miraculous movement,
aid, jerked a trifle by the big horse's reins, 'Are you Mr
Crawford of Lymond?'

'I am Mr Bailey's great-nephew,' said Lymond coolly.
And you, I suppose, are my cousins?'

There was a chorus of jeers from the gate. The faces
were grinning.

'I had hardly expected such a welcome,' said Lymond.
'And on such a wet day. Have you been waiting long?'

'Long enough,' said the spokesman, who had handed
the two horses to someone else who was holding them,
for nothing. 'You took your time at the "Chicken".'

'And the rain, I expect, has been making you thirsty?'
Lymond said.

The spokesman, one of the smith's big helpers, shifted
his feet. 'Ah well, yes. But the old man, he's paid us to
watch him.'

'A contract,' said Lymond, 'must be honoured. I want
to watch him too. I think we should all go in there and
watch him. But you must have a boy somewhere who
could go for the ale?'

There was a boy. He pocketed the money Lymond
gave him and ran off, while the gate swung open and
the pikes and hatchets moved back, to make way for the

lady and escort the gentleman into the house. The fir
that Leonard Bailey knew of the arrival of his grea
nephew was the tramp of many thick boots on the stai
and the crowding into his study of half the yeoman
Buckinghamshire, bearing with them the insolent gi
who had been there before, and a man whose name h
had no need to ask: a man with a beautiful doubl
under his long, rainsoaked cloak, and fair hair and lash
as long as a cow's.

'The Semple by-blow!' said Leonard Bailey.

If Lymond was still suffering any disability wha
ever, only the practised eye of Philippa Somerville cou
detect it. He looked carefully at the elderly, powerfu
man rising from his desk by the window: at the fraye
cap and big jowls and short, open gown, creased wher
he had been sitting. 'Yes,' he said regretfully. 'Whicheve
way you look at it, your poor sister had extremely ba
taste. Good evening, Uncle.'

'This is the man,' said Leonard Bailey, and looke
round grinning at all the interested faces. 'You see? Th
insolence? This is the cunning rogue who would tric
me.'

'I am known for it,' said Lymond repressively. 'I stea
linen off hedges.' The sapphire on his right hand, Philipp
calculated, must be worth at least four hundred gol
pieces. The pikemen breathed heavily, their gaze switch
ing from one man to the other. Lymond said, 'You di
invite us to come? Uncle?'

'I told the girl to tell you to come,' Bailey said, 'Sh
gets no welcome from me. And neither do you. Yo
came – I can tell! – to prove me wrong, or pay me t
keep my mouth shut. You'll do neither.'

'Heaven forbid,' Lymond said blandly, 'that I shoul
provoke hard feelings between nations on your accoun
An envoy from the Tsar of All Russia and one of th
Queen's Majesty's ladies in waiting, here to murder a
Englishman! Think of the uproar!'

'Here,' said the smith's lad, exchanging the role o
audience unexpectedly for that of chorus. 'You're not
Rus, you're not?'

Lymond surveyed him. 'I'm not a Rus, I'm not,' h
agreed, 'I'm Crawford of Lymond, a leader of mercenarie
and I work for the Grand Prince in Moscow. And if :
weren't that I've no mind to take you away from you

weethearts, there are some likely lads among you there
vho would do well in Russia. They roof their houses
vith gold.'

The eyes of the pikemen became large as pipe-hoops.
'That be damned for a tale,' said his great-uncle quickly.
'That wasn't what I heard.'

'When were you last in Russia?' Lymond said. His
hand emerged from his cloak and in a single smooth gesture, he opened and upended his purse over his great-
uncle's desk. Gold pieces, new minted and shining, trilled
from it like the song of a blackbird and created, in
seconds, a hillock. 'Be the nest roofed or lined, what does
it matter? But I came to talk about family business. And
for that, we nephews like our moment of privacy.'

'No!' said Master Bailey loudly. 'No, you'll not get these
lads to leave me. They're good English lads, and they're
here to protect me and mine.'

'From Mistress Philippa?' Lymond said hopefully.

'From you and your mercenaries, you contrary churl!'

'But I have no mercenaries with me,' Lymond said.
'They must have told you about that. And I gave these
gentlemen here my sword and my knife when they asked
for them. I am harmless, and innocent, I promise you,
of reprobious inventions. Besides, I have already explained. I have my position to think of. I couldn't possibly kill you.'

'Could you not?' Bailey said. 'I can see what you're
at. Humiliate me; steal my books; throttle me, for all I
know, and then claim exemption as the Tsar's favourite.
Ah, no. I'll not ask these lads to leave me.'

'What a pity,' said Lymond. Moving circumspectly, he
walked round the back of the desk and stood, looking
through the closed panes at the garden. 'I had hoped you
would allow them to pass downstairs at least. The ale has
arrived.'

And so it had, in a large keg rumbling erratically up
the winding, flagged path, propelled by the boy, along
with one or two helpers. 'I am sure,' said Lymond to the
smith's lad, 'that your master would release you to continue your guard duties below. Consider me, if you will,
as your prisoner. I shall not expect to walk out of that
door until you have all assured yourselves that your
master is alive and well. Assuming that he is alive and
well, that is, to start with. Are you alive, sir?' he said,

turning with interest to Master Bailey. 'We seem to have heard remarkably little of you in Scotland. But your manor, if I may say so, is very fine. I find that gratifying. They nearly gave it to me.'

Behind his back, an apologetic exodus was going on. With one eye on the detestable face of his great-nephew. 'Stop!' said Leonard Bailey. 'I haven't said— You've been bribed!'

'Just a barrel of ale, sir?' said the smith's man, who suddenly seemed to be the only one left 'And as he says sir. He can't get away with it, sir : no matter what he may do.'

'Who nearly gave what to you?' Philippa said, against the noise of Master Bailey's cane ill-temperedly thwacking his desk.

'Gardington was made over to me once, by the Crown. It's one of their standard good-conduct prizes for espionage.'

Philippa said, rather blankly, 'I thought you were spying at that time for Scotland.'

'Well, I wasn't spying for England,' Lymond said. 'But there was a small campaign afoot to make everyone think I was. A long time ago. But it makes it all the more interesting to find that when I no longer qualified, my great-uncle was presented with Gardington. What loyal service brought this reward, Uncle?'

Leonard Bailey laughed. He glared round the empty room and flung his cane to the floor, and sitting back in his chair gave vent to a bark of fleering, furious laughter. 'I nearly sent you to the headsman,' he said.

'I thought so,' said Lymond. His manner, perfectly courteous, was such that Philippa, biting her lip, found she preferred not to watch him. With the same exquisite manners he lifted over a chair, and placed her in it. Then he closed the door, and seated himself, on the other side of the desk from his great-uncle.

'Now,' said Francis Crawford. 'Before we talk, there is a small matter I wish to bring to your notice. In a moment, you are going to explain to me what you know of my birth. Since there seems little goodwill between us, I am sure that the explanation, whatever it is, will be one painful to me and my family. I merely wish to warn you that if in the course of it you speak slightingly or with the least disrespect of my mother, I shall indeed

hrottle you, and tell the men below that you died in a
it.

'Further' – as Bailey, his face suffused, lifted himself
to his feet – 'if you call back your men, you will see not
a crown for your pains.'

Bailey stopped, his hand on the window.

'Sit down,' Lymond said. 'And tell me how much my
mother has been paying you. For how long? For thirty
years?'

'What?' said Philippa; and Lymond, impatient, turned
round and looked at her.

'But of course. Or why else have both he and the Lennoxes forgone the chance to make all this public? He hates
and despises the Crawfords. But he has been living off
them – haven't you, dearest great-uncle? – all his life.'

'It was the woman who sinned—'

'Uncle!' Lymond said gently.

'Who made the mistake, and the woman who paid the
price. She could afford it.'

'But since she is not so young now, and not so well, it
seemed a good time to insure your income with the
next generation.' And as Philippa stifled an exclamation
Lymond said, his blue eyes still on Bailey, 'That is why
he asked you to bring me. You thought it a matter of old
grudges and hatred. It is, of course. But it is also a very
English matter of trade. You promised me proof,' Lymond
said to the other man.

'I have it,' said Bailey. On his big-lobed nose and his
cheeks, rather pale, the veins stood out like cracklure on
china. 'But not in this room. And I'll not leave it either,
with those light fingers near. No. Dorcas will fetch it. . . .
I take it I can ring my hand bell for Dorcas?'

'Provided only Dorcas comes,' Lymond said.

The old man set his jaw. Then, seizing his desk bell, he
rang it. And a moment later, the door opened to reveal the
thin, aproned form of the housekeeper. She was flushed.

'Master Leonard : did you send for that ale?'

'I sent for it, ma'am,' Lymond said. 'And I hope you
will share it, with my compliments. Your master has a
message for you.'

'Which he is capable of giving with his own tongue,'
Bailey said angrily. 'Dorcas, you recall the papers I told
you of? Get them.'

'And while she has gone,' said Lymond, as the door

closed behind the housekeeper, 'you will answer my question. How much of a pension do you accept from my mother?' And as the big man drew breath, he added calmly, 'I can, obviously, confirm what you tell me. I would save time therefore to give me the truth.'

Leonard Bailey had recovered his confidence. 'A peppery young man!' he observed. 'A very assured young gentleman, accustomed to the obedience of louts and ruffians in the field, and ruffling it at foreign courts, in great favour and pomp. Dorcas will tell you of the recipe she has for such as you. Take a peacock, break his neck and cut his throat and flay him, skin and feathers together.

'I am not sure, Master Nobody, if I care to do business with you, or answer your questions, or jump to your bidding. I have had an arrangement with pretty Mistress Sybilla – chaste Mistress Sybilla – spotless Mistress Sybilla – for thirty years now as you say. It is a trifling matter of a few coins. Had Honoria lived, she would have cost your family as much in a week. But she died giving birth to poor Gavin who was not, of course, and never could be the equal of your glorious, impeccable mother Sybilla. It seems but right that the family should pay for the mourning rites.

'It has been a long mourning, poor Honoria. And now the 1st Baron has gone, and his son Gavin has gone, and none is left to remember her but Sybilla and one of her sons. If we do business,' said Leonard Bailey, the saliva winking at the corners of his strong lips, 'I trust you will be generous. Or I shall have to try if the other son thinks Honoria deserves better remembrance.'

'How much?' Lymond said. He had made no effort to interrupt. But his eyes, all the time Bailey was talking, had been wandering, Philippa noticed, along the book shelves, marking the thick rolls, the leather and velvet bound volumes of his great-uncle's remarkable library.

'I receive a pension,' said Leonard Bailey, 'of three hundred pounds per annum.'

'I don't believe it,' said Lymond.

'Nevertheless, it is true. Does it seem so much for an old man to live on?' said Bailey. 'But if you wish, I can show you papers. Her last payment' – and he pulled open a drawer of his desk – 'is there. Signed by the noble and virtuous lady herself.'

From where she sat, Philippa could not see the paper, but she watched Lymond read it. Three hundred pounds a year – six times what the Queen's Latin secretary earned to keep himself and his wife at Court, including his prize money. And spent on nothing, so far as she could see, but this miserly gathering of books. She could not believe he ever opened them. They lay undisturbed, as they had lain when she came to Gardington last: an insurance: a treasure safe from most robbers, for what country labourer would know the value of these six perfect volumes of the works of St Augustine? She wondered thinking rapidly of the libraries she knew – Sidney's, Ascham's, Pole's, that of John Dee – what this collection was worth, and put it, at its lowest, at three thousand marks. Then Lymond laid the paper down carefully on the desk and turned, as the door opened and the woman Dorcas came in, with a locked metal box in her hands.

'Ah!' said Leonard Bailey. 'Put it there. What is it, Dorcas?'

The housekeeper's lidless, angry eyes stared at the two unwanted visitors and then at the flushed face of her master. 'Your friends below,' she said, 'are already crapulous. Am I meant to sit in the same kitchen with the scum?'

It reminded Bailey of his fears. 'The devils!' he said, starting up. 'Will they take my fees and leave me here to be killed?'

'If you guard your tongue,' said Lymond pleasantly, 'you have nothing to fear. The papers, please.' And Leonard Bailey, after glancing round them all again, drew a key from his drawer and, unlocking the box, took from it the only two papers it contained, and held them fast in his powerful hands.

'These are copies,' he said. 'These are signed by the Semple woman – by your dear lady mother – but they are copies. You will get nothing by stealing them. But they will prove to you what I told the girl here is true. There, dear Master Nobody, is what you came for. There is your certificate of bastardy.' And he threw them on the table before Francis Crawford.

He rose, and picking them up, took them across to the low window. The housekeeper, after hesitating for a moment, had gone. After a moment Lymond said,

'Philippa?' And rising with rigid composure, Philippa walked to the window and joined him.

There were two papers which he handed to her, one by one. On each was a single paragraph written in the same hand, with the same wording exactly, save for the child's name which had been filled in on each. The first paper he gave her bore the name of Eloise Ann Crawford, his younger, dead sister. The second carried his own.

I, Sybilla Semple or Crawford, Baroness Culter of Midculter Castle, Scotland, do swear before these witnesses below listed that the child born of my body this day and to be named FRANCIS CRAWFORD *is not the son of Gavin Crawford, 2nd Baron Culter of Midculter Castle but the true offspring of . . .*

And there followed a blank. Below, there were two signatures, one of a man and one of a woman, and Sybilla's own name, signed in thin, faded ink. It was dated 1 November 1526. She looked at Lymond, who was not, it seemed, the same age as her mother.

Lymond said, his voice perfectly steady, 'But the father's name is missing on each.'

'Ah, yes. She would have that,' said Bailey. 'It is on the originals. Or so I believe. But she wouldn't risk keeping a copy of that in the castle, would she?' And he laughed.

'You stole these from Midculter?' Lymond asked.

'I came across them,' said Bailey. He looked pleased. 'You recall. It was no part of my promise to tell you your parentage. Only to give you proof that you were got out of wedlock. There you have it.'

'But,' said Lymond delicately, 'it seems to me that nothing as yet has been proved. These are copies, you say. Where are the originals? And how do I know this is my mother's signature? Of all people, I have reason to believe that you may have talents as a forger. Am I right?'

'I have a gift,' Bailey said. 'But that writing is genuine. Hold it beside the paper I showed you, with my pension. As to the originals, I have no idea where they are. You are welcome to look for them. Or you could ask your mother, if you think it is worth it. But ask yourself first' f she would have paid me all these years to keep a lie private.'

'Another question occurs to me,' said Lymond. 'Why were these certificates written? And when written, why copied?'

Bailey shrugged the massive, stained shoulders. 'You know the lady – the gentle, excellent lady – better than I do. Perhaps she wished to hold your father – your nameless father – to his duty. There must have been accouchement expenses to pay. Perhaps – whoever he is – he has been helping her with your upbringing, my pension, her pins and ribbons and sweetmeats. He may be a grieve at your own—'

He broke off, and not before time. Lymond said, 'No. My patience has quite well-defined limits. You talk of 'he'. Does that mean that my sister and I shared the same father?'

The lord of Gardington was afraid, but he covered it still with bravado. 'I am terrified to speak,' said Leonard Bailey. 'I can only say that I do not know. And that you know the lady – the dear lady – better than I do.'

'Yes,' Lymond said. His face, Philippa saw, marked the stress more by its altering planes than by any dramatic displacement of colour. She knew her own face was pale and her stomach tired and painful within her. She walked back and sat down, while Lymond laid the two papers again on the desk and remained, surveying his relative.

'Now,' said Lymond, 'you will listen to me. From this moment, the payment from my mother will cease and I shall order a similar sum paid to you monthly, from my bankers in London. I shall leave with them such an amount that, whatever happens to me, there should be a pension secure for your lifetime. I shall also leave instructions that the day this information becomes public, from whatever source, the pension will cease. Is that understood?'

'But—' said Leonard Bailey.

'*Is that understood?*' said Lymond again, and this time Bailey said, 'Yes.'

'I am glad. You will now take paper and pen and write a letter to my mother at Midculter telling her that your health is failing and that you intend to go overseas. You will thank her for all the financial support she has

553

given you hitherto, and say that you now have enough to serve the remaining years of your life, and do not wish to have this matter more on your conscience. She may take it upon your honour . . . your honour, great-uncle Bailey . . . that her secret will remain quite safe with you. You will sign it, and I shall see that it reaches her.'

The letter seemed to take a long time. Outside, the rain beat, noisy as straw on the window panes and the vice candlestick, newly lit, threw its light on the littered desk and the worn, damp-smelling books as they waited. It was late: too late to make much of their journey back to London. They would have to stay, as Lymond thought, at the 'Chicken'. No . . . not at the 'Chicken', Philippa suddenly recalled. For that inn harboured the underpaid ostler who had sent Bailey word of their coming. Mr Crawford would not want to return there. Well, there were other inns.

She looked at him, standing by the desk watching Bailey painfully writing his letter. He had not touched the old man, or even threatened him, except to protect Sybilla from his foul tongue. She wondered what part Bailey had played in his past, when outlawed and sought by both England and Scotland Lymond had come eventually to stand trial in Edinburgh, on the evidence which Bailey must have helped manufacture. It took a self-denial approaching to Calvinism not to take revenge for that kind of malevolence, because a man was old, and alone, and a kinsman. . . . No. Not even a kinsman. If all this were to be believed, Leonard Bailey was no kin at all.

The rest of it, of course, was all done for Sybilla. Sybilla who, having broken her marriage vows, had been too proud to tell this son whom she had drawn so close, but had left him to find out, like this. Who must know, or suspect, why he turned his back on her, but still had done nothing to put matters right. Because, one was bound to suppose, she dared not face the one question he was certain of right to ask her: the name which the paper left blank.

And then the letter was finished, and laboriously signed and dusted, and the direction written, and Lymond, putting it away, had removed also the glittering pile of gold coins, followed by Bailey's covetous eyes, and had slung on his cloak. She rose as well, and Bailey, behind

554

his desk, stood also, and backed a little into the corner, his veined eyes wary, the linen damp round his neck. Lymond stood perfectly still, and looked at him.

'I wonder,' he said, 'in all my life what reason I have had before to take a man's life. The house you were brought up in was a Crawford house. The money which fed and sheltered and educated you was Crawford money. You reached man's estate and still you stayed there, in this circle you found so despicable: stayed until the child born there to your sister was man enough to marry in turn; and only left when at last it was made clear your presence was unwanted. You told Mistress Philippa you were flung out. I do not think that, even if you were, you have cause for complaint.'

'Do you not?' said Leonard Bailey. 'You do not remember my sister's husband. Or did he dandle you on his knee? He never did as much for me, a child of eight, when my sister died.'

'But that was not his offence,' Lymond said. 'His offence was his charity. It takes a great man to accept alms, and be grateful, and honour the giver with love and honest achievements. It has been done. But you did not even accept the gift of your manhood and then turn your back on the Crawfords. You devoted the rest of your life to injuring them.'

'You move me to pity,' his great-uncle said. 'Show me again your purse, and the ring on your finger. I see how I have ruined you. I see how your mother sits, bereft in the poorhouse. Look, sir, about you! Is this Midculter?'

'No,' Lymond said. 'It is the tomb of a scavenger. The last station in a journey which should have been stopped long before, had you fallen among any but upright people, and men of good faith. They are not my kin, but I shall not disgrace them. Live your life, if you think it worth living. Spend my money, since you do not despise it. I shall only make one stipulation and since, unlike you, I am a man of my word, it will do you no injury. I wish, before I go, to see these papers burnt.'

'What?' said Bailey. He strode forward, snatching them up from the table and held them, protectively, behind his shabby gown. Lymond, the desk tinder box in his hands. was already occupied in lighting a spill. Bailey reached for the handbell. 'Ho! Billy—!' and then halted abruptly. The flame in Lymond's hands, nursed, ran along the middle bookshelves, causing a little charring on the nearest calf bindings. A wisp of smoke, coiling, lifted. 'Or I turn your books into ashes. Don't call,' Lymond said.

Bailey's hand, shaking, put down the bell. He swore. 'This lying family! Upright, you said! And now—'

'But you will get your pension,' Lymond said. The flame in his hands, rising, touched the books above. He shifted his grip on the spill. 'For, after all, you could still start a scandal, a rumour; and the originals, you claim, still exist. In any case, as I say, I keep my word. Your money will come. But it would be sad if, instead, you were to lose all your books.'

The smell of singed calf filled the room. A vermilion light flickered. A roll had taken fire.

Bailey cried out. 'There! There, God damn you! There, son of a harlot, begot in the brake! There is your birthright!' And he flung the documents over.

Lymond's hand, disregarding the heat, closed upon the bookroll, and extinguished the small flame. And then, picking up the two papers, he reduced them to ashes.

Then he said, 'Come, Philippa,' and, moving forward, she let him take her downstairs.

There was hardly a man capable of climbing up to see if Master Bailey was in his room, alive and unharmed by his visitor, but Lymond waited until Dorcas, with Billy stumbling beside her, had clattered up to the study, and when they came down, he threw the man another gold piece and, collecting his sword and dagger, left the house with not a few of them following him, and asking his interest for them in Russia, where the rooftops were all made of gold. He answered them smiling, and rewarded the lad with the horses, and lifted Philippa up, and then swung into the saddle himself. His hands, gripping Philippa, sent a rapid, vibrating pulse into her arm; but he appeared otherwise perfectly collected, and spurred off with exemplary vigour.

She followed him as best she could, for he rode very fast and the way was now almost dark. He passed the 'Chicken', as she had expected, and it was only an increase in the downpour and a realization, she supposed, that he could not expect her, as he would himself, to endure the hazards of a rough road in the dark that made him rein in at the next inn they came to, and, dismounting, find that there were two rooms to be had for the night.

Then he came back with a groom, who handed her down, so that she could not detect his state of mind by his touch. Inside the inn however, by the light of the lamps, it was a different matter. She climbed the stairs without speaking, and without speaking heard him wish her good night. She was to have a light meal, he said, served in her chamber.

The door to her room was beside them. 'Come in for a moment,' said Philippa. And as he made no immediate response, she added, 'I know. My company isn't going to help, but my medicaments might. I had a word with one of the maids there myself. Short of executions and violets and even the brain-pan of the blessed St Michael there are a few humble remedies which might make the thing a little less crippling. What does it spring from? The opium?'

He did come in, but not to sit down. She shut the door with a bang and knelt to improve the inn's idea of a fire. 'Lack of self-control, I thought,' said Francis Crawford.

'Yes. Well, I deserved that,' said Philippa grimly, getting up. 'I have seldom seen such an exhibition of howling restraint. And if you want to shout and smash things, please do. I should have been better pleased if you had smashed Master Bailey.'

'On the contrary,' Lymond said. 'I think you were the restraining element. For which I am grateful. Philippa, I am better alone. You must forgive me.'

'In a moment. Do you think he knows?' said Philippa abruptly.

'Who my father is?' He moved incessantly, drifting from the table to the window to a chair, and back to the window again. 'I don't think so. Or my mother would not be paying him.'

Philippa said, 'Do you want to find out?'

'It seems a little late,' Lymond said.

Philippa said, 'Except that we both know Sybilla. Whoever he is, he must be a remarkable man. Your blood is not Gavin's, which would please anybody: do you not want to know whose it is? You need to understand yourself better than you do.'

'I have enough difficulty,' Lymond said, 'trying to understand your tortuous reasoning. You want my leave now to track down my father?'

'That was by the way,' Philippa said. She had a mild headache herself and wondered whether he had actually envisaged her sitting down, arms akimbo, to attack even the lightest of meals. 'I was about to suggest that you must next find the originals of these certificates, and destroy them.'

He said, 'Your mind works too well, doesn't it Philippa? I thought today we should come to the end of it.'

'Something happened today,' Philippa said. 'You shared Sybilla's burden. You didn't want to do that before.' She paused. 'You can't look for the papers yourself : you'll be in Russia. Unless you want to confide in Nick Applegarth, let me do it. Or if there are things you don't want me to know, tell me, and of course I'll do nothing more.'

And she looked, candidly, at the place where he had come to rest, his arm on a chairback in the shadows.

'I know no more than you do,' Lymond said. 'The papers will be in France, I should think. Perhaps Sevigny is a clue. . . . It was in the family, and Sybilla perhaps stayed there. One might look among the Dame de Doubtance's papers, or seek the witnesses, or question priests and wetnurses and midwives. . . .' He broke off. Then he said, 'I don't think I can stand the thought of that particular kind of prying. No. I don't want you to do it.'

'Because of the prying?' Philippa said. 'Or because of the certificate that wasn't there?' And as he looked at her without speaking she said, 'For there should have been three papers, shouldn't there? There was no certificate for your other sister, whom we know was illegitimate. There was no paper for Marthe.'

She did not know that her headache showed too : that the fresh colour had gone from her cheeks and had left behind it two half-circles of strain under her thinking brown eyes, and a single line across the clear brow, between the sheer, silky falls of her hair. She stood lost in worried contemplation and was only moved to look up when a sound told her, to her surprise, that he had found his way without warning to the door.

Francis Crawford stood with his back to the doorpost and said, '*Yunitsa*, forgive me. My ailment will be the worse for it, and so shall I, but I am going to leave you.'

She had seen him look like that before once, at Volos,

nd she made no move to stop him. Only, '*Yunitsa?*, she aid.

He smiled, a glimmer in his darkened blue eyes. 'What, fter Best's Russian teaching? It means *heifer*,' he said. Good night. And thank you, wise Philippa.'

The maid came soon after that, with the food and the potion for headaches. Philippa sent the meal back, and, rather desperately, took the mixture herself.

*

The idle fellow from Dover, aghast at his ill-timed sleep by the road-side, set off in the dawn light to Gardington and was fortunate enough to find an inn called the 'Chicken' just short of it, where Mr Crawford had ordered beds for the night. He and the lady, it seemed, had failed to occupy them. The innkeeper, discussing the matter, began to have hopes of compensation. When none was forthcoming the innkeeper, disgruntled, recalled something else. A reward, Mr Bailey had said, for every soldier of Crawford's whom he managed to detain on the way.

There had been no soldiers so far. But this was a powerful fellow: not the kind of man an old gentleman would like for a visitor. The inn host, switching the talk to refreshment, showed his unwanted visitor into a chamber and, slamming the door, turned the key on him briskly.

*

Waking next morning wan, limp, but full of persevering good sense, Philippa Somerville was surprised to find, passing Mr Crawford's neighbouring bedroom that the door was standing ajar, and inside there was no sign of an occupant. From the innkeeper she heard what she might already have guessed. Mr Crawford had ridden out early, having paid for them both and having arranged for two trustworthy grooms to accompany the lady to London. He had also left her his apologies.

Considering this, she came only slowly to realize what the innkeeper was also explaining. 'It'll be the news, mistress. Everyone is going to London. They say it will be war, within days.'

559

'What news?' said Philippa hardily. And listened in silence to the account of Mr Stafford's ill-timed Scarborough raid.

'They say,' said the innkeeper, 'that the French have already been warned to fly from the country. And the Scots will declare war soon, so they expect. All the high officers are called back to London. War. . . . It's a dreadful thing, Mistress.'

He sounded pleased, Philippa thought. *A longing for novelty, peculiar to this nation.* Or so the Venetians said.

She didn't want breakfast. She left the inn while he was still exclaiming and rode with her two grooms to London with a premonition, and a fear, in the back of her sensible mind.

CHAPTER TWELVE

There was rumour of war at every halting-place between Gardington and London. By the time he reached Fenchurch Street, it occupied Francis Crawford's mind to the exclusion of almost everything else : the French had sent five hundred Gascon foot soldiers to Scotland and were to dispatch three thousand more; Scotland had been asked by France to raise fifteen thousand French-paid Scots infantry. The Queen Dowager had been voted sixty thousand pounds by the Scots Parliament. On the Border, the English were planting fifteen hundred reinforcements at Berwick and Carlisle, Norham and Wark. . . When war came, Richard Crawford, who was not his brother, would be fighting for Scotland.

But he, the Voevoda Bolshoia, would be in Russia. He had reached Dimmock's house before he was reminded by the bustle outside, of the thing he had contrived to lose sight of : that today, Thursday 29 April, he was to attend the great banquet to be held by the Muscovy Company to mark the departure of the first Muscovite Ambassador. His coat for it, already chosen, was Russian and made by Güzel's staff : it was so heavily jewelled that Dimmock's servants, terrified, had offered a special case with three locks to keep it in.

Güzel had made no such provision. It is only the poor man, said Güzel, who counts his belongings. The rich man guards himself, and lets his goods fall where they may. . . .

On Saturday Ely and Petre would come, with the royal letters and presents. And by Monday the four ships, towed downstream, would await the Muscovy party at Gravesend there to take their leave of England.

So by Monday he must complete all his arrangements, receive the last papers, organize the last interviews. Four days so planned that it might be done, at the cost of a little hard work. But there would soon be time enough on the *Primrose* to rest and reflect. And it allowed no time – no time at all for personal business.

Adam Blacklock met Lymond at the door of Dimmock's house. 'Nepeja is going mad. You know that it is only an hour to the banquet?'

Lymond stared at him. 'Calm! Calm,' he said. 'They are not likely to begin it without us.'

'Well, they're likely to begin it without Ludo and Danny,' Adam said, who, no longer in Russian employ, had rebelled against Russian edicts. 'They both rode out of London yesterday, and neither of them has been heard of since.'

Someone had taken Lymond's horse. With Adam at his side he was already running upstairs to his room when the implication of that statement reached him. He stopped. 'Together?' said Lymond.

'No,' said Adam, his uneasiness suddenly crystallizing. 'Danny first, and then we found Ludo had gone later. Neither of them left any message.'

'Blackheath?' Lymond said.

'No. I sent there,' said Adam. He added, worrying, 'Have you come straight from Gardington?'

'Forty miles. I am unlikely to live,' said the Voevoda, with an air of abstraction. 'Did Hislop receive any message, that you know of?'

'I asked that as well,' Adam said. 'It seems someone did call and ask for him. There is an impression Danny sent him straight away. I wondered if he had dispatched him to you.'

'Well, if he did, he didn't reach me,' Lymond said. 'Good God : is that Nepeja?'

'He has been ready,' said Adam, 'for the last hour and a half.'

561

'You look very pretty as well,' Lymond said, and disappeared into his room.

He was, astonishingly, ready in time, with no trace of the dust of his journey, and the work of Güzel's sempstresses and goldsmiths and embroiderers like a riza adorning his person. There was a ceremonial ride, this time through Lombard street and Lothbury to the towering oriel windows, painted, gilded and carved, of the Drapers' Hall, hired by the Muscovy Company to do justice to the splendid occasion.

Inside, gathered in heated bales of fur and velvet and brocade, were the Governor, consuls, assistants and sad, discreet and honest Members of the Muscovy Company, waiting to convey their guests to their places at the long, laden tables before the blue cloth of state with its shield showing a ship in full sail, with the lion of England above, and round it the motto of the Company: *Refugium Nostrum In Deo Est.*

'If the war comes,' said Sir George Barnes on Lymond's left hand, ''twill be the only harbour we may trust. They say England will pay the whole cost of it, and all for King Philip's purpose, not for our own. Trades suppressed, new taxes imposed. . . . How else will we finance the foot and horse they say the Queen has promised to send. The King can't collect any more money in Brussels or Antwerp; they say Ruy Gomez can't even raise it in Spain, or why else does he delay?'

It was all they could think of, the merchants crowding here to do public honour to the Ambassador, although they chatted and joked and called across the tables to one another between the entertainments: the jugglers and the singers and the acrobatics, and the one-act interlude by players in false heads, between the blubber dainties and the darioles. There were no Sumtuous Hores.

The Voevoda Bolshoia, a civilized and entertaining companion, for a Scotsman, kept afloat the cross-conversations all about him, as deftly as the jugglers their balls, and gave no sign of the two, and three, and four other subjects which were occupying the rest of his mind in the meanwhile. Most of the senior officials were there. At the head of the table, old Master Cabot, with his broad face and broken nose and long, white forked beard. The knights, Andrew Judde and Will Chester, part owners of the *Primrose* and the *John Evangelist*, and

ohn Dimmock his host, owner of the *Anne*, now waiting
leave St Botolph's Wharf with the *Trinity*, fully-laden
ith twenty-one bales of cotton stuff and two hundred
rting cloths and five hundred pieces of Hampshire ker-
y in sky blue and red and green and ginger and yellow,
ith sugar and with nine casks of pewter of Thomas
asel's making, the cloth alone being worth £3,400. And
low the casks and the crates and the bales, another
rgo whose worth was not public knowledge, and whose
ntents had not been broadcast at all.

Sir Henry Sidney, soon to go back to Ireland, with his
iend Edmund Roberts, newly back from his labours in
cotland, from which five hundreds pounds of cargo of
e wrecked *Edward Bonaventure* had been recovered
nd was now on its way south in a hired English ship.
etween them, Sidney and Roberts had given him the
en and the advice he needed to mine the iron in Russia,
nd work it, and in time give them, he hoped, a steel
rpassing that of the Turks and Persians. In time. . . .

Anthony Hussey, whose cousin Lawrence had had such
signal success with the Queen Dowager in Scotland. As
on as he left Russia, Lymond knew, a letter would be
n its way from Scotland to the Queen Dowager's dearest
ster, Mary of England, regretting that she could not,
ithout her dearest daughter's advice, dispense with the
bellion of the sometime Earl of Lennox, and that there-
re, as the wife of a man without civic rights, Lady
ennox's claim to the Angus estates would instantly be
opped.

John Buckland, Master under God of the new flagship
e *Primrose*, with Tony Jenkinson, who would sail in
hancellor's place and do as well, probably, as Chan-
ellor. And whom he, the Voevoda Bolshoia, would come
know in the long journey north, and either tolerate or
islike, it did not matter which. There had been good
ews for the Company that day, John Buckland had
ld him. They had had word that the *Searchthrift* was
fe and had wintered at Kholmogory : the pinnace which
tephen Burroughs and Richard Johnson had taken to
ardo, hoping to sail east past the Ob. This they had not
one, but this spring they were to set out again. So the
ompany were not without their adventurers, or John Dee
is pupils. . . .

William Garrard, who had told Philippa how to reach

Bailey's house: a good thing, or a bad? Robert Best, wh
knew as much as anyone about the Voevoda's activitie
in Russia, but who was going back to Russia with him
and therefore had to be circumspect. Philip Gunter, whom
he had met with Sir Henry and Harry Becher, with th
harem of drakes, whom he had not met at all.

Those with office near to the Queen: Sir Henry Jer
ningham, Vice Chamberlain and Captain of the Guard
the Earl of Arundel, President of the Council; Sir Willian
Cecil; Sir William Petre, who left the chamber unex
pectedly with Dimmock beside him, and did not com
back for ten minutes.

The speeches began. Wine, in a loving cup, was passe
back to back through the whole company to pledge th
departing Muscovite Ambassador; and then the old man
Cabot himself, made the announcement they had al
come to hear. To Osep Grigorievich Nepeja, first Am
bassador to England from the Tsar of all Russia, th
Company here present were agreed to bear the whol
cost and charges incurred by the Ambassador and thos
travelling with him from Scotland to London, and als
during his stay until sailing, as testing and witness o
their good hearts, zeal and tenderness towards him and
his country.

There was a touching display of appreciation, as thi
generous offer was translated by Rob Best and receive
by the Ambassador with hands clasped over his sturd
pearled chest. He embraced Master Cabot. He embrace
Sir Andrew Judde and Sir George Barnes. He almos
embraced Rob Best until he remembered that he, a mer
servant of the Company, would be returning to Russia
Then, in rolling tones, the Ambassador started hi
answer.

It was launched into respectful silence, broken onl
by the obedient echo of Robert Best's English. It pro
ceeded with a little less clarity, against some whisperin
which was making itself heard at the foot of the tables
The whispering, spreading, became a subdued murmu
punctuated by hissing noises as the merchants so fa
ignorant tried to hush, from politeness, the merchant
more favourably placed.

Francis Crawford, watching and listening, could sens
only one thing. Whatever news had arrived, it concerne
the merchants, not the Russians or his own affairs in an

f their various aspects. And the news, whatever it might
e, was good.

Then it reached the top of the table and Osep Nepeja,
uzzled, brought his speech to a more rapid conclusion
han he had intended while Best rushed through the
ranslation and was applauded almost before he had
lone, so eager were his audience to get rid of him.

And in the end it was Sir George Barnes who stood and
nade the announcement, from a piece of paper passed
long from his fellows; perhaps because he had the
oudest voice; or perhaps because, with Judde, his had
een the vigour which had launched the Muscovy ships
nto their first, fateful journey to Russia.

The statement was brief. 'My lords; gentlemen; the
Philip and Mary has arrived safe in London.'

The answering roar rose to the hammerbeam roof, and
ats and gloves leaped vying after it. Men jumped to
heir feet. Barnes and Cabot and Judde, leaning over the
able, shouting answers, exchanging embraces and slaps
nd hand-wringings of joy had, every man, a tear in his
ye. Nepeja, his massive head jerking to and fro sat
jaculating until Best, taking pity, explained it. The fourth
f Richard Chancellor's fleet of small ships, given up as
ost with the others at the entrance to Trondheim, had
nade its way safely to harbour, and, after wintering
here, had now crossed the ocean to London. Intact, with
very man well, and her whole cargo, including ten
housand pounds of wax, to the value of over four thou-
and pounds.

Lymond did not rise to his feet. Nor did Henry Sidney;
r Adam Blacklock or John Buckland, or Robert Best.
Across the jostled tables, strewn with meats and over-
urned glasses, the eyes of the five men found each other,
nd met. And the look they exchanged was not one of
oy yet, nor of thanksgiving, but a recognition of
nourning.

Then Sir Thomas Jerningham's hand touched Francis
Crawford on the shoulder, and the Vice-Chancellor said,
I hesitate to call you away in the midst of such rejoicing.
But there is a matter my colleagues and I would wish
o discuss. Will you follow me?'

And since he could recognize, also, the touch of fate
vhen it came, and its inevitability, Francis Crawford rose,
nd followed him out of the room.

Sir William Petre was in the small room they took hi
to, and his host John Dimmock, and the Earl of Arunde
the President of the Council, and a great many other mer
armed, whom he recognized as Jerningham's, and wh
closed in behind him as he walked through the door. A
he moved forward there was another step on the threshol
and Lymond, glancing back, saw that Adam Blackloc
also had been ushered into the room, followed rathe
quickly by Sir Henry Sidney. Petre said, 'Henry! Th
does not concern you.'

'Nevertheless, as a member of the Muscovy Compan
also, I should like to stay,' Sidney said. 'This is our roc
and Mr Crawford is our guest beneath it.'

'Let him stay,' the President said. Henry Fitzalan, 10t
Earl of Arundel, could afford to be magnanimous to
man married to a Dudley, the family he had helped t
overthrow when Queen Mary came to the throne. '1
does not affect the course of our business. Mr Crawfor
you have two servants named Daniel Hislop and Ludovi
d'Harcourt?'

'I have,' Lymond said. The Russian coat, long an
close-fitting and sashed with Persian silk burned in th
afternoon sunlight with its gold wire and jewels : th
buttons were emerald cameos. The eyes of the men a
arms, like cats in a jungle, reflected the points of gree
fire. Lymond said, 'They are officers of rank in Tsa
Ivan's army, and much esteemed by him.'

'I have no doubt,' said Arundel smoothly. 'It is to giv
your opinion as to their integrity that we are asking yo
to leave this hall and favour us with some of your tim
this afternoon. There has been an unfortunate incident.'

'I am disturbed to hear it,' Lymond said. After the fir
glance, he had not looked round and Adam, conscious c
Sidney beside him, did not look sideways either. He coul
feel his heart beating.

'Yes. It seems that our very good friend the Dean c
Salisbury and late English Ambassador to the Doge an
Senate of Venice, travelling from Dover to London to mak
his duty to her Majesty at Westminster, suffered a
armed attack on his baggage, in the course of which tw
of his men were killed and three injured. The initial rai
I am told, was launched by the officer Ludovic d'Ha
court, and subsequently a further attempt was made b
your other servant, Master Hislop. Both men are now i

566

custody and we have not, alas, been able to persuade them to give us an explanation. It appeared to us that your presence might help.'

Francis Crawford, allowing his gaze to wander round the chamber, returned it at leisure to Arundel and said, pleasantly, 'Do I gather that I am conceivably in custody as well? And Master Blacklock?'

It was Sir Henry Jerningham, Vice-Chamberlain and Captain of the Guard who cleared his throat and replied, 'Unlike your hosts the Merchants, the people of England are not so understanding in their dealings with foreigners,' he said. 'Men have been killed, and it is known that men in the Ambassador's train are implicated. The Ambassador cannot speak English and we accept that he is unaware of what has happened. But—'

'Master Blacklock and I are to be protected for our own good?' Lymond said. 'I am touched by your forethought. I should certainly like to talk, as soon as possible, with d'Harcourt and Hislop.'

'Unfortunately,' the Earl of Arundel said, 'they received some rather brisk handling, but naturally you will see them as soon as they have recovered sufficiently. Sir Henry Jerningham has kindly offered to shelter you : you will find some friends of yours, I think, already at his house. Mr Dimmock here will undertake any commissions you wish to give him regarding unfinished business or your engagements. He also joins me in regretting that your special mission from your master the Tsar has not after all been successful.'

Sir William Petre, who was neither a stupid man nor, as it happened, a cowardly one, met Lymond's eyes. 'Ah. The shipment of arms?' Lymond said.

And Sir William replied. 'Unfortunately, news of it came to the ears of King Philip, and he has ordered all the materials of war to be removed from the ships, and has cancelled the passage of all your trained men save for Master Gray's seven ropemakers and Master Standish, the physician. It was, if you remember, a hazard against which we were unable to guarantee you any protection. No blame will attach to yourself or the Ambassador. But the cargo of arms will not be allowed to leave England.'

'I see,' Lymond said. He did not, surprisingly, make either protest or counter-threat : he seemed, indeed, to be giving all his attention to Petre and Dimmock. Then he

said, 'It is a matter of deep regret to me also. In view o
its importance, and also as a matter of courtesy, I shoul
be glad of your leave for a few moments to speak t
Master Nepeja.'

None of the pikemen behind him moved, and the doc
remained shut. 'During the banquet? It would be
pity,' said Sir Henry Jerningham, 'to disturb him, si
There will, I am sure, be ample opportunity for speakin
to the Ambassador later.'

And that, too, Adam saw Lymond accept without re
monstrance. It was while he was still staring, bewildered
at Lymond's back that the Voevoda said, 'Sir Henry wi
tell Master Nepeja, no doubt, what has occurred, whic
is all I intended. I see you are anxious to leave. Ma
I know, before we do so, the names of the friends I am t
meet at Sir Henry Jerningham's?'

Arundel looked at Jerningham, and Jerningham in tur
pulled a piece of paper from his waist pouch and passe
it over. The President said, 'Ah, yes. You may look fo
ward, Mr Crawford, to an unexpected reunion. On boar
the *Philip and Mary* were two further officers of you
master the Tsar, who boarded her, we understand, durin
the winter at Trondheim. Their names are Alexande
Guthrie and Fergus Hoddim. I understand,' said the Ea
of Arundel, passing the paper gracefully back, 'that yo
will hear tidings of great changes in Russia. Affairs ar
not, Mr Crawford, as they were when you left Mosco
ten months ago.'

There was mild interest on the Voevoda's face. H
bowed, acknowledging the information; he bowed, smilin
to Sidney and waited for Adam, hesitating, to walk to h
side. A second door, leading away from the Hall, ha
been opened on the far side of the room and Jerningha
stationed there was waiting, his sword at his side.

Lymond was wearing no sword, and neither was Adam
one did not take weapons as honoured guests to a banque
Even had they been armed, they could do nothing again:
such a number of soldiers.

You might argue, thought Adam sardonically, that the
had not as yet been accused of any crime, or eve
officially arrested. But as Lymond must have realized a
once, the indiscretions of Danny and Ludo, whatever i
God's name they were, could never account by then
selves for this sudden and cavalier handling. After near

ree months of unalloyed, obsequious conduct, England,
seemed, no longer cared if she offended. What had
anged?

Not, at least, Guthrie and Hoddim, jumping to their
et in the small room allotted them all in Sir Henry
rningham's house. Or Lymond's manner, greeting them.

'Carpets!' said Lymond. 'And you are going to have to
ep three to a bed: what a pity. But at least it is better
an Maidstone Gaol. . . . What has just happened in
ussia is, I am sure, very exciting, but if you had
anaged to keep it to yourselves, we none of us should
 here.'

And Alec Guthrie, whom he had last seen at the
eglinna Bridge outside the Kremlin of Moscow, said, 'It
as Howlet, the sailing-master, who spread the news . . .
r. Why are we all here? Not, I take it, on vagrancy
arges.'

'Don't be caustic,' said Lymond lightly. 'My buttons
ay save us all yet. We have been nailed, as they say,
r horabull lyes and sedyssyous wordes, and because
aniel Hislop and Ludovic d'Harcourt have made a
tch of something between them.' He sat down on one
f the pair of low beds and looked from Guthrie's
earded face to Hoddim's lined one; and his eyes were
y no means as carefree as his voice. 'Then tell me,' he
id, 'what *has* happened in Russia?'

'The Tsar is mad,' Alec Guthrie said.

'He is not an Englishman,' Lymond said.

Guthrie said with some bluntness, 'There are strains in
is nature which are due to his race. There are others
hich are not. Since you left, the vagaries have increased,
nd the violence. He has become quite unpredictable. The
an he adores today he will have cut for the hounds to
at the next morning. He will not be governed by the
uncil you left with him. It must be one soul who
eaks to his soul; one man who helps him undress; one
ho prays with him and one who reads to him of an
ening. . . .'

'Vishnevetsky,' said Lymond. He paused, his eyes, blue
s stones, moving from Guthrie to Hoddim. Adam, stand-
g forgotten by the door, did not move or speak. Lymond
id, 'But Vishnevetsky could not win a place next to the
sar, or keep it, alone.'

'He is not alone,' Guthrie said.

There was no need, with Lymond, to mention Güze name. He was understood. Lymond, his considering ga resting on Guthrie showed nothing on his face but th pure, mechanical process of thinking. Since he did n speak, Guthrie added after a moment, 'You perhaps d not know it, but all your possessions were sent to Nicholas and loaded on the *Philip and Mary*. Vences saw to it. She knew you were not going back. A matt she said, of a prophecy.'

'But I am going back,' Lymond said.

And then Alec Guthrie said quietly, 'Dmitri Vis nevetsky has been made Voevoda Bolshoia. And the Ts has said that if you return to Russia without the munitio you were sent for, you will be executed as you step Russian soil.'

'Then I must run the risk,' Lymond said. And, anger revealing itself only in the coolness of his voi 'But you did have the army, Guthrie. Hoddim, Plumm and a group of first-class Russian captains. The army, t weapons and the money. Were they all powerless aga a Lithuanian princeling and a woman?'

'They were powerless against the Tsar,' Guthrie sa The red of anger showed also, in his cheeks. 'Do y think I allowed it to happen, like a sergeant surprised an alehouse? The Tsar impounded our money a weapons, imprisoned my captains and gave us the choi of fighting under Dmitri Vishnevetsky or leaving t country. We were lucky to get away with our lives.'

'And Plummer?' Lymond said.

'Plummer is already building the Tsar a new summ palace. Plummer has retired from the rude exchanges the battlefield,' Alec Guthrie said. 'He will stay in Russ We left. We crossed Sweden and Norway to bring t news to you. And when we got to Trondheim, we fou the *Philip and Mary,* wintering there, with all your g aboard.'

'Still?' said Lymond. 'They will have impounded it.'

'No. It is safe,' Guthrie said. 'And ready to go wherev you want St Mary's to go.'

Fergie Hoddim, cleared his throat, spoke for the fi time. 'Assuming, that is, that the present litigious busine whatever it may be, is happily concluded for all parti May we speir the nature o' the process, and the cond scendance, and the name o' the pursuer?'

'The Crown is the pursuer,' said Lymond. 'And the
latter is treason and espionage. I had asked both Hercules Tait and Hislop to waylay some compromising papers
being brought from Venice to London. They both seem
to have failed. And d'Harcourt, who to my knowledge
had never heard of the matter, seems to have got himself
arrested as well.' He wheeled round suddenly, so that
Adam started, in his dark place by the door. 'Did you
know of these papers?' Lymond said.

Adam Blacklock shook his head. Then he said, 'But
you told Danny?' Danny was the only one I did tell,'
said Lymond. He was still looking at Blacklock.

'Then d'Harcourt may have followed him,' Adam said.

'But,' said Lymond gently, 'didn't you hear Arundel?
D'Harcourt launched the attack first. There is another odd
thing. Why did the Ambassador manage to reach Sittingbourne unimpeded before he was attacked, and before
Hislop was apparently warned he was coming? There
were men hired to await him at each possible stopping-
place, with orders to steal that casket, no matter what
happened.'

'I think I can answer that,' Guthrie said. 'The box was
probably too heavily guarded. Your Peter Vannes must
have been on his guard already, by an unsuccessful
attempt to take the box before they ever landed in England. I thought you knew: the men who brought us here
told us about it, though not about Vannes and the papers.
They have Hercules Tait in London, also a prisoner.'

Lymond turned. 'Ah,' he said at last. 'Now, that *is* bad
news.'

'Compared to all the good news?' said Adam bitterly.

'One thing at a time,' Lymond said. 'I shall deal with
the news from Russia when I am free to go there. I shall
be free to go there when that casket has been opened and
the contents found innocuous. But—'

'But if Tait and Hislop and d'Harcourt have all failed
in their efforts, the papers are still in their casket, undisturbed?' said Guthrie dryly.

'It seems so,' said Lymond. 'And three of my officers
are now implicated. I have still to find out what happened at Sittingbourne. I should like to know something
else as well. How long is it since the *Philip and Mary*
made her first landfall on English soil?'

'Ten days,' said Fergie Hoddim, after some thought.

'Near enough. They sent a party on shore for water at Orwell Haven. We didn't go.' He paused. 'Why, sir?'

'Why?' said Lymond transferring the question to Adam. And Adam, looking at the furious blue gaze knew suddenly what the answer implied.

'Because,' said Adam slowly, 'when the English Privy Council agreed to let you have the arms and men you wanted for Russia, they already knew you had been supplanted, and they could withdraw whenever they wished.'

'Yes,' Lymond said. 'Whose is the wily head, I wonder? Petre? Pembroke? Paget or Arundel? We shall have a chance to find out. When Hislop and d'Harcourt have recovered; when all the witnesses have been assembled, we shall certainly be given a chance to find out.'

Guthrie said, 'You may be lucky. If the evidence is not against you, what will you do?'

'Sail to Russia,' Lymond said.

'But Nepeja is boarding the *Primrose* four days from now,' Adam said. 'Do you imagine they will have finished with you here by that time?'

'No,' Lymond said. 'But on the other hand, they don't want me in this country. Or in Scotland. Or in France. If the case against me looks like collapsing, they will make sure I am on board the *Primrose* when she sets sail for Russia.'

'And if the case against you holds?' said Fergie Hoddim.

'Then my problems, I imagine, will disappear altogether,' Lymond said. 'And you may track down my possessions and enjoy them. Unless you think Güzel is likely to require a small pension?'

But although he looked at them all with raised eyebrows, no one replied.

*

The other person whose predicament was occupying all his thoughts, he did not mention. But Sir Henry Sidney, as Lymond had hoped, went straight from that ill-fated banquet in the Drapers' Hall to take a barge to Lady Dormer's and there found and told Mistress Philippa all that had happened. He also told her what he had learned later from Sir William Petre. 'Mr Crawford will not be returning to Russia. The Tsar has put another in his

ace, and has sent word that if he returns without these
unitions, he will be executed.'

Philippa considered him. 'Has Mr Crawford said that
: is not returning to Russia?'

Sir Henry began to realize that there was more to the
oblem than had at first appeared. 'No,' he said. 'But
hen I was there, the Council had very cleverly re-
ained from telling him that he had no credit left. For-
nately for the sake of his dignity, he guessed, I think,
at something was wrong other than this foolish business
: Hislop and d'Harcourt.' He paused. 'Did you know
out that?'

'Yes,' said Philippa. 'But I think the less said about all
at, the better. If they can prove Mr Crawford was the
istigator of the assault, then they may be able to sen-
nce him: he no longer has the protection of the Tsar.
the case against him fails, you can expect him, I think,
go to Russia.'

Sir Henry Sidney was watching her closely. 'In spite of
hat is virtually a sentence of death? Will he not take
mployment in Scotland? Heaven forbid poor Shrewsbury
hould have that to contend with on the Borders, but he
ould be a godsend to that remarkable woman de Guise.'

'The one thing you may be assured of, in Mr Craw-
ord's singularly erratic life,' said Philippa gloomily, 'is
hat he will not go back to Scotland.'

'But *Russia*?' said Sir Henry impatiently.

'Yes, Russia,' said Philippa. 'Of course he won't relin-
uish Russia. He ploughed it; he sowed it. He now feels
is mission, without doubt, is to weed it. Besides, Güzel is
here.'

Sir Henry Sidney drew a long, tactful breath, and
xpelled it. 'The lady also,' he said, 'was apparently con-
inced that Mr Crawford would not return.'

'Oh,' said Philippa. A little colour grew in her cheeks,
and went on increasing; it vanished leaving her a little
pale, as she had been before. 'In that case,' she said
prosaically, 'I think he most certainly will insist on
returning to Russia.'

'You may be right,' Sidney said. 'But meantime, we
have to make sure of your safety. The case against Mr
Crawford may hold. And you are his wife. A diplomatic
illness, I think, is indicated. You must quietly disappear.'

'Leaving my mother to take the brunt?' said Philippa

acidly. 'Or should she disappear too, leaving Fla[...]
Valleys to be confiscated while we wander romanticall[...]
penniless through the Channel Islands, handy for flyin[...]
in any direction? Whose idea was this? Mr Crawford's[...]

Henry Sidney gave a sigh. 'It was more in the natur[...]
of a pious hope that if anything untoward happened [...]
him, I should advise you to take to the heather. Or th[...]
equivalent.'

He was a very likeable man. Philippa Somervil[...]
grinned at him. 'Well, I won't take to the heather,' sh[...]
said. 'But you can trust me to plunge wildly into th[...]
equivalent.'

Sidney was uneasy when he left, having persuaded h[...]
to accept none of his help to leave London. He woul[...]
have been a great deal more uneasy had he returned fiv[...]
minutes later, to find she had left the house by boa[...]
quickly, to visit the home of the Venetian Ambassador.

From there she went to John Dee's. It was on he[...]
return from that unpublicized residence that she found [...]
courteous gentleman waiting for her at the landing stag[...]
at the Savoy, and three more in the garden beyond.

They were Henry Jerningham's men, and they wishe[...]
her to accompany them, they said, on a small matter [...]
royal business. She was not allowed to change her dre[...]
but was taken, just as she was, to the Westminste[...]
apartments of the Countess of Lennox who treated he[...]
as she had once before, as a much-cherished guest. Bu[...]
as before, there was an armed man before every doo[...]
and the Queen, invoked by courier, merely returned kin[...]
messages commanding her sweet Philippa to remain [...]
Lady Lennox's loving care until the current matter con[...]
cerning her husband had been fairly examined.

The heather, as it proved, was extremely comfortabl[...]
but Philippa, growling, did not take to it.

*

Several days passed. In Henry Jerningham's hous[...]
Lymond bore the waiting with equanimity; his officers [...]
good deal more uneasily. In another part of Londo[...]
Hercules Tait conducted himself with decorum, as h[...]
had since his unfortunate arrest, and awaited, with som[...]
resignation, the exposure of his folly to Lymond. Els[...]
where in the same building Ludovic d'Harcourt an[...]

Danny Hislop, incarcerated together, were no longer speaking to each other. Or if Danny, revived, thought of something wittily abusive to say, d'Harcourt no longer answered him.

On the first of May Sir William Petre and the Bishop of Ely called at Fenchurch Street with royal letters of recommendation under the Great Seal of England for the Sovereign Grand Prince of Russia; and with gifts for the Tsar and his Ambassador, offering goodwill and friendship between the Queen and King and the merchants and fellowship of the adventurers for and to Russia.

Accepimus literas vestras amoris et amicitie plenas per dilectum Virum nuntium et legatum Osiph Nepeam ad nos delatas, said Ascham's elegant Latin. . . . *Speramus hoc fundamentum mutue amicitie, hoc modo bene et feliciter jactum et stabilitum magnos et uberes fructus tum fraterni inter nos et successores nostros, amoris et amicitie firme tum perpetui inter subditos nostros commercii coniunctionem allatuvum. . . .*

To Master Nepeja, the Queen gave a chain of gold of one hundred pounds weight, a large basin and ewer, a pair of pottle pots and a pair of flagons, all made in the western style which did not in the least take his fancy, and all of gold, gilt or silver gilt, which did.

To the Tsar of Russia his cousins the monarchs of England sent two rich cloth of tissue pieces, one piece of scarlet cloth, one of azure and one of fine violet in grain. They also sent a set of body armour with helmet adorned with red velvet and gilt nails; and a lion and lioness, living.

The lions roared in their wagon outside Master Dimmock's fine house through all the handsome exchanges, translated by Rob Best, and a crowd of some size had gathered by the time Sir William Petre and the Bishop emerged, duty done, and rode away, empty-handed and smiling.

The merchants were not smiling. Nor were the mariners at Gravesend, as the news travelled there as by drumbeat. With some misgivings Anthony Jenkinson, worthy gentleman and great traveller, stood in the street and looked at the lions from Affrik which he, in truth, had to translate to a contrary heaven across two thousand miles of fierce ocean and deliver, roaring, to their new and sensitive master in Moscow.

On Monday as planned, the Muscovy Ambassador left London for Gravesend, accompanied by the city officers and the merchants, who set him aboard the noble ship *Primrose*, with many tears and embracings. He had been told how, having lost the Tsar's favour, his former colleague Francis Crawford had not yet decided whether to sail back to Russia as expected. And that a small infringement of law had detained temporarily the rest of his party.

Robert Best translated it all, impassively, and John Buckland made no comment either, in public. But when Henry Sidney came on board the flagship, Jenkinson took him below and with Best and Buckland beside him said 'What of Mr Crawford?'

And Sidney succinctly replied, 'There is a legal case pending. And Crawford is tangled with it as well.'

'But can they hold him?' Jenkinson said. 'He is still officially, an envoy of the Tsar.'

'Officially,' said Sidney dryly. 'But should they deal with him less than gently, I doubt if the Tsar would trouble to lodge a complaint. My guess is that the Privy Council want Mr Crawford as a witness against other eminent conspirators here in England.'

'So we sail without him?' said Robert Best. 'And without Danny or Ludo?'

But the eyes of Henry Sidney and Tony Jenkinson met. 'Ships are strange creatures,' said Sidney, 'and cannot be ordered like house dogs. A ship may wait a long time for the tide or the wind that will suit her. I think you will be given your orders.'

Rob Best groaned. 'Lions,' he said, 'do not necessarily understand orders. And, my God, how shall we explain to Nepeja?'

'You've forgotten,' said John Buckland calmly. 'Once out into the estuary with a freshening wind, and there will be no need to explain anything to Osep Nepeja.'

CHAPTER THIRTEEN

With Osep Nepeja on board, the *Primrose* waited at Gravesend for a week with the three other vessels freighted for Muscovy. At the end of that time the Earl

f Arundel, having opened and perused with his fellows
ie contents of Master Peter Vannes's box, decreed that
n inquiry should be held into the attempts to purloin
ie chest on its travels, and that all the accused and their
ipporters should be brought to one room for that purpose.

This was, in the event, one of the many small cham-
ers used for justice in Westminster and was furnished
ith no more than a long table for the commissioners
nd/or judges, and with a few unpadded stools and long
enches. Inside and out, it was thoroughly guarded.

There were no more than seven commissioners and five
f these were, Adam Blacklock noted, members of the
Iuscovy Company. It was the first thing he saw as he
ame in out of the sunshine, with Guthrie and Hoddim
nd Lymond : the long bench with the grey-haired men
tting behind it, in their flapped hats and thick robes
nd long, bushy beards. The President of the Council,
rundel again; with Griffin, the Attorney-General, and
erningham, as you would expect. Sir William Petre, of
ourse. And two other powerful figures : William Herbert,
ie 1st Earl of Pembroke, and Paget, the Lord Privy
eal.

And someone he had not expected : a man also grey-
earded but tall and thin and elegant in black silk as an
nion skin. Don Juan de Figueroa, the Spanish nobleman
nce Ambassador at the Emperor's Court and lately King
hilip's excellent observer and high officer in England.
he Queen was represented by her officers of State, but
id not care personally to interfere in matters which
light be prejudicial to her merchants. The King had
:nt his eyes and his ears.

The Tsar's officers were not asked to sit. They had to
:and in their small circle of guards and watch Hercules
'ait appear, escorted. Tait saw Lymond but showed no
:cognition : Lymond's face expressed a hard-tried but
:ill polite patience. All that any of them had been able
 discover from that nerve-shattering week in his com-
any was that he was virtually unbeatable at card games.

Then Ludo and Danny were brought in, looking rather
l-groomed, with bruises still yellow on their faces and
rists. Danny stared round the room until he found
veryone, and then rolled his eyes until a yeoman told
im to stop.

D'Harcourt looked round once, gave a kind of grimace

577

in Lymond's direction and then stood, holding his wea
arm with the other, his head bent in thought on hi
chest.

Lady Lennox came in, with her secretary John Elde
and Philippa Somerville, employing the stalk she ha
learned balancing sherbet jars on her crown in th
Seraglio. After a reasonable length of time her hea
swam round on its neck and she bestowed a vigorou
grimace on her husband. Then she was given a stoo
beside Lady Lennox's chair while John Elder stood
holding the chairback behind them.

Since the two women had come in, Lymond had beer
standing remarkably still. He returned Philippa's greet
ing, Adam noticed, with a look which was both ques
tioning and guarded: Margaret Lennox with a smil
was studying him in her turn. And from across the room
oddly enough, Ludo d'Harcourt had lifted his head and
was watching also, first Philippa and then Francis Craw
ford, until Lymond in turn became aware of it; then
d'Harcourt, reddening, looked away. The Presiden
banged with his gavel. 'We are waiting for Maste
Vannes.'

But he was already at the door, the long-awaited Peter
Vannes, Dean of Salisbury, the swarthy Italian now in
his sixties who for six years had been Ambassador for
England with the Doge and the Council of Ten. And a
he came in and bowed to the Council, Adam noticed
that he also smiled towards the clerks' table, where a man
sat at the head of the scriveners who was obviously, from
his clothes, of some consequence. And that, one took it
must be the Queen's Latin secretary, Roger Ascham, with
some of his staff, ready at need to translate any necessary
evidence in that tongue.

And on the desk before Ascham was a battered
wooden box, nailed all over with yellow nails and barred
strongly with iron, which had been splintered open, one
would guess, with a chisel; and beside it some thirty
papers in an irregular bundle; some rolled, some folded;
none of them very neatly or efficiently kept. One or two
were small notes, of the kind which might accompany a
parcel. Some were letters running clearly to many pages,
in thick dog-eared sheaves. The private papers of the
late William Courtenay, Earl of Devonshire, with all the
578

amning evidence they must contain of conspiracies and
those engaged in them, on the lady Elizabeth's behalf.

Peter Vannes seated himself and, without preamble, the
Earl of Arundel began.

'I do not mean to spend long over this matter. You are
here to explain three attempts to steal or interfere with
the coffer you now see before you. The three men concerned are in this room, and from none of them have
we been able to discover their reasons, or on whose
behalf they have been acting. We have not so far used
force, since it seemed that the answer might quite simply
be in the contents of the coffer itself.

'We have now read these papers. As I have said, we
have not so far used force. I shall not hesitate to use it
now, if I do not receive the answers I require. So I now
ask you again. Master Tait, on whose instructions did
you attempt to prevent these documents from reaching
their proper destination?'

And Hercules Tait, man of taste and garrulous correspondent, drew breath to answer and was spared the
necessity by Lymond, who had played chess with better
men than Henry Fitzalan, 10th Earl of Arundel.

'Master Tait acted under my instructions,' Lymond
said.

Everyone turned. Beside him, Adam heard Guthrie
swear; and across the room Danny Hislop's empty
stomach gave a croak of despair. Philippa, allowing her
head to drop back, stared at the ceiling inhaling and
reviewed, speechlessly, a number of telling ejaculations in
Turkish. The Earl of Arundel said slowly, 'Indeed? And
the attacks by the men Hislop and d'Harcourt were made
at your orders as well? May I ask why, Mr Crawford?'

Her husband's manner, thought, Philippa approvingly,
was quite perfect: deferential without being obsequious;
serene without being flippant. Lymond said, 'The severity
of these attacks I regret. They were made under my
orders and I in turn have been acting, Lord Arundel, on
behalf of my employer the Tsar.'

He paused. Philippa, keeping her gaze on the ceiling,
heard someone near her swallow, quite audibly. 'Go on,
sir,' Arundel said.

And Lymond went on in the same, undisturbed voice.
'As you know, important trade agreements were in project
between your country and Russia. My Tsar was about

to cast aside the long-standing connections he already possessed through the Hanseatic ports and other parts of the Baltic, and rely instead on a new route and a new agreement with England. The stability of England, her prospects and the hazards which might threaten her woollen trade, her finances and her shipping, were therefore of great importance to us. For this reason, since I spoke the language and had many connections in Europe, I was asked to find out what I could about the present condition of England.

'It was not, naturally, something I wished widely known. It is however a mode of insurance which we thought essential, in view of the many rumours of disturbances reaching us.'

'I see,' said Arundel. He did not look surprised.

Sir William Petre, glancing at him, added a question. 'We are to understand therefore that you wished to study the Earl of Devonshire's papers to find out what plot might be afoot which threatened the security, as you thought, of this throne? The man is dead; the plots, if there were any, long abandoned. Why then go to such trouble, Mr Crawford?'

'Because I, too, had corresponded with William Courtenay,' Lymond replied. 'I sought information about England, which on occasion he gave me. I was not anxious that this traffic should be made public. You will have seen the letters, no doubt, in the casket.'

There was a long pause, during which the eyes of Arundel and Pembroke met and parted. It was Pembroke who finally spoke. 'There were no such letters here in the casket,' he said. 'There were no letters, notes or reports of any consequence whatever. You have had your trouble and these men have died, Mr Crawford, for nothing at all. For less than nothing, since your interest in our domestic affairs was already known to us. Your correspondence over the years with Master Lychpole has been no secret. As you say, nations must make their own safeguards. I am surprised that you underrated ours so seriously.'

'You astonish me,' Lymond said. 'May I know what directed your attention to Master Lychpole?'

The Earl of Pembroke smiled. 'You have taken us, under duress, into your confidence, Mr Crawford,' he said. 'I do not think we need take you into ours. Especi-

lly as it will be our melancholy duty to regard what you
ave told us as a matter for prosecution. The Attorney
eneral cannot lightly overlook espionage, nor yet vio-
nce and murder in our quiet English lanes.'

Adam Blacklock stared at the man. *Quiet English
nes.* There was a smugness in Pembroke's voice, not only
riumph. And if you looked closely at the others, you
nsed the same thing: an air of satisfaction; of superi-
rity. It came to Adam suddenly that these men had been
oncerned with the casket not only to seek evidence
gainst the lady Elizabeth; against Dee and his friends;
gainst all those conspirators paid by the King of France
ho had entangled William Courtenay so foolishly, so
ften in their tortuous intrigues. They had been afraid,
ach of them, for himself.

And it was then that Lymond said, 'You had better
nen cultivate Venice, whom the Pontiff is wooing so
eartily to his cause. For I have Master Tait's word that
ou were not the first to open the box there, since the
ailiff of Padua sealed it. The papers you found inside
ere harmless because all the rest of William Cour-
enay's documents have been extracted and kept by the
)oge and Senate of Venice.'

No one spoke. Prowling like fire, comprehension, vibrat-
ng and hideous, ran through the judicial chamber.

Venice. Venice, seduced by the Pope and publishing
broad those very secrets the Council had dreaded to
neet with in these papers. Not the plots and counter-
lots between France and Elizabeth – those would be
lestroyed or suppressed. But the rest. . . . The polite,
robing exchanges between William Courtenay and the
nen now in high office who had not been so certain of
igh office when the death of one young king led to such
lrastic changes in religion and government.

Men who made their availability known and who
erhaps went even further, in the early days, before the
Queen took her throne with all King Harry's courage
nd pride at the start of her realm: *What I am, ye right
vell know. I am your Queen, to whom at my coronation
ou promised your allegiance. I cannot tell how naturally
he mother loveth a child, for I was never the mother of
ny, but certainly if a prince and governor may as
naturally and earnestly love her subjects as the mother*

581

doth love her child, then assure yourselves that I do
earnestly and tenderly love and favour you. . . .

She had overthrown the rebels and begun her reign
on that blaze of splendour and success, and those who
had hesitated became, warmly, her men. They did not
wish to be reminded, now, of what had gone before.

Then the Earl of Arundel, rallying, said, 'I do not
believe his serene highness the Doge would stoop to con
fiscate an Englishman's papers.'

And a Spanish voice; a dry, accented voice which had
not spoken in that conclave before said, 'But it is true.'
And opening the leather box on the floor at his side, Don
Juan de Figueroa, representative of his Majesty King
Philip, drew out a thick bundle of pages tied with tape
and placed them on the table beside those other, inno
cent papers from Vannes's splintered box.

'It is true, my lords,' said the Spaniard; and, lifting
his sharp eyes, met Lymond's unreadable blue stare and
then, switching, the brown, owl-like gaze of Philippa
Somerville. 'The Doge is our friend : he was anxious that
none of the effects of this important Englishman should
fall into unauthorized hands and prove an embarrassment to us. A selection of papers was therefore withdrawn from the casket at Venice, and the box resealed
and sent on to Padua. I have the missing papers here.
The Venetian Ambassador, of his great generosity, has
made them available to King Philip and myself. Do you
wish to see them?'

There was another, ragged moment of silence. Then the
Earl of Arundel said, speaking as if to a deaf man, 'We
were not made aware of these facts. Are we to take it
that King Philip has already perused these documents?'

'He has,' said the Spaniard.

'And,' said Pembroke, 'perhaps Don Juan de Figueroa
would tell us whether His Majesty considers them a
subject for action?'

Gazing, one by one at each of these avaricious, important Englishmen, Don Juan pursed his pale, bearded
lips. 'His most serene Majesty,' de Figueroa said, 'is of
the opinion that these papers are of no importance, and
may well be destroyed without further action. He also
recommends that, under the circumstances, the case
against these men should be dropped, provided they
leave the country immediately, and provided that Mr

rawford agrees that his talents and his destiny will be
est fulfilled by a speedy return to his master in Russia.
onfronted with a man of such ability, we cannot believe
at the Tsar will deal harshly with him.' And he raised
is eyebrows, halting.

There was a short silence. Beside Adam, Guthrie moved
arply and then was still. Tait and Danny were grin-
ing; Ludo looked, thought Adam, aghast. Lady Lennox,
ho had shut her lips, opened them again and said, 'And
Ir Crawford's wife?'

The Spaniard turned and looked at Philippa Somer-
ille, who recalled the sophisticated maxims of Don
lfonso Derronda and favoured him with a long, cool
nd haughty regard.

'It seems to us,' said de Figueroa, 'that Mistress
omerville has not been implicated in anything detri-
ental to her country, and that it will suffice if she with-
raws from the Queen's Court.'

Philippa inclined her head. Out of the shattered
lence along the ranks of the eminent, the Earl of
rundel said, 'Mr Crawford. You have heard what has
ist been said. Are you prepared to sail back to Russia
ith the fleet presently leaving from Gravesend?'

'I shall be happy to do so,' said Lymond. He had,
dam noted in the midst of his own voiceless consterna-
on, a faint colour under his skin. He added, 'I shall
ave, if you wish, straight from this place. My baggage
in follow me.'

'Then,' said the Earl of Arundel, moving his eyes
owly along the faces on either side of him, 'I think we
re in accord with you, Don Juan. The papers burn; the
risoners are freed; the matter is ended. Mr Crawford—'

'It will give me pleasure,' said Don Juan de Figueroa,
ising, 'to assist Mr Crawford to fulfil his generous
ndertaking to board ship immediately. My lord presi-
ent, have I your leave?'

Arundel, half rising, nodded. Vannes, wisely reticent,
ood up, but could not refrain from saying, 'And the
risoners, my lords? When are Master Tait and the
thers to leave the country?'

It was Pembroke who answered. 'They are mercen-
ries. They will have no trouble in finding employment,
r a ship to carry them wherever they wish to go. Some,
take it, may wish to return with Mr Crawford to

Russia. The rest have three days in which to leave thi
island. Meanwhile Sir Henry Jerningham, I am sure
will continue to see to their comfort.'

Guthrie said, 'We wish to go back to Russia.' Adam
looked at him.

'All of you?'

Adam opened his mouth. 'All of us,' said Fergie Hoddim

'Except me,' said Hercules Tait. 'I am no longer, alas
a man of the sword.'

'All of you, except Master Tait?' said Arundel once
more. Philippa's face was expressionless : Lymond's was not

Ludo d'Harcourt said flatly, 'If Mr Crawford goes, I
will go.'

'Then it seems,' said Lord Arundel, 'that we shall re
quire river transport for six people. Don Juan?'

'It can be arranged,' said the Spaniard, and, com
pleting his walk over the floor, called for his captain and
secretary, and spoke to them. Sir William Petre, gather
ing his robes, walked round the table to Lymond.

'Provided you wished indeed to return to your Tsar, I
must congratulate you, sir, on this outcome. And on
possessing a master so alert to the value of information
I doubt if any western nation could command such a
distinguished espionage service.' He smiled, his eyes un
smiling. 'When did you have your audience with King
Philip, Mr Crawford?'

'I cannot quite recall, my lord,' Lymond said. 'But I
think shortly after we concluded the agreement con
cerning the munitions of war. It was a pleasure to revive
my rusting Spanish.'

'Ah. You speak Spanish,' said Petre. 'It is a gift some
on the Council would envy you. . . . You exercised care
I take it, in stowing the pewter?'

'Master Dimmock,' said Lymond, 'was most generous
with advice concerning the pewter. I trust the lion and
lioness will prove no more dangerous. It is my conviction
that, in matters of trade, the English and Muscovites will
deal well together.'

And Sir William Petre, bowing with something close
to a genuine smile, straightened and said, 'You are in
deed serious about returning to Russia. I see that. Do you
expect to recover the ground you have lost? May we
look to see you stand friend to our merchants in
Moscow?'

'So far as I am able,' Lymond said. 'My first duty is the realm and its ruler.'

'And Scotland?' said the voice of Lady Lennox beside [h]m; and as he turned, the black eyes looked into his [wi]th bitterness and with anger and with something else [t]o well hidden to identify. 'Scotland may slide at [Fr]ance's petticoat tails, losing her men, her pride and her [na]tionhood, and you no longer care for it?'

Lymond returned the challenge standing at ease, self-[po]ssessed from the sheen of his hair to the fall of his [ex]quisite robe. 'Would she have fared better, do you [su]ppose, at England's petticoat tails, which seem to be [slid]ing with equal haste in a different direction? Or do [yo]u mean that Scotland should rise and overthrow her [Fr]ench rulers and appoint a King of her own, with [St]uart blood in his veins as strong as that of the little [Q]ueen Mary? But would such a king not constitute a [th]reat in himself to your monarchy? And where, be-[si]des, could one find such a paragon?'

Pembroke and Arundel, Paget and Petre were all [wi]thin range of that deliberate, carrying voice. Margaret [Le]nnox did not look at the other men round her. But, [he]r colour high and her carriage stiff and erect and [un]yielding, she said, 'Mr Elder: I think we must go. [T]he whims and humours of his unfortunate master [ap]pear to have affected Mr Crawford's whirligig brain.' [A]nd turning her head, 'Where shall we find you next?' [sa]id Margaret Lennox to the boy from long ago who [w]as now so obdurately a man. 'In New Spain, perhaps, [in] a mantle of feathers, running errands with knots on a [st]ring? Before you die, there must be nothing you have [no]t experienced. When you die – and I shall be there – [it] will be an experience which no man has savoured. [G]uard your health, Mr Crawford. I should not like you [to] leave us too soon.'

For a moment longer, she held his eyes. Then, waiting [n]either for Elder nor Philippa, Margaret Lennox brought [he]r train round to her hand and, gathering it, walked [fro]m the room.

'Talking of feathers,' said Francis Crawford conver-[sa]tionally to his elegant, seraglio-trained wife.

'Or feather-brains,' said Philippa Somerville furiously. [H]er eyes, glassy with rage, glared at her spouse. 'You

585

heard what the Tsar threatened. He'll have your hea
in a blood-bowl like Cyrus.'

'Not Cyrus,' said Lymond. 'I'm the other one. *H
pincheth and spareth and pineth his life. To coffer
bags to leave to his wife.* The pay is good. And I'
remembered another quotation about Greeks.'

'I don't want to hear it,' said Philippa.

'You can try it on Master Vannes. *Greeks in be
Italians at table, are most neat.* It doesn't mentio
Spanish. Which will you have, Philippa? I like yo
Austin. I haven't met your Don Alfonso.'

'Earrings,' Philippa said. 'And eyes like dome-head
rivets. I don't know which I shall have. I can't have an
until someone annuls this—' She broke off. 'How am
going to get this marriage dissolved if you go back
Russia?'

'Desertion?' Lymond suggested easily. 'Which remin
me. There were one or two mysteries about these la
proceedings which I can see are going to be for ev
unexplained. I think I owe you another debt. I owe y
a great many debts, it would appear: it is time I r
moved myself and allowed you to allot your endowmer
where they are better deserved. Goodbye.'

He smiled, but did not kiss her cheek, as Don Alfon
would have done; or take her hand, as Austin effected
gracefully, or hug her, as Jane or Kate would have f
impelled to do.

He said again, without the smile, 'Goodbye, *Yunits*
and turning walked out of the room.

Ludovic d'Harcourt, come to take his wistful leav
stood beside Philippa, as Lymond vanished. '*Yunitsa*
he queried.

She smiled, bringing her gaze back to her hand as I
lifted and kissed it. 'A stupid joke. It means heifer, I
tells me.'

'It means heifer,' d'Harcourt agreed; and, since th
others were becoming impatient, pressed her hand an
abandoned the subject without informing her how mu
more it meant.

*

The barge which Don Juan had commanded for N
Crawford and his five friends was a fine one, with a ga
canopy aft, and eight oarsmen in livery, who made th